SCOTIA,
Regnum.

Miliaria
Scoti
ca

Orcus

MARE

GERMANICUM

Per Gerardum Mercatorem
Cum Priuilegio

MICHAEL PHILLIPS

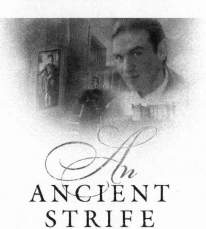

An
ANCIENT
STRIFE

This Book Belongs To:

Dee

Olivers

MICHAEL PHILLIPS

CALEDONIA

An

ANCIENT
STRIFE

BETHANY HOUSE PUBLISHERS
MINNEAPOLIS, MINNESOTA 55438

CONTENTS

⁜ ⁜ ⁜

MAPS
AND
ILLUSTRATIONS

※ ※ ※

CALEDONIA

AN ANCIENT STRIFE . . .

In the year 1314, the most significant battle in the history of the land called Caledonia was fought on Scottish soil, between a small river called the Bannock Burn and the town of Stirling. This is the story of events and personalities leading up to that decisive moment in the ancient strife . . . and of that portion of the drama which may yet be waiting to unfold.

CALEDONIA

Cuimhnich có leis a tha thu.

Remember the men from whence you came.

—OLD GAELIC PROVERB

PROLOGUE

Tꜧe Legend and
Tꜧe Prophecy

Saturday, June 22, 1314
Near Stirling, Scotland

An unsteady flame flickered low in the summer's late night.

The company in the tent was not comprised of many men, but the strategy they were devising would change the history of their land forever.

"I argue against your going out alone, my lord King," said one of the party, a loyal nobleman of his ancient clan and lieutenant of the division commanded by Walter the Steward. "They may send an entire regiment against you."

"They will lead with their heavy cavalry," replied the King. "I am sure of it."

"I salute your courage, my lord," rejoined Douglas, "but the risk of harm befalling you is too great."

That Douglas had perhaps been emboldened to speak thus because he had been knighted by the King himself earlier that same day in no wise lessened the pluck required to raise the specter of doubt on the night prior to battle.

"If you die, my lord, Scotland is doomed," he added in honest tribute. "No one else can unite the country and lead its nobles as you have done."

The tent grew silent.

Douglas had voiced the reservation that several of the highest-ranking officers held in their hearts concerning the King's final suggestion. The English, so the scouts said, would be coming north along the Roman road from Tor Wood tomorrow with numberless troops. King Robert the Bruce commanded but six thousand Scotsmen.

The silence continued several minutes.

At length the King turned his head unexpectedly toward the youngest of those present in the tent, a lad of less than twenty years, who looked more the part of armor-bearer or groom than general.

"And you, young MacDarroch," he said, "what advice would *you* give your King on the eve of battle? You have heard the objection. What does your stout heart tell you in the matter?"

Whatever may have been the reaction of the elder nobles around the table to the King's asking such a one to render opinion on the momentous proceeding, their faces displayed nothing.

The ensuing wait was brief.

"My lord Douglas speaks wisely, my lord King," replied the young man with a confidence in excess of his years, "when he warns care on your part. Your courage will be required as long as the battle wages."

A brief pause followed. He appeared to be siding with Douglas.

"And it *shall* be so given, I am confident," Donal MacDarroch went on even more boldly. "Let them ride against you. Let them discover whom they have chosen for an adversary—and what manner of man rules over this land."

"Bravely spoken," commented Bruce.

MacDarroch said nothing.

"Would you ride beside me to await them, MacDarroch?" asked the King.

"With honor, my lord King."

The Bruce waited but a moment more, then turned the piercing gaze of his strongly chiseled face back to the nobles seated with him.

"It is decided then," he said firmly. "If this stalwart youth places such confidence in me as to answer thus without a note of fear in his voice, shall I doubt myself? No—I will meet them as proposed, whomever they send to dispatch me. If we can entice Edward's army across the river bridge and lure them into the bog . . . the battle will be ours."

He glanced at his four commanders—his own brother Edward, Thomas Randolph, Walter the Steward, and James Douglas. Each in his turn nodded solemn consent.

The candle burned low.

Robert the Bruce spoke once more. His voice contained the accumulated tradition of one hundred fifty generations of the inhabitants of his land. Upon his shoulders, in that moment, did the legacy of that history and the destiny of his kingdom come to rest.

He was a man standing alone at the apex of his nation's history. He was at that moment *himself* authoring the legend for a race and a nation to follow.

"The time has at last arrived," he said softly, but with the fervor of the great warrior heart rising in his breast, "when the interloping Sassenach must be sent back across the border—not for a mere day, or year, or season . . . but forever. The moment has come for us to claim once more the land of our fathers, the land of our Kings, the land of our heritage, the land of our birthright."

Another pause, this time brief. Then Bruce spoke again, calling his beloved land by its ancient name:

"*Hail, Caledonia!* We pledge here and now that you shall not be taken from your own people again!"

1

INTRIGUE IN
HIGH PLACES

❈ ONE ❈

Fog clung soupy and thick to an isolated stretch of rocky coastline. Whatever ancient Viking explorer first discovered these lonely islands between Scotland and Scandinavia, few had found them habitable through the centuries. Even now their population was sparse, and no visitor walking their isolated moors and coastlines could realize from the lonely topography their strategic importance to the future of that once proud land whose nationhood had been taken from it two hundred fifty years before.

Through the dusky fog of evening strode two men whose attire and demeanor could not have been more out of place in this region where fishermen, poor crofters, and birdwatchers on holiday made up 98 percent of the resident population. The expensive suits and faintly discernible gleam of opportunity in their eyes gave them away as entrepreneurs or politicians, perhaps both. One was of medium build, the other tall and uncommonly slender, though muscular—a physique that to an unwary observer masked his power and the danger in which one stood who dared to cross him.

This particular location had taken them two days to reach. To keep out of the public eye, they had discreetly boarded an overnight ferry, then remained in their private cabin for the fourteen-hour northward crossing. It was about as far removed from civilization as either had been in their lives. But for what the latter of the two had long been planning, this remote parcel of land represented the focal point of all he hoped to achieve—an objective that currently hung in precarious balance, owing, as he judged it, to the stupidity of his associate. Despite recent setbacks with regard to the fabled Stone of Scone, however, he still hoped to pull the thing off.

If they succeeded, both would become rich and powerful men—more powerful than the one had been only a short time before, and perhaps even more powerful than the other still was.

"They're looking for me everywhere," said the shorter man, whose standing in public affairs had suddenly plummeted. "I'm leaving the Isles directly from here."

"To the Continent?" asked the taller man, whose prestigious position remained intact.

"Right. Then to our friends down under."

"They should be able to arrange to keep you out of sight."

"It will give me a chance to firm up that aspect of our plans."

"After what happened, perhaps it might be best if you disappeared permanently. They should also be able to set you up with a new identity."

"I'm not sure I like the sound of that. Don't get the idea of trying to cut me out now."

"Whatever your involvement," rejoined the tall man, "your political career is certainly over. Scotland Yard is sniffing about high and low for you."

"Have you been questioned?"

"Not yet. Our association has so far escaped attention."

"Just make sure when everything falls together—whether a year from now or ten—that my share does not disappear. I may have been taken out of the political game, but I am still a member of the committee."

"Don't worry. You will be provided for."

"I expect to be more than merely provided for."

"I assure you, there will be plenty for all. In the meantime," said the tall man, glancing around, "the next step will be getting our hands on this piece of ground."

"Do you seriously think this is the only place that will work?" asked the other, scanning the lonely site. "One stretch of rock around here looks about the same as any other."

"This protected inlet could be the key. Look around—it would make a perfect harbor. Not only that, but preliminary tests reveal a strong likelihood that the field extends under the coast exactly here. The rights will be everything."

"Have we been successful yet in contacting the owner?"

"My people have traced it to some Highland Scots. Apparently it has been in the family for years. It is not even certain whether the present fellow, a low-level laird somewhere in the Grampians, is altogether aware of what he has. Management of the parcel has been in the hands of an Aberdeen solicitor's firm for a century."

"What is the property's status? Doesn't appear to be worth anything."

"They lease it on behalf of the owners for two hundred fifty pounds a year."

"That's a ludicrously small sum!"

"Precisely. Once preliminary investigations into the matter are concluded, our solicitors will undertake inquiries to see if this so-called laird will sell."

"They would surely be willing if it brings in no more income than you say."

"Exactly how I see it. But you know these Highlanders—they can be a stubborn lot. We must walk carefully in the matter. In any event, now I've seen it for myself. You are flying out, I take it, from Lerwick?"

"Right. Tomorrow."

"All right, then, we'll stay in touch through the normal channel."

They stood a few more minutes in the fog, listening to the sea, each silently contemplating the new developments in their scheme that had suddenly and dramatically altered their personal fortunes.

Then they turned for their separate cars and parted in the night.

⊠ T W O ⊠

The pavement in front of the Palace of Westminster was congested with tourists and passersby, even though the House of Commons was in the middle of its summer recess. On an equally busy side street two blocks away, Scottish Nationalist Party Deputy Leader Baen Ferguson walked briskly toward his office. He had remained in the capital most of the summer thus far, trying to keep reasonably in the public eye, giving an occasional interview, speaking at various clubs and banquets on the changing face of Scottish politics since devolution and the seating of the new Scottish parliament.*

---

*A move, instituted by the Labour government of Tony Blair and given impetus by favorable referendums (nonbinding votes of public opinion) among the voters of both regions, to "devolve" more self-governing authority to Scotland and Wales, resulting in new parliaments and First Ministers for both regions. The overall effect is a system perhaps similar to the federal system in the United States, in which power and decision-making authority is divided between the federal government and that of the individual states. The states have significant powers, yet are still ultimately responsible to the authority of the federal government. Such parallels the newly altered regional relationships in the UK. There are those, however, who advocate far greater autonomy, even full independent nationhood and withdrawal from the United Kingdom altogether. For this vocal minority, devolution has been little more than a token gesture.

It wasn't that he was particularly interested in all that right now. He had other things on his mind. But he wanted to do nothing to convey to the watchful eye of Scotland Yard that he was nervous or about to make a break for it. He must exude perfect nonchalance, even dropping by the Yard every week or ten days to inquire about the investigation, making sure Inspector Shepley knew that he was only too willing to help however he could. In that vein, he had decided not even to go north to visit his district quite yet. He would have to eventually, of course, but he must walk carefully . . . and hope no one else talked.

Shepley had grilled him more than once about the Glencoe cottage where he used to meet Fiona. But he had continually denied any knowledge of the Stone's theft, insisting—convincingly, he thought—that the clue linking the Abbey drain to the cottage had been merely a plant to implicate the SNP.

Which it had been. He wouldn't have made such an idiotic mistake as to drop his own phone number in plain sight at the very site of the theft. Besides, he had been in the boat out on the Thames the whole time, waiting for Fiona and the others to bring the Stone out through the tunnels that ran beneath the Abbey. So the dropped clue had obviously been a decoy—even though the information it contained was true enough.

He didn't like to think who it was that had double-crossed him.

If it was Fiona, had she planned it from the beginning? The very thought of it made him crazy with rage and jealousy.

Or was it one of the others?

Shepley was buying his denials for the present. But Ferguson knew the inspector remained suspicious.

He was in an interesting position—a suspect of sorts, but also the only committee member still in the clear who knew the identity of the others. So, in a sense, he held others' fate in his hands. But that fact probably wouldn't do him much good. He couldn't blow the whistle on anyone else without implicating himself in the process. And he didn't know where Fiona, Reardon, Malloy, or any of the others were, anyway, or what good trying to blackmail them would do him now that they no longer had the Stone. Nevertheless, the thought of turning the tables was tantalizing.

He reached the building, nearly deserted, went upstairs, and unlocked the door to his own office.

If he could just find Fiona and talk to her—perhaps they could get back to how things were before. But he had not heard from her in weeks. Why had she made no attempt to contact him, he thought, his anger rising again.

And there was still the matter of the death of his parliamentary colleague Eagon Hamilton hanging like a cloud—

Ferguson's thoughts were interrupted by the ringing of the telephone on his desk. He strode across the floor to answer it.

"Baen—hello. It's Miles Ramsey," said the familiar voice of his Tory colleague in Commons. "I'm glad I managed to catch you."

"I'm one of the few still left in town," replied Ferguson to the powerful opposition leader of the Conservative Party.

"And your SNP colleagues?"

"Mostly in Scotland."

"Ah . . . celebrating Scotland's rising status in the world, no doubt," said the opposition leader good-naturedly.

"We're not celebrating quite yet, Miles," replied Ferguson. "The SNP's objectives are much loftier than a mere regional parliament."

"Independence?" queried Ramsey. "Do you seriously think it will happen?"

"Of course, Miles. Times are changing."

"We shall see, my friend. In the meantime," Ramsey went on, "I would like to get together with you to discuss a matter of mutual concern."

"If you are thinking of a coup, Miles," said Ferguson wryly, "I'm afraid our SNP block of twenty-one votes won't give you a majority as long as the Liberal Democrats remain in Richard Barraclough's corner. You really ought to be talking to Andrew Trentham. He's the one who holds the key to the coalition in Commons."

"Let's leave the LibDems out of it for the moment," laughed Ramsey. "And the prime minister. But for the record, I'm *not* planning a coup. What I have to talk to you about is, let us say, of a more personal nature."

"Well, then, I shall be happy to oblige."

THREE

Patricia Rawlings, known to her friends as Paddy, knew she could not rest on her laurels. An American who had lived in London seven years and worked most of that time for the news division of BBC 2, she was acutely aware that her place in the fiercely competitive world of British broadcast journalism was far from secure.

True, she had broken the biggest story to hit London since the Queen's abdication. She had even managed a bit of cloak-and-dagger, following Liberal Democrat Deputy Leader Larne Reardon to Ireland and tracking down the famous Stone of Scone, which had been stolen from Westminster Abbey on the eve of King Charles III's coronation. And telephoning her editor Edward Pilkington—from the home of the prominent MP* Andrew Trentham no less—to report that she and Trentham had indeed uncovered the Stone in Ireland had been one of the highlights of her career.

Pilkington had done as promised—let the story run with her by-line instead of going to her rival Kirk Luddington. But he still had not put her live on the national evening news with the on-camera interview she coveted.

All that had happened more than a month ago. Her star had shone brightly for a week or two. But none of the suspects in the theft had been apprehended. Reardon and noted druid Amairgen Cooney Dwyer were both still missing, as well as the others who had taken her captive at the druid compound before Mr. Trentham had arrived to rescue her.

And the related case—the murder of former MP and LibDem Leader Eagon Hamilton—remained unsolved. Paddy knew Luddington was working feverishly to scoop her by being the first to uncover the next big piece of the puzzle.

Paddy feared her career would be right back where it was before—stalled and going nowhere—if she didn't come up with a dramatic scoop pretty soon.

Her thoughts, as they often did, drifted to the man responsible for drawing her into all this in the first place.

Andrew Trentham, Hamilton's surprise successor to the helm of the Liberal Democratic Party, had been at home and out of touch ever since her return to London. He had telephoned two weeks ago to see how she was getting on, but their conversation had been brief.

She could hardly think of him as *Mister* Trentham now. After their harrowing experience together in Ireland and their drive back through southern Scotland to his Cumbrian home—when he had spoken so personally about his quest for his Scottish roots—she knew he would always be her friend. He was that sort of man, once he let you get to know him—warm and personal, even vulnerable in a way. She realized he sometimes had to guard that side of himself because of the public fishbowl he lived in. He had been cautious with

---

*Member of Parliament, specifically one elected to the House of Commons.

her at first too, the politician and journalist sparring with one another, each wondering what motives the other was hiding.

But all that was behind them now. Journalists weren't supposed to worry about the feelings of public figures. But she was thinking less and less like a journalist these days when it came to Andrew Trentham.

Andrew had become her friend, and she liked to think he considered her a friend as well. He would make some lucky woman a great husband someday.

Paddy allowed herself a moment of melancholy at the thought. *If only everyone could be so . . .* She shook her head to shake off the gloom and forced her thoughts in other directions. She glanced toward her coffee table, where sat the two Scottish history books Andrew had lent her, insisting that she read them.

Paddy smiled. Andrew could get anyone interested in the tales and legends of Scottish history, she thought, if they listened to him for five minutes. The ancient Picts . . . St. Columba . . . the maiden of Glencoe. According to Andrew, the men and women of Scotland's past were as alive today as ever.

And she had to admit, she had found everything she read as captivating as promised. The other day she had bought a CD, a collection of Scottish ballads drawn from the poems of Robert Burns, at the Scotch House in Knightsbridge. Every time she listened to it, the haunting, mystical music penetrated a little more deeply into her soul.

Was she being infected by the Scottish bug, as Andrew called it? Maybe he was on to something after all. What if it turned out that *she* had Scottish ancestry too!

Gradually Paddy's thoughts returned to the more pressing matters before her. Actually, she reflected, no one really knew whether the two crimes—the theft of the Stone and the murder of Hamilton—were related. But it seemed so.

One thing was clear, Paddy said to herself, if she was going to get anything, she was going to have to uncover it on her own.

FOUR

Harland Trentham rode slowly up the slopes of the Skiddaw mountain near his home on one of the prized horses of his stables, which included thoroughbreds as well as a half dozen other specialty breeds. Halfway up, he paused to gaze down upon his family home, Derwenthwaite Hall. From this height he could easily see the layout of the ancient gray stone house and stables, the treelined drive, the well-kept but unfussy gardens, the green paddocks where spring foals chased each other about. Behind the kitchen he spotted their cook bending over the wheel-shaped herb garden—a basket on her arm. Then the kitchen door opened and his wife emerged. She walked over to meet the other woman, her gait purposeful but halting. Harland watched as the two of them conversed in the sunshine—discussing dinner, no doubt.

For long minutes he sat gazing down, transfixed by the beauty and comfort of the scene. How could he have taken it all for granted for so long? he wondered. Here he was in his sixties, and thinking for the first time about so many things . . . like roots. Was his wife's stroke of a month before responsible for his new outlook? Or was it his son's sudden interest in their family's Scottish lineage? Who could say? And it didn't matter, really. Each had done its part to turn his thoughts a little more inward.

And his old friend Duncan MacRanald had certainly been influential as well. Harland had neglected his boyhood friendship with the Scots shepherd too long, and he was grateful to Andrew for helping him renew it and discover its importance.

He was proud of Andrew, thought Trentham. Not merely because of all his accomplishments, of who he was in the public eye, but because he was a young man with the right kinds of priorities, who valued the right kinds of things.

He loved his wife more now too. He had not been much of a praying man throughout most his life. But he had prayed more this last month than ever before. And the fact that Waleis was recovering more rapidly than their doctor expected had caused him to think twice about more things than just prayer.

Harland turned his head back toward the hillside before him and urged his mount on in the direction of Duncan's cottage. He had been listening to the old Scottish sheepherder's stories for several weeks now, along with Andrew, and was ready for another round. After all, if the family was indeed of Scottish extraction, as was clear, then as a branch of the ancient Gordon clan tree he ought to know more about it.

Twenty minutes later, the elder Trentham approached the stone crofter's cottage at the corner of the Derwenthwaite estate that his own father had essentially given MacRanald's father many years prior.

Duncan, who had been outside with his few sheep, saw him coming from a good distance off, and was waiting for his arrival at his cottage with a hearty greeting.

⛉   F I V E   ⛉

That same night, as Harland Trentham and Duncan MacRanald and most of the United Kingdom slept, the people of Auckland, New Zealand—half a world away and twelve hours ahead of Greenwich mean time—were gathering to cheer the arrival of King Charles III. It was the new King's first state visit to Australia and New Zealand since his coronation. Though no longer linked formally to the British Empire, New Zealanders remained loyal to the royal house that had once ruled them. Despite the chill of the southern hemisphere winter, they had turned out in droves for the processional through Newmarket.

Not everyone in the crowd, however, shared in the enthusiasm of the occasion. One man in particular, a newcomer to the city, had no interest in the motorcade, or in the King either for that matter. But the processional had overtaken him as he left his hotel for the appointment he had set up the evening before. His timing could not have been worse. Once engulfed by the throng, he had little choice but to wait it out.

Across the street, another expatriate who had arrived in the New Zealand city less than a year before observed the approaching motorcade, camera to his eye, snapping photographs in rapid succession as the entourage slowly rolled toward him. One didn't get many opportunities down here for a major piece of free-lance work, and he was trying to make the most of this one that had come his way.

⛉   S I X   ⛉

Inspector Allan Shepley of Scotland Yard sat at his desk looking for the hundredth time at the small torn piece of paper he held between his fingers.

When it was first brought to him, he thought it a breakthrough, this scrap linking the theft of the Scottish Coronation Stone to Baen Ferguson's place in Glencoe. But he had been able to pin nothing on the man. The Scottish MP had done nothing to show the slightest hint of complicity in the affair.

Still, Shepley intended to keep watching him. What could Ferguson be hiding, he asked himself for the two-dozenth time. Who else could be involved that might lead him to the missing four individuals identified by Trentham and the Rawlings woman—the druid, Dwyer, the MP, Reardon, some bloke the American woman said they called Malloy, and the blond woman known either as Blair or Fiona?

All had disappeared without a trace. Reardon and Dwyer were probably the only ones they had any chance of finding, but no one at any of the major airports, ferry terminals, ship lines, or the entrances to the Channel Tunnel had seen either of them. There was no record of their having come back into the country from Ireland. So he had nothing to go on at this point but Ferguson and this scrap of paper.

In his gut, Shepley was sure that high-ups were involved—even higher than Ferguson himself. Whether they represented the Scottish Nationalists, Irish interests, or some other point of view, he didn't know.

He leaned back and exhaled slowly, more puzzled than ever over this high-profile case. The stolen Stone had been recovered—thanks to Andrew Trentham and his reporter friend. But although no positive links existed between the theft and Hamilton's murder, he *knew* they were somehow connected. He was almost as certain that Ferguson knew more than he was telling. In this business you had to trust your gut instincts, and that's what his were telling him.

Meanwhile, Prime Minister Richard Barraclough was badgering him for some kind of progress, if not closure, on the matter.

But as yet, Shepley had to admit, he had nothing to tell him.

2

CALL OF ANCIENT ROOTS

The summer in Cumbria had been a warm one. Northern England's Lake District was inundated with its usual flood of tourists, many walkers traipsing across the dozen or more public footpaths that crisscrossed the Derwentwaite estate. But for Andrew Trentham and his parents it had been a peaceful two months, with Andrew and his father attentive to Lady Trentham's recuperation from her stroke.

As much as was possible for a member of Parliament who had been so visibly in the news of late, Andrew managed to distance himself from the frantic pace of what he referred to as "his other life." It certainly didn't take much for him to enjoy the country setting, and being at home with his father and mother.

Despite his ongoing concern about his mother's health, he marveled at the healing that had come about in their family relationships. Not many months before, he had felt the weight of his formidable mother's disapproval in every conversation. She herself had once been an MP, and the need to live up to her expectations had hung over him most of his life it seemed.

But something had changed in her since her illness—perhaps because so much had changed in him. At any rate, for the first time since his sister died, he felt comfortable and relaxed in her presence, felt her keen interest in his life as supportive rather than critical. He actually looked forward to his times at home.

He attended two or three gatherings a week throughout Cumbria as his position demanded and found such meetings with his constituency all the more enjoyable because of the knowledge that the wide spaces of Derwentwaite awaited him less than an hour away. Perhaps he enjoyed them more now too for the sense of belonging and personal roots that had made him love this place more than ever. Nor could it be denied that he was more at peace than ever in his life. For one of the first times in his thirty-eight years, he felt content with who he was and with his lot in life. Not merely content with them . . . finally thankful for them.

It felt good. He was grateful to God for the recent changes in his life, even for the pain that had been part of them.

As he crested the slope behind the house on his customary morning walk following breakfast, he glanced out northward to where Scotland lay in the distance over the Solway Firth. A similar sight on a walk not so very long ago had sent him rambling off to Duncan's cottage and had plunged him into an adventure with this ancient land called Caledonia—an adventure from which he had still not emerged.

And now, as a result of the incredible string of circumstances that had landed him at the leadership of Parliament's third largest party in a coalition government, the future of *present*-day Scotland might well rest, at least in part, on his own shoulders. For the issue of how the Scottish state would be governed and what level of self-determination would be allowed to the Scottish people was rapidly becoming a critical one in Parliament.

But he would worry about that when he returned to London. For now, his personal quest would concern itself with Scotland's ancient past, the times when Caledonia had been a free and sovereign land.

▧   T W O   ▧

Patricia Rawlings sat at the window of her Georgian flat enjoying her morning cup of coffee and reminiscing on the day, just like this one, when she had spotted Andrew Trentham walking at the base of Primrose Hill off Regent's Park and then had gone dashing off after him.

What a crazy thing to do! But in retrospect, she wasn't sorry. That had been the beginning of an adventurous series of events she wouldn't trade for anything.

She picked up her morning paper, opened it, and took a sip of coffee as she scanned the front-page headlines and photographs.

Her eyes caught sight of a photo of the King on his travels in Australia and New Zealand. Below it, the credit for the photograph jumped off the page at her.

A slow smile spread over her lips at sight of the name—a smile of pleasant nostalgia tinged with reminders of melancholy. But she didn't have long to reminisce. Suddenly her eyes shot open, and she drew the paper toward her for closer inspection.

She jumped up, flew to her desk, and within seconds returned with a magnifying glass, which she now focused three inches above the newspaper photo, squinting through the thick glass.

It only took a second or two to make up her mind. It was him all right—there could be no mistake. Bill's 350-millimeter Nikon lens had caught the face only slightly blurred in the crowd watching the motorcade.

Was it an incredible coincidence . . . or something more?

The next moment, Paddy grabbed the telephone from the reading stand beside her chair and was punching in the number she hadn't called for months but still knew from memory.

It was seven in the evening of the same day when the familiar voice answered.

"Bill . . . hello."

"Paddy!" came a surprised exclamation on the other end. "I can't believe it. I was just thinking about you."

"Well, here I am," replied Paddy. There was a brief, awkward silence on both of the lines, then she continued, "Listen, I saw your photo of the Auckland motorcade in this morning's *Times*."

"They've run it already!"

"It's there, your credit line beneath it. But listen—there's someone in the crowd I'm interested in."

"I was trying to get the King in the picture!" laughed the photographer.

"You did. It's very good. But I need to know about someone behind him that your camera caught, I assume by accident. Are you familiar with the name Larne Reardon?"

"Doesn't ring a bell."

"Deputy leader of the Liberal Democratic Party. Or *was*, I should say. He's sure to be ousted now. He was involved in the theft of the Stone of Scone—"

"I remember that. And *you* were involved too! I wanted to call, but—"

"I'll tell you all about it someday," interrupted Paddy. "In the meantime, I have reason to think he may also have been involved in the murder of Eagon Hamilton."

"Whoa!"

"So . . . what's he doing in New Zealand?"

"Haven't a clue. You're right—if my lens caught him, it was entirely by accident. I had no idea he was there, or even who he was if I had seen him."

"Do you suppose you could keep an eye on him for me, and let me know what he does?"

"Uh . . . what—you mean *spy* on him?"

"I don't know . . . something like that, I guess."

"What exactly do you suggest I do?"

"Well . . . it looks like there's a building of some kind in the photo."

"Yeah, the Auckland Towers Hotel. The motorcade was passing in front of it."

"Maybe he's staying there—could you check for me, Bill?"

"What's his name again?"

"Larne Reardon," she answered.

"Although come to think of it," Paddy added, "I doubt he's using his real name."

"I'll see what I can do. All right, but I'm no sleuth—don't expect much."

"Thank you, Bill. I appreciate it."

The line fell momentarily silent again.

"It's good to hear your voice, Paddy," Bill said after a moment.

"Thank you," she replied, a slight cooling in her tone. "But I can't go there right now."

Another pause followed.

If Paddy could have seen the look of pain on the man's face, she might have chosen to end the call differently. But he would respect her wishes, and therefore said nothing further.

"All right, then . . . that's fine. Good-bye, Paddy."

"Good-bye, Bill."

※   T H R E E   ※

As the summer passed and his mother's condition steadily improved—and without any apparent break in Scotland Yard's investigation into the Hamilton murder—Andrew's thoughts again turned toward the north. Perhaps it was time he resumed his long-planned summer tour of Scotland, which had been interrupted first by his mother's stroke and then by Paddy's frantic telephone call from Ireland.

He couldn't shake the feeling that it was important to complete his "up close and personal" exploration before the summer recess ended and he had to return to London for the fall. It would help him resolve in his own mind some of the issues he was sure to face when Commons resumed in November, especially those related to the role of Scotland's Parliament and the questions of greater Scottish autonomy that the SNP was certain to lobby for.

He was also eager to visit several sites he hoped would further his own personal search into his family's roots, as well as shed additional light on some of the historical periods he had been researching. He had already devoted much of the past eight weeks at home delving more deeply into his family's past, drawing on the wealth of information available to him in the library at Derwenthwaite, with frequent inquiries to the Society of Genealogists on Goswell Road in London.

A number of visits to Duncan MacRanald's cottage, with tea and oatcakes and a good dose of the Scotsman's stories, had whetted his appetite all the more.

"I say, Dad," he mentioned one morning at breakfast, "would you like to ride over to Duncan's with me today? I'm returning a book and want to borrow another."

"With pleasure, son . . . sounds splendid."

"Cook baked some shortbread yesterday aft . . . aft . . . afternoon," said Lady Trentham. "I'll . . . have her make up a . . . a box for Duncan for you to take . . . to him."

By ten o'clock the two men were at the stables saddling two of their favorite mounts—a light bay Danish Warmblood and a black three-year-old Furioso—and soon struck out over the hills toward Bewaldeth Crag in the warm summer morning.

"Greetings to the baith o' ye!" exclaimed Duncan MacRanald from the doorway of his stone shearing shed as they rode up twenty minutes later. A wide grin creased the granite face under the wild mop of white hair as the old sheepherder strode out to meet them, his confident gait belying his years. Behind him trotted a shaggy black-and-white border collie. She eyed the visitors with interest but did not bother to bark, for these two men were well known at the cottage.

"Good morning, Duncan," returned Mr. Trentham. "A fine day, wouldn't you say?"

" 'Tis indeed, though a wee bit warm fer my tastes. Can ye bide fer a wee drap o' tea?"

"Always, Duncan, my friend!" answered Andrew's father. "It's nearly time for elevenses anyway. And we brought shortbread, compliments of my wife." He dismounted and handed the package to the Scot while he and Andrew saw to their mounts.

"An' hoo is the dear lady?" asked Duncan, leading them inside.

"Recovering wonderfully," replied Trentham. "We still don't know how complete will be the use of her one arm, but her spirits are good."

"I'm aye glad t' hear it."

Duncan ambled to the stove and put water on to boil. In the winter, he made his tea in an iron kettle over the peat fire in the fireplace. On warm summer days such as this, he consented to use the small electric cook stove Andrew had insisted on installing—though he still refused to consider the possibility of a microwave.

"Hoo goes the readin', lad?" he said, noting the volumes Andrew had toted into the cottage.

"Fine, Duncan. I'm bringing back the book about the expansion of Christianity in Scotland in the seventh century. I'm ready to move on. But I'm growing more and more curious about something more recent."

"What's that, laddie?"

"Scottish independence . . . when was it lost?"

"If ye're still readin' in the seventh century," chuckled Duncan, "ye haena even gotten t' where Scotland's a nation at all. Dinna ferget—'twas jist tribes battlin' amongst themselves back then, the Picts an' Scots an' the rest o' them. An' noo ye're jumpin' ahead t' the loss o' oor national freedom— 'tis a bit of a leap."

"I'll read how it all began later," said Andrew. "But right now I want to know how it was lost."

"Surely ye studied yer history, lad. Dinna they teach ye aboot sich things in yer English schools?"

Andrew laughed. "I know, the Act of Union in 1707," he said, "the creation of the United Kingdom. But why . . . why did Scotland agree to join with England in the first place? What led up to it? What was the real story?"

Duncan took a seat and was quiet some moments before answering. A pensive silence settled over the cottage.

"Do ye mind," he began at length, "back when I told ye that t' unner-stan' the Scot, 'twas t' Glencoe ye maun gae?"

"I remember it well," replied Andrew. "The story of Ginevra and Bro-chan started me on all this, leading me back to the Wanderer and then forward through Scottish history on up to Columba's time."*

"In the same way," Duncan went on, "gien it's the Scot's thirst fer freedom from England ye're wantin' t' unnerstan', 'tis t' Bannockburn an' Culloden ye maun gae. There's more than four hundred years atween the twa—years o' strife atween the English and the Scots that tell the story o' liberty won and liberty lost. 'Tis what I call the ancient strife o' Caledonia."

"Bannockburn and Culloden," repeated Andrew thoughtfully.

"Ay—the beginning an' end o' Scottish freedom."

Andrew nodded. "Were Gordons involved?" he asked.

"Ay, they were," replied Duncan.

"Our own ancestors?" said Andrew, glancing toward his father, then back at Duncan.

"It wouldna surprise me," answered the Scot.

As Andrew and his father rode back across the rolling Cumbrian hillside an hour later, both were thoughtful, reflecting quietly and inwardly on Duncan's words. Little conversation passed between them.

They arrived back at the Hall and parted, each still engrossed in his own private pensive mood. Andrew slowly moved toward the stairs with the vague idea of walking up to the library to look up the two events Duncan had mentioned.

He paused at the gallery, then stopped to note once again the portrait of the kilted Highlander that had so fascinated him when he first discovered it not many months ago. He took in the stoic expression, the green-and-black Gordon tartan, then at last the name on the brass plate beneath it: *Kendrick Gordon, Earl of Cliffrose.*

Who was this man? Andrew wondered yet again. What was he like . . . what might be his relation to the Lady Gordon of his own ancestry who had migrated to Cumbria in 1866 to marry his own great-great-grandfather John Trentham? Might this very portrait have come from Scotland in that year with Lady Fayth?

For a long minute or two, Andrew continued to reflect upon the old face.

What was significant about that date beneath his name? Why did it seem familiar? Was it something Duncan had mentioned?

Andrew heard his father's footsteps ascending the stairs behind him. He turned.

"Still puzzling over the old Highlander, eh, my boy?"

---

*These stories can be found in *Caledonia: Legend of the Celtic Stone.*

Andrew nodded with a smile. "Ever since I first noticed this portrait," he said, "I've been haunted by the look in those eyes. The old fellow seems to have a story to tell, a story that mustn't be forgotten."

Harland Trentham drew alongside Andrew and paused to look up at the figure gazing silently down on them from the wall.

"I see what you mean," he said. "The eyes are unusually alive for a portrait, aren't they? As if they were trying to speak out over the centuries."

"That's it exactly, Dad," rejoined Andrew. "Do you recognize that date underneath?"

"Which one?"

"1746."

"It does have a familiar sound, now that you mention it. Something important happened then."

Andrew nodded. "But I've not been able to quite put my finger on it."

"Why don't you look it up in the *Epitome*?"

"Great idea!"

Already Andrew was off for the stairs, continuing his way up to the library on the second floor.

▧   F O U R   ▧

Paddy Rawlings, journalist and amateur private investigator, had not been expecting a return call in regard to her request quite so soon.

"Hey, Paddy, guess what?" said Bill without benefit of additional greeting the moment she answered the phone. "Your friend *is* staying at the Auckland Towers, just like you thought."

"No kidding!" replied Paddy excitedly. "How'd you find out?"

"Believe it or not, he is registered using his own name, just backwards. For some reason, on a whim as I was walking up to the counter, I thought of it. So I just asked if they had either a Mr. Reardon or a Mr. Larne registered. And the fellow replied, 'Why yes, sir. We have an R. Larne with us.' "

"Good work, Bill!" exclaimed Paddy. "And he is still there?"

"As far as I know."

"Then we've got to notify Scotland Yard—"

Paddy paused.

"No, wait," she went on. "Bill, you've got to see what he's up to first."

"What do you mean *up to*? He's just at the hotel."

"But what's he doing in Auckland?" persisted Paddy. "I've got to find out. Bill, you've got to trail him . . . follow him."

"What—you've got to be kidding! Asking if a man is registered at a hotel is one thing. Running out, hailing a taxi, and crying, 'Follow that cab!' is something else. That James Bond stuff just isn't me!"

"You can do it, Bill! Besides . . . we've got no choice. I can't just fly down there. It would take me a week or more to arrange."

"Not that I wouldn't love to see you, but even if you were here, what could you do?"

"I'd follow him and find out what he's up to."

"You're saying you could actually do that?"

"Of course. It just takes a little daring. That's how I located the Coronation Stone."

"By following Reardon?"

"All the way to Ireland. I even cut my hair and put on a disguise."

"So *you* are becoming a sleuth! I don't know, Paddy—that kind of stuff is dangerous. I'm a photographer, not a PI."

"Come on, Bill. I've *got* to know. Reardon could be the key to everything."

The line was silent for just a minute. Paddy realized she was chewing on a fingernail. Then Bill's voice came back on the line.

"Give me a night to sleep on it."

⌘   F I V E   ⌘

Andrew stood in front of several rows of books, scanning the titles on their spines. He spotted the one he had been looking for, Ploetz's *Epitome of History*, then scanned through the timeline history of dates to 1745–46. There his eyes fell on the entry "Second Jacobite Rebellion."

Of course. Now he remembered . . . the dispute over the rightful heirs to the British monarchy. Old Alisdair MacIain of Glencoe—fiercely loyal to the ancient Stewart dynasty of the early Jameses and Mary Queen of Scots—had been murdered along with most of his village both for his Jacobite sympathies and his fierce Highland independence.

Just thinking of the story sent a poignant shiver running down Andrew's back. It formed the backdrop for the first story Duncan had told him, the story that had captured his heart and piqued his interest in the story of the northlands. His own story, as he was coming to realize.

But that had been back in 1692, half a century earlier than the dates he was interested in. Then had come the Act of Union in 1707—and Andrew knew from his Eton history lessons there had been considerable bitterness in the north over that.

Did the date on the portrait mean that Kendrick Gordon had some connection to the Jacobites? Was that the year the portrait had been painted? And how did the portrait wind up here? If it had come with Lady Fayth in 1866, what was her connection to Kendrick Gordon of Cliffrose?

Andrew replaced the *Epitome* and fell to thinking. As he walked about the library he attempted to dredge up memories about the Jacobites from Duncan's tales and his school history lessons.

His recollections of the strange group were hazy. MacIain of Glencoe had been an early Scots Jacobite. But were all the Jacobites Scots? It seemed that there might have been Jacobites in France and England too. . . .

Andrew continued to scan the shelves. A minute or two later he took down another thick volume, this one entitled, *A History of Clan Gordon*. He sat down beneath the tall window in his favorite reading chair in the library, switched on the lamp beside him, opened the large book in his lap, then turned to the table of contents.

It required but a few seconds for him to locate what he wanted: "Clan Gordon and the Jacobite Rebellions."

He turned to the page indicated and immediately began to read.

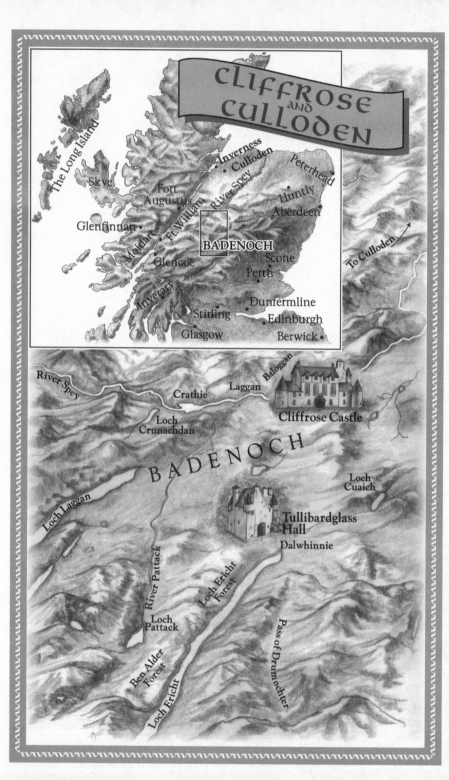

3

LEGACY OF THE KILTED HIGHLANDER

─────────── ▨ ───────────

A.D. 1746

▨   O N E   ▨

The Highlands of central Scotland, Spring 1715

A thick fog had descended during the night. The airy mist now hovered like a shroud over the land, producing a silent dripping cascade off the tip of each leaf and branch and blade of grass in the Scottish Highlands.

From every fence rail, every cow's nose, every goat's horn, every pig's tail, every sparrow's wing, and from every strand of every sheep's woolly coat the drizzle fell, for the atmosphere hung heavy with the moist dews of heaven.

A solitary woman made her way slowly through the thick morning, breathing the wet air deeply into her lungs. The dampness and the spring chill felt good on her flushed face.

Behind her, the smell of peat smoke drifted from two or three chimneys of the massive stone edifice that was her home. But no smoke could be seen. The instant it reached the cool air, all evidence of fire below disappeared as smoke and fog mingled in one filmy mass of whiteness.

That the walker was in a woman's way was obvious from her somewhat uneven gait. The fact should have made her happy. She had already carried this child months longer than any of the three she had lost before birth. She well knew this might be her only chance. The midwife Sarah MacGregor had pronounced the likelihood good for a normal delivery.

But Aileana Gordon, mistress of Cliffrose, walked with tears of apprehension rather than joy slowly falling down her weathered, stately cheeks.

She had awakened before dawn from a terrifying apparition. Her tongue was silent, not even able to scream out in the night. She started up from her bed in a cold sweat, panting heavily. Obscure images filled her with dread—claymores dripping with blood, torn bodies and red-drenched tartans lying in heaps as far as the eye could see. Even as her wide eyes stared into the blackness and she gradually came to herself, she could not rid her brain of the visions. What horror could the awful sight portend?

She eased back, gradually calming, and continued to lie for more than an hour. But sleep did not return. The deathly ghosts of her vision would not go away. Finally she rose, dressed warmly, and went out into the dawn.

She had always tended to deny the visions that sometimes came to her, considering them more a curse than a gift. Her grandmother, distantly related to Ginevra Maclain of Glencoe, though she did not know it, was said to possess the second sight, and some maintained it visited alternate generations. As a young woman, Aileana had once prayed that God would give her eyes to see what was important in life. Were the visions that sometimes came to her His answer . . . or simply a reminder of her Highland heritage, which seemed to bestow such mystical abilities in its children from time to time? She would never know.

But there was no denying that she occasionally foresaw with uncommon clarity sights that chilled her soul. She had walked through the snow to sit with Sally MacKenzie three winters ago, knowing in her heart that the woman's husband would not return from the blizzard then blanketing the Highlands. The poor man had never been seen again. And just months ago she had gone with Sarah to help with Eliza Munro's delivery, knowing that the child would be stillborn and that Eliza would need the comforting of one who had suffered a similar loss.

Women often sensed things, she told herself. Everyone had dreams. All brains spun out imaginative fancies. Her intuition was nothing to be wondered at.

She walked away from the castle, shivering not from dawn's chill but from the sight that refused to leave her mind's eye—the remote and lonely plain, wet, boggy, and cold, overspread with the silence of death.

Unconsciously her palm sought her bulging stomach as she went, as if to protect the infant within her from whatever harm life might try to bring into its path. With her other hand, large and callused, she pulled the woolen plaid more tightly around her broad and muscular shoulders.

The woman who walked alone in the morning called Aileana—whose name meant *from the green meadow*—was one whom the men and women of the region knew as Lady Gordon.

There were Forbeses on her mother's side who had risen high. One of her cousins was on his way even now to becoming one of Scotland's most influential men. But cleavage in the family fortunes had been sharp, and none of it had come to her mother.

The former Aileana MacPherson was thus no aristocrat by birth. She was the third of five children born to a poor MacPherson who took a poor Forbes woman for his wife, then raised their family in a small glen to the west. For most of her first twelve years, no tongue but ancient Gaelic had sounded in young Aileana's ears. But her intelligence had always been as remarkable as her intuition, and she had quickly picked up that unique Scots form of the English tongue which every year encroached more and more from Lowland Scotland toward the north and west. She could now speak comfortably with Highland commoner and English lord alike.

How and why a young man like Kendrick Gordon, the future earl of Cliffrose and the most handsome youth for miles, had been drawn to a peasant such as she was still a marvel to her. He had always said it was her smile that won his heart.

Even as she walked, Aileana's lips parted in a hint of that same smile, remembering their meeting on the shores of the River Spey.

———————

She had actually first seen him the day before. Aileana and several friends had been laughing together in the small marketplace in Baloggan, where they had traveled from their homes in the surrounding hills to sell their handmade items. Her back had been turned, and she had not seen him dismount and walk toward them. But as her friends stopped laughing and stared behind her, she turned, still smiling, and saw him standing in front of her small display of baskets.

Her face flushed.

"I had to see the face that went with the beautiful sound of that laughter," he said. "And now I realize that the smile is just as pretty as the sound."

She didn't know what to say, or who he was, and was relieved when he began looking over her wares.

"I would like to find something for my mother," he said, picking up first a wool basket, then a creel, both of which she had woven herself. "Hmm . . . how about this ciosan?" he went on, now picking up a round basket with flat bottom. "It looks sturdy and well made—I think she would like it."

He took out two silver coins and laid them before her.

"Oh, but, sir," she said, finally finding her voice, " 'tis far too muckle."

"I always pay a fair price, and unless I am mistaken, that basket took a great deal of time to make. Consider one of the coins for the ciosan and the other for the laughter that drew me to it."

Her face flushed again at his words. She glanced up, their eyes met briefly, then she looked away.

"Thank ye, sir," she said. "Ye're verra kind. I am sure baith oor mithers will be weel pleased."

He turned and mounted his horse, basket in hand, and rode away. The instant he was out of earshot, her two friends began chattering at once.

"Aileana, du ye ken wha it was ye were speakin' t'?"

She shook her head.

" 'Twas the earl's son," said the other. "Isna he the most handsome man ye've e'er seen!"

The next day, while she was collecting bent river grass beside the Spey for more baskets, she heard in the distance the splashing sounds of a fisherman tromping along the river's edge. She glanced toward the sound, but saw no one—the tromping came from just around a bend, where the river was lost to her sight. Maybe it had been a deer, she thought as she returned to her work.

Another few minutes went by, when suddenly another sound startled her, this time close by. She glanced up again. There stood the handsome earl's son. Recovering her momentary fright, she smiled and nodded.

"Guid day t' ye, sir," she said.

"Ah," he replied, smiling now in turn, "I hoped I would be so fortunate as to see it again."

"An' what wad that be?" she said, tilting her head in confusion.

"Your lovely smile."

She felt her face grow pink. She dropped down to cut some more grasses.

"What is that you're doing?" he asked.

"Gatherin' grasses fer oor wee baskets."

"You weave the baskets yourself?"

"Ay, me an' my mither."

"Did you make the one I bought from you in the village?"

"Ay, that I did."

"Then that makes it all the more special. My mother was very pleased with it, by the way."

"Then I am aye pleased too," she replied, venturing another look in the young man's direction.

"If you will show me what to do," he said, stooping down beside her, "I will help you. I have my own knife, and if we work together, you shall have twice the grass by day's end."

"Ye're verra kind, sir. Thank ye."

———

Now for eight years she had been his wife, mistress of Cliffrose. In those years, he had made a lady of her, and she had worked hard to be a good wife to him. In one thing only had she failed. She had not been able to give her Kendrick a son. And now that at last the time seemed at hand, she dreaded what it might mean.

She stared ahead into the mist, as if with physical senses trying to make out more detail of the impressions that had awakened her. They were good eyes that squinted into the morning fog, of light blue tinged at the edges with green, eyes that when they saw suffering tried to meet it with compassion. Even without an accompanying smile from the lips, they were eyes that would yet for many years to come cause men to pause for a second look. The visage out of which gazed the orbs of blue-green light, and which an occasional smile turned to radiance, was a mysterious face in its own way, beautiful with the beauty that increases, not fades, with age. Her beauty held the elegance of the Highlands, whose features love imbues with subtle enchantment. Faint lines of the years were becoming evident in neck, forehead, and the corners of those remarkable eyes, the severity of the climate hastening their approach by several years. But they were lines that added character and enhanced the mystery. If the thick mass of unruly light brown hair was already streaked with a strand or two of coming gray, that too, in the eyes of her husband and every Highlander for twenty miles who loved her, gave Aileana Gordon yet the more stature and dignity. They loved her for who she was—the earl's wife—and also for the peasant she had been. But they loved her most that her heart was true, and all knew it.

Even for those who dwelt in castles, however, life in the Highlands was difficult in the eighteenth century. Age seemed to advance more quickly here. Nearly as tall as her husband, Aileana was large and powerful of frame, but no ounce of fat was to be found on her. She had worked hard as a child and had continued the practice all her life.

She crested a small rise. Gradually the white morning brightened, though the river down the slope to her left and the snowy peaks in the distance behind it remained invisible even to one possessing the second sight. As she gazed into the mist, she saw mountains and water only in her imagination.

In truth, the handsome wife of the young earl of Cliffrose was not as common of ancestry as she supposed. Though she would never know it, in her veins pulsed reminders of the fierce Viking stock that had invaded and impregnated this land with its Scandinavian vigor in the tenth century. So too did her carriage bear hints of an even more ancient heritage. If the Pict inhabitants of prehistoric Caledonia were now a breed of humanity all but lost to the sight of their descent, nonetheless did their blood continue to energize the race they had founded. Aileana Gordon carried herself with an inborn stature reminiscent of those from whom she had sprung, the Pict warrioress, Deargicca, and her daughter, Turenna, who, with the man who would become her husband, had led the Pict attack to repulse the Romans from their land. The blood of these ancients, therefore, which might be detected in the pale blue of her farseeing eyes, interwove the threads of her own Celtic lineage, though faintly, with those of her husband.

She was a Celt. Had she lived in another era, she would likely have taken her place in the forgotten annals of prehistoric legend. But most of all, Aileana Gordon was woman. *This* was the day, not some age long past, when destiny had chosen for her to walk upon the earth. And she was afraid. Afraid for what bringing a son into this world at such a critical hour could mean. Was she to suffer the heartbreak of birthing a child, only to lose him to the sword?

She knew of the Queen's death. She knew of the King over the water, and what the men of her country had on their minds when they toasted his health. She sensed the direction in which the unrest was building, and the very thought filled her with dread. She was as deeply a Scot as any of them—a MacPherson and a Forbes by birth, a Gordon by marriage, a Highland Catholic by upbringing. She had longed to be a mother of one who would share her Highland blood and that of her husband and uphold their way of life. But all she could envision on this morning was the shed blood from both their legacies staining the cold and desolate moor of her waking nightmare.

This was no time to bring a son into the world.

Sons went to war. Sons spilled their blood. And no cause was worth such a legacy to a heart that longed to be a mother. Now that her dream seemed about to be fulfilled, she could not bear the thought that the nationalistic passions of her nation's men might take that dream from her.

She walked awhile longer with undefined thoughts filling her breast.

"Holy Mother," suddenly burst from her lips, "pray for me, that I might have a daughter, not a son!"

T W O

August 1715

Three months later, another walker made his way across a wide moor in the crisp sunlight of early morning.

High summer had come to the Highlands, though it would be another hour before the sun's rays altogether removed the brief night's chill from the ground. As the man went, he detected a thin wisp of white probing its way skyward in the distance, spreading out lazily as it rose above the ridge of a low range of hills bordering the moor to the north. Faintly now invaded his nostrils the singular aroma of peat burning in the hearth of the cottage toward which he was bound. His nose told him fresh peats had recently been added to the fire—sure evidence that the midwife's husband had followed his usual custom of rising early.

The walker's thoughts were interrupted by the dull sound of a horse's hooves faintly reaching his ears through the still morning.

He paused to listen. The beast and its rider were coming this way, along the road half a mile south. There could be little doubt, both from the speed and the direction, who was astride what sounded to be an enormous creature. His cousin Murdoch Sorley from nearby Tullibardglass

Hall was bound for Cliffrose Castle.

He thought a moment. His guest would wait, he decided. He would deliver his message to the cottage, then hurry back to see what had brought the viscount across so many miles this early in the day.

The man turned back to the path and continued on his way. His step was vigorous and strong, for he walked with the exhilaration of knowing his newborn son would carry his name into the next generation.

In another five minutes he approached the stone cottage. He gave the door a single rap with the thick flesh of his fist, then opened it and strode confidently in without awaiting reply.

"M'lord," cried a raspy voice the moment his foot had crossed the threshold. "I was aboot t' set oot fer the castle. Hae ye news?"

"Ay, Robert—I've a son."

" 'Tis good news ye're bringin'!" exclaimed the man with wide smile, taking two gigantic strides forward across the hard-packed earthen floor. He clasped the hand of his visitor with a grip that could break the fingers of many a Lowland aristocrat. "My hertiest congratulations, m'lord!"

"Thank you, Robert. You are the first I've told. The boy's no more than half an hour old. I brought a bottle to give you, and to have a wee dram with you."

"Ye bring honor t' my humble cottage, m'lord."

"Your own wife brought my son into the world. Drinking a toast with her husband and my friend is the least I can do. Will you drink with me?" asked the earl, withdrawing a bottle of whiskey from the large pocket of his coat, where it had rested for the journey across the moor from castle to cottage.

"Wi' pleasure, m'lord," replied the shepherd, turning to find two glasses. "We'll toast both the bairn an' his father."

"And the future of Scotland," added the earl, thinking of events that were gathering themselves about the land of his birth. Though his son was but an hour old, the earl already found himself wondering into what manner of Scotland his son would grow to become a man—a free nation again or a servile one.

Robert returned a moment later, extending two small glasses. The earl poured out generous portions of the amber brew into each, then set the bottle down on the table.

"To the future earl," said the old Highlander, holding his glass aloft, "an' to the lad's father, Kendrick Gordon, the present earl o' Cliffrose an' friend t' all, be they rich or poor."

"And to Robert MacGregor, friend to earls, be they young or old!" added Gordon.

A light chink of glass and two or three sips followed. Then came a pause. As of one accord, both men lifted their hands again, more seriously this time. As had become common practice throughout the Highlands in the past several years, one final toast had to be added.

"An' to the King o'er the water," said MacGregor.

"To James Edward," added Gordon.

The nobleman and the shepherd, friends who loved one another deeply despite the vast gulf that stood between the stations into which each had been born, now emptied the remaining contents of their glasses in two long swallows of warm satisfaction.

⬛ T H R E E ⬛

It had only been twenty-three years since the bloody massacre in the tiny Highland glen called Coe, but much had changed since then. Most significant for Scots, William of Orange—the Dutchman who had become King William III of England and had engineered the massacre at Glencoe—was dead. Enthusiasm for the Stuart dynasty he had ousted in 1688 was again gaining support throughout the Scottish Highlands. It seemed at last that Maclain's death at Glencoe might be avenged, if not with his murderer's blood, at least with vindication of the cause he had died for— the freedom of his beloved Caledonia from southern domination.

But while the hope of that liberty was perhaps more realistic now than in 1691, it would be difficult to win. For English politicians now looked to measures even more permanent than the extirpation of a Highland clan to keep the Scots in their place.

The ancient strife between the two neighbors could lead to but one inevitable conclusion: one of the two must be vanquished. To eradicate Scotland as a sovereign political entity had long been the unspoken goal of a certain political faction—mostly represented by the Whig party—in England. The most certain means, in its view, to achieve such an objective was to do away with its nationhood.

Toward just such an end had Caledonia's history inexorably been drifting for a century.

Upon the death of Elizabeth I of England in 1603, Scotland's King of twenty years, James VI, son of Mary, Queen of Scots, had been declared Elizabeth's successor. Remarkably, the King of one nation now became also the King of another. James VI was crowned James I of England. The throne of the two rival nations now rested in a single monarch—James Stuart.

Thus the situation remained for eighty-five years. When James's Catholic grandson James VII of Scotland (James II of England) fell into disfavor with the Whig-dominated Protestant English Parliament in 1688, they deposed him from the English throne in favor of William of Orange, the King's son-in-law. But the ousted monarch did not, as might have been expected, retreat north from London to carry on his Scottish monarchy in Edinburgh. Instead, he fled with his family to France. This appearance of abdication left William of Orange unopposed to declare himself King of *Scotland* as well.

The two nations remained essentially separate, and most Scots begrudgingly accepted the new monarch. But while James remained in exile in France, a small loyal following continued to look to him as Scotland's rightful King. The most ardent support for the fading Stuart dynasty—changed from the Scots *Stewart* to the French spelling of *Stuart* after Mary, Queen of Scots' upbringing in France—clustered in the predominantly Catholic Highlands. These loyalists to the ancient Scottish house of *Jacobus*, Latin for James, were known as Jacobites.

The massacre at Glencoe in 1691 had put an effective, if temporary, end to active Jacobite opposition to William III's reign. Even in the Highlands after Glencoe, resistance to the new order gradually quieted. But William's death in 1702 threw open once again the question of the rightful monarchy—and began to stir up Jacobite sentiment in Scotland once more.

Queen Anne, William's sister-in-law, immediately succeeded to the thrones in both London and Edinburgh. But she was aging and had no direct descendent. Whenever her death came, the obvious heir to both thrones would be James VII's fourteen-year-old son, James Edward, who had been living in France with his father most of his life. In the opening decade of the eighteenth century, therefore, the Stuart line seemed about to reassert its claim to both thrones. Upon the death of James VII, in fact, King Louis XIV of France publicly declared young James Edward to be James III of England.

But the young descendent of the royal Stuart line, like his father, was a Catholic. The English Parliament had ousted his father for just that reason and was no more likely to accept the son now. Instead, they looked to another branch of the royal Stuart family tree—a line descending from the firstborn daughter of James I (James VI). The present progeny of that line was a German princess, Sophia of Hanover. Her claim to the throne was less direct than that of young James Edward, having come through the female line. But her claim was legitimate and, more important, she was a *Protestant*. So it was to Germany that the Whigs of England now looked for a solution to their dilemma.

Fearing a Jacobite uprising to establish James Edward on either or both thrones, steps were taken in London to guard against a Stuart claim. The English Parliament passed an Act of Settlement, declaring that upon Anne's death the English Crown should pass *not* to James Edward but to Sophia of Hanover—now called the Electress Sophia.

Having made that declaration to insure that a Stuart Catholic would not take the English crown, English parliamentarians sought to close what they called "the back door." Regardless of what happened in England, as long as Scotland remained a separate national entity, the possibility would remain of a Stuart restoration upon *Scotland's* throne. The only true resolution, from the Whig standpoint, was a national union between England and Scotland. The *crowns* had been one since 1603. It was now time to fuse the two *nations*.

An English *coup d'état* for complete control of Scotland was now set in motion. The lead player in the scheme was, fittingly, none other than one of the most powerful men in all Scotland, head of the ancient clan that had already proved itself so accommodating to the English on so many occasions.

He was John Campbell, duke of Argyll.

❈   F O U R   ❈

Even as the two Highlanders lifted juice of the barley to their lips, back at the castle, Robert MacGregor's wife was bringing the object of their toast gently to his mother's bedside. Aileana Gordon had fallen asleep in utter exhaustion thirty minutes earlier, almost before the delivery was complete. She had only moments before begun to come awake, glancing groggily about for the midwife. Sarah now laid the child, whom she had washed and dried, into the mother's arms.

"Ye've got yersel' a muckle wee son, my lady," she said as she bent down over the bed and tucked the swaddled infant under the weary arm.

A thin gasp sounded from the mother's lips. Her pale eyes widened, seeking first the midwife. As at last she came fully to herself, she glanced to her side.

"A son! Sarah . . . is it—"

———

In the passing of an instant, a new image came into Lady Gordon's memory.

She was only six. A rider came slowly toward the cottage. She heard the approach. She crept to the window and looked outside. A stranger reined in and began talking to her mother.

Suddenly her mother's hand went to her mouth, and young Aileana heard a forlorn wail in a voice she hardly knew. Now the stranger leaned down and handed her mother a folded plaid—a tartan blanket. He reached and drew up a corner, showing that the plaid was wrapped around a Highland dirk.

Her father's dirk . . . her father's plaid!

The horseman straightened himself in the saddle and now turned and rode away. A few moments more her mother stood, then walked back toward the cottage. Her face was red, her cheeks glistening with tears.

Aileana shrank back, sensing that some awful change had come to their lives. The door slowly creaked open. Her mother entered, said nothing, only sought a chair, where she sat many long minutes holding the plaid and dirk in her lap, quietly weeping. One of Aileana's older sisters and her two younger brothers approached with eyes wide like her own.

At last the poor widow spoke. From her mouth came words that pierced young Aileana's heart as surely as had the tip of a razor-sharp *sgian-dubh* been plunged into her flesh.

"Guard yer herts, my lassies," she said in prophetic tone. "'Tis no land where women should let themselves love. 'Tis an evil land that takes its men frae its women. Sons grow an' become husbands. Husbands fight

an' dee, an' tis jist the women wha are left t' grieve . . . alone an' desolate."

———————

"Ay, my lady," came Sarah MacGregor's voice. No more than a second had passed. "He's a healthy wee bairn."

Lady Gordon turned her face away. The courage of the Pict warrioress
shrank from sight. For the present she could summon only the mother side
of her nature—and the mother in her mourned. But she could not let Sarah
see the tears falling from her eyes at what should be a joyous occasion.

After a moment she heard the midwife tiptoe from the room. She cradled the child close, reached under the blanket and offered the tiny mouth
her breast, then closed her eyes and continued to weep.

❈ F I V E ❈

Hae ye named the bairn yet, m'lord?" asked MacGregor.

"Ay, Robert," replied the earl. "It's Alexander—Sandy we'll call him."

"Sandy Gordon—'tis a braw name, m'lord. There'll be nae mistakin'
the lad fer any but a Scot."

Gordon laughed, thinking that neither would such a mistake be made
about the shepherd MacGregor.

"An' Lady Aileana—is she weel?"

"Asleep when I left," answered the earl. "Your wife came to me with
the boy and said Aileana had fallen asleep without yet laying eyes on
him."

"She'll ken soon enough, I'm thinkin'," rejoined MacGregor, "an' be
rejoicin' wi' ye, nae doobt."

Even as they spoke, the sound of a horse galloping toward the cottage
interrupted them. Both men went to the door to see a man of obvious
noble bearing dismounting from an enormous steed, the same whose thun-
dering hooves Gordon had heard earlier.

"Ho, Murdoch!" cried Gordon, "you couldn't wait for me to return to
the castle to offer me congratulations! But how did you know? I was planning to ride over to Tullibardglass as soon as—"

"I offer congratulations, my friend," interrupted the newcomer, striding forward and shaking the other's hand. "But I knew nothing of the birth until I arrived at Cliffrose."

"Then what brings you out at—"

"I fear my journey was not on account of your son," again interrupted Murdoch Sorley.

"What then?"

"Bobbing John has heard from James Edward in France. King James has called him to raise the clans."

"Has the rising come?" said Gordon, his expression suddenly grave, though there could be no mistaking the heightened pitch of excitement in his tone. Behind him, MacGregor inched closer.

"Lord Mar has summoned Scotland's nobles to a *tinchal* on the Braes of Mar. I only heard of it last evening and set out this morning to tell you. We shall both receive invitations within days."

"When is the event set?"

"Next week. The word is that we shall likely muster in Braemar and march on Perth within the month. You had better sharpen your sword too, MacGregor," Sorley added, turning to the shepherd. "The new King will need every man who is loyal to the Jacobite cause."

MacGregor would need no persuading. His eyes were already aglow for the chance to fight for the cause of the Stuart kings against the Hanoverian usurpers.

"Come, Kendrick," Sorley said, "we must return to Cliffrose. Notwithstanding the birth of your son, we have much to discuss. Time is short."

Gordon nodded, bid MacGregor farewell, then turned toward the door.

"And *your* wife, Murdoch?" he said as they walked. "Any news?"

"Feeling well, but no news. It is yet early."

"Perhaps by our return from Perth, she will have given you a son as comrade to my own bairn."

Sorley laughed and slapped Gordon affectionately on the shoulder.

"So we may hope, my friend," he replied.

"What could be better," added Gordon, "than to see our own two firstborn grow and ride and romp together over the Highlands of a Scotland again free from the tyranny of the south?"

Sorley leapt onto the back of his giant horse, then reached down with his hand and pulled his friend up behind him. The moment he felt the earl's arms clutching his midsection, he dug his heels into the horse's side. Within seconds, the two were flying back over the heathland toward the ancient stone castle of Cliffrose.

MacGregor watched the two nobles disappear, then turned back inside. The open bottle of whiskey yet stood on the table beside the two empty glasses. Thoughtfully he recapped it and then placed the bottle on the single shelf of the nearest wall.

He would not drink a drop of it until Lord Kendrick returned to visit his humble cottage again—when the two could raise a toast to James Edward Stuart on his throne in Edinburgh . . . and when all in Scotland called him their *King.*

❈ S I X ❈

In the duke of Argyll, the English had a powerful and persuasive Scottish ally. He, therefore, had traveled to Edinburgh in 1705 as Queen Anne's personal representative. His assignment had been straightforward: to set before the Scottish Parliament the advantages of entering into a treaty of union with England and thus to form a single nation.

Debate throughout Scotland on the matter had been heated—and not surprisingly, for nationhood itself was at stake. The Jacobites objected fiercely to the treaty, as did a number of other Scots who held dear the cause of Scottish independence. And yet many in the cities and Lowlands believed Campbell's claim that in the new nation Scotland and England would be equals and that the union would prove greatly to Scotland's benefit.

The chief argument in favor of union was financial. Scotland was nearly bankrupt from a tragically failed colonial venture that had taken place between 1695 and 1700 for the purpose of boosting Scotland's trading prowess in the world. The Darien Scheme, as it was known, had involved an attempt to establish a Scottish trading port on the isthmus of Panama, from which goods would be transported overland between the Atlantic and Pacific, thus effectively shrinking the distance between Europe and the Far East. Vast sums of Scottish money—by some estimates, up to half Scotland's available capital—had been invested in this scheme. But everything, along with thousands of lives, had ultimately been lost. The failure of the Darien Scheme was by some accounts the greatest single disaster in Scottish history and had reduced the country to the direst of financial straits.

Five years later, Scotland was still reeling from the repercussions of the affair, and financial confusion had provided the English just the opportunity they needed. Campbell came to Edinburgh promising a lifeline that would enable Scots to recoup their staggering losses.

The agreement offered by the Queen and the Whigs was relatively simple. Scotland would retain its own legal system and church structure—since the Scottish Reformation in the middle of the sixteenth century, the official Scots church had been Presbyterian—and would be brought into English commerce as an equal trading partner. Shareholders in the Darien Company would be recompensed in the amount of four hundred thousand pounds, paid directly out of England's coffers. In exchange, Scotland would be required to agree to only two conditions—first, to disband her Parliament and join in nationhood with England, and second, to bind herself to the Hanoverian succession for the united throne. The two countries would link together and become one nation, henceforth to be called Great Britain.

Even though the Jacobites themselves represented a minority within Scotland, however, hatred toward England in the north had long been widespread. The measure could never have hoped to pass by a vote of the people. Mustering the necessary votes in the Scottish Parliament had seemed equally doubtful. But Campbell was persuasive. And the inducement of four hundred thousand pounds was great for those who had been stung in the Darien Scheme. Moreover, those who had lost most heavily were the same men who held the strings of power and who stood to profit most from union.

In the end, money carried the day, and the measure passed. Thus by the hand of Scotland's own guardians of power was its sovereignty relinquished. Caledonia's own children, remarked one sad opponent, had dealt the country its fatal blow. The proud and ancient nation—independent since 1314—was handed over to its bitterest enemy for four hundred thousand pounds.

The Act of Union was signed in 1707 and took effect the following year. The Scottish Parliament met one final time in March of 1707, conducted some last minor business, then adjourned. Lord Seafield, the Lord Privy Seal, was heard to say, "There's ane end of ane auld sang."

The Scottish crown, the sword, and the scepter were wrapped in linen and put away in a box in Edinburgh Castle.

"We are bought and sold for English gold," the Jacobites had lamented ever since. By the time Sandy Gordon came into the world in ancient Cliffrose Castle, Scotland as a nation was no more.

❖   S E V E N   ❖

A week and a half after the birth of his son, Kendrick Gordon, earl of Cliffrose, rode with his second cousin and friend, Murdoch Sorley, viscount of Tullibardglass, southward through the Pass of Drumochter into Glen Garry. At Pitlochry they would turn east through the Atholl hills, then northward to Braemar and the site of the hunt to which they had been invited.

The Act of Union of eight years earlier had by no means ended Jacobite sentiment in the north, but it would now require rebellion, a coup, or a civil war to regain what Caledonia had given away. The once mighty land conquered by the Wanderer's grandsons, peopled by the ancient progeny of Cruithne and Fidach, held by the blood of Foltlaig and Maelchon against the Romans, and brought into the family of faith by Columba and Diorbhall-ita had become little more than the northernmost county of England. For Caledonia's proud heritage and sovereignty to be regained, a hero needed to rise up from within its ranks like the great Bruce of old.

Unfortunately, these were times when heroes were scarce. James Edward, the would-be King who commanded the loyalty of the Jacobites, was more French than Scot, and had never set foot in the land he would rule.

Yet if a time for him to claim his birthright arose, no more propitious moment could be imagined than the present—only a year before, in 1714, both Queen Anne and her cousin the Electress Sophia had died. An attempted Jacobite coup had only been prevented by the swift declaration by London's Whig government that Sophia's son would become King of England. George of Hanover, a German through and through, thus became King George I of Great Britain. Discontent with the union and offense over this obvious slap in the Stuart face had spread throughout Scotland, and Mar's correspondence with James Edward in France had been the result.

"What do you think about Argyll?" asked Sorley as they rode.

"In regard to what?" rejoined Gordon.

"I meant, do you think we might be able to convince him to throw his loyalties to the cause?"

Gordon laughed. "Are you serious, Murdoch?" he said. "John Campbell!"

"Times change. Perhaps as old friends we might be able to reason with him now that a German is on the throne."

"The duke of Argyll is your friend, Murdoch, not mine. I am no ancient and territorial Highland chief. I consider myself a tolerant and modern man. But I still consider the events of 1707 treason against Scotland, and John Campbell's role in it was, in my eyes, just as vile as that of Campbell of Glenlyon against the Glencoe MacDonalds. He will never join the Jacobite cause. If it comes to a contest, I have no doubt that he will take the government's side whatever the circumstances."

"Strong words, Kendrick," observed Sorley thoughtfully. "But Glencoe was another time. Those days are long past."

"Not so long, Murdoch," said Gordon. "Only twenty-three years."

"It might as well be a century ago, Kendrick," rejoined Sorley. "I do not think we have anything to fear from Argyll."

"The Campbells have cost us our nation," said Gordon emphatically. "Yes . . . strong words—and deservedly so."

The viscount of Tullibardglass did not reply. In the future, it would be best for him to keep his own counsel in matters having to do with his friend the duke.

The hunt in the middle of August had been called by the earl of Mar to let his allies know what was in the wind—that the moment they had been waiting for was at hand. For two days they hunted together, they feasted, and they planned. Then they departed to carry word of the impending uprising throughout the Highlands.

They would gather again in two weeks, said Mar, this time bringing the supportive clans of the Highlands with them.

EIGHT

The scene on September 6, 1715, at Castletown in Braemar, could not have offered a more colorful display of Highland regalia and pride. A hundred or more weaves of tartan had come from nearly as many separate clans and septs.

After the morning's great hunt across hills and moors, and with the pleasant aroma of roasting venison, grouse, and boar rising from several fire pits, the earl of Mar solemnly raised the old Stuart flag. This was the second hunt he had called within two weeks. The first had been for the purpose of garnering support. This second was to announce rebellion.

The symbolism of the flag raising was lost on none of those hundreds present. As the banner ascended, however, suddenly the ornamental golden ball atop the flagpole came loose and crashed to the ground.

"No harm done," cried Mar with a laugh, trying to make light of the incident, though he had been shaken by it like the rest. "Raise the standard, and may the Jacobite cause triumph!"

This time the flag rose to the top. They watched for a minute or two as it blew in the breeze, then Mar began to speak.

"We are all in agreement," he said, "that the Act of Union of 1707 was a blunder and mistake. By it Scotland's ancient liberties were delivered into the hands of the English. With my own hand I signed the act, along with many of my fellow countrymen, not realizing that English promises for equality were but disguises for servitude. We were wrong, my fellow Scots, and it is time we redressed our error. Our rightful monarch is James Edward, and I proclaim him here and now King James VIII of Scotland and King James III of England. I have been in touch with our King, and as soon as those who will gather for him can secure Scotland, he will sail from France and take his rightful place on the throne that was snatched from his father by the usurper William of Orange."

Despite his impassioned speech, however, John Erskine, sixth earl of Mar, was hardly the hero the Scots needed. Here was no William Wallace or Robert the Bruce of ancient time, no Montrose or Dundee of more recent years, or even a white-haired giant martyr like MacIain of Glencoe. Rather, Mar was chubby and lackluster, an indecisive leader. Even among his followers, he was known as "Bobbing John" for his tendency to shift political allegiances. James Edward had thus doomed the rising from the start by selecting as his general a man ill equipped to capture the imagination of Caledonia.

Only James Edward's son, it would turn out, would be capable of that.

"But he is a Catholic," objected one when Mar concluded his opening statement.

"Ay, and what of it?" objected another, a Highland Catholic himself.

"He is still our King," soothed Lord Mar, "and has assured me that he will make no attempt to force his faith on either Scotland or England."

His words were confident. Unfortunately, by this time many in Britain suspiciously viewed the Stuarts as more French and Italian than British, and James's Catholicism did nothing to dissuade them.

⊠   N I N E   ⊠

With the Highland clans behind him and armed support throughout the Highlands in excess of twelve thousand men, the earl of Mar marched south to Perth. With something less than a third of that number, he took the city without difficulty. Throughout the north, many cities and towns declared their support and their allegiance to King James. The Stuart uprising seemed well begun.

But as Kendrick Sorley had foreseen, the duke of Argyll, arguably the most powerful man in Scotland, remained loyal to King George. With two thousand government troops at Stirling, he now blocked Mar's way south to England. Though Mar could easily have overrun him with decisive action, instead he delayed at Perth. Throughout Scotland individual clan leaders led sporadic and independent battles and sieges of various towns and castles, but for weeks their leader did nothing.

Valuable time and opportunity passed. The impassioned momentum that had lit the flame of unrest so brightly at first began to slow.

And then came the word that finally stirred the earl of Mar to action. Strong government reinforcements were on their way from Holland to join Argyll. If the Jacobites did not capture Stirling before the reinforcements arrived, they would probably not take it at all. And if they failed to take Stirling, they would lose all hope of moving south and accomplishing their objective.

The quagmire of swampy lowland running west to east between the firths of Clyde and Forth essentially bisected Scotland with a line of impassable terrain. In only one spot, at the head of the Firth of Forth, could this morass be crossed. At Stirling a ridge of rock and solid ground—overlooked by the natural fortress of stone upon which its castle had been built—had allowed passage in former times to explorers, in these latter times to armies. Whoever held Stirling, therefore, controlled access to the only land bridge between north and south. It was the most strategic site in all Britain—as the earl of Mar knew all too well.

Quickly rallying his Highlanders, Mar set off with a large force in the direction of Stirling with the intent of taking town and castle before more troops could arrive. John Campbell in turn moved out from Stirling to meet him.

The two armies met on November 13 at Sheriffmuir, north of Dunblane. As he looked out on the line of hated Campbells, Maclean of Duart, a veteran of Killiecrankie, where the first blood had been shed for the Stuart cause in 1689, addressed the men of his clan. "Gentlemen," he said, "this is a day we have long wished to see. Yonder stands MacChailein Mor for King George. Here stands Maclean for King James. God bless Maclean and King James. Gentlemen . . . charge!"

The attack of Highland clans was fierce and forced Argyll to retreat. Yet this apparent victory proved indecisive, for the government troops simply fell back to Stirling and continued to hold it. The battle had been won, but no objective gained. The land bridge remained blocked, and the rebels still could not penetrate into England. Mar retreated again to Perth, where Kendrick Gordon and the viscount of Tullibardglass remained among his number.

The battle of Sheriffmuir changed nothing. The Jacobites still had no way into England. Meanwhile, the government troops from the south arrived. The force at Stirling doubled, with more soldiers on their way. Gradually the Highland Jacobites, bored from inactivity and concerned about the coming winter, drifted back into the hills. Soon government troops in Scotland outnumbered Mar's dwindling army three to one.

In the third week of November, a messenger rode into Perth from the north. He had traveled all the way from Tullibardglass Hall with an urgent message for the viscount: His wife had given premature birth to a daughter. It appeared that the tiny little girl was healthy and would live. His wife, however, was in desperate straits.

Murdoch Sorley immediately sought his cousin and showed him the hastily written message from the doctor. Within an hour, both men were on their horses riding for home.

When they arrived two days later, it was too late. Lady Sorley was dead, the infant in the hands of a nurse.

⊠   T E N   ⊠

The snows came to Scotland early as fall gave way to winter in the year 1715. Fortunately for Caledonia's wives, those snows kept Campbell's hugely increased army bottled up at Stirling. But the cold did nothing to assuage the bitter grief in the heart of Murdoch Sorley of Tullibardglass.

After spending a day at the hall following their return, doing his best to console his friend, Kendrick Gordon returned home to Cliffrose. After joyful greetings, tinged with sorrow for the devastating loss of Murdoch's wife, the earl filled Aileana in on all that had happened since he had seen her.

"The English were outnumbered to begin with," he said. "A swift decisive stroke into England, a rapid march to London . . ."

He paused and shook his head in frustration.

"I tell you, Aileana, we were so close. Stirling could have been ours. But Mar is the most indecisive man I have ever met. Sitting in Perth all that time, waiting for the government to gather its wits and catch up. Even by Sheriffmuir, had we pressed our advantage, I think we might have taken the castle. But now I fear it is too late."

"What will you do?" asked Aileana carefully.

"I don't know," replied Kendrick. "What can I do but await events? The rebellion is in other hands than mine. I can only watch . . . and hope."

Meanwhile, at Tullibardglass Hall, Murdoch Sorley was thinking not of the rebellion, but of the bitter turn his life had suddenly taken. His grief gradually turned dark, hard, malicious.

As he sat for hour upon hour, whiskey glass in hand and bottle on the table beside him, the viscount of Tullibardglass fell to brooding caustically on the very different ways fortune had treated his cousin Gordon and himself.

Both had longed for sons to carry on their legacies. And Kendrick had been granted his wish with a son who was healthy and well. But not only had the viscount been given no son, he had been deprived the chance of ever having one! Now his wife was dead, along with the one thing he had hoped for above all else.

If only she had given me a son! he thought, cursing inwardly at the irony of it. At least then his life might go on with some purpose. But a shriveled, red, smelly little creature who would probably not live through the month. . . !

The introspective depression deepened. He sat for long hours in darkness, speaking hardly a word, drinking more and more heavily as the winter's cold closed in around his soul.

Occasionally the nurse ventured near with tentative step, asking if he would like, perhaps, to hold his daughter. A look of disgust and a shaking of the head was his only response.

Gradually he began to resent the whole Jacobite cause as responsible for his wife's death. Surely, he thought, had he not been away, he might have done something to prevent it. With such thoughts increased the silent creeping resentment of his cousin, who still possessed what he should now be enjoying—a wife and family, an heir to his name, a warm hearth. What a bitter Christmas this would be!

Had their mutual great-grandmother's *blessing* come to Kendrick and her *curse* fallen upon him? wondered Sorley, meditating on the possibility with another sustaining swallow of whiskey. Now that he thought of it, an incident came to mind when the two boys had been standing before some old man ancient beyond years—was it his own grandfather or Kendrick's? . . . he couldn't recall—with Kendrick receiving a kindly pat on the head while some harsh word was dished out to him.

It had always been that way, Sorley thought. Kendrick the favorite . . . his title higher . . . Cliffrose the more desirable of the two estates.

Sorley continued to brood, the resentments biting deeper and deeper, slowly consuming him.

He took another long swallow, emptying his glass and pouring it full again to the brim. What was it that his father had told him about some complication in the family finances—that Kendrick's side had originally been without land but had purchased Cliffrose? There was more to it than that—what was it? A loan with ambiguous terms . . . a lien on the property?

He had all but forgotten over the years. But now thoughts of the incident began to come back to him . . . his father's deathbed disclosure that

Cliffrose had belonged to them for centuries ... and that Kendrick's grandfather had been nothing more than a mere baron at the time he bought it ... and that the manner in which his son had risen to an earl was a suspicious affair. He possessed the original deed to Cliffrose, the old man said, though he had never pressed the claim. His son could do with it all what he wished. But he had died before divulging anything further.

He remembered it all clearly now. How could he have forgotten?

In the dark winter hours of lonely silence within the walls of Tullibard-glass Hall, Murdoch Sorley's brooding thoughts returned to his father's words. Over and over they repeated themselves in his whiskey-soaked brain, and he resented Kendrick all the more because of them.

❈   E L E V E N   ❈

In mid-December, a messenger arrived at Cliffrose with the news that James Edward was on his way from France.

Immediately the earl set out for Tullibardglass Hall.

"Let me go with you, Kendrick," said Aileana. "I haven't yet seen the little girl."

They rode to Tullibardglass that same afternoon. While Aileana sought the nurse, her husband went upstairs to find his friend and tell him the news. Tullibardglass took it disinterestedly.

"I am leaving for the north in the morning," said Gordon. "Will you join me?"

Sorley shook his head.

"It might be good for you to get away," suggested his cousin.

The words of advice grated on their listener's ears. Everything in his life had been swept away, thought Tullibardglass, and now he had to undergo the humiliation of listening to Kendrick preach at him as well!

"Perhaps," he replied, keeping his irritation to himself, "but the north coast in the middle of winter doesn't interest me. And, frankly, I've begun to lose interest in the cause."

In the nursery, Aileana gently rocked the month-old infant girl in her arms, whispering into its tiny sleeping face, wondering at the tales the infant's nurse had just passed along about the father's neglect.

"You precious dear," she said softly, little realizing that she would herself become the answer to her own prayer, "may God give you special care to make up for the loss of your mother. And may he soften your father's heart to love you as a father should. You dear, dear little girl!"

A faceful of mother's kisses and the soft words of an ancient lullaby followed, of which the baby felt nor heard none, but all of which went deeply into the mother's heart.

Thirty minutes later, Kendrick and Aileana Gordon stood at the door taking their leave of Tullibardglass Hall.

"I am sorry again, Murdoch, about Jean," said Aileana.

"Thank you, Lady Gordon."

"Your sweet little daughter is lovely."

To her final comment Sorley gave no reply.

————

James Edward, the heir to the Stuart legacy, arrived by ship at the northeastern seaport of Peterhead on December twenty-second. Kendrick Gordon, earl of Cliffrose—without his cousin Murdoch Sorley—was part of the small group of Jacobites that gathered there to meet him. By the time Gordon returned again to Cliffrose in early February, the uprising had come to an inglorious end.

"It was terrible, Aileana," Kendrick explained to his wife. "James Edward was sick and unimpressive, dour and cranky. From the moment I saw him I knew there was no chance of our prevailing. I tell you, Mar is no leader, but James Edward was even worse. I don't know how he imagined retaking his father's throne without at least some attempt to raise the spirits of his supporters. Some of the men called him old Mr. Melancholy rather than His Majesty, and I'm afraid the name is apt."

"What did you do?"

"After getting him ashore and recovered from the voyage for a day or two, we marched to Perth to join the army."

"Were there plans of an invasion?"

"I don't know. I was not admitted to the inner circle. But I can hardly imagine Mar and James planning anything. There was no leadership whatsoever. Then at the end of January the snow melted somewhat, followed by news that Argyll was advancing north from Stirling to engage us, and with a far superior force. We retreated to Aberdeen. Then suddenly Mar and James fled to France."

"What do you mean, fled?"

"They simply left without a word. I didn't know of it in advance. Neither, I think, did anyone."

"They just left the army on its own?"

Kendrick nodded. "A message from James Edward was read out to those who remained."

"What did it say?"

"Basically we were told to shift for ourselves. I immediately left for home," sighed Kendrick, "as did most of the others. If our *King* is not ready to fight to gain the throne, his supporters certainly aren't about to risk their lives."

───────

After the failure of what came to be known as "the Fifteen," the union between England and Scotland became even more unpopular in the north. Though Scotland as a nation had not exactly risen up of one accord behind James Edward, his ignominious retreat, followed by an even more heavy-handed response by Parliament toward its northern province, inflamed resentments as in days of old.

Once again, as they had done for a century, clan Campbell had chosen sides shrewdly and continued to profit by its alliance with the crown. But some of the leading Scottish nobles who had helped spearhead the rebellion found their houses and lands taken from them and titles stripped away. And Parliament went so far as to attempt to disarm the Highlands and do away with the Gaelic language. In the eyes of most English men and women, Scottish Highlanders were backward savages who would continue to rebel until they were entirely quashed. And though most Lowland Scots might have tended to agree about their northern neighbors, they bitterly resented London's condescending attitude toward the whole of Scotland, savage Highlanders and cultured Lowlanders all together. Thus pro-Jacobite, anti-Hanoverian sentiment continued to foment.

A minor Jacobite uprising flared up in 1719, this time with Spanish support. But a storm prevented most of the Spanish vessels, which carried more than five thousand troops, from landing. Those who did come ashore were easily beaten back by government forces. Yet again, the Jacobite cause seemed doomed by ill fortune and went underground.

After both the Fifteen and the Nineteen, it was clear that neither the earl of Mar nor the King over the water possessed the leadership necessary to reinstate a Stuart on the throne of Great Britain. If that time were to come, new leaders would have to arise to carry the Jacobite cause forward.

One of those new leaders would be Kendrick Gordon of Cliffrose.

❈ T W E L V E ❈

Summer 1721

The retreating sound of horses' hooves had not yet completely faded away when suddenly the playful shouts of children filled the large kitchen of Cliffrose Castle. Aileana Gordon turned from the door toward the youngsters. Her son was holding out two yard-long pieces of wood.

"Take this stick, Culodina," cried Sandy, "it will be your claymore."

"What's a claymore?" asked the girl, taking one of the sticks, but without much interest in putting it to use.

"A sword, what else? The kind the Highlanders use. Defend yourself!"

"Be careful, Sandy," said Aileana.

"He won't hurt me, Lady Gordon. Look, I'm bigger than—"

Suddenly Sandy's blunt weapon crashed against the girl's unprepared stick, nearly knocking it from her hand.

"Ouch!" she cried. "That hurt."

"I warned you to defend yourself. Lift it up again."

"Sandy, please," interposed his mother, approaching quickly before serious injury resulted. Knowing her Sandy, the next blow could land on top of their guest's unsuspecting head!

But not to be caught unaware a second time, Culodina had already grabbed her stick with both hands, not realizing that in so doing she had indeed turned it into a Scottish claymore, and hoisted it to shoulder level. A sharp whack followed against both Sandy's calves with one well-aimed blow. He yelled in pain and leapt back. He hadn't expected quite such a vigorous counterattack from a girl!

"I think that is enough sword fighting for now, Sandy," said Aileana, stepping between the two combatants. "Even the mightiest of Highlanders don't use their claymores in the kitchen."

"My father says Highlanders are savages," said Culodina.

"Your father doesn't know what he's talking about," rejoined Sandy a little angrily. His legs still stung from the blow. "We have to win our freedom back. I'm going to fight the Sassenach when I'm old enough."

He raised his pretend sword in renewed challenge.

"Why don't you and Culodina give me your claymores for now," said Sandy's mother, "then go outside and find a more gentle game. I hear some of the other boys."

"Come on, Culodina," said Sandy, throwing down his stick and dashing for the door. "We'll play Killiecrankie!"

He was outside the next instant, and his cousin followed.

Sandy's mother watched them go with a wistful look. Why did everything in this country have to revolve around battles and swords and fighting?

Soon she heard shouts from outside as Sandy and Culodina joined three or four of the sons of Cliffrose's servants and two more youngsters from Baloggan a mile away. Being son of the earl certainly did not prevent Sandy from having many lads to play with, and his parents encouraged his associations with them. If he picked up an occasional bad habit or an expression unbefitting one of noble fatherhood, mingling with the families of the region still kept him in touch with the humble roots of his maternal stock.

Aileana sighed at the sounds of pretended battle, helped the cook with cleaning up after the men's breakfast, then went outside and walked slowly away from the castle. It was a warm morning, and she knew her husband and his friends would relish the day's hunt in the forests south of Tullibardglass Hall. Kendrick had been anticipating this day for weeks. He and Murdoch had seen one another but infrequently since the rising, mostly on social occasions or at a rare hunt with other men of the region. She was glad he had this opportunity to enjoy a hunt with two or three other friends.

The children were now six. Murdoch's little Culodina had grown so much in the year since Aileana and Kendrick had last visited the Hall. It hardly seemed possible that the little girl stood nearly three inches taller than their own Sandy. But Sandy made up for the difference with his rambunctious nature.

Aileana glanced back as she walked, listening to the happy yells and cries of the children at play. Poor Culodina, she thought with a smile. It wasn't easy to be the only girl in a company of boys. But Culodina could run faster than any of them, so that should keep her safe enough from mischief for now. And tomorrow, perhaps Aileana would invite some of the village girls to the castle for Culodina to play with.

The viscount would disapprove, of course. Murdoch Sorley wasn't as eager as they to mingle with the commoners of the region. She more than half suspected the statement that had popped out of Culodina's mouth earlier about Highlanders had indeed come straight from her father.

Murdoch had changed over the past few years, Aileana thought. She knew Kendrick had noticed it too, though they never spoke of it. He was not the same man Kendrick had grown up with. In any event, the exposure to some of the local girls would be good for his daughter.

Aileana sat down on a rock as she continued distractedly to watch the youngsters in the distance. She tried so hard to dissuade Sandy from battle play. Her dream prior to his birth was ever before her. But it was no use. Fighting was in his blood, in the blood of all Scots' youths. He would never know what anguish the sight caused her, or the fears she harbored concerning his future. Sometimes it nearly broke her heart.

She sent her eyes gradually around in an arc from the northern mountains of Monadhliath down toward the two triangular glens that met at the northern end of Loch Ericht at Dalwhinnie. She strained to see if she could make out her husband and the other riders making their way along the easternmost of the two southern roads.

While she was still gazing in the distance, her thoughts were interrupted by the sound of a voice behind her.

"Why do boys always pretend to fight, Lady Gordon?"

She turned to see little Culodina standing beside her with a confused expression on her face.

"I don't know, Culodina," Aileana replied, mustering a smile out of the midst of her own similar reflections. "It is something all boys seem to do."

She reached up and took the girl's small, soft, warm hand.

"I don't like it. That's why I left."

"Neither do I, dear. But you may call me Lady Aileana if you like," she added as Culodina sat down beside her, still keeping hold of her hand, "or Aunt Aileana."

"What is an aunt?" she asked.

"An aunt means something like your parents being brothers or sisters," replied Aileana. "Your father and my husband, Lord Kendrick, are actually second cousins."

"What is a cousin?"

Aileana laughed lightly. "That means that your papa and Lord Kendrick had the same great-grandmother."

Culodina seemed to take the idea in thoughtfully, though how much she understood of the conversation was unclear.

"I wish I had a mother, Aunt Aileana," she said suddenly after a moment. "I wish I had a mother like you."

The poignant simplicity of the words sent a stab of affection into Aileana's heart. She pulled Culodina toward her, took her in her arms, kissed her, then set her down in her lap amid the folds of her dress.

"You poor dear," she said. "I will be as much a mother to you as you will let me be."

They sat awhile in contented silence. How ironic, Aileana thought, that she had once prayed for a daughter and had none, while this darling child wanted a mother but had lost hers. Perhaps they could each be for the other what neither possessed of her own.

Gradually little Culodina relaxed back and leaned her head on the mother's breast. Aileana held her in her arms, gently caressing the small head and hair with one hand, rocking slowly back and forth. Softly she began to croon an old Gaelic fairy lullaby her own mother had used many a time to soothe and calm her at the end of the day.

> *Dh'fhàg mi'n so 'na shìneadh e,*
> *'Na shìneadh e, 'na shìneadh e;*
> *Gu'n d'h'fhàg mi'n so 'na shìneadh e,*
> *'Nuair dh'fhalbh mi 'bhuàinnam braoileagan.*
> *Hòbhan, hòbhan, Goiridh òg O, Goiridh òg O, Goiridh òg O;*
> *Hòbhan, hòbhan, Goiridh òg O, Gu'n d'fhalbh mo ghaol 's gu'n*
> *d'fhàg e mi.*

Gradually Culodina's breathing slowed and deepened. The haunting Highland melody softened.

> *Fhuair mi lorg na h-eal' air an t-snàmh,*
> *Na h-eal' air an t-snàmh, na h-eal' air an t-snàmh,*
> *Gu'n d'fhuair mi lorg na h-eal' air an t-snàmh,*
> *'S cha d'fhuair mi lorg mo chóineachain.*
> *Hòbhan, hòbhan, Goiridh òg O, Goiridh òg O, Goiridh òg O;*

*Hòbhan, hòbhan, Goiridh òg O, Gu'n d'fhalbh mo ghaol 's gu'n
d'fhàg e mi.*

I left my darling lying here,
   A-lying here, a-lying here,
I left my darling lying here,
   To go and gather blueberries.
Hovan, hovan, Gorry og O, Gorry og O, Gorry og O;
Hovan, hovan, Gorry og O, I've lost my darling baby, O.

I found the track of the swan on the lake,
   The swan on the lake, the swan on the lake;
I found the track of the swan on the lake,
   But not the track of baby, O.
Hovan, hovan, Gorry og O, Gorry og O, Gorry og O;
Hovan, hovan, Gorry og O, I've lost my darling baby, O.

Aileana realized Culodina was asleep. Her voice faded. The sounds
of the distant play had now all but left her ears. She remained quiet and
still, as full of motherly love even as she felt for her own son, unable to
prevent tears of grateful contentment rising in her eyes to hold this child
in her arms.

How she loved this precious, lonely little girl!

If only she might be allowed to give her a tenth of what swelled in her
heart at this moment, it would make her a happy woman for the rest of
her days.

Later that night, after the sounds of pretended battle had faded from
young boys' lips and the cooling mists of the summer gloaming had overspread the Highlands with its subtle hues of orange and pink, Aileana
Gordon went to both children's rooms for final kisses and prayers. She
tiptoed softly into the room where she had tucked Culodina in ten
minutes before and crept to the bedside. Culodina lay just as she had left
her, staring straight up at the ceiling with eyes still wide.

"Are you ready for a hug and kiss, dear?" she said.

"Yes, Aunt Aileana," replied the girl, turning toward her with a sweet
and peaceful smile.

Aileana sat on the edge of the bed, bent down, and stretched her great
strong arms about the tiny body. Culodina leaned up from the bed and
kissed her on the mouth.

"I wish I could stay here forever," she said.

"But wouldn't you miss your papa?" said Aileana. "I know he would miss you very much."

"I am always cold at the Hall."

"Then whenever you are with us, we shall try to make you warm."

"Will you pray with me, Aunt Aileana?"

The words took Aileana by surprise. The viscount's sentiments toward Catholics were well known. Though he had always treated her with courtesy, out of respect for her husband, she strongly doubted he would want a Highland Catholic such as she praying with his daughter.

"What would your father say?" she asked.

"I won't tell him. Please pray with me, Aunt Aileana. Father never prays with me."

"All right, dear," consented Aileana. "I will say an Our Father. Surely there will be no objection to that."

She glanced down. Already Culodina's eyes were closed.

Uor fader quhilk beest in Hevin, she began, lapsing into a mingling of her childhood tongue with the Lowland speech she now used. *Hallowit weird thyne nam. Cum thyne kinrik. Be dune thyne wull as is in Hevin, sva po yerd. Uor daile breid gif us thilk day. And forleit us uor skaiths, as we forleit them quha skaith us. And leed us na intill temptatioun. Butan fre us fra evil. Amen.*

Aileana quietly made the sign of the cross upon her breast, leaned to kiss the girl again, then rose. "Good night, dear," she said softly.

"Good night, Aunt Aileana," murmured Culodina in reply.

Aileana left the room, walked down the hall, turned a corner, and entered Sandy's room. He was already nearly asleep. She sat on his bed and leaned down to embrace him. This was her favorite time, with the day behind and his boyish energy spent. Toward whatever destiny his manhood might lead him, she would treasure these precious quiet moments as long as she could.

"Did you have fun today?" she said.

"Yes, Mummy. How long will Culodina be here?"

"Until her papa is back. A few days perhaps."

"Good. I like her to be here. I pretend she is my sister."

"Do you think she might like to play something other than fighting?"

"Why?"

"Because she is a girl. Girls like other kinds of games besides fighting. Quieter games."

"Not me."

"Perhaps you could show her the rabbit warren. Girls like rabbits."

"All right. I like rabbits too. Will you sing me the lost little baby song, Mummy?"

Aileana smiled, then softly repeated the lullaby she had already sung once today, this time singing it through to its end.

Fhuair mi lorg an laoigh bhric dheirg,
  An laoigh bhric dheirg, an laoigh bhric dheirg;
Gu'n d' fhuair mi lorg an laoigh bhric dheirg,
  'S cha d'fhuair mi lorg mo chóineachain.
Hòbhan, hòbhan, Goiridh òg O, Goiridh òg O, Goiridh òg O;
Hòbhan, hòbhan, Goiridh òg O, Gu'n d'fhalbh mo ghaol 's gu'n
  d'fhàg e mi.

Fhuair mi lorg a'cheò 'sa bheinn,
  A'cheò 'sa bheinn, a'cheò 'sa bheinn;
Ged fhuair mi lorg a'cheò 'sa bheinn,
  Cha d'fhuair mi lorg mo chóineachain.
Hòbhan, hòbhan, Goiridh òg O, Goiridh òg O, Goiridh òg O;
Hòbhan, hòbhan, Goiridh òg O, Gu'n d'fhalbh mo ghaol 's gu'n
  d'fhàg e mi.

I found the track of the yellow fawn,
  The yellow fawn, the yellow fawn;
I found the track of the yellow fawn,
  But could not trace my baby, O.
Hovan, hovan, Gorry og O, Gorry og O, Gorry og O;
Hovan, hovan, Gorry og O, I've lost my darling baby, O.

I found the trail of the mountain mist,
  The mountain mist, the mountain mist;
I found the trail of the mountain mist,
  But ne'er a trace of my baby, O.
Hovan, hovan, Gorry og O, Gorry og O, Gorry og O;
Hovan, hovan, Gorry og O, I've lost my darling baby, O.

Aileana tightened her squeeze slightly, then silently prayed, "Holy Father, keep Sandy tonight, and be with his papa and Culodina's papa. Help us to sleep well. Protect Sandy, dear God. —Good night, Sandy dear," she added. "I love you."

"I love you, Mummy."

Aileana rose, stooped down to kiss the tiny mouth, then tucked him in one last time and left the room.

❈   T H I R T E E N   ❈

October 1728

King George died in 1727 and was succeeded by his son, who became George II of Great Britain.

As time passed, hostilities quieted. The majority of Scots gradually accustomed themselves to an inevitable future as a province of Great Britain, and Jacobite sentiment slowly waned. The economy of Scotland improved as well during the two-decade administration of the first British prime minister (1721–42), Sir Robert Walpole, and this further quieted insurrectionist activity. Under his ministry, though it required heavy taxation to do so, the government built roads and bridges and schools throughout the north.

During the same period, the personal fortunes of the earl of Cliffrose and the viscount of Tullibardglass were changing. They were not the same men as they had been in their youths, though only the latter was aware how great had become the difference between them.

Tullibardglass had channeled his secret resentments into ambitions after both wealth and power. His deepening association with the duke of Argyll gave him opportunities to rise high in certain English circles of which his cousin was unaware. He knew that the wave of the future lay south of the border and saw how the Campbells had prospered from alliance with the English. Certain dubious investments had forced him to sell off portions of the Tullibardglass property exactly as his grandfather had, causing him to covet his cousin's estate all the more. He had, however, managed—though it remained unclear exactly how he had done so— to obtain a small though expensive estate south of the border near Carlisle, as security in case his fortunes in Scotland suddenly shifted. With the help of a shrewd solicitor, the property was purchased in his daughter's name so as to render it untouchable should financial reversals on other fronts present themselves. His new outlook, it need hardly be said, had swayed him entirely away from past loyalty to the Jacobite cause.

Kendrick Gordon, on the other hand, had become increasingly a quiet and conscientious man, well thought of by other Jacobite nobles as a level-headed Scot whose words one did well to heed. He was viewed as an individual whose loyalty would be important if the Jacobite cause ever hoped to be rekindled at some future time.

———

It had been a quiet day at Cliffrose. Aileana Gordon sat in her favorite chair, mending a torn tartan blanket, when the sound of a horse approaching outside interrupted the silence of the morning.

The servants were busy elsewhere in the house. She went downstairs to answer the door herself.

"Culodina!" she exclaimed as she opened it.

"Hello, Aunt Aileana," replied the daughter of her husband's second cousin.

Culodina had just turned thirteen. And though she had not added so many inches as Sandy in the last several years, she had begun to grow in those subtle and mysterious ways that distinguish girls from women. Her hair had lightened almost to blond, making one wonder if she possessed more Viking blood than Aileana herself. It fell down around a face gradually defining its features into maturity—high cheekbones, well-set intelligent eyes of gray, and glistening teeth that showed themselves from time to time in a gentle smile or well-considered comment. Her demeanor had quieted. Though she was prepared to laugh if occasion presented itself, a certain sadness conveyed by the shape and expression of forehead and eyes hinted at the dreary prospects of life alone with her father at Tullibardglass Hall. That she thought about life even at such an age was evident from the way she looked at people—taking in, absorbing, reflecting on what she observed, but rarely revealing what passed through her mind.

"It is wonderful to see you," said Aileana, "but—"

She glanced behind the girl.

"I am alone, Aunt Aileana," said Culodina. "My father let me come by myself."

"All this way?"

"He rode with me as far as the road toward Crathie. He had to go south for a few days, perhaps a week. I asked if I could come visit you."

"Oh, that's delightful! I'm so glad you did. Come in, dear. Just a moment . . . I'll call Daimhin to see to your horse."

"I hoped you might help me with a dress I am trying to make," said Culodina when Aileana returned half a minute later. "Nurse helps, of course, but she . . ."

"Of course! I cannot think of anything I would enjoy more.—I will set water boiling for tea," Aileana added as they entered the kitchen. "We shall enjoy some biscuits with cream together first. Where is the dress?"

"On my horse with the things I brought," Culodina answered. She glanced about and sensed that the castle felt unusually quiet. "Where is Sandy?" she asked, a hint of shyness in her voice.

"He and his father are hunting across the river in the Glenshirra Forest."

"Oh," replied Culodina in a disappointed tone.

The conversation was briefly interrupted by the appearance of the groom at the door.

"Miss Sorley's bag, Lady Gordon."

"Thank you, Daimhin," said Aileana as she took it.

The two women, so different in age yet friends of the heart, went upstairs together, where Aileana began gathering up her mending things and putting them into a worn basket on the table, so that they might work on Culodina's dress.

"That is a curious basket, Aunt Aileana," said Culodina as she watched. "I don't remember seeing it before."

"You probably just didn't notice, dear," said Aileana. "It has been here for years. It's called a ciosan. The women of the Highlands weave them," she added with a wistful smile as she thought of her mother. "If you like it, I could show you how to make one."

"Oh, would you, Aunt Aileana? I would very much like to."

"We shall go down to the river tomorrow and gather grasses."

"Do you really know how to weave baskets, Aunt Aileana?"

Aileana smiled. "Yes, dear—I wove this very basket when I was not so much older than you. You might even say that it was this basket that made me fall in love with Sandy's father."

"How could it do that?" said Culodina, eyes brightening.

"He bought it from me in the village, to give to his mother," answered Aileana. "It was the first time we ever saw one another."

When Sandy and his father arrived home that evening, they immediately heard more feminine laughter coming from somewhere up the stairs than could be accounted for by Aileana or any of the servant women.

"By my guess, I would say we have a guest at Cliffrose," said the weary earl, glancing with curious expression toward his son.

Already Sandy was bounding up the stairs two at a time. When he entered the large sitting room on the first floor, he immediately perceived the change in Culodina since the last time he had seen her, though he did not pause to define its cause. A momentary flutter passed somewhere in the region of throat and chest. But it lasted only an instant. Then he was a boy again and she his occasional playmate. Thirteen is a very different age for a boy than for a girl. And though Culodina was halfway toward becoming a woman, Sandy had hardly yet begun the corresponding journey toward manhood.

"Culodina," he cried, running forward. "Come downstairs and see the deer I killed!"

With an inward shudder, she glanced grimacing toward Aileana, then rose and followed Sandy toward the stairs and outside.

The next morning Sandy was up at dawn. The moment Culodina made an appearance, he fairly attacked her with his enthusiastic plans for their day together, which included fishing in the River Spey and a hunt along its banks for otters or deer in the forest. Perhaps they would visit the cave on the slopes of Ben Alder or even search for the fabled great white stag of the Highlands up on the high slopes of Marg na Craige.

As much as Culodina had always enjoyed such adventures in the past, on this day they did not sound quite so inviting. She was still thinking of her dress.

✺　F O U R T E E N　✺

Meanwhile, the appointment to which Culodina's father was bound had more to do with Cliffrose than either she or Sandy's family could have imagined. Several days later and farther south, at the Campbell stronghold of Inveraray on Loch Fyne, Murdoch Sorley was engaged in private counsel with his longtime acquaintance, the duke of Argyll.

"Another rising is sure to come, Tullibardglass," John Campbell was saying. "I need eyes and ears throughout the north to detect any hint of Jacobite activity."

"There is always talk," replied Sorley. "Surely you are aware of it."

"Talk is harmless. I was referring to activity that might have potential to rouse itself into a full-fledged uprising."

"I think you will find me dependable. What do you want me to do?"

"Your friend Cliffrose has become an influential man. I seriously doubt any move will be made by the Jacobites without his knowledge. He may even be a prime mover in the affair when the time comes. I want to know what he is up to."

"Kendrick Gordon no longer confides in me."

"Then find a way to reinstate yourself in his good graces."

"Are you suggesting I spy on my cousin . . . betray my country?" said Sorley with a wry smile.

"Come, come, Tullibardglass, you've gone beyond that now. Your country is Great Britain. And as you know, those Scots who were most instrumental in effecting the union, though called traitors by the Highlanders, were heroes in London. Most were given honorary titles and fat pensions for the rest of their lives."

"So the Jacobite complaint that Scots loyalties were bought is true?" chided Sorley with pretended surprise.

"Of course. Most of 1707s ayes were secured by, shall we say, material incentive. Nearly every man who voted for the measure in the Scottish Parliament was paid to do so. I am merely suggesting that you look at matters realistically with regard to your *own* future."

Tullibardglass eyed the duke carefully. There was no mistaking Argyll's meaning.

Murdoch Sorley's jealousy with regard to his cousin had by now become all but irrational, possessing him with thoughts of getting his clutches on the Cliffrose estate. He had turned Tullibardglass Hall upside down looking for the papers his father had mentioned, but to no avail. If the documents had been stolen, they were no doubt now lying in some vault at Cliffrose to keep the truth hidden. He would find the papers once he had his hands on the place. He had already devised several schemes to install himself at Cliffrose, but had not been able to clear away the snags in each case.

Slowly Sorley began to nod.

"I thought so," smiled Campbell. "What is it that would insure your, ah . . . allegiance and confidentiality?"

"I want Cliffrose," said Sorley after another brief pause.

"That could possibly be arranged," answered Campbell. "Timing would of course be important."

"I have waited this long. I can afford to be patient."

"And your daughter?"

"I have plans for her that will keep her out of it. When the time comes, she will not be a problem."

"Then perhaps, my friend Tullibardglass, you should hope for another Jacobite rising. That may be just the thing to provide you the opportunity to gain that which you desire."

※   F I F T E E N   ※

May 1733

Four more years passed, and Sandy Gordon at last shot up and filled out, developing a man's broad shoulders and frame and muscular chest. The boyish exuberance had not left his eyes, nor had his love for hunting and battles and the out-of-doors. He would have been equally as at home on any of the mountains surrounding Cliffrose as in front of the fire in his mother's kitchen. His hair matched his name and was as thick a mane as ever graced a lion's neck. Dark blue eyes, almost black, gazed out from beneath it—eyes ever on the move, not the eyes of a scholar that paused to dwell on some thought or another, but active eyes that constantly anticipated life's next adventure.

When the invitation arrived at Cliffrose for a ball at Tullibardglass Hall to be held in honor of the birthday of King George's German wife, Caroline, Kendrick Gordon tossed it on the table and shook his head.

"I don't understand it, Aileana," he said. "What is Murdoch thinking, making so much of the fact that Argyll and Forbes of Culloden will be in attendance? Not many Highlanders in these parts would show their faces at such an affair—especially not with those two of the King's men on hand."

"Perhaps that is Murdoch's intent," suggested his wife.

"How do you mean?"

"Maybe he wants no Highlanders to come, though he feels duty bound to invite them."

"But why, Aileana?" asked the earl in frustration. "Why does he seem intent to consort with these crown lackeys? *In honor of our great and worthy King George II* . . . the invitation smacks as an insult against Scotland itself."

"Murdoch has been changing for many years," remarked Aileana.

The earl nodded. "I have noticed," he sighed, "and it disturbs me. What has come over the man, Aileana? I thought I knew him. Sometimes a word will fall from his lips that makes me think I am with a total stranger."

They were silent a few moments.

"Will you attend?" asked his wife at length, glancing toward the invitation where it still lay.

"I don't know—what if I am one of those, as you suggest, whom Murdoch felt obligated to invite but would rather stay away?"

"I cannot believe that, no matter how changed he may be."

"I suppose you are right. But I am loath to show my face to either Campbell or Forbes—with all respect to your mother. The dukes of Argyll have been more English than Scot for a century. And this present Campbell, along with your mother's nephew, the Lord Advocate, has displayed all too clearly that he is intent on pursuing a course that is anything but in Scotland's best interest."

He paused, then glanced seriously at his wife. "On the other hand," he went on, "if I refuse, Murdoch may take it as a slap in the face. He is my friend and my cousin, after all. Will you go with me?"

"If you ask me to, of course. And Duncan Forbes is my cousin, just as Murdoch is yours. What has Scotland come to when families must take sides against one another?" she added pensively.

"The invitation also includes Sandy. I wonder what he will think."

"I'm sure the politics of the situation will weigh less heavily on his mind than they do on yours," replied Aileana. "He is only seventeen."

"And will be eighteen in three months. The politics of Scotland will draw him in eventually."

Inwardly Aileana shuddered. "Nevertheless," she said, "at present I imagine he will see it as an opportunity to peruse all the young women in attendance."

Gordon laughed. "No doubt you are right. Maybe we should attend, if only for his sake. Perhaps we shall find him a wife."

"I am not quite ready for *that*," said Aileana. "Especially not the daughter of some English sympathizer. I've heard that Samantha Forbes can turn any young man's eye, and I would prefer she not set her sights on our son—he has become too handsome for his own good. On second thought, I'm not sure we *should* take Sandy with us!"

"I doubt we shall prevent his going, whatever we do!"

"Then we shall attend, if only so that I can keep a mother's eye on him!"

"You will have to release him to the world of women sometime, Aileana," laughed Gordon.

"Yes, but not a moment sooner than necessary," rejoined his wife playfully, though with more sincere intent in her tone than a stranger might have noticed. "I am a Highland mother after all."

⧉   S I X T E E N   ⧉

The event, as predicted by Aileana Gordon, was not highly attended by those with Highland sympathies. But both Forbes and Campbell had many friends who made the journey from Kingussie, Pitlochry, and Fort William, even from as far away as Inverness and Perth. Thus a good-sized crowd, mostly with, as they judged it, sophisticated Lowland sensibilities, was on hand.

Aileana had dressed in white, with a tartan shawl of a blue, green, and white pattern, accented with thin stripes of yellow, draped over her right shoulder and held in place at the shoulder and left waist with brooches of silver thistle set with amethyst stones. Her husband and son both wore black wool jackets above matching dress kilts in a darker blue, green, and yellow plaid, high woolen stockings pulled up below the knee, and silver and leather sporrans hung around their waists. Kendrick and Aileana made a stunning couple, with Sandy following and no less dashing to all the young ladies who glanced his way.

The music as they entered the ballroom at Tullibardglass Hall was certainly not Scottish in character. The small orchestra was playing a series of decidedly English minuets and hornpipes by the younger of the two Purcells. Then followed a "Trumpet Tune" and a "Saraband" of his father's. Not a harp or a bagpipe was to be seen, nor were more than a handful of kilts in evidence.

"Are you certain we are in Scotland?" Aileana whispered to her husband as she walked in beside him on his arm. "Or did we cross the border without knowing it? He's even taken down the tartan from the wall where it usually hangs, over there between the stag's head and shield and crest."

Her husband followed her nod toward the far wall and noted the change with a dark creasing of his forehead. "We had better keep our mouths shut," he answered, attempting a sardonic smile. "I can scarcely make out a single broad Scots tongue in the place. Sandy, what do you—" he began, turning to his right.

But already Sandy had left them in search of companions his own age.

A stately young woman approached with radiant smile.

"Good evening, Aunt Aileana . . . Cousin Kendrick," said Culodina, greeting them each with an embrace. "Welcome to Tullibardglass Hall."

"Hello, Culodina, you look positively radiant this evening!" said Aileana. "A new dress?"

"Yes, Aunt Aileana," Culodina replied. "I finished it just yesterday. I used some of the stitches and other ideas you showed me for the last one. Do you like it?"

"It is beautiful, Culodina dear. And so are you." She gave the viscount's daughter a warm hug, holding her a bit longer than usual perhaps. Her mother's heart could not help but go out to this poor lass, who was so obviously caught between a young girl's dreams and her father's politics.

"I concur, young lady," added Kendrick. "I know nothing about dresses, but I consider myself well qualified to comment on their contents. And the contents of the dress you are wearing would certainly attract my attention if I were twenty years younger."

A good-natured jab from his wife into his ribs followed, and he quickly added, "If I were not *already* at the side of the most beautiful woman in Scotland, that is!"

"Thank you, Cousin Kendrick," laughed Culodina.

"Have you seen Father yet?"

"We just arrived."

"He is glad you were able to come. He was afraid you might not."

"How could we not?" said the earl. "Is that not what I said, Aileana?" he added, glancing to his wife.

"Is Sandy with you?" asked Culodina.

"He was a moment ago," replied Aileana. "Then we looked up and he was gone."

"Well, I hope you have an enjoyable evening," said Culodina. "But I should mingle. Father says I must try to greet everyone and play the part of hostess. I will see you again later, I promise."

She smiled, then glided off toward more newcomers.

Before he had a chance to speak to anyone, Sandy himself had been spotted by a set of roving young eyes that looked out from the middle of a dazzling though calculating face. The figure of its owner, though youthful, had long since filled out in all the right places, and the girl knew it. By this time she had surveyed all the other available young men in the hall and found them lacking. She now began maneuvering his way.

"Hello, Sandy," said the silky voice, as he was glancing about to get his bearings.

Sandy turned to see his beautiful second cousin oozing toward him.

"Samantha—I didn't expect to see you here," said Sandy. "It is a long way down from Inverness."

"Oh, but I couldn't miss it," rejoined the girl, slipping her hand through Sandy's arm and subtly leading him away from any competitors for his attention. "It has been positively boring since I returned from London. I made Papa promise he would bring me. Dance with me, Sandy," she said, now leading him to the center of the floor.

Near the door, walking forward to greet Baron MacLeod and his wife from Skye, Culodina saw the incident out of the corner of her eye. A pang surged through her at sight of Samantha Forbes on Sandy's arm. She had hoped she might be able to dance at least once with Sandy. But if she knew Samantha, she would somehow manage to keep him to herself the whole evening. She glanced back toward Lady MacLeod, forced a smile, and tried not to think of it.

Meanwhile, from the conversation in progress to one side of the orchestra, it was clear that not everyone of anti-English sentiment had declined the viscount's invitation. Even now one Lehrin Morey of Aberfeldy, also kilt-clad and with a second drink in hand, was taking his host to task, as others on both sides gradually gathered around to listen.

"I couldn't help but notice the flag, Sorley," said Morey, a loyal Jacobite in every inch of his massive and muscular frame. He nodded toward the Union Jack on the far wall. "Isn't the Scottish flag customary as well?

And as I recall, the last time I visited Tullibardglass, the Stuart colors were flying outside."

"That was a long time ago, Morey," replied Murdoch Sorley. "Times change, and we must change with them. The era of the Stuarts is past, their cause long dead."

"Yet you once considered yourself a Jacobite, did you not, Sorley?" now asked Cameron of Spean, of more moderate views than Morey, but still an unrepentant Jacobite and sporting the red-and-green tartan of his clan.

"A youthful indiscretion, Spean," laughed the viscount. "I have come to my senses since then. It is a new era, and Scotland is the better for it."

"Unless you are a merchant of salt and malt," quipped Morey, draining the whiskey from his glass and absenting himself from the gathering momentarily in search of another.

"I too am curious about the flag, Sorley," interjected MacDonnell of Fort William. "What about our identity as Scotsmen? What about pride in our past?"

"Don't you know, there is no Scotland now, only Great Britain," commented the staunchly unionist Douglas, coming to Sorley's defense.

"Precisely why I fly the colors of the united nation," rejoined Tullibardglass.

"An uncomfortably English gathering for so far north, wouldn't you say, Gordon?" whispered Morey at the earl's side, a few paces away from the others. The talkative Highlander was returning with a new glass in his hand filled with the amber fire of the north.

"I must admit," replied the earl softly, "that I have noticed a distinct absence of the pipes at this gathering, not to mention the kilt. If I didn't know better, I would think we were in Coventry," he added with a light laugh.

"There are English sympathizers wherever you look, Gordon," whispered Morey, a little louder this time. "It's an evil pass when our bonnie land has come to this."

"It may not last forever, Lehrin. We must be patient and bide our time. We can only—"

The end of his sentence was cut off by the sudden appearance of Duncan Forbes.

"There might be some who would take your words as treason," remarked the Lord Advocate as he approached from the other side.

"Ah, Lord Culloden," said Morey effusively, lifting his glass toward Forbes and downing a healthy swallow.

"Forbes," nodded Kendrick Gordon, shaking the hand of his wife's cousin. MacDonnell, Spean, Douglas, and the few others present all now shook Forbes's hands as the two coteries intermingled.

"I would be curious to know what you were implying a moment ago, Gordon," said Forbes after a moment. "I would not like to think that my aunt's daughter has fallen in with traitors."

"Certainly I meant no treason, my lord," replied Kendrick, "only love for my homeland."

"I for one would consider treason in King George's eyes a badge of honor," said Morey. The whiskey was taking its toll on both his brain and his good sense.

"Even if it resulted in hanging?" said one Sean Lyle, a friend of Morey's who had come all the way from Edinburgh for the occasion. His tone was attempted tongue-in-cheek, though the words carried a more somber meaning than he had intended.

"The King hasn't a rope strong enough to hang Lehrin Morey of Aberfeldy!" said Morey. "And you can tell him so."

"You don't think the King would listen to me, do you, Lehrin?" laughed Lyle.

"Nevertheless, Lyle has a good point," commented Forbes. "It would be well no such words reached the court of King George."

"He wouldn't understand them, anyway," laughed Morey with derision.

"That was his father who spoke no English," said Lyle.

"That's right," added Spean. "George II claims to be a thorough Englishman." The sarcasm in his tone, though subtle, was not lost on any of those present.

"He is still a Hanoverian and a German," insisted Morey, "whatever else he is."

Now John Campbell approached and joined the discussion. But his presence did nothing to moderate Morey's remarks. If anything, Argyll's appearance further inflamed Morey's whiskey-soaked tongue.

"Are you saying a Stuart should be on the throne instead of His Majesty?" asked Campbell.

"You can hardly deny that King George is a German and we are not," interjected Lyle in hopes of keeping his friend Morey out of further trouble. "We should be ruled by one of our own kind."

"As I said earlier," added Tullibardglass, "we are one land now, not separate countries. And we are ruled by one King."

"Perhaps the nation is not as unified as the Act of Union dictates," suggested the earl of Cliffrose. "You cannot deny that there are legitimate disputes, Murdoch . . . the rightful monarchy among them."

"Here, here!" chimed in Morey, lifting his glass again. "To the King over the water!"

Spean, Lyle, MacDonnell, and a few others began to lift their glasses in response.

"We'll have no such toasts in my home, Morey," warned Tullibardglass sternly. "We have our King, and he's no Stuart."

"Come, Gordon," said Argyll with condescending tone, turning toward the earl, "the Fifteen is done with and past, the Pretender living out his years in Rome. And the Hanoverians are proving able monarchs. You and your Jacobite friends must eventually join the modern times. This is the eighteenth century."

"Some in the north find the tax increase on salt and malt excessive, Campbell," suggested Lyle.

"The King is within his rights," rejoined Argyll. "There have always been taxes. But the smuggling that has become epidemic in the cities of the north—outlaws treated as heroes, excise men as public enemies . . . the rioting—I tell you it must stop. Otherwise the King will be forced to crack down."

"As his predecessor from Orange did at Glencoe?" shot back Gordon.

The strong words pierced the atmosphere of discussion like an icy dagger and clearly annoyed the evening's host. A brief silence followed.

"He will do what he must to maintain the union," said Argyll after a moment. The threat in his tone was unmistakable.

"And with the help of men like you and Forbes, I'm sure he will succeed admirably," spat Morey. "I should have known better than to come to a den of English sympathy like this. I don't know what kind of Scot you think you are, Tullibardglass.—Gordon, Lyle, Spean, MacDonnell, MacLeod . . . good evening. To the rest I say, good riddance!"

He turned and strode angrily toward the door.

The beginning of a waltz put a fortunate end to the tense situation. A few wives approached. Kendrick looked about for Aileana, then, spotting her talking with a small group of women, excused himself and made his way across the room toward them.

⌘   S E V E N T E E N   ⌘

Would you like to dance?" Culodina heard a familiar, though deeper, voice than she remembered say behind her. She turned.

"Sandy!" she exclaimed. "I thought you were—"

She paused, embarrassed for what she had been about to say.

"With Samantha Forbes?" he grinned. "I was, but—"

He stopped and pulled her to one side. As he did he bent down close to her ear.

"I escaped when she wasn't looking!" he whispered.

Culodina snickered, though her heart fluttered at the feel of Sandy's warm breath in her hair and against her ear.

"I've been looking for you," he went on as he led her onto the floor, then slowly put his right arm around her waist and took her hand with his left. They began dancing to the music of the waltz. "But I couldn't get away," he went on. "Besides," he added with a carefree grin, "you've had people clustered around you all evening. This is the first time I've seen you alone."

"No, it's not. I've been free all the time."

"What do you mean?" said Sandy with a mischievous smile. "Everyone is talking about you. You're the belle of the ball."

"I am not!" laughed Culodina, feeling red rising from her neck into her cheeks. "It's you all the girls are whispering about."

Sandy roared, attracting more than a few glances from the other dancers.

"Culodina, now it's you who are talking nonsense!" he said, continuing to laugh.

"Why else do you think Samantha nabbed you the instant you walked in? She wanted to make sure everyone was looking at her."

"Well, now they're looking at *me*," said Sandy, "because finally I am dancing with the prettiest girl here."

Culodina glanced away, glad for the quick spin Sandy had just effected. She didn't think she could bear his eyes right now.

Not all love springs instantly into the human heart. The blossoms of some flowers are slow to reveal themselves and grow invisibly through years of tender nurturing. The youth and the maiden had known each other all their lives. But now suddenly the friendship of their youth began to take the affections of each in directions neither had expected.

The remainder of the dance, and the several that followed, were quiet. Hardly a word passed their lips, though books unwritten passed between their eyes and hearts.

Across the hall, Culodina's father took note and watched the two with concern upon his face plainly evident. The girl was growing up more rapidly than he realized.

Already irritated at Aberfeldy's unseemly display and at Sandy's father, as he supposed, for assisting the drunken Morey in making him appear the fool in front of Forbes and Argyll—whose favor the evening had been intended to curry—he grew more and more annoyed as he watched. He would put a stop to what he feared was developing before his eyes on the dance floor. Now that his former friend's sympathies were out in the open, he could not allow a closer approach between the son and his own daughter. Such an alliance could damage his chances of improving his standing in the eyes of—

"Your daughter seems to be a hit with the son of our Jacobite friend," remarked Campbell, as if he had been reading Sorley's mind.

The viscount turned quickly from his reverie to see Argyll at his side.

"Forbes tells me his daughter is outside venting her wrath at this very moment," Campbell added.

"I will put a stop to it," said Tullibardglass.

"That would be advisable. It would not be seemly for the King to hear that your daughter is on friendly terms with one so openly scornful of both King and union."

"It will be seen to, my lord Argyll."

Campbell turned and eyed the evening's host significantly.

"I must say, Tullibardglass," he said after a long moment, "whatever the ultimate outcome concerning the dispute over his estate, I hoped you would have been more successful in turning Cliffrose from his folly by now."

Sorley winced at Argyll's reproof. "To do so is my highest ambition, my lord Argyll," he said.

"It would certainly assist toward a favorable ruling by the King in the matter of the Cliffrose property," rejoined Campbell.

As they danced, over her shoulder Sandy saw Culodina's father in close counsel with Argyll. From the occasional glance in their direction, he knew they were talking about him.

He did not like the look in either man's eyes.

※   E I G H T E E N   ※

A week later Sandy Gordon called at Tullibardglass Hall.

"Hello, Swayn," he said to the manservant who answered his knock. "I am here to see Lady Culodina."

He was shown into the drawing room and left alone.

The next voice he heard was that of Culodina's father.

"So, young Gordon," he said coolly as he entered, "what brings you to Tullibardglass again so soon? Misplace something at the ball, did you?"

"I hoped to pay my respects to your daughter, sir."

"Your . . . respects? Hmm, I see. Well then, I shall certainly see she is informed that you are here."

Sorley nodded stiffly and left.

It was several minutes before Culodina appeared. Her eyes were red, and Sandy saw instantly that something was wrong.

"Would you like to go for a ride, Culodina?" he said cheerfully. "It is a wonderful day out, and—"

"Thank you, Sandy," she replied, keeping her eyes to the floor. "I am afraid I will be unable to."

"A walk, then . . . in the garden perhaps."

"I am sorry. I am really very, very busy. You must excuse me."

She turned and half ran from the room.

A moment later Swayn appeared. "I was instructed to see you to the door, sir," he said. Sandy did not argue, but followed the silent manservant outside and to his horse, whose reins the Tullibardglass groom held in his hands in the middle of the entry. Baillidh had clearly been advised that the visit would not be long enough to require oats, water, or other provision for the animal.

Bewildered, Sandy mounted and began the ride back to Cliffrose.

Ten days later, a tearful Culodina Sorley sat silently beside her father the viscount in a luxuriously appointed coach pulled by four black Holsteiners imported from King George II's breeding farms at Celle. The animals were Murdoch Sorley's pride. All Culodina knew or cared about was that they were bearing her away from her home and from the land of her birth.

That same afternoon, Sandy Gordon called again at Tullibardglass. Sufficient time had passed, he judged, for the situation, whatever it was, to have cooled. He was determined this time to speak with Culodina.

Again the door was opened by Swayn.

"Good afternoon, Swayn," said Sandy. "I have come again to see Lady Culodina."

"I am sorry, sir. She departed this morning with her father."

"Departed . . . bound where?"

"For my lord's estate in England, sir."

"England!"

"That is correct, sir."

"Why?"

"My lord did not confide his plans to me, sir. I did overhear talk that my lady Culodina is to be a lady's companion near Carlisle."

"For how long?"

"The carriage was loaded full of boxes. I was not told when to expect her again at Tullibardglass."

Stunned, Sandy Gordon turned and began a long, slow ride home, revolving many things in his mind.

※   N I N E T E E N   ※

Despite a generally improving economic outlook, there were those Scots who continued to despise the House of Hanover. King George II's German wife, Caroline, did nothing to ease these resentments when in 1736, acting as regent while her husband was in Germany, she passed a vituperative series of measures against the City of Edinburgh for hanging a condemned English officer her husband had pardoned. The measure was called the Bill of Pains and Penalties, and though in the end, through the duke of Argyll's pleading, most of its extreme penalties were not enforced, it inflamed Scottish resentments anew.

In 1739 England went to war with Spain, and in 1740 against France. Soon most of continental Europe was involved in the widening conflict, and by 1742 most of the British army was engaged on the mainland. The crown demanded ever higher taxes to fund its activities abroad. Talk began to circulate of a new Jacobite rising. With England's army committed elsewhere, there could be no more perfect time. And now the support of powerful allies, particularly France, was likely.

Indeed, as a result of the war, France was poised to invade England in 1744. If a Stuart rebellion could be mounted simultaneously, a new personality was now on the scene to lead it—none other than James Edward's magnetic, energetic, courageous son, Charles Edward, now representing a third Stuart generation since the ouster of his grandfather in 1688.

Living in Rome with his father, Prince Charles Edward had been raised in the belief that the Stuart cause was right and just and that it was only a matter of time before his family's house would fight to regain the throne that had been wrested from it now more than fifty years before. His years on the Continent, where many of the royal houses of Europe still regarded his father as rightful King in exile, had strengthened this view as he grew into adulthood.

Now, with France at war with England, that time seemed nearly at hand.

When news of the planned French invasion reached him, Prince Charles left Rome for France, determined that it now fell to him to take up his father's cause.

Meanwhile, Gordon had seen none of the family nor heard from Culodina Sorley in eleven years. Numerous letters had gone out from Cliffrose to the Sorley estate near Carlisle. But silence had been the sole reply.

Other communications, however, had proved more successful, though the letters between Paris and the Highlands had to be guarded with vigilance. Should the Stuart prince's plans become known, danger for everyone could result.

Word began to circulate that the son of the King over the water was planning to sail from France in the wake of a French invasion of England, to mount a rebellion and seize the Scottish throne on behalf of its rightful royal family. Furious messages flew back and forth in the north as the clans of the Highlands began to line up on one side or another.

Tensions mounted between England and Scotland, and again the Jacobite flame burned bright.

When Kendrick Gordon left Cliffrose with his son in August of 1744, even Aileana was not told that from Aberdeen they planned to sail for the mainland with a small contingent of Scots bound for France. When they returned a month later, both Kendrick and Sandy had met the young prince and were more confident than ever that success only awaited the right moment.

⊠   T W E N T Y   ⊠

November 1744

The clattering, bouncing sound of a large passenger coach echoed faintly along the enclosing high slopes of the Boar of Badenoch. Four wood-and-metal wheels crunched unevenly along the narrow pitted road as the weekly coach between Perth and Inverness rumbled through the Pass of Drumochter east of Glen Garry.

The rumbling of sixteen shod hooves, the snorting from fleshy lips and noses, the occasional shout and crack of whip, and the creaking of wood and straining of leather harnesses and reins gave loud and unmistakable evidence of the vehicle's approach—though along this deserted section of the road, no one seemed likely to hear.

Then suddenly a horseman appeared halfway up the slope. He sat astride a spotted gray in the midst of a thick stand of pine. As the sound came closer, at last he urged his mount forward. Within seconds he was galloping down at great speed on a bearing to intercept the carriage. A moment later appeared behind him three riders, well armed with long swords. They had come as out of nowhere and now rode down the hill out of the Dalnacardoch Forest behind their leader.

The coachman glanced up warily. The front rider displayed too noble a bearing as he lifted a hand, thought the coachman, for a thief. But one could never be certain. He reined in his team of four, hoping he was right.

Pounding hooves and slowing wheels, whinnies and stretching leather, rearing and stomping and a few shouts mingled with the dust of the road as riders, horses, and coach gradually ground to a noisy halt. The horses continued to stomp, shuffle, and snort uneasily.

More slowly now, the horseman eased his mount at a walk toward the scene.

"Gien ye intend any harm," called out the coachman, "either to the coach or my passengers, be assured that the King's—"

"No harm will come to any of you," interrupted the deep voice of the leader of the four riders. "We are expecting something. I must ask that you hand over your mail pouch."

"Ye can wait till it reaches Dalwhinnie like the muckle rest."

"I am sorry, I cannot wait. If it has not been confiscated already, it will be there. We are expecting a communication from France."

"Wha are ye, then?" asked the coachman.

"A friend of ancient Caledonia, and one loyal to her rightful King."

"Jacobites!" exclaimed the coachman.

"Say only friends of Caledonia."

"But is a new rising aboot—"

"Keep your tongue, man!" barked the rider.

"Ay, sir! Here be the mail!" he added, tossing the leather bag toward him.

———————

Inside the coach, a young woman sat with pounding heart.

She had recognized the voice. Not in eleven years had her imagination allowed her to envision that this day would come. Now as she neared her home for the first time since her father had sent her away, suddenly she heard the voice she had longed for all that time.

She could hardly dare bring her face to the window.

He sounded so old, so commanding. Perhaps it was not he at all! Or if it was, perhaps he had changed.

A thousand *what ifs* overwhelmed her brain.

What if he didn't know her . . . or didn't want to see her? What if he despised her for what she had done? What if he was married? What if he hated her because of her father?

She had not heard a word from him all that time. Perhaps he no longer even remembered.

The rider tossed the mail pouch back to the driver.

"Did ye find what ye were luikin' for, lad?"

"Ay, we did! And I thank you . . . for all Scotland!"

"Can ye tell me noo?"

"I can't say a word, driver. There are ears everywhere. Just keep your claymore at the ready if you love freedom!"

He spun his horse around and dug his heels into the great beast's flanks. Already his three companions were galloping back up the slope into Dalnacardoch.

———

At the carriage windows, the pounding in the heart of one of the three passengers had risen to thunder within her breast.

She had summoned courage to look out. But her mouth was too dry to speak.

He was starting to ride away!

She *must* know!

With trembling hand she reached for the latch, then rose from her seat. Slowly she stepped out and down to the ground.

On the box, the coachman had been about to shout a new command to his team. All at once he detected movement in the corner of his eye. He eased back on the reins.

"We're aboot to be on oor way, lass," he said, "gien ye wouldna mind stepping back inside."

She did not reply or even glance up. She gave no sign that she had heard a word. She just stood, pale and gazing after the retreating form of the rider who had caused the delay.

At last she opened her mouth and half raised a hand to beckon him. But no words would come. She remained mute as a statue.

———

Halfway to the stand of trees in which he had waited for the coach to arrive, some inner impulse caused the rider to glance back.

Why was the coach still sitting where he had left it? And why was that woman—

A chill swept through his frame.

The same instant he yanked on the reins, still looking back over his shoulder. The great horse reared, then felt the leather pulling it around. The gray mare wheeled, and within seconds was pounding back down the hill.

Still fifty yards away, the rider reined in, then leapt from his saddle and ran toward the coach. The figure beside it had found her legs and was now running toward him.

Ten yards from each other, as of one mind, both began to slow . . . then stopped.

For long seconds they stood . . . staring . . . hearts pounding . . . a hundred thoughts of doubt and eagerness fighting for supremacy . . . uncertain, surveying faces that were the same, yet which were so changed.

All the Highlands fell still and silent in waiting expectation.

At length the man's mouth slowly opened. *"Culodina . . ."* he said in tone of lingering hesitation, "is . . . is it really *you!*"

The spell was broken. Culodina rushed forward and fell into his waiting arms.

"Sandy!" she breathed, eleven years of pain and sadness swept away in an instant.

How long they stood embracing, neither knew. Nor were they conscious of the stares and whispered comments behind them from the coach.

"How . . . but what are you doing here?" said Culodina at length. "I cannot believe it!"

"I hardly recognized you," laughed Sandy.

"Nor I you. You have grown, Sandy."

"No more than you. You are a woman now . . . a lady."

"And you a man. Is what the man said true—is there going to be another Jacobite rising?"

Sandy pressed a finger to her lips.

"If I still mean anything to you, Culodina, you must promise not to breathe a word of what you have seen or heard to your father."

"Of course, Sandy. I would never dream of it. He is still in England for a few more days."

"For that I am glad. It means I shall be able to see you. I must go, Culodina," said Sandy, backing toward his horse. "But I will call soon at Tullibardglass."

"Let me come to Cliffrose, Sandy. Most of my father's servants are very loyal. I would rather you not be seen."

"At Cliffrose, then! My mother will die of joy to see you!"

※   T W E N T Y - O N E   ※

June 1745

The French invasion never came. But King Louis XV of France continued to assure Charles Stuart, not many years younger than himself, that he would have France's full backing—both money and soldiers—for a Stuart restoration.

Growing impatient, and encouraged by continued promises of French help, Charles finally decided to sail for Scotland. With or without the French fleet, he would launch his rebellion. Fate had destined him, he believed, to precipitate events. Once he began to move, support throughout England, Scotland, and France was certain to rally to his cause. There were reportedly thousands of eager Jacobites not only in Scotland, but also in Wales, Ireland, and England. After the movement was under way, he had no doubt that an army of ten or fifteen thousand would swell behind him. Then would follow an invasion by the French army, and before long the throne would be his.

Kendrick Gordon knew it was probably no use. But he had to see his old friend one more time before events began moving too fast. He had received word just the night before that the prince had sailed. This would be his last opportunity.

When he called at Tullibardglass Hall, the whole place seemed run down and lifeless. Culodina opened the door. She looked sad and tired, Kendrick thought—not at all herself. Her face immediately brightened at sight of him.

"Cousin Kendrick!" she exclaimed.

"Hello, Culodina," he said, embracing her warmly. "Is your father home?"

"He is up in his study."

Gordon thanked her and walked toward the stairs.

The familiar door stood open. He knocked lightly, then entered. His cousin stood at the far end of the room with his back turned, shoulders drooped, drink in hand, gazing out a tall window.

He turned at the sound. "Ah . . ." he nodded in greetingless acknowledgment. "What brings you so far from Cliffrose?"

"To see an old friend," replied the earl. "And it is not really so far. We used to ride it twice a day."

"Times were different. We were younger then."

"Do you remember when you rode to tell me of Mar's invitation, the day Sandy was born? Those were the days, eh, my friend!"

Resentment surged through Murdoch Sorley at the supposed gloating mention of his son. But he kept his thoughts to himself and merely nodded without returning his cousin's smile of enthusiasm. The glint of bitter envy in his eye was barely discernable, though it had grown to consume him in recent years. Kendrick's very sense of courtesy and goodness angered him.

"I recall that we spoke of our sons' riding together . . ." he said after a moment, then paused.

"Ironic, isn't it," he continued, "you have your son, but I . . ."

Again he stopped, looked away, and drained his glass.

"And you have a lovely daughter," added the earl.

Sorley made no reply. He moved to the sideboard to pour himself another whiskey, then lifted the bottle toward the earl in silent inquiry. Gordon nodded. Sorley poured out a second glass and handed it to him.

"Times of change are coming again, Murdoch," said the earl after taking a sip. His voice grew serious.

"What change?"

"You must have heard the rumors as well as I."

"About the boy prince, the Young Pretender they call him?" rejoined Sorley. "Bah—I don't believe a word of it!" In truth, he had been apprised of stirring within the Jacobite ranks in recent weeks, though had been unable to learn any details. He hoped feigning ignorance would loosen his cousin's tongue.

"There may be more truth in it than you think, Murdoch."

"Such as?" said the viscount, one eyebrow arching slightly upward.

"I only say that perhaps the reports are reliable. It may be time for you to reconsider your wavering from the cause that so stirred our blood thirty years ago."

"As I said before, times change. Scotland has changed."

"And perhaps will change again. It is not too late to rekindle your passion for the legacy of our Highland heritage."

Tullibardglass eyed him as if reflecting seriously upon his words.

"If only I could be sure," he said slowly, "that such a rekindling, as you call it, would reap the rewards of a wise choice. I must know more."

The earl thought for a moment, then replied. "Murdoch," he said seriously, "Prince Charles has sailed from France."

Sorley took in the words with affected astonishment.

"He is actually bound for Scotland!"

"The Stuart restoration is coming, my friend," Gordon continued. "I do not want to see you dispossessed along with those who sided with Argyll and the Hanoverians. It is not too late."

"Where is he set to land?"

"There is no word yet. Probably somewhere in the Hebrides."

"And when?"

"That I do not know either."

Tullibardglass nodded with interest. "Hmm . . . perhaps you are right," he said. "I would not want the new King Charles to hear I had not toasted his success at the critical moment."

"Shall we then toast the cause together," suggested the earl, "as we did of old?"

Sorley nodded, raising his glass toward his cousin. "To the King over the water," he said.

"To the prince *on* the water," added the earl.

The next morning Murdoch Sorley was on his way to Inveraray—vowing during the entire ride that he would get the best of his condescending cousin in the end—to tell the duke of Argyll what he had learned.

※   T W E N T Y - T W O   ※

Sandy will be thirty later this summer," said Aileana Gordon to her husband a week or two after his return from Tullibardglass. "I would like to have a portrait painted."

"Of Sandy?" asked the earl. He began to laugh as Aileana nodded.

"Envisioning him sitting for a portrait," said Kendrick, "stretches my brain beyond what it can bear! How will the thing ever be done? He could never sit still long enough."

"That is where you come in, my dear husband," answered Aileana with a smile. "I thought you and I would sit first, then present him with our portraits on his birthday. He will not be able to deny my request then."

"You are a shrewd one. And your scheme also puts *me* in front of the painter's eye, a position I will relish no more than Sandy."

"But you will do it for me, will you not, Kendrick?"

"For you, my dear—of course. But is not one portrait of me enough?"

"The one in the hall downstairs is twenty years old. You are much more handsome and distinguished now, with your head half gray and your wise eyes gazing out from under it."

Kendrick roared. "You have a most cunning tongue!"

"And the previous one is but from the waist up. I would like to see a full portrait in the kilt."

"Ah, I see it now—you would make a thorough Highlander of me for all posterity to see! Well, my dear, to make you happy, and if by it we might contrive also to get our son's face on canvas, I will don the kilt, sporran, and dirk and consent to your plan. When do you propose this project to begin?"

"I have a painter coming to Cliffrose tomorrow," answered Aileana.

He roared again. "How did you know I would consent?"

She only smiled in reply.

"And he will begin with you, no doubt?"

"Oh no," she said. "*You* are head of this family—he will begin with you."

※   T W E N T Y - T H R E E   ※

August 1745

As Kendrick Gordon, earl of Cliffrose, rode away from the castle with his son, Sandy, tears filled the eyes of their wife and mother. Were her worst fears about to be realized? wondered Aileana as she watched them disappear northward through the glen toward Newtonmore.

How well she remembered that season exactly thirty years ago when she had carried Sandy in her womb. The spring of the dream, the summer of Mar's failed uprising.

Now the men of the Highlands were at it again. Her husband was too old to fight, and her son was in the prime of his youthful manhood. What did it matter who was King? Women needed their sons alive!

Hardly thinking, she fingered the smooth beads of the rosary at her waist, breathing a prayer for protection.

She did not think she could bear it if she lost him!

She turned and walked slowly back inside, the weight of a woman's worst fears bearing heavily upon her. She was less than three years away from sixty. Age had stolen upon her gracefully, as it did not to many of this region. The lines around her mouth and eyes had deepened, and her full head of hair showed but a few strands of fading light brown among the gray. But her eyes shone with even more luminescence than before for what the years had taught her.

The beauty of Aileana Gordon was that of inner character made strong by life, not bitter by it. Her peasant roots made her heart soft, but her noble marriage brought out character fashioned into grace by her faith in God. In spite of the secret anxieties she had never even shared with her husband, she was a woman at peace with herself and her place in the world. Could she script the remaining years of her life, the story she would write would be one of growing old with husband and son, and enjoying grandsons and granddaughters in abundance at her knee, singing lullabies to them as she had for her own Sandy.

But if such things were not to be, she *would* bear it. Well she knew that it is not given to mortals to write the stories of their own lives. Life *had* to be borne.

The next day, as if in response to the sudden loneliness within the castle's desolate walls, Culodina appeared at Cliffrose. No angel's visitation could have been more timely. At sight of her, Aileana broke into tears.

"Aunt Aileana . . . what is it?" said Culodina.

"Oh, Culodina . . . they're gone!"

"Gone . . . gone where?"

"There is word that Prince Charles Edward has arrived from France."

"He has really come?"

"Kendrick received word that he had landed in the Hebrides and was on his way to the mainland. He and Sandy left almost immediately."

"For where?"

"They have gone to Glenfinnan, where the MacDonalds are awaiting the prince. Word has been sent out to the rest of the Gordons too, and Kendrick and Sandy will meet them there to muster."

"When will they be back?"

"I don't know. Oh, Culodina . . . I am afraid!"

It did not occur to Aileana that the portrait of her husband was still unfinished until Monsieur Beauvelais arrived the next day for a session with the earl.

"Oh no!" she gasped, drawing in a breath when she saw him at the door. "I'd completely forgotten."

"Forgotten what, Madame?" he asked, puzzled.

"About the portrait. I am afraid the earl is gone."

"For how long, madame?"

"I don't know when I will see him again. Oh, and I had so wanted one of Sandy!"

She began to cry at the horrid realization that the opportunity now might never come.

"As for Monsieur Sandy," said the painter, "I am afraid I must await his return. But have no fear regarding your husband's portrait, Madame Gordon. The face is nearly done. If you will allow me the liberty of continuing to work in his absence, I shall be able to complete it most satisfactorily."

TWENTY-FOUR

Fall 1745–Winter 1746

With a mere seven companions, Prince Charles Edward Stuart landed on mainland Scotland on July 26, 1745. They came ashore at Moidart, directly west of Fort William.

Initial enthusiasm for the prince's cause, even in the Highlands where Jacobite support had always been strongest, proved now almost nonexistent. Assuming the country would welcome its rightful King, the twenty-five-year-old prince found to his astonishment that not only had French support all but vanished, so too, to a great extent, had that of Highland

Scotland. The Act of Union was by now thirty years old. Scotland on the whole had accustomed itself to the new regime of a Great Britain ruled by the Hanoverian dynasty. And after a difficult decade or two, by now the Union's economic benefits to Scotland had begun to trickle northward. No one in the Lowlands, and few in the Highlands, was eager to wage war for a cause whose purpose had faded with the years.

None realized, however, the power of the young prince's charm to capture the imaginations and stir the hearts of a nation.

Weeks before, Prince Charles had first landed in the western isles. As he was in Clanranald territory, he had sent for the highest MacDonald in the region, who promptly told the prince to go home.

"I *am* come home, sir," Charles replied. "My faithful Highlanders will stand by me."

Now on the mainland, Prince Charles sought the backing of the powerful head of Clan Cameron, Donald of Lochiel.

Lochiel, like Clanranald, was against an uprising.

"Put your objections in writing," warned his brother, who knew of the young man's dynamic magnetism. "If this prince once sets his eyes upon you, he will make you do whatever he pleases."

Lochiel, however, set up a private meeting with Prince Charles. He voiced his objections sternly, criticizing Charles for sailing without actual French support, and suggesting that he return to France to arrange a properly funded, supported, and armed invasion.

"In a few days," replied the prince, "with the few friends I have, I will erect the royal standard and proclaim to the people of Britain that Charles Stuart is come over to claim the crown of his ancestors, to win it or perish in the attempt. I have been brought up since the day of my birth to believe that our cause is right, indeed divinely ordained. He who calls himself the King in London is a usurper. I *must* pursue the Stuart cause. My father has often told me that Lochiel was our staunchest friend in the Highlands. However, he may stay at home and learn from the papers the fate of his prince."

Charles's persuasive gifts won the day. Cameron of Lochiel sighed and shook his head.

"No," he said after a moment, "I shall share the fate of my prince, and so shall every man of my clan over whom nature or fortune has given me power."

Quickly word of Lochiel's promise of support spread to other clans throughout the Highlands. Within weeks the handsome young Stuart heir was well on his way to the stature of legend which would thereafter follow his name.

On August 19, at Glenfinnan on Loch Shiel, fourteen miles west of Fort William, in front of nine hundred assembled Camerons and Mac-Donalds, Prince Charles Edward Stuart raised the red-and-white silk flag of the House of Stuart and proclaimed his father, James Edward, King of Scotland and himself regent in his father's place.

The Jacobite uprising that would become known as the "Forty-Five" had begun.

Word of the event quickly reached Edinburgh and London. In London, King George II immediately offered a reward of thirty thousand pounds to anyone who would "seize and secure the said son of the said Pretender, so that he may be brought to justice." In Edinburgh, the commander in chief for Scotland, Sir John Cope, roused his army and marched north out of the city toward the Highlands, prepared for battle.

By now, more clans had arrived at Glenfinnan—including a contingent of Gordons that included Lord Kendrick and his son Sandy—and twelve hundred to fifteen hundred men had rallied behind the prince.

In the beginning they were supporting the cause of the Stuart monarchy. As the weeks passed, however, the newly gathered army grew devoted to the prince himself. Slight of build and boyish in countenance, he nevertheless walked with a soldier's long stride and an irresistible enthusiasm. Though his bearing was habitually aristocratic, his manner was unpretentious and down to earth. He loved to spend time with the troops, and was always ready with a question, a pat on the back, or a word of encouragement.

Before long, the men in Charles's army were writing home with words of praise for their "Bonnie Prince," and more Jacobites arrived by the day to swell his ranks.

It was with this growing army that the young prince moved into Corrieyairack Pass to encounter Cope. The English commander, however, realizing that the mountain pass would not suit his straight-line battle tactics, turned north to Inverness. Suddenly the whole interior of the country was undefended, and a straight road all the way past Stirling to Edinburgh lay open to the Highlanders.

"Will we actually move down into England?" Sandy asked his father one evening while they sat together beside their cook fire.

"If our objective is to restore the rightful King," his father answered, wrapping his plaid more tightly around his shoulders to ward off the evening chill, "that is where we must go. And it is not really so far, once we get to Edinburgh."

"It is hard to imagine," Sandy mused, "taking London. I've never even been to Edinburgh!"

"We'll be there," added a Gordon cousin who was sharing their fire. "If anyone can do it, our Bonnie Prince can."

"Ay, he's a braw one," answered his father. "And well-enough trained in the art of war. But I am a bit concerned about who has his ear these days. Murray's a good man, but some of the others, I'm not so sure of. I hope he stays his course and won't be led astray."

"Ach, don't worry," scolded the cousin. "Our King will have his throne."

———————

They marched through Atholl, took Perth and Stirling, easily routing what small opposition they encountered, and on September seventeenth entered Edinburgh still unopposed. By the following morning, Prince Charles was in control of the city and had proclaimed his father King James VIII. The Jacobite army by now had grown to twenty-five hundred.

But Cope, meanwhile, had marched from Inverness to Aberdeen, then sailed south and landed in Dunbar with twenty-five hundred men of his own. Calling the prince's troops "a parcel of rabble, a small number of Highlanders, a parcel of brutes," he approached Edinburgh on the twentieth.

The prince led his troops out of the capital in the early hours after midnight on the morning of September twenty-first, moving silently in a thick mist, which hid them from view until they were nearly upon Cope's easily visible red-coated army at Prestonpans.

The attack, when it came, was so sudden and ferocious that it sent panic as well as destruction into the English ranks. The screaming Highland charge came clan by clan, unit by unit, led by the various chiefs and urged on by the deafening skirls of bagpipe and drum. It was the only tactic that had proved capable anywhere of routing the orderly red lines of the British infantry. Coming from all directions—down hills, from out of hollows, and behind trees—the wild charge rendered both muskets and bayonets impotent. The Highlanders flew forward with bull-hide shields in the left hand to absorb the first thrust of bayonet. The rifle-knives were brushed or wrenched aside by the shield at the same moment that great Highland broadswords cut down their owners from the right. It was a devastating strategy that few English armies had successfully repulsed.

With shield on the left arm and dirk clutched in the left fist, the clansmen now ran three-deep into the midst of Cope's surprised force, firing what muskets they possessed with right arms, those without guns wielding great basket-hilted broadswords or claymores.

The onslaught was terrifying and brutal. Cope's lines were shattered in eight minutes. He never had the chance to use his artillery. His ranks fled or surrendered, and the cavalry units known as Dragoons retreated all the way across the border to Berwick, Cope with them.

In the first decisive battle of the campaign, Prince Charles and his strategists—and the Highland army itself—had won a stunning victory. Now indeed did King George II in London begin to tremble, realizing for the first time that his throne was seriously threatened. Quickly he began recalling troops from the mainland to bolster his army and placed them under the command of his son, William Augustus, duke of Cumberland.

The initial success of the Highland rebels brought in more clan leaders from throughout the north, and the momentum of the uprising continued to mount. But rather than strike quickly on the heels of the victory at Prestonpans, Charles delayed for six weeks, hoping for more reinforcements. Meanwhile, he was treated as a conquering hero, and the city of Edinburgh was his. Unfortunately, the delay also allowed King George to regroup and field a sizeable army at Newcastle under Field Marshall Wade.

In early November, with five thousand foot soldiers and six hundred cavalrymen—Kendrick and Sandy Gordon among them—Prince Charles led his army across the English border and marched south. The prince wanted to engage General Wade at Newcastle. But his lieutenant general, Lord George Murray, argued against it, urging that they move west instead by way of Carlisle. Entering England through the west, he reasoned, would help rally Welsh and English Jacobites to the cause before significant fighting occurred. Charles finally agreed.

Success continued to follow the Jacobites, although the expected support from England and Wales did not materialize. The army grew in size by dozens and hundreds, not by thousands.

As it turned out, many English Jacobites who enjoyed drinking toasts to "the King over the water" were reluctant actually to shoulder arms for the cause of a Stuart Restoration. The same could be said within Scotland herself. Had every available man throughout the north rallied to the prince's cause, his army might have been thirty to forty thousand strong—easily enough to regain the throne. His army of a mere five thousand showed how little practical support the cause actually had.

Nevertheless, the city of Carlisle surrendered on November 15, and Charles entered triumphantly on a white charger preceded by a hundred bagpipes. They took Manchester on November 28 and continued south. Finally, by December 4, the Jacobite army had reached Derby. London lay only 130 miles away.

Prince Charles now anticipated victory. His army had been almost unopposed all the way from Scotland. London itself was in a panic. Word had spread south that the Highlanders were savages and cannibals. The very word *Highlander* seized the London heart with no less fear than the words *Chippewa, Creek,* or *Crow* would present to American colonialists who heard that New York was under siege and every citizen in danger of losing his scalp. London shops closed, and a run on the Bank of England began. George II made contingency plans for an escape to Hanover, and the royal jewels were packed up to accompany him.

Charles was ready to strike the decisive blow at the very heart of the capital. But Lord George Murray saw disquieting signs. He shared his concerns at a council of war held on the fifth of December.

"We are losing men and gaining none," he said. "The weather is against us. Our rations are poor and will not get better. Fatigue is severe among the men. And what is worse—Wade is approaching from the midlands and Cumberland from the southwest."

"We have not been defeated once," objected O'Sullivan.

"Because we have not been seriously opposed," rejoined Murray. "There is also said to be a militia at Finchley of five thousand. We are badly outnumbered and far from our lines of supply."

"But if we reach London, I am confident of Welsh and French support," insisted the prince.

"Perhaps, my lord. But if they have not supported us till now, can we be sure of it then?"

"What do you suggest, then, Lord George?" asked Charles, perturbed at such a negative report.

"Retreat, my lord."

"Retreat! But we have been unopposed, I tell you. London is before us."

"And Wade and Cumberland are closing in with thirty thousand combined troops. We are virtually surrounded."

"If we strike decisively—"

"We haven't a chance of victory, my lord. We would face annihilation. Desertions continue. Winter is setting in. Every day we delay, our conditions grow more risky."

"There is nothing to be gained by retreat," the prince argued. "Rather than go back, I would wish to be twenty feet underground."

"Our only hope of victory lies back in Scotland," insisted Murray. "There might we raise further support throughout the winter and use the time to appeal again to France."

The debate continued bitterly. In the end, the prince was outvoted by his advisors. On December 6, retreat was ordered for the Highland army. A depressed and moody Prince Charles quit mixing and talking with soldiers and kept to himself. Lord George Murray conducted the retreat as shrewdly as he had orchestrated the southern march, beating off several attacks from the rear. On December 20, with the duke of Cumberland marching north behind them, the Highlanders waded a hundred men abreast through the flooding River Esk back into Scotland.

By this time the size of the army had shrunk to thirty-six hundred infantry and five hundred horsemen. In the meantime, during their absence, Edinburgh had been taken back by the government and was in the control of General Hawley with eight thousand troops. Cumberland, with several thousand more, now took Carlisle and there had paused his northern march.

After a respite in Glasgow, Charles marched to Stirling and took the town on January 8, 1746, then began a siege on the castle. In response, General Hawley marched out with his eight thousand men from Edinburgh to put an end once and for all to the uprising. But again the masterful generalship of Lord George Murray proved victorious. Occupying the high ground south of Falkirk, the Jacobite army was in a much better position. When Hawley ordered his army to attack during a fierce winter downpour, several successful Highland charges dispersed them in panic.

King George sent orders to his son Cumberland in Carlisle to march north and take charge of the government army.

Meanwhile, the Highlanders continued in the attempt to take Stirling

Castle. Two weeks passed. Aware of Cumberland's advance with an
army of well over seven thousand, and knowing that their victory over
Hawley at Falkirk had not been decisive, again the prince's advisors recommended retreat from Stirling, this time into the Highlands.

"Good God!" Prince Charles exclaimed bitterly at still another counsel of retreat. "Have I lived to see this!"

But by now, sick with a cold, he had no choice but to allow his officers
their way. The shrinking and dispirited Highland army began its retreat
from Stirling on February 1, 1746.

✖   T W E N T Y - F I V E   ✖

Early February 1746

Through scattered reports and an occasional brief letter from the front,
Aileana Gordon had been able to keep track of the movement of Prince
Charles's troops. As the army reached Scotland, more and more refugees
and returning soldiers carried news that spread up and down and across
the land—news that both armies were on the march.

Then came word that the Highlanders had laid siege to Stirling Castle and beat back an attack of government troops at Falkirk. But still it
had not been the decisive battle that would put an end to the conflict.

For two long weeks afterward Aileana heard nothing. She was nearly
beside herself for fear of what might have happened.

Finally one afternoon the despair nearly sank her spirits altogether. It
was far too early for bed, but darkness fell early in the north, in the dead
of winter, and she was too cold and sick of heart for normal activity. Only
sleep brought comfort.

After a soothing cup of tea, she took to the stairs and sought her bedchamber. A few minutes later she blew out the remaining candles and
turned down the lantern. She lay down, crept inside, and tried to find
some pocket of warmth in the lonely bed under the thick covering of blankets.

But she lay wide awake. Slowly the minutes passed, finally an hour.

Something sounded outside. She started up.

Had her ears deceived her? But could it have been . . . horses?

There it was again . . . yes, someone was approaching!

Aileana threw back the coverings, leapt out of bed, grabbed her dressing gown, and proceeded to grope for the lantern. Within seconds she was flying down the stairs.

With trembling hands she fumbled with the latch and bar of the front door, then flung it wide to the night. Only pitch black met the squint of her eyes.

Slow, heavy steps shuffled toward her. She held up the lantern, directing its light outward. The face that gradually came into sight in the pale glow of the flickering wick looked like a ghost's.

"Sandy!" she exclaimed in mingled joy and shock. "You look—"

She could not say it. She glanced momentarily away with heart in her throat. The next instant she was pulling him inside and lavishing him with kisses of which he scarcely seemed conscious.

He was gaunt and pale, his eyes red from lack of sleep and almost bulging out of their thin sockets. Behind him, his father now also approached, bearing the same general appearance.

"Oh, Kendrick!" exclaimed Aileana. Quickly she set down the lantern and took her husband in her arms. "You look *so* exhausted!"

"Exhausted and cold," he said, forcing a wan smile. "The rest of the army is only a few days behind us. We won battles at Falkirk and Stirling—"

"Yes, I heard," said Aileana, leading her husband inside.

"Now the army is heading north toward Inverness."

"How many men have been lost?" she asked, closing the door behind them.

"Actually, very few," he replied. "There has not been a great deal of fighting—only marching, long marching, nearly the whole length of Scotland and England and back, without enough food or clothes for the men, worn boots, thin coats. We have not lost numbers to battle, but to fatigue and exhaustion."

"And now?"

"Most eventually just became too tired. In ones and twos they have gradually left for home, simply worn out and unable to continue. Especially since we arrived back in Scotland, the lure of the fires of home has become stronger and stronger."

"I am glad you two joined them. It is so good to have you back," she said eagerly, leading them into the kitchen, where she immediately began to stir the banked coals.

"Prince Charles can have his rebellion," she went on, "but I want my husband and son back."

"I'm afraid you don't have them back quite yet," sighed the earl, slumping into a chair.

"Why . . . what do you mean?"

"We are not here to stay, Aileana," said the earl as he watched his wife throw two or three fresh peats on the fire. "We have only come for a few days—to rest and enjoy some warm food and get new clothes."

"No," Aileana wailed, feeling the tears well up as she turned again to face him, "you can't mean—"

He nodded. "We will rejoin the others when they come through the pass and turn north. If you want to meet the prince—"

"I don't want to meet him!" interrupted Aileana in tearful frustration. "His rebellion is not mine!"

"I am sorry. I know it is difficult for you."

"But why, Kendrick . . . *why*?"

"Aileana, we have to."

She looked away. It would be pointless to argue. Sometimes men and their principles of honor were more than she could understand . . . more than she *wanted* to understand.

"Have you seen Culodina's father anywhere?" she asked after a moment.

Kendrick shook his head. "The occasional rumors of his activities and loyalties are not encouraging."

"Worse than that," added Sandy. "He is reportedly one of the duke's chief advisors."

"What duke?" asked his mother.

"The duke of Cumberland—King George's son. The new commander of the King's army. Reports are that he is advancing north from England after us with reinforcements."

※   T W E N T Y · S I X   ※

Even as they spoke, at Tullibardglass Hall less than ten miles away, Culodina's father was pouring a drink for the newly arrived son of the King, whose girth gave evidence that the supply lines throughout his drive into Scotland had remained more than ample. He and a few trusted advisors had retired secretly into the Highlands for a strategy session following the defeat of the Hanoverian army at Falkirk.

"Where do you think the rebels are heading?" asked Cumberland.

"It's hard to say, but scouting reports indicate Inverness their likely destination," answered the duke of Argyll.

"Then we shall pursue them. That is your country, is it not, Forbes?" said Cumberland, turning to the new Lord President.

"Precisely, my lord," replied Culloden, shifting uneasily in his chair.

"If I may be so bold as to propose a recommendation, my lord . . ." now began Murdoch Sorley.

Cumberland lifted his glass and nodded, indicating for his host to proceed.

Despite his cool demeanor, Murdoch Sorley had begun to have a few second thoughts about his choice of allegiances. This Cumberland was but a fat twenty-four-year-old who knew next to nothing about military strategy. What if the fool of a so-called Scottish prince actually succeeded in his gambit for the throne? Where would he be then? He could be sent to prison for treason, all his financial dealings uncovered, both estates taken away. He had a great deal at stake, and had thus given the outcome of this conflict much thought.

"The winter snows will be less severe near the coast," Tullibardglass began. "If you lead the King's army northeast from its present encampment in Edinburgh toward Aberdeen, you can, if needed, billet the troops there. Let the fierce winter ravage the Highland army. Then, when the time is right, you can advance northwest through Elgin, engage the rebels, and put an end to this folly."

"Well spoken, Tullibardglass," replied the duke, "and possibly a shrewd plan. If what I have seen thus far is any indication, I would certainly approve of anything that will lessen winter's bite on my men. This is a dreadful place, this Scotland of yours. One wonders why we fight for it. Are the fires warm in Aberdeen?"

"Yes, my lord," smiled Tullibardglass. "There will be plenty of dry peat in the northern city, I assure you."

"Then Aberdeen shall be our objective."

"What you suggest could result in a battle between Inverness and Elgin," now put in Forbes. "That is boggy and treacherous ground. I would be loath to see—"

"Are you worried about your own estate, Duncan?" interjected the duke of Argyll with hint of a smile.

The pointed comment rankled Forbes.

"And if I am?" he challenged.

"The cause is greater than one man's fortunes."

"That is easy for you to say, Argyll, when your own assets and property lie safely to the south."

"Tut, tut, gentlemen," interposed Cumberland. "I had heard that you Scots were a fractious lot. But such disputes settle nothing. I like the plan. We will meet the Highlanders when and where fate determines."

Forbes remained silent, inwardly irritated at both Argyll and Tullibardglass.

"Meanwhile," the duke went on, "reinforcements from the ranks of your Campbells are on their way to Edinburgh even now, are they not, Argyll?"

Campbell nodded.

"Upon their arrival, then, we shall set out for Aberdeen. We will billet the troops and wait for the fool of a Stuart. His army is shrinking by the day, they say. I have no doubt the rebels will overplay their hand—if the winter doesn't kill them first."

———

Four days later, never realizing how close they had come to the duke of Cumberland's private enclave, the Highland army marched through the Pass of Drumochter. Their northward journey would take them through the valley of the River Spey as far as Aviemore, then northwest to Inverness.

Feeling rested and much better than when they arrived at Cliffrose, at last Kendrick and Sandy Gordon prepared to rejoin their companions.

"*Please* don't go," insisted Aileana one last time, with tears in her eyes.

"We must, Aileana."

"Oh, Kendrick . . . what difference will two men make?"

"Father is one of Prince Charles's commanders, Mother," said Sandy, coming alongside them. "Lord Murray needs his help. The prince has several Irish counselors whom he favors, but often their advice is disastrous. Father and Murray are the only two of his leaders with any sense, I think."

"And the prince has a stubborn streak," added the earl with almost a sad smile. "His knowledge of Highland methods of battle is not the best. He needs wise counsel if the rebellion is to succeed."

"Then *you* stay, Sandy."

"How can I, Mother? It is a matter of honor."

"Honor, honor!" she said, weeping bitterly. "What honor does a man's death bring his wife!"

Father and son looked at one another disconsolately. How could they make her understand what was in a man's heart?

Gently Sandy placed his hands on her shoulders. "Mother," he said, "we love you. But we *must* fight for Scotland's honor, even if every one of us dies in the effort."

"Don't say such a thing!" she cried. "Oh, Sandy . . . Kendrick—you must know how foolish such words sound!"

She turned away weeping. Kendrick took her in his arms. She turned and laid her head on his chest. He stroked her hair, then bent down and kissed her gently one last time.

Aileana said no more. Father and son left the house for their waiting horses and soon were gone.

About midnight, as she slept, Aileana's nightmare from so many years ago returned, this time with even more graphic horror.

❋   T W E N T Y · S E V E N   ❋

Early March 1746

Culodina Sorley had scarcely seen her father in months.

When she did he was distant, distracted, irritable, in and out with strangers. Soldiers and nobles came and went—some English, some Scots. She kept to herself, and he scarcely took notice of her. During his most recent soirée with the fat Englishman and his Scots officers, she hardly left her room.

Now he was gone again. Tullibardglass Hall had been silent as a tomb ever since, for weeks on end. Even the servants acted as if they hardly dared speak for fear of breaking the silence.

Finally she could stand it no longer. She packed two bags, gave them to Baillidh the groom, and told him to saddle her favorite horse and tie them behind. Then she sought her father's manservant.

"Swayn," she said, "I am going to Cliffrose. Whenever my father returns, if he should happen to care or inquire about my whereabouts, you may tell him I am there—or not tell him. I really do not care."

"Very good, my lady."

As Culodina rode away, somehow she sensed she would not be back for a long time.

※   T W E N T Y - E I G H T   ※

April 14, 1746

In mid-April a letter arrived at Cliffrose. It was dated some three weeks earlier. Aileana tore apart the envelope and opened the single sheet. Culodina read over her shoulder.

Dear Mum,

We are encamped near Elgin. Our force temporarily swelled after our return to Scotland, with new recruits and the arrival of a few French troops. But as we retreated north after leaving you, our beleaguered force melted away again. I doubt we are now six thousand men, perhaps less.

Father is well, but I read anxiety on his face whenever I see him.

The prince is behaving as if this were the London season. Father fears he does not grasp the gravity of our situation. Father does what he can, but often he and Lord Murray are the only two voices of reason. When we arrived, against Father's counsel, Inverness Castle was captured and destroyed. Then Culloden House several miles south of the town was taken and has since been used for the prince's quarters and command. I have wondered what poor Samantha thinks of her father's enemies tramping about in her own house. She is probably in London.

Father is at Culloden House with the prince and other leaders.

Occasionally we men are able to spend a night at the Cairngorm Arms in Inverness, but mostly we remain encamped in the park and precincts spreading out across the moor near headquarters, or in Elgin and Inverness.

I hope you will be able to give my love to Culodina when you see her.

Culodina broke into tears at sight of these words and leaned closer to Aileana, whose own heart grew cold as she read. She shivered involuntarily. Then tears filled her own eyes as she continued to read the blurred words in her son's familiar hand.

Something must happen soon. An end is surely coming, whatever it brings. I sense that spring will not arrive without a decisive change.

The prince sponsors dances and entertains the local ladies, many of whom are smitten with him. Whatever his ability as a commander and leader, he is the most charismatic and engaging personality I have ever met.

Even though we have seen nothing of Cumberland's army, conditions among the men remain terrible. The winter has taken its toll. Gradually our numbers evaporate as men continue to return home.

Just a day or two ago we heard word that Cumberland's army in Aberdeen is preparing to march at any time.

It is so cold. But spring is on its way and, as I said, it will all be over soon.

Father sends his love, as do I.

Your son,
Sandy Gordon

They had no more than read the final words before Culodina had turned and was running upstairs to the room she occupied whenever she was at Cliffrose. Almost without realizing what she was doing, she began stirring frantically among her things, pulling out a small bag. She hurried down the corridor to Sandy's empty room and opened the door. She had never been inside it before, but she did not stop to think of that now. She ran inside, looked quickly about, then grabbed at some of Sandy's shirts and trousers. They were far too big for her. But they would have to do. With a warm plaid belted over them, perhaps no one would notice.

When Aileana saw her ten minutes later, bag in hand, dressed in men's clothes she recognized as Sandy's, wearing a hat and with a pair of Sandy's old boots on her feet, she gasped. Immediately she knew what was in Culodina's mind.

"Don't try to stop me, Aunt Aileana," said Culodina. "I have to follow him."

"Culodina, please—" Aileana began.

"I want to be with him. His letter sounded so forlorn . . . I can't bear it!"

"But, Culodina, you can't! It's winter . . . a woman . . . alone . . ."

"I must go to him!" Aunt Aileana. "Please understand. Don't you know . . . I love him."

Aileana turned away, weeping again. A few seconds of silence filled the room.

She felt a hand on her shoulder. She turned. She and Culodina embraced.

"I couldn't bear to lose you both," said Aileana, almost in the whimper of a child being bereft of everything she counts precious.

"I love you, Aunt Aileana," whispered Culodina, holding tight in her arms the only mother she had ever known. "You won't lose us, I promise. But I have to go . . . I *have* to try to find him."

Aileana felt the arms release, but she could not look up. Her mother's heart was breaking. When she looked up a few moments later, Culodina was gone.

TWENTY-NINE

April 15, 1746

After months of waiting, word at last reached the rebel army that the duke of Cumberland was on the march toward them.

On the fourteenth of April, a Monday, the King's son encamped at Nairn, fourteen miles from Inverness. The Highland troops were hurriedly rounded up from about Inverness to gather on Culloden Moor, four miles out of town. All indications were that Cumberland would attack the next day. The prince gave orders to muster by clans on the moor after dawn.

That night the candles in the parlor of Culloden House burned low. Discussion had been heated and lengthy. The cautions of Lord George Murray were falling on deaf ears. His brilliant generalship had outwitted both Wade and Cumberland in November of the previous year, and his tactics were responsible for the victory at Falkirk in January. But Murray had also been responsible for the retreat from Derby, and that decision, as well as the more recent retreat from Stirling, still irked the prince. His Irish favorites again had his ear—particularly now that Murray was suggesting yet another retreat into the hills.

They had been retreating for months, and the prince had finally had enough. On the advice of his Irish colonel, the notorious John O'Sullivan, Prince Charles Edward Stuart now determined to stand and fight.

"I tell you, my lord," Murray insisted with urgency, "with all due respect to Colonel O'Sullivan, the moorland is disastrous ground. Cumberland outnumbers us at least two to one."

"I must voice my agreement with Lord George," now added Kendrick Gordon. "Our only hope is surprise, with a choice of terrain that favors rapid slashing attack and withdrawal. The wide, boggy moor will prevent the kind of charge that shattered Cope's army. In the open, our forces will be no match for their superior muskets and artillery."

"Precisely," rejoined Murray. "We must have cover from which to launch repeated wild bursts. If I might just suggest—"

"I have brought the army to Drummossie Moor to await Cumberland," repeated the prince. "And here we shall engage him."

"But it is a parade ground, my lord," said Cliffrose, "and a boggy one at that. An orderly advance of troops with bayonets will crush us."

"Don't you understand, my lord?" insisted Murray. "This is no field for the clans. It is suicide. I tell you, we must seek the hills and then swoop down on Cumberland where he will be unable to marshal his ranks in order."

"The army will remain on the moor," repeated the prince firmly. "We will await Cumberland there."

In disbelief, and fearing what lay ahead, Gordon and Murray saw that as long as O'Sullivan opposed them there was no hope of convincing the prince to reconsider.

At six o'clock on the morning of the fifteenth, some six thousand Highlanders took up their lines clan by clan, from MacDonald on the far left at the north to the men of Atholl on the far right, and waited for the first glimpse or sound of Cumberland's red-coated army.

But only silence filled the morning. George Murray and Kendrick Gordon put the hours to use riding together to scout out more favorable battle terrain in the hills and across the River Nairn to the south, still hoping to redeploy the army elsewhere. Another brief meeting was held, at which they argued their case yet again. But despite continued entreaties, neither the prince nor O'Sullivan would change his mind. On the open moor the army remained in ranks all morning . . . and waited.

But Cumberland did not come.

Shortly before noon, the prince dismissed the lines to refresh themselves. Sleep they might, but what they really needed was food, and there was none. In their hasty assembly out of Inverness the previous day, the food carts had been left behind. A few biscuits were to be had, but no more than one apiece.

In the afternoon, word came that Cumberland's army, still encamped at Nairn, was celebrating the duke's twenty-fifth birthday with brandy, cheese, ale, and what was left of their meat. Again, Lord George and the earl of Cliffrose sought the prince.

"My lord," began Murray, "we have been discussing our plight and have a new recommendation—a night attack, this very night. Let us march to Nairn and launch a surprise attack while the enemy sleeps, drunk from the birthday brandy."

Prince Charles reflected, then sought his Irish advisors. After a brief discussion, he returned, nodding and enthusiastic. The plan was authorized. By eight o'clock that evening, the hungry ranks were again assembled and the march begun.

☷   T H I R T Y   ☷

April 16, 1746

Sandy Gordon had not spoken with his father in two days, though he had seen him in the distance on his horse, riding with Lord George. Now he could not see him at all. It was past midnight, and the night was pitch black, misty, and cold. Rain threatened, though his nose told him that, if it came before morning, it could well be snow that fell on them.

They had been marching, if such it could be called, for more than four hours.

How many struggled along in the frigid night, he didn't know. He had seen dozens drifting out of rank and back toward Inverness throughout the previous afternoon after receiving the single-biscuit ration for the day. They could be shot for desertion, they said, but they were not going to fight without meat in their bellies. Sandy had no doubt that a thousand or more had eventually broken ranks.

Sandy had remained on the moor, his plaid wrapped tightly around him, and with only the biscuit to sustain him. His stomach was gnawing at him even now. But it had been so long since it had been full of anything that the growl of hunger was no different than the shivering of his legs and chest—they were with him every moment except perhaps for the three or four hours in every twenty four when sleep might briefly take them away.

As he trudged along, scarcely able to make out the form of the man in front of him, visions of Culodina filled his brain. Would he see her again? Would he ever have the chance to tell her how he felt? Or would shot from an English musket or some screaming cannonball rip his body in two and leave him dead on the moor, face down in his own blood?

All night he plodded resolutely forward, unaware of the bitter arguments taking place ahead of him between his father and Murray and the Irishman O'Sullivan. Nor could he know that behind him, led by the prince, half their force was lagging badly behind and already rendering the entire night's march useless. They had hoped to attack by two in the morning. But they would be nowhere near their objective by then.

Throughout the wintry night, the exhausted Highlanders peered ahead for signs of the English campfires. With every step their water-soaked boots gurgled to ankle depth in the boggy sod, and with great effort were sludged out, sucking mud and water up in their wake. Then the same exhausting process was repeated ten thousand more times, with packs and swords and shields feeling more like lead weights every hour.

No one spoke. The pipes were silent. Only an occasional sudden pool or quagmire that claimed a leg to the knee might cause yell or curse or squeal from terrified horse to break the night silence.

All the while, progress remained agonizingly slow. The prince's rear guard fell further and further behind. Gradually a bitter wind whipped up in their faces from the sea ten miles to the north.

By half past two, they were still two, perhaps even three miles from the enemy.

There could be no surprise now. It was too late. Dawn would soon be upon them. Attack was impossible.

"Back to Culloden!" came word of the order through the ranks. The Highlanders sought the road, and once again—fell to retreat.

Slowly came first hints of dawn, a faint line of gray at the horizon beneath the covering of black clouds overhead. On came the thin light from the east until forms and figures of their clansmen could be seen all about them.

All at once, faintly in the distance behind them, sounded the roll of Cumberland's drummers, calling his army to wakefulness.

In the increasing dawn and with solid ground under their feet, they made quick return work of the six miles they had come. As they went, many fell by the wayside from lack of sleep. Some collapsed alongside the road; others stumbled into open fields and dropped; still others crept into wet ditches or beside stone dykes in utter exhaustion. Eventually most made it back to the moor and slept there.

The hour was somewhere between five and six, the temperature hovering between zero and three degrees Celsius.

After a scant hour or two of what fitful sleep might be had on the open ground, the shrill skirl of bagpipes blared through the morning. Exhausted and hungry to faintness, crawling and struggling up on frozen feet, they groped their way into clan groups. A few men were sent into nearby villages to see what food they could buy. Then, as if in final insult, the sleet and rain and a few flakes of snow finally began to empty from the sky.

It had been a miserable night and would prove an even more miserable day. How many were left of the six thousand that might have been on the moor two days ago no one could say—perhaps four thousand, at most five. Many still slept or had scattered into the surrounding countryside.

As the Jacobite troops stood frozen to the bone, stomachs empty, wind pelting their cheeks with specks of ice, rain gradually drenching kilts and tartan cloaks, sleet and an occasional slashing attack of hail pummeling bare legs beneath the knee, the Highlanders were as dispirited an army of men as ever had rallied for a cause whose meaning had long since abandoned it.

Murray and Gordon knew it was madness to fight thus. Not merely their own personal forebodings, but reasonably accurate scouting reports told them that they were seriously outnumbered. Yet the prince rode among his sleepy men on his gray gelding trying to buck up their spirits as if victory were sure. His judgment and maturity had proven itself wanting at this final desperate hour of his cause. But no one, not even his enemies, could deny his courage and determination.

As they watched him try this one last time to prepare his men for what lay ahead, both Murray and Gordon could not but admire this prince of the House of Stuart to whom they had given their allegiance, though inwardly they also cursed his foolhardy obstinacy.

All morning the Highland army stood on icy legs, with blocks of ice for feet, staring into the icy wind that gusted into their faces . . . waiting.

THIRTY-ONE

Around eleven in the morning, the roll of drums, beginning faintly, then steadily increasing, could be heard some distance away through the stormy air.

What terror the sound struck into the hearts of the Highlanders as they stood waiting, none would divulge to those next to them. All knew what the sound meant—that ten or twelve thousand well-fed and rested Englishmen and Campbells were coming to kill them. But stoically they stood their ground. If they must die, they would not die cowards.

By infinitesimal degrees the ominous sound grew. The crisp beat of a hundred drums was rhythmic, unending, maddeningly efficient and precise, echoing the cadence of seventy-five paces a minute at which Cumberland's army had pursued the Bonnie Prince all the way from England and around the opposite sides of Scotland.

At last the first glimpses of red appeared in the east.

After many long months, the prince and the duke—each a mere boy alongside most of the men whose lives they held in their hands—met face-to-face. Each sat astride their respective royal mounts behind their front lines, peering toward one another in the distance. They were two cousins of twenty-five years—the slight handsome Italian rogue and the fat German son of a King, both descendents of Mary, Queen of Scots, and both commanding armies that on this day would achieve immortality in their fight for control of Britain.

Steadily the thick red line advanced.

Between noon and one, the massive red-coated army drew close enough that individual soldiers could be seen across the moor. The English King's drums grew louder. The Scottish King's pipers blared out a shrill call to readiness.

The drums rolled. The pipes screamed.

Suddenly the drums ceased. The bags of the pipes replied, gasping and wheezing to emptiness.

A moment of stillness. Only the sleet peppering the hats and bonnets of both armies sounded in the ears of the fifteen thousand men about to make history.

Sandy Gordon gazed at the line of red across the moor at a distance of two or three hundred yards. He stood among one of two Gordon regiments of three hundred men, made up of recruits from the region of Strathbogie under the command of seventy-two-year-old John Gordon of Glenbucket.

As suddenly as had fallen the silence, now erupted a soundless puff of white smoke tinged with yellow against the low black sky. Almost instantly, several more bursts followed. All across the line now the deafening explosions of Cumberland's artillery reached Jacobite ears. At the same instant, the volley of iron balls began blasting through the front lines. The cannon fire quickly accelerated into continuous succession, its explosions relentless as smoke rose from the field in a dense, lung-burning cloud.

Antiquated Jacobite cannons attempted to answer the barrage, but without effect. A few rounds went off, then Charles's cannons fell silent—powder, touchholes, cords, and linstocks all soaked from the rain.

What had always been the Highlanders' most devastating weapon— the frenzied attack—never came. From such an open position, the Highland charge could have no effect. In their mustered ranks, the Highlanders stood helplessly awaiting orders, while the screaming iron from Cumberland's artillery fell in such unrelenting assault that neither escape nor charge could prevent it from decimating their ranks. The three-pound roundball shot killed and maimed in a single blow, blasting arms and legs from above and below the kilt, gruesomely pelting those who survived with flying human limbs. The smaller accompanying grapeshot—which spread out after leaving the cannon's forty-inch barrel—peppered the ranks and sprayed the clans with the warm blood of their own kith and kin.

Within twenty minutes, five hundred, perhaps a thousand Highlanders were dead.

The clans could wait no longer. Brave men of their number were dropping by the second. They would attack without an order from prince or chief. They must attack or die where they stood!

One clan, now another, broke ranks toward the enemy. With left hands maintaining shields as well as could be managed, they yanked kilts to the thigh and surged forward, swords aloft, their lungs erupting into frenzied Gaelic war cries. But the slaughter was on, and no ferocious charge by scattered clan groups could now stem it.

As the belated attack finally broke upon the field, it was answered with the musket fire that made the thick red line of the orderly British infantry such an effective killing machine, feared on the continent and wherever the wars of its nation took it.

The musket of the eighteenth century was an inaccurate weapon at more than a hundred or hundred and fifty yards. But when a hundred muskets were fired simultaneously, the collective onslaught of shot could halt almost any attack in its tracks.

As the Highlanders came flying toward them came the command, *Make ready!*

The first rank of musket infantry dropped to one knee.

Present!

Rifles jerked to the shoulder and squinting eyes sighted down the barrel. What they saw was a charging line from Clan Chattan, the first to sprint across the moor.

Fire!

No more than a second passed after a hundred triggers had been squeezed before the first rank had sprung back to its feet even as the second rank heard its *Fire!* and unleashed another hundred rounds. The first rank hurried to the back to reload, prime, and cock their weapons while rank three now took the knee, aimed, and . . . *Fire!*

Along the red line of six battalions, company by company, platoon by platoon, ranks one, two, and three sprayed their shot into the Highland charge—the discharges kept orderly by the beat of the drum. They released such a massive volley of tiny iron, with grapeshot and cannonballs continuing to soar overhead from the cannons, that a Highland force of three times the size could not have survived.

At the first crack of musket, dozens from Clan Chattan fell. At the second, dozens more collapsed. Their kilted lines sprinted hopelessly into a hailstorm of mutilating iron shot unleashed by the alternating ranks of musket fire.

Clan Chattan and the others behind them ran bravely, choking on the white-yellow sulphurous smoke, stumbling over their dead as they fell. Those few who chanced to reach the enemy faced a solid wall of bayonets ready to plunge them through if close-range musketry missed. Of several hundred Chattans who had led the Highlanders in attack, only a dozen or two survived.

Within minutes of the charge, the clans staggered, then spun about into frantic and scattered retreat. The charge had been hopeless, and they knew it. Now the English dragoons, waiting astride their horses on the west flank along with two regiments of Campbells, swept in from the side to slaughter with sword and hoof those attempting to get away. As the horsemen bore in from the west, the regiments of musketry rose from the knee to pursue on foot—to shouts of "After the dogs!"—with five thousand shiny bayonets thirsty for blood. The infantry soon swarmed the moor toward the Highland position like a surging tide of red in pursuit of the fleeing tartan remnant.

Kendrick Gordon sat astride his horse beside Lord George Murray watching the butchery unfold. The hearts of both men were breaking. Both knew the cause was lost. Cumberland's army had overrun and scattered the lines of the clans a mere twenty minutes after the lines had broken. All around, the Highlanders fled in panic. The entire rout had taken less than three-quarters of an hour.

But it was not just for the failed Stuart cause that Kendrick Gordon wept. Fear for his son, whom he had not seen since morning, nearly consumed him. His heart dreaded what might already have happened. If only he could catch sight of—

Suddenly in the distance he saw what might be the familiar form. The next instant he was galloping over the battlefield toward it.

"Where are you going?" shouted Murray after him.

"To my son!" cried Gordon.

Neither did Lord George sit observing the catastrophe any longer. He now urged his horse into the thick of combat with sword in hand. He was a commander no more, but merely one man among those who remained, ready to give his own life if he might thereby save one of his fellows.

❖   T H I R T Y - T W O   ❖

For twenty minutes, Sandy Gordon had been fighting for his life.

After the third wave of musket fire fell upon the Gordon ranks, he had joined the charge toward the enemy.

Clutching sword in his hand, he knew he would never reach the impenetrable red wall. All around him, those who made the attempt were falling over the bodies of those who had preceded them into the blistering musket fire. That he was about to die did not actually enter his mind as a definite thought, only the vague sense that he would never again see his father or mother or Culodina. He felt no sense of courage as he flung himself into the battle, screams of men falling and dying on his right and left, the explosion of musket and cannon fire rending the air in continual barrage. He ran only because he was here and he must do what soldiers did—fight the enemy and die when the bullet split his skull or, should he survive the musket fire, when an English bayonet plunged through his heart.

He was afraid, not of death but of pain, not of *being* dead—he had already reconciled himself to that—but of *dying*.

Suddenly amid the cacophony of death and mayhem, he heard his name called. The voice was familiar but strange, like some long-forgotten memory from another life.

"So, young Sandy Gordon of Cliffrose," came the words, "how fitting that we should meet like this."

Sandy paused in flight and glanced toward the sound. A horseman was approaching.

Murdoch Sorley, he thought. Momentary confusion rushed in upon his sleep-starved brain. His heart leapt in brief recognition. Was Culodina here too! If only it might be. The hint of a welcoming smile broke upon his lips.

But just as suddenly his brain cleared. Culodina's father was riding toward him from the ranks of the enemy!

Sorley saw the bewilderment pass over Sandy's face. A wide smile spread over his own lips, and he broke into laughter. The sound was bitter, cruel, mirthless. The next moment he raised the pistol in his hand and aimed it toward the ground.

"It should have been I who had the son," he cried. "It was I who deserved an heir, not your cowardly father! But what he had will soon be mine!"

Suddenly the truth of the man's treachery was clear.

Inflamed by the words, Sandy rose up and burst toward the horse in a frenzied charge. If he was going to die by the hand of his father's cousin, he would not do so without a fight!

Through the ranks of death Kendrick Gordon galloped, urging his horse over bodies, galloping where possible toward the middle of the moor where the remains of the rebel army was battling sword against bayonet.

Suddenly he saw his cousin before him in the colors of the enemy, pistol raised against the son whose birth they had celebrated together. He reached across his body and pulled out his long Highland dirk.

"Tullibardglass!" came a great roar across the ground separating them. So fierce was the sound that it echoed even above the dwindling explosions of musket fire.

Culodina's father looked up to see the Gordon mount pounding across the turf. An evil glint came into his eye as he saw his mad Highland cousin attacking in full flight, dirk waving.

He took his aim off the son, and slowly raised his arm.

At the cry from his father's mouth, Sandy turned. Behind him the shattering report from the pistol intended for him exploded. A splotch of red spewed out from his father's chest. The eyes of father and son met but for an instant. Then the light faded from the rider's face. He toppled backward off his horse onto the reddened moor, adding his own to the blood of thousands.

"Father!" cried Sandy in horror, sword falling from his hand. He ran forward in desperation. Behind him sounded a wicked laugh. He glanced over his shoulder. But already Murdoch Sorley had wheeled his mount and was galloping back toward the English line.

Sandy reached his father, knelt beside him, and gently eased his hand under the beloved head. The eyes opened a feeble crack. "Sandy . . . oh, Sandy . . . my son," came a gasping whisper.

Tears streamed down the young man's mud-caked cheeks.

"I . . . I love you, Sandy, my boy . . . tell your mother . . ."

The voice was weak. He choked, struggling for breath, ". . . tell her that—"

The final moments were too few for all that was in the good man's heart to say. The memory of his life would have to speak for him now.

Sandy burst into a howl of agony. Slowly the echo of his wailing voice was swallowed up in a thousand other cries of death this evil day had brought. He leaned down and kissed the warm dead face.

But the tender moment of farewell could last but a moment. Before the son could utter a whispered *I love you*, another of the enemy was upon him.

Sandy jumped to his feet and glanced about for his sword. But there was no time to find it. He broke into a run away from the scene even as piercing pain slashed through his leg from the tip of a bayonet thrust behind him.

He struggled another three steps. Vaguely the thought filled his seared brain that death would now be welcome. Any instant he expected the full bayonet to split his back and puncture through to his chest. But ahead of him two kilted Highlanders tore past, screaming and wildly waving their claymores. In seconds they had dispatched the owner of the bayonet that had just crippled him.

Sandy did not look back again. He was heedless of the fight now. His only thought was to flee this terrible place.

His life was over. There was nothing to do but run until he dropped . . . and then hope he would never wake.

T H I R T Y - T H R E E

When Culodina Sorley rode into Inverness in the drizzly cold of early afternoon, chilled to the bone from the rain and sleet that thankfully now had stopped, she sensed an ominous stillness. Something was wrong. No soldiers were to be seen. Somewhere in the distance sounded an occasional ominous rumble of cannon and a faint thudding crackle as of gunfire.

The first thing she must do, she thought, was find an inn. She had ridden that day from Tomatin, which had not been so very far, but she was tired and cold. Perhaps she would have something to eat. Then she would find out where Culloden House was located—or the place called Cairngorm Arms. She had to find Kendrick Gordon. She could not hope to locate Sandy among thousands of men, but his father was sure to know his whereabouts.

An hour later, warmed and fed, her horse stabled, and with directions to the Cairngorm Arms, Culodina walked back out into the town.

She had not gone far before she heard shouts.

Two men on foot raced past her with looks of terror on their faces. Both were caked with dirt and blood. Looking right and left, they darted into a nearby well house. Moments later a rider galloped toward her, nearly skidding his horse to a stop at the point where he had seen the rebels run in to hide.

"Come here!" he shouted at her. Culodina ignored his command and backed away in terror.

"Girl . . . hey, you!" he shouted to a servant girl who had just emerged from a house. He leapt to the ground. "Take my reins and don't move from this spot."

Too surprised and terrified to refuse, the girl stood paralyzed to the spot. The rider ran into the well house, knife in hand. Screams sounding from inside moments later brought the girl to her wits. She dropped the bridle and ran away. The next thing Culodina saw was the same man running back out, blood dripping from hands and wrist and knife.

Her stomach wrenched at the sight. By now dozens of galloping horsemen were entering the town. Commotion broke out everywhere. Highlanders were running frantically, kilts and bodies splattered with blood, desperately trying to hide from the shouting red-coated English soldiers.

"After the rebels!" cried the riders. "Cut the Highlanders down!"

Then there were more soldiers . . . the clatter of hooves on cobblestones, now in greater numbers . . . breaking down doors, rudely searching houses and inns and hotels.

"I saw two or three this way!" yelled a soldier to the riders behind him, yanking his reins to the right along an adjacent street. His companions galloped after him.

As she watched in shock, Culodina slowly crept toward the shadows of an alleyway. Suddenly before her a young man who could not have been more than sixteen darted past. He glanced toward her, eyes wide in terror, then dashed across the street.

A deafening crack of gunfire exploded behind her. Blood splattered across the young man's back, and he fell face down with a dull thud in the middle of the street.

Culodina screamed. But the red-coated officer paid her no heed. Already he was galloping after another.

She fled into the alley, running as fast as she could. She emerged at its far end into a street less congested with soldiers, not realizing she was sobbing. She wiped at her cheeks and across her stinging eyes. Breathing hard, she did her best to collect her thoughts, then tried to follow the directions she had been given.

Six or seven minutes later, keeping to the shadows and side streets and managing to avoid most of the riders, she approached the Cairngorm Arms.

A kilted figure hurried limping out of the building twenty yards in front of her, dark splotches on his skin and clothes, a dreadful gash on one leg.

Culodina's feet froze, eyes widened in mingled joy and horror.

He ran across the street toward an alleyway.

"Sandy!" she cried out.

He stopped and turned. She ran toward him. As she drew near, Culodina beheld the horrible sight more closely—his clothes muddy and torn, blood on shirt and kilt. And the huge wound on his thigh, still oozing dark crimson, his eyes red from bitter weeping.

"Oh, Sandy . . ." she said, breaking into fresh tears at the sight. "It *is* you!"

She stretched out her arms to embrace him, heedless of mud and blood, relieved to ecstasy that he was alive.

"I was so afraid! I thought I might not—"

Suddenly a grotesque expression of horror on his face stopped her. His mouth seemed trying to speak. His lips quivered. He took a step or two backwards, the look of revulsion spreading to eyes, then turning to hatred.

"Get away from me!" he shouted, not even recognizing his own clothes on her body nor pausing to question how she had come here. "Get away . . . get away!"

The voice was strange, foreign, and empty. It was not the voice of the Sandy Gordon she knew.

"Sandy . . . Sandy," she said, continuing to walk toward him. "Don't be afraid. It's me—Culodina."

"I know who you are!" he spat, continuing to back away. "Get out of here—go away!"

"Sandy, why . . . what are you talking about . . . I want to help—"

"Help?" he shrieked like a wild man, then howled in a tormented laugh. "I want none of your help! I never want to see you again. Do you think I don't know who you are, Culodina Sorley, daughter of the traitor Tullibardglass. I know you well enough!"

"But . . . but why, Sandy . . . what are you talking about?"

"My father is dead!" he shouted.

"Oh, Sandy!" exclaimed Culodina, breaking again into tears of heartbreak, "I am so sorry!"

Again she started forward to embrace him.

"Get away from me!" he spat out yet again. "My father is dead, I tell you—dead by your father's hand!"

"Sandy," she exclaimed in horror, "what are you saying!"

"That your father killed the best man in Scotland. He shot my father, who is lying on the battlefield. I can't even bury him! And if one of the redcoats finds me here, I'll have my own throat slit or a sword run through me."

"But when . . . where. . . ?" Culodina whimpered in a voice about to fail her. Tears streamed down her face.

"Culloden . . . on Drummossie Moor," replied Sandy, "—the moor of death!"

He burst into a wail of remorseless sobbing, then ran for the alley . . . and was gone.

❈　T H I R T Y - F O U R　❈

How Culodina Sorley found the evil battlefield, she could not have said.

She tied her mount to a shrub and walked among the dead from that afternoon's slaughter, her broken heart weeping with a bitterness deeper than any feeling she could have imagined—for Sandy and his father, as well as for what her own father had become. She had seen signs of it for years. But the love of a daughter for the only parent she knew had prevented her admitting what kind of man he had gradually turned into. Now that she saw it, she realized she could never love him again.

Never had she felt such desolation. Her mother had been taken from her before she could remember. Now the only other people she cared about were gone too. Sandy, whom she loved, hated her. His father was dead. And her own father had become a murderer to despise rather than a father to love.

What was left for her? Where would she go, to whom could she turn? How could she face Aunt Aileana again and look her in the eye after what her father had done? The poor dear lady, left a widow for a cause she would never understand . . . and she did not even know it yet.

As Culodina wandered senseless among the dead, stepping over corpses, wails and moans from the wounded and dying sounding from every direction, her feelings were frozen senseless. She did not stop to consider her own danger, nor that the afternoon's killing was by no means ended. In her stupor she had given up the effort to disguise herself as a man. She had long since lost Sandy's bonnet, and her light hair fell free on her shoulders. But for present, few paid her heed.

Dead horses and overturned carts and wagons, swords and clothes and tattered tartans were strewn everywhere. Bodies had fallen so thick that in places she had to walk around mounds of dead men, boys no more than fourteen or fifteen, mutilated parts of arms and legs—indescribable sights no human should have to see. And blood . . . blood . . . blood everywhere.

In every direction for miles, what remained of the massacred Highland army fled, while its prince, now a fugitive, made his way across the river to safety with a small escaping band of rebel horsemen. Prince Charles had not left the field in cowardice. He had watched the horror unfold, weeping for the army that had stood with him till the end, reluctant to depart the scene. Finally O'Sullivan had grabbed the reins of his horse and pulled him away.

Those of Cumberland's infantry ordered to remain at the site for the rest of the afternoon took a break on the battlefield to enjoy a midday dinner of biscuits and cheese, laughing and talking amongst themselves in a spirit of grisly sport. A few glanced her way as Culodina passed fifty yards away. One rose, took a step or two toward her, then seemed to reconsider and returned to the cluster of his comrades. One of their officers would later write of the scene, "The moor was covered with blood, and our men, what with killing the enemy, dabbling their feet in the blood, and splashing it about one another, looked like so many butchers rather than Christian soldiers."

As they ate, the Englishmen kept watch for jerks of movement from the piles of dead and took turns walking toward such remnants of humanity to shoot or bayonet whatever form of life might be struggling beneath them.

As horrifying as the battlefield was, Culodina could have no idea what other atrocities were going on even then throughout the surrounding countryside, though in the distance an occasional scream or report of gunfire evidenced clearly enough that the killing was not done.

A certain farmer by the name of Alexander Young was plowing in his field a mile or two away that afternoon and did not even know there had been a battle. Suddenly clansmen came running across his field. Whatever was going on he didn't know or care, but it looked dangerous. Young dropped the plough and ran for his house. But he was spotted by some English dragoons, who galloped after and shot him as he tried to open his door. Bleeding, he ran into the house. The horsemen dismounted and followed him inside to finish with the sword what they had begun. They killed his eight-year-old son in the same manner, while the boy's brother darted to safety through a hole in the cottage's earthen wall.

In a farmhouse in Culwhiniac, the wife of a certain farmer named MacDonald had been mixing, kneading, and baking bread all morning for the poor hungry young men she had been helping feed for days. She knew no other way to cope with the terrible sounds outside than to keep her hands busy, and she had kept up her baking all through the battle.

Suddenly through her door burst one of Prince Charles's faithful, who had lost his hand to an English sword only minutes before. In horror she watched as he ran across her floor, blood gushing from the stump at his wrist, and thrust the bleeding end of his arm straight against the burning stones of her fireplace to staunch the wound and stop the bleeding.

From the surrounding farms and hamlets and villages, spectators had come out that morning to watch the battle, only to be themselves swept up in the tragic drama. Once the butchery was on, the English soldiers had little sympathy for innocent bystanders. Their curiosity on that day cost hundreds their lives.

A traveler that fateful evening between Nairn and Inverness, had he lived to tell about it, would have seen hundreds of dead bodies, only a few of them belonging to rebel soldiers. He would have seen women stripped and shot, lying in the fields or at the side of the road in indecent positions that testified to the morbid lust of their murderers . . . a boy of twelve in the middle of the road, his skull crushed and the features of his face unrecognizable . . . naked, castrated men with their private parts placed in their dead hands . . . bodies everywhere . . . men, women, children all slaughtered together. Perhaps the soldiers of Cumberland's army and the Campbells who fought with them were humane individuals who had wives and children of their own to whom they would return to live normal lives again when this terrible day was but a memory. But on this afternoon, for a few hours, they became wild beasts intent on perverse cruelty toward their own kind.

Back at the battlefield, Culodina continued to walk through the carnage, gagging as she surveyed the dead faces, looking for that one familiar form she sought. She could not keep her stomach still for the revolting sight of bodies and screams and moans and cries. The stench of death had not yet begun, though in her nostrils she could smell the blood that she was trying to keep from Sandy's boots and trousers as she stepped over and walked around the dead. She gagged again, then finally lost the dinner she had eaten earlier, vomiting uncontrollably over a pile of four or five corpses.

How she found the one body among more than two thousand dead she would never know—any more than how she had got to the battlefield. But at last she found herself standing over the lifeless form with the familiar face. Mercifully the eyes were closed.

At last Culodina's emotions gave way and she sobbed bitterly, falling to her knees beside this man she had loved. That her own father had done this was a grief more miserable and horrible even than the fact of Sandy's poor father lying dead on the ground beside her.

She gathered her courage, then reached down and slid her hand under the lifeless shoulders. She was able to lift the stiff body enough to unwrap the cloaklike plaid, its tartan weave of green and black stained dark with blood, and pull it from around him. Through the torn and tattered shirt she felt the death chill of his body on her hand. She shivered with a cold whose memory would never leave her. The pale look of the dead face, whiter than any snow, was so terrifyingly different than a face asleep—a ghastly, empty shell that looked *almost* human, but whose soul was no longer within sight beneath the skin.

Kendrick Gordon's hand still clutched the dirk. Had he been defending himself, she wondered. Or perhaps defending Sandy? If she knew Kendrick Gordon, he would never have raised it against her father.

With great effort she spread apart the cold, lifeless fingers one at a time, shivering again as she touched them, forcing the stiff joints to release their death grip on the great Highland knife. All at once she spun about again to vomit, though there was little left inside her to spew on the ground, then continued what she had begun until the knife was loose.

With one final tearful look of farewell, she rose and left the battlefield for her waiting horse.

❊   T H I R T Y - F I V E   ❊

April 19, 1746

Culodina Sorley returned to Glen Truim, though she hardly knew how. She did not later remember the route she had taken, how long it had taken her, where she had stopped to eat or sleep, or if she had done so at all.

Hours and minutes, days and nights all blended into a blur of waking stupor—grief, anguish, tears, and forgetfulness, Sandy's stunning and horrifying words still searing her brain.

Men came and went, running, riding, escaping, pursuing. That she was herself in grave danger she did not reflect on. If she were to die now, what was that to her? Death would be a welcome reprieve to stop the images in her brain and prevent her having to do what she had to do. But even now that she was dressed in her own clothes, no one bothered her. All the people she encountered seemed to have other things on their minds. Thus, death did not come to release her from the dungeon of her silent torment.

At length she found herself approaching Cliffrose Castle. It was Saturday, though she did not know it. She had been gone five days.

She saw the beloved castle in the distance, then reined in her horse. For long minutes she sat, wondering if she could go through with what she must do. She had only one friend left in the world. Yet the news she

had to bring that dear one was sure to crush her heart to ashes and perhaps make her scream just as Sandy had. How could poor Aileana do
otherwise? How could she not hate the daughter of the man who had
murdered her husband?

But her steps had brought her this far. She could not ride away now.

With the resigned air of one approaching her own doom, Culodina
slowly urged her horse forward.

Inside Aileana heard the approach.

Fear seized her heart at the slow sound of hooves. She ran to the window.

A single rider . . . it was a woman . . . and it looked like—

Again Aileana's heart leapt inside her, but this time for joy at Culodina's return! She flew toward the door.

Culodina dismounted, then drew in a deep breath of agony, full of the
horrible image of the beloved white face on the cold moor. With slow,
trudging steps she walked toward the castle.

Aileana hurried out into the cold afternoon, a relieved smile spreading
over her face, and ran to greet her young friend.

Gradually her step slowed. Her smile faded as she took in the tears
and the red eyes . . . the anguished expression on Culodina's face?

Slowly Culodina came forward, lifting her hands with the folded
bloodstained plaid and dirk lying on top of it.

"Oh . . . oh, Aunt Aileana," she began, "I'm so sorry . . ."

With sudden horror, Aileana Gordon knew all.

A great disconsolate wail filled the glen. The next minute, the two
women fell weeping into one another's arms, the great tartan cloak falling
to the ground, the dirk clattering onto the stones beside it.

"And Sandy?" Aileana finally ventured to ask, though her heart was
terrified to utter the words.

"He is alive," whispered Culodina. It was enough for now. She would
not add to the poor woman's grief just yet by telling her at whose hand
her husband had fallen.

Aileana's arms clutched Culodina tightly again, feeling a surge of mother's relief in the midst of the wife's despair. She broke into passionate sobs against Culodina's shoulder.

Even as she stood weeping with the one she had always called her aunt, Culodina knew she would have to leave Cliffrose. Where she would go, she hadn't an idea.

Returning to Tullibardglass Hall, however, was out of the question.

✖   T H I R T Y - S I X   ✖

April 21, 1746

That evening they spent tearful but together, bearing in each other's company the old curse of Scotland's women that now had visited Cliffrose.

All the while, a terrible stone of ice sat at the pit of Culodina's stomach for what she knew. She *had to* tell her, but she could not bring herself to it. She did not think she could bear the disgrace of the truth in Aileana's eyes.

On Monday morning, about an hour before noon, they heard the approach of horses. From the sound it might have been a small army. They were moving rapidly, their business urgent.

Both women hurried to the door. A dozen riders approached, more than half dressed in the red coats of government troops. At the sight, Culodina's stomach lurched. Horrifying visions of Culloden swept through her brain. It was all she could do to keep herself from hating every one of them for no reason other than the red they wore. She recognized but one among them.

"We are in search of the outlaw who calls himself Prince Charles Edward Stuart," announced the lead rider. The contingent behind him sat stoically in the saddle. He scarcely acknowledged their acquaintance as he spoke. A momentary glance toward the younger of the two women was the only sign he gave of recognition. "We have reason to believe he is hiding in the western Highlands," continued Culodina's father. "Have you seen him?"

Though Aileana did not yet know the full truth, the demeanor of her husband's cousin and the expression on his face told her something was seriously wrong. "Of course not," she replied cautiously, summoning from some reservoir of strength the dignity of her husband's name. "He is certainly not here."

"Where is your son, Lady Gordon? He was seen with him somewhere south of Fort Augustus."

"Neither have I seen my son," replied Aileana. At last she gave way to the humanity of their long association. "Oh, Murdoch . . . please," she began, "you know—"

"I have no time for that now, Lady Gordon," he interrupted.

Culodina's father lifted his hand, and from inside his coat pocket now pulled a folded paper. Once the victor in the contest for Scotland had been decided, he had wasted no time in claiming his portion of the spoils. He urged his horse forward a step or two and handed the paper down to her. She took it, but kept it folded in her hand.

"I am possessing myself of Cliffrose Castle," he said coldly. "That paper indicates forfeiture of the property and has been duly signed by the duke of Argyll. It is your husband's doing, Lady Gordon, that it has come to this. He was a traitor, and this is the price for treason.—Culodina, come with me."

Both women were so stunned by the words they could not immediately reply. Tullibardglass nodded to several of the men behind him, who immediately dismounted and came forward. Before Culodina could utter a peep of protest, her hands were tied, and she was mounted on a horse from the stables for which the viscount had sent one of his men.

"You have twenty-four hours to vacate the premises, Lady Gordon," said Tullibardglass. "I will return with troops at this same hour tomorrow. At that time, I will take possession."

He spun around and led the contingent away. In desperation Culodina managed one final glance over her shoulders. There stood the tall figure of Aileana Gordon, forlorn and alone in front of the castle. With her hands bound, Culodina could not even manage a tiny wave of good-bye.

She had still not told her the terrible truth of what had happened on Culloden Moor.

Spring 1746

From Inverness, Sandy Gordon fled south by the shores of Loch Ness. He found an abandoned horse, which made travel easier, and met here and there a few companions who, like him, were trying to keep one step ahead of the duke of Cumberland and his pursuing hoards. He skirted around Fort Augustus at the head of the loch, where government troops were already prowling about, and made his way to Invergarry Castle, hoping there to find a friendly welcome. The place, however, was deserted, and night was falling. Sandy took refuge in one of the stables for the night.

At two in the morning, he was awakened by the sounds of horses outside. Thinking it must be government soldiers, he jumped to his feet, crept stealthily to the ledge of an open window, and peered out. Four or five horsemen with lanterns were dismounting. They apparently had access to the castle.

Suddenly his eyes focused on the familiar form on one of the mounts. It was the prince!

Immediately Sandy ran outside from his hiding place and toward them. Drawn swords from the prince's comrades nearly ended his life before he could identify himself.

"Hold, Burke!" cried Prince Charles. "I recognize this man.—Identify yourself," he added toward Sandy.

"Sandy Gordon, my lord," replied Sandy, bowing. "Sandy Gordon of Cliffrose."

"Yes . . . yes, of course. In the darkness, I could not see your face. Put away your weapons—this man is our friend, Earl Gordon's son."

The prince now dismounted himself, and welcomed Sandy with a shake of the hand. He had all but forgotten the bitter arguments of his war counsel, during which Sandy's father had persistently taken the side of Lord George. Perhaps he was inclined more favorably toward him in that he now realized how right Murray and Sandy's father had been.

"Come inside with us, Gordon. Mr. Burke here has promised to cook salmon for me. I have not seen your father since the battle. Is he with—"

"No, my lord," replied Sandy as they walked toward the castle, the door of which now stood open. "My father is dead."

"I am very sorry to hear it," said the prince. He stopped and turned toward the young man, a dignified sorrow evident on his handsome face. "We lost so many brave men today . . . yesterday, that is. Your father was a fine man, and his death is a great loss. But we will rally the army again. I intend to gather the clans at Fort Augustus at the soonest opportunity and make full amends for Cumberland's recent butchery."

The next day the prince's small band, Sandy Gordon now with them, rode on southwest to Glen Pean at the western end of Loch Arkaig, hoping from there to make plans for a counteroffensive.

What remained of the Jacobite army, meanwhile, some fifteen hundred men, had managed to gather itself south of Inverness near Ruthven. More than two thousand others had been taken prisoner in and around Inverness, a number that would grow in coming months as Cumberland's parties widened their search throughout all of northern and western Scotland.

From Ruthven, Lord George Murray wrote an angry letter to the prince, resigning his post. He laid blame once again on Charles for coming to Scotland in the first place without French help and for stubbornly relying on the counsel of John O'Sullivan, who, he said, was hardly fit to look after luggage, much less an army. As for the Jacobite cause, he was through with it and was going home.

The letter was dispatched by horse to Charles's small group at Glen Pean. O'Sullivan's Irish face turned red with fury upon hearing its contents, but the prince stood grimly frozen, his boyish features pale. If such was the state of his command, he realized, there was nothing for it but to escape.

He wrote a terse reply back to the army, signed and sealed it, then handed it to the rider to take back to Ruthven and be read aloud by Lord George or whoever might be in charge. The message from the prince was simple: "Let every man," he wrote, "seek his safety in the best way he can."

The uprising was over. It was every man for himself.

That same afternoon, the prince and his small band of five companions set out on foot across the boggy ground toward the Sound of Sleat. It took them several days to reach the coast and make arrangements. Finally, nine days after the battle, they were on their way in an eight-oared boat piloted by sixty-nine-year-old Donald MacLeod from Skye, tossing across seventy miles of treacherous water toward the town of Rossinesh on the island of Benbecula.

They had been spotted, however. Almost immediately the King's ships were after them. For the next five months, Prince Charles Edward Stuart would wander as a fugitive in the western Highlands and the coastal islands, a bounty of thirty thousand pounds still on his head.

Sandy Gordon remained with him for two of those months, on what was called "the Long Island"—that tight chain of more than five hundred islands, most tiny and uninhabited, stretching from Barra Head in the south to the Butt of Lewis in the north and now known as the Outer Hebrides. That Cumberland's soldiers could track the furtive prince so far offshore and managed to dog his footsteps every step of the way revealed how quickly allegiances could change. With the Jacobite cause now failed, spies and treachery were everywhere. But in cottages and caves, constantly moving, with many friends still loyal to his father and dedicated to the Highland code of hospitality, the prince managed to elude capture.

And Charles also had his faithful spies, who learned in June of a government scheme to land men on Lewis and South Uist. While ships patrolled the waters of the Minch, the government troops planned to march and sail north and south the entire length of the Long Island—eventually, it was hoped, capturing the prince and returning him to the mainland for hanging.

The prince and his friends now hatched a daring scheme of escape. They would sail the prince through the government net right under the noses of the redcoats who were closing in on him. To be successful, however, the prince would need to don the dress and appearance of an Irish servant girl and leave his faithful companions behind.

Sandy Gordon was ready, at any rate, to give the prince his farewell. He was tired of being on the run. And for months he had been haunted by two images in his brain: Tullibardglass killing his father and his outburst at Culodina. Would he ever be able to see her face-to-face, to take her into his arms and beg forgiveness?

He also must return to his mother. She was alone now and without a husband. In his concern for the welfare of the prince, he had waited far too long already. He had discharged his debt as a soldier, but the prince's fate now rested in other hands. His duty from henceforth lay at Cliffrose.

On June 28, Sandy left the man whom posterity would call Bonnie Prince Charlie—in quilted petticoat, blue-and-white dress, and hooded cloak—on the shores of the isle of North Uist. For good or ill, the prince's future was now up to a brave young woman of the MacDonald clan by the name of Flora. An eighteen-foot boat with four oarsmen splashed from side to side behind them, in readiness to brave the turbulent waters of the Minch and, if they could stay out of sight of government ships, carry the prince across to the island of Skye.

"If fortune should bring you back to Speyside," said Sandy, "you will always have a friend at Cliffrose, my lord."

"I will not forget all you have done for me, Gordon," replied the prince. "You are the earl of Cliffrose now. I wish you all the best."

"Godspeed, Prince Charles."

They shook hands and parted, the prince to become Flora Mac-Donald's servant girl, Betty Burke, and Sandy Gordon to find his own way back through Cullin Sound and thence to Mallaig on the mainland of Scotland.

THIRTY-EIGHT

Summer 1746

Sandy Gordon arrived in the village of Baloggan in the third week of July.

On his way to the castle, he spotted old Robert MacGregor, the midwife's husband and his father's longtime friend, in the fields near his cottage. Now over seventy years of age and stooped with the years, the man was still out with his dog and a few sheep. Sandy paused for a brief visit to tell him he had returned and inform him about his father.

"We aye heard, laddie," said MacGregor, "an' many were the tears shed roun' aboot fer the puir man."

"Have you seen my mother, Robert?" asked Sandy.

"Ay, I see her noo an' then. She's weel, ye can count on that."

"I'm happy to hear it," replied Sandy. "I'm on my way to Cliffrose now to see her." He turned and began to walk in the direction of the castle.

"But ye canna go home, lad," Robert called after him. " 'Tis all changed noo."

Sandy paused in his step and turned.

"What are you saying, Robert?"

"Yer mither's not at Cliffrose."

"What!—where is she, then?"

"In Baloggan," replied the shepherd.

"She is in the village for the day? You've seen her?"

"Lad, ye're not graspin' my meanin'. She's *livin'* in Baloggan noo."

"*Living* there! Why? Where is she . . . tell me where, Robert."

"In one o' the wee cottages in a row behind the kirk—ken ye the place, lad?"

"I know the kirk well enough. But I don't understand a word of what you're saying."

"She's in the third cottage, Sandy lad. She'll be wantin' t' explain the thing to ye hersel'."

"Old Dughall MacPherson's place?"

"He was killed in the battle, lad. His Effie left t' her sister's in Aberdeen. 'Tis yer mither's cottage noo."

Sandy turned again and hurried away across the grass.

"But, laddie," MacGregor called out behind him, "watch yersel'. There's soldiers everywhere, an' they're luikin' fer ye, lad. There be a price on yer head. Ye're wanted by the croon, so ye mauna let yer face be seen. The village is changed, lad. Ye dinna ken wha be yer enemies, an' wha be yer frien's."

Still bewildered by the man's cryptic words about his mother's plight but sobered by his warning, Sandy made his way toward the village. Because the day was already advanced, and knowing he must do nothing to endanger his mother, he waited until the gloaming had brought its summer's dusk down over the land, then sneaked behind the village from the north and crept toward the cottage Robert had described. He did not knock, for fear of neighbors, but gently tried the latch. It was open. He walked inside.

The lone occupant heard the sound and turned her face toward it.

"Sandy!" gasped Aileana. She was out of her chair and flying toward him the next instant.

"Hello, Mother."

"Sandy . . . oh, let my arms hold you, my son!"

She fairly attacked him with arms that had ached for this moment for months.

"I am sorry for not returning sooner, but—"

"Say nothing about it, Sandy. You are here now, and safe, and that is all that matters. Oh, it is so good to have you back!"

"You . . . do you know about Father?"

"Yes," answered Aileana. "Culodina was here."

Sandy winced at mention of her name. They fell apart. Sandy glanced about the cottage. Now for the first time he became aware of his surroundings. Had he not known otherwise, he would have thought this the hovel of the poorest peasant woman for miles. The cottage had but two rooms, its furnishings sparse. On the hearth boiled a few potatoes which, as far as he could tell, might be the only food his mother had. He saw not a single recognizable possession of her former life save a handful of books, her treasured prayer book on a shelf set into one of the walls, her rosary beads beside it, and a curious old worn basket made of local grasses, badly frayed at the edges, that had once belonged to her mother-in-law.

He began to walk slowly about, shocked at what he saw.

"But . . . but, Mother," he began, sweeping his hand about the cottage, a look of bewilderment on his face, "what is all this? Why are you here? What has—"

"Don't you know, Sandy?" she said. "I thought, but . . . then, how did you find me?"

"Know . . . know what? Robert MacGregor told me you were here."

"The rising changed everything," replied Aileana seriously. "Government troops were here less than a week after the battle. They took everything, just as they have done throughout Scotland."

"What do you mean, they took everything?"

"Cliffrose has been forfeited, Sandy. It is no longer ours."

"What! And the servants . . . the animals . . . our possessions?"

"The servants were turned out. The animals, our possessions—I assume they all remain and are—"

She faltered momentarily.

"—in the hands of the new owner," she added. "There was nothing I could do."

"The new owner!" exclaimed Sandy. "Who can that be? I will go there right now and—"

"Sandy!" interrupted his mother, placing her hand on his shoulder as he made for the door. "Sandy, please listen to me. All through Scotland, property is being seized and Jacobite supporters arrested. Your being gone these few months is the best thing that could have happened. I was watched night and day for the first month. Please . . . do not add to my grief the moment I have you back. Going to Cliffrose will do no good. That would be just what he wants. You are in danger."

"What are you saying, Mother? Just what *who* wants?"

"Murdoch Sorley . . . Culodina's father."

"What has he to do with it?"

"He is now the owner of Cliffrose," replied Aileana with reluctance, knowing the disclosure would enrage her son. "He served me the forfeiture nearly three months ago."

"Tullibardglass—the scoundrel!" exclaimed Sandy, in a passion of wrath. He made for the door again.

"Sandy!" cried Aileana, her voice filled with pleading. "Do not go!"

Again he paused and looked at his mother.

"It is no use, Sandy," she said. "The viscount has risen high since the rebellion. He is a powerful man. And there are new laws now—the old Highland ways have been forbidden. Sandy, they've made it against the law to wear the tartan or to play the pipes or even to speak in the old tongue. Weapons have been confiscated all over. Sandy, the old way of life is gone."

At last the truth began to dawn on her son that foolhardiness would only get him killed. Shaking his head, he sank into one of the two chairs in the room.

"But I have to avenge what he has done," he said at length, "not only to you, but to Father."

"Your father?"

Sandy glanced at his mother with eyes of question. "Culodina did not tell you?" he asked.

"Tell me what? That he is dead?"

"That it was Tullibardglass who killed Father at Culloden."

Aileana's eyes filled with tears. It took several long seconds before she could reply.

"I knew Culodina was trying to tell me something in those two days after her return," she said softly. "She would look at me and start to cry, but then turn away and grow silent. Oh, the poor dear . . . the grief it must cause her."

"Where is she, Mother?" said Sandy. "I must see her. I was very cruel when we met after the battle. I had watched hundreds die, was wounded myself—I'd seen Father die in my arms. I was out of my mind with despair and hatred."

"I don't know where she is," replied Aileana. "I've heard nothing since that day her father served me the paper and took her away. I have assumed that she is at Tullibardglass Hall."

It fell silent for several long minutes. At length Sandy spoke.

"I will get Cliffrose back, Mother," he said.

"Then you must take care, Sandy. I fear Culodina's father will expect you."

"Is he at Cliffrose now?"

Aileana shook her head. "It is being maintained by a factor by the name of Fearchar. He has men on hand."

"I will get it back," vowed Sandy a second time, "and I will avenge Father's death."

"There is no profit in revenge, Sandy. We must go on with our lives. Nothing you do will bring your father back. You mustn't become a murderer yourself."

"You don't understand, Mother," he said, growing heated again. "I *have* to redress what he has done!"

Sandy rose and paced the small room, then went out into the dusk to be alone with his passion, while his mother prayed that in time reason would return to his tormented mind. When Sandy walked back in an hour later, subdued but obviously still agitated, Aileana had a supper of boiled potatoes, tea, and brown bread on the table waiting for him.

THIRTY-NINE

The following night, under cover of darkness, Sandy stole out of his mother's cottage in Baloggan and rode to Tullibardglass Hall.

He knew every hill and stream, tree and rock, between his old home and Culodina's. Heeding the warnings of both his mother and old Robert MacGregor, however, on this occasion he kept off the valley road and instead skirted the mountain around the edges of Loch Caoldair, thus approaching toward the Hall from behind, down the hill and through the trees, with the light of a half moon eerily shadowing the ground beneath him.

The place seemed asleep. Flickers of light glowed in a few of the windows. If he could just find a way to get inside, or find Culodina's window and tap on it to rouse her attention . . .

He crept around the base of the Hall, looking for a way in.

All at once a sound came from the direction of the stables. Sandy ducked out of sight beneath a large shrub. A figure slowly emerged from the shadows.

It was the old groom! Sandy jumped to his feet and hurried forward before the man reached the house.

"Baillidh," he whispered.

"Who is it?" exclaimed the startled man.

"Baillidh, it's me—Sandy Gordon."

"By the heavens, m'lord!" exclaimed the groom in a low voice. "Ye mauna be seen, or ye'll be arrested on the spot."

He turned. "Come wi' me," he whispered, walking quickly back into the nearest of the stable buildings. Sandy followed. As soon as they were safely inside, the loyal Jacobite, whose master had never suspected his allegiance to the Stuart cause, turned toward his surprise visitor.

"What are ye doin' here, m'lord?" he asked. " 'Tis not safe."

"I only now returned and learned what the traitor Tullibardglass has done to my mother," replied Sandy. "I came to see Lady Culodina and perhaps kill her father at the same time."

"Ye're too late on both accounts, m'lord," replied Baillidh. "My lord whisked the lass away directly after the battle."

"Away . . . away to where?"

"His estate near Carlisle."

An exclamation of frustration burst from Sandy's lips. His foe had outsmarted him yet again. No wonder his mother had heard nothing about Culodina. Tullibardglass was keeping her south of the border in England, with no Jacobite loyalists for miles. If he hoped to see her, the peril would be even greater than coming here on this night.

"We had heard that ye escaped the sword yersel'," said the groom. "But my hert aye grieves fer yer puir father, bless him. He was the best man in Badenoch."

"Thank you, Baillidh," said Sandy. "I will tell my mother what you have said. It will comfort her."

"An' the Bonnie Prince, m'lord?"

"He was safe when I left him," replied Sandy, "bound for Skye. But they were searching for him everywhere. We may yet see him again—who can tell?"

"Ye maun tak care, m'lord Sandy. My lord's factor is under orders not t' spare yer life gien ye show yer face at Cliffrose."

Sandy nodded. They shook hands and parted.

✖   F O R T Y   ✖

Sandy tarried two weeks with his mother, making sure she had what she needed, acquiring for the cottage what few additional items of furniture he could without raising suspicions, and using the time to secretly renew old friendships and find how many in the area he might still be able to depend on. At the end of that time, well disguised and with false identity papers made up for him during his two months with the prince on the Long Island, Sandy said good-bye to a tearful Aileana and set out for England.

It took him most of another week to reach Carlisle and discreetly inquire into the location of Tullibardglass's estate. His mother and Baillidh had been right. Soldiers were everywhere near the border. The very sound of his speech was often enough to arouse suspicion and send uncomfortable glances his way. But the disguise, which he hoped made him appear ten years older, and the papers proclaiming him to be a Glasgow linen merchant, in most cases proved sufficient to deflect undue questions.

In the dead of night, the moon temporarily hidden by clouds, he finally scaled the wall surrounding Murdoch Sorley's estate. A warm wind was blowing the trees about in a mounting frenzy. He hurried through them, then sprinted across an open lawn to the two-story stone house, ducking hastily into the shadows beside it.

The front door was bolted fast. He crept around the circumference of the place, trying doors and windows, glad there were no dogs about and that all the inhabitants, however many there might be in addition to Culodina and her father, were sleeping soundly.

Unsuccessful, at length he found a rock the size of his hand, crept for a second time to the back of the house, and stopped at what appeared to be a service entrance. With one quick blow he shattered the lowest pane of the nearby window. Reaching carefully through, he managed to get hold of the edge of the door latch. A minute later he was inside.

He sat down to wait. If the sound had disturbed anyone, he would let sleep return before proceeding further.

He remained where he was for twenty minutes, hearing nothing. At last he rose again, his eyes now accustomed to the blackness, and took stock of his surroundings.

He had obviously entered some kind of storage room off the kitchen. From the exterior layout of the house, he had judged the private quarters to be on the first floor, probably facing the front. He crept out of the room, feeling and inching his way. The main staircase should be easy to locate.

Ten minutes later he stood on the first floor, at the top of the stairs. A thin light had broken in through a window on the landing, from the moon now partially visible in the blustery night sky.

He glanced about, glad for the illumination. Three doors presented themselves as likely to lead from the wide landing and adjacent corridor into Culodina's room.

There was nothing for it but to silently probe the latches of each one. If they were unlocked, he hoped the hinges were well oiled and that no creaking floorboards gave him away. He should be able to tell within a second or two whether he had guessed correctly, had stumbled into someone else's room, or worse, had blundered into the viscount's chamber. In any event, after two attempts he should know where Culodina slept.

Stealthily he crept toward the first door.

Suddenly footsteps sounded behind him. The landing flooded with light.

Sandy spun around.

There stood Culodina's father, lantern in one hand, sword in the other, a wickedly cunning smile spreading over his lips.

"You young fool," he said with disdain. "Did you really think I didn't know you would eventually try something foolhardy like this?" He set the lantern down on a sideboard and slowly approached. By degrees the point of the sword rose menacingly toward Sandy.

"Tullibardglass," said Sandy. "It pains me that it has come to this. But when we last met, it was not as friends. We were enemies, and you were a murderer."

"Say rather a patriot who honors and obeys his King," spat Sorley angrily.

"It is only the lowest of men who betrays his own," replied Sandy to Sorley's statement. "And when you killed my father, you forced me to defend my family's honor."

"Your family has no honor!"

"To prove you wrong, I will either kill you or spill my blood on your floor in the attempt."

Tullibardglass laughed in derision, then strode forward clutching his sword in readiness. Sandy's hand moved toward the handle of his dirk.

But Culodina had wakened from the harsh words. Confused and frightened at first, she had quickly thrown on a wrapper and come to her door, not dreaming who was arguing with her father. Now, seeing what was happening, she dashed from her room.

"Sandy!" she cried, running between them.

Startled by her sudden appearance, her father paused momentarily. "Stay where you are, Culodina!" he shouted.

But she continued to Sandy's side. Keeping his eyes locked on her father, Sandy stretched out his free hand and drew her to him.

"I'm so sorry for what I said to you," he said softly. "I was not myself."

"I know," she replied. "We will not speak of it again."

"Culodina, come here!" demanded her father, inching forward again. "Get away from him before you are hurt."

"No, Father, I won't!"

"He is a traitor and a wanted man. If I do not kill him, he will hang from Argyll's gallows."

"Father, you are the traitor," said Culodina. "I know what you did at Culloden. You killed your best friend!"

"He was never my friend. His grandfather was a thief who stole Cliffrose from us."

"That's a lie, Tullibardglass!" rejoined Sandy heatedly.

"I don't believe you either, Father."

"Silence, you little—" began Sorley, advancing quickly toward them with heavy stride. The fire in his eyes indicated clearly enough what was in his mind.

"Sandy, quick!" cried Culodina.

She yanked him by the hand toward her room. A lethal *whoosh* of her father's sword whizzed through the air behind them, its tip missing Sandy's back by inches. Sandy followed her inside. Culodina slammed and bolted the door. The next instant her father's fist exploded upon it.

"Culodina!" he shrieked in a rage. "Culodina, open this door or suffer the consequences. I will not be able to protect you if you continue this madness!"

Even as he pounded, shouting curses and threats, Culodina grabbed a dress and cloak, then led Sandy to the open window. Within seconds they were climbing down the slope of the roof. Sandy leapt to the ground, then did his best to break Culodina's jump as she followed. By the time Tullibardglass realized he was yelling at an empty room, they were sprinting through the trees for the perimeter wall.

Enraged yet further as the truth dawned on him, Sorley spun around, sent the sword clattering across the floor, and stormed down the stairs, hurriedly rousing every available man in his employ and the three soldiers he had arranged to be stationed on the premises. The gates of the estate swung open five minutes later, and the viscount of Tullibardglass galloped off after the renegades with eight armed men.

Their orders regarding Sandy were "kill on sight."

❋   F O R T Y · O N E   ❋

Racing on the back of Sandy's horse across several miles of rolling hills, then through the deserted streets of Carlisle, with Culodina holding on around Sandy's waist for dear life, the two fugitives turned onto the northern road and were galloping back over the Scottish border within an hour. The southern Lowlands, however, were no safer than the English countryside. Anything out of the ordinary was sure to raise the suspicious eyebrows of Lowland Scots eager to curry the favor of the nearby redcoats.

The first thing they had to do was procure a horse for Culodina. Then they might travel as brother and sister, calmly, and without apparent fear or urgency. These days, the worst thing a Jacobite who was desirous of staying out of jail and off the gallows could do was look like a man on the run.

Pausing for several hours in a protected hollow, they managed to get three or four hours of sleep. They bought a horse in a nearby village the following morning, then struck out east across the southern mountains, where they knew Culodina's father would not look for them. But Sorley was certain to know their eventual destination. Therefore, Sandy was in no hurry as they made their way back to Speyside. Along the way, they tarried at what Jacobite homes still existed, gathering what news he could of the failed cause and the prince's plight.

Two weeks after Culodina's rescue, they finally approached the familiar glen. The hour was late. They left their horses in Robert MacGregor's byre and stole to Aileana's cottage sometime after midnight.

Again the door was not locked. They walked in.

Waking suddenly from the press of her son's hand against her mouth, Aileana was nearly frightened out of her wits.

"Mother . . . Mother," said Sandy in an urgent whisper, "it is me—do not be afraid. I did not want you to cry out." Slowly he released her mouth.

"Sandy!" she exclaimed, trying to rise from bed. "What are . . . but let me light a candle."

"No, Mother, please. We mustn't be seen or heard."

"But who is that behind you?" said Aileana, sitting up and noticing a figure in the shadows of the thin moonlight that fell through the one window.

"Aunt Aileana . . . it is me," said Culodina softly.

"Culodina! Oh, my dear child!" exclaimed Aileana, bursting into tears. The next moment they were in one another's arms. "But . . . how did—"

"We will tell you all in the morning, Mother," said Sandy.

"Your father was here, Culodina."

"I thought as much," nodded Sandy with concern. "How long ago?"

"Ten days, perhaps. He was furious and full of threats. But eventually I think he believed me that I knew nothing of your whereabouts. After that, as far as I know, he left Tullibardglass Hall and returned south."

Sandy sighed. The situation remained dangerous. "At the moment we are near exhaustion," he said. "If we might simply have some oatcakes and milk, and then sleep, we will think what to do in the morning."

Already Aileana was on her feet and gathering her wrapper about her. The opportunity to minister to their needs with her hands and heart acted as a tonic to her spirits.

Suddenly she had a family again!

FORTY·TWO

September 1746

Having committed Culodina to the care of his mother so as to make sure neither of them would be endangered by his presence, Sandy again made preparations to leave Baloggan.

"I have made arrangements with Baillidh at Tullibardglass Hall," he said. "He will know if Sorley returns again and will get word to you, Mother. If that should happen, take Culodina to Sarah MacGregor or Sally MacKenzie. Baillidh will find a way to alert me. If I hear of danger to you, I will return immediately. But until such time, you are both better off if I am not here."

Sandy disappeared into the night. He was gone for ten days. When he returned, the glow in his eyes told his mother he was preparing for a fight. She feared what might be the result. Dissuading him, however, proved useless.

"I must do what I can to clear my name, Mother, and to get Cliffrose back. What kind of man would I be to just let things remain as they are?"

"A man who is *alive*, Sandy, and free," urged his mother. "Why can you not at least give my way a chance?"

"Your way—what is that?"

"While you were gone, I wrote to make appeal to my cousin, Duncan Forbes, who is now the Lord President," explained Aileana. "With your father gone, I am hopeful he will feel I have paid a sufficient price for his involvement."

"Bah! Forbes was Cumberland's lackey, like all the others. Why should he care?"

"My mother was a Forbes, remember, and Duncan's own aunt. He saw well enough what it was like for her after his uncle, my own father, died at Killiecrankie. Duncan always loved my mother, though their stations in life were vastly different. I think he will have sympathy with my similar plight."

Sandy took in her words thoughtfully.

"Your father was well thought of on both sides of the conflict," Aileana added. "And there are rumors that Duncan and the duke of Argyll have had a falling out since the battle."

Sandy nodded. He had heard the same thing from his own contacts.

"I am hopeful that Argyll's name on the forfeiture document," continued Aileana, "and the fact that it was so hastily drawn up will weigh favorably on my cousin's mind."

"You are a crafty one, Mother, I will say that," laughed Sandy. "I will think about what you say. But I make no promises as yet. Cousin or not, the good Mr. Forbes supported Cumberland, and that is something for which I will have difficulty forgiving him."

Even as they were speaking, a soft knock came on the door. Sandy and Culodina jumped up from their chairs to hide in the next room. Aileana went to the door.

There stood the longtime groom of Tullibardglass Hall.

She gasped in alarm. "Baillidh!" she exclaimed. "Has Murdoch returned?"

"Not yet, m'leddy," he replied. "Word is, hooever, that we're t' be expectin' him soon."

"That is a relief for now, at least."

"I'm sorry to be so late, m'leddy," the groom went on, "but gien ye ken the whereaboots o' yer son—"

Sandy now appeared in the doorway.

"Baillidh, do you bring news?" he said.

"Ay, m'lord. 'Tis aboot the Bonnie Prince . . . he's comin', m'lord, jist like ye said."

"Coming where?"

"He's bound fer the glens. He's in the care o' Lochiel. But one o' his men has come sayin' he needs oor help t' hide him while he waits fer transport t' the Continent."

Sandy thought a moment.

"We'll hide him in the cave on the loch," said Sandy. "They'll never find him there."

"I'll pass word back t' the chief, m'lord."

"Tell Lochiel to bring the prince to Gordon's Cage. All the provisions he needs will be supplied. Tell him to wait for me there."

"Ay, m'lord."

When the word came some days later, again Sandy prepared to depart, leaving the two women yet again alone in the small cottage.

"I know it is a trial for you," he said, "but Culodina, you must remain inside and not be seen in the village. Your father has many friends. Word must not leak out that you are here.—Mother, you do understand how important—?"

"We will be safe, Sandy," she said. "I am more anxious about you."

"I must still be loyal to our prince. Whatever has happened, his father remains the rightful King and is still due our allegiance."

"Be careful, Sandy!" said Culodina.

They embraced and held one another tightly for several long seconds. Then Sandy kissed his mother and walked out the door into the night.

For the next eight days, between the third and tenth of September, Sandy Gordon played host to Charles Edward Stuart at the prince's final lodgings in Scotland. They were also the most unusual quarters he had occupied during the long sojourn that had begun the previous year or any place he had slept during his recent five months of wandering the Highlands and islands. The great cave, high on the cliff edge of the southern slope of Ben Alder, overlooking Loch Ericht, had been a favorite haunt for Sandy in his youth. Some ancient Highland wanderer had no doubt first discovered the place in an era long past in Caledonia's history. Now it was known as Gordon's Cage.

After eight days came word that the French privateer l'Heureux was awaiting the prince in Loch non Uamh. Again the two young men parted, the prince and his three guides embarking overland to the coast. Having eluded every effort by the British government to capture him, the prince finally sailed for France on September 20. He would never again set foot in Scotland.

Sandy Gordon, meanwhile, returned to Baloggan.

The moment he walked into the cottage, his mother greeted him excitedly.

"I have heard from Duncan!" she said.

Sandy glanced around. He saw no sign of Culodina.

"I took her to Sally's two nights ago," said Aileana in answer to his unspoken question. "There was a rumor her father may be about. But, Sandy!—the Lord President has agreed to rescind the forfeiture . . . *if* we can produce the deed that proves our ownership."

"I thought the property was seized because Father was a Jacobite."

"The actual wording of the forfeiture was based on Murdoch's claim that Cliffrose rightfully belonged to him, *not* treason to the Crown. In his haste to grab Cliffrose, Murdoch created a loophole that may come back to strangle him. Duncan also apparently very much dislikes Murdoch, and that helps our cause as well. But we must have proof. If we supply it, Duncan said, he will void Argyll's order."

"But you have no papers, do you, Mother?"

"I thought nothing of such things when I left."

"Where are they, then?"

"I don't know, Sandy. I've never seen a deed to the land or the castle."

"There must be one somewhere."

"Your father kept his important documents in his study on the third floor. But I am afraid I don't know where. I was never curious about legalities and records."

"Even if a deed had existed, Tullibardglass has no doubt destroyed it by now."

"It is our only chance."

"What about the charges against me?" asked Sandy.

"That may be more difficult," replied Aileana. "But for my sake, and since Kendrick is dead, Duncan has promised to consider a pardon, if only to get back at Culodina's father."

FORTY-THREE

As Sandy approached Cliffrose Castle, where he had spent the happy days of his boyhood and youth, a host of emotions flooded his heart and brain . . . images of his father's smiling face, memories of so many things they had done together, the sound of his father's low voice, the ring of his laughter.

He looked up at the beloved stone walls and towers. Even if what he had come here to do succeeded, could this place ever be a home again?

The place was so desolate, so quiet. The grounds had not been kept up and were overgrown. How quickly, he mused, a place could run down when love was taken away.

But he could not tarry with such reflections. He must be about his business. He had spent the early evening finalizing the arrangements and making sure all was in readiness. Now he must do his part to prevent unforeseen danger to the others.

He ran toward the castle, skirting the entry wide by staying under the row of large beech trees, then crept toward the front door.

He saw nothing of Fearchar as he approached, or no one else, for that matter. If the factor indeed had men about, they must have all retired early.

The key that had lain hidden as long as he could remember still lay buried in its place . . . the lock was also unchanged. In less than a minute, he was inside.

How strangely familiar everything appeared. He had been gone only a year, yet it seemed a lifetime ago. How strange, too, that the interior had hardly been altered. Chairs and sideboards and carpets all sat exactly as he remembered them. The walls looked identical . . . the same portraits and tapestries . . . the faint smells so powerfully nostalgic. Did anyone actually *live* here? The place felt lifeless.

He approached the stairs and tiptoed gently up. He reached the first floor safely, pausing at the top to gaze at the year-old portrait of his father. The poignant sight of Kendrick Gordon in full Highland regalia brought a lump to Sandy's throat. His father looked again so vibrant, his eyes bright and alive, just as Sandy had always known him.

The other two portraits his mother told him they had planned were never even begun. They hardly seemed to matter, Sandy thought, now that his father and Cliffrose had been taken from them. Why would Tullibardglass have kept the image of his father hanging here? Why had he not destroyed it? Or had he even taken notice?

As he gazed up at the image, a voice sounded behind him. He spun around. There was Tullibardglass standing in the darkness, again with sword in hand. The man seemed to anticipate his every move!

"He could have been a great man," he commented, "had he not turned traitor in the end."

"He *was* a great man," stated Sandy. "Certainly greater than his traitorous cousin."

Tullibardglass received the pointed rebuke without further reply, and now took a step or two forward out of the shadows.

"I always knew it would come to this in the end," he said as he came. "This fight was destined to be decided between you and me, young Gordon, no one else."

Sandy glanced about, took several steps to his left, then carefully removed a sword from the wall mount where his father's collection of weapons still hung. Tullibardglass chuckled. But if he thought that his young adversary was still a boy he was badly mistaken. The son of his cousin was no mere youth now, but a man who was more than his own equal.

"I urge you to reconsider, Tullibardglass," said Sandy, adjusting the sword in his hand. "I do not want to have to kill you, if for no other reason than for Culodina's sake."

"You are being extremely foolish," replied Sorley with a condescending laugh.

"Don't underestimate me," Sandy said evenly. "I know how to use this. So I will ask you once very calmly—will you reinstate Cliffrose to my mother?"

Tullibardglass did not laugh this time. Instead, the fire of hatred flashed in his eyes.

"Never!" he said. "Cliffrose is mine. It should always have been mine!"

He lunged forward and suddenly aimed a wicked circular slice toward Sandy with his blade. Sandy leapt back and at the same instant raised his own weapon. As he met the oncoming blow, a great clank echoed of steel upon steel. Both men's hands jarred them in pain, and each realized they were in a fight to the death.

───

Outside the castle, Culodina stooped behind Aileana through a low cellar door. Both felt their way toward the stairs in the blackness. It was the only entrance through which Aileana was sure she could gain access to the house without being seen, now that her son had gone in through the front.

A few minutes later they stood in the darkened kitchen. A flood of emotional memories surged through her at sight of the homely room, its working surfaces far less grand than the rest of the house. But Aileana could not pause to let the memories distract her just now. Instead she hurried across the familiar floor and unbolted the locked rear door. Two men entered hastily from the night and carefully closed the door behind them. Both clutched large claymore swords dug recently out of the peat where they had hidden them three months earlier rather than relinquish them to government soldiers.

The unlikely trio now quietly followed the former mistress of the house through a black corridor to a narrow, little-used staircase at the northeast corner of the place, then ascended slowly up the circular stairs. Above them they could already hear shouts and sounds of combat.

On the darkened landing, the only light being that from the moon through the windows, the young man who had grown up within these walls and the older man who had taken them from him continued to swing and jab their blades at one another in a more dangerous contest than either had seen since Culloden. Though the quiet man whose silent eyes now overlooked the battle from his portrait on the wall had never himself taken a human life, the blood of either his cousin or his son seemed likely to be spilled upon the oak slabs of floor before many more minutes had passed.

Suddenly a vicious thrust came straight at Sandy's chest. He leapt to the right as he parried to avoid it, momentarily losing his balance. A clanging horizontal whack from Sorley's weapon followed before he could right himself and ripped the sword from his hand. It clinked over the floor in two or three bounces, coming to rest four feet from his enemy, who stepped over and secured it with his foot.

Seeing his dilemma, Sandy darted across the floor in the opposite direction.

"Not running away like a coward this time, Gordon?" taunted Tullibardglass.

"The only coward, Sorley," rejoined Sandy, inching along the wall, "is he who betrays his country and his friends . . . and his own kin."

At the words, emboldened at what he considered his imminent victory, Culodina's father now rushed forward, sword outstretched. But the gesture was unwisely considered. He had not apprehended Sandy's objective.

Before Tullibardglass could prevent it, Sandy had caught up another sword from the wall. Seeing Sorley's hand outstretched, he grabbed the weapon's hilt in both hands, as if the lighter-weight saber were a claymore. Before his adversary could correct his foolish lunge, a great blow crashed against the extended blade and knocked it from Sorley's hand. It clattered noisily to the floor with the other. Tullibardglass stumbled sideways from the unexpected power of the jolt and fell. The next instant Sandy's foot was on his chest, the tip of the saber poised against the skin of his Sorley neck.

"Go ahead, Gordon," spat Sorley, "run me through—unless you are a coward. You bested me. Now kill me as you said you would."

Sandy clutched the hilt of his sword tightly. His hand was trembling.

"Stay your hand, Gordon," commanded a voice behind him from the top of the stairs. "I have a pistol pointed at the back of your head."

Light gradually lit the room as two more men clambered up the stairway behind the factor, one of them carrying a lantern.

"Fearchar, you fool!" gasped Sorley from the floor. "What took you so long to get here?"

"You told us to follow him in after he arrived," replied the factor, inching his way in a semicircle away from the landing until he came directly into Sandy's sight. His two accomplices followed. "But we never saw him," he went on. "It wasn't until I heard your swords that I realized he had slipped past us into the house."

Still Sandy's hand clutched the sword, whose tip remained tingling Sorley's neck.

"You are a greater pack of idiots than I thought!" cried Tullibardglass. "What are you waiting for? Shoot the—"

Suddenly behind them sounded the crash of a door. Footsteps pounded across the floor, then burst out a great cry of pain and an explosion of gunfire. The blunt end of Robert MacGregor's claymore had come down on Fearchar's wrist, sending the pistol flying and discharging its shot into the nearest wall.

Even as its echo was dying out, Aileana, Baillidh, and Culodina had rushed in behind him.

Before either of the factor's two lackeys could draw their swords, they found themselves backing against the wall behind them, on either side of the portrait of Kendrick Gordon, unexpectedly staring at the points of two smaller sword blades whose opposite ends were held by two trembling yet very determined women. MacGregor followed his blow to the wrist by turning the tip of his giant weapon against Fearchar's unwieldy stomach.

In the middle of the room, Murdoch Sorley's groom prowled the floor with his own claymore clutched in both hands and lifted as high in the air as his strength could maintain it, ready to bring it down on the head of any of the three who dared make a move.

Sandy's eyes now met Sorley's. The entire room fell silent. Softly his mother's words came back into his mind: *There is no profit in revenge, Sandy. . . . You mustn't become a murderer yourself.*

Slowly he pulled away, then removed his foot from Sorley's chest.

"Where are the others?" Sandy asked, glancing toward Robert MacGregor.

"Munro, MacPherson, and Murison are outside the front door, clay-mores in hand," answered MacGregor.

"You are through here, Tullibardglass," said Sandy. He reached down, grabbed him by the shirt, and yanked him to his feet.

"Don't forget, Gordon," replied Culodina's father, in no way humbled by his recent brush with death, or grateful to Sandy for sparing his life, "this little game of yours means nothing. Cliffrose is still mine," he added spitefully. "You have not heard the last of this."

"We shall see, Tullibardglass. For now, I am ordering you to get out. As for you, Fearchar—you and your men are no longer welcome on my mother's property."

Culodina's father straightened himself as best he could under the cir-cumstances. He nodded to the three fools, as he judged them, who had allowed themselves to be overpowered by two women, an old groom, and an even older shepherd, and strode toward the door.

"Culodina," he said turning, "I will give you one final chance to save yourself. If you come with me, no harm will come to you. Otherwise, I cannot help you."

"I'm sorry, Father, but my life is with Sandy and Aunt Aileana now."

"Even if it means going to jail with them?"

"Sandy Gordon has asked me to be his wife."

Tullibardglass burst into a laugh of scorn. "I might have expected it!" he said. "I suppose you two young fools deserve one another. But even if he manages to elude the law, he will be a pauper at best. You will be throwing away everything to marry him, Culodina. And you may well be a widow before the year is out."

"I would rather be the wife of a pauper in Scotland, or even the widow of a hero, than the bride of the richest man in all England. I am sorry, Father, but I intend to marry Sandy, and nothing you can do will stop me."

Seething, Culodina's father clattered down the stairs and out the heavy door. Carefully Aileana, Culodina, and MacGregor eased their swords away from his three henchmen, while Baillidh's claymore remained poised above his shoulder in the event any of them made a sudden move. But without incident the others followed Tullibardglass from the house.

The moment they were gone, Culodina rushed into Sandy's arms. Baillidh let down his heavy weapon. "No doobt after this," he said, "I'll be findin' mysel' turned oot o' Tullibardglass Hall."

"You shall henceforth be our groom at Cliffrose," laughed Aileana.

"*If* Cliffrose becomes ours again, Mother," now added Sandy. "We need to find those papers." He stepped away from Culodina briefly in order to replace the swords on the wall. "The viscount may be back with a small army before morning. At present he is still the owner and could throw us out, not to mention arrest me and send me off to the duke of Argyll."

"We shall have to work quickly, then," said Aileana. "I don't know what we will be looking for, but we should see what there is in your father's study."

They left the landing and hurried in the direction of the third floor. As she went, Aileana paused at the portrait. A few tears formed in her eyes as she returned her husband's gaze. Then she nodded quietly, as if speaking to him the resolve in her own heart and echoing her son's determination from weeks earlier. She, too, would not rest, for the sake of her husband's memory, until Cliffrose was once more in Gordon hands.

They succeeded in finding Kendrick Gordon's cache of important documents, though without immediately being able to distinguish among them those of singular importance. Gathering every scrap of paper to take with them for safekeeping and further perusal, they left the place, this time together by the front door, where they met their three faithful guards—MacPherson, Munro, and Murison.

Neither seeing nor hearing further signs of the enemy, the eight members of the brave if unorthodox Highland force that had retaken the castle without a drop of blood being shed returned in the darkness to their own homes.

Four days later Sandy and Aileana Gordon, along with Culodina Sorley, left by coach for Inverness and an appointment with the Lord President for Scotland, Duncan Forbes.

❖   F O R T Y - F O U R   ❖

November 1746

Winter was on the approach in the north when Sandy Gordon, now recognized as earl in his father's stead, approached Tullibardglass Hall. The place was full of significance for him, though not so full of memories as it was for the woman who rode at his side.

They reined in their mounts, dismounted, then walked hand in hand toward the front door. They had reason to be confident that Culodina's father was in residence.

The door opened to their knock.

"Hello, Swayn," said Culodina. "Is my father at home?"

"Yes, my lady. I will tell him you are here."

Sandy and Culodina waited in the entry. What was going through Culodina's pounding heart Sandy suspected well enough. Neither had seen her father since that fateful night. She was fearful, detached, relieved. Her daughter's heart hoped he might yet learn to accept her *as* she was and for *who* she was, although she knew him too well to be optimistic. It was unlikely they would ever be close, but she had determined to try to learn to love him again.

At length they heard the heavy familiar step of Murdoch Sorley descending the staircase. Culodina's heart began to beat a little more rapidly.

His form came into view. He seemed to have aged since they had seen him last.

He approached without greeting, without even expression of recognition, came forward, and stood before them waiting.

"Viscount Sorley," said Sandy, addressing him soberly and formally, "I have here papers from the Lord President nullifying the forfeiture of Cliffrose and reinstating it into the hands of myself and my mother. Be assured that Mr. Forbes has had the deeds and documents pertinent to the case submitted to the scrutiny of the King's solicitors. You will find all scrupulously in order, including the deed to the property legally transferred to my great grandfather."

As he spoke, Tullibardglass stood stoically, giving no sign that he heard so much as a word that was being said.

"As you had long suspected, there were certain irregularities in the case, dating back to the year Cliffrose was purchased by my ancestors from your great-grandfather, who was at the time suffering financial setbacks. As it turns out, a sizeable loan was made to your great-grandfather, which was added to the proceeds from the sale. This apparently was never repaid by Mr. Sorley, nor by his son, or by your own father when the property, and its debt, came down to him. It would appear, therefore, though it grieves me to be the bearer of the news, that according to the original terms of the sale and loan it is actually Tullibardglass Hall that stands in forfeit to the earl of Cliffrose."

Sorley winced slightly, inwardly cursing his father and grandfather and all the rest of them for being so careless as to pass on their financial difficulties to him. He did not know whether to believe any of this nonsense or not. He would certainly look into it.

"I have my solicitors looking into the matter further to determine the exact amount that stands in arrears. Until the matter is resolved," Sandy continued, "you are welcome to remain in residence. And be assured that you will be more than generously provided for, whatever the outcome. I will see to it."

Sandy now handed him the paper, which Sorley took without looking at it.

"Now, finally, we would like you to know that we two were married two weeks ago in Inverness. We will be hosting a Christmas ball next month at Cliffrose for all the people of Baloggan and the community. It will be our first social event as husband and wife. And we would like you to attend as a special guest of honor."

By now tears were flowing from Culodina's eyes—tears of happiness to hear Sandy refer to her as his wife, tears of sadness to see her father so alone and sad. She gathered her courage, then stepped forward and kissed him on the cheek.

"I am very happy, Papa," she said. "I want you to be happy too. If I can try to forgive you for what you have done, is it not time that you let forgiveness into your heart also?"

He gave no sign of response. Culodina gazed at him a moment, then stepped back to Sandy's side. Sandy now extended his hand. But the offered gesture of farewell was not taken.

After a moment, Sandy and Culodina turned and left the house. As they walked to their waiting horses, Sandy stretched his arm around Culodina in loving reassurance. It had been a difficult interview. A few final tears glistened down the daughter's cheek. But she had made her choice, had chosen her happiness. No fatherly bitterness could take that from her.

They rode back to Cliffrose quietly, thinking of many things.

The next morning, Murdoch Sorley was on his way from Tullibardglass Hall back to his English estate. He did not attend the Christmas ball at Cliffrose.

———

As Aileana Gordon's hair continued to gray, her remaining years at Cliffrose were among her happiest. As those years went by, she found herself gradually surrounded by a joyous quiver of granddaughters and grandsons and by the most loving and attentive daughter-in-law every woman could hope to have, who now called her *Mother* Aileana.

Slowly the old clan life of the Highlands passed into history. But the memory of the Bonnie Prince who had given Caledonia a bright and shining moment of hope lived on in the hearts of those who remembered the days when Scotland was free. And the cause for which he had been willing to risk all, for which many Jacobites had given their lives, grew to symbolize far more than merely the rightful kingship of a nation. Over the years, it would come to represent the idea of liberty for all people and the hopes and dreams of future generations.

In afteryears, when Lady Aileana Gordon sat her grandchildren round about her and in her lap, with a voice full of mystery and with crooning lips that occasionally lapsed into the old Scots tongue or even the Gaelic of her youth, she told of the cause for which her husband and their father had fought, the cause the one had died for. Young ears listening and eyes wide, they took in the poignant tales and the plaintive melodies. Their favorite was the soft ballad of a Highland legacy now lost—remembering him who left his royal dynasty, and their hearts, on a lonely battlefield called Culloden Moor.

> Bonnie Charlie's noo awa;
>   safely o'er the friendly main.
> Mony a hert will break in twa,
>   should he ne'er come back again.
>
> Will ye no come back again?
> Will ye no come back again?
> Better lo'ed ye canna be.
> Will ye no come back again?

4

NORTHWARD TOWARD
THE PAST

What a moving story!" whispered Andrew to himself, closing the book and setting it on his lap. He was close to tears but wasn't sure why.

How could human beings treat one another with such . . .

His thoughts trailed off indistinctly. There were no words to give definition to the feelings rising within him.

Was it any wonder many Scots resented what had happened? As if Glencoe weren't enough! No wonder the Scots wanted their freedom back.

Andrew rose, left the library, and walked back down to the gallery. Again he sought the portrait, whose meaning he finally understood.

Kendrick Gordon, Earl of Cliffrose, 1688–1746.

Now the date of the man's death contained such poignant significance.

Duncan's words of a few hours earlier returned to Andrew's mind.

"Gien it's the Scot's thirst fer freedom from England ye're wantin' t' unnerstan', 'tis t' Bannockburn an' Culloden ye maun gae. . . . 'Tis what I call the ancient strife o' Caledonia."

Andrew realized it really was time to resume what he had begun earlier. He had to go to Culloden and Bannockburn, just as Duncan said. He had to walk the historic battlefields for himself. If he could not resolve the ancient strife of the past, he must at least ask what role he might play in its future.

And he wanted to see the rest of Scotland too!

⚅   T W O   ⚅

In early September, as he had three months before, Andrew Trentham set off for the north. His mother hugged him warmly as they said final good-byes at the door. He couldn't help but remember the tension that had hung between them on the eve of his first departure. So much had changed since then.

"I know you're planning to travel incognito and let the spirit lead, my boy," said his father. "But do keep us posted on your whereabouts."

"No problem, Dad," replied Andrew. "I'll call every night. But you might not recognize me when I come back—I didn't pack my razor!"

"When you say incognito, you go all the way!"

"I can't blend in and get to know the people if they recognize me."

"Well, every man has to grow a beard at least once in his life, I always say," laughed Harland Trentham. "We'll do our best not to let the sight of yours shock us."

Andrew left Derwenthwaite in high spirits, especially buoyed by the changes in his mother's countenance. Though she walked with a limp and had not regained complete command of either speech or arm, he thought she was happier and more at peace than he had ever seen her. Who could have imagined a stroke to be a blessing in disguise? She smiled warmly as he got in the car and kept her right hand raised, waving in gentle poignant fare-well, until he was out of sight along the drive.

Andrew followed the same route as before through Scotland's southern uplands, skirting Glasgow and again making his way northward to the plain of Rannoch, then down the narrow pass into the valley of Glencoe. In his mind, as he traveled, the stories he had learned from Duncan unreeled themselves once more. There on the plain he saw Foltlaig and his son Maelchon laying their plans to counter the northward expansion of the Roman legions. And then, as he descended toward Glencoe, the dreadful events for which the tiny valley had become known to the world came back to him as if he had heard from Duncan's lips only yesterday the tale of the doomed village and the strange maiden with the second sight who managed to save the young man she loved from the carnage. The high slopes of the mountains stretching high on both sides as he drove added a sense of awe, even quiet terror, to the place.

The day was a warm one. He parked his car and hiked along one of the several streams tumbling down off the slopes of Bidean Nam Bian. Before he knew it, several hours had passed, and he had climbed to a height where the wild, desolate, uninhabited glen spread out below him.

Was the place of Ginevra and Brochan's meeting somewhere on these slopes near where he walked?

For long minutes he stood, no sounds entering his ear but the silence of height and isolation and the gentle whisperings of the Highland winds. All looked so peaceful now, so different from that terrible night more than three hundred years before.

For the first time he understood how intrinsically the two tragedies of Glencoe and Culloden were linked, providing the foundation for present Scottish passion to regain what had then been lost.

An impulse toward prayer stole over him.

"God," he whispered, his voice tentative to address the Almighty aloud, though he was miles from any other human creature, *"help me know what to do. Show me what is the right thing to do in the matter of Scotland's future. Give me courage to see the truth and to be bold to act upon it. Show me what is right to do for the people of this land and for our whole nation."*

The walk back the side of the tallest of the Three Sisters was a quiet one. Three-quarters of the way back to his car, he began to chuckle as the thought came of a photographer from one of the tabloids positioned somewhere on a hilltop out of sight with a 500mm telephoto lens.

Wouldn't *The Sun* love that! Or Ludington of the BBC? Rumors had begun to fly about him the previous spring. A picture of him praying on a mountain would cap it off—he could see the headlines now!

"MP Seeks Scottish Mountaintop to Find Peace with Soul."

In a light mood, he drove on to Fort William, where he spent the rest of the day browsing in shops, walking the streets and waterfront, observing, listening, thinking, and finally locating a bed-and-breakfast for the night.

The following morning, outfitted with a dozen cassette tapes of Scottish folk music and historical ballads, he drove west to Mallaig and ferried across the Sound of Sleat to the island of Skye, to which Bonnie Prince Charlie had escaped following Culloden. What remained of the afternoon and that night was taken up at the Clan Donald Study Centre and hotel at Armadale, though he had little time for more than a quick stroll to make initial acquaintance with the gardens and ruins of Armadale Castle before dinner.

Rising early the following morning, he walked up the narrow roadway behind the castle, then bore off left up the slope, exploring for a high vantage point from which he could look down upon the ruins with the blue waters of Sleat behind them. A brief walk through the sheep farm of the estate followed, and then a return down the hill and slowly through the gardens, with their varied collections of pine, fir, and rhododendron contributed by MacDonald clan members from all over the world.

A sudden rain shower erupted, nearly drenching him as he sprinted for the cover of the gift shop in the former castle stables. But it was over almost as soon as it began, and he continued his explorations.

As a sense of the history of the place grew upon him, his curiosity mounted to delve into that portion of his ancestry hinting at connections with that ancient and most powerful clan MacDonald, whose chief had originally been known as Lord of the Isles.

As a result of his readings—from the ancient days of the Wanderer and Cruithne up to medieval times—and his genealogical research, he had discovered, he thought, a link by marriage between Fintenn, boy-convert of St. Columba, and the MacDonald line—through Domhnall, the man who became Fintenn's sister's husband.

"I am all but certain," said Andrew later that morning to the director of the Study Centre, "that Fintenn's brother-in-law was connected with the line that would eventually become the Clan Donald."

"You may well be right," nodded the kindly young woman, intrigued by the connections Andrew had discovered, but without the remotest idea that she was speaking with one of the most important leaders in the House of Commons.

"If so," Andrew went on, "then Domhnall would be ancestor to Somerled and his grandson, Lords of the Isles—"

"Now you're touching on *my* roots," she said excitedly. "Somerled's sons and grandsons walked this very ground—and from them the MacDonald name sprang in the thirteenth century."

"Right," agreed Andrew. "But is it truly possible to establish verifiable bonds between the present and such ancient times?"

"That's why we are here," rejoined the woman, pulling several thick volumes of ancient genealogies down from a shelf. Her detective's nose was already after the scent.

But as yet the name Gordon had made no appearance in Andrew's research to link those first millennium Celts to the family of Kendrick Gordon of the eighteenth century and thence to him. When the name *Gordon* first came to Scotland, he had not yet discovered.

From the Clan Donald Centre, Andrew's travels took him from Kyle of

Lochalsh and the magnificent Eilean Donan Castle eastward to Loch Ness. Instead of turning north toward Inverness, however, first he made his way south along the lake's bottommost tip toward Fort Augustus. As he drove beside the narrow, enigmatic body of water, Andrew thought back to Columba's first approach along this same route to the land of the northern Picts, recalling the story he had read about the saint's encounter with the legendary sea monster Nessie. He wondered how much truth existed in the tale. Was it but one more embellished myth which had gathered around the old saint?

Andrew pulled over at the next parking turnout and retrieved the *Life of Saint Columba* from his briefcase. Again he read the fascinating passage.

On another occasion, when the blessed man was journeying in the province of the Picts, he was obliged to travel up the River Nesa. When he reached the bank of the river, he saw some of the inhabitants burying an unfortunate man, who, according to the account, was a short time before seized, as he was swimming, and bitten most severely by a monster that lived in the water; and his wretched body was, though too late, taken out with a hook, by those who came to his assistance in a boat. The blessed man, on hearing this, was so far from being dismayed, that he directed one of his companions to swim to the farther bank. Hearing the command of the excellent man, Lugne Mocumin obeyed without the least delay, taking off all his clothes, except his tunic, and leaping into the water. But the monster, which, so far from being satiated, was only roused for more prey, was lying at the bottom of the loch, and when it felt the water disturbed above by the man's swimming, suddenly rushed out, and, giving an awful roar, darted after him, with its mouth wide open, as the man swam in the middle of the stream. Then the blessed man observing this, raised his holy hand, while all the rest, brethren as well as strangers, were stupefied with terror, and, invoking the name of God, formed the saving sign of the cross in the air, and commanded the ferocious monster, saying, "Thou shalt go no further, nor touch the man; go back with all speed." Then at the voice of the saint, the monster was terrified, and fled more quickly than if it had been pulled back with ropes, though it had just got so near to Lugne, as he swam, that there was not more than the length of a spear-shaft between the man and the beast.

One fact could not be denied, he thought as he gazed out over the icy depths: the legend of the mysterious Loch Ness monster was as ancient as the mysterious Picts themselves.

❖ T H R E E ❖

From Fort Augustus, Andrew drove south through Glen Albyn, then turned northwest at the town of Spean Bridge. Though his route had been circuitous in order to visit all the places he wanted to see, at last Andrew came into that region he had been most eager to visit. Through Glen Spean he now approached Glen Truim and the valley of the River Spey, where his ancestors Kendrick and Aileana and later Sandy and Culodina Gordon of Cliffrose had dwelt.

He visited Cliffrose Castle, now in ruins. Was this his own ancestral home, he wondered. Did some of his familial roots originate here? Was he not only of Gordon blood, but also, through Aileana, of Forbes and Mac-Pherson? Who owned this land now—some distant relative perhaps? He would have to find out later.

After a stroll through the village of Baloggan, he continued on his way, feeling more a Scot than ever in his life.

From Glen Truim he drove north, along the route of Prince Charlie's army and following Culodina's footsteps as she followed Sandy that fateful April in 1746.

After a quick detour to Inverness, where he made lodging arrangements, he drove out of the city west and to Culloden's historic battlefield.

Could a more fitting place exist, thought Andrew as he stood gazing across the moor of massacre, to contemplate the future of Scotland. Here had the long feud between the Scottish Highlanders and the English Crown been finally decided. Caledonia had lost its independence in that century so long ago. Now here *he* stood, three centuries later, contemplating whether the Parliament of King Charles III should give it back.

He was still so full of the story he had read in the library back home that he almost imagined he could hear the ominous roll of Cumberland's drummers from the east, answered by the shrill cry of Prince Charlie's pipers from Drummossie Moor to the west.

For an hour he walked alone across the desolate open spaces, gazing pensively down at the stones marking the mass clan graves scattered across the countryside, reliving the tale of Sandy and his father. What must have been the horror for Culodina to find the body of the man who was to be her father-in-law! Was his own Jacobite ancestor buried somewhere under this ground, Andrew wondered, beneath the stone upon which were carved the simple words *Clan Gordon*.

He moved on the following day. Andrew's travels then took him to Ullapool, around the desolate far north to Thurso, John O'Groats, Wick, and Dunbeath. All the stories he had read now mingled together, tumbling back in time from Culloden to Glencoe all the way back to Cruithne and the Wanderer. From what he could sketchily make out from the place names and the geography of the legend, he felt sure that Cruithne and Fidach had grown up in the vicinity of the Highlands of Easter Ross. Somewhere in the triangle represented by Lairg, Ullapool, and Dingwall, he was convinced had once existed the hill-fort of Laoigh.

If only there were still ruins of the broch of Caldohnuill that he might actually set his eyes upon! And what a thrill it would be to find the stones of the ancient monument of burial from which the sacred Coronation Stone had been cut by Columba's Pict companions and taken back to Iona—the very stone that he and Paddy Rawlings had recovered in Ireland.

But alas, wherever the ancient Caledonii had lived, and wherever Cruithne and Fidach had dragged their commemorative stones, and wherever Maelchon had buried his father Foltlaig near the grave of the ancient Caledonii chief who had longed for peace among the tribes of Caledonia—all was now lost with the passage of time, just as was the Culloden grave of Kendrick Gordon.

Andrew tarried three days at a bed-and-breakfast in Invershin, driving and walking the desolate Highland moors and hills from early morning until late every afternoon and retracing, not in fact with his feet but within his soul, the journey the two Caledonii brothers Cruithne and Fidach had taken with Domnall, son of the bard. He was drinking in the spirit of the Highlands and allowing Scotland's historic past to enter yet more deeply into him.

Surely, he thought, these empty, unpeopled, windy, rocky places captured the essential mystique of this land!

On the third day, knowing he would be leaving the region in the morning, he drove into the wilderness along the River Carron, parked his car at Alladale Lodge, and struck into the remote hills on foot, climbing up the slopes toward the peak of Carn Chuinneag.

The blanket of heather on the mountainside had nearly reached its full glory, spreading its color out across the otherwise barren slopes.

He stooped to pluck a tiny sprig, then sat down and gazed at the mixture of purples that surrounded him, reflecting on its subtle hues and its hardy nature.

Would the Scots, he wondered, hold their heads so high in the world without the immortality they gave their heroes? The romantic mist surrounding the legend of the Bonnie Prince, for instance, added almost an aura of triumph to the chronicle of that heroic time, even in the face of his defeat.

What a fit symbol was this heather—characteristic plant of the expansive lonely moors and the vast, rugged, mountain—for the prince whose rule over the land as son of his father, the last Stuart king of Jacobite legend, was so poignantly brief. Both burst into their royal explosions of color for but an instant and then were gone, left to elicit sonnets and ballads that elevated both blossom and prince to the stature of legend.

As short-lived as was the prince's shining moment, Andrew thought to himself, out of the fading bloom of Stuart royalty in the years following Culloden grew a legend that gave new hope to the very land the prince could not conquer.

And though the purple robe of the prince's royalty broke into flower like the heather—for a mere flicker of time—English swords could not entirely destroy its power. The spirit of Prince Charles lived on in these Highlands, giving life and warmth and hope, and like the heather, becoming greater in death than in life.

As winter leads to spring and death to life, so, in the seeming end of his cause, Bonnie Prince Charlie had infused what would become a yet deeper life into Caledonia's consciousness—a final victory, in the imaginations of Culloden's descendents, over those who had slain them.

Andrew gazed about at the subtle robe of Caledonia's majestic royalty waiting again to be donned, perhaps by some future Stuart king. There was no other place quite like this, he thought. Scarce wonder Robert Burns, a Lowlander, made the claim that his heart was in the Highlands.

His brain full of many such thoughts, with a smile Andrew now pulled his well-worn green volume of Burns from his jacket pocket and read the words over slowly and thoughtfully again. He must have read this poem a dozen times back in London. Never had it carried the depth of meaning it possessed on this day. It was time now for *him* to bid this region farewell, and he would let Burns's melancholy love anthem to the wilds express the sentiments of his heart.

> Farewell to the Highlands, farewell to the North,
> The birthplace of valor, the country of worth!
> Wherever I wander, wherever I rove,
> The hills of the Highlands forever I love.

Farewell to the mountains high cover-d with snow,
Farewell to the straths and green valleys below,
Farewell to the forests and wild-hanging woods,
Farewell to the torrents and loud-pouring floods!

As he sat, he was reminded once more of the legend of the white stag—first sighted by Son of Wanderer, then spotted by the brothers Fidach and Cruithne in just such a setting of forests and "loud-pouring floods." Would indeed one day the majestic creature return to Scotland . . . and bring with it the unity and brotherhood it promised those early Celts? Or would the return of the stag perhaps be symbolic of a return of Scotland's sovereignty?

He bent again to the page and finished the poem:

My heart's in the Highlands, my heart is not here,
My heart's in the Highlands, a-chasing the deer,
A-chasing the wild deer and following the roe—
My heart's in the Highlands, wherever I go!

He rose, placed the sprig of heather in the book and closed it, then began the long walk back to his car. As he drove south again, the taped music of pipers, harpists, accordions, fiddles, and tin whistles wove a magical spell, now with a ballad, now with a dance tune, now with the sad lament of a poignant historic Burns verse, infecting him with a melancholic nostalgia. Never, he thought, did the folk music of a nation so perfectly harmonize with the evocative sensations caused by the land itself. If these Highlands, these streams, these forests, these bare and rocky mountains, these jutting and jagged seascapes—if they could produce music *of themselves*, if the sounds of symphony could arise from out of the places where hidden melodies haunted the ground and rocks and lifted their strains to the heavens, then surely that glorious symphony would be composed of the melodies, rhythms, instrumental combinations, ballads, and harmonies the musicians of Scotland had been giving her people through the years.

As the cassette of music continued, now came the haunting words:

Bonnie Charlie's noo awa;
	safely o'er the friendly main.
Mony a hert will break in twa,
	should he ne'er come back again.

Will ye no come back again?
Will ye no come back again?
Better lo'ed ye canna be.
Will ye no come back again?

What might the future hold for the legacy of Prince Charlie's land? mused Andrew. The Bonnie Prince himself could not come back again . . . but perhaps his cause, maybe even one of his own descendents, might "come back again."

Whenever that time came, surely the spirit the Stuart prince had come to represent would rise again in the hearts of Scots everywhere.

▨ F O U R ▨

This was the craziest thing he had ever done in his life, Bill Rawlings said to himself.

Paddy and her ridiculous sleuthing!

After their last talk, he'd thought to himself, "If she can do it, I can." After all, the Reardon fellow didn't know him from Adam. What would it hurt to poke around a little? Especially if it was as important as Paddy said.

So he had hung around the lobby of the Auckland Towers for several days, on and off, thinking maybe he'd get lucky.

Reardon showed himself a time or two, walking through the lobby and getting into a taxi out in front, then disappearing as Rawlings emerged behind him. Thus far he hadn't summoned the courage to do the Bond imitation with a "follow that cab" scenario.

But today he'd decided to go for it. If he lost his nerve, or if Reardon showed signs of becoming suspicious, he'd just tell the driver to stop and he'd get out and be done with it.

He followed Reardon's taxi through the city, across the Harbor Bridge, and eventually to Bayswater, where Reardon got out in front of a six-story office building of modern design. Rawlings told his own driver to stop, got out and paid him, then followed Reardon inside at what he judged a safe distance. The elevator doors across the lobby were just closing as he walked in. Bill glanced at the second hand of his watch, then hurried forward and pressed the *up* button.

Rawlings stood waiting. Forty seconds later the doors opened in front of him. The elevator was empty.

He held the door open with one hand and thought a moment, then stepped inside, pressed *one* for the first floor, and hurried out. The moment the doors closed behind him, again he pushed the *up* button.

The elevator took eighteen seconds to climb one floor, then return and open its doors.

He stepped into the elevator again, now pressing *two* and stepping out quickly.

Twenty-six seconds this time before the doors opened in front of him.

Again for the third floor . . . thirty-two seconds.

Fourth . . . forty-one.

And floor five . . . fifty seconds.

That was it—Reardon had exited on floor four.

He didn't want to follow him and risk being spotted, even if he and Reardon were strangers. He glanced about the lobby. There was what he was looking for—a building directory. He hurried over and scanned the entries. Only one tenant appeared to be occupying the entire fourth floor. That was all he wanted to know for now. He'd let Paddy figure out what to do with it.

He turned, left the building, signaled for another cab, and returned to his flat.

F I V E

Andrew's sojourn now took him along the northern coast of the Grampian region of Scotland, through Elgin, Cullen, Portsoy, and Banff. Here the texture of the landscape changed from lonely Highland moors to bustling tourist and fishing towns. As it did, so did Andrew's mood. The great variety enriched yet further his sense of the land and its people which seemed to evolve daily in new and unexpected ways.

One morning he drove past a colorful blue sign near Huntly that read, "The Gordon District." A surge of identification went through him at the sight. Did his family have roots *everywhere* in Scotland!

Rounding the cape to Peterhead, he headed south to Aberdeen. He had never before visited the great seaport and historic center of learning for the north of Scotland. Walking the deeply rutted cobblestone streets of its Old

Town near the original university buildings sent new and quietly pensive feelings through him, a sense of nostalgia for a bygone era in which he felt comfortably at home.

He walked into the King's College chapel. The bronze plaque by the entrance set a mood for reflection that had become more common within him these days:

> Here one may
> Without much molestation
> Be thinking
> What he is
> Whence he came
> What he has done
> And to what
> The King has called him.

The chapel was empty at midday. He took a seat in the darkened sanctuary, the thin light streaming through the colorful stained-glass windows. He sat for some minutes quietly wondering where his travels would take him next.

From the gray granite city, Andrew followed the River Dee up through the Royal Deeside region. His route took him past the Bridge of Feugh—where he stopped, walked out midway across, and there stood above the rushing, turbulent brown peat-fed river gazing down at the frothy display—and thence to Ballater, Balmoral Castle, and eventually Braemar, where the earl of Mar had once gathered his friends to plan an uprising.

It was there, in the heart of southern Grampian's most royal and poetic hills, that Andrew's life would change in yet another way he could never have foreseen.

⚅ SIX ⚅

"Paddy, it's Bill . . . I may have something for you."

"You followed Reardon?"

"I know it's loony, but I did."

"And?"

"From what I could tell, he met with some bigwigs at a company in Auckland called World Resources, Limited."

"What do you know about them?"

"Not much. But I did ask around. It's a multinational corporation that's into investments, land leases, bonds, offshore drilling . . . all sorts of things."

"Interesting, but . . . hmm, I don't see much unusual in that."

"Their main interests, according to a friend of mine," Bill went on, "involve North Sea oil."

"Oil!" exclaimed Paddy. "That could be significant. What about the ownership?"

"Seems to be well shielded."

"Good work! Keep at it. If you can find out anything more about what Reardon is up to, I'll . . ."

"You'll what?" said Bill with playfully significant tone.

"Let's just put it this way," said Paddy, "—I'll owe you one. In the meantime, I'll see what I can dig up on World Resources on the Internet."

⊠ SEVEN ⊠

Leaving Braemar after breakfast, and without a planned destination for day's end, Andrew drove south on the A93 through Glen Clunie. Suddenly, on a narrow straightaway of only some four hundred meters, an expensive BMW of a near-black shade of rich maroon zoomed past him on the right. It seemed to come from nowhere. Briefly unnerved, Andrew watched as within seconds it disappeared from sight.

Half an hour later, upon cresting a ridge of the mountainous drive, he found himself overlooking a flat cultivated valley where many cars were parked and several hundred people were assembled. The village called Spittal o' Ballochallater stood just beyond. From the small size of the village, Andrew judged that all the residents, and more besides, must have come to the gathering.

He made his way on down the winding road toward it. As he neared the site he saw the large maroon car that had passed him parked near a rectangular stone residence that was the closest thing to a castle this out-of-the-way region seemed to possess. On an impulse, his curiosity aroused, he pulled in and drove slowly past the BMW, then parked in a group of two- or three-dozen automobiles about thirty meters away.

He glanced toward the BMW. The glass shielding the rear seat was darkened. He thought he could faintly make out a figure seated inside, but he wasn't positive. The driver's seat was empty.

What was such an expensive vehicle, and one so obviously in a great hurry, doing at what appeared some kind of rustic gathering? It was the kind of car one saw in London. In fact, now that he thought about it, he halfway thought he recognized it, although he couldn't pinpoint where he might have seen it before.

Andrew got out and maneuvered through the clump of parked cars in the direction of all the activity. Before long, he found himself walking amongst a diverse conglomeration of tents, tables, and booths where all manner of local handcrafts and woolen items were displayed for sale. Bagpipes sounded in the distance. Moving beyond the handcrafts, Andrew was drawn toward a sheepshearing contest and for the next fifteen minutes watched the proceedings with fascination.

All at once, Andrew's eyes shot open. Beyond the hubbub of bleating and yelling in the distance, two men were talking, one of them heatedly. He was obviously a local, dressed in kilt and full Highland regalia. Andrew could make out nothing of what he was saying, but the animated gestures of his hands made clear that he was upset. The other, dressed in the only suit for miles, dark blue and of obvious expensive cut, was none other than one of the four vice-chairmen for the Conservative Party, a man he knew on a passing basis, Robert Burslem.

What in the world was he doing here!

Andrew shrunk out of sight amid the cheering spectators of the shearing display, intuitively realizing he did not want to be seen. Then he fingered his new growth of light brown beard, wondering if he could be recognized anyway.

The interview between Burslem and the Scotsman lasted but a minute longer. The Tory MP now turned and walked back in the direction of the small car park and the castle. It came as no surprise when Andrew saw him get into the BMW and drive off, not quite so rapidly as before, but obviously wanting to waste no time getting to wherever he was going next.

While Andrew was still pondering the strange coincidence of seeing one of his colleagues in this remote village, a loud speaker interrupted his thoughts, announcing several events about to begin. He glanced up, then toward his car, debating briefly with himself whether to hurry out and try to follow Burslem. Almost as quickly he realized he would never be able to catch up with a speeding BMW. Maybe he could discover what Burslem had been doing in the village by hanging around awhile, perhaps learning who was the fellow Burslem had apparently angered. Andrew couldn't say why, but it seemed important that he know.

As a result of the announcement, some half the crowd had by now turned and was walking toward the middle of the open field beyond the display area. Unconsciously he found himself accompanying the human tide.

"What is this?" he asked an older fellow moving in the same direction beside him.

"Hoo's that?"

"What is this . . . what's going on here?"

"They're readyin' fer the races," answered the old Scotsman.

"I mean the whole thing," said Andrew, sweeping his arm around the entire gathering. "What is going on here today? I was just driving by and happened to stop."

"Ay, I git yer meanin' noo!" laughed the man. "Why, 'tis oor Highland Games, laddie—fer the region o' Ballochallater an' Lochnagar. We hold oor ain Games every year."

"May anyone participate?"

"Ay, laddie. Ye luik like ye're fleet o' foot. Why dinna ye pit yersel' agin the rest o' the laddies?"

Andrew laughed at the thought of competing. He hadn't done anything of the sort for years!

Ten minutes later, however, as much to his own surprise as anyone's, having succumbed to the hearty expostulations of his new friend and several others and having grabbed his sneakers from the car, Andrew found himself removing his shirt and approaching the starting line for a 2.8-mile run.

This was not what he'd been thinking when he pulled off the road thirty minutes before!

He glanced around at the group. One fellow looked to be in his forties; three appeared about his own age, in their midthirties. There were a couple of young men in their twenties, three in their midteens, and two boys not more than ten or eleven—comprising a total field of an even dozen.

The gun exploded with a sharp report.

Suddenly the parliamentary leader, who an hour before had been contentedly driving down a country Highland road singing along with his car's cassette player, found himself sprinting across a flat grassy field in a madcap effort to keep up with the rest of the runners and not embarrass himself too badly. They dipped slightly downward for some two hundred yards, then came up the gradual slope of the opposite side. Suddenly Andrew realized that their course was bound straight for a monstrous hill looming ahead across the valley floor!

Already the lead runners were onto its slopes. Within another few seconds, Andrew realized he had bitten off more than he had bargained for! What had he been thinking? He was in the Highlands . . . this hill was steep!

When he crossed the line nineteen minutes and forty seconds after the gun in a surprising third-place finish, he felt as though his lungs were about to explode. But he was nevertheless unable to prevent an exhausted smile—not because of the well-placed race he had run, but from the exhilaration of what he had so spontaneously done.

Bent over, hands on knees, trying desperately to get his breath and chastising himself for allowing himself to get so out of shape, Andrew heard a cheery feminine voice approach beside him.

"Congratulations!" it said with heavy Scottish accent.

Still unable to bring himself fully to a standing position, Andrew did his best to glance around toward the sound.

"Ye took third place—I'm t' take yer name t' the judges."

Slowly he stood, still gasping for air, and turned to see a young woman standing before him. Scot was written over every inch of her ruddy, chiseled face and determined expression, even had the thick accompanying brogue not announced that these Highlands could be no other than her lifelong home.

He smiled and laughed in the midst of the pain.

"The way I feel right now, I don't consider myself deserving of a prize," he said. "To tell you the truth, I may be about to get sick. I haven't run that far since I was at university."

He bent down and again clasped his knees for support.

"Weel, university or no, sick or no, ye won third place. So . . . what's yer name?"

"First tell me yours," rejoined Andrew, standing again and gradually coming to himself. His face, however, remained pale. "Then I won't feel like such a stranger here."

"Ye're no a stranger, whoe'er ye be, though ye be a mite stubborn aboot givin' oot yer name when it's asked fer. But there are nae strangers here at the Gordon Games. In this country, all's kin an' all's weelcome."

"The *Gordon* Games?" repeated Andrew, half in question, half astonishment.

"And why not? Isna the Gordon name as guid as ony ither?"

"Of course . . . it's only that I was surprised. I'm sure you have noticed from my speech that I'm not from this country."

"I maun admit I detected a slight somethin' t' gie ye awa," said the young woman.

Though she could not have been more than an inch or two over five feet or weighed more than seven and a half stone, a bouncy vitality gave her appearance a stature that, in the right circumstances, might prove equal to any man's. Her smile was as full as her green eyes were large, with teeth white and glistening. From beneath the ribboned tartan of her Glengarry bonnet tumbled out the most notable and undiluted example of bright red hair Andrew had ever seen.

Now that his wits began to gather themselves more firmly, in fact, he realized what an altogether picturesque Highland image the young woman presented. She wore a kilt skirt, as did most of the other women he had observed, with a white cotton blouse. A plaid to match skirt and cap—blue and green interlaced with wide-spaced thin yellow bands—draped over one shoulder and diagonally across both back and front, meeting just below the waist, where the two ends were pinned together by a great silver-and-feathered brooch. Even the two shaggy terriers that accompanied her—and were now busily sniffing his heels—added to the picturesque effect. He judged the spunky young woman as being somewhere in her late twenties or early thirties.

"But . . . ye still haena told me yer name," she insisted.

"Because you have not told me yours," rejoined Andrew, now managing a smile of his own as he bent over to greet the little dogs.

"Gien ye aren't a stubborn one for an Englishman!"

Andrew laughed outright. Seeing the fun in his expression, she could not help joining him.

"All right, gien ye will hae it . . . it's Leigh Gordon—there! And these lads here"—she indicated the little dogs—"are Faing an' Fyfe."

"All right, then," said Andrew, extending his hand. "I'm Andy Trent. And I am pleased to make the acquaintance of all three of you."

It was the first time he had actually spoken the pseudonym he had been using on lodging registers throughout his travels, and he didn't know quite what to make of the feel of the words as they left his lips.

"Then come wi' me, Andy Trent," she said, shaking the hand vigorously, then turning and bounding off. "Come an' collect yer prize, an' be a weelcome guest o' the Gordons o' Lochnagar."

⊠   E I G H T   ⊠

The next three hours passed more quickly than Andrew could have believed possible.

As the only nonlocal present at the annual village celebration, he had enjoyed more lavish Scottish hospitality than he had experienced during the whole of his travels.

He had participated in two more races—a fifty-yard sprint and a two-hundred-yard lap around the grassy perimeter of the field, reminiscent of Eric Liddell's booted sprint around the grass in *Chariots of Fire*. Having seen *Chariots* three times, he was amazed to find himself engaged in such Liddell-esque activity.

In neither of the races had he come close to winning a prize, however, though he was nonetheless applauded and congratulated by the crowd for his good-natured efforts. And he had thoroughly embarrassed himself—going up against the most burly of the local he-men—in the caber toss, nearly allowing the nineteen-foot-nineteen-inch, 132-pound pole to crash down upon his head!

Weariness and near concussion notwithstanding, however, he had had the time of his life. By the time a light afternoon's snack was laid out, he was thoroughly caught up in the festive local atmosphere and warmed by the way the inhabitants embraced and welcomed him into their midst—even while knowing nothing of his own Gordon ancestry.

The Gordon clan apparently stretched all the way from Strathbogie down to the region of Cliffrose. Now he had stumbled upon a cluster of Gordons in the center of the Grampian Highlands—a friendly, boisterous, fun-loving, kindly, hospitable community of men and women who still, this late in the twentieth century, showed such deference to their leader that a few of them called him *chief.*

What could it all mean?

Had he been caught in a time warp? Had he driven over a hill and suddenly discovered himself in the early 1700s, before such Highland display had been outlawed by the English Crown? He felt almost as if he'd slipped into *Brigadoon*. Kilts and tartans, dirks and sgian-dubhs, bagpipes and Highland flings, sheep shearing and an outdoor bonfire of peat at the edge of the small valley—for effect, apparently, and not for heat, since the day had grown into a warm one, although there also appeared to be preparations under way for some kind of food associated with the fire. On the adjacent hillsides grazed longhaired bulls and curl-horned, black-faced sheep. The Highland clan heritage here seemed as close and personal and vibrant as if the twentieth and twenty-first centuries had never come to this place at all!

His thoughts drifted back to Sandy and Culodina. If he closed his eyes he could just imagine—

"Another glass o' stout fer ye, young Trent?"

Andrew glanced up to see the kilt-clad, gray-bearded man they called chief—the very man with whom Burslem had been arguing—striding toward where he sat. He grasped a tall foaming glass in his left hand for the guest in whom he had taken a personal interest, while he sipped at the one he held in his right as he walked.

"I'm afraid this must be my last!" laughed Andrew. "I'm no more accustomed to this ale you people drink than I am to your Games."

As he sat, he had been watching the young girls in the sword-dance competition, sweat standing on his face, trousers splotched from a fall or two he had taken, shirt sleeves rolled up, and messy blond hair going in a hundred directions.

"Weel," rejoined Finlaggan Gordon, slapping Andrew on the shoulders with his hand as soon as he had delivered him of its contents, "ye've handled yerself right weel today, fer a Lowlander. We Highlanders admire a man wi' grit, an' ye've shown ye got yer share by gettin' in there wi' oor ain brawly lads an' doin' yer best t' beat 'em at their ain game."

Andrew laughed. "Thank you very much, laird," he said. "Coming from you I take that as a compliment of high praise. Although I must say I didn't handle the colors of my own country all that well."

"What! What mean ye, lad . . . yer ain country? Ye're among the Gordons noo. It doesna tak us mair'n a day t' mak a Scotsman o' a man wha's willin' in hert an' limb! Ye're a Scot now, lad, ye hear!"

Again Andrew laughed heartily. If only Duncan MacRanald could be listening to the conversation. His old friend back home had been trying to make a Scotsman of him for years, and now this Gordon Highlander was doing his best to complete the project!

The afternoon's activities had taken Andrew's mind completely off the reason he had stopped here in the first place. Talking now with the chief reminded him of it.

"I couldn't help noticing you talking with a man in a suit when I arrived," said Andrew. "You appeared to be arguing . . . there's nothing the matter, I hope."

"Only a Sassenach tryin' t' git his clutches on what disna belong t' him," rejoined the chief.

"A *Sassenach*?" repeated Andrew.

"An Englishman."

Andrew laughed. "But I'm English, as I'm sure you can tell. Yet you invite me to drink ale with you."

"There's Sassenach an' there's Sassenach," said the old man. "When we use the term, we mean an Englishman wha's tryin' t' use the Scots fer his ain gain. Honest English are as weelcome under my roof as honest Welshmen or honest Scots or honest men o' ony ither kith an' kin or clan."

"Even a Campbell?" suggested Andrew with a twinkle of fun.

"A guid one, that! Ha, ha!" laughed the chief. "Ye aye ken yer Scots history, lad! I'll hae t' think twice hoo t' answer ye. Not that the Gordons harbor the same spite o' the Campbells as the sons o' Donald. But they slaughtered oor fathers at Culloden too, jist like Glenlyon did MacIain's at the wee glen. So ye may be right—the Campbells may be worse than the Sassenach. Though one o' my best friends is a Campbell, so I'll hae t' consider the matter further. But *ye're* no Campbell, I ken that weel enouch, and ye'd be weelcome under my roof whate'er the sound o' yer tongue."

"You are a kind man, laird," said Andrew, "and I thank you very much."

They tipped glasses, then followed with a long swallow of the frothy cold brew.

"Papa!" called a voice. Both men turned to see the diminutive redhead whom Andrew had met earlier—and whom he had learned to be the eldest daughter of the chief—bounding toward them with the little dogs still at her heels. "Ye're wanted at the judgin' tent."

"What for, Ginny?" replied the laird, whose hefty size and robust carriage would give no immediate indication that the two were related. "Canna ye see I'm enjoyin' a pint wi' oor guest?"

" 'Tis time for the final awards, Papa, an' nane but the laird'll be able t' name the final prizes."

"Then keep oor guest happy," said Gordon, rising to his feet. "An' mind,

Ginny, that my stout's here when I come back."

The moment he turned his back, with a naughty expression of fun, she took a sip from his glass, though she followed it with a grimace of displeasure.

"I canna weel stand the stuff," she remarked with a laugh, "but I like to tease Papa. He still treats me like I'm fifteen."

"A common ailment among parents," said Andrew, laughing lightly.

"Do yours do the same?" she asked.

"Not so much now," replied Andrew, taking a slow, thoughtful sip from his glass. "But I'm thirty-seven, so they've had plenty of time to get used to my being an adult."

"I'm thirty-two," she rejoined, "but gettin' used t' it hasna helped Papa. Mummy's better, but Papa's still tryin' to make me into his son wha'll be laird after him," she added, laughing.

Andrew thought of his sister Lindsay and his own similar, though opposite, struggle with his mother's expectations.

"Do you have brothers and sisters?"

"Ay—a yoonger o' each."

"Are they here?"

"My brither's aboot someplace—my sister's married an' bides in Glasgow."

"Tell me—what's the Ginny for?" asked Andrew.

"My middle name—Ginevra. But folks call me Ginny."

Andrew's heart leapt. Had he heard right? *Ginevra!*

"Ye're luikin' at me like ye seen a wee ghostie!" she exclaimed in response to his wide-eyed stare. "Did I say something t' flaucht ye?"

"No . . . no, sorry," replied Andrew. "It's just that hearing your name startled me."

"Why for that? Isna Leigh Ginevra Gordon as guid a name as any ither?"

"Yes, of course. It is a beautiful name—majestic, just like the mountains and hills all around. Do you know of the maiden of Glencoe?"

"Ay, I've heard the tale. But I doobt many o' the wives o' the village—or the men for that maitter!—I doobt they'll be thinkin' o' Ginny Gordon as majestic!"

She laughed at the very thought.

"Majestic," she added, "is the place we like oor sma' clan t' be known by—Lochnagar there yonder."

She pointed vaguely toward the hills to the northeast.

"But the laird's daughter," she went on, "the maist o' them'll be callin' her a wee-shankit quean wha canna right grow up 'til a lady like she ought."

Andrew laughed. "I'm sorry. I'm afraid I don't understand you."

"I said they a' call me a short-legged girl wha'll never grow up t' be a lady."

"I see," smiled Andrew. "Is your father really a chief?"

"Not o' a' the Gordons! Na, na . . . there's a heap o' Gordons all o'er the world. An' they got a Gordon in Aboyne, jist doon the Dee, that dresses up in fancy kilts wi' silver bits an' buttons all aboot 'im an' sits fer his picture t' be taen—an' *him* they call the chief o' the whole lot. But this wee corner o' the Gordons came doon here back in the last century an' made their hame around the great mountain an' then spread oot doon Glen Clunie an' Glen Shee. My father's great-great-gran'papa cam down frae Strathbogie—his older brother was made ninth marquis o' Huntly when the fifth duke died, an' was known then as the chief o' the clan. An' since then his gran'papa, an' noo my ain papa—they hae all been called the lairds and chiefs o' *this* region. But Papa says nobody holds by all that nowadays."

"But you *are* related by blood to the titular head of the whole clan?"

Ginny nodded. "Ay. But Papa doesna keep touch wi' ony o' the important folks 'cept at Aboyne Castle. I dinna doobt nane o' them in Strathbogie or Haddo Hoose in Aberdeen or them that's in Gight an' Canada ken the wee clan Gordon o' Lochnagar exists at a'."

"Are you by any chance related to the Gordons of Cliffrose?"

"Ye'll hae t' ask Papa. I'm no aware o' any connections mysel'."

Fascinated, Andrew took the information in without further comment.

"Weel, the laird's made his decision!" boomed a voice behind them.

The two looked up to see Ginny's father walking briskly back toward them.

"Who won the gran' prize, Papa?"

"Alastair again, jist like last year," answered the laird. "A braw young man," he added, turning to Andrew. "Him it was wha tossed the caber oot there sae far, an' whas heels ye was luikin' at yersel' on the way back doon the ben there yonder."

"I remember him now!" sighed Andrew. "A fine athlete."

"Ay . . . an' one wha's got his eye on my daughter here, doesna he noo, Ginny lass?"

"Everyone in Ballochallater kens weel enough, Papa," replied Ginny, with more annoyance than embarrassment. She did not seem capable of embarrassment.

The conversation soon ended with the necessity of the laird's presence for the Games' award presentation and the final piobaireachd*, or piping, competition. With Ginny accompanying him, Andrew started to walk toward the gathering crowd. But they were interrupted as they walked by a breathless middle-aged woman in Wellingtons who laid a big hand on Ginny's shoulder and pulled her around.

"I've aye been tryin' to catch up with ye' fer maist of the day," she blurted out, then stopped briefly to catch her breath. "I wanted to tell ye' little Nellie's much better this mornin'. Fair wolfed doon her brakfast and was askin' fer mair."

"Weel, that I'm right glad t' hear't," replied Andrew's companion with a smile. "An' will ye be bringin' the little darlin' to see me next week?"

"Ay. We'll baith be aluikin' forward t' it. Ye ken yer Nellie's favorite."

"She's a darlin'," commented Ginny as she and Andrew continued on their way.

"I take it you like children?" Andrew said.

Ginny glanced at him, puzzled. "Weel, ay, but . . ."

He gestured back toward the woman, who was weaving her way through the crowd away from them. "I mean Nellie. The little girl."

The confusion on Ginny's face now vanished in a hearty gale of laughter. "Ach, oor little Nellie!" she said. "She's a fine'un, that's fer sure, but she's hairdly a wee bairn. Mr. Trent, Nellie's a potbellied pig!"

Now the confusion moved to Andrew's face. "But she said she'd bring Nellie to see you. . . ."

"Ay," she answered, "in my surgery. Dinna you see? Tis what I do. I'm a veterinarian."

Andrew was intrigued. This lively woman bore little resemblance to the burly middle-aged man who took care of the animals back at Derwenthwaite. "Do you take care of the horses and cows too?"

"Ay, an' dogs an' cattle, though my partner helps w' the large animal work, on account of my bein' sich a dwarf. Tho' I do ken my way around a horse."

Andrew was beginning to wonder what other interesting things he would find out about his fiery-haired companion.

They were still in lively conversation when they sat down on the grass to watch the proceedings.

---

*Pronounce pee-broke.

Before Andrew was aware of it, the afternoon was nearly gone.

When the ceremony was over, they rejoined Ginny's father. Unconsciously Andrew glanced down at his watch.

"It's going on five o'clock," he exclaimed in astonishment. "I've got to be on my way or I'll be stuck in the middle of the Highlands tonight with no place to stay."

"On yer way, laddie?" rejoined the laird. "What would ye be meanin'? Ye're stayin' wi' us in the castle tonight. I thought Ginny'd already speired ye aboot it."

"I haena had the chance yet, Papa," said Ginny.

"Weel, laddie," the laird went on, "then I'll speir ye mysel'. Oor hoose is open, an' ye'd be weelcome. We'd be pleased t' hae ye bide the night wi' us."

"I . . . I don't know what to say. That is very generous of you."

"Besides, ye canna weel go noo," Ginny added. "Ye see that great peat fire yonder—the men are already roastin' the lamb, an' there'll be lots o' food an' drink. Ye maun stay wi' us."

How could he pass up such an invitation!

❈   N I N E   ❈

It took but a dropped word or two that evening among the Gordon family that he was vaguely traveling through Scotland to learn more about the country and its people for the mat of hospitality to be rolled out for Andrew in full measure.

Thinking he would resume his travels after breakfast the following morning, Andrew was in for more surprises when he came downstairs to discover that Ginny and her father already had his whole day planned. Thought of his leaving was out of the question now. If he had come north to learn of Scotland, then he must remain with them long enough to do so.

He found in Mrs. Gordon the combination of the laird and his feisty daughter. Ginny's bright hair had obviously come from her mother's orange mane, which was now fading to a soft golden shade. She was not so slight of build as Ginny, being of medium height and stockier. But occasional hints of Ginny's smile could be seen when her lips parted in fun.

"You have been very kind to a stranger, Mrs. Gordon," said Andrew as his hostess poured him another cup of tea. "Surely it cannot be the custom around here to take in every traveler who wanders into your village. I saw the laird arguing with another man yesterday who looked more out of place than me. He didn't seem to be receiving such an invitation!" added Andrew, laughing.

"He didna need no hospitality frae my hand," put in Ginny's father a bit irritably. "I told ye, he was naethin' but a Sassenach tryin' t' git his clutches on a wee parcel that's been Gordon land longer than anyone alive noo kens."

"Land . . . near here?"

"Way up t' the north, in the Shetlands. I've ne'er seen it mysel'. No worth muckle, the way I hear it. It's jist come doon through the years t' this strain o' the Gordon line in Ballochallater, an' it seems I've ootlived all the ither cousins an' kin whas names were on some will or anither. I dinna ken a thing aboot it."

"But it is valuable property?"

"Not so valuable. We jist get a wee check once a year from a solicitor whas got the papers."

"And the fellow wants you to sell?"

"Ay. An' what a dapper suit like that wants wi' a worthless piece o' island rock I canna weel think. I wadna mind sellin' it, I suppose, but I jist dinna trust the man."

"What does he want it for?" asked Andrew.

"I haena ony idea. But I'm certain in my own mind jist from luikin' in his een that he's hidin' somethin', and I told him so."

While Andrew was puzzling over the affair, Mrs. Gordon spoke up again.

"Perhaps we're not quite so hospitable as t' tak in everyone wha comes along, I'll grant ye," she went on again in the previous vein. "But when a man says he's learnin' aboot Scotland, that's all my man needs t' tak him under his wing."

"Well, I am very appreciative. It is certainly more than I expected."

———

The day went by more quickly than Andrew could have imagined, with conversations with each of the members of the family, walks about the castle and surrounding hillsides, and a midday visit to the local pub, the Heather and the Stout, with Ginny's father. Her lanky twenty-four-year-old brother— whom they called Shorty in spite of the fact that he stood half a head taller than the laird and two taller than his sister, and whose given name Andrew never did learn—invited him into the hills and the next minute was shoving a rifle into his hands. By midafternoon, the parliamentary leader was traipsing through trees and heather on the highest peak overlooking the castle, with a young man he hadn't even known twenty-four hours ago, in search of rabbit and pheasant and whatever other wild game might chance their way.

By the time they returned, not realizing how quickly it had passed, the day was drawing to a close.

"Whew, what an afternoon!" sighed Andrew, easing into a chair. He glanced around but saw no sign of Ginny. He supposed she was still busy at her surgery. "I'll sleep well tonight. And I'll need it, too, so I can be off in the morning."

"Ah, ye canna rest yet, lad," expostulated the laird. "There'll be time for all that later. An' we'll hae no talk o' yer leavin' quite so soon. Noo ye maun git yersel' cleaned up an' dressed so we can hae oor supper an' be off."

"Be off!" laughed Andrew, remaining in the chair, unable to imagine what additional activity the evening could hold. "Off where?"

"The ceilidh."*

"What's that?" rejoined Andrew.

"Ye'll see weel enough. 'Tis jist a wee ceilidh t' finish oor Games weekend."

An hour and a half later, Andrew was again entering the Heather and the Stout in the company of the laird and his wife. The establishment was hardly recognizable from its lazy midday trade. It was nearly filled with men, women, and children and loud with festive atmosphere. Andrew was included in the round of greetings and handshakes as if he had been part of the community all his life.

Fifteen minutes later, Ginny walked in with a man Andrew recognized. They made quite a picture—the huge burly chap of at least six foot two and sixteen stone and the tiny red-haired lass of half the weight and a foot less in stature. Ginny introduced her companion to Andrew as Alastair Farquharson.

"My caber opponent," laughed Andrew, remembering as he shook the gigantic hand. "I'm sorry I wasn't able to provide you more competition."

"Fer a Lowlander," replied Farquharson, "ye handled yersel' right weel, Mr. Trent. Ye're not exactly o' the proper build t' toss the caber, gien ye unnerstan' my meaning."

"I believe I do," laughed Andrew.

---

*Pronounced *Kay*-lee.

The place continued to fill. Musicians arrived, and a few fiddles began to tune. An accordion came out, then another. The crisp shrill of a tin whistle sped through a warm-up octave or two. Gradually the diverse sounds began to adjust and blend with each other, drifting into an occasional harmony, until suddenly, as if unplanned, Andrew realized the small band had actually launched into a tune, accompanied now by the drummer who had completed arranging his drums and high hat during the tuning phase. He could identify no moment when the melody had actually begun. Rather it seemed to emerge gradually out of the scattered and random warm-up sounds of the instruments. Obviously these musicians knew one another well.

A few feet began to shuffle and move and tap the floor to the beat. Here and there a clap or two could be heard. Before long, music filled the room, and the floor in the middle began to clear.

Then came a great chord of finality. Everyone seemed to know what was coming, for a great scurrying ensued. Couples hurried onto the dance floor and took up positions in sets of eight.

Another chord, followed by graceful bows and curtsies . . . then suddenly band and dancers erupted into a frenzy of melody and motion to a Scottish reel.

Andrew watched spellbound and continued to sit through the first several dances at the table with the laird, thoroughly mesmerized by the intricate patterns of Scottish country dance, though without the vaguest idea what sort of complex foot patterns were involved. But he did his part to enter in with the rest of the spectators—clapping in time, whooping, cheering, and encouraging the dancers on.

After three reels and a strathspey, the band paused briefly. Another great scurrying throughout the room followed. Whatever was about to happen, as before, everybody else seemed to know. Suddenly Andrew was pulled to his feet. He turned to find himself being led onto the dance floor with Ginny's mother firmly attached to his hand.

"Wait . . . stop," laughed Andrew. "I don't have a clue what's going on!"

"Jist follow me, Mr. Trent," she said, clamping down yet more firmly, if possible, on his palm.

"But I don't know—"

"Jist watch the feet an' follow along. 'Tis called the Gay Gordons—'tis the simplest dance o' all. Jist follow aroun' the circle, wi' a wee waltz thrown in atween. Come, here we go!"

The music began. Standing at his side, she took his two hands in hers, arm over arm, and led as they and the other couples began marching around in a great circle in time with the music. This he could do, Andrew thought—walk along with the music!

All at once came a change. A brief waltz maneuver . . . twirls and twists . . . then he felt his hands lifted high, Mrs. Gordon spun under them and released herself, and suddenly he found himself walking along in time again, hand over hand with someone else. How the change had happened or where the large woman had come from who was now at his side, he wasn't quite sure.

Then just as before, suddenly the circular march came to an end. He felt himself turned and pulled into the huge-bosomed chest of his new partner. She must have been Alastair Farquharson's sister. If there had been a women's caber toss yesterday, this lady would certainly have walked away with the prize!

She clenched Andrew with both hands and pulled him toward her in a robust grip as the waltz phase began. Even had he known what to do at that point, he could have done nothing but follow the woman's lead. He stumbled over her feet once, then again, but her powerful arms kept him upright.

He felt himself, as before, spun about through a brief series of twirls. Then his arms were hoisted up, she ducked her bulky frame under them and was suddenly gone. Now he found himself marching along with the woman who had been ahead of them in line. Knowing what was coming now as they walked, he tried to prepare himself for the waltz-step phase, which he now realized would lead to another change of partner.

Two more cycles went by. By degrees Andrew began to catch on to the pattern of the Gay Gordons enough to enjoy himself. Suddenly he saw a splash of bright red marching along with the man in front of him and realized its owner would be his next partner.

Again came the waltz step, the twirl, and suddenly the tiny woman who danced as lightly over the floor as Alastair's sister had lumbered across it was smiling and offering her hands.

"Ye're doin' right weel, Mr. Trent," said Ginny with a sprightly nod as their four hands joined and they began walking forward to the music.

"I have stumbled over every poor woman here!"

"Ye're doin' fine fer yer first time. All the young ladies are talkin' aboot ye."

Andrew laughed. "It's no wonder," he said. "My cloddish feet must be quite a sight."

"'Tisn't yer feet they're luikin' at, Mr. Trent. They're sayin' ye're the handsomest Englishman they've ever seen."

Before Andrew could think what to say, again came the brief waltz. Ginny slipped gently into Andrew's arms. Miraculously the few bars of music were accomplished more gracefully than any of his previous interludes. Then came a twirl under his arm . . . she flashed him a smile . . . and as soon as the nymph had come, she was off to the man behind him, and he was greeting his next partner in line.

This was beginning to be fun!

When the dance was over, perspiring and laughing in triumph for having survived it, Andrew again joined the laird at his table, where new glasses of thick, frothy ale were poured as a new dance began.

"That was quite an experience," he laughed.

"Ye'll aye be a Scotsman afore we're weel dune wi' ye, Mr. Trent," said the laird. "Maybe we'll even make a Gordon o' ye too."

The words caught Andrew off guard. Though they represented exactly what he had come to Scotland seeking, his Gordon roots, he had almost forgotten that he was actually still an outsider.

While he was still pondering the laird's words with a sip from the glass in front of him, their conversation was interrupted by the approach of a middle-aged Scottish gentleman, newly arrived at the pub, and just back after two days in Aberdeen.

"There—what think ye noo, Finlaggan Gordon?" said the man, slapping down a newspaper onto the table in front of them as he sat down, and paying the stranger no heed. "Didna I tell ye nae good'll come o' it e'en wi' the Hamilton traitor gone."

Andrew glanced down at that morning's copy of the *Express*.

The glass nearly fell from his hand as his eyes shot open in stunned surprise. There on the front page was a four-inch picture of his *own* face!

Beside it, the black caption read, "Liberal leader Andrew Trentham stalling on home rule, says SNP's Dugald MacKinnon." The article, at which Andrew managed to sneak quick glimpses over the next few minutes, alleged that he had deliberately waffled on the Scottish issue through the spring with the motive of attempting to sway Prime Minister Barraclough to exclude the Scottish Nationalist Party from his coalition when Parliament resumed in the fall.

In the ensuing moments, as he attempted to swallow his astonishment and keep from flushing red, Andrew did his best to give attention to the conversation which followed. Once the newcomer had a full glass in his own hand and introductions had been made, the discussion focused for several minutes more on the implications of the erroneous information in the article.

Andrew did not speak until he had recovered his composure.

"I take it, then," he said, trying to sound casual, "that the two of you are in *favor* of Scottish independence?" he asked.

"Ay, laddie—spekin' for mysel', I support it wi' every drap o' blood in my Highland veins," said the newcomer, Angus MacLeod.

"And you, laird?" asked Andrew, turning to Ginny's father.

"Ay, I cast my vote wi' Angus. Scotland's been ruled too long, gien ye'll pardon me sayin' it, by yer English frien's in Lonnon. They pay nae heed t' us in the north even wi' this new business they call devolution. They dinna care aboot Scots an' what we're thinkin' nor wantin'."

"Do you think that's true with all the MPs in Commons?" Andrew asked carefully.

"Ay, 'tis true, laddie," interrupted MacLeod, who obviously felt passionately about the subject. "—What'd ye say was yer name, laddie?"

"Uh . . . Andy," stumbled Andrew. "—Andy, uh . . . Trent."

"Weel, I'll tell ye, young Trent. They dinna care, an' they dinna care that they dinna care! The Parliament's a' fer England, 'cept fer a few o' oor ain lads down there, but the rest pay nae heed t' them. An' fer this new Parliament up here in Auld Reekie, I canna weel say yet, but seems likely t' me 'tis jist a plot o' the Sassenach t' quiet us doon wi' oor talk o' independence."

"Auld Reekie?" repeated Andrew.

"Edinburgh, man—that's Edinburgh!"

The conversation continued on amid the music and dancing, though eventually, to Andrew's relief, a few others joined them around the large table.

"What do ye think, Angus," commented one, "—that Scotland can stand alane wi'oot England a' t'gither?"

"An' why not?" rejoined Angus feistily. "We didna need its help fer centuries."

"That was before industry," replied the other. "Scotland's still a mite small land t' support itself wi'oot—"

"Ye'r spekin' blasphemy agin yer ain land!" interrupted Angus.

"I'm spekin' common sense, man. We're not enouch people for it t' be itherwise. The land's not guid for much farmin'."

"Geordie's in the right, Angus," now put in another. "We got oor Glasgow an' Reekie, t' be sure, an' the fishin' an' the oil in Aberdeen. But it still isna enouch fer five million folks t' keep up wi' the rest o' the world. We split off frae England, an' we'll be headin' doonhill faster'n Alastair can run doon the ben."

"I canna weel believe what I'm hearin' oot o' the mouths o' two Scotsmen!" exclaimed Angus. "There's plenty o' oil fer us all, lads. We'd be a wealthy nation gien we cud keep the oil fer oorsel's."

"I tell ye, the same year we get oor independence," insisted Geordie, "is the year oor taxes go up. Wouldna be no ither way Scotland could support itself."

"Ach!" exclaimed Angus in frustration. "'Tis oor freedom that's wanted, man. Disna matter a' that ye say gien we be not a free an' independent nation. What's become o' *Scotland* these last three hunnert years! She's disappeared frae the face o' the earth, and I say 'tis time we bring her back."

The beginning of yet another dance, with several wives coming to claim their husbands, brought the discussion to an end.

TEN

Mornings, thought Paddy Rawlings, were the times she liked best. Early mornings, when the intoxicating smell of coffee from her two-cup pot permeated her London flat, when the light poured in through the high top-floor windows, when morning traffic was just beginning to stir on the street below and walkers and joggers were beginning to fill the park across the way.

Mornings had always been her favorite times to sit quietly and lose herself in the possibilities of a new day. To dream dreams and rehearse the ambitions that brought her here to England and kept her here.

But no, she reminded herself now as she sat by the window and brought her coffee to her lips. *I've always had my ambitions—but it was Bill who kept me here.*

Even at the thought of him, she felt the wave of uncertainty sweep over her that she had worked hard and long to keep at bay. Uncertainty that could bring her ambitions to a dangerous stall. Memories she really didn't have time to remember.

Bill . . . the cheerful Englishman who had beguiled her heart on her first visit to London . . . who had christened her Paddy because of her fondness for Irish music . . . who had talked her into staying in England and cheered her and encouraged her in her rising career, then asked her to leave it all again and go with him to New Zealand.

But at the time she hadn't been able to agree to such a change. It was hard enough to start over again in a new country. She couldn't do it a second time—especially with no idea where his wandering spirit would take her next.

Or could she?

Paddy sighed. She was accustomed to cutting off such doubts before they could interrupt her concentration. Yet she knew she couldn't put Bill on ignore indefinitely. He had already been gone almost a year, and she was less sure than ever of what she wanted.

A year ago, it had all seemed so clear. She had felt so focused, so sure of where she was going—and of what she had to do to get there. So what if she had to put a huge chunk of her life on hold while she achieved it. That had always been her strength—the ability to keep her mind on one thing at a time and put everything else on the back burner.

She took another sip of the hot, fragrant coffee. *Focus, Paddy*, she reminded herself. *You've got to keep your focus.*

First, wrap up the Stone story, she told herself sternly. *Get back in touch with Andrew and see what he knows.*

After that . . . maybe there would be time to think about Bill.

※   E L E V E N   ※

Two more days had passed since Andrew Trentham had arrived in Spittal o' Ballochallater.

He felt almost as if he had stumbled into a Scottish fairy tale. But this fairy-tale world was not filled with dragons and witches and dwarfs—this was no Narnia or Middle Earth—but solid and real . . . an actual place! Would the magic last only for a day, as it had for Van Johnson in *Brigadoon*? Or would his future perhaps be like Gene Kelly's?

Andrew's hostess and guide and companion for the day just past had been the chief's daughter, who had arranged for her partner to take her calls— "What's the use o' havin' a partner," she laughed, "if ye canna cover fer one anither!" After a brief tour of the surgery, where he met a variety of four-legged patients and the two ginger cats that lived on the premises, she had taken him to the hills. They had ridden and romped and walked and hiked all over the Highland countryside through the environs of Ballochallater, talking about Scotland and its history. Andrew told her the tales that had so fascinated him in recent months. His free-flowing questions had not thus far caused her to wonder why he was so curious, or what might be at the root of his preoccupation with Scottish politics, history, and the Gordon genealogy.

His wonderful hours at the small castle—talking late into the previous two evenings with Finlaggan Gordon, his wife, and his two grown children—had offered such a broad and personal perspective to the observations Andrew had gleaned from Duncan MacRanald.

But most of all, it could hardly be argued, did Andrew find himself bewitched by the vibrant personality that accompanied the wild red hair of the engaging Leigh Ginevra Gordon. She was the fairy-tale princess, but of a sort that could only be discovered in a story of the untamed north.

With amusement he found himself contemplating walking into a black-tie reception in Chelsea with Ginny on his arm. She was so refreshingly intelligent and knowledgeable, yet in such an unrefined Highland way. Was hers something of the savagery that so intimidated the English two centuries earlier? He could almost imagine her storming into a room full of MPs or lords and drawing a sword, declaring, "Independence for Scotland . . . and we want it now!" And the sword, if she chose a claymore, would be as tall as the warrioress!

What an enchanting combination of toughness and femininity had somehow fused into a single personality with a double portion of energy and vigor!

She was the chief's eldest, and he was as proud of her as he would have been had she and Shorty been born in reverse order. She could run faster for her size and ride a horse harder and shoot a hunting rifle more accurately than any young man for miles, including Shorty and Alastair Farquharson—and yet she danced lightly and gracefully, could hold her own in any discussion of current events, and knew how to take care of sick animals to boot. Her bright mane and the fire in her black-green eyes, fair ruddy complexion, and accent so thick he had to ask her to repeat half of what she said, all combined to draw around her an aura of mystery and delight in the young Englishman's eyes.

Here *must* be a chief's daughter from some other time—a modern personification of Ginevra of Glencoe or Culodina of Culloden—come back to rouse the Scots' hearts to their ancient pride in their nation.

Her deepest regret, she said, was that she was not a boy. If only she might become the Lochnagar Gordon chief—for *she* would have no qualms about using the old word!—after her father. She loved her brother, but it was the one thing in life she begrudged him—his sonship.

And how could Andrew know that his own presence had already caused things to awaken within her that no local-bred man like Alastair could stir. To the young daughter of the laird, the visitor who had suddenly appeared at their Highland Games represented wider expanses and further horizons than the small world of the glens and hills of her home.

Beyond her university days in Glasgow and brief holidays with friends, she had rarely visited far from home. Even today, London seemed almost as foreign to her as Antarctica. The very sound of Andrew's English tongue spoke to her of adventure, of faraway places, of cities, of romance and drama and possibility, filling her vision with . . . she knew not what.

Ginny *too* was being drawn into a fairy tale. But hers was of more traditional flavor involving a prince and a chieftain's daughter—a story whose central figure was a bearded knight who appeared one day in the land of the princess, his shirt off and running up the hill chasing after her own Alastair, and then was too exhausted a few minutes later to give her his name.

▨   T W E L V E   ▨

Ginny had been called out that afternoon to a couple of nearby farms. As Andrew strolled leisurely through the small village reflecting on his days with her, the faded label of a box of chocolates in the window of the tiny post office and notions shop caught his eye. A sudden impulse possessed him, and he walked inside.

"Do you have any more of those chocolates I see in the window there?" he asked the buxom, red-faced woman behind the counter.

"Ay, I du, sir—ahind ye there on the wee shelf wi' the magazines."

"Ah, right . . . I see them," said Andrew. He took a box down and placed it on the counter.

A minute later he was enthusiastically on his way back up to the castle.

"Is Ginny back yet, Mrs. Gordon?" he asked as he entered, trying to keep from giving away his excitement.

"No, Mr. Trent," she answered. "She said she'd likely be gone the day."

"Where is she, then? I'll surprise her. Is it within walking distance?"

"Ay, in a manner o' speikin'."

"How do you mean?"

"Only that ye'd hae t' climb the hill o'er yonder," she replied, pointing vaguely with her hand, "the one ye ran up at the games—"

She paused. Andrew nodded in indication that he was following the information thus far.

"—then over the next ridge an' doon into the wee glen on the ither side," Ginny's mother went on. "'Tis James Gregor's place. She's checking his milkers fer wee ones. Ye canna miss it, though it'd be a walk o' two or three miles, I'm thinkin'. Why dinna ye speir Shorty t' take ye?"

"No, I'd like to find it myself," replied Andrew. "If I get lost, I'll just come back. It'll be an adventure. I'll enjoy myself."

He turned and left the castle in high spirits. Within minutes he was bounding and puffing up the steep hill whose acquaintance he had made on his first day in Ballochallater.

About an hour later, after a brief detour along a path which led him in the wrong direction, he came upon what he took to be the Gregor farm. There was Ginny's little red mud-splattered truck parked beside the barn. Led by an occasional moo, he made for the building.

Carefully he slipped through an open side door and crept in. Ginny and the farmer were busy with a row of cows, although from his vantage point as he entered Andrew could not see at first what their business with the bovines actually was. He took a step forward.

The black-and-white animals stood calmly swishing their tails along the railing, munching the oats placed in front of them to occupy their attention as each waited its turn to be checked by the diminutive young woman moving about amongst and behind them. Ginny and the farmer seemed to be deep in conversation about one of the animals. Andrew paused and watched in admiration as Ginny, all hundred and ten pounds of her, now maneuvered around the next Holstein, easily ten or twelve times her weight, gently stroking its head and speaking a few soft words to reassure the creature. She returned to the back of the animal and extended herself up on her toes. Then, to Andrew's sudden shock, she plunged her gloved hand and arm all the way up to her shoulder into the cow's backside.

Andrew's stomach lurched momentarily and he glanced away. Then he had to look again. He couldn't believe what he was seeing.

The procedure was over in less than a minute. After a brief palpitation of the uterus to see if it was enlarged, she removed her hand.

"Okay, James," said Ginny. "No wee one here. That's still only two so far that need to be calved in."

Hearing the words, Andrew realized what test she was conducting. Now her mother's words to him made sense. By this time he'd completely forgotten the purpose for his romp over the hillside.

Summoning the courage to look again, he saw Ginny change her gloves, go through the same ritual of speaking a few gentle words of reassurance to the would-be mother, then shove an arm into the next awaiting rump.

"Ay . . ." she said slowly, "I think . . . ay, James—Nora here's aboot t' be a mither again. She's growin' nicely already!"

"'Tis good news," said the farmer, noting the information on the sheet he was holding.

Ginny retracted her arm with a soft, liquid *whoosh*. Turning toward her next patient, she glanced up to see Andrew in the shadows fifteen feet away.

"Andy!" she exclaimed. "What on airth are ye doin' here?"

She walked toward him beaming in her dirty work jeans and red-and-yellow plaid shirt, heavy rubber boots stomping across the floor, unpeeling the dripping latex glove from her arm and tossing it aside.

"Uh . . . your mother told me where to find you," Andrew replied, taking a step or two forward, then pausing briefly to still his queasy stomach. "I walked over."

"Hoo did ye find the place?"

"She gave me directions. I only made one wrong turn."

"So noo ye *really* see what I du fer a livin'," she laughed, glancing down at her mud-splattered trousers and manure-coated rubber boots.

Tentatively Andrew continued forward as Ginny turned back toward the cows and pulled on a fresh glove.

"James an' I had a time," she said as she stretched it up her arm as far as it would reach, "coaxin' a few o' the ladies back into the barn in the middle o' the day fer their testin'.—Meet James Gregor . . . James, this here's oor guest, Andy Trent."

"Ye'll hae t' pardon the dirt, Mr. Trent," said Gregor, vigorously wiping his palm on his thigh, though by the look of his trousers he was unlikely to accomplish much from the action by way of cleaning it.

"No problem, Mr. Gregor," said Andrew, extending his hand.

The two men shook hands.

"Wha's next, James?" asked Ginny.

"Clover," replied the farmer, patting the next in line on its fleshy mid-section.

"I winna be much longer, Andy," she said. "Then ye can ride back doon wi' me. So, Clover lass," she went on in a soft voice, "this wee test will jist tak a second or twa an' ye'll hardly feel a thing. Jist enjoy yer oats an' pretend I'm not even here."

She turned back and ducked under the rail to begin the probe. She paused briefly, noticing for the first time Andrew's left hand behind his back as he stood, seemingly embarrassed in front of the wizened dairyman.

"What's that ye're hidin' ahind ye?" she asked, tiptoeing up again and plunging her hand inside the cow.

"Uh . . . nothing," replied Andrew, gulping a time or two in order to keep his lunch in place.

"Ye got somethin' there—I can tell that," persisted Ginny.

"Well, I was in the village," began Andrew, then pulled the box out from behind his back. "Actually . . . I brought you a box of chocolates," he said. "I thought I would bring them out to you, but it doesn't seem . . . that is, I wasn't exactly expecting . . ."

"Chocolates!" exclaimed Ginny as she stretched yet deeper into the abyss and felt for the uterus. "Hoo thoughtful o' ye. I'm starvin'!"

Unable to comprehend in his brain the thought of eating at a time like this, Andrew continued to stare at the spectacle before him while fumbling unconsciously with the lid of the box.

"Open it up, Andy," said Ginny, "and pop one in my mouth."

Grimacing, as he ventured a step or two closer, Andrew took one of the candies between thumb and two fingers and stretched it forward between Ginny's waiting lips. "Hmmm, thank ye!" she exclaimed. "Chocolate is one o' my worst weaknesses. I canna git enough. Hmm, 'tis a good one!"

Almost the same instant, at Clover's side and with her own test behind her, Nora decided to get rid of some of that morning's grass.

Two or three loud splats sounded on the concrete floor. Andrew glanced down to see his trousers and shoes splattered in smelly brown.

Still munching on the chocolate, Ginny broke into laughter as she turned to Gregor. "Negative fer Clover, James," she said, then pulled out her arm with another long *schlooorsh*.

It was enough. Andrew turned green, lurched several steps to one side, hastily set the box of chocolates on a nearby stool, and proceeded to lose the ploughman's lunch he had enjoyed an hour earlier at the Heather and the Stout.

Ginny removed her glove and walked toward him as he recovered.

"I'm sorry, Andy," she said. "I guess I forgot what sich a thing must be like gien ye haena seen it afore."

"Not exactly the sort of sight one runs into in—" began Andrew. "I mean, no, you're right . . . I've been around animals, but I confess I have never seen a cow's pregnancy test before now. I don't suppose I was quite prepared for it, especially with, you know, your little snack."

Ginny laughed. "It was delicious, though!" she said. "An' I thank ye fer it. Now, why dinna ye come outside. Ye can wait fer me there. I'll only be anither ten minutes.—James, I'll be right back. I'll tak Andy outside an' git him some fresh air."

Andrew drew in two or three breaths as they left the barn and emerged into the sunlight. Gradually he came to himself, and the color returned to his cheeks.

"Whew!" he said, "I didn't know how weak my stomach was. I would never have been cut out to be a vet."

"Ye git used t' the sights an' smells," laughed Ginny. "Actually, some o' them ye actually come t' like."

"I'll take your word for it!"

That evening when Andrew arrived at the dining room for dinner, he found the laird and Mrs. Gordon awaiting him, but Ginny had not yet made her appearance. He took his chair and was chatting informally with them, telling them of his embarrassing experience in the Gregor barn, when she entered.

After seeing her at her work, unabashed by and even relishing the earthiness of her job, the sudden contrast of her present appearance nearly took Andrew's breath away. She was wearing a green tartan skirt and white blouse, completed with a lace jabot. A green ribbon was tied in her freshly washed and bouncy red hair, and a hint of eye shadow and mascara accentuated the deep green of her eyes. But her freshly scrubbed and radiant face needed no additional color, for her cheeks possessed a natural glow all their own.

"Hello, Andy," she said sprightly. "I du hope ye're feeling better."

A subtle wave of perfume followed her as she sat down in the seat next to him. It was at that moment, with the two enchantingly different images of her that he had seen that day swirling in his brain, when Andrew suddenly realized that had she not already been spoken for by the blacksmith Alastair Farquharson, his heart might well have been in danger.

✖   T H I R T E E N   ✖

Andrew was down from his room early the following morning. Ginny and father and mother and brother were already seated in the kitchen. The smell of fresh-brewed tea rose from the table as he approached, though the unmistakable aroma of fish emanated from the frying pan to mingle with it. As might have come as no surprise, he found them talking about him.

"Are ye weel recovered frae yesterday's mishap?" said Ginny, smiling as he entered.

"I think so," sighed Andrew sheepishly. "At least my appetite's back."

"I'm aye glad t' hear it. I wouldna want t' be responsible fer makin' an Englishman think ill o' Scotland."

"Little chance of that," replied Andrew. "Let's just say that I am enjoying more experiences here than I anticipated when I came!"

"We were jist wonderin' amongst oorselves, Mr. Trent," said Ginny's father, motioning for him to join them, "what an Englishman sich as yersel' thinks aboot the notion o' Scottish home rule. 'Tis all folks here hae been talkin' aboot since we got oor own Parliament."

Andrew smiled and gave a shrug.

"Ye been speirin' a heap o' questions," said Mrs. Gordon, pouring him a cup of tea, "but I canna say as I recollect hearin' what ye think o' the maitter yersel'." She turned to the stove to begin poaching five eggs to accompany the *finnan haddies* already frying.

"Ye see, Andy," put in Ginny, "we're interested in hoo an Englishman might see the thing, as ye seem t' be jist as interested aboot what *we're* thinkin'."

"I don't know that I'd be your *typical* Englishman," laughed Andrew.

"Weel, ye'll jist have t' leave that t' us t' figure oot. Ye've com t' be oor frien', an' we'd like t' ken yer mind on the maitter regairdless," said her father.

"*Do* you think the English are against Scottish home rule for the most part, laird?" asked Andrew.

"That I dinna ken," Gordon replied. "All I ken's what I read in the papers, whaur it seems naebody south o' the Tweed cares what we Scots think one way or the ither."

"I don't think that is true, laird," said Andrew. "Generally speaking, I imagine you'll find the English very fond of the Scots."

"Tak that Trentham fellow, then," the laird went on, "him that's in the papers—"

Andrew had just raised his cup to his lips and now choked momentarily.

"Is the tea too strong fer ye, Mr. Trent?" asked Ginny's mother.

"No, no," replied Andrew, coughing again and struggling to take a breath. "A swallow went down the wrong way, that's all."

He continued to take a few more sips from the edge of his cup while attempting to steady himself, thankful to have something to hold in front of a face that had suddenly grown very red and very hot.

"—as I was saying," the laird continued, "the fellows in Parliament, first Hamilton—and I wish the man nae harm now he's dead, but there's no denyin' he was no frien' o' the Scots—an' now this new upstart Trentham—they've been doin' all they can t' keep us frae havin' oor ain say in the maitter."

"How do you *know* that?" pressed Andrew.

"MacKinnon says so," now put in the laird's younger son.

"Who's MacKinnon?" Andrew, wincing inwardly as he pretended ignorance.

"Why, he's the leader o' the Scottish Nationalists, laddie," exclaimed Gordon. "He's jist aboot the maist important voice Scotland's had in Lonnon fer generations."

"Dinna ye follow politics nane at all, Mr. Trent?" asked Shorty. "Ye speired so many questions when we were hunting, I figured ye kenned all aboot it."

A slight cough of discomfort followed.

"Uh . . . not really—uh . . . not too much," lied Andrew. How was he going to get out of this conversation and keep his skin?

"If we Scots arena entitled t' make up oor ain minds in the maitter o' whether we want t' be free or no, that's hardly a democracy t' my way o' thinkin'—what say ye t' that, Mr. Trent?"

"I don't know, laird," replied Andrew, still hedging.

"Whaur's the differ' atween that an' what they did t' the American colonies? Whaur's the differ' atween that an' what they did t' India . . . or the

African colonies or all the rest? England's had a way o' takin' over ither coontries, and it's had a heap o' 'em through the years. But now America's free, an' so is Canada an' New Zealand an' even South Africa an' Zimbabwe an' the rest. All we're sayin' is, *What aboot Scotland?*—why dinna we deserve the same consideration oorsel's? When's *oor* turn fer the same kin' o' treatment?"

"You make a persuasive argument, laird," said Andrew thoughtfully.

The tone of his voice did not convey how strongly he meant the words. He had never thought of the issue in such a light before, but always as if England held a proprietary *right* to sovereignty over Scotland. But if, from the Scots point of view, Scotland was another country altogether, with a *different* heritage, its *own* history and culture, even an essentially *distinct* bloodline and language—then what was to distinguish Scotland from, say, India, in its right to self-governance?

It was an astonishingly simple, yet profoundly new perspective to bring to the matter of home rule.

"Would ye care for a fresh haddock, Mr. Trent?"

"Oh . . . uh—oh, yes . . . thank you," replied Andrew, suddenly realizing Mrs. Gordon had been standing at his side holding the plate of fish for several seconds. "I'm sorry—I was thinking about your husband's words."

"What I want to ask," said Andrew after she had laid the fish on his plate, "is why do Scots feel so strongly about independence after all these years united with England?"

As if the question itself bordered on being an affront, Ginny's father nearly rose out of his chair.

"Because Scotland's its ain coontry—'tis as simple as that," he replied. "Scotland's not England. Scotland's *Scotland*. Nae mair, nae less. Scotland's no just a state, like New York or California over in America. Scotland's a *nation* o' its own. Ye want t' know aboot independence, laddie, I'll tell ye— it's aboot when they made a single nation oot o' this land we ca' Scotland. Ye ever hear o' Kenneth MacAlpin?"

Andrew nodded his head. "Sounds familiar . . ."

"He it was that united Caledonia. MacAlpin's the name—he made ane independent kingdom here afore they did in half the coontries o' Europe. We were a nation o' oor ain back then . . . so I figure we've as much right as ony coontry t' be independent noo, since we was one o' the first t' become a nation at all."

" 'Tis true, what Papa says," added Ginny now with the emphasis not merely of a proud daughter, but of a staunch advocate in her own right.

"We've the right t' have oor ain say aboot it, same as all the ither coontries."

"Yes . . . yes, it is an argument I must confess I hadn't heard before. We ought to make you a national spokesman, Mr. Gordon," Andrew added.

"*We*—who do ye mean, laddie?"

"Oh . . . nobody . . . I mean . . . they—*they* ought to make you their spokesman. The Scottish Nationalists," replied the flustered MP.

Ginny's father broke into a roar of laughter.

"Naebody in England wad listen t' an auld Highlander like me," he said. "No maitter hoo much sense I might bring t' the discussion."

"I don't know, laird," rejoined Andrew. "You might be surprised."

"Weel, as I was sayin', auld King MacAlpin's the one wha did it."

"I would enjoy hearing about him."

"Weel then, laddie—I'll tell ye. It was back in the 800s, jist aboot the same time as the Vikings cam oot o' the north wi' their ransackin' an' pillagin' an' the like. Ye see, laddie—"

"Oh, Papa," Ginny broke in impatiently. "Dinna ye start tellin' Andy one o' yer lang stories noo. We're gaein' fer a ride."

"He said he wanted t' hear't, lass—didna ye hear him wi' yer ain twa ears?"

"Ay, Papa, but—"

"You shall tell me everything this evening," said Andrew, stepping in as the diplomat before the argument could escalate further.

The laird nodded, satisfied.

"I'll jist git started while we finish oor brakfast," he said, "fer Caledonia's got a lang, lang history . . . an' it taks some time t' tell it aright. Ye got nae objection t' that, do ye, daughter?"

"Nay, Papa," smiled Ginny.

▓   F O U R T E E N   ▓

After breakfast and what turned into a fascinating hour of listening to Finlaggan Gordon, Andrew and Ginny saddled two horses and set out across the countryside.

A brief rain had fallen during the night, the only remaining evidence of which now lay underfoot rather than overhead. As they rode away eastward from the castle, the brilliant day reminded Andrew of the morning back at

Derwenthwaite not so long past—yet in another way for the searching parliamentarian, a lifetime ago—during those weeks when he had first begun thinking more personally about Scotland. His overnight visit with Duncan MacRanald had followed, and his reading of the legend of the brothers Cruithne and Fidach. And now, such a short time since, so much had changed.

They had packed a lunch, for Ginny said they would be gone most of the afternoon. It was warmer today. Both horses and riders were perspiring freely before they were an hour toward their goal.

"Where are we going?" asked Andrew soon after they had set out.

"I want t' show ye what oor clan is named fer!"

"Oh yes! What is it—Lake something or other?"

Ginny laughed.

"Lochnagar," she said. "But 'tis a mountain, not a lake."

"I thought a loch was a lake."

"It is. I dinna ken why it's called that—but that's its name . . . Lochnagar."

They rode on and reached Loch Callater, a proper lake, in about an hour and a half. There they stopped for ten minutes to water the horses, then continued gradually up and onto the slopes of the great mountain itself. They passed a number of smaller lakes as they made their way through valleys and across wide bare expanses of heath, bearing northeast and constantly upward. They splashed through dozens of brown, foaming streams tumbling down their rocky courses and passed through three or four dense pinewoods, from which their way opened onto meadowlike moors with still pools scattered throughout. Eventually they began ascending steeply again, now around giant boulders and up rocky inclines, leveling out finally to a long steady slope of treeless heath. This side of the mountain would lead to the summit.

It was just before one in the afternoon when they at last drew in sight of the crest. Ginny reined in her mare and stopped. Andrew drew alongside.

"Why are we stopping?" he asked. "It looks as if we're nearly done."

"Ay, we are—I thought maybe ye'd like t' race t' the top, there yonder."

"Race!" laughed Andrew. "I'm no jockey on the back of a horse. And this hardly looks like safe terrain for a gallop."

"Ay, but these twa horses know every inch o' the way. There's no worry o' them stumblin'. Ye can tak yer pick o' the two, whiche'er one ye think the faster."

"I suppose I'll stay where I am."

"A canny choice. Are ye ready, then? I'll gie ye a head start—hang on!"

As she said the words, Ginny lashed the rump of Andrew's mount with the small leather whip in her hand and gave a bloodcurdling shout to go along with it.

The beast leapt forward and lurched into a gallop, nearly throwing Andrew from the saddle. He recovered himself, then hunched forward and did exactly as Ginny had told him—hang on!

Regaining his balance, he glanced back. Ginny still sat where she was, laughing with glee. The spirit of the race now possessed him. Looking now the part of a wild man in the saddle, Andrew kicked at the sides of his steed, shouting exhortations to greater speed.

When he had measured about a third of the distance, Ginny suddenly exploded after him.

Andrew had not seen his companion in full gallop all morning, nor did he see her now. Had he glanced back, however, he would have observed her mare gliding over the uneven heath as if it were the trimmed and mown grass of Kensington Gardens. The perfect motion could be gauged by the steady position of the great head, whose flared nostrils worked in rhythm with the blurred invisibility of the hooves, sucking in huge drafts of oxygen to power the mighty equine lungs.

Leaning forward, her own back parallel to the ground, the beast's mistress required no whip now, nor shouts, to urge her steed on. Fingers and heels and whispers were sufficient, for the creature was well acquainted with her voice and her touch. The two moved across the earth as one, with a speed marvelous to behold. Ginny's eyes glowed with the fire of her race, red hair flying windily about as an extension of the mare's auburn mane, wide exhilaration spread across her face.

Had he seen it, Andrew would have witnessed an expression he would never have forgotten the rest of his days. As it was, he would have to make acquaintance with the Celtic fire of those eyes in other ways. The only indication of the great velocity of the pair was given by the occasional clumps of sod that shot up from behind the powerful hooves as they flew across the ground.

Steadily Ginny gained upon the horse and rider ahead of her as if Andrew were out for a mere leisurely canter.

When she galloped by, hair streaming behind, and without so much as a glance to the side, Andrew was astonished at how swiftly she passed. How could she have suddenly found such speed in her horse's legs? Unless his was an old nag, and she had been setting him up for this moment. . . . No, that could not be, since she had given *him* his choice of mounts.

Before he had even completed his thoughts, she was past him and pulling away. She glanced back briefly, and the wild exuberance on her face revealed itself. Andrew beheld it only for an instant. The next, she had turned forward again and was increasing her lead up the slope.

By the time Andrew reined in at the summit, Ginny sat easily atop her heavily breathing mare, watching his arrival with the joy of fun across her face.

"Were you trying to make me look bad!" shouted Andrew as he rode up.

Ginny threw her head back and broke into laughter of pure delight.

Andrew could not help joining her.

"Alastair canna keep wi' me either," she laughed.

"Can anyone?"

"Not yet."

"I thought as much!"

Again Ginny laughed, then dismounted her mare. Andrew followed. For several moments, the only sounds to be heard were the great expansions of two huge rib cages, accompanied by the alternate puffs and inhalations from the distended dragonlike nostrils of the two beasts.

Andrew and Ginny caught their breath more easily as they gazed slowly about them, where all directions sloped downward.

Still without speaking, Ginny unfastened the bags from the two horses and began unpacking their lunch. The horses had recently watered in a stream they had passed, and a bagful of oats would soon occupy them as well.

Fifteen minutes later, Andrew and Ginny sat and nibbled contentedly on oatcakes and cold kippers while some distance away the two mares grazed about for what grass they might find.

"It's so beautiful here," sighed Andrew, who had still not stopped his wide-eyed exploration of the distant horizons.

"It has always been one o' my favorite places," said Ginny.

"But . . . but what *is* it," Andrew went on, as if carrying on a dialogue with himself that had been in progress for some time, "—what is it that *makes* it so alluring?"

"What du ye mean?" asked Ginny.

Andrew smiled. "I suppose for someone like you, who's grown up in the Highlands, perhaps it's not so unusual," he said. "You're used to it."

"Used t' what?"

"All this!" replied Andrew, rising to his feet and swinging his hand in the full gesture of a circular arc, as if no more than the gesture were required to illuminate his meaning completely. "Don't you see? It's so different than anywhere else! So desolate, so wild, so open, so huge! I don't know how to explain it! It's more splendid than the tidy gardens and lawns and flower boxes in England. Even though my own home isn't really like that, either, out here you feel you're touching something ancient, something . . . almost—I don't know—something holy, as if this must have been how it looked when God was halfway through His creation and hadn't yet gotten everything neat and orderly for human beings to live in."

Ginny laughed.

"Now that's a way o' describin' it I've ne'er heard afore! Are ye sayin' the Creator didna git altogither finished wi' Scotland?"

"That's not it," laughed Andrew, kneeling back down to the ground. "It's not incomplete—it's even better! Because it's older, maybe *nearer* to what God might have intended. Not that this is how it looked when He was halfway through, but how it looked before humans came along and tamed everything."

Ginny laughed again. "Maybe it's 'cause I've always lived here, but it doesna seem sae unusual t' me."

"It *is* unusual—believe me," rejoined Andrew. "There are not many places on the earth that can compare with the majesty of where we are sitting right now. Just listen."

He stopped. Both were silent a long while.

"I dinna hear a thing," said Ginny at length.

"Exactly! It's the peaceful silence as well as the wild aspect of the terrain and scenery. We're miles from any other human being. No airplanes, no cars or trucks or busses, no city, no voices. Find a place in *England* where you can say such a thing."

"It isna *always* sae quiet an' still—ye ought t' see Lochnagar when all this is covered with thunderclouds, an' when the storms are flyin' an' the snow's pilin' high an' the wind is blawin'!"

Andrew nodded. "I *would* like to see it then!"

" 'Tis too wild for man when it's like that," said Ginny. "When the snow's flyin' aboot Lochnagar, that's when I bide in the castle!"

Again Andrew rose and began walking softly about, breathing in deeply, as if the air itself were imbued with the quality of reverence he had spoken of.

He walked about alone for some time, feeling a gathering of the same mystique he had felt so many times in his northern journey.

When again he joined Ginny, his heart was calm and full. There was no other place in the world right then that he would rather be.

They sat for two hours and spoke of many things.

The ride back down the mountain was leisurely and slow. Neither seemed inclined to bring the pleasant afternoon to an end.

※   F I F T E E N   ※

That night Andrew paced back and forth in his room replaying the wonderful day's events in his mind.

They had arrived back from their ride around five that afternoon. After a bath and rest, followed by a most satisfying meal, Andrew listened while Chief Finlaggan Gordon regaled him for another three hours with tales of ancient Caledonia. As a storyteller, Andrew decided, Ginny's father was every inch the equal of Duncan MacRanald. He even managed to keep Andrew's attention off the subject that increasingly occupied his mind: Ginny.

Now, alone and weary but unable to sleep, Andrew fell to inspecting the contents of his room, while gradually a pensive and introspective mood came over him.

In one corner leaned a walking stick. Andrew picked it up and began to examine it. The round brass top-ball unscrewed into two half-spheres, revealing a compass inside.

"Clever," thought Andrew, "and handy if you get lost walking in these hills."

Fiddling with it further, he discovered the entire walking stick comprised of three equal lengths, each of which could be unscrewed by means of a brass fitting inset into the wood.

"For traveling, I take it," mused Andrew, "to take apart and put in a suitcase."

He replaced it in the corner and continued about the room.

A bookshelf full of intrigue claimed his attention, though it was too late and he was too tired actually to read. Robert Burns, Sir Walter Scott, Robert Louis Stevenson, Ian MacLaren, and George MacDonald all were well represented. Most of the books were old and apparently well read. What a treasure trove of the great Scots literature of the nineteenth century—and how he wished he had a month to explore it!

He meandered to a glass-enclosed case, upon whose several shelves were displayed items of apparent sentiment: an old doll clad in tiny kilt, a faded strip of tartan, a small set of decorative bagpipes, a knife of the sort that kilted men wore sticking out of their stockings—a scian-dubh, Andrew knew by now—several small porcelain figures of no obvious significance, a thin and very old book of poetry bound in leather, a framed photograph of a man and woman of nineteenth-century vintage, a plainly bound book that resembled several he had seen in the bookcase, and finally a length of heavy chain. Old, pitted, and discolored, it consisted of some eight or ten double links, each oval and some three-quarters of an inch in width, and with the links at one end apparently having been cut in half and then crimped together so the cut links would not fall out of the rest. An ornate and very old connective latch was fastened to the uncut end, with some undecipherable markings upon it.

The case was unlocked. Andrew opened one of the doors, then took out several of the items one at a time and examined them reverently. He wondered about the old couple in the photograph—they must surely have a story to tell! He would ask Ginny.

The book was something he had never heard of before, with an odd title: *Warlock O'Glenwarlock*. He opened the cover.

There before his eyes stood the reason it had been placed in the case rather than with the others on the bookshelf!

In what was clearly an old hand, under the date October 1882, the inscription inside read: *To Laird Finlaggan Gordon, Lochnagar, a man who occupies a singular place of honor in my eyes: For those born and bred in the Gordon region of Strathbogie, the name is one to be esteemed, its great men most of all—and this laird in particular the author counts it a privilege to call his friend.*

Beneath the words was the personal signature of the author. The autographed volume must have been presented to Ginny's great- or even great-great-grandfather, thought Andrew, replacing the book with care. He would ask her about that too.

He removed the curious link of old chain. From the weight and color he judged it must be forged of pure silver. But what could be its significance?

He closed the door of the case, still clutching the chain with the latch and the oddly cut end, absently jingling it in his hand as he pondered its origin, and continued slowly about the room.

On the wall opposite the case, a framed poem now caught his eye. He began reading, only to realize that it was an ode to the very mountain they had ridden up today, written by an Englishman, no less—none other than Lord Byron!

Why was an *Englishman* penning such words about one of *Scotland's* mountain peaks? Had *he* been bitten by the Caledonian bug as well?

But of course—now that he thought of it, it made sense. Lord Byron's family name had been Gordon as well!

Andrew read through the verses twice.

Away ye gay landscapes, ye gardens of roses—
In you let the minions of luxury rove;
But restore me the rocks where the snowflake reposes,
If still they are sacred to freedom and love.
Yet, Caledonia, dear are thy mountains,
Round their white summits tho' elements war,
Though cataracts foam 'stead of smooth flowing fountains—
I sigh for the valley of dark Lochnagar.

Ah, there my young footsteps in infancy wandered,
My cap was the bonnet, my cloak was the plaid;
On chieftains departed my memory pondered
As daily I strayed through the pine-covered glade.
I sought not my home till the day's dying glory
Gave place to the rays of the bright polar star;
For fancy was cheered by traditional story,
Disclosed by the natives of dark Lochnagar.

The words penetrated deeply into his soul, as if completing all the unspoken feelings and sensations he had felt this afternoon on the mountaintop.

Andrew walked toward the window, opened it, and gazed into the stillness of the night.

In the distance, he imagined he could see the peak of Lochnagar, though he knew it was only in his imagination. He drew in another deep sigh of pleasure.

What a land was Scotland—how wide, how open, how magnificent in its very starkness, how wild and untamed . . . how *free*!

But these very thoughts reminded Andrew of who he was and what was his mission. Suddenly he was aware that his life was not as unencumbered as the wide-open spaces of Lochnagar. His picture had been in the paper, and Scotland's future had to be decided.

He would eventually have to resolve in his own mind whether Caledonia's freedom should also include the right to be its own land, its own nation.

His thoughts strayed to Ginny, though in truth during these last few days she had hardly left them.

He *had* to tell her. He couldn't leave this place without telling her who he was.

He would tell her right now, in fact . . . tonight.

It was late—ten-thirty or eleven. He glanced at his wrist and hesitated. But he couldn't wait. It had to be done.

Andrew turned and left the room. He walked down the hallway, then gingerly knocked on Ginny's door.

He waited.

Several moments passed.

Then the door opened a crack, and Ginny's face appeared. She was clad in a white-and-blue robe.

"May . . . may I talk to you a minute?"

"I . . . yes . . . o' coorse," Ginny answered. "—Bide a wee."

She ducked back into her room, then returned a minute later with a light coat over her robe. She stepped into the hallway and closed the door behind her.

Andrew followed as Ginny led him down the main stone stairway to the ground floor.

"Shall we go ootside into the garden?" she asked. "'Tis a warm evening."

Andrew nodded.

A three-quarter moon, along with what remnants of the sunset would remain all night at the horizon in this northern locale, cast a pale red glow over the simply laid-out lawn, bordered with a short-trimmed box hedge and containing four or five divided sections where Ginny's mother grew different types of flowers, notably—notwithstanding Byron's indication to the contrary—a nice rectangle of colorfully blooming roses.

They sat down on a stone bench.

An awkward silence followed.

At last Andrew rose and began pacing.

"Ye dinna hae t' be afraid o' whatever ye hae t' tell me," said Ginny.

"You're right," replied Andrew. "There *is* something I have to tell you. But . . . but it's not so easy."

"Jist say't."

Another pause. He felt her nearness intensely.

"I want you to know that these last several days—today, especially—have meant more to me than I can say."

"Thank ye. But that sounds like a fareweel."

"I'm afraid it is. I have to leave in the morning."

Now it was Ginny's turn to be silent.

"Will ye be back?" she finally asked.

Andrew had no answer.

"After I tell you what I came out here to tell you," he said, "you may not *want* to see me again."

"I doobt that."

"You haven't heard it yet."

"Then I'll tell ye again . . . jist say it."

Suddenly realizing he was still holding the silver links in his hand, Andrew glanced down at it.

"What is this?" he asked, glad for a reprieve from his awkward stalling.

"I dinna ken—jist an odd bit o' chain."

"But what's it from? Why is it in the case in my room with what look to be family mementos?"

"I dinna ken. Jist something that's always been there."

"Does your father know?"

"I asked him aboot it when I was a wee lass, but he didna ken either. He said it was here when he was a laddie too."

"Hmm . . . curious."

"But what was't ye had t' tell me?"

"Oh . . . oh, nothing—I just wanted you to know how much I enjoyed today's ride," Andrew finally replied, unable to bring himself to make the disclosure.

They talked a few more minutes. The emotional atmosphere was strained, however, and soon they returned inside. They walked upstairs to the first floor in silence. Both knew something was amiss.

They parted in the corridor, bidding one another good-night for the second time that evening.

"I'm sorry for getting you out so late. Good night, Ginny."

"Good night, Andy Trent," said Ginny, trying to hide the slight quiver in her own voice.

Andrew walked slowly back to his room. Once more he began pacing about. He read again through the words of Byron's tribute to the Highlands hanging on the wall.

> Shades of the dead, have I not heard your voices
> Rise on the night rolling breath of the Gael;
> Surely the soul of the hero rejoices,
> And rides on the wind o'er his own Highland vale.
> Round Lochnagar while the stormy mist gathers,
> Winter presides in his cold icy car;
> Clouds therein circle the forms of my fathers:
> They dwell midst the tempests of dark Lochnagar.
>
> Years have rolled on, Lochnagar, since I left you,
> And years must elapse e'er I see you again;
> Though nature of verdure and flower has bereft you,
> Yet still you are dearer than Albion's plain.
> England, thy beauties are tame and domestic
> To one who has roved o'er the mountains afar;
> Over the crags that are wild and majestic,
> The steep frowning glories of dark Lochnagar.

When he had completed it, again he sought the window, as if looking out into the night might stop the pounding in his chest.

The silence was heavy, full of the mystery of the hills stretching away in the thin darkness, full of legends from the past, full of memories of this day . . . and perhaps full of something in his heart he was afraid would be destroyed before it even had a chance to bloom.

When Andrew turned back inside toward his bed, moist drops stood in his eyes. The Highland hills drew tears from his soul . . . though he could not explain why.

▓   S I X T E E N   ▓

The next morning Andrew awoke early.

He had to leave. Even though he was not on a tight schedule, he sensed that to remain longer could not help but draw him and Ginny more closely together. He must not allow that to happen as things presently stood.

She had to know.

He had always believed in truth, or so he thought. He was here in Scotland because he wanted to do the right thing for the future of this land.

But what had he been doing these last days but living an *untruth*? Even if the falsehood over his identity had begun almost by accident, it had gone on far too long. He should have stopped it sooner. But like all falsehoods, the longer it went on, the more difficult it had been to correct.

But he could not let it go on any longer.

He *had* to tell her—he had to tell them all—the truth . . . come of it what may . . . even if she never wanted to see him again.

He gathered his things. When he heard the sounds of activity below, he descended the staircase and made his appearance for breakfast, suitcase in hand.

"What—ye're no leaving us sae soon!" exclaimed Ginny's mother, walking out of the kitchen toward the dining room.

"I don't want to presume on your hospitality, Mrs. Gordon."

"Dinna ye say sich a thing, laddie!" she exclaimed. "Wouldna be nae way for ye t' do sich a thing."

"And it's hardly so soon," he added with a nervous laugh. "I've been here four days."

"An' we've been privileged t' hae ye."

"Nevertheless, I really must be on my way."

"Weel, set yer bag doon an' eat a good brakfast afore ye gae. We'll be eatin' in the dining room this mornin', though Shorty's done an' gane."

Andrew followed her into the room, where Ginny's father was already seated. Ginny appeared a minute or two later.

A quiet descended on the room and continued throughout the meal, which each present explained to his or her own satisfaction by the sad fact of Andrew's impending departure. Andrew, however, knew there was more to it.

At length, he summoned his courage and spoke.

"I . . . I have something to tell you all," he said, with difficulty.

He paused and took in a deep breath. Ginny stared down at the table, avoiding his face. She could not have known what was coming, yet a sense of impending doom seemed to hang over her. Somehow she seemed afraid.

"I want you first of all to know how greatly I appreciate your hospitality," he began. "You have truly made me feel at home. I have had the most enjoyable time of my entire trip through Scotland with you here."

"Dinna say a word more aboot it, laddie," said the laird. "Ye're as guid as family noo."

Andrew sighed. They weren't making this easy!

"But I have something else to say," he went on, determined to do what he needed to do no matter what, "something that might not be altogether pleasant for any of us."

He paused. Silence surrounded the table. The other three seemed at last to suspect the approach of a thundercloud, though they yet knew not what it contained.

"I have not been altogether honest with you," said Andrew. "I am sorry for that. It was never my intention to deceive you or anyone. It just . . . it just sort of *happened*. . . ."

Again he paused, gathering himself for what must finally come. He had taken on the UK's toughest politicians and newsmen with little difficulty. But this was excruciating!

"What I'm trying to say is that . . . that my name is not really Andy Trent. I . . . I came north to Scotland not *merely* for a holiday. I came . . . as part of my job as well. And that's where, as I say, I haven't been honest with you."

Slowly all three faces rose. Six eyes bored into him. Knives and forks and mouths were suddenly motionless.

"You see," he went on, "I'm actually . . . I'm a member of Parliament myself. My name is really Andrew Trentham."

At the words, the eyes of the chief shot open wide in shock. He knew the name well enough.

Andrew Trentham was the political enemy of the SNP!

The stunned silence lasted ten or fifteen seconds, which to Andrew seemed an eternity.

"Weel, laddie," Ginny's father said in a voice of authority which Andrew had never heard before, "ye've told us yer name, but that hairdly explains yer mission! Ye got a heap o' explainin' t' do. I dinna wonner that ye're in league wi' the other wha was here. Are ye his lackey, pretendin' t' be oor frien' sae we'd sell the land? It luiks like a bit o' treachery t' me!"

"I . . . I'm sorry," fumbled Andrew, "I—"

"What did ye think," interrupted the laird, his red face holding back his rising fury, "t' come here an' spy on us simple folk so ye cud go back t' yer

English frien's an' laugh at the backward Scots that cudna rule themsel's if they *were* given independence?"

"Honestly . . . it wasn't like that at all," Andrew struggled. But before he could say another word, Ginny's voice erupted.

"Ye lied!" she cried, her face the same shade as her hair. "Ye lied t' us a'!"

"I didn't mean—"

"Ye're jist a lyin' Sassenach! I wouldna doobt if ye're a Campbell too! Ye're nothing but—"

She could not continue. Instead, she cast him a darkly furious look and stalked from the room.

The laird rose up to his feet and spoke as one declaring the solemn pronouncement of a magistrate.

"Ye're no longer weelcome in this hoose, sir," he said in the voice of stern command. "My wife an' daughter an' son an' I—we'll thank ye t' gather yer things an' leave us at once."

Andrew rose, more mortified than he had ever been before in his life, and left the room in silence.

He retrieved his suitcase, walked to his car, then drove away from the place where he had known such brief happiness.

He saw none of their faces again.

░░   S E V E N T E E N   ░░

As he drove south out of the central Grampian Highlands, Andrew Trentham's heart was heavier than he ever remembered.

He had been what is commonly called *misunderstood* hundreds of times. In politics, that went with the territory.

But never had there been anything like what he had just been through. It was more than merely being called a traitor and liar. He had grown to *love* these people. He had also grown to love their land, its heritage, and the legacy of its history.

But in their eyes he was a liar and a traitor. Just like Campbell of Glenlyon, he had partaken of their hospitality while deceiving them. He would never betray them, of course, but they had no way of knowing that.

How could they possibly see what was in his heart—when everything they had heard about him seemed to say the opposite?

He had tried harder than many of his colleagues to keep from becoming cynical about the press. Incidents like this made it difficult. The story he had seen the night of the ceilidh, which he assumed to be the cause of Laird Gordon's intense reaction against him, had misrepresented both his position and his motives.

For the moment he saw no way to rectify what had happened. Anything he might say could not help now but sound hollow in their ears. And judging from the heated and unequivocal responses of Ginny and her father, trying to explain further by telephone would be useless. He would call or write later, after they had a chance to cool down.

Andrew sighed, drawing in yet another deep breath. He would just have to hope that *time* did indeed possess the capacity to heal this particular wound.

Until then . . . there was still a great deal of Scotland yet for him to see. He would try somehow to make sense of what had happened. It was time now to continue on with what had brought him north in the first place. Perhaps it would all fall into place as he learned more of Ginny's land and people.

He was driving through some truly remarkable scenery southward through Glenshee toward Kirkmichael. As he forced himself to take it in, gradually he found himself reflecting once again on the Caledonian saga that stretched so majestically through the centuries.

He had to laugh—Ginny's father had been so animated when talking about independence! No wonder the English always found Highlanders difficult to deal with!

Andrew thought about the tale the laird had told last evening about the era when—by violence and bloodshed—Scotland had been compelled into nationhood. *A kingdom won by the sword* had been the laird's words.

And Andrew was not far, he suddenly realized, from the traditional seat of that ancient kingship. He would stop and visit it.

Less than an hour later Andrew Trentham entered the town of Scone just north of Perth where the ancient Stone of Destiny had received its name. Here had the Stone rested for more than four hundred years before being taken south by King Edward I—and long before recent events had brought it back into the limelight.

This was where the kingdom of Scotland, as Ginny's father said, had begun—far back in the ninth century, when the land had been occupied by warring Celtic peoples.

Andrew recalled his drive along the north Buchan coast of a week or more ago. It was from across those waters—from Scandinavia to the northeast—that the invading evil had come which sparked the events that eventually led to Caledonia's nationhood.

Over the sea had sailed *Vikings*—the seafaring pirates of whom an ancient Irish historian said: "Neither honor nor mercy for right of sanctuary, nor protection for Church, nor veneration for God or man was felt by this furious, ferocious, pagan, ruthless people."

For good reason had church litany in the ninth and tenth centuries along the coastal regions of Britain included the prayer: *A furore Normannorum libera nos, Domine.* Deliver us, O Lord, from the fury of the Norsemen.

The Danes and Norwegians had accomplished what the might of imperial Rome had been unable to. They had subdued a Celtic race and helped bring an end to the kingdom of the Picts that had dominated northern Caledonia for nearly a thousand years.

In the process, they made it possible for the people of Caledonia to become, for the first time in history, a sovereign nation.

5

FORGING OF A KINGDOM

A.D. 843

✻ ONE ✻

805

Two cousins were born to Caledonia in the early years of the ninth century—in the royal lines of two Celtic peoples who made northern Britain their home.

The boys would never meet, and their diverse natures would take them on different paths. One would become a man of peace, the other a man of war. One would give Caledonia its future name. The other would give the land its spirit.

Their destinies would approach at a critical moment in the founding of Caledonia's nationhood but then ultimately diverge. One would be known as a mighty ruler and the father of a nation; the other would be forgotten to history. Whether true greatness would be thus determined by the annals men later wrote of this land, only eternity would determine.

The infant born in the south, in the kingdom of Dalriada, was named *Kenneth*, or "handsome," by his mother. Her husband was Alpin, King of the Scots.

The infant of the north, born fifteen years later in the small Pict village of Steenbuaic, was given the name of *Dallais*, or "wise." The boy's father was Donnchadh, of ancient Caledonian descent—a seventh great-grandson to the sister of Columba's Pictish convert Fineach macAedh—and bard to his people. His mother, Ghleanna, was first cousin to Eoganan, King of the Picts at Fortriu.

Both boys grew strong, became men, and awaited their mutual destinies.

That they were distant cousins would not be sufficient to insure peace for their two Celtic peoples. For Dalriada was expanding and beginning to look hungrily at the territories of its neighbors. And at the same time, a new menace was fast approaching—a terrifying wave about to break over all of Caledonia.

▩   T W O   ▩

833

A girl was also born in Steenbuaic, six years after the bard's son, to the sister of the Pict King. Seonaid named her daughter Breathran.

As the girl grew, the mother wondered if something might be wrong with her daughter, for she was slow to speak, and even at the age of five or six she opened her mouth but rarely. Yet her eyes sparkled with intelligence and animation and a lively interest in all about her, and she loved animals with an unusual tenderness and sense of identification.

One day the mother came upon seven-year-old Breathran some distance from the village, on the plateau between Steenbuaic and the sea. As she approached, Seonaid heard her daughter's voice. She slowed her step and listened. The girl was speaking words such as her mother had never heard from her lips—and in a voice utterly different from anything she had heard before—a soft, soothing voice as if talking to one much younger.

As she watched and listened from behind, Seonaid suddenly realized that Breathran was speaking to a tiny bird that had alighted several feet away, trying to coax it toward her. Then Breathran began softly to mix melody with her words, and even her own mother found herself mesmerized by the sound.

> *Air feasgar ciùin Céitein's me teurnadh an tsléibhe.*
> *Hug óro is eutrom mo cheum air làr.*
> *Tha ghrian anns na speuran a' dèarrsadh gu ceutach.*
> *Is eunlaidh nan geugan a' seinn an dàn.*
> *Th'n tallt ruith do'n abhainn le caithream 's le ceòl,*
> *Na craobhan fo'n duilleach 's na lusan 'nan glòir.*
> *Na beanntan 's na gleanntan 'nam maise ro òirdheirc.*
> *Is thall air a' chòmhnard tha òigh mo ghràidh.*

The stars are burning cheerily, cheerily.
   Ho-ro, little one, turn you to me.
The sea mew is moaning drearily, drearily.
   Ho-ro, little one, turn you to me.
Cold is the storm wind that ruffles your breast,
   But warm is the downy plume here in my nest.
Cold blows the storm there, soft falls the snow.
   Then ho-ro, little one, come you to me.

Whatever the villagers might think, it was obvious the girl lacked for nothing in the way of expressiveness, but only reserved the deepest expressions of her heart for the animals she loved.

The bird fluttered and bounded a step or two toward her. Breathran continued softly to croon the strange melody, moving not a muscle, not flinching a finger. How long she had sat here waiting, her mother had no idea.

Seonaid now took a step toward her. A thin twig snapped beneath her foot. The bird flew into the sky and away.

Breathran stopped her melody, turned, saw her mother, and her innocent face lit into a smile.

"Did you see the little bird, Mother?" she said.

"Yes I did, Breathran dear," answered Seonaid.

"It almost came to my hand—did you see?"

"I am sorry I disturbed it."

"It will come again, Mother. I like the birds. I think they like to hear me sing. That little one was nervous. But I will see him again."

She rose, and they returned to the village together.

✕   T H R E E   ✕

839

Two children playing some years later on a high rocky promontory jutting into the sea first spotted the sleek vessel plowing through the blue-gray water several hundred yards offshore.

Excitedly they clambered down and scampered across the narrow expanse of sand onto the mainland, then up the steep bank and across the heath plateau toward the slope of *Nochd Brae,* or the "bare hill," at the base of which their settlement of stone and earthen houses was situated.

As they ran toward the settlement, they passed a thirteen-year-old girl sitting quietly on the ground inspecting a tiny patch of heather blossoms, wondering how they gathered their color from out of the earth. The two boys ran past, taking no notice of her. Breathran rose and ran after them for a while.

It took the boys twenty minutes to reach the village from the coast. Before their shouts had died in the wind, one of the stout young Pict men of Steenbuaic had scrambled atop the highest of the granite stones from which the settlement took its name. He peered northward with a hand shielding his forehead from the sun. But the sea was some three miles distant, and he could see nothing.

He climbed down, joined his comrades who were already gathering what weapons they could carry, and ran toward the sea.

On the way they passed the King's niece walking back toward them. Confused first by the shouts of the two boys running by and now by the commotion involving what seemed to be every man left in Steenbuaic, she paused and watched as they flew past her.

Now came her cousin, a great strong lad in her eyes. He slowed when he saw her and saw that her eyes were filled with confusion.

"Aod and Cein saw strange boats, Breathran," he explained. "We are going to see if there are more."

"But why, Dallais?"

"We must know if they are friends or enemies."

"An enemy?"

"I will explain it to you another time, young cousin," laughed Dallais. "I must go."

He turned and sprinted to catch up with the others.

It was a long distance to the sea for men lugging spears and swords. To save their village from the sea intruders, the men of Steenbuaic would run five times as far. By the time they reached the bluff above the great northern waters, however, not a sign of the boat was to be seen.

From what the youngsters said, they could not tell much. But from the shape, length, single square sail, and high-curving prow the boys described, the men of the village surmised it had been a Norse craft.

They stood at the edge of the hill overlooking the sea—Pict husbands, fathers, and warriors—and held serious counsel together. They had to know if the Norse ship had ventured here alone or in number, and whether it would continue following the coastline or put in at the nearby River Linn. Finally they decided to send their fastest runner, nineteen-year-old Dallais, along the shore to the river's mouth. At the same time they would post young Obtreidh to watch from here for other ships that might follow.

This being decided, those who remained hoisted their weapons once more, adding those of the runner, and began the hurried return to the settlement to make what preparations were possible should either of the two carry back grim news. With injunctions of haste from the others, Dallais set off westward at a brisk run. Within moments his cousin Obtreidh was left alone on the bluff, peering into the distance, ready to begin his sprint back to the settlement should his eyes descry a gathering of ships approaching.

They would also have to send a messenger to the battlefront, where most of their able warriors were engaged in war against Alpin of the Scots. Their King, Eoganan, must know that a new enemy approached from the north.

FOUR

This day of danger was not unexpected.

The first explorations by Danes and Norwegians from across the two hundred miles of sea in the previous century had been relatively peaceful. But with the perfection of a new type of vessel—long and slender, heavy of keel, utilizing both oars and sail, fast and maneuverable for stealth or battle or flight, strong enough for ocean sailing yet with shallow draft equally able to navigate shallow inland waterways—these initial traders were followed by dangerous men bent on plunder and conquest. Foreboding tidings had been spreading through Pictland for three or four years—black tales of a marauding and wicked people from across the sea landing in increasing numbers on the shores of every coast, rowing up the rivers, killing and ravaging throughout the land.

Now the year was 839, and never had the clans of the Picts found themselves in greater peril—not only from the Norsemen across the sea, but also from the Scots of Dalriada to the south, who were taking more of their land every year.

The village of Steenbuaic was typical of Pict settlements of the ninth century, facing dangers from all sides. But it was uncommon in that among its number dwelt two close female relations to the King—both his younger sister, Seonaid, and his first cousin, Ghleanna. And because of Pict matrilinear tradition, under certain circumstances both women might play intrinsic roles in the succession of the kingship after Eoganan.

Steady encroachment from the strengthening race of Scots from the southwest had pushed the descendents of the Caledonii toward the northern and western extremities of the land they had completely dominated four centuries earlier. *Pictland,* as it was now called, had shrunk to less than half its former size. The Picts and the Scots were in truth not distinctive races. Both came from nearly pure Celtic stock. But for millennia the waters of the North Channel had separated Eire and the Scots from Caledonia and the Picts. With the waters now easily navigable, the reuniting of their common roots was not a peaceful one.

❊   F I V E   ❊

In those days, peoples were in flux throughout Europe.

By the eighth century, the *Angles* and *Britons* from the south had penetrated northward to share the land north of England with the *Picts* and the *Scots*. None of the four tribal groups yet possessed superiority. Ultimately nationhood would form out of the struggle of these diverse peoples for dominance. But supremacy could only be won by the shedding of all their blood.

The religion called Christianity, brought to the region by Columba and his followers, continued to strengthen its own forms within a framework of tribal paganism and steadily took on greater aspects of the Catholicism of Rome.

These religious developments did little, however, to obviate the tribal barbarism of the times. Notwithstanding the so-called spiritual inclinations of their leaders, kingdoms were won by the sword, not the cross. These were dark days upon the earth. Savagery among men was everywhere, and the heavens wept for what man did to man.

Throughout the sixth century, the various Celtic groups maintained a kind of standoff in numbers and strength. Early in the seventh, however, the Scots extended their reach far into the north, while in the southeast the Angles pushed across the Forth and the Tay. The Pict kingdom shrank rapidly on both sides. The Scots ruled from Dunadd, while the Pict kingdom was centered in Fortriu, near Scone. But Dalriada was on the rise, and Pictland on the wane.

Through intermarriage between the two Celtic bloodlines, gradually the distinction between *Pict* and *Scot* blurred as the strains intermingled. Nowhere was this fusing more visible yet confusing as in the connected bloodlines of the two royal houses. This coalescing of Pict and Scot blood was hugely complicated by the fact that Scottish succession was determined by an essentially patrilinear system called *tanistry,** while Pict succession was traced through the *mother's* line. This latter arrangement produced conflict and open warfare between rival brothers and cousins because eligibility was open to the vagaries of interpretation. The Pict system also encouraged outsiders with Pict mothers to lay claim to the Pict throne.

The inherent weakness of the Pict system inevitably led to constant disputation and infighting. The Scots system, on the other hand, tended toward stability and strength. It was only a matter of time before the stronger would come to dominate the weaker. By the ninth century, Pict matrilinear succession was breaking down under Scots influence.

Steadily the power of the Scots grew, while that of the Picts declined. When in the ninth century the Picts found themselves confronting a new foe from the sea, they no longer possessed the might to triumph over strong enemies on two fronts at once.

᙭   S I X   ᙭

For the moment, however, the young Scot named Kenneth, called the "hardy one," had little concern for either the Scottish or the Pictish succession, much less for the menace to the north. He knew only that his arm

---

*From *tanaiste rig*—"second to the king"—in which an heir chosen during the king's lifetime then succeeded to the throne upon the king's death. It was not strictly a father-to-son arrangement because it could move *laterally* as well as generationally forward, with brothers and cousins coming in for their share. It was patrilinear, however, in that it followed the *male* side of the genealogical chart.

ached, that sweat was pouring from his chest and forehead, and that a young Pict warrior was descending upon him with a bloodcurdling scream and an upraised sword.

The sword in his own hand sounded with a dull clank against his foe's weapon, jarring his heavy wrist. Recovering quickly, he lurched to the left, deftly dodging another slashing blow, and the next instant, while his opponent was off balance, hurled the whole of his might into a forward thrust.

The red-stained tip of his sword found its deadly mark, as it already had many times this day. The youth he killed hardly made a sound. The body fell to the ground and pulled the instrument of death down with it.

The thirty-four-year-old son of the King of Dalriada had come east with his father, Alpin. In the mountainous region north of their seat of power—but far to the south of the coast where the Viking menace had just appeared—they were now engaged in combat with the Pict King, Eoganan. The fact that the two royal families were related had not prevented war from breaking out the year before. It was a royal link that stretched back to Kenneth's own grandmother, who had been sister to Eoganan's grandmother. So they said. But notwithstanding the Pictish blood in his veins, Kenneth considered himself a Scot, loyal only to his father and his plans to expand the scope of their kingdom.

At daybreak this morning they had mounted an attack against Eoganan's army of two or three thousand. Though they had only eighteen hundred men of their own, Kenneth's father had hoped to surprise the enemy and drive the northerners back into the river beside which they were camped.

"I do not like it, Father," Kenneth had said, expressing caution about the plan. "I fear the apparent weakness of the enemy's position could be a trap."

Alpin shook his head.

"I tell you, Father, it is their hope to lure us down the hill into an attack."

"I am convinced it is we who will hold the element of surprise," rejoined his father. "We shall attack as planned—with the sun's first light."

The man had been a mighty warrior in his time. But though Kenneth did not like to think it, his father was aging. He had feared for the plan's success from the beginning. And indeed, his premonitions were well founded.

As the Scots abandoned their secure position and came down toward the river, suddenly the Pict camp came awake, howling and attacking with two descending flanks from the right and left that had been hiding in the woods.

It was a trap, cleverly sprung. And they were now in its teeth!

Within moments the Scots were surrounded, every man among them fighting desperately for his life. Any thought of conquest instantly gave way to mere hope for survival.

The battle went badly from the start. At least five hundred men had fallen. Now, at midday, Kenneth was stumbling over bodies and sloshing through blood, trying desperately to lead his left flank in slow retreat back up the hill. His father was attempting the same on the right. Kenneth had himself received a deep gash on the left arm. But its pain had long since gone numb, and he could still wield the sword with his right.

The son of the King stooped forward and jerked his sword from the chest of the fallen youth he had just slain.

That the dead warrior was but eighteen, and his own fourth cousin, were two facts Kenneth, son of Alpin, neither knew nor cared about. The boy was an enemy, had tried to kill him, and had paid for it with his own life. This was no time when blood of kinship mattered, but only the skill to keep one's own blood from staining the earth.

A scream of death suddenly sounded in his ear.

It was followed the next instant by a tremendous blow crashing against his back. Kenneth stumbled and fell against the body of the boy whose life he had just taken.

Keeping to one knee, he spun about. He had narrowly missed being run through by an iron-tipped enemy lance, the point of which had found its mark only a few feet from him. As his comrade slumped sideways to the ground, the shaft of the spear protruding from his back had swung around and dealt Kenneth the unexpected blow.

Regaining his balance, he leapt up and dropped his sword. With great effort he grasped the lance with both hands and yanked it from the dead warrior. A second later he sent it flying silently through the air. His target was the Pict King, who at that moment was leading an attack on horseback across the body-strewn field toward Alpin's flank. Kenneth did not wait to see how accurate was his release. Already he was retrieving his sword and swinging it against the steady onslaught of numberless Picts.

A shrill whinny of pain told him he had missed his mark and had instead pierced Eoganan's mount. Had he looked up from his fighting, he might have taken some pleasure in seeing that he had pinned the Pict King's leg to the dying horse's side.

As the beast fell, the lance broke clean in three pieces and threw Eoganan clear, crippled by the chunk of Pictish lance that protruded from his calf.

Seeing the Pict King down and wounded by his son's throw, the Scots King Alpin rushed out from the ranks of his men to dispatch the leader of the Picts.

Eoganan, however, was a younger man than Alpin. He was on his feet the next instant. And in spite of the blood flowing from his leg, he was soon having the best of it over Kenneth's father.

The son of Alpin, however, saw none of this, nor was he witness to the fate of the two kings, each of whom sought to rule the land called Caledonia. He was frantically attempting to keep his head atop his *own* shoulders. He had just been alert enough to raise his sword against the blow of another Pict warrior, whose side he slit with a vicious sideways stroke of his own blade.

Blinking hard to prevent sweat from blinding him, Kenneth now glanced across the hill. His father was clearly losing his struggle against the Pict King he himself had wounded. Even now the Pict King was lifting his sword, as if in slow motion, and bringing it down with deadly force. Kenneth's heart pounded. Red rushed through his brain and a great cry escaped him, even as he realized he could do nothing to help his father. All round the frantic sounds of pain and death sounded in his ears.

"Retreat . . . back up the hill!" he yelled to his men for the tenth time, the words now bitter in his mouth.

Yet even Kenneth himself could manage but a few steps in that direction before another Pict warrior was upon him, eager to be the one to kill the son of the Scots King.

Kenneth spun to face him and raised his blood-dripping sword to the attack.

Dallais, son of Donnchadh, returned from the mouth of the Linn with an evil report.

The raiders from the north had indeed put in at the river, and they were not alone. A hundred or more burly Viking warriors were already encamped at the site. When or how they had arrived, Dallais did not know, perhaps from the north or west. Three or four of their longships were tied some distance inland from the river's mouth. They appeared to be establishing a base. They might, he said, be making preparations to advance inland. But it was impossible to tell for certain.

Obtreidh, too, had brought dire news. He had witnessed another six, perhaps eight, ships like the first sailing offshore toward the west.

Eoganan must be alerted. Fortriu, indeed all of Pictland, was in danger.

A counsel of the elders of the settlement convened within the hour. Only a few men of fighting age were present in the village. Most had gone south to wage war against the Scots. Alone, the remaining villagers could never hope to withstand the Norsemen. Runners must be sent south to Fortriu to warn Eoganan and beg the Pict King for help. Though the mouth of the Linn was less than ten miles distant, they could only hope the marauders did not locate Steenbuaic before help returned.

"Dallais and Obtreidh must set off this very afternoon," said one.

"There is not an hour to spare," added another.

If only they had a horse. But the King had summoned most of the men and all the beasts to the battle in the south.

Quickly the two fleet-footed teens gathered food in leather pouches to strap to their backs. When preparations were complete, Dallais's father called him aside.

The roles of priest and bard, through the centuries since Columba's arrival at Iona, had grown nearly indistinguishable. In Steenbuaic, Donnchadh—descendent of Domhnall and Anghrad through their daughter Frangag, and of ancient Caledonian warriors Foltlaig and Maelchon—was spiritual leader, historian, musician, and father of four.

Father and son made their way together some distance from the settlement.

As they went, they passed young Breathran walking outside the cluster of stone homes. Donnchadh was bard enough to recognize in the girl uncommon gifts and perceptions not unlike his own. But this was a time he must be alone with his son, and they could not tarry.

He smiled and placed a gentle hand on her head as they passed, then he and Dallais continued away from the settlement.

It was a flat, rocky heathland over which they now walked, toward the shore and away from the boulders beside which their stone homes had been constructed and toward the granite sentinels a little distance away. They had always taken pride in these five huge chunks of stone that had been heaped upon one another in apparently random fashion, though they knew nothing of the prehistoric convulsive quakings of the earth that put them there. The villagers thought of the rocks as protective guardians who stood watch a little outside the gathering of their homes.

Breathran stared after them, curious at the somber expressions on the faces of the two men. A chill slowly came over her. She shivered, but continued to watch until they had disappeared among the shadows of the granite pillars.

What were they doing there, she wondered. Why had they walked alone to the great slabs of rock at such a time?

Neither Donnchadh nor Dallais knew of the wandering father and son of whom they were descended, who had crossed over to this land before that same quake made of it an island. Other legends, however, more recent, clung vaporously to the traditions passed down by bards to their sons, to keep alive the heritage of the Caledonii. Donnchadh had from a young age taught Dallais what he knew of their story.

What he had to say in these few moments was more personal.

In the father's heart as they walked pulsed the fear that the huge slabs, visible in the midst of this flat plateau stretching inland from the sea, might attract unwelcome notice by the strangers in the Norse ships and thus betray the very village they guarded.

Donnchadh spoke in soft tones to the boy who was not many years more than a child. He spoke of things men think of when mortal danger is at hand. And he gave him that which would always remind him of the legacy of his heritage.

"*Cuimhnich có leis a tha thu,*" Donnchadh said to Dallais in the old tongue. "Remember the men from whence you came, my son."

They did not have long minutes to spend together. Time was short.

They returned to the settlement.

Tears stood in Dallais's eyes when he departed Steenbuaic soon thereafter.

"God go with you, and protect you, my son," said Donnchadh.

Dallais embraced father and mother again.

With final farewells from the elders and many injunctions to haste, the two cousins began the easy canter they would continue on and off for three days. Dallais did not see his mother, Ghleanna, turn away weeping. She kept her tears from him, for she would not slow him down with thoughts of her sorrow.

As Steenbuaic retreated from sight behind them, a dreadful foreboding sat in the stomach of the son of Donnchadh. But he would summon what courage he had learned in his nineteen years. He must do his duty to his people.

It was time to be a man.

Donnchadh had told him not to fear, that the God of their fathers would watch over them . . . and he trusted his father.

❈   E I G H T   ❈

After his eldest son disappeared from sight, Donnchadh proceeded to carry out certain other necessary preparations. Entering the small stone enclosure that was his home, he walked quickly to the corner of the tiny building. There, in a vault buried under the floor and concealed by several stones, which he now lifted aside, sat the reliquary he had carried here many years ago. It had been his charge, and his father's and grandfather's before him, all the way back to Fineach's time. No one knew when it had been taken from its original site of fabrication, the monastery of Kailli-an-Inde.

His grandfather said that the box—a much larger replica of the tiny, nearly identical, reliquary at Iona—had at one time contained St. Aidan's bones, and had made its way from Kailli-an-Inde to Lindesfarne. Whether the legend was factual, Donnchadh's father never knew. No bones lay in it now. The true value, he told Donnchadh, lay not in the contents, but in the reliquary itself, which was priceless, and whose secret he could never tell another soul if he valued his life, especially during these troubled times.

Donnchadh brought the box with him here to Steenbuaic, where he had kept it well concealed ever since. No one in the settlement knew of it. The one item he had already removed from it, his son now wore about his neck.

If only he could get the box away, to one of the monasteries. It was too valuable for one man alone to possess. He would arrange for its return to Lindesfarne at the soonest possible moment.

Unfortunately, that moment was not now. Danger approached, and he must make sure the reliquary of Kailli, fashioned by his many-times great-uncle of St. Columba's time, did not fall into pagan hands.

Now, with attack possible, his was a sacred duty to guard the box, to protect it against defilement, and to make sure, whatever happened, that it was not discovered by the pirates of the sea. It would have to remain here in Steenbuaic.

He had already determined to hide it in the earth. He would be able to find it again, even if thirty years should pass. The huge granite sentinels would make sure of that. No other man but his son, whom he had minutes ago told of his plan, would know its location. When the danger was past, they would transport the box and the items it contained to Lindesfarne.

Donnchadh knew evil times were at hand. He was bard of the clan. On him rested the legacy of their ancestors. The lineage of both blood *and* spirit was his to preserve—a birthright of kinship *and* spirituality. Past generations untold depended on him. He must not allow the heathens, if they came, to desecrate their spiritual and familial clan heritage.

Reverently Donnchadh drew the box from its crypt in the floor, then carefully opened it.

One by one he took out the items—a number of jeweled ornaments, three silver chalices, four coins, two penannular brooches, a silver cup, two crosses, several smooth stones, three silver spoons, four bowls, and the one item which he had always found most curious of all the contents, a small plain gray rock. That the box no longer contained written documents did not seem strange to him. He had never seen the manuscripts that had originally been placed within it.

When the container was empty, he took a blanket from the corner where he and his wife slept and laid it carefully in the bottom of the box, then replaced the original contents. To these he added what few items he counted of value in what he himself possessed—two knives, a piece of a sword hilt, a chape, a pommel, and a small but heavy pair of silver candlesticks. Now he took another blanket, laid it over the top of the contents, then reclosed the box. He would wait until the sun was far away and the rest of Steenbuaic was asleep.

When the night was black, a man, unseen by others of the settlement, made his way with great difficulty outside the wall to the base of the granite pillars, now illuminated against the moon. His burden was of exceeding weight, and he moved slowly.

He crept under the natural door through the stones into the protected portion of the hollow below. Children played here by day, but no one witnessed his activity this night.

He eased down his load and, as silently as possible, set about excavating a cavity that would safely hold the box, upon which he could pile stones when he was done.

How long it might have to remain buried here, Donnchadh did not know. He must do his work carefully and leave not a trace of evidence behind him.

❋   N I N E   ❋

Dallais and Obtreidh had been in the settlement at Fortriu only a few hours when the first messengers arrived back from the battle against the Scots, bringing news of a great victory.

Eoganan and the rest of the Pict army returned the next morning. Exultant, though pale and badly wounded in the leg, the King himself rode at the front of his triumphant throng.

Shouts and cheers and great celebration welcomed the army home. In his hand Eoganan held aloft his spear, upon which sat the grotesque and decaying head of the Scots King Alpin.

The whole army was full of the tale of their King's courage and skill: Only moments after being run through in the leg by a lance and thrown from his horse, Eoganan had recovered himself, stabbed the Scots King through the heart, and chopped off his head with a single blow. Impaling the skull upon his spear, he had thus carried it to his settlement to celebrate the rout of the Dalriadic foe.

Even the news brought from the two youths from Steenbuaic in the north could hardly diminish the revelry of his celebration. Eoganan, however, had lost much blood. Infection to the leg had already set in.

"We will rest two or three days," the weak King declared, "then set out with the army and defeat the Vikings as we have the Scots!"

The elders of Fortriu counseled against the King's leading his army out again so soon. "You must recover from the wound," they said. "Your face is pale. You need rest."

"Would you make me an old woman in my prime?" he roared. "I will not be left behind when we send the Norsemen fleeing back across the sea!"

Meanwhile, far to the south and west at his home of Dunadd, the son of Alpin was vowing revenge.

He had himself nearly killed the Pict King. Instead, death had come to the house of Alpin.

That he would succeed his father and soon himself be King of the Scots and ruler of all Dalriada mattered not half so much as the thought of one day slicing through the neck of the Pict King with his own sword.

TEN

While their runners were gone, the feared Viking attack came.

Shouts and screams of panic erupted in the thin light of dawn, and suddenly it seemed that the plateau of Steenbuaic was filled with hundreds of the cruel marauders from the sea. Against the mere dozen men who had not gone with the King to fight the Scots, the outcome was brutally swift.

Breathran had risen early, not because she sensed what was coming but because she knew the predawn hours were the best for visiting her creature-friends of the fields and wooded areas around Steenbuaic. In those hours, the rabbits that scampered about looking for food were less likely to run at sight of her, and the occasional deer that ventured out of the forest seemed to accept her presence.

This morning, however, she heard the yelling in the distance and was seized by a premonition of dread. She immediately began running toward her home. But the shouts and screams that continued were hideous, and before she was halfway back, she knew that something evil had come upon them. She dared not continue toward the village, but in her confusion, she knew not what else to do.

She stood for some minutes listening in horror, then took a few more tentative steps forward, tears already filling her eyes. She realized she was listening to the sounds of death. She thought she heard her mother's voice.

All at once she seemed to come to herself. Genuine panic seized her. She glanced around.

The sentinels!

The image returned to her of Dallais and his father leaving the village together and talking quietly as they passed her and smiled. They had been going to the granite pillars.

All at once she was running toward the great stones as well, not realizing exactly why, but with an undefined sense of following the bard and his son, as if their memory would lead her to safety. She would hide there!

A minute later Breathran was scrambling down the incline beneath the shadow of the giant stones.

❈ E L E V E N ❈

Breathran crept into a tiny rock cave and lay still—for minutes . . . then hours.

Even after the screams of death had long faded, she heard occasional men's voices in strange tongues and the tramping of many feet and evil-sounding laughter. Then time began to lose its meaning as sleep and wakefulness faded into a continuous dreamy blur.

A day passed—two days . . . four days. She grew weak, but dared not leave the tiny hole she had made for herself. Not even bird or rabbit or mouse came to comfort her.

The horrifying sounds she had heard paralyzed her into such shock that she became incapable of movement, incapable of thought. The only relief was sleep. But before many days had passed, even that sleep grew dangerous, for if she did not find sustenance soon, she would surely drift into that deeper sleep from which mortals never wake.

But suddenly Breathran did awake!

A sound had stirred her brain . . . closer than before. Footsteps!

Someone was near, right above her. She could tell from the sound that it was no beast.

A gasp escaped her parched throat. The murderers had returned. They were looking for her!

She could not help it . . . try as she might to keep silent. There in the darkness, Breathran began softly to whimper.

※   T W E L V E   ※

Dallais, son of Donnchadh, and his cousin, Obtreidh, returned north to Steenbuaic with the northward advance of the Pict army some ten or twelve days after he had left the village.

Sensing a premonition of what he might find, Dallais left Eoganan's force before daybreak of the final day's journey. He ran the remaining twenty miles alone.

While he was yet far off, he knew that destruction had visited the settlement. He stopped on a hilltop to look down over the plateau sloping westward into the fertile valley of the Linn. No sounds of life rose anywhere. A sense of eerie desolation spread out before his gaze.

The King's army was too late to save Steenbuaic from the sea pirates.

His father had known what was about to happen even as he set out. Dallais had been able to tell from the way he spoke.

Now tears filled his eyes as he gazed down toward the granite sentinels of the settlement. He knew it was vain to hope that human breath remained, for the Vikings' methods of conquest were well known among his people. No longer would the giant stones signify life. Henceforth would these pillars mark the scene of butchery, rape, and murder.

He did not find his father among the bloated bodies that lay unburied in the village, nor did he search long. The corpses of mother and sisters lay outside their hut. His young brother's body was inside. Dallais vomited at the sights and smells that assaulted his senses. He could not prevent hatred from rising within him.

Half the women of the settlement were rotting naked where they had been attacked. How shamefully had they been brutalized, then sliced apart as carrion for whatever prey might desire their remains. How long ago the slaughter had taken place he could not know exactly, probably three or four days.

Sobbing without shame, Dallais turned retching from the carnage. He ran some distance onto the plain and there threw himself on his face in mortal anguish. Never again would this place be home to any of the race of men. Innocent blood had spilled upon this ground . . . and loudly could the silent weeping of the heavens be heard.

An hour later—though he had lost all sense of time—Dallais forced himself to his feet. He walked back and climbed atop the highest of the giant boulders. He had played here as a child. Now he gazed southward into the distance to see whether his eyes could descry the approach of Eoganan's host coming too late to save the settlement.

He saw nothing.

Suddenly a tiny sound came to his ear from below!

Could it be? . . . a human voice . . . the faintest whimper.

Dallais scampered from his high perch. Listening, he detected the sound again. It came from under the boulders!

He hurried down the sides of the ledge, squeezed through the narrow opening between the pillars and jumped the final several feet to the ground.

Another whimper sounded. Yes, there was a human form!

He rushed to it and stooped down in the darkened hideaway under the overhang of a granite slab. The huge rock leaned at an angle against the wall of rocky earth that created the depression in the plateau. Under it, hiding in the tiny cave only a short distance from where his father had buried the reliquary, lay the weak, terrified, dazed form of his cousin. Half dead from lack of water and nourishment, Breathran knew not whether it was day or night, or whether she was even still alive.

At his touch she started feebly, then turned a dreadful face toward him. She recognized her cousin and crawled, weeping with relief, into his arms. He lifted her off the ground.

He could tell that she was half dead. In other respects she seemed unharmed.

Dallais kissed her and stroked her hair, pressed her head gently against his chest, and whispered words of comfort into her ears to re-awaken the will to live. Suddenly energized by the possibility of *giving* life in the midst of so much death, he set her down and fumbled for his skin of water. He initially gave her but a few sips. He could not hope to find much food. It was all his own stomach could endure to search for it among the ravaged homes and rotting bodies of the settlement. But the girl must have sustenance to live.

Within an hour he had put enough down her throat to begin the recuperation process. A few of her wits seemed to have returned. Still she had not spoken, but Dallais was confident she could hear and understand him.

"I must leave you," he said tenderly.

Breathran's face revealed no hint of response other than an imperceptible widening of the eyes.

"But I will return. I will not leave you for long."

Again Dallais searched the distraught face for sign of comprehension. "Do you understand?"

Breathran nodded feebly.

"You must remain in the protected hollow," Dallais went on. "If you hear voices, you must creep back under the stone overhang and hide in the cave without a sound—do you understand?"

Again she nodded.

"When I come, I will call out your name."

Breathran nodded.

"I will leave you food and water enough until I return. You must *not* leave the hollow."

After a few more tender assurances, Dallais climbed back up the stones out of the hollow and onto the plateau.

By now was Eoganan's approach visible. Dallais set out at a brisk run to meet the army, thinking what he should do. To tell the King of his niece might endanger her. Eoganan would bring her into the camp with the army. But if the battle which was surely coming went badly, Breathran would be left at the mercy of the same Viking marauders who had killed the rest of the village.

I must say nothing of her to the King, thought Dallais. *She will be safer where she is.*

If the battle went well, then he would tell the King of Breathran's survival. Then she could return to the safety of Fortriu. For now he would report that the massacre at Steenbuaic had been complete and that the family of the King's sister had all been killed. They must march straight to encounter the Vikings and come back to tend to their kinsmen later.

When he reached the army, Obtreidh greeted him warmly, but sensed the truth. The boy, younger by a year and a half, immediately set off in a run toward Steenbuaic, now only two or three miles away.

Dallais chased after him, overtook him quickly, and restrained him with a hand.

"No, Obtreidh," he said, "you must not go."

"I have to—I must find my father . . . my mother," insisted his cousin.

"You must not."

"I must see what I can do for them."

Again he turned and ran off.

"Obtreidh!" cried Dallais after him. "Obtreidh . . . they are all dead!"

❈ T H I R T E E N ❈

The army of Pict King Eoganan met the Viking force west of the mouth of the Linn.

The battle lasted but one day.

Pict scouts had vastly underestimated the number of longships that had come ashore in the short time since the children of Steenbuaic spotted the first two weeks earlier. A huge invading host of Danes had by now arrived. By the time the bloody confrontation was over, Eoganan, King of the Picts, would not have to worry about the worsening wound in his leg, for he lay dead along with almost five thousand of his ablest warriors.

The power of Pictland was broken.

Even before the fighting was over, Dallais, son of Donnchadh, had slipped into hiding in the thick forest which lay south of Linnmouth.

He was no coward. But what would his own death accomplish now, when there was another life to save? The King was dead. Most of the Pict army was dead. Those who remained were fleeing back to Fortriu.

As for Dallais, Fortriu was not his home. He had no family, no home left anywhere. There was but one glimmer of purpose that remained for him—and she lay vulnerable and alone where he had left her under the granite sentinels.

Dallais's hand unconsciously went to his neck, where his fingers touched the silver chain his father had placed around it. He knew well enough what it meant—that this chain was the royal neckpiece of the ancient King of the Caledonii. He also knew that, with Eoganan now dead, he and Breathran were the only two remaining of that royal line. He knew to what claim his mother's blood entitled him.

Yet none in Fortriu would know whether they were alive or dead, whether life yet breathed in them or whether their bodies were among the numberless slaughter.

Perhaps, he thought, fingering the ancient links, *it is best that way.*

Dallais knew this lush wood called Dorchadas, the place of mystery, like the back of his own hand. Many a day and night he had spent hunting in its shadowy depths. He would be protected here until today's carnage was past. Tonight he would slip back to Steenbuaic to rescue Breathran. He would bring her here too, to the Dorchadas. Here they would be safe. Here he would nurse her back to strength.

When she was well and strong and thinking clearly, he would tell her what calamity had befallen Pictland—her own mother and father and two brothers, and her uncle the King. He would leave it to her whether she wanted him to take her to Fortriu to make known their royal claims.

❖ F O U R T E E N ❖

843

Four years had now passed since the death of Alpin, King of the Scots. The year was 843.

Kenneth the Hardy, now known as the son of Alpin, or MacAlpin, had desired to take the life of the Pict King Eoganan by his own hand.

Unfortunately, that possibility never came. The Vikings had done it for him. So Kenneth intended to exact his revenge by taking his cousin's throne instead.

The son of Alpin was now King over Dalriada. It had taken him two years to secure his hold on his father's throne and another two to consolidate his power and raise an army. Kenneth was now confident he could overrun what was left of the Picts with little opposition.

The arrangements were complete. The army was assembled. And Kenneth, son of Alpin, was prepared to set off for Fortriu with the rising of tomorrow's sun.

There were, to be sure, any number of his own Scots relations who might lay an equal claim to the Pict throne, not to mention dozens of Pict offspring who might squabble for a piece of it. Easily ten or a dozen Dalriadic earls had made noises about *their* connections to the Pict kingship.

Only when he had overrun Fortriu, therefore, and was in an unassailable position would he publicly lay claim to the Pict kingship.

The most important thing was to seize Fortriu while the Picts were without a King. Reports had come to Kenneth of several temporary leaders since Eoganan's death, but no one had yet emerged to take the throne. If he waited too long, the Picts would no doubt install a pretender through some woman's bloodline.

Now was the time to move. He must seize power quickly. There was word of a nephew or some such distant relation to the former King who had survived the Norse slaughter. Why he wasn't already King, Kenneth didn't know, but he wanted to take no chances. He would find the nephew and dispatch him later. At the same time, he would need to institute measures to insure that none of his own kinsmen ran him through with a sword to take the Scots throne he *already* held.

Morning came, and the army of Kenneth MacAlpin set out from the west. From Dunstaffnage in Argyll, where it had been taken in the century following Columba's time, MacAlpin brought with him by cart the fabled Highland stone, hewn from one end of an ancient burial slab. Upon it a long line of Scots Kings had been crowned. Kenneth planned to use it soon for the first time in the coronation of a *Pict* King—MacAlpin himself.

The army of MacAlpin passed nearly unopposed through what remained of the territories formerly held by the Picts. A modest battle was fought at Fortriu. But the badly outnumbered Picts were not inclined to see what remained of their people wiped out, and soon surrendered.

The Scots force quickly occupied the settlement of Fortriu. Kenneth called a great assembly of his own conquering army and all the people of Fortriu. On the basis of being the great-grandson of King Eoganan's great-grandmother Ealasaid, and thus by Pict matrilinear law the legal successor to the throne of his second cousin, Kenneth MacAlpin declared himself King of the Picts.

Few were inclined to contest MacAlpin's claim. It was, after all, not without credibility. He was indisputably descended, through his mother Mor, his grandmother Moibeal, and his great-grandmother Ealasaid, of the Pict royal line.

Most of the Picts, furthermore, were weary of bloodshed. Since no strong chief had asserted himself from any of their own tribes since Eoganan's death and the slaughter at the Linn, there was no *stronger* claim to the kingship.

MacAlpin therefore encountered little resistance to his claim.
The kingdoms of Dalriada and Fortriu now shared the same King.

⊠   F I F T E E N   ⊠

The new joint King of the Picts and Scots summoned the important men from the kingdoms of Dalriada and Pictland to nearby Scone for a banquet.

He had taken control of the throne with a minimum of bloodshed. Now he must consolidate his power. What more fitting place to establish his new united kingship than here, at the center of the Pict kingdom?

Though only legends survived concerning the origins of the legendary Celtic stone he had brought from Dunstaffnage, the King of the Scots considered it sacred. Upon it for almost two centuries, since the enthronement of Aedan by Columba himself in 574, had the Dalriadic Kings been crowned and their dynasty perpetuated. Upon the same stone Kenneth now took his seat for coronation, symbolically uniting the kingdoms of the two Celtic strains that had grown long ago from the Wanderer's seed.

The stone did not scream out as he sat down, as it was said to do for the rightful ruler. Notwithstanding its silence, Kenneth declared himself King. Here at Scone the stone would remain to make Kings of his sons and grandsons after him.

Following the ceremony came a feast such as had never been held in Scone.

Word had gone out through Fortriu declaring an end of hostilities between the two peoples. The time had come, the edict said, for Picts and Scots to join and celebrate with one another their common heritage and their common King.

When great quantities of roasted boar had been consumed and the meal was well past, and when most of those present were more than half intoxicated with strong ale, MacAlpin stood to toast his own kingship and the future of a united land.

"Men of Dalriada and Fortriu," he said, "many have been the struggles between our kingdoms. We have been enemies, but it is now time we look to the joining of our kingdoms in peace. We must together resist further onslaughts from the Norsemen—and the Angles and Britons from the south. Henceforth we shall be a single people. Caledonia of the Picts and Dalriada of the Scots shall henceforth be known as *Alba*—the kingdom of the north."

He paused while his guests took in the information. The name was not new to any of those present—it had been used to refer to the northern territory for hundreds, if not thousands, of years—though the fact that MacAlpin had so unceremoniously done away with ancient Caledonia was of some concern to the older Pict men present. None spoke, however, for the King yet wore a huge double-edged sword at his side. Everyone knew well enough his skill in wielding it. And no one had forgotten that the former Pict King had killed MacAlpin's own father. They would provide him no excuse to exact revenge.

In truth, Kenneth's revenge was already nearly complete. The fact was, he was far less worried about a Pict challenge to his authority than about one from the *Scots* side. There had been grumblings and threats from many of his own kinsmen as he had prepared for the banquet, complaints about his bold move upon the throne. There were several, in fact, who considered their *own* claims to the Pict royal line as well founded as his. Most of these were present this afternoon, according to Kenneth's cunning design.

For it was in view of eradicating this most serious remaining threat to his kingship that Kenneth had consumed little of the stout which for three hours he had been encouraging down the throats of the rest of the assembly.

"My friend and cousin, earl of Ardanaiseig," now called out Mac-Alpin, "please rise and toast with me the kingdom of Alba."

The surprised earl eyed the King from across the ground where he sat. Slowly he rose and lifted his cup, then took a great swallow of the dark brew within it.

"You are a man of prowess with the blade," the King went on in jocular tone. "Let us demonstrate to our good brothers of Pictland what allies they now have against any who might oppose them."

The earl stood, cup in hand, bewildered at what his fool of a cousin might intend.

"Draw your sword, man," said MacAlpin in a clear voice of command.

Slowly the earl set down his cup and complied with the King's request.

The next instant MacAlpin's sword was likewise aloft. He began to approach his cousin.

"Lift your weapon, Ardanaiseig," commanded MacAlpin, "and defend yourself. Let us, I say, demonstrate our skill to our Pict brethren. We have feasted. The hour for entertainment is at hand!"

He pointed the tip of his own sword menacingly at the earl, smiling widely as if in fun. But his eyes glowed with the fire of evil intent. The earl saw the look, recognized his peril, and finally lifted his own weapon. It clanked against MacAlpin's as it knocked the blade aside. None mistook the sound.

Only now did the assembly realize the seriousness of the King's sport. The game did not last long. The earl, though a fair swordsman, was far too near being drunk to swing the heavy blade effectively.

Blood gushed first from his left shoulder. A glancing blow off the neck followed, which drew more red but still did not endanger his life. The earl was about to throw his weapon to the ground and beg for mercy, but did not have the chance. With a mighty thrust, MacAlpin's blade shot straight through his belly, the tip emerging three inches out his back.

With gruesome display, MacAlpin held the body upright for a moment. Then he yanked his blade swiftly out. The former earl of Ardanaiseig slumped limply to the dirt in a pool of his own warm blood.

There was not a man among them who had not killed, who had not seen the blood of kinsmen shed in battle. Yet shocked gasps now spread throughout the company, for the King's brutality had come under cloak of friendship and shared blood.

Argyll, it seemed, bred treachery. And such betrayal under the guise of kinship would come from its regions again.

Behind him, Ardanaiseig's brother leapt to his feet with an outraged cry. His sword was already in his hand, and he flew upon the King.

But MacAlpin's temperance kept him light on his feet. He also knew precisely where each of his seven rivals were seated, and had been shrewdly watching them all afternoon, paying special heed to their consumption of ale. Thus he knew from which directions the attacks were likely to come.

He spun quickly, met the charge, and seconds later the two brothers lay dead beside one another on the ground.

A third was already on his feet—the earl of Clanbreck, brother-in-law to Ardanaiseig's brother.

This battle was waged more evenly and went on several minutes. As the others watched in silence, several clutched the hilts of their own swords and considered rising to join against the King.

None succumbed to the temptation. The clanking and slashing and footwork of the King and the earl sent dust flying from under their feet. The fire in their eyes left no doubt that theirs was a battle only death would resolve.

Suddenly a great blow fell from MacAlpin's blade onto the arm of the earl. A cry of anguish echoed from Clanbreck's mouth as his sword clattered to the ground. The arm had nearly been severed, and blood spewed from it in a torrent.

Aghast at the sight of his own life pouring out of him onto the grass, the earl of Clanbreck staggered backward, then collapsed. MacAlpin was upon him in a second. He placed a great booted foot on the dying man's chest, while the tip of his blade tickled the skin of his neck.

"So, you would challenge my right of kingship?" said MacAlpin angrily. "You and your two brothers would be King in my place!"

"No . . . no, my lord," murmured Clanbreck.

"Even now you lie! Do you deny that you three had plotted my death?"

"Please, my lord . . . I beg of you—"

"You beg for my mercy—yet you would kill me if you could. Do homage, Earl—make submission to your King. Perhaps I shall let you live."

Realizing he was dying, a spirit of defiance rose up in the prostrate earl.

"You . . . you misbegot," he sneered with what choking voice he still could manage. "I will *not* submit . . . rather I spit on your—"

Whatever final words he had intended were drowned in a faint gurgling sound, as MacAlpin pinned his neck to the ground with a cruel thrust of his razor-sharp blade.

No others jumped up to challenge the son of Alpin, though the day's murder was far from complete. What had begun as a festive celebration ended in slaughter. At day's end, the bodies of seven earls of Dalriada— each a potential rival for the throne MacAlpin had seized—were dragged outside Scone for burial. Thus was put to rest any further disputation of the joint kingship which had been created.

But MacAlpin was not entirely at peace on the night of his victorious slaughter. There was still the matter of the missing grandson of Eoganan's aunt to resolve. He had eliminated threats from the Dalriadic side. But he must prevent any future Pict uprising behind one who claimed descent from the old King.

It would not do to have a potential pretender with a valid claim to his throne lurking about, one who might come forward at any moment.

He would continue making inquiries.

※   S I X T E E N   ※

King Kenneth MacAlpin had no need to be anxious. Dallais, son of Donnchadh, had no interest in presenting himself as King.

In the days following his flight from the battle between the Pict army and Viking horde, Dallais's sole purpose had been to bring his young cousin back to health.

He carried Breathran to the wood know as Dorchadas. The warmth of summer would be with them for another month or two. But he knew winter would come quickly, and thus he immediately undertook to fashion a shelter to keep them dry throughout its coldest months. This for a time, would be their new home. Here they would be safe.

If the weather became too harsh, the snows too heavy, they could return to the stone buildings of Steenbuaic, though Dallais hated the thought of doing so. Already he had removed from the settlement what they would need to live—tools, supplies, peats, wood, buckets, line, spears, fishing and hunting implements, weapons, blankets, skins, carts, utensils, bowls, and what dried food remained.

He had also buried the members of their two families. On his second visit to the village, he had discovered his father's corpse, thankfully in one piece, and committed it to the earth with great reverence and many tears. But he could not bury all of Steenbuaic and had no choice but to leave many to the elements.

He hoped, therefore, that he and Breathran would not have to return to Steenbuaic. And he had good reason to believe they would not have to. He knew how to live from the land. They would have fire. Their hut of stone and turf would soon be finished, and the forest itself was lush with vegetation to provide them with food and fuel. In the future, if the Vikings did not remain nearby, the surrounding fertile valley might allow them to grow a few crops. For the time being, though, he sought the forest for the cover and protection it afforded.

It was a wondrous place, this new home of theirs. No paths wound through the solemn splendor and tangled undergrowth of the magnificent wood. Not many men had set foot on the soft mosses which carpeted the forest floor, nor had many eyes beheld the seemingly infinite array of flora which flourished in its depths. Oaks and sycamores and giant beeches appeared to have been growing already for centuries. In truth, Dorchadas was but a distant extension of the ancient primeval forest, formerly known as Muigh-bhlaraidh Ecgfrith, which had once covered huge expanses of the region. In it grew also thousands of seedlings that would provide future generations with wondrous sights when time came for their discovery. Ferns, rotting logs from past ages, and a multitude of variable shrubbery grew in and around the trunks of the giants.

There were not yet many flowers here, though in time, Dallais and Breathran would bring many bright-colored species to the sunlit glades that opened up unexpectedly within the forest. For now, they walked among a thousand shades of lush green. It seemed as though the Creator, finding himself with a bit of paint remaining after stretching the first rainbow across the sky, mostly from the middle of the bow, had paused from His work, then given His brush a few vigorous shakes. Down into the valley of the Linn had tumbled ten million droplets of colorful, growth-producing energy, there to sprout into a living rainbow of green.

The seasons to come would bring other colors as well. During the autumn months, the Dorchadas would explode in a resplendent profusion of reds and golds and yellows and browns—the same warm hues brought by the spectacular summer sunsets. In August the blooming heather would add blues and purples to the celebration, as would the rhododendrons in spring, providing reds and whites as well. Then indeed would the rainbow of promise be complete!

In the meantime, the green of life and growth surrounded them and helped them heal and grow. Returning from the horrible task of burying his father, Dallais received a sign that all would indeed be well.

He had walked slowly and silently all the way from the ruined village, ever watchful for signs of lingering Norsemen. As he descended the ridge toward the forest in which he had already begun their new home, Dallais suddenly froze in place, breathless before a stunning sight—no rainbow on this day, yet for him imparting the same message: an enormous, many-tipped stag of the most pale velvety gray coat imaginable.

He might have called it white had he not known that the white stag was but a thing of ancient legend.

The wondrous beast stood gazing at him unmoving, unafraid, as if attempting to convey a message which, because of his animal nature, could be accomplished only through his eyes. The distance between them was wide, yet Dallais could see *life* in the creature's eyes . . . and knew he had likewise been *seen*.

He glanced back toward the village of his former home, pausing as if between the dead past and the unknown future, then looked again to the valley before him and the green and beckoning woods.

Already the stag had turned and was walking slowly into the forest. The majesty of its movement beckoned Dallais to follow, urging him to look back no more upon the destruction, but rather to leave yesterday forever behind. Never again, the silvery beast seemed to say—as the bow had said to Noah—would such devastation be visited upon the seed of the Wanderer.

Dallais broke into a run. A few minutes later he entered the wood at the same spot where the stag had disappeared, pausing only long enough to glance about for sign of the hoof, for the ground beneath his foot was soft. He found no print, however, and though he searched the rest of the day and most of the next, he could discover no further sign of it.

That the stag had entered Dorchadas there could be no doubt, though never again did Dallais observe sign of its presence. From that day forward, a peacefulness descended upon both human dwellers of the forest. It enveloped them whenever, after being away, they entered again under the leafy canopy. Dallais attributed the sense of peace to the stag's presence, which both of them could feel within the enclosure of the wood.

Within two weeks his young cousin began to regain her strength, and she began helping Dallais ready their shelter for the approach of winter. The spirit of the loner had always resided latent in her young breast. And now indeed did the two find each within the other the kindred spirit most needed at such a time of loss.

Their mourning gradually turned to a sense of adventure. They were young and resilient of body and soul. The two youths came to relish their shared life, working hard but laughing as they sweated and hauled and lifted and planted and cut. Were they not *alive*—and was not life a precious thing? What could they do but rejoice in it?

Thus did summer give way to autumn, which at length yielded to winter.

Dallais and Breathran, comrades in the shared struggle against the elements, survived in the mysterious forest called Dorchadas and grew to love their new home almost as much as they grew to love one another.

The Norsemen who had put in at the Linn were gone before the first snows fell.

Thus the smoke that drifted up from the wood-and-turf hut through the tops of the trees in the forest of Dorchadas was seen by no other living human.

✖   S E V E N T E E N   ✖

Three more years went by.

The two increased in vigor of limb and mind and purpose, waxing older, larger, and wiser during the years they remained in the forest in the valley near where they were born.

As Dallais grew, he conquered his hatred toward the enemy of his people, and transformed it into love—for land and animals and the forest, and later for the mountains—and into the care he showed for Breathran. And yet he continually sought the open spaces, shying away from his race. A spirit of the nomad entered into him at sight of what cruelty man was capable of toward his fellow man. Never again would he and his young cousin seek the companionship of their kind.

In time the forest could no longer contain the rising spirit of adventure and exploration blossoming within the young man and woman. Nor, as long as they remained in the valley of the Linn, could they erase the gnawing reminder of what had happened such a short distance away.

By the time MacAlpin was feasting with his new subjects and slaying his potential rivals, Dallais and Breathran had taken to journeying together far from their forest home, exploring great distances to north and west, yet still for some years returning to the valley of the Linn for the cold months of winter.

Dallais was now in his mid-twenties and master of mountains and forests. He knew at sight every animal of the Highlands, large and small. Roe came and nibbled berries from his palm. Squirrels and other creatures scampered unafraid where Breathran sang beside sparkling mountain burns, even approaching and occasionally allowing her to stroke their soft furry coats. Birds fluttered down to perch upon her shoulder, as if drawn by her soothing voice and eager to blend their own chirping happy melodies with hers.

Dallais came to know where was food and water, where shelter could be found. The girl Breathran was approaching her own maturity, and never more devoted friend, servant, and companion did man have. She knew he had saved her life. She also knew he was a great man, a man of the earth—powerful and swift, knowing and considerate, brave and wise—a *true* King among mortals . . . and she loved him.

One day Dallais came upon Breathran while she was softly singing a haunting melody, apparently to a small flock of sparrows pecking about and feeding near her.

"What is that you are singing?" he asked.

"Just a little song from when I was young," she answered, "telling the birds to come sit in the nest of my lap."

"And do they?"

"Not always, but sometimes."

From that day on, the heart of the young man began to see his cousin differently than he had before, and he loved her as she loved him.

The Highlands were Eden to these two, and they explored their world as if not merely their own settlement but their entire race had been destroyed—as if all the earth had been given to them anew, that they might rediscover all its wonders.

During these years of their innocent solitude together, never did Dallais touch Breathran wrongly or with thought to gratify himself. He would not be like other men of his time. He had witnessed man's evil. He had seen how easily man could *take* life and destroy innocence. He was determined instead to *give* life and preserve innocence. His hand reached to her only as that of a compassionate brother. When she was older, perhaps, when she was ready, he would love her more completely. Then, gently and tenderly, he would make her his wife.

Dallais had heard the name of the Scots King Alpin, and he knew something of the exploits and prowess of his son. He knew also well enough the significance of the silver chain he still wore around his neck, and that he might himself fight to lead the kingdom.

But Dallais had set himself upon a different path than Kenneth, son of Alpin. The son of Donnchadh would rule over that which had been given as man's dominion, but not over his fellows. He would tend the raven's broken wing and share the warmth of his winter's fire with squirrel and rabbit and fox who might venture near. He did not encourage such friendship with the wolf, bear, or wild boar, but neither did he fear them. Even such beasts as these seemed to know of his authority in their realms, and they never threatened his family or camp.

But Dallais, son of Donnchadh, would not rule man. He would leave earthly kingships to his many-times distant cousin who now sat upon the sacred Stone at Scone. Dallais would wear the regal necklace, reminding himself of his father's words the last day they had been together. He would remember the legacy that had been passed down to him. That right of sovereignty which flowed in his veins he would exercise over himself first, then over his family, and lastly over the land upon which they set their feet.

Thus the man who would be known to posterity as the King of Alba—the first King of a united Scotland—never wore the silver chain of monarchy that had been passed from the old Pict King into the hands of the holy man, nor even did he know of its existence.

Neither would MacAlpin ever gaze into the eyes of the stately white stag whose visits since antiquity had signaled peace and brotherhood among the peoples of the north. For the stag's eyes were not for his kind, but for stature in another kingdom altogether.

Kenneth, son of Alpin, became a mighty ruler, the self-proclaimed King of all the Scots and Picts.

But Dallais, son of Donnchadh, became a mighty man of the kind who possesses the world's true riches and thus who inherits the earth.

And the Highlands were his home.

EIGHTEEN

843–858

Dallais and Breathran returned less and less to Dorchadas as the years passed.

In time, all northern Caledonia became their home. They lived from the land. The land was good to them, because they cared for it.

King Kenneth MacAlpin, in the meantime, established the center of his kingdom at Scone, and spent the years between 843 and 850 crushing occasional Pict resistance to his leadership, then leading raiding bands north and south to pillage and increase his wealth. By the year 850, the united kingdom of Alba was secure north of the wide mouth of the Great River.

A man concerned that his kingdom be bolstered by the tradition of the church, King Kenneth brought many Columban relics from Iona to the monastery of Dunkeld on the River Tay north of Scone. There the King established the religious center for his kingdom.

Among the items brought from Iona was the *Brecbennoch* Reliquary, which was said to contain some of St. Columba's bones. Legends persisted that there had been another reliquary as well, one that had disappeared long ago. But it was never unearthed in Kenneth's time.

When Kenneth MacAlpin died in 858, he was buried on Iona as *Ardrigh Albainn*, Supreme King of Alba. His brother succeeded him, then his son, then a second son.

❖   N I N E T E E N   ❖

Dallais and Breathran had three sons and two daughters.

They taught them all in the ways of peace and harmony with the land, and to reverence, fear, and worship the Creator of the heavens and the earth, as had been passed down to them. Every living creature of the Highlands, except those who kept away, knew this gentle man and woman as friend. They did not kill except to draw fish from the lochs to eat, which practice their two older sons learned with masterful cunning before they were ten.

Nor would their descendents forget this legacy. While their cousins to the south waged war to conquer, the progeny of Dallais and Breathran roved the wild spaces of the land of Caledonia in joyous freedom. Truly they *possessed* it, for they had no desire to *own*.

Never, however, did Dallais return to exhume the box laid to rest by his father under the high granite sentinels on the plateau west of the valley of the Linn. There would it remain, awaiting discovery by some distant future generation.

In time, the sons and daughters of Dallais and Breathran grew and took to themselves wives and husbands. They were fruitful and multiplied, and their progeny inhabited the north country.

Dallais was revered by wife and sons and daughters, and in time by all who followed them. His descendents spread out and filled the land. As his hair grew white and his eyes glowed with the fire of his wandering forebears, future youngsters of his brood came to call him not King, but *chief*.

Thus did Dallais and Breathran, as their sons and grandsons after them, spawn *new* clans out of the devastation that had come to the settlement of Steenbuaic, preserving the purity of their shared Celtic bloodline for all time to come.

✦ T W E N T Y ✦

888

Never again did Dallais set eyes upon the white stag, though its message of hope deepened within him as the years went by. Then, during his sixty-eighth year, a peculiar sensation came over him that the stag was beckoning. He set out two days later with his three sons, grown now, and his seven grandsons—though he knew not where.

It was summer and warm. They wandered into regions far to the north, regions the white-haired Highland chieftain had never visited. Yet even from a great distance, the moment he saw the three great stones on the slope of the hillside, they seemed familiar. They reminded him of those at his home of Steenbuaic.

The pilgrims set off across the flat valley before them, then up the rise toward the great stone sentinels. Immediately, as they drew closer Dallais knew they represented a monument of some kind, from an ancient time. A great silence descended over the band of eleven men as each set to examining the carved markings upon the stones, a few of which they could decipher, but most of which were strange to their eyes.

Feelings indescribable filled the breast of the son of Donnchadh as he laid his hands upon the ancient surfaces. Something was *here*—he knew it, he could sense it. He had been *led* to this place.

Wandering about, he discovered first one, then a second oblong mound of stones set some distance from the two pillars and horizontal slab. He knew them instantly as graves.

A great wave of antiquity came over him. A feeling, somehow, of recognition. He could not explain why, but somehow he knew he belonged to this place.

They remained several days, piecing together fragments of the story which had been carved in the stones centuries before so that they would know what breed of man had conquered Caledonia. They discovered the ruins of an old hill-fort. Norsemen had apparently been here too, for destruction was evident. The sons and grandsons of Dallais left every stone as it was.

When at length they made ready to return to their families, Dallais gathered his sons and grandsons around him. It was his wish, he said, to be buried in this place, beside what could only be the resting places of ancient kinsmen, possibly kings or chiefs. Solemnly they nodded in assent. None protested the impracticality of such a request. They too sensed somehow that it was right.

As the small band descended the hill known to their ancestors as Beinn Donuill, stopping often to look behind, from across a great distance beside the waters of Aethbran nan Bronait, two gleaming eyes of a huge, pale, and much antlered creature gazed upon them.

After several minutes, his work completed, he turned, sprang across the narrow river in a single majestic bound, and disappeared in the direction of Muigh-bhlaraidh Ecgfrith.

⁜ T W E N T Y · O N E ⁜

909

Many years passed.

Dallais grew old. His hair was now white as the winter's snows, for he was almost ninety. By then indeed the inhabitants of Scone had heard legends of a mysterious old man who roamed the Highlands, whose voice the animals knew and even understood, whose wife was nearly as old as he, though more beautiful than any goddess, who sang sweetly over the hills while birds and rabbits flew and scampered to her feet, and whose grandchildren and great-grandchildren populated the mountainous regions with clans innumerable and prolific settlements in every valley and strath where man might survive.

Some believed the tales. Others said they were mere fancy.

None knew, however, that the new Highland wanderer, with hair as white as the snowcapped hills and with a Highland Eve for a wife, wore around his neck the ancient royal chain that might have given him a claim to the throne of their land.

▨   T W E N T Y - T W O   ▨

The house of Alpin continued for two centuries to fill its throne with descendents of the man who, by the might of the sword, had unified the kingdoms of Picts and Scots. By such constant bloodshed did fourteen kings come and go, and murder became the normal mode of succession to the sacred seat of Scone. Over time, the kingdom of *Alba* became known as *Scotia*, then finally, by the tenth century, as *Scotland*.

MacAlpin's Scots at last conquered and gave their name to the land of Caledonia.

But in the Highlands, the pure spirit of the Celt lived on. The descendents of the Wanderer and Cruithne, now also the sons of Donnchadh, Dallais, and Breathran, would come to be known by many, many names . . . and would keep the legends of their fathers alive.

6

SLEUTHING ON THE WEB

As he motored southward from Scone through Edinburgh, and then through Scotland's southern uplands back toward his home in northern England, Andrew's thoughts drifted back from the ninth century to the present.

The incident at the Gordon castle still stung. Along with the mortification he felt over his own deceptiveness, he could not prevent a mounting annoyance at the press.

That was the frustration of public life—nothing was ever your own. Privacy was nonexistent, and worse, the journalists so often seemed to misrepresent the facts.

He had been lucky enough to enjoy his morning walks in London without intrusion. But it would hardly surprise him to learn that some enthusiastic reporter had been dogging his steps all summer. He half expected to open a paper a few days from now to find a slanted account of his Scottish sojourn in one of the rags.

The more he thought about it, in fact, the more annoyed he became. He had thought he was accustomed to press intrusion, able to take them in stride, but now they had managed to sabotage something he really cared about!

Paddy Rawlings came into his mind. Well, she was different, he thought. She was one journalist he could trust.

Then he found himself thinking once more of Ginny Gordon, of her jaunty carriage, her crown of fiery russet hair, her intriguing mixture of naive innocence and earthy professionalism. And, as he had witnessed all too recently, her passion for truth.

Well, so much for the truth! he thought wryly. Now he might never be able to set things right with her. And knowing that the fault had been entirely his only worsened his mood.

Andrew had calmed a little by the time he entered the long drive into the Derwenthwaite estate three hours later. He saw an unfamiliar auto parked near the door. He pulled in beside it, got out, and entered the house.

Voices were coming through the open door of the large sitting room adjacent to the foyer. One of them he recognized as his mother's. He approached and walked in.

"Andrew!" she said in surprised greeting as well as astonishment to see the four-week beard on his face.

A woman was sitting with her, cup of tea in hand, her back to the door. The visitor stood and turned as Andrew strode forward to hug his mother where she sat.

He stopped in his tracks the instant he saw the face.

"*Paddy!*" he exclaimed, half in question, half in disbelief. "What . . . what are *you* doing here?"

"Patricia and I were just . . . enjoying tea and . . . conversation together," said Lady Trentham slowly.

Andrew hardly heard the words. A sudden sense of betrayal filled him, fueled by his musings on the road. The next words out of his mouth were unplanned and he would long regret them. But they were gone before he could retrieve them.

"I thought you were different, Paddy," he said indignantly. "I trusted you—and now you come here, to my home, behind my back . . . to get something on me."

"Please, Andrew," said Paddy in an almost pleading tone. "It's not that at all. I didn't mean—"

"Just what *did* you mean, Paddy?" interrupted Andrew.

"If you'll just let me explain."

"Explain what?" he shot back. "That you spotted a story while I was gone? Have you been talking to Dugald MacKinnon too?"

"Andrew . . . please. Of course not. I thought we settled all that a long time ago. I told you I would never print anything without your permission."

"Well, you can forget about any further interviews with me. The book on this particular member of Parliament is hereby closed."

He spun around and stormed from the house the way he had come. Allowing the door to thud shut behind him, he strode rapidly through the garden and toward the open heathland that rose toward Bewaldeth Crag.

❁   T W O   ❁

It did not take Andrew long to cool off and to realize that whatever Paddy's reason for being here, he had been a complete chump to take out his frustrations on her. He hadn't allowed Paddy any more chance to explain *her* motives than Ginny and her father had given *him*.

What was he thinking? Paddy was not the enemy. She was his friend. He *could* trust her, just as he had been thinking a few hours earlier.

He turned and went back to the house, entering through the back door.

He walked straight to the sitting room. There stood his mother, her back to him, staring out one of the large windows. She was alone.

"Where's Miss Rawlings?" asked Andrew sheepishly, not relishing having to apologize in front of his mother.

"Where do you think she is . . . after the fool you . . . made of yourself?" she replied slowly, not turning to face him. "She is gone."

"Where?"

"I don't know—probably . . . to London. She was in tears."

Andrew drew in a deep breath and slowly exhaled. He turned and left the house once again.

When he returned an hour later, he found his father and mother seated in the dining room for tea. He entered, walked forward, and sat down to join them.

"Hullo, Dad," said Andrew, shaking his father's hand. He then turned to his mother.

"I'm sorry, Mum," he said, pouring himself a cup of tea. "You're right, I did make a fool of myself." He buttered a slice of wheat bread. "I'm sorry you had to see it."

"What's the trouble, Andrew?" asked his father seriously.

"I suppose I was on edge," Andrew replied. "I had an unpleasant experience in Scotland that had to do, at least partially, with the press. It was really eating at me on the way back, and then when I saw Paddy—well, it just all came back. What was she doing here anyway?"

"She said she had new information about the case," answered Mr. Trentham.

"The case," repeated Andrew. "Do you know what she meant?"

"No, I assumed you would. But when she learned that you were gone, she asked your mum if she could do an interview with her."

"I am so sorry, Mum," said Andrew again. "Looks as if I spoiled things for you. I'll talk to Paddy and try to set something up."

"Talk to her . . . how?" said Mr. Trentham.

"Hmm . . . you're right. And you have no idea where she's staying?"

"We would have invited her to stay here again, but . . ."

"Yeah, right, Dad—if I hadn't opened my big mouth. No doubt she's on her way back to the city. I probably ought to go down for a few days anyway, check in at the office, catch up on correspondence and calls. It will be a chance to forget what made me snap at Paddy."

"Pretty fair growth of beard there, son," said Mr. Trentham, trying to lighten the heavy mood that had marred Andrew's homecoming. "You plan to keep it?"

"I don't know, Dad," laughed Andrew. "I was just trying to disguise my appearance while traveling. What do you think—should I take it with me to London?"

▧   T H R E E   ▧

Paddy Rawlings sat at her desk in the large noisy newsroom.

She had been back on the job in London several days, doing her best to put what happened in Cumbria behind her. When she did think of it, mingled feelings of humiliation and confusion filled her. Here she had thought that she and Andrew—

A low hubbub caught her ear from the other side of the open room.

The imposing figure of a man strode across the floor, leaving in his wake low murmurs and staring eyes from the newsroom staff. He was well dressed in an expensive suit, clean-shaven, and carried nothing in his hands. His walk was purposeful, and he comported himself with obvious poise and breeding.

Paddy's eyes took but a second to focus. Her face immediately reddened.

It was Andrew Trentham!

She turned and bent her head low to her desk, hoping to prevent his seeing her, not sure if she could face him again.

Andrew did not see her. He walked straight to the office of Edward Pilkington. As the Honorable Gentleman paused to knock on the open door, the sound of conversation between Pilkington and Kirk Luddington immediately ceased.

"Mr. Trentham," said the news chief, rising and extending his hand, "it is an honor to see you. I am Edward Pilkington."

"I am pleased to meet you," replied Andrew, shaking the other man's hand. He turned to the reporter and gave him his hand as well. "Luddington," he said.

"Please, have a seat," said Pilkington a little too enthusiastically. "What can we do for you?"

"I'll only be a minute," said Andrew, remaining on his feet. "Could you direct me to where I might find Patricia Rawlings?"

"Uh . . . Ms. Rawlings is one of our *junior* staff members," began Pilkington. "Whatever your business, I am certain either I or Mr. Luddington here—"

"My business is with Ms. Rawlings alone," interrupted Andrew crisply. "I'm afraid neither of you would be able to help me."

"She is also—" put in Luddington, in a voice pretending to be helpful but with an unmistakable air of condescension.

Here he lowered his voice.

"—an *American,*" he added. "Her knowledge of British politics is, shall we say, limited. If you—"

"I am quite aware of that fact, Luddington," interrupted Andrew again. "Now please, Mr. Pilkington, I must insist that you direct me to the young lady."

The veteran newsman pointed beyond his office door and toward the other side of the room, where Paddy sat listening to every word.

Andrew turned and walked straight toward her, unaware that both Pilkington and Luddington had risen from their chairs and now followed, and that a small cluster of six or eight others throughout the room likewise inched forward from their positions.

Unable to make a dash for it, Paddy rose and awaited the arrival of the MP and the gathering entourage behind him.

Andrew walked straight to the front of her desk, then stopped and looked her straight in the eye.

"Paddy," he said. "I am sorrier than I can say for how I behaved the other day. My words were utterly uncalled for—and untrue, besides. I was very rude, and I am extremely sorry. I beg your forgiveness."

"Of course, Andrew," replied Paddy softly. "Certainly I forgive you."

"Thank you," rejoined Andrew. "I had an unfortunate experience in Scotland, and I hadn't expected to see you. I am afraid I took my frustrations out on you."

"Does what happened have anything to do with the article in the *Express*?"

"That wasn't all of it," nodded Andrew, now allowing a wry smile to his lips, "but it didn't help."

"I saw it," said Paddy. "I knew there wasn't a word of truth in it."

"I knew you had nothing to do with it, of course. I'm afraid it was just a matter of guilt by association," Andrew went on. "—But my father said you have new information . . ."

"Uh . . . perhaps," replied Paddy, cautiously glancing around at her curious colleagues as they slowly meandered back to their desks and workstations. Luddington, however, continued to hang around a little too close for comfort. Andrew saw the reason for her reticence.

"What would you say to telling me about it over dinner this evening?" he asked.

"I think that sounds wonderful . . . and I think I just *might* have an opening in my schedule," she added with a smile.

"Good—I'm glad you can fit me into your packed social calendar on such late notice."

Paddy laughed.

"Seven o'clock?"

"That will be perfect."

"I'll come by your place then."

Andrew turned and strode from the room, leaving the newsroom in astonished silence, with every man and woman dying to know more about whatever incident had precipitated the unusual visit. Even Kirk Luddington, usually at no loss for words, found himself in no position to offer comment.

❖ FOUR ❖

I am so relieved to know we're still friends," Paddy said as the waiter left them. "These last two days have been miserable for me."

"I am sorry again," said Andrew. "I hope we can put it behind us. At least I want to put it behind *me*, since I am the one who caused it!"

"All right," laughed Paddy, "consider it forgotten."

"Now, I am eager to know what you have," said Andrew. "My father said there was new information."

"I don't know whether it's important or not," replied Paddy. "But I've located Reardon . . . he's in New Zealand."

"New Zealand!" exclaimed Andrew. "Don't tell me you followed him all that way, just as you did to Ireland!" he added, laughing lightly. "With haircut and sunglasses and everything . . ."

She laughed too, remembering her past attempt at detective work. "No . . . I didn't follow him this time."

"But you located him? How?"

"I have my sources," smiled Paddy.

"As far away as New Zealand?"

"A long story," answered Paddy evasively. She paused seemingly on the verge of saying something else, then changed her mind and said instead, "As far as I know, Reardon is still there."

"What's he doing?"

"All we can tell so far is that he seems to be meeting with people who have heavy interests in oil."

At the word *oil,* Andrew snapped to attention. Instantly came into his brain the vision of his first minutes at the Ballochallater Games, the maroon BMW, and Robert Burslem's brief argument with Ginny's father. Quickly followed memory of the laird's words:

" . . . a Sassenach tryin' t' git his clutches on a wee parcel . . . up t' the north, in the Shetlands."

The north . . . that was where Scotland's oil was.

"We can't be certain it's anything underhanded," Paddy continued. She went on to explain briefly the visits of Andrew's former deputy leader to the Auckland investment firm.

Andrew pondered the development thoughtfully.

"And is your . . . uh, your friend still keeping an eye on him?" he asked.

"As much as he can," answered Paddy. "But he hates it. He's just a photojournalist temporarily on assignment in New Zealand. He's uncomfortable following someone around he doesn't know. He—" Again she paused, as if on the verge of telling him something.

"He what?"

"He—oh, nothing. He's just not a spy, that's all."

"One thing's for certain," said Andrew, giving her a puzzled look, "we've got to learn more. And we really ought to notify Inspector Shepley. Since Reardon is an active suspect in the Stone theft, Shepley has to know what you've found out. I'll talk to him tomorrow."

"I'm glad you're back," sighed Paddy. "I feel much better now that you know all this. I wasn't sure what to do."

Their conversation was interrupted briefly while the waiter brought their starters, then gradually drifted into other channels as dinner progressed. Andrew gave Paddy a brief account of his time in Scotland. He did not dwell long on his visit to Ballochallater, which had ended so painfully.

Actually, he had been about to tell her all about it when she floored him with the thing she had been trying to say all night.

It didn't come easy for her. In fact, it required several minutes of fiddling with her fork, rearranging her napkin, clearing her throat.

"Your mother thought I should tell you something," she began hesitantly. "I don't know why I told her, except she was so kind and interested in my career and all, and—I usually just keep this kind of thing to myself, you know.—Not that it's anyone's business, really, but you're a friend, and I thought, well . . ."

Andrew was intrigued. He had never seen his confident journalist friend this nervous.

"Why don't you just tell me what it is?" he prompted gently. "I promise I can take it—even if you turn out to be Larne Reardon's long-lost daughter."

She managed a weak smile. "No, it's nothing like that. It's not even that big a deal, only . . . it just seems strange to work so closely with you and you not know."

"Know what?"

"Well," she told him, "did I ever happen to mention to you that I'm married?"

❊   F I V E   ❊

It was later that same evening. Their dinner was long behind them, their long discussion about Bill wound down to a comfortable conclusion. Now Andrew sat beside Paddy at the desk in her flat, staring at her computer screen.

"I'm not as versatile with the Internet as I would like to be," she was saying, "but earlier I managed to track down World Resources, Ltd. . . ."

She was clicking in commands as she spoke.

"There it is—but you can see this is just a generic sort of informational website. It was probably generated by their PR department—I doubt it will tell us much."

"Can you probe more deeply into the company itself," asked Andrew, "—ownership, board of directors, when and where founded, holding companies, sub-branches, finances . . . that sort of thing?"

"Theoretically we should be able to find out whatever we want. *Everything's* on the Internet if you can figure out how to get to it. Let's trace some of the keywords and see what links we can find. . . ."

She rapidly moved her mouse across its pad and began clicking options.

"Dead end . . . we'll try another. . . ."

"That looks interesting," said Andrew, watching the screen intently as she worked. "Can you follow up on that?"

"I'll try. Let's see what we get when we ask for more information . . . there we go—a company menu. Okay, which option do you like—Investment Opportunities, History, Employment Opportunities, Financial Rating—"

"Try Corporate Structure," said Andrew.

A few minutes went by as Paddy continued to explore different directions in the various files.

"Board of Directors . . . recognize anyone?"

Andrew shook his head. "What about that?" he added, pointing to the screen, "—UK Division?"

"All right."

Paddy clicked on the link.

"Looks like another generic web page."

"Wait—that looks interesting there," said Andrew, "—on that small menu to the right . . . try Exploration Committee, and maybe Land Lease Holdings."

Paddy clicked the word *Exploration*. The screen filled with new information. Gradually she scrolled down as they scanned the listings.

"What . . . look!" exclaimed Andrew, "—there's Robert Burslem! I don't believe it!"

She shook her head. "Name sounds familiar, but I'm not sure . . ."

"One of the Conservative vice-chairmen," he reminded her, "an MP. I ran across him in Scotland a few days ago—under, shall we say, interesting circumstances."

"*Suspicious* circumstances?"

"I'm not really sure. They struck me as odd at the time, but I'm not sure why—nothing I could put my finger on."

"Did you talk to him?"

"He never saw me. Actually, I was growing a beard at the time, so I was well camouflaged."

"I remember the beard—now there's a news story!" She grinned. "May I run an exclusive?"

"Not on your life!—But what could Burslem be doing buried in the UK division of World Resources, Ltd.?"

"You think there's a connection to Reardon?"

"I don't know. But I am more than a little intrigued. Can we get a look at their real estate holdings, oil leases? Let's look at that Land Lease thing for a starter."

Paddy returned to the previous menu, then clicked on *Land Lease*.

"Looks like they are all over the UK," she said.

"I would like to see an actual map of their holdings and leases."

It took Paddy a few minutes, but eventually she was able to produce exactly what Andrew wanted.

"Good—wow, that's super. Zoom in closer. Let's isolate the Shetlands."

Paddy did so.

"From this I would think they control half the islands. Can you print this?"

"No problem," replied Paddy, entering the command.

"I wish I knew where the laird's property was," reflected Andrew aloud while they waited for the printout to emerge.

"The laird?"

"A Scottish fellow I met—sort of chief to a small branch of Gordons tucked away in the Highlands. He controls a parcel of land in the Shetlands that Burslem has been trying to get his hands on. The laird is none too happy about it."

"I see what you mean . . . it is interesting."

Suddenly Andrew became quiet. A strange, almost shocked, expression came over his face, as if the thought that had just flown into his brain had caught even him by surprise.

"What is it?" said Paddy. "I can tell you are thinking something."

"Don't laugh."

"I promise."

"I know it's a long shot," said Andrew, his voice soft and serious, "but I just had a wild idea."

"I'm listening."

"I don't know if the Internet is the way to go, or old newspapers, or other records you might be able to dig into at the BBC . . . but I want you to look into something. I think it's better I not be visible at first. If anything comes of it . . . we'll cross that bridge later. . . ."

"What do you want me to find out?"

"The crazy idea that just came to me is this—that we ought to see if there might be a hidden link between Burslem and Eagon Hamilton."

Now it was Paddy's turn to gaze at Andrew with an expression of astonishment.

"That is quite a leap," she said. "What makes you think such a thing might be possible?"

"I have nothing whatever to base it on," answered Andrew. "The idea just came to me and I thought, why not?"

"What would be the point?"

"I don't know . . . maybe to see if we might—"

Andrew paused and shook his head slowly, as if the idea was too far out there to say aloud. Paddy waited.

"—to see if we might discover a motive for murder," he continued after a moment.

It was silent a few seconds as the word hung in the air.

"Are you suggesting that Robert Burslem—" began Paddy.

"No, not at all," replied Andrew. "I'm suggesting nothing. But *if* there are hidden connections, hidden motives, hidden involvements in something like oil . . . who knows what *else* might be involved? It's possible we may have just uncovered the tip of the proverbial iceberg here."

Paddy nodded as she took in Andrew's comment with interest.

"I mean, look at it," Andrew went on. "We know that Reardon's been up to no good, but we don't really know what his motives are. And we've got Reardon in New Zealand with a company involving Burslem, a company heavily invested in oil and with holdings all over the Shetlands. Then I see Burslem in Scotland in heated conversation trying to buy a piece of Shetland real estate that its owner says is worthless. Let's just say all that strikes me as one coincidence too many."

"But there's nothing here even remotely suggesting murder," said Paddy.

"Not yet . . . but there is money in oil—"

"Not to mention power," added Paddy, picking up the scent.

"Two powerful motives."

"But why would Hamilton have been murdered?"

"Who knows? I haven't a clue. I just—"

"And what connection could they have—Burslem and Hamilton, I mean? Their politics are all wrong. On the face of it, everything would suggest *no* connections. What would a Conservative like Burslem and a Liberal Democrat like Hamilton have in common? They were opposite on everything, from the Scottish question to free trade, from taxes to welfare."

"I see what you mean—the look of the thing is all wrong," nodded Andrew with a sigh. "You're probably right—how could there be anything? It makes no sense. I just thought it was an avenue we might explore."

☒ S I X ☒

The next morning Andrew went to Scotland Yard to see Inspector Shepley. He told him briefly what he had learned.

"Do you know where Reardon is staying?" asked Shepley.

"The Auckland Towers," replied Andrew.

"All right . . . good work, Trentham. I'll make a call immediately, and we'll have him picked up. Whatever is going on, we have two eyewitnesses to his involvement with the Stone—you and the Rawlings woman. If we can get our hands on Reardon, then perhaps he will lead us to Dwyer and the rest."

"Keep me posted, Inspector," said Andrew as he rose to leave.

"Are you back in the city now?" asked Shepley. "I thought I heard you went north for the recess."

"I'm here only briefly," replied Andrew. "But you have my numbers if you need me."

"And likewise," said Shepley. "So far you've uncovered more in this case than I have! So call me if you happen to crack it wide open."

Andrew laughed. "That's your job, Inspector. But right, I'll let you know if I learn anything more."

☒ S E V E N ☒

SNP Deputy Leader Baen Ferguson read the brief message through a second time, then tossed the slip of paper into the fireplace.

Ferguson,

Meet usual place. Midnight Thursday. Bring Fiona. Next phase may require woman's touch.

R

Bring Fiona . . . right! As if he had any idea where she was! He thought she was with Reardon, so what was this all about?

Two evenings later, at twenty minutes before midnight, well bundled and with a wool cap pulled tightly down over the tops of his ears, the SNP Deputy Leader walked slowly over the bridge across the Thames toward his appointed rendezvous. A thick fog prevented visibility from one end to the other, in spite of the numerous light poles lining the walkway.

As he neared the far end, a tall, slender silhouette came gradually into view under the pale yellow glare of a bridge-lamp above him. Ferguson continued on. It was not until he was nearly upon the figure that he suddenly realized it was not whom he had expected.

"What are *you* doing here?" said Ferguson in surprise.

"I sent you the note," replied the man.

"What? I thought it came from Reardon. How did you know about the bridge?"

"He told me how to contact you. He's hot, so it's up to you and me now."

"You're in on this?"

A slight nod was the only reply. "Where's Fiona?"

"I haven't the slightest idea," snapped Ferguson, irritated at the now obvious fact that he had been left even further out of the loop than he realized. First Fiona had double-crossed him, as he saw it . . . and now this. He hardly knew what to make of it. "I haven't seen Fiona since June," he said. "Look—I want to know what you have to do with this. What's going on?"

The tall man laughed. "Don't be naive, Baen. Do you think things happen without connections . . . *high* connections? We're not talking about some penny-ante theft of a chunk of Highland sandstone, but a major restructuring of the European power alliance. I've been involved from the beginning."

"But what about—"

"Reardon? Let's just say circumstances required a partnership, so we brought him in some years ago. But he was never running this operation."

"Maybe I don't like these kinds of surprises. Did you ever think that so far I'm the only one in the clear, and that I could blow the whistle on you all?"

"You're not going to blow the whistle on anyone, Baen," rejoined the man, a hint of threat creeping into his tone. "You're not as in the clear as you think. If you make one false move, the Yard might suddenly discover that they missed a fingerprint on the sgian-dubh that killed Eagon Hamilton—*your* fingerprint."

"That's ridiculous—I was nowhere near Aberdeen."

"Tell it to the Yard. I am only telling you that your fingerprint is *already* in the files; they just don't know it yet. All they need is a little nudge to reexamine the evidence, and they'll find you everywhere they look. I happen to have inside information that Shepley still has you at the top of his list because of your Glencoe cottage. So I suggest you keep your cool.—But enough of this. Things are starting to move fast, and I need Fiona."

Reeling from the devastating string of sudden disclosures, Ferguson returned his colleague's stare with as much composure as he could muster.

"I told you," he said, "I have no idea where she is."

"I know where she is, all right," replied the other. "I just can't afford to make contact."

"Where then?"

"Ireland. I'll tell you where. I want you to go there personally."

"I'm a busy man. I can't just drop everything and—"

A raised hand silenced him. The look in the man's eyes told him he had better guard his tongue.

"I'm not giving you a choice in the matter," the man said. "Tell her you came from me. Bring her to the Grand Hotel in Lerwick."

"Lerwick! You can't be serious!"

"Another young woman has become involved," the man went on, ignoring Ferguson's outburst. "She could prove a handful, and I may need Fiona to handle the situation. I will contact you with details. Be there and wait."

"And if she refuses?"

"She will come."

"What does any of this have to do with the Stone?"

"At this point, nothing. Unfortunately, that aspect of our plans fell through. But there is more than one way to open the doors of power. The Stone was but symbolic anyway."

"Not according to Dwyer."

The man chuckled in the yellow darkness. "Dwyer is a fool," he said.

"We had no intention of letting him keep the Stone indefinitely. He was a mere convenience, but the ultimate prize was much greater than his ridiculous little ring of stones."

"But . . . why *you*? You have all the power a man could hope for."

"Not quite *all*. . . . That's why long ago I decided to cast my fortunes with the future of the north."

"Where is Reardon now?"

"You have no need to know that. But you will see him in the Shetlands."

"And Hamilton?" probed Ferguson.

But already the tall man had turned and was walking away in the opposite direction into the night.

❧   E I G H T   ❧

The telephone rang at nine o'clock in the evening at Andrew's flat.

"Andrew, it's Paddy," said a voice when he answered. "Can you come over?"

"Now?"

"I've got something on my screen I think you should see."

"I'll be right there."

Andrew hung up. He had put on his jacket and made for the door when the phone rang again.

"Trentham . . . Allan Shepley," said the caller. "I just got off the phone with Auckland. Reardon's skipped. Checked out yesterday without a trace. We're tracking the airports, but if he's already left New Zealand, I'm afraid we've lost him again."

Andrew hung up, then left his flat. He arrived at Paddy's at 9:25.

She led him straight to her computer desk. Two chairs were waiting for them. Andrew sat down.

"Do you remember when we were glancing through World Resources' main menu?" Paddy began. "On a hunch I tried the History file—remember, we skipped over it before? I want to show you what I found . . . look—the company actually began in Liverpool—"

"Liverpool?" repeated Andrew.

"Right, in 1969," Paddy went on. "It grew rapidly due to some very favorable parliamentary regulations. But get this—there are two very interesting names on the founding documents."

Paddy showed Andrew the printout.

A low whistle escaped his lips.

"It seems I was wrong about Burslem. He *wasn't* involved. But . . ."

His voice trailed off, and he slowly shook his head.

"What can this mean? Like you said earlier, the politics is backwards."

"Unless," reflected Paddy, "they used their political differences as a smokescreen to obscure deeper motives and long-range objectives so that no one would link them."

"Surely they couldn't have foreseen all the implications way back then— or the political shifts that have occurred during that time. That was back when there was still a Soviet Union. Back before the EU. Before devolution."

"I know it's a stretch, but stranger things have happened."

"The world has completely changed," Andrew went on. "Eagon would have only been . . . let me see—he would have been twenty-five at the time."

"Unless the whole scheme was even more far-reaching than we yet realize," suggested Paddy. "I'm only thinking aloud—you know how journalists are—but what if the ultimate design wasn't just control of oil itself, but control at a higher level . . . perhaps even control of a nation? What if the oil cartel was only a means to that ultimate end?"

"Control . . . of a *nation*?"

"Remember, I'm just brainstorming . . . but I was thinking of a nation not yet in existence—not in 1969, not even today . . . but getting closer all the time."

"Are you thinking what I think you're thinking?"

"I just might be."

"But the North Sea oil fields weren't discovered until—"

"The late sixties," said Paddy. "I already looked into it. And just a few years later, in the early seventies, when World Resources began growing rapidly and started buying up land and leases in the Shetlands—that's when Eagon Hamilton's political career took off."

Andrew nodded in thoughtful amazement.

"You may be on to something," he said. "I see what you mean—there are tantalizing coincidences. But how could they have foreseen the rise of nationalism throughout the world way back then? If you're right, that obviously plays into their hands."

"But the politics still puzzles me. Eagon Hamilton was on the record as being *against* greater autonomy for regions such as Scotland."

"Exactly," replied Andrew. "He was no friend of the SNP. That he would be involved in a scheme to use the potential clout of an autonomous Scotland as a stepping-stone to power throughout Europe, even in the EU . . . it just strikes me as inconceivable."

"As I said before, perhaps a smokescreen. Or," added Paddy in a more serious tone, "maybe that's what eventually got him killed."

"And the Stone—if the two things are linked, that continues to puzzle me," said Andrew. "What could be the connection?"

"But think about it," said Paddy. "What better way to legitimize their efforts than with one of the most sacred objects in Scotland's history?"

"Are you talking about an actual coup?"

"I don't know . . . more like gaining control over Scotland's economy and hoping the politics would follow. The oil provides control of the economy, and perhaps the Stone was to provide a symbolic foundation for political power."

"Wild ideas, Paddy!" said Andrew. "You reporters have fantastic imaginations."

"Investigative journalism—a wild imagination is the name of the game. But you're the one who started all these wild imaginings—with your speculations about Burslem and Eagon Hamilton!"

"True enough," he laughed, "but you have to admit this is getting crazier and crazier. At any rate, if you can find me a more solid connection than just being involved with starting a perfectly legal corporation," he added, "I'll be more than happy to listen to your conspiracy theory."

He paused thoughtfully, then went on. "You know what I ought to do," he said, "is talk to my mother. She's an old-school Tory. She may remember something from back in the seventies when all this was getting under way. I need to go north again soon anyway."

"While you do that," said Paddy, "I'll talk to my friend Bert Fenton, the computer whiz. I'm sure he'll be able to help me dig a little deeper into the personal backgrounds of Hamilton and Reardon and the others."

"Now that some pieces are beginning to fit together," said Andrew, "I should also try to see if I can find out anything more about the laird's Shetland property. We'll stay in touch. Ring me if you find anything."

⊠   N I N E   ⊠

Even as he was driving home from Paddy's that evening, Andrew realized that he needed to go farther north than just Derwenthwaite. He had to go back to Scotland for more reasons than to investigate the laird's Shetland property. He could not let much more time go by without making another attempt to explain and apologize to Ginny and her family. Already two letters of his had been returned unopened. He felt he had no choice but to go in person and try to resolve the issue.

Meanwhile, on the evening of his arrival back in Cumbria, while he and his parents lingered over a late tea, Andrew asked his mother about her former Tory colleagues.

"Yes," said Lady Trentham, "now that you mention it . . . remember odd rumors from time to time."

"About what?" asked Andrew.

"Nothing substantiated . . . connections to left-wing organizations."

"What kind of organizations?"

"You know the kind," she answered, and in the lift of her chin he caught a glimpse of the old fire that had made her such an effective politician. "—anti-union . . . split up the UK . . . four separate states . . . all a bunch of nonsense, you know."

Andrew took in the information with interest. His mother's words reminded him uncannily of Paddy's brainstorms of a few days earlier.

"No one believed it," Lady Trentham went on. "Miles and I and all the rest of us . . . we were on the right . . . we were Maggie Thatcher's Tory base. But rumors . . . were persistent."

"And Robert Burslem?"

"Never knew him well . . . just arriving on the scene as I was leaving."

"And Hamilton's connections with the Tories?"

"Nothing out of the ordinary . . ."

Andrew's mother paused.

"Now that you mention it," she went on slowly in a more reflective tone, "recall an occasion . . . Miles disappeared . . . some secretive trip . . . people said Australia or New Zealand. When he came back . . . more rumors . . . he and Hamilton on junket together. Afterward he pushed through a bill . . . seemed odd at the time."

"Did it have to do with oil?"

"Can't remember now . . . may have. . . . vaguely familiar. Remember overhearing someone ask Miles about Hamilton. He snapped . . . out of character, I thought."

❋   T E N   ❋

After two days at home, Andrew drove north again to Scotland, retracing his route across the southern uplands and central Highlands toward Spittal o' Ballochallater.

As he entered the tiny village from the south, it was with a multitude of thoughts and feelings far different than his previous adventurous outlook. He felt a part of this place now, a part of Scotland, no longer a stranger.

Yet sight of the village, and the castle on the hill behind it, brought pangs of uncertainty. Would Ginny and her family see him? Would he even have a chance to explain himself?

He stopped in front of a bed-and-breakfast, one of three in the village. A small sign outside read *Craigfoodie*. He went inside to make arrangements for a room. He signed the register *Andrew Trentham*.

The stout proprietress glanced at his name, seemed to recognize it, and started to say something, then evidently thought better of it and led him to his room in what seemed to Andrew a sudden chilly silence.

An hour later Andrew walked back outside. He glanced again toward the castle, then down at his watch. It was three o'clock. He might as well get right to his business.

As he walked through to the outskirts of the village, the once friendly and embracing atmosphere he had felt during his visit of only a short while earlier had evaporated. Only silent stares now greeted him. Not a soul spoke, not a smile came his way, even from the two or three individuals he recognized from his previous visit. The air itself was cold too, he thought with a shiver, with the early darkness of autumn already approaching.

He reached the castle after a walk of ten or twelve minutes and approached the front door. He lifted the brass knocker and let it fall heavily on the huge oak door, then a second time.

A long minute went by. At last the door opened slowly, and there stood Ginny's mother. Surprise at seeing him registered on her face, but otherwise she gave no sign of recognition.

"Hello, Mrs. Gordon," said Andrew. "I've come back hoping you and your family will give me the chance to apologize and try to explain myself."

She took in the words, nodding slightly.

"Is, uh . . . your husband at home, and Ginny—could I talk to the three of you for a few minutes?"

"Bide a wee here," she said matter-of-factly, then turned and disappeared inside. She returned two minutes later.

"The laird's awa in Braemar wi' Angus MacLeod," she said, "so ye winna be seein' him. An' Ginny says she doesna want t' see ye jist noo."

"But if I could only have a minute to—"

"Good day t' ye, Mr. Trentham," said Mrs. Gordon. With the words, Andrew saw the door closing in front of him.

Dejected, he returned to the village. What was the use of his staying any longer? He might as well start for home immediately. He went to his room and lay down on the bed to think.

Forty minutes later, just as he was dozing off, a knock sounded on the door. Andrew rose to answer it, surprised to see the huge hulking form of Alastair Farquharson standing in the corridor. His first reaction was to assume that he was about to be beaten to a pulp by Ginny's boyfriend. Instead, now it was Andrew's turn to receive the same question he had posed to Mrs. Gordon.

"Cud I hae a word wi' ye, Mr. Trentham?" asked Farquharson.

"Of course," replied Andrew. "Please—come in."

"How did you know I was here?" he asked after they had shaken hands and taken chairs opposite one another.

"Ev'yone kens, Mr. Trentham. The whole village is talkin' aboot yer bein' here."

"But I've hardly been here more than an hour."

"Ay, but word travels fast in a wee place like Ballochallater."

"And everyone thinks I am a liar and a traitor?"

"Somethin' like it," answered the big man with hint of a smile.

"And you?"

"To be honest wi' ye, Mr. Trentham," replied Alastair, "I didna think ye'd come back gien the things they're sayin' aboot ye were true."

"It is kind of you to say so," said Andrew. "You are right. I came back to try to apologize and explain, though I haven't had a very successful time of it so far."

A brief silence fell. The big Scotsman shifted uncomfortably, then looked at Andrew with serious expression.

"The reason I came t' see ye," he began, "—an' dinna think me too much a loon fer sayin' it, Mr. Trentham, but I canna help thinkin' that ye're the only one wha can help."

"Help . . . help with what?" said Andrew.

"The laird . . . Ginny's father," replied Alastair.

"What about him?"

"I'm thinkin' he's in some kind o' trouble."

"Trouble—how do you mean?"

"There was two men here when we had oor Games—ye may hae seen 'em."

"I saw one fellow who looked out of place. Do you mean the man in the suit who came in the expensive car?"

"Ay, that's him. Actually there was twa o' them, though I didna see the man in the car weel enough. But they were back, Mr. Trentham—jist a few days ago. I heard them an' the laird togither. They was threatenin' Ginny's father gien I heard them aright."

"Where did you see them?"

"I had come oot of the Heather an' Stout an' was walkin' up the hill. I was gaein' t' the castle hopin' t' see Ginny, but I came o'er the hill instead o' by the road. They were standin' in front o' the castle, by that fancy car o' theirs. They didna see me, cause when I heard their loud voices, I stayed ahind the wall. They luiked like the kind o' men who would do maist anythin' to git what they wanted. They're after something o' the laird's, I ken it, though I'm no sure what."

"And you don't think he will give it to them?"

"They were offerin' him a heap o' siller, I ken that," said Alastair. "They were talkin' aboot thousands an' thousands o' pounds. But the laird can be a stubborn man, an' gien he gits it int' his head that they're up t' nae guid, he wouldna take their siller gien it were a million pounds—that's jist the kind o' man he is. That's all I heard. But I don't mind tellin' ye—I'm afeart fer the laird, an' fer what they might do t' him, an' his family as weel, gien they git too angered at him."

Andrew thought for a moment.

"I don't know what I can do, Mr. Farquharson," he said. "Especially from England—and I'll probably be heading back south tomorrow. The laird is apparently gone, and Ginny won't see me."

"She's aye a mite stubborn too," nodded Alastair. "I'm afeart the lass has got more o' her father's Highland blood in her than is guid fer her."

Andrew took out his wallet and handed Farquharson a card.

"This is my private card," he said. "It has all my telephone numbers, including my mobile phone. If these men return, or if you see anything you think is suspicious, I'd appreciate it if you would ring me."

Alastair nodded.

"Do not hesitate," insisted Andrew. "Do you understand? I don't mind your calling. Day or night."

Alastair nodded again. "I'll du it. Ye can count on it."

He rose and again offered his hand.

"Thank ye, Mr. Trentham," he said, nearly crushing Andrew's fingers in his gigantic palm. "I kenned I cud trust ye. Thank ye."

⌘   E L E V E N   ⌘

It was too late in the day to start for Cumbria.

Andrew went out again, this time to the Heather and the Stout. Though none of the patrons were particularly friendly, he managed to enjoy a tasty pub meal of beef pie and fried potatoes.

That evening he spent in his room. As much as possible, he tried to put the events of the afternoon out of his mind so that he might engross himself in eleventh-century Scotland, reading about the changes that had come to the isle of Britain with the Norman invasion.

––––––––

Even as Andrew sat reading about Scotland's famous Queen Margaret—and as Leigh Ginevra Gordon stewed about her room a mile away trying to convince herself to walk down to the village and see him—Paddy Rawlings sat before the computer in her London flat, wading through more Internet files than she could keep straight in her mind. Her friend Bert had given her enough leads and pointed her in so many new directions that she almost felt she was starting over.

"Okay," she said to herself, "half the solving of any crime is establishing links, even if on the surface they don't seem to mean anything. So what were they both doing in Liverpool in 1967, two years before the foundation of World Resources, Ltd.?"

She clicked back to the file she had put together, with Bert Fenton's help, on Eagon Hamilton, then perused the screen, continuing to think aloud.

"Born Ireland, Queens University Belfast, various student organizations . . ."

She read through the list again.

". . . came to Liverpool summer of 1964 . . . returned to Belfast, graduated Queens 1965. No apparent IRA links. Returned to England after graduation. Took up residence in Liverpool . . . elected to Commons at age 31, in 1975 . . . rose in prominence . . . leader of Liberal Democratic Party at time of death . . ."

She sat back, shaking her head. If something was there, she wasn't seeing it.

"All right, Bert, let's see if I can do what you taught me . . . let's look into the backgrounds of some of the other principle players. We'll start with our old friend Larne Reardon and see where it leads us . . ."

An hour later Paddy had two detailed newly created personnel files printing out and had now begun to gather information for a third. Fenton had taught her well. She was beginning to move through the Internet like a pro.

"What's this?" she suddenly exclaimed. "Born . . . *Glasgow!*" She would never have expected that. "So the loyal Thatcherite was a Scot. But that didn't necessarily make him a closet nationalist," she said to herself. "Especially in that nothing during his entire political life has given any hint in such a direction . . . but still, it's an intriguing fact."

She waited as more information came up.

"Moved to England with mother at age three . . . educated University of Manchester—"

Suddenly Paddy's eyes lit up.

"What?" she said. "Is that the same . . ."

She turned to grab the printouts recently completed on Hamilton and Reardon and compared them with what she was looking at on her screen. Suddenly she realized she had a lot more research to do, perhaps a trip to the London Library . . . and another Internet session with Bert!

She was getting close to what Andrew had asked for—a solid connection between the two men and World Resources, Ltd.

She couldn't stop now!

⁂   T W E L V E   ⁂

The following morning about ten-thirty, a diminutive young woman known to everyone for miles walked with determined stride down the hill from the imposing stone edifice of her home, red hair bouncing in the sunlight, toward the village of Ballochallater. Her two companions, the terriers Faing and Fyfe, took frequent detours to investigate interesting smells, but she marched straight to *Craigfoodie*, Mrs. Stirrat's bed-and-breakfast, still not sure what she intended to do when she actually got there.

Whether she would yell at him and call him a liar or apologize for her rudeness the day before at not seeing him—neither possibility had exactly focused itself in her brain. She only knew she had to do something.

"Guid day to ye, Mistress Stirrat," she said when the proprietress opened the door. "I'm here t' see one o' yer guests."

"If ye're meanin' the Englishman, lassie," replied the rotund woman, "ye're twa hoors late. He's gane back t' England."

Ginny stood staring, her face growing as red as the top of her head.

"And why'd ye let 'im go then?" she cried. "Didna ye ken I wanted t' talk t' him!"

She turned and stormed away, wiping at her eyes as she went, angrier now with Andrew than she had been before.

Not imagining for a moment that he was the object of a new round of consternation in the north, this time for his absence rather than his presence, Andrew drove the now-familiar route across southern Scotland and arrived back in Cumbria around noon.

He remained at Derwenthwaite for several days, visited Duncan Mac-Ranald once more, then continued south to London. By now the autumn was well advanced, and though the opening of Parliament was still several weeks away, he could no longer put off important planning for the new session and the press of his duties as leader of the Liberal Democratic Party.

On the final leg of his trip, Andrew's mobile phone rang.

"Andrew . . . Paddy—where are you?"

"On the M1 between Nottingham and Leicester."

"Hold on to your hat—when can you get here?"

"To your place—three hours, maybe four depending on London traffic. What's up?"

"I may have the connection we've been looking for—predating the current political lineup that's had us so bewildered. If you look at it only with today's political eyes, it all seems backward, like we said. But if you go back thirty-five years—it all makes sense. . . ."

"I think I'm going to have to see this in person," he told her. "I'll be there as soon as I can!"

Planning to stop briefly by his office on his way to Paddy's, Andrew drove along the Millbank, where he spotted a dark maroon automobile ahead of him. It pulled into the gated entrance to the Palace of Westminster. For a moment Andrew thought of following it, but decided to continue on. As he drove past toward the Norman Shaw building, however, he looked to his right as the gates began to close. From a quick glance he couldn't make out whether it was a BMW or not, but the similarity to the vehicle he had seen in Scotland was striking.

Three hours and forty minutes after her call, Paddy excitedly met Andrew at her door. They went straight to her computer desk, where Paddy had printouts of the three personnel files she had prepared spread in readiness.

"Look," she said, pointing to each in turn. "All three were members of the same organization at university—S.E.E.D."

"What in the world—"

"The Society to End English Domination of the UK. Ever heard of it?"

"No, I haven't," replied Andrew, smiling. "Sounds like some daft student group. What's it all about?"

"I did some more digging," said Paddy. "It was a left-wing group popular in the sixties, now defunct. It was tied in with some of the African nationalistic movements, especially in Rhodesia—very anti-British."

"How active was it in the UK?"

"Scattered university campuses. Not particularly influential."

"Considering devolution, maybe they were just ahead of their time."

"They tried to generate the same kind of interest in autonomy for Wales, Northern Ireland, and Scotland," Paddy went on, "as was stirring in Africa at that time. If Tanganyika, Kenya, and Rhodesia could throw off English rule, why not Wales and Scotland? That was their basic philosophy anyway, simplistic as it sounds. But it wasn't a movement that gained much traction in the UK. But here's the interesting thing—they advocated violence to a certain degree, and the theft of artifacts as necessary symbolic acts to secure the statehood they sought."

Andrew let out a low whistle. "What about our three men?" he asked.

"Well, Reardon wasn't involved at first. As you can see, his university years don't jibe with the others. He came into it later. But these two—"

Paddy picked up the two printouts for emphasis.

"—both attended a conference of the group in '67, in Liverpool no less. As far as I can tell, that was their first meeting. And—get this!—they stayed on for a few days afterward together . . . apparently talking plans and strategies for their mutual goals of seeing Northern Ireland and Scotland, in particular, and Wales to a lesser degree, become free and sovereign nations again."

"Wow, Paddy—dynamite work!"

"They met on and off several times. Then, just two years later, World Resources, Ltd., came into being, with its oil interests in the North Sea."

"You obviously think all this has continued on until today. So what is your conjecture about their motives now?"

"This is where I really start guessing," admitted Paddy. "But I think there's a certain logic to my progression, so just bear with me . . . now, Scotland has one of the world's newest parliaments, and Scotland is being given VIP treatment as a result. So if, as the SNP hopes, Scotland eventually achieves national sovereignty, then entry into the EU could follow, which would mean greatly increased status for Scotland on the world stage. That status would be all the greater if Scotland controls a major portion of European oil reserves—and given the oil fields in the north, that certainly appears likely. So whoever controls Scotland would have genuinely serious clout, might even be a bigger player in the EU than the British prime minister."

She pointed to the third printout she had prepared. "And that is how I think our friend here decided to play his cards. He hopes to become one of the most powerful men in Europe—first through oil, then through Scottish statehood."

"You obviously think he planned to leave Parliament in London eventually?"

"I think he would make a break at some point, going back to the land of his birth in hopes of becoming Scotland's first prime minister when and if that day comes."

Andrew shook his head, trying to take it all in.

"Your scenario is pretty out there, Paddy," he said, "but . . ."

His voice trailed off.

"Guesswork, like I said," added Paddy. "But it seems to make sense—that is, if all the pieces of his scheme fell together."

"And Hamilton?" said Andrew.

"Again, I'm only guessing . . . but I wonder if the recent changes in Scotland threw some kind of glitch into what they had been planning. Who knows, maybe the Stone theft isn't connected—but if it is, there might have been a falling out over that. Or over something we don't know about yet . . . something Hamilton got cold feet about going through with . . . or even some kind of a love triangle."

Immediately Andrew thought of Blair, alias Fiona. With her lively gold hair and elegant smile, she was certainly capable of turning any man's head. He ought to know!

"And by *falling out*," continued Andrew, "you are hinting at a possible motive for murder?"

"I suppose that's what it boils down to," nodded Paddy.

"In any event, you've uncovered enough that it's about time to see Inspector Shepley again," said Andrew. "Whether it means anything or not, these links are too strong to ignore."

"Give me one more day," said Paddy, "to see if I can learn anything more."

"All right. One more day. But then I'm going to Shepley."

※   T H I R T E E N   ※

Two mornings later, about nine-thirty, the telephone rang in Andrew's flat.

"Mr. Trentham, it's Alastair Farquharson," began the voice Andrew recognized immediately. "I wasna certain which number t' ring ye at . . ."

"You guessed right, Mr. Farquharson," he said. "You caught me just as I was heading out the door. Is something up?"

"Do ye mind the danger I told ye aboot?"

"Of course."

"I'm no sure, Mr. Trentham, but Ginny an' her father was jist by my blacksmith's shop not ten minutes ago t' tell me they were leavin' fer the Shetlands."

"The Shetlands!" exclaimed Andrew. "Why?"

"The laird said a solicitor rang frae Aberdeen sayin' he needed him t' sign some papers aboot his land—that some kind o' what he called on-site inspection was required afore signin'. It sounded a mite oot o' the ordinary t' me."

"Yes, hmm . . . I see what you mean," said Andrew seriously. "I can understand your concern. But I'm not sure I understand why Miss Gordon went with him."

"They said the solicitor said that gien the land came t' Ginny in time— an' it would when the laird died—then she'd hae t' inspect it eventually, so she might jist as well du it noo so he wouldna hae t' trouble her again."

"Hmm . . . I suppose that makes some sense."

"But, Mr. Trentham," Alastair went on, "what made me run straight doon t' the telephone at the post t' ring ye, was that jist as they left Ballochallater in the laird's wee Vauxhall, I saw that same dark car comin' along the road, then followin' them north on the A93, but keepin' a ways back so it wouldna be seen."

"The BMW!"

"Cudna say fer certain, Mr. Trentham. But its back windows were the kind ye canna see through. I'm thinkin' it's nae good, Mr. Trentham."

Andrew thought a moment.

"Is Mrs. Gordon still at home?" he asked.

"Ay."

"Get what you can from her about the exact location of the property. Ring me back on my mobile telephone—do you still have my card?"

"Ay."

"Good—call me. Meanwhile, I'm on my way to Scotland Yard."

※   F O U R T E E N   ※

Andrew Trentham walked into Scotland Yard and proceeded straight to Inspector Shepley's office. The inspector glanced up from his desk and knew instantly from the expression on the MP's face that something was up.

"Trentham," he said with a nod.

"I may have the missing link," said Andrew. "The name behind the whole thing—the one that ties the loose ends of this case together."

"Let's have it," said Shepley eagerly.

"You won't believe it when I tell you."

"Try me," said Shepley.

"I can't even bring myself to say it aloud," said Andrew.

He took a slip of paper from the inspector's desk and wrote down two words. He handed it across to the inspector.

"You have to be joking!" exclaimed Shepley as he looked at it. "Do you have facts?"

"I admit it's mostly conjecture," said Andrew. "But when you put every-thing together, there are just a few too many coincidences."

Andrew now pulled from his vest pocket the printout Paddy had prepared listing the connections. He unfolded it and handed it across the desk to Shep-ley, who perused it seriously.

"All right," said Shepley, "you have my attention. But if I make a move and we're wrong about this, it could cost me my job."

"And mine," added Andrew seriously.

A brief silence fell as they pondered the implications, not only for them-selves but for the country.

"There are two facts I would like you to look into that will confirm to me that we're on the right track," said Andrew at length. "One, the current stock holdings of World Resources, Ltd. We hadn't gotten that far yet with our Internet search."

"All right," said Shepley, making notes as Andrew spoke. "And the sec-ond?"

"I would like to know what kind of automobile the Right Honorable Gentleman drives."

"That one's easy," answered Shepley. "It's the envy of everyone around here who pulls parliamentary duty—a splendid custom BMW."

"And the color?" asked Andrew.

"A specially mixed very dark maroon."

"That's what I was afraid of," said Andrew. "In that case, Inspector, I think you had better find out where my Right Honorable Colleague is at this minute."

Shepley picked up his telephone and made the call. Andrew waited, listen-ing.

"And when was that?" asked the inspector after a few questions had gone back and forth. He listened briefly.

"Right . . . I see . . . thank you very much."

He put down the receiver and glanced up at Andrew.

"According to his office," he said, "it seems our friend left London late yesterday afternoon."

"Did they say where he was going?"

"They didn't know for certain, said he was a little vague . . . but some-where in the north."

Andrew rose. "Inspector," he said, "how fast can you get us on a plane to the Shetlands?"

"The Shetlands?"

"I think that's where we'll find the answers to this whole thing . . . that is, if we're not too late."

⁂   F I F T E E N   ⁂

As their plane for Lerwick rose in the sky, Andrew sat back and tried to relax.

His mind filled with images of Ginny, just as it had been filled for weeks now in unguarded moments. Ginny racing past him on her horse, her bright hair a flag in the wind. Ginny bouncing lightly across the heath with her little dogs at her heels. Ginny businesslike in her white veterinary smock or her grungy work clothes, yet managing somehow to look like a little girl dressed up in a doctor's costume.

He smiled without even knowing it, then frowned as he imagined what might be happening to her. Whatever danger she and her father were in, he couldn't prevent the nagging idea that it might have been avoided if he had handled things differently.

But what was done was done. They had to do what they could now to help. He just hoped they were in time.

Behind him in the plane sat half a dozen agents from Scotland Yard, as well as Inspector Shepley.

Whatever was going on up there in the Shetlands, there was nothing he could do to help now. All he could do was wait—and worry—until they arrived.

Thoughts of Ginny brought with them remembrance of the eleventh-century Scottish King named Malcolm, whose impetuous Celtic nature seemed as fiery as Ginny's, though not nearly so beguiling.

He pulled out the book he had brought with him. Maybe reading would help him get his mind off the danger Ginny and her father might be in. He had put off finishing the story ever since the evening at *Craigfoodie* in Ballochallater. Since then, he hadn't felt the right mood come over him to get back into it.

But now he had two hours before they landed. With Ginny on his mind, perhaps this was the perfect time.

7

ROMANCE THAT CHANGED A NATION

A.D. 1068

※ O N E ※

It was a bright sunny day of early summer. The sky shone radiant blue, reflecting off the deep blue-green waters of the sea. For farmers, fishermen, and soldiers alike, the air seemed alive with promise. Even King Malcolm III of Scotland, descendent of Kenneth MacAlpin and known as the Great Head, or *Canmore*, in significance of the extent of his reign, felt similar stirrings in his blood. And with them came an eagerness to do what he loved best—fight and conquer.

He had no inkling that the news brought by the messenger that bright morning in 1068 would indeed lead to conquest, but of a very different kind than he could have expected.

"My lord."

The King's attendant waited.

"My lord," he repeated, "there is word from the coast."

The King stirred, then suddenly came awake, his eyes for a moment wild and threatening.

As accustomed as he was to the King's behavior, the attendant unconsciously took a step back out of his master's reach. He had never personally been struck, though he was only too well aware of the sudden and occasionally violent moves of the King.

"Yes, what is it?" grumbled the King, "—what is the report?"

"A vessel appears to be entering the firth from the sea, my lord," answered the man.

"What are its colors?"

"English. And it draws near, my lord."

"Near—how near?"

"It has cleared Fife Ness and now seems making for our own harbor."

"And what—" began the King, then paused. He was on his feet now and fully alert, buckling on his sword as he spoke. "Better yet," he added, "—bring the scout to me. I will hear the report from his own lips."

The attendant disappeared, returning some three minutes later with the rider, who still had the dust of travel and the smell of horseflesh about his person from his ride to Dunfermline Castle from the lookout at Elie. The King was pacing his quarters when the man arrived.

"Give me your report," he demanded. "How many vessels—does it look to be an invasion force?"

"No, my lord. It is but a single ship."

The King took the information in with puzzled interest. "Keep me informed. I want to know the instant they put in."

Messenger and attendant left the King alone. What could it mean? Malcolm asked himself. He was expecting no one.

The word he awaited came to the castle an hour and a half later. The ship had continued its course up the narrowing firth into the river, the King was told, and had just weighed anchor in the protected bay to the south.

"Give me information that is useful," shot back the King. "How many boats did they unload? What is the disposition of their men? Do they bring horses ashore as well?"

"From what can be seen, the travelers appear well-to-do but are not protected," replied the rider. "No armed force is visible. One horse only was observed on deck, and two boats were let over the side, my lord."

"Are the travelers armed? Do they appear intent upon battle?"

"They are just now putting ashore and are certainly unprepared for an attack. They appear weary and worn. That they are from Wessex is likely, my lord."

"Are they preparing to march upon the castle?" asked the King, still bewildered.

"It is doubtful, my lord. They move slowly—there are women among them."

Malcolm's face momentarily showed a thoughtful expression, then broke into a smile.

"Saddle my roan!" barked the Scottish King, "and gather my band.

We will see what ransom we may collect . . . and *then* we will hear what these seek who sojourn to our land."

⧉ T W O ⧉

The land of France, far across the waters to the south, was just as distant from the King's mind that sunny summer morning as the land of Wessex, from which his visitors fared. Certainly he had no fear of invaders from the south. After all, if the mighty Roman Empire had been unable to subdue Caledonia in years past, surely the French had even less hope of accomplishing such a feat.

And so Malcolm had not been anxious when forces from the Norman region of France had breached the English Channel two years before and taken over the English throne. How could the landing on the south coast of England of a Norman nobleman—even a cousin to the former English King who considered himself entitled to the throne—in any way affect the secluded, mountainous land north of Hadrian's Wall?

But when William the Conqueror breached the Channel in 1066, the ancient Celtic kingdom now called Scotland, along with the rest of Britain, was destined never to be the same.

In the eleventh century, rule was achieved and maintained by force, not law. He with the strongest army reigned. Most thrones of Europe were transferred by murder, not peaceful succession. The ideas of constitution, law, and the orderly flow of power from generation to generation were notions that still lay in the distant future for civilized societies. In those days, only might insured rule.

Alfred the Great of Wessex had held the south of Anglo-Saxon England under his sway from 871 until 900 because he was the mightiest man of his time. But by 975, under increasingly less powerful successors, the kingdom he forged had grown weak and vulnerable to invasion.

Meanwhile, both in the north of England and on the Continent, a new people of mingled native and Viking stock were flexing their collective muscle. The Scandinavians were the strongest and most energetic race of peoples in Europe at the end of the first millennium A.D. As the Vikings had conquered and pillaged a century and two centuries before, their descendents had continued to subdue native peoples wherever they went.

England had fallen under the rule of Danish kings in the early years of the new millennium. And in France the Norman (or *Northman*) state had been founded by Danes and Norwegians who intermingled with the native French.

But whereas ultimately England, though still weak, had managed to throw off the Danish yoke, the Norse influence on the Continent had grown stronger and stronger, and Normandy had grown into a powerful, highly organized, and efficient feudal* state under a single strong ruler. By early in the eleventh century, in the face of England's growing disarray, expansion of the Norman juggernaut was all but inevitable.

The English crown passed in 1042 to Edward the Confessor. Having spent more than half his life in France with his Norman mother, in customs and tastes Edward was more Norman than English, and he brought many Normans with him to London to serve in his court and in the church. Thus the invasion of Britain by their racial cousins of Normandy had begun long before the later military conquest.

The fact that Edward had no children insured that a dispute over his throne would one day be inevitable. In 1054, he decided to make his nephew and the former King Edmund II's son, also named Edward but called the Ætheling* his heir. This Edward was at the time living in Hungary with his wife, Agatha, daughter of the Hungarian king and niece of the German emperor. Upon the announcement of the Confessor's choice, the Ætheling and his Hungarian family—son Edgar and daughters Margaret and Christine—left Hungary for England in order that Edward might assume the throne upon the Confessor's death.

Edward the Ætheling, however, died prematurely three years later. Rather than return to the Continent, now that they were comfortably established, his widow Agatha and her three children remained in England.

There now remained two potential successors to the Confessor's throne: Harold, earl of Wessex, the Confessor's brother-in-law, and Princess Agatha's son Edgar, now called the Ætheling in his father's place. On his deathbed in January of 1066, Edward named Harold his successor. Harold therefore became King of England, with Edgar designated as the probable next in line to succeed him.

There was, however, a third claimant to the English throne: William,

---

* *Feud*—land or property held from a lord in exchange for service or fee rendered.
* *Ætheling*—of royal blood, of noble stock, indicating a potential heir to the throne.

duke of Normandy, the Confessor's cousin. The duke considered his ties of blood closer than either of the other two, especially closer than Harold's, who was not linked to the royal house by blood at all, but only by marriage. William of Normandy, therefore, immediately began preparing for an invasion to take the throne he felt rightfully belonged to him. He landed on the southern coast of England eight months later.

The dispute over succession to the English crown was settled swiftly. The new King Harold, even with superior forces, was no match for the organization and generalship of the duke of Normandy. The fighting was over in a day.

By the time word of the invasion battle reached London, the message was stark and unmistakable: King Harold II, along with much of the English nobility, lay dead on a low ridge north of Hastings. William, duke of Normandy, had become William the Conqueror of England.

The news was especially significant for one particular family. Agatha knew immediately that her son must flee England. Otherwise Edgar the Ætheling, grandson of Edmund II, descendent of Alfred the Great, and the nearest English claimant to Harold's throne, would surely fall by the Conqueror's hand.

Her fears were well founded. Immediately William began consolidating his rule according to the law of the time—the sword. He ruthlessly harried the south of the island, subduing England's aristocracy with violence and an iron will and installing his fellow Normans in positions of leadership. All property was confiscated and became the King's. William then redistributed the land in tenancy to his friends and loyal supporters to manage on his behalf. Much of Normandy had already been effectively subjugated according to this feudal system of land management, and now William quickly began to institute the same system throughout England.

William was especially determined to leave no vestige of the former English royalty, no rival claimant to the throne. He would root out all other scions of the royal bloodline that had ruled Wessex, Essex, Sussex, and Kent for two centuries.

In 1068, therefore, two years after William I's landing, the dispossessed royal family of Edgar the Ætheling, half English, half Hungarian, sailed for the Continent, bound once again for Agatha's native land and the birthplace of her children.

In Hungary they would find refuge from the Conqueror.

⁂ T H R E E ⁂

Twenty minutes after receiving word of the strange ship that had dared anchor in his waters, King Malcolm of Scotland rode south out of Dunfermline with his men.

They were a wild band, well accustomed to raiding and pillaging, resembling more a band of Vikings—the warring stock whose blood had been infused into their veins in the past two centuries—than a King's regiment. It had been months since Malcolm had raided in the southland. He was agitated and eager for action. His weapon had remained sheathed too long. His hand itched for adventure.

They did not have far to ride. The wide waters of the Firth of Forth were but three and a half miles distant from Malcolm's castle. As they rode, however, the Scots King's enthusiasm for plunder cooled. Upon reflection, he half suspected who might be aboard the vessel.

They reached the overlook from which the narrowing waters of the sea and the expanding waters of the Great River were visible. There below, in the protected bay, sat a ship at anchor, exactly as reported.

The colors of Wessex flew from its mast, though the flag as well as most of the sails, was in tatters. There had been violent winds the past week, and the ship had obviously been caught in some weather.

The King urged his horse again into a canter. His men followed down the incline toward the river. A few minutes later, at sight of a single horseman, he drew up and waited. Malcolm knew well enough by now that no threat was intended by this landing—and little plunder was to be had. At first glance toward the man, his suspicions were confirmed.

Malcolm sat on his roan and waited. This was his land. He would let the newcomer draw near.

"I come in peace," said the lone rider as he approached, then stopped in front of the King, "—seeking the refuge of your court."

"Who are you?" asked the King of the Scots. He knew well enough who the fellow was, but he would prepare him to do homage by pretending ignorance and forcing him to identify himself. He had not seen the man for years. At last meeting they were both scarcely out of their teens, but Malcolm recognized him instantly.

"I am Edgar, of the royal house of Wessex," replied the visitor, keeping up the formality, "from the house of King Alfred, called the Great."

Malcolm nodded with apparent disinterest. In truth, Edgar was smaller than he remembered, and with a higher-pitched voice. He had not come into manhood, he thought with satisfaction, with altogether the same vigor and brawn as had he himself.

"Our land has been overrun by Normans," Edgar went on. "Our lives are in danger."

Malcolm was well enough aware of what was going on in England. He had had dealings with the duke of Normandy already.

"We were bound for the Continent," the English heir went, "but the summer storms have thrown us off course. We had little choice but to put in. Our vessel is unable to continue."

There came a momentary pause.

"Surely you cannot have forgotten me, Malcolm," said Edgar, with a hint of exasperation at the King's disinterest and apparent nonrecognition. "We rode and hunted together. Why do you say nothing and look at me so?"

Malcolm nodded, as if begrudgingly indicating his remembrance of their youthful affiliation.

Edgar sighed in frustration.

"We throw ourselves on your mercy," he said with sarcasm, "O great and mighty King Malcolm, lord and sovereign of Scotland and all the realms of the north."

"You have entered unbidden into my lands," said Malcolm. "Give me reason why I should not kill you all and take your horses and your goods for myself."

"Come, Malcolm!" replied Edgar now in open frustration and annoyance. "How long will you play this game? *Why should you not kill us!*" he repeated in disbelief. "Because we are your friends! You were sent to the court in London for refuge yourself. You received every consideration. I seek only the same." He gestured behind him toward the firth. "See, my mother is rowing toward the shore even as we speak. What shall I tell her—that you *refuse* the lady, the princess of Hungary and Germany and England, who loved you as if you were her own son?"

If Malcolm was shocked by the outburst of his companion of many years earlier or the overstatement regarding the affections of Edgar's mother, his countenance did not reveal it. Most of his band, however, expected any second to see the great sword at his side drawn in a rapid stroke and plunged with powerful blow straight through the puny Englishman's chest. None of them would *dare* address the King in such a manner! King Malcolm's temper was legendary. He had killed Macbeth, his own father's murderer, to gain the throne eleven years before, and he had been burning and plundering Northumbria without regard for life or property ever since. Surely he would now dispatch this unassuming ingrate, and then follow with an order for them to kill every man, woman, or child on board the vessel.

A long and tense silence followed.

Still without revealing more than a gruff and slightly irritated nonchalance at the whole affair, the King suddenly urged his horse forward and galloped toward the river where the small boat which had brought the Ætheling and his horse to land had now been joined by a second at the shore.

Malcolm's rough band of men followed, leaving the vexed Englishman to eat a cloud of dust, then turn his own mount and do his best to catch up.

▨ F O U R ▨

The distance to the water was not great. But in the ten or twenty seconds following the interview, Malcolm's mind relived his thirteen years in England—the memories stirred by Edgar's unexpected appearance. He had been sent south at the tender age of ten to protect him from Macbeth, his own father's rival, and returned north in the year 1055, at age twenty-four, to set about regaining his father's throne.

About those formative years, most of what Edgar said was true—Malcolm had learned to fight in England, to wield a sword with deadly skill, to ride any horse, to outrun any challenger on either his own two feet or the four flying hooves of mare or stallion. His association with Edgar's family had not been a long one, however. Malcolm was already grown and raising an army in preparation for his return to Scotland by the time Edgar and his family arrived from Hungary. In that year, however, they hit it off reasonably well. He almost talked Edgar into joining his cause. And for a time, the two heirs to the Scottish and English thrones had indeed ridden and romped throughout Wessex and Kent together.

One thing he had *not* learned to do any better in England than he had in Scotland was to read, despite the most persistent efforts of Edgar's mother to teach him. Malcolm smiled to himself at thought of the princess Agatha's frustration over his overgrown boorishness and his disinterest in her attempted lessons.

"Malcolm," she had upbraided him more than once, "if you plan to be the King of a nation, in these modern times when scholarship and education are necessary for those who would lead their people, you *must* know how to read and write!"

The Hungarian princess had done her best to refine his rough and backward ways, but he had frustrated her at every turn. He was always more interested in conquest than study. At any rate, the tutoring was sporadic, for Agatha had two young daughters to care for. Reminded now of Agatha's family, he wondered briefly if the two little girls were on board with her.

Within a year after her arrival in England, Malcolm had left for Scotland to seize his father's throne. He had gone south as a brash and cocky boy and had returned as a huge, hulking, and confident young man ready to kill for his right to rule Scotland. He had grown to manhood in England. He would never forget those years.

When Edgar arrived in Wessex, talk immediately began to circulate that these were the two young men who would one day rule the northern and southern realms of Britain. But fate had not treated Princess Agatha's family kindly. Her husband was dead, and now her son had been deprived of the English crown by a Norman. Malcolm had his throne, while Edgar's chances of gaining his seemed slim.

If the truth were known, in spite of the bluster Malcolm tried to show as a twenty-three-year-old, the thought of seeing Edgar's mother intimidated him. The fact that she was multilingual, refined, a princess of three dynasties, and spoke with a Hungarian accent all produced an air of mystery in the young man's eyes. When she spoke, he felt the combined royal houses of the world commanding the obedience of all who heard her voice. In Agatha, princess of Hungary, was personified the ancient, dynastic power of the Continent . . . and the mysterious east.

The Scottish King reined in his roan at water's edge. His reminiscences immediately vanished. The band of horsemen slowed behind him in a flurry of dust and hooves.

Edgar's boat was held by his groom. The second floated at the shoreline, four sailors holding the ends of their slack oars and three ladies sitting inside, impatient to set their feet on solid land. A burly-looking fellow stood, then jumped ashore, holding the bow of the small boat with a thick line of hemp rope.

The lead horseman glanced briefly over the party of newcomers, and an awkward silence followed. He instantly recognized the aging Hungarian princess. The years had done nothing to diminish her elegant stature, the air of royalty emanating from her presence. The look on her face, as she gazed toward him, was at first warm but quickly gave way to impatience and displeasure.

"How long will you force us to sit here waiting, Malcolm?" she said in an exasperated tone. "Dismount that horse and help my daughters and me ashore!"

Again Malcolm's men sat in stunned silence to hear the rude familiarity with which these people spoke to their King. Did they not know that one look of command from his eye could mean instant death? How long would he endure such debasing treatment, allowing himself to be ordered about—by a woman?

Only a moment did the silence last. At the sound of her voice, the great brute of a Scottish King was an awestruck young man again, and she was the princess from the great east who commanded obedience.

Like a compliant child, the King dismounted, handed his reins to one of his attendants, and approached the boat, to the astonishment of his men. He splashed into the water to knee depth, then gently offered his hand.

In the small boat, the three women stood. He did not recognize the other two.

Demurely the one nearest took his hand, then glanced into his face.

"Malcolm," said Princess Agatha behind him, "you remember my daughter, Margaret."

The light, white hand touched his huge, dirty rough fingers. A tingle of current surged through Malcolm's arm. He took the soft tiny thing, then his great palm closed gently around it. Now the huge man let his gaze wander up the arm attached to the hand.

He beheld a face staring down into his with a look of innocence such as he had never seen. His whole kingly being was instantly swallowed into it.

The two pale eyes, dark-lashed and slightly narrow, held him in a spell that caused time and surroundings to evaporate. He knew only that face, and the haunting eyes and delicate mouth which gave it life. His earlier, ill-fated marriage to the Norwegian Ingibjorg, now dead, had not once caused such feelings to swell inside him. His heart began to pound wildly. He feared his men would hear it and know how this creature had undone him.

In the second or two of that touch and the glance of those eyes, Malcolm Canmore, King of Scotland, was smitten more deeply than had a sword been run through his heart.

He pulled the dainty thing gently toward him. With childlike trust she yielded to his touch. He let go the wondrous hand, placed his two giant paws on either side of her waist, while she rested a steadying hand upon his shoulder—ah, what delight the feathery touch!—and with a single motion pulled her over the edge of the boat and through the air, landing her lightly on the bank.

A smile now broke from the heavenly lips.

"Thank you, Malcolm," uttered a light, sweet voice.

In three words, and the trailing smile that remained, a kingdom was conquered.

🕸 F I V E 🕸

Agatha, princess of Hungary, found refuge in the castle of Dunfermline, but she also found the King of the Scots a more bestial man than the invading Conqueror she and her family had fled England to avoid.

Her memory of Malcolm was nothing like the reality of seeing him as a grown man in his own rustic surroundings. She had always known him as crass and uncouth, though she had not been able to resist the attempt to civilize him. Perhaps more English culture had rubbed off on him when he was in the south than she had realized at the time. If so, he had certainly regressed upon returning to *this* backward environment.

And the land of Scotland was indeed backward in her eyes, filthy and inhabited by barbarians and savages.

She was eager to continue the voyage to Hungary at the soonest possible opportunity!

That her eldest daughter—a gentle, refined, and devout young woman who was making preparations for a life of devotion to the church—actually found the heathen Celtic warrior interesting was beyond the powers of Agatha's comprehension. In her opinion Malcolm was nothing but a crude brute, every inch the giant hulking savage he looked.

But Margaret had always seen life in her own unique way. As a child, she was sensitive and compassionate—eager to rescue hungry sparrows, to see the beauty in mangy stray pups. As she grew, her reclamation projects extended to a variety of unfortunates—orphans, beggars, anyone in need who crossed her path. Even now, upon arriving in the north, she immediately set out finding people to help. Yet Agatha knew her gentle, loving daughter could be headstrong as well as compassionate, and she doubted there was much she could do to persuade Edgar's sister to see the vulgar Scottish King as he really was. She knew of his reputation after he had left the refinement of their court, that he had gone back to Scotland bent upon murdering Macbeth—and had done so. She would have no daughter of *hers* involved with such a man.

"It is obvious Malcolm is infatuated with her," remarked Agatha to her lady's maid one day, not especially because she trusted the woman as a confidante, but because she was simply unable to contain her frustration.

"Yes, my lady."

"Obvious, that is, to everyone but the girl herself!"

"Does my lady Margaret still plan to take the veil, my lady?" asked the maid.

"Yes, and becoming a nun will be our salvation from this Scottish King!" said Agatha. "At first I wondered at the decision. But now nothing could suit me better!"

A brief silence filled the room. The maid busied herself with the dress they were fitting.

"Margaret is so innocent," said Princess Agatha after a moment. "She doesn't even seem to notice how changed Malcolm becomes whenever she is around. The monster becomes a puppy dog—but he is still a monster. Is my own daughter so naive at twenty-two that she does not recognize what a churlish lout the fellow is?"

❇   S I X   ❇

Agatha and her family did not set out as soon as she would have liked for Hungary. Repairs to their vessel dragged on, and the delay increased. Within a year, Edgar was making plans for a return, not to Hungary at all, but to England.

William had encountered more resistance than anticipated, and Edgar was now involved in a planned rebellion against the Norman King. He was determined to return to Wessex and retake Alfred the Great's throne. Mother and sisters would accompany him. The repaired and re-outfitted ship was to sail with the morning's tide.

The spring evening was warm, though a chill approached. The King and the young woman who had been guest at Dunfermline for almost a year strolled alone out from the castle toward a favorite haunt, a small dense wood beside a rocky burn which flowed down into Loch Fitty. Margaret wore a long robe of white and purple—mostly silk, with brightly colored embroidery along the hem and sleeves—her long, wavy auburn hair spilling over her shoulders. Never, thought Malcolm, had he seen her more lovely. The King—bare-kneed, with red kilt and cape, green tunic partially covered with coat of mail, soft leather boots tied up over his calves, and wild beard—walked at her side. He looked a giant beside the lithe form of the English princess. He kept his huge hulking strides in check, as a powerful workhorse beside a newborn colt.

She carried a psalter. A massive sword hung at his side. The devout young woman and the warrior were as different as any two individuals could be. Yet as they went, it was the great hulking King who appeared tentative of step and timid of speech, while the graceful form beside him carried herself with poise, dignity, and self-assurance.

Reaching the burn, they took seats on two of the many large rocks which lay scattered about. The gnarled trunks of several massive old trees grew out of the ground behind them, reaching upward and overspreading the peaceful place with their hundred woody arms and fingers. The two sat quietly for a few minutes, listening to the gentle trickling of the water through its rocky course.

At last the King broke the silence. "Must you go tomorrow?" he said.

"You know Edgar sails at sunrise," replied Margaret.

"Yes, but . . . but must *you* accompany him?"

"He may be the King of England within a month. He must have his family near."

"If the rebellion is successful, you could join him later," persisted Malcolm. "I do not like to see you in danger. You could remain here, in safety, until—"

"Malcolm," laughed Margaret, "you know I cannot do that. Mother would not hear of it."

Malcolm sighed.

"Your mother is not fond of me," he said nodding. "But she hardly needs to protect you from me."

"She thinks it her duty."

"I weary of her watching my every move with a scowl."

"I know, Malcolm," smiled Margaret. "But she does think you rough."

"You are a grown woman and may come and go as you choose."

"She insists I sail with them. I must respect her wishes."

Another silence fell. Again it was the King who broke it.

"Do you?" he said.

"Do I what?"

"Do *you* think I'm too rough?" said Malcolm.

Margaret laughed the merriest laugh Malcolm had ever heard.

"Not to me," she replied. "Though sometimes, I must admit, I shudder a bit when you talk to your men."

He did not answer, nor did she seem to require it. After a moment, Margaret opened her book and read the first psalm aloud. Malcolm listened quietly, gazing down at the book as the melodious voice entered into one ear in harmonious accompaniment to the sounds of the stream in the other.

"I hoped you would stay," said Malcolm at length.

Margaret sighed. "I thought perhaps I might remain. There is so much to be done, and I will miss the children—did I tell you that three of them are already reading the psalm I just finished, in Latin?"

Malcolm nodded. Something other than orphans was on his mind.

"I have such hopes that they will all read soon—oh, I *will* miss them! Malcolm, you have not forgotten your promise that you will make sure someone looks after the French lessons?"

Again Malcolm nodded, which movement of the neck was accompanied by a few barely discernible grunts indicating the affirmative.

"Is . . . is that all you will miss?" he said tentatively.

"Oh no—it is so wonderful and peaceful here. I shall miss the country and the castle . . . everything."

"Is that all?"

"Of course I shall miss our rides together."

Malcolm nodded. "Nothing more?"

A brief awkward silence intervened. Suddenly Margaret realized his meaning. Her face reddened, and she glanced down shyly.

"Oh, Malcolm," she exclaimed after recovering herself, "you are as stray and forlorn as an orphan child!"

A great roar of laughter erupted from the mouth of the King of the Scots.

"Do not worry," said Margaret, joining him in laughter. "I shall be back. I shall *have* to return, to see to my children . . . and you among them!"

"I am glad to hear you say it! But I shall miss you every day you are away."

Again a silence fell. This time it lasted longer, and Malcolm feared he had offended her.

"You must not miss me *too* much, Malcolm," said Margaret at length.

"Why?"

"Because if you miss me too much," answered Margaret, "it will mean my mother is right, and then I shall have to stay away forever."

"But . . . but why?"

"Malcolm, do you not yet understand? My heart belongs to another— I have given myself to the church."

The silence which now followed was awkward. Soon they rose and returned to the castle. Had she been anyone else, the King would have been furious at having his wishes so thoroughly denied. But he could not be angry with Margaret. She was too good to be angry with.

By noon the next day, Dunfermline was empty and quiet. Its temporary English residents were already within sight of the Isle of May and making for the south ahead of the sea winds.

※   S E V E N   ※

No one had seen the King like this since Lady Margaret had arrived the previous summer.

Malcolm Canmore was his old self again—storming about in one rage after another. He was *worse* than his old self! The calm that had come over him from her presence was gone. The old fury of his tempestuous nature had returned in full force.

Malcolm knew well enough what everyone in his court said—that he was a crazed fool, whom a woman had turned into a docile child one minute and a maniac the next.

What did it matter what people said? He was beside himself—he knew it as well as they! Everything they said was true. She had undone him!

His marriage to Ingibjorg had been one of convenience and politics. He had never known what love could be until the moment Margaret placed her hand on his shoulder and allowed him to lift her lovely foot onto Scotland's soil.

Now she had sailed south . . . and was gone!

What if she does not return? Malcolm asked himself a dozen times a day. *What if they succeeded in ousting William the Conqueror? What if Edgar becomes King of England and his sister remains in the south?*

If that happened, Malcolm thought, he would have no alternative but to invade England and conquer the whole country for himself! If such measures were required to make her his Queen, he would do it!

The fact that she was still set upon becoming a nun . . . well, he would have to somehow talk her out of it. He would command her obedience! Who was *she* to refuse *him*?

He spun about and paced again across the large floor. What was he thinking? Compared to the rest of the world, Margaret was a saint. She was no woman *anyone* could command—not him, not her mother . . . no one but God.

She would never agree to marry him. Malcolm knew he could not force love from her heart. And he would not attempt it.

She was *Margaret.* She would be ruled by no man.

In the meantime, he could not remain cooped up in this castle pining away. He needed something to do!

At the same time, in England, Margaret, daughter of Agatha and princess of England, found her thoughts occupied with the north country she had left behind, especially the orphans, the children she was teaching to read, and the women of the court who knew so little of spiritual things. There was so much she had wanted to teach them while she was there. And the church in Scotland was so primitive and disorganized. Its abbots and bishops were a disgrace—their rituals imbued with pagan practices. If only there were some way she could help.

But besides all this, to Margaret's surprise, she found that whenever she recalled the wild but peaceful hills and moors of the north, images of King Malcolm also intruded into her thoughts. At first she merely wondered whether he would make good on his promise about the children and their studies. But gradually the memory of his face, his laughter, and his robust enthusiasm rose above thoughts of French lessons and Scottish bishops.

Back in Scotland, a large band of riders clattered off the barge which had taken them across the Forth from Dunfermline to the opposite shore. They rode through Dunedin, then galloped south toward Northumbria. They were led by a large man who bore himself with an aspect of command and authority, and whose only distraction in a time of lonely heartache was to turn his attention to plunder.

Every knight had a sword at his side, and in their eyes was not the look of peace.

EIGHT

The short-lived rebellion against William the Conqueror was quickly rebuffed. The throne of William 1 of Normandy was at last secure. The kings of Wessex would not lead England's future, but rather the dynasty from the Continent. Edgar the Ætheling would never become King.

Now again did the family of Agatha, princess of Hungary, set out for the north. This time, however, Scotland was their intended destination.

As they sailed, an uncharacteristic anxiety began to be visible in the older of Edgar's two sisters. None knew its cause. No one had observed her like this before. It might be seasickness, some thought, though the Channel was much calmer than before.

Her mother began to worry. She had an uncomfortable suspicion as to the cause of Margaret's peculiar moods of alternating gaiety and melancholy. But she held her peace and hoped she was wrong.

In her stateroom, Margaret stared out the small round window at the gray-green waters of the sea. She could barely make out the shoreline of Northumbria as they passed along. This would be their last night on board. Tomorrow they would reach Dunfermline!

Though she was doing her best to quell her rising anticipation, she still felt herself aquiver with it.

The stray puppy that had been hanging around the castle kitchen came unexpectedly to her mind. She had fed it scraps, and it had attached itself to her. Margaret wondered if it would remember her now. In her mind's eye she stooped down to pet its furry back, smiling as she envisioned the wet tongue licking her hand and the high-pitched yelp of greeting to an old friend.

Suddenly Malcolm's hairy face replaced the puppy in her vision. He was just like a stray dog too, she thought with a smile. She had even told him so. Would *he* be as happy to see her as the puppy?

Now that they were almost back she could admit it—*yes, she had missed him.* Maybe Malcolm needed her too, just like the puppy. How could she resist one who depended on her so? But there was her vocation to consider. Ever since childhood, she had known she was called to do the Lord's work. Could she give that up to follow the call of her own heart? Or was it possible that her call was simply changing—that she could live for Christ in a Scottish castle as well as in a nunnery?

Margaret slept fitfully that night.

Midway through the following morning, the splash of the anchor sounded overboard. Skiffs were lowered. Margaret scanned the shoreline as she waited. Neither man nor beast was in sight. Why had no party been sent to meet them?

When the rowers were in position, she and her mother and Edgar and Christine climbed down over the sides. They rowed to shore, waited for the horses to be unloaded, then rode inland to the castle.

Margaret urged her mount into a canter when they were half a mile away, reaching the castle before mother, sister, and brother. She jumped off her horse, quickly tethered it, and ran inside. The sound of her footsteps echoed softly on the floor with vacant lifelessness. It was obvious the castle was empty. One by one a few servants began to appear.

"Where ... where is Malcolm?" exclaimed Margaret, with hardly a greeting to the familiar faces.

"The King and his army are away, my lady," answered one of the men.

"How long?

"They have been gone a month."

"And due back?"

"No one knows when to expect them, my lady."

Margaret sighed, tried to manage a smile, then walked to the kitchen, continuing out the back door, glancing this way and that. There was no sign of the little dog. He would no longer be a puppy anyway, she thought with a disappointed smile.

She returned inside as her mother, sister, and brother were entering and greeting the servants. Margaret walked upstairs to her previous guest quarters, but stayed only a few minutes. She ate a silent meal with her family, the little group dwarfed by the all-but-empty great hall. In the afternoon, she went walking toward the village, but was in no mood to visit her children and friends. She could not shake off the doldrums. The rest of the afternoon and evening passed drearily.

The next day, shortly before noon, suddenly Margaret heard the thunder of many hooves approaching. She ran to her window.

The army had returned!

There was Malcolm riding at the head of it. How majestic he looked with his armor gleaming, his wild beard flying in the wind!

The next instant she was flying down the stairs. Then, trying to calm herself, she slowed to a swift walk. But her effort to retain her composure was altogether useless.

Malcolm burst through the tall oak doors of the castle as if he were a dozen men, making more noise than a legion, the scabbard of his sword clanging against the doorpost, his great boots echoing across the wood floor.

Margaret flew down the last of the stairs as he crossed the wide entryway. He galloped forward with great strides, face aglow.

"Margaret!" he exclaimed.

Without realizing what was happening, she found herself swept up and in his arms. She did not resist his embrace.

"Our scouts informed me of the arrival of your ship," he said. "We turned immediately for home."

"I am happy to see you again, Malcolm," she said softly, her heart beating a little too quickly. She could not have imagined how good it would feel to be swallowed up in such manly strength.

"Oh, Margaret—you cannot know—"

Heedless of Agatha's descending appearance now on the stairs, Malcolm's great fingers tenderly stroked Margaret's long hair as he spoke.

Sensing her mother's presence, Margaret came to herself. How could she have allowed this to happen? She tried to take a step back, but only felt the answering pressure of Malcolm's huge frame clutching her tightly.

"Margaret," he said, now whispering in her ear. "Please say you will marry me."

Margaret's face reddened. Her heart began to pound even more rapidly than before. The hot awareness of her mother's stormy approach mixed fear and confusion with what Malcolm had said.

What words had she just heard?

But Agatha now paused on the bottom step and came no farther, as if no longer daring interfere with her daughter's destiny.

Once more Margaret tried to step back. This time Malcolm yielded and gently released her. But he continued to gaze expectantly into her face for an answer to his question. Nervously Margaret glanced down. Now for the first time did she notice his appearance.

"What is that on your tunic?" she gasped.

"Oh," Malcolm fumbled, glancing down. "Only dirt and grime."

Margaret took another step back, now glancing up and down to behold more closely the dark red splotches covering him.

"Malcolm," said Margaret, her face suddenly ashen, "—it's . . . it is blood!"

The King did not reply. He was a soldier. What was the harm in a little—

"It is dried *blood*, Malcolm," repeated Margaret. "*Whose* blood is it?" Her face was suddenly full of a very different kind of passion than what he felt.

"I don't know—we were . . . we have been—"

"*Where* have you been? I must know!"

"We were in England."

"Doing *what*, Malcolm?"

"There are rebels—those who oppose my kingship. There are regions that are rightfully mine."

"Malcolm, that is England, not Scotland. You are not King there!"

"I have lands where I must maintain control of—"

"Oh, Malcolm—how could you!" Her voice was low but intense.

"I am King of this kingdom," he explained, his voice beginning to rise, "and there are times—"

"Oh, you wicked man," she murmured, appalled at the brutality now all too evident on every inch of him. "I cannot stand the sight of you!"

"But I just asked you to be my Queen."

"How can you even think I would marry a man who takes killing so lightly!"

Margaret spun around and ran across the floor, past her mother, who stood watching the explosion in mingled shock and delight, and up the stairs to her room.

His face red, he yet uttered not a word. The instant the echo of Margaret's steps were gone, Malcolm turned and strode from the castle in angry mortification.

Upstairs, Margaret threw herself on her bed and sobbed. A hundred emotions she had never felt surged through her. Nuns never encountered things like this!

At the stables, the King stormed about fuming and cursing.

"I was an idiot to love such a pious woman!" he cried. "I will send them all back to England the moment their ship is turned around! I should have known better!" he cried. "Me—love a nun! The thing is preposterous!"

Even as the words exploded from his lips, however, he knew that even if Margaret was the most unreasonable, religious, prudish woman he had ever known, he couldn't help loving her.

He continued to rant across the dirt floor, kicking wildly, sending tufts of straw flying about, grabbing tools and whips and hurling them across the floor. Aware of the storm with their master in its eye, the nervous horses moved uneasily in their stalls.

Yet . . . he couldn't help it, cried Malcolm as a shovel crashed against the wall opposite, its handle splintering—he *loved* her!

NINE

An hour later Margaret heard a tentative rapping on her door.

She continued lying on the bed, her face buried in two pillows. The knock sounded again. Still she did not respond.

She heard the door open.

"I . . . I came to apologize," she heard a voice behind her.

She turned and lifted her head.

There stood Malcolm, the most timid, sheepish, and irresistible expression spread across his face. He had changed his clothes and washed. No sword hung from his side.

"I am sorry you were offended," he said softly. "We Scots are not as refined as you English."

Margaret forced a smile.

"I am sorry for my outburst," she said, wiping at her tears. "I was confused. I know being King must be difficult, with rebels everywhere. I will try to understand."

Margaret rose from the bed and stood before him.

"Could we try again," said Malcolm, "and pretend I only just now rode in . . . wearing a clean tunic?"

Margaret smiled, then could not prevent a musical little laugh.

"I am willing," she said.

"Then I shall say it again—I missed you."

"I missed you too, Malcolm," she replied softly. "I am happy to be . . . back home."

His heart soared.

They gazed into one another's eyes a long moment. At length Malcolm opened his arms in invitation. Margaret approached, slowly reaching around the great waist with her arms as the huge embrace of the King closed gently around her.

This time she did not pull away.

King Malcolm III of Scotland and Margaret, princess of England, were married at Dunfermline Castle in 1070. The kingdom rejoiced. Already his subjects had grown to love the new Queen almost as much as her husband did.

⬚ T E N ⬚

As the peat-ambered burns of the Scottish mountains trickle and flow downward, their waters mix with that of lower rivers and eventually tumble into that great repository where all waters end. There the concentrated brown of the Highlands must yield up its individuality to the blues and greens of the sea.

So the Celtic blood of Pict and Scot merged in time with that of Angle and Saxon and Briton and Scandinavian—each contributing its rich and ancient hue to the amber stain of Caledonia's stream of descendnts. And with the passage of yet more generations, they would mingle as well with the Norman strain from the Continent. Thus were infused six founding, interrelated bloodlines to flow in the veins the people the world would come to know as Scots.

And as no stream or river can hold back the surging ocean's tide, neither can the hand of man hold back the flow of love. And it was the love of a man for a woman which eventually would allow the southern Norman sea to flood the Celtic rivers and peat streams of the north, known now only to the fading memories of its bards as *Caledonia*.

In the mid-eleventh century, most of Scotland spoke a mixture of Gaelic and ancient Pictish. Malcolm, however, brought the English tongue back with him from the south. Thus did the *language* of Scotland—that first and most vital cultural foundation stone—begin to shift. Margaret accelerated the cultural diluting of Caledonia's ancient waters by adding the Latin and French tongues to the Scots court.

And her influence was felt in many other areas as well. She influenced the land—as Jewish Esther of old, who, by marriage to the merciless Persian Xerxes, influenced the direction of *her* nation—because she won the favor of everyone who knew her.

How Margaret grew to love a ruthless man such as Malcolm was as great a mystery to many as it remained to her mother. Yet love him she did. And with Margaret Queen in Scotland, many English men and women, displaced by the Norman invasion, came north to settle in Lothian. Their presence gave English custom and taste a fertile environment in which to flourish.

If she was not exactly given Esther's gold scepter with which to execute her will, Margaret influenced the north country in subtler ways. Fine clothes and food were to her taste, along with ornate decorations and beautiful silks and tapestries. Fine French wines were substituted for Malcolm's strong ale. Balls, dancing, banqueting with English and French music, entertainment by the harp and the ballad—all these and much more took their place in her court. And it could not be denied that Malcolm, when he was not plundering England, encouraged the changes instituted by his wife and enjoyed their pleasures.

Religion no less than culture flourished during Margaret's reign. Though she had given up her dreams of a church vocation when she married Malcolm, she remained a woman of deep faith, and her personal piety could only influence the nation toward good.

In Margaret's view, the practices, customs, and piety of the Celtic priesthood had become so lax since Columba and Aiden's time as to border on infidelity. She therefore set out to reorganize and restructure the Scottish church and to restore the priesthood, scattered over the years, to the isle of Iona. She built a tiny chapel for herself high on the castle rock at Edinburgh and oversaw construction of a church at Dunfermline, later made into a Benedictine abbey by her son, David.

But Margaret's faith did not limit itself only to ecclesiastical reform and personal worship, it also extended itself in service. The poor were her special concern. Almost daily was she among them, ministering to those about her with no less dedication than if she had taken the vows of chastity instead of those of marriage.

Those who lived in the few hamlets and throughout the countryside within the environs of Dunfermline, poor though most were, were proud of their beautiful Queen and mighty King. He was fearsome to behold, it was true, rumored to possess a fierce temper. Yet one glance from the lady Margaret's face was enough to swallow any anxieties one might harbor concerning her husband. A smile from her lips could melt the countenance of the surliest grouch in the kingdom.

The people did not have to gaze upon the Queen from afar, for Margaret was in the habit of walking and riding among them nearly every day. She would sit on her favorite rock outside the castle, encouraging any who wished to visit with her. If no one came, she sat and peacefully read her Bible, always ready lest any shy man or woman might desire an audience but take longer to approach.

Whenever the royal entourage was seen leaving the castle, men, women, and children alike would pause in their work, hoping to catch a glimpse of the lovely young Queen from the south. She was ever ready with a kindly smile to cast abroad to any and all—be they King or beggar—and her subjects coveted the privilege of being the recipient of such a treasure. The Queen was so gentle and beautiful that it was all they could do not to stare when she chanced to pass by. If she rode near enough and an onlooker had the good fortune to catch her eye, even briefly, it was a moment never to be forgotten.

Margaret's influence over her monarch husband was as powerful and mysterious as her sway over the people of the land. At one thing, however, was Margaret as utterly unsuccessful as her mother had been—teaching Malcolm to read. Yet in such reverence did the King hold his wife's scholarship that he kissed her devotional books and, upon occasion, stole some of her favorites when she was away, that he might present them back to her, bound and decorated in gold and precious jewels.

❧   E L E V E N   ❧

The advancing sophistication and polish of his court, however, and the spirituality of his wife, did not end Malcolm's raids into Cumbria and Northumbria. Great as was Margaret's influence over the King in certain areas, he yet remained a cruel warrior.

These were times when authority was demanded and submission given. *Homage* determined rule, authority, and the extent of sovereignty. Whoever commanded the power to compel his peers to bow the knee and do homage—he it was who ruled the land. If an oath of loyalty would not be given, the sword decided the matter.

When Kenneth MacAlpin formed the kingdom of Alba out of the Scots and Picts of ancient Caledonia, it had been comprised of that region north of the Firths of Forth and Clyde, just south of Stirling and north of Edinburgh. Likewise, the kingdom of England had first been created out of the ancient southern kingdoms of Wessex, Sussex, and Kent. As the years passed, England had expanded northward, Scotland southward.

By the reign of Malcolm's father, Duncan I, the kingdom of Scotland had grown to include the regions of Lothian, Strathclyde, and even Cumbria, the latter of which had been leased to Scotland by English King Edmund in 945.

When the two strong kings came to their respective thrones in the mid-eleventh century—William I, *the Conqueror*, in England and Malcolm III, *the Great Head*, in Scotland—no distinct boundary between England and Scotland existed. Armies of both invaded and counter-invaded, ravaging the middle lands in a bloody arena of conflict—Northumbria, Cumbria, and southern Lothian. The provinces of northern England were called slaughterhouses for good reason; corpses by the hundreds had been left to rot on the open ground after raids by both kings.

As was the case with all strong military leaders, conquest was as important as rule. William was not satisfied to have placed all England beneath his feet. The fact that a strong King of fierce reputation existed in Scotland meant that eventually he must be conquered too.

Once his English conquest was secure, therefore, just two years after Malcolm's marriage to Margaret, William the Conqueror led a great army of horsemen north, accompanied by a fleet of ships sailing up the coast. He invaded Scotland in huge force, led his army to Stirling, forded the great river, and rode on to the Tay.

Malcolm was a warrior, and courageous. But he was smart enough to know that in this instance resistance was futile. His army was severely outnumbered. To fight would mean annihilation. He therefore sent word ahead to William, announcing his surrender. He met the Conqueror at Abernathy, at the heart of ancient Caledonia, and performed a formal act of homage to the English King, bowed his knee, kissed the Norman's hand, and declared himself King William's man.

Satisfied, William returned with his army to England. Malcolm had preserved his life, his throne, and Scotland's peace.

But what did his submission mean? The answer to such a vital question was perhaps unclear even at the time. And it grew even murkier as years passed. The ambiguity would confound and torment English-Scottish relations for hundreds of years thereafter.

The question was: Did Malcolm submit to William as the King of *Scotland*? Was his act thus a tacit subordination of the entire kingdom of Scotland to the English King? Or did Malcolm intend submission only with respect to those lands he held in English territory—namely, Cumbria and Northumbria—giving, therefore, merely the loyalty a feudal landholder owes his King?

Was he surrendering *the independence* of Scotland?

Or was he merely acknowledging his feudal subordination to William for territories *outside* Scotland?

Three hundred years of warfare would demonstrate that in the eyes of English kings the answer was the former: Scotland fell *within* its realm . . . *Scotland was one of England's rightful provinces,* over which the kingship of England extended. The King of Scotland, accordingly, was necessarily and forever subordinate to England's King.

In the eyes of Scotland's rulers, however, the independence of Scotland was inviolable. The King of Scotland ruled as monarch of a separate, autonomous, and *independent* nation, over which English kings had no right of jurisdiction.

This dispute between the two interpretations would continue—sometimes to simmer, at other times to rage. Indeed, an eventual climax seemed inevitable to determine whether Scotland was a free nation or a mere vassal state and province of England.

Notwithstanding his pledge of loyalty, after the odds for success became more favorable, Malcolm invaded northern England twice more.

⬚ T W E L V E ⬚

A certain old woman who dwelt in a small cottage on the edge of a wood east of Dunfermline Castle hurried home from the western forest one gray autumn afternoon.

Fionnaghal was not actually as old as she looked, for she was bent over as much from the cares of the world pressing upon her as from the bag of kindling sticks upon her back which she had collected this day. Somewhere deep within her bosom a remaining spark of Celtic flame remained aglow. But like the peats in her hearth after a long cold night, something was needed to rekindle her fire and fan it again into life.

She had seen neither husband nor son for five weeks and her heart had grown anxious as the time wore on. They had departed with their old horse and cart to cut and gather a winter's supply of peats from a distant valley. Her husband had said they would perhaps be gone two or three weeks. He desired to see, and for their sixteen-year-old son to witness with him, certain ancient stones of their Caledonii ancestors, which he had seen with his father when, as a boy, he himself had made his home in the mountains. It could wait no longer, he said. They would collect their peats as they returned.

Perhaps it was good they had gone when they did, Fionnaghal thought, for they had missed the sickness that had come upon her daughter five days ago and was now threatening her as well. Yet still she was worried about them. They should have been back long before now.

Fionnaghal and husband came from the Highlands, and both spoke the old tongue. They had ventured down into lower regions when times were hard and food was scarce. Here, near the sea, her husband could work and fish and hope to feed the four mouths in their family. That she was descended from the Highland nymph Breathran, through one of her eldest sons, she had not an idea, nor did she guess that others like her and her husband had likewise migrated from out of the Highlands and carried their ancient bloodline in all directions throughout the land.

As Fionnaghal, unknown daughter of Breathran, now trudged her way through the small village through which she must pass to reach her cottage, her spirit was as bent over with anxiety for her loved ones as was her back under the load of fagots. Thinking only of making haste back to her sick daughter, she was scarcely conscious of the noise of the royal entourage as it returned to the castle from an afternoon's hunt.

By the time she realized she was in the middle of their path, Fionnaghal threw herself up to the wall alongside which she walked, frantic to avoid horses and riders. There she leaned against the stones, panting for breath, waiting for the commotion to pass that she might continue on her way. Never once had she looked up to see who had thus interrupted her solitary steps.

By the time poor Fionnaghal realized that the ten or fifteen horses had stopped and that two people had descended to the street and were walking toward her, a sudden wave of fear swept through her. Had she unknowingly trespassed on castle grounds!

A sweet voice sounded.

Trembling, she looked up. The Queen stood not two feet away, gazing into her face with the most heavenly smile.

Again the Queen spoke. At last Fionnaghal managed a timid smile, which conveyed clearly enough that she could not understand the English words.

"Malcolm," said Margaret, turning to the huge, stern-looking man beside her, "would you please ask this dear woman if we might help her?"

Now sounded the King's voice—soft, though as terrifying as the expression on his face—in her own native tongue. She understood the King's

Gaelic clearly enough, though it accomplished nothing to loose her own tongue. Still she stood speechless, aware that fifty or more eyes were upon her.

Again the Queen's lovely voice spoke—first to Malcolm, then to one of her attendants—ordering that water be found from one of the nearby cottages and that a basin be brought. The King took a great step forward. He stretched out his massive arms and lifted the burden from Fionnaghal's back, setting it beside him on the road.

All consciousness now floated about in a dream to the bewildered woman—all, that is, except the eyes of love and the gentle smile upon the face of the Queen.

The lady who could be nothing but an angel took Fionnaghal's hand and made her sit down on a rock beside the road . . . now the lady Margaret knelt in front of her and was unwrapping her weary feet . . . now came the attendant with water and basin . . . and suddenly Fionnaghal realized—but how could such a thing be!—the Queen was washing her feet!

The soft, gentle touch of her warm hands was more soothing and healing to the tired soul than any touch of human kindness she could remember.

The companions of King and Queen, on horse and on foot, waited patiently. None were surprised at the delay, for they had come to know that their Queen felt such profound compassion for her fellow creatures that it was hardly possible for her to lay eyes on man, woman, or child in need but that she must go and see what ministration might be offered. Wherever Margaret turned her eyes, those upon whom she looked were instantly engulfed in peace. In truth, this was her greatest ministry of all.

The King himself had witnessed similar occurrences many times. These were not the only feet his wife had washed. The first time he saw her kneel down before a beggar woman seeking alms in front of the castle, he had been stunned into speechlessness. He had done nothing, however, but stand awkwardly to one side until the humiliating ordeal should be done with.

Thereafter he had always stood by—stoically, silently . . . enduring while not altogether condoning his wife's acts of charity.

All at once on this day, however, a breeze of gasps began to go through the courtly entourage, followed by what could only be described as the descent upon those same astonished mouths of a holy hush. Before them the King now knelt beside his wife and proceeded himself to bathe the second foot of the awestruck woman in the basin of water. What was it about this Queen who could so tame the wild beast in their King . . . and even transform *him* into a ministering angel?

Quietly Fionnaghal began to weep.

Margaret saw the tears and was moved yet more deeply. She set aside the basin, now dried both the feet within the folds of her own robe, then reached forward with both hands and tenderly cradled the weeping face in her palms. The words she spoke needed no translation, for they were the gentle words of love, and Fionnaghal understood them clearly enough. King and Queen now each wrapped the feet of the woman back as they had been.

Malcolm eased himself back, still on his knees. Margaret turned and glanced deeply into his eyes. A look of sheepish boyishness was on his face. Margaret smiled, tears now standing in her own eyes. She wept not only for Fionnaghal.

"Thank you, Malcolm," she whispered. No other soul ever heard the words. "This means more to me than I can say."

Malcolm smiled but had no words. He was almost as surprised at what he had done as everyone else was. Margaret turned back to Fionnaghal.

"What is your name?" she asked gently.

Malcolm repeated the words in Gaelic.

Fionnaghal answered.

"Where do you live?"

"In a cottage . . . it is not far, my lady."

"We will help you with your fagots. Do you have a husband?"

Fionnaghal briefly explained, and now—looking not nearly as old as before, her face softened by the kind treatment she had received—began to weep anew. The three continued to speak quietly—the King of the realm, his saintly Queen, and the poor Highland woman who was their subject. Gradually the whole story came out of the long absence of husband and son, as well as the ailing daughter.

Malcolm now stood, turned, and barked out brisk commands to several of his men.

They came forward. One caught up the bundle of sticks, two were sent off to the castle with orders to bring back a full cartload of dried peats. Malcolm turned back, and now he and Margaret assisted Fionnaghal to her feet and into one of the horse-drawn traps, where she might sit comfortably. Sending the rest of their attendants on to Dunfermline, Margaret and Malcolm now escorted the bewildered Fionnaghal home.

Within an hour the blissful woman was resting comfortably. A huge supply of peats and kindling sticks had been stacked outside, and Margaret was returning from the castle with what provisions she judged would make the lives of Fionnaghal and her daughter easier until the return of their men. She sent one of her women from the castle back to stay with the two peasants, mother and daughter, in the cottage and care for them until the sickness was passed.

Before she left them, Margaret slipped one of her rings from its finger, placed it into Fionnaghal's palm, then closed the woman's fingers around it, clutching her hardworking hand in the middle of her own.

"I want you to have this, dear Fionnaghal," she said through the interpretation of her maid, also a transplanted Highlander. "If you ever need me, this ring will be a token between us of our friendship. You may call upon me anytime."

Again Fionnaghal wept. What words of gratefulness could she possibly utter? An angel had come to her this day. Forever would this humble cottage seem to shine with the memory of the heavenly visitation.

⌗   T H I R T E E N   ⌗

During Malcolm III's reign, shifts occurred *away from the Celtic past* and *toward the Norman future*—in three areas: language, custom, and religion. These changes signaled the beginning of a major division that would divide Scotland and make harmony among its peoples increasingly difficult.

From the twelfth century forward, because of these changes, the most serious enemy to Scotland's unity would be the Scots themselves.

Ann an aonachd tha bràithreachas—"In unity is brotherhood"—would fade as a prescription for nationhood ever more distantly into the past, and become a vision long forgotten and unfulfilled by the descendents of those two Caledonii brothers who first dreamed it.

Through no fault of either Margaret's or Malcolm's other than the desire to bring beneficial change and learning to their people, Gaelic language, clan customs, and Celtic religion were gradually pushed back into the regions of their origins—toward the ancient Caledonia of the mountainous north and west.

Two Scotlands began thus to emerge and develop distinct cultures—the *Highlands* of the north and west, where the Celtic and Gaelic heritage of Caledonia remained vital and alive, and the *Lowlands* of south and east, which continued to grow more courtly, more genteel, more *English*. And as England itself became more Norman, the Norman influence of Scotland would become more pronounced. The brown peat waters of Celt and Scot and Pict would retreat deeper into the Highlands while the Norman sea completed its conquest, flooding the Scottish aristocracy and Lowlands with the clear waters of continental and English change.

Though Malcolm himself was of Celtic ancestry—never a more anti-Norman could be imagined than the King of the Scots—the fact that he took to using the English tongue evidenced the shifting direction of Malcolm's cultural loyalties. Perhaps without intending it, and because of his great love for his angel-wife, he turned his back on his Celtic heritage and threw wide the door for change. With strange irony, the fiercest of Celts and his Anglo-Saxon/Hungarian wife thus ushered in refinements that would speed the Normanization of his nation.

Ever after Malcolm's reign, therefore, a rift would exist, invisible at first but steadily widening, between the Gaelic-speaking Celtic Highlanders—ancestors of former Scots and Picts, in whose veins flowed the rich amber heritage of mountain peat—and the English influence of crown and nobility—in whose veins flowed blood blue as the Channel over which the Norman had crossed to achieve his conquest.

This fissure revealed itself periodically at the deaths of various monarchs. Then would old Celtic forces rise to exert claim to the kingship according to the former complex Scottish system of tanistry, pitting itself at odds with Saxon, English, and Norman linear succession. Possession of the crown of Scotland would thus—as an ongoing legacy to the Picts and Scots—remain divisive for the next seven centuries . . . until the right of self-rule was taken from Scotland altogether.

Malcolm had fathered one son, Duncan, by his previous marriage to Orkney princess Ingibjorg. He and Margaret produced six sons and two daughters of their own. Even in the naming of these children, Margaret's influence over the King was not difficult to observe—all were given English, biblical, or classical names: Edward, Edgar, Edmund, Ethelred, Al-

exander, and David. The daughters were Matilda and Mary. No reminders of the House of Alpin were thus passed into the twelfth century
through the names of the offspring of Scotland's King. Though Mac-
Alpin's Pict and Scot blood still flowed in its veins, henceforth would
Scotland's royal line be Norman, not Celtic, in its orientation.

Malcolm would not be the last son of Caledonia to forsake the heritage of his fathers for the lure of the south and all its manifold attractions.

※   F O U R T E E N   ※

Rains came to Scotland every year in the fall. It was the established
pattern of nature in the north. This particular autumn, however, they came
in more than usual earnest. They began in early September and did not
let up for three weeks, steadily increasing to the point where danger became evident in the lower regions.

Still the downpours persisted. By the end of the month most rivers
and burns of Lothian, Fife, and inland along the Rivers Tay and Earn were
swollen beyond their banks. Serious floods threatened.

Within another week, brown water swirled everywhere, spreading
across valleys, over farms, through streets of villages—rivers meeting
other rivers, carrying trees and animals and shrubs and carts and even
cottages helplessly to the sea. In all low-lying regions, the homes of the
poor were flooded, some swept entirely away by the deepening currents.
Many were left with no place to find shelter, and their numbers increased
daily.

One by one, then by fives and tens, they began gathering outside the
castle gates of Dunfermline. Their Queen would tell them what to do.

Before Malcolm was aware what was happening, his wife had turned
the great hall of his home into a refugee center. Messengers were sent out
to all the noble houses within fifty miles where passage was possible, re-
questing blankets and food and other supplies. By the middle of October,
two hundred people of all ages, mostly peasants who had lost their
houses, now called Dunfermline Castle their temporary home.

Dunfermline had not been the center of so much activity since the
King's marriage to Queen Margaret! Children scurried about everywhere.
The poor knew their Queen would care for them, and none were disap-

pointed. Margaret served her huge new family with an indefatigable energy and joy. Truly did nobility now become servant to the people. Even the most hard-bitten anti-English Highlander could admire this new kind of royalty, which actually cared for its subjects.

Four of Margaret's most dedicated and hardest-working assistants were the peasant woman Fionnaghal, along with her husband and son and daughter. Their own cottage next to the wood sat on high ground and was safe from the calamity of the surrounding lowlands. But with happy hearts they now eagerly repaid the Queen's kindness during their own time of need. Each morning they rowed across a newly created lake of brown water, then took the high road leading to the castle and spent the day helping to care for the masses of homeless citizens. Each evening they would walk and row back again to their own home.

At long last the rains began to abate and the floodwaters to recede.

Now, however, did even greater work begin, for the loss of property and crops had been great. Many of those without shelter were taken in by friends and relatives. King Malcolm ordered that new cottages be built to replace those lost to the flood.

Great was the happiness when the villagers and crofters and fisherfolk began returning to their homes, both old and new. The King and Queen continued to lodge some of their flood guests throughout the winter months. As new cottages were slowly completed, gradually the great hall of Dunfermline was restored to its original state.

As winter gave way to the next spring's thaw, a great hope filled the people for a good season's growth following what was already being called the year of the Great Flood. The affection between the people and their King and Queen deepened all the more from having weathered a crisis together. That next year, Malcolm himself was seen frequently walking in the village, chatting with workers and peasants whose friendship he had gained during the rainy winter.

Nine waifs remained behind at the castle, orphaned by storm and flood, with neither parents nor relatives to look after them. During the flood days, the Queen made them her personal charges. Now, with the crowds gone, she adopted them into the household of the castle, seating them at her own table, at times feeding the younger ones at her side with her own spoon.

⬚ F I F T E E N ⬚

William the Conqueror died in 1087.

His son William the Red, called *Rufus,* came to the throne even more determined than his father to secure Cumbria and Northumbria against Scottish hands. Four years after the Conqueror's death, Malcolm once more invaded across Northumbria's border. But William Rufus proved as able a general as his father. He drove Malcolm back and, following in his father's footsteps, forced the Scottish King again to do homage.

The English King then accelerated the policy which would ultimately complete the Normanization of Britain. He began to colonize Cumbria and Northumbria, exactly as his father had the south, by deeding large tracts of land to Anglo-Norman knights and nobles who built great houses and castles, then occupied and defended them in the name of the King. Thus did the feudal system, already so lucrative for landholders in Normandy and newly successful in the south of England, arrive in the north.

Rufus's expulsion of Scots from northern England and the restoration of Carlisle into English hands at last brought definition to the Solway-Tweed line (drawn between the Firth of Solway and the mouth of the Tweed River) as the recognized border between the Scottish north and the English south.

A meeting was scheduled between William Rufus and Malcolm in 1093. They would come together at Gloucester to discuss the yet unfulfilled terms of their agreement of 1091. In exchange for Malcolm's oaths of loyalty to the English King, restoration had been promised *to* Malcolm of lands in England that were rightfully considered possessions of the Scots King.

Before leaving for the south, however, Malcolm ordered a great celebration throughout Scotland. Crops were coming in, the country was at peace, and no English troops were on northern soil. It was Malcolm's desire to eat, drink, and be merry with his people.

⊠   S I X T E E N   ⊠

The event had been heralded all summer.

Messengers had ridden to all corners of the land. They were sent to proclaim in every village and croft and in the land, that by royal decree all inhabitants of the kingdom—rich and poor, women and men, Highlanders, Lowlanders, Scots, and English—were invited to be guests of King Malcolm and Queen Margaret on the lawns of Dunfermline Castle during the second week of August, in the year 1093. They might bring tents and wagons, carts and blankets, and sleep in the open air in the fields and hillsides surrounding Dunfermline.

Feasting and celebration would last the entire week. A great country holiday was organized. Food of every sort would be on hand. Tents and tables were being set up. Carts were already arriving at the castle with pigs and deer and rabbit for roasting, and an unending supply of meat pies and steamed puddings was being prepared.

And entertainment—there would be music and jugglers, jousting and a variety of tournaments. Margaret would see to the dancing, and there would be all manner of song and merrymaking.

As the summer advanced and the date drew near, Lothian, Strathclyde, Fife, and Tay were in a state of unprecedented anticipation. Guests were even expected from such distant regions as Moray and Buchan in the north and the Highlands and isles of the west.

When the people began to arrive, the King and Queen greeted each man and woman as friends and walked daily through the village of tents and carts and wagons. Steadily the countryside around Dunfermline filled.

What a happy time for the inhabitants of Scotland!

No one remembered its like before. The sounds and smells of summer floated in the air. Violets abounded, and bees buzzed from the prickly thistle's hairy purple centers, then flitted toward big yellow dandelions. No heather was yet in bloom, but the hillsides were splotched with the bright gold of broom.

Down from the mountains came hundreds of Highlanders, and from along the seacoasts arrived the fisherfolk. Crops had been good. People were gay. Priests were again respected, and the church, flourishing under Margaret's patronage, was more highly regarded than at any time in memory.

The King gave several speeches throughout the week, congratulating the farmers for their successful harvest and the fishermen for their good season of catches. French wine and local ale flowed abundantly, and the King and Queen, demonstrating to their nobles how royalty could mix with peasantry, at week's end had more greatly endeared themselves to their subjects than ever.

Malcolm had set up a race for all willing boys and young men. He would himself start the contestants at the castle gate. Thence they would run along the entry road, up the hill northward to its crest, halfway down the other side, around the great boulder, and then back, a distance in all of some three miles.

When the twenty or twenty-five athletes—including the royal couple's own sons—were lined up and had received instructions personally from the King, Malcolm drew a line across the dirt road with his sword. The contestants walked toward it. Malcolm stepped several paces back, then lifted his royal sword high into the air.

A long pause came while each waited at the line.

Suddenly the great sword slashed downward. A great shout from the mouth of the King accompanied the motion. Off the young men tore to the enthusiastic cheers of five hundred spectators.

A broad smile spread across Malcolm's face as he watched their retreating heels. He turned to Margaret, then impulsively grabbed her hand and pulled her after him.

"Come!" he cried. "Let's run to the ridge where we can see Alexander and David on their way back!"

He grabbed two fruit tarts as they dashed by one of the tables, to the laughter of the servants, who still took delight in the King's obvious and manifest love for his Queen.

"What about Edgar, Edmund, and Ethelred?" she asked as she hurried beside him to keep up.

"They'll be so far ahead," Malcolm replied, huffing and chewing together, "they will be back before we get a good look. But the two younger ones—I think we'll arrive in time to see them."

Before they were halfway to the ridge, breathing more heavily than he had in years, Malcolm slowed to a walk.

"I had been thinking about joining the race myself!" he laughed. "It is a good thing I didn't. I am too old for this!"

▨   S E V E N T E E N   ▨

They reached the overlook as the lead runner crested the hill and began his return back down to the castle.

"Who is it—can you tell?" asked Margaret as she tried to catch her breath.

Malcolm squinted into the distance. "I can't tell yet," he replied. "It may be Ethelred."

Margaret laughed. "Edgar won't appreciate being bested by his younger brother."

They stood and watched as one by one the rest of the runners spilled over the opposite hill, then trudged on tired legs downhill back toward the line of the King's sword.

"Oh, Malcolm," Margaret sighed, throwing herself onto the ground with a lovely smile of contentment. She was in no hurry to leave this peaceful spot. "This reminds me of the tales my nurse used to tell me of the days of King Arthur, when everything was so peaceful in Camelot. That is how I feel today—as if you will never go to war again, and all the disputes with other kings will disappear, and we will live happily and content in our own little northern kingdom."

Malcolm smiled, then sat down beside her. It was a lovely daydream.

"Maybe it will always be so," he mused dreamily, though he knew better. "Perhaps Rufus will prove cooperative."

Margaret rolled over on the warm grass and bent her face down to the earth, then plucked two or three of the tiniest, most delicate flowers hidden amongst its green blades.

"Look at the faces of these violets, Malcolm. Aren't they the most gorgeous you've ever seen?"

Malcolm smiled. He loved his Queen as much now as on the day she had let him help her out of the boat.

"Was there really a Camelot?" he asked after a moment.

"Of course," replied Margaret.

"And King Arthur?"

"Malcolm, how can you even ask such a thing? Of course! And his beautiful Queen Guinevere." Margaret's face fell. "But it was she who brought the beginning of the end of those happy days," she added.

"We Scots have stories of our own," said Malcolm. "There are some who say Arthur was really a Scot."

"I know," replied Margaret. She paused briefly, then added, "You may become a legend one day yourself, Malcolm."

Malcolm laughed. "And perhaps so shall you! But my beautiful Queen will not bring *my* kingdom to an end."

They chatted another few minutes. When again a brief silence intervened, Malcolm grew pensive.

"I do not feel that I should go to Gloucester," he said.

"Why?"

"What good can come of it? Maybe you are right, and we ought to let this happy time go on and on. I do not trust the red English King. If I have to pay him homage one more time, I think I shall vomit, then rise up and run him through with my sword."

"Malcolm, please don't talk so . . . not on a happy day like this."

Malcolm grew silent, as if at sixty-two he had just been scolded by his forty-seven-year-old mother.

"I am sorry," he said after a moment's reflection, "but you cannot know what it is like for a man to bow the knee before such imbeciles as the English allow to rule them."

"I think I may have some idea," smiled Margaret. "But do not forget, my brother was almost King."

"You, Margaret, are cut from a different piece of the human cloth than most English nobility," replied Malcolm, committing himself in neither direction concerning an opinion of his brother-in-law. To himself, he doubted Edgar would have made any better king than the rest.

"In any case," Margaret went on, "I think I know what homage must mean for one such as you. I have been your wife for twenty-three years. I know what kind of man is my husband."

"It turns the stomach," persisted Malcolm. The memory of bowing before the English King made him angry every time he was reminded of it.

"William *did* agree to return your English lands."

"Which he has not done yet," rejoined Malcolm.

"I think you *should* go to Gloucester," said Margaret. "Mind your manners, and then insist he honor the terms of the treaty."

Malcolm nodded.

"Perhaps you are right," he sighed. "The meeting is arranged. But I don't know if I can stand the sight of Rufus's ruddy face again."

Margaret laughed.

"You are man enough to handle even such an ignominy as that," she said, then jumped up and offered the King her hand.

"Let us go down and congratulate the racers, especially our five stout sons."

"It was a good test of endurance, was it not?" said Malcolm. "Perhaps we shall make it an annual event."

"I heartily consent. And now the celebration wants its King!"

Malcolm allowed Margaret to pull him to his feet. Hand in hand they descended the slope back to the castle.

EIGHTEEN

Two and a half weeks later, Malcolm arrived in Gloucester for the meeting with the English King.

William Rufus, however, refused to see him. He would let his own courts decide, he said by messenger, whatever disputes might exist.

The legendary rage for which he was known filled Malcolm III, *Ceann Mor*, at this insult. He stormed home to Scotland, still furious when he arrived.

Margaret did her best to calm her giant of a husband, who paced their chambers like a caged tiger. She knew of his temper, but only rarely had she seen him like this.

"Perhaps it is best that the decisions are made without your armies."

"He is nothing but a liar! He has no intention of keeping the agreements," cried Malcolm, pacing about with giant stride. "Bah—the courts, he says! *His* courts—they will obviously weigh more heavily for English interests than mine!"

Notwithstanding his wife's strenuous pleas, Malcolm immediately gathered his army for yet another invasion of Northumbria. By early November he was ready to lead his men south.

His four oldest sons would now accompany him. Edward, eldest at twenty-two, would ride at his side. That fact alone caused the Queen many sleepless hours during the final week before their departure.

"I am afraid, Malcolm," said Margaret as her husband and sons prepared to depart. "I now say to you the words you once spoke to me—do you remember? You asked me if I must return to England. Now I say that to you, my dear husband—*must* you fight again?"

"The honor of our nation is at stake," replied Malcolm. "Rufus has not only broken the terms of the treaty, he has humiliated Scotland. He agreed to the meeting, then refused to see me. So I answer you as you answered me then—yes, I must."

"You are not as young as you were," she reminded him. "And I have heard that Rufus's forces far outnumber ours. Please, Malcolm—stay with me."

The King could not mistake the pleading tone in the Queen's voice. He glanced away. He could not let her eyes find his just now, otherwise his resolve might be undone. Neither could he mistake the paleness of Margaret's countenance. She had been feeling unwell ever since his return from Gloucester.

But he was warrior and King first, husband and lover second. He would take back his lands in England.

He *must.* It was the way of kings, the way of the warrior, the way of Scotland. Then he would return and see to Margaret's comfort.

"I am sorry," he said after a moment, turning back toward her but still not quite able to meet her eye. "I would not be a man if I let Rufus humiliate the King of the Scots."

He kissed her, then turned and left the room. From a high window she watched him join his mounted men where they waited outside the wall.

Margaret wept a few dry tears. Dark forebodings filled her heart. She took to her bed that same afternoon.

Her ladies waited on her with fearfully eager yet helpless hands. They loved her, but none knew what to do for her. She could not eat.

NINETEEN

Malcolm marched his inadequate force past Berwick and into Northumbria uncontested, arriving at the castle at Alnwick inside English territory on November 13.

It was rumored that William's army was two days out and advancing to meet him. The castle, he decided, would give his men a good place to rest and await the battle.

At the head of his column Malcolm marched toward the gatekeeper's cottage that sat some hundred yards in front of the castle, then slowed and raised his hand. The column behind him reined in their horses. The keeper came out and eyed him belligerently.

"In the name of Scotland, I am taking occupation of Alnwick," said Malcolm from astride his mount. "Open the gate, and hand over the keys to the castle."

"And who might you be?" said the man, apparently not cowed in the least by sight of Malcolm's army. Malcolm did not like the expression in the fellow's countenance.

"I am Malcolm III, known as Canmore—King of Scotland!" barked Malcolm. "I order you to surrender the castle."

A canny glint flashed from the man's eye. He turned and walked slowly back inside the cottage. When he returned a moment later, he held a long lance with sharp iron tip.

Instantly the clatter of thirty swords being unsheathed sounded behind the King.

"Tell your eager Scotsmen to relax," growled the man. "I merely bring you the keys as you asked." Even as he spoke, however, two or three dozen armed men emerged from the castle behind him.

The gatekeeper walked slowly forward. He stopped, then pointed the spear up in the direction of Malcolm's face. Dangling from the tip was a small chain which held three large keys.

The Scottish King bent forward, leaned down from the saddle, and stretched out his hand to take them. . . .

⊗   T W E N T Y   ⊗

It was two days later when her second son, Edgar, aged twenty-one, was shown into the ailing Queen Margaret's chamber.

He was exhausted, covered with mud and grime from the hard retreat north.

Margaret greeted him with a wan smile. Even before he stuttered out the message, his mother knew, from his bearing and visible pain to bring such tidings, that her husband was dead.

"Edward . . . Ed-Ed-Edward himself sl-slew the . . . the k-k-keeper," Edgar tried to say. "The . . . the instant he had thrust the lance . . . in-in-

into F-Father's eye, Ed-Edward was off his horse and had r-run . . . r-run the m-m-man through."

He tried to collect himself with a deep breath and then managed to spill out the dreadful news that in the skirmish which followed, his eldest brother, Edward, had also been killed.

The Queen received the news calmly, obviously stricken with anguish but pale and unweeping.

Later that day, with her remaining five sons and two daughters in her room to join with her in prayer, Margaret thanked God for sending such a bitter grief, in the last hours of her life, with which to purify her soul from remaining worldly concerns.

Two days later she went to join her earthly and heavenly husbands—both kings, though ruling over vastly different realms—to each of whom she had all her life been so lovingly devoted.

The beloved body of her whose name in Greek, *magaron,* meant "pearl" lay in her chapel on the high rock for three days.

Then Margaret, the Pearl of Scotland, was laid to rest beside her husband Malcolm III, called the Great Head, and their son Edward at Dunfermline. There had the King and Queen met and married, and there had they spent all their happy years at one another's side.

At Dunfermline would they thus remain entombed together . . . forever.

8

ANOTHER SHAKE-UP
IN WESTMINSTER

※ O N E ※

This is Patricia Rawlings reporting live from outside the Palace of Westminster. . . ."

The little-known American journalist had finally landed a scoop big enough to justify her being put on live camera before the nation. A cold winter drizzle stung her cheeks but could not dampen her spirits as she looked into the camera and began her report.

These were the most talked-about stories to break since Kirk Luddington's reporting of the Queen's abdication a little more than a year before. And the fact that Rawlings herself had been instrumental in the cracking of the two related cases meant that Pilkington had had little choice.

Suddenly the young woman who had awkwardly put her foot in her mouth at this same spot for mistaking the English political term *division* was, for a few days at least, the most famous journalist in London. Her detective work in the matter of the Stone, the solving of a murder, and the breakup of an international conspiracy had made of her, if not exactly a hero, certainly a newswoman who would have plenty of offers on the table by next week if her BBC producer did not give her the airtime she wanted.

All at once Rawlings' American accent had become a trump card rather than a liability.

So here Paddy was—while her rival Luddington cooled his heels in the crowd—her heart pounding in fear lest some other Yankee blooper pop out of her mouth, and doing her best to look calm and collected as she conveyed details to a listening world.

"After secret machinations and hidden relationships behind these walls on the very eve of Parliament's opening for its new year," Paddy continued, "involving Liberal Democratic leader Andrew Trentham and colleagues from several parties in the House of Commons—"

As she spoke, Paddy could not prevent another momentary glance toward Andrew, where he stood among the crowd of notables present.

"—late yesterday afternoon investigators at last broke wide open the case involving last year's murder of the Honorable Eagon Hamilton. As suspected, the murder was connected with the theft of the fabled Stone of Destiny, which was recovered several months ago from the Celtic Druidic Center in County Carlow, Ireland, and is now once again safely in the Crown Room of Edinburgh Castle."

▓ T W O ▓

William Rawlings sat with a cup of black coffee—a habit he had picked up in the States and had enjoyed ever since—in front of the television set in his small rented apartment in Auckland, New Zealand. He was watching the time-delayed unfolding of events back in his homeland with both disbelief and pride.

"Well, Paddy," he said with a rueful smile, "you did it . . . you actually did it."

There was his wife in front of the BBC's cameras, conducting herself with as much poise as if she'd been an anchorwoman for years. He knew otherwise, and as much as he was pulling for her, he had not honestly expected to see such a thing so soon in her career.

He glanced down at his watch. He was already late for his assignment. But what did it matter? He would be leaving this place in a week or two anyway, and no darkroom work was going to make him miss this. He didn't have another photo shoot scheduled for two days.

He sat back and smiled, recognizing the blue suit Paddy was wearing. He'd helped her pick it out at a shop near Harrods. She had said at the time that she would save it for her first on-camera assignment. Now that moment had come.

She was a determined one, that American wife of his. He had been drawn to her the moment they met on the other side of the pond, as the saying went, while he did a stint as a visiting newspaper photographer working out of the Atlanta office. He could still see Paddy hurrying after her boss, insisting she listen to some hot lead. Paddy hadn't even seen him at the time, but he had certainly taken notice of her.

How did you manage this, Paddy? Bill said to himself. *How did you get yourself in front of the camera on such a huge story?*

▨   T H R E E   ▨

In what appears to be a far-reaching scheme," Paddy was now saying, "originating more than thirty years ago, connections were recently uncovered between the late leader of the Liberal Democratic Party and Conservative Party leader Miles Ramsey.

"The two business associates, whose opposite political orientations were apparently designed to disguise their long-range objectives, had a falling out earlier this year that may have led to the death of the Liberal Democratic leader. Mr. Ramsey was arrested by agents of Scotland Yard just days ago in the Shetland Islands and has been charged with Mr. Hamilton's murder, which has remained unsolved since early this year.

"Also indicted at the time were Larne Reardon, former Liberal-Democratic deputy leader, and Baen Ferguson, SNP deputy leader. Both men denied knowledge of the murder, but were allegedly working together with unnamed others in the theft of the Stone of Scone. Their willingness, even eagerness, to cooperate with Scotland Yard in exchange for leniency in the matter of the murder enabled investigators to fill in details of an intricate plot to take over Scotland's oil industry. Without such cooperation, these details would doubtless have remained cloudy or altogether unknown. Exactly what charges will be filed has not yet been determined.

"Still at large in connection with the theft is noted Irish druidic leader, Amairgen Cooney Dwyer.

"Motives in the complex double crime are still fuzzy, but apparently the theft of the Stone was part of the larger plan to gain control of the North Sea oil reserves of an independent Scottish state through development of certain vital sites in the Shetland Islands. The international cartel, World Resources, Ltd., is under investigation at this time, their assets frozen until the inquiry is complete.

"How these developments will affect the Scottish situation remains to be seen. Prime Minister Richard Barraclough, meanwhile," Paddy went on, "issued a brief statement from Number Ten Downing Street, expressing shock at the developments. . . ."

As Paddy spoke, she glanced in Andrew's direction, but neither she nor the Cumbrian MP gave any sign of their direct involvement in the case.

⁂   F O U R   ⁂

How well he remembered, thought Bill Rawlings as he watched, the inner anxieties Paddy tried so hard to hide when she found herself in new or uncomfortable circumstances. She had certainly matured as a newswoman. If she was nervous now, she didn't show it.

After she'd come to London to visit, three months after his own return from Atlanta, he had set her up with her first job in England. There were a lot of memories . . . those early days in London . . . their first evening together. He had called her *Paddy* for the first time that evening too, because of that silly little Irish song she used to sing.

Even then she had said her one goal was to do a major story on the BBC evening news, American accent and all.

Now she'd done it. He had to hand it to her. She had a job to do, and she had done it. Whereas he'd really been drifting, unsure what he wanted out of life, content to follow any possibility that occurred to him.

In the end, he realized now, that was why she hadn't come with him. Not because she didn't love him, but because she couldn't just drift along in the wake of a man who didn't know what he wanted.

But I do now, he reflected, with another sip of the American coffee that reminded him of his wife. *I know exactly what I want.*

And what he wanted more than anything else was Paddy.

Meanwhile, Paddy drew in a steadying breath, gradually feeling more comfortable as the cameras rolled.

"All the United Kingdom," she went on, "indeed, the entire world, is now waiting to see how these events will affect the growing debate over the future of Scotland. No statement from Liberal Democratic leader, the Honorable Andrew Trentham, who has become a de facto spokesman regarding the cause, has yet been released. Sources close to the Cumbrian MP suggest that an announcement may be forthcoming within a few weeks."

Another look followed in Andrew's direction. This time Paddy could not help curling the edges of her lips in the hint of a smile at the veiled reference to herself in her own report. Andrew smiled, then chuckled lightly at her words, as most of the cameras broke from the reporter's face to his.

After a pause, again Paddy continued.

"We will update you with more details as they become available," she said. "According to Scotland Yard spokesman Jack Hensley, more arrests are expected. Scotland Yard will issue a full report within forty-eight hours, Hensley said. Shaken as it is by the implication of its own in these events, the House of Commons must now prepare for what may prove to be one of its most extraordinary sessions in decades. No statement has yet been issued by Buckingham Palace. It is not known whether or not the King's speech will address this serious shake-up within Parliament.

"I will be back tomorrow with a live interview with the Honorable Andrew Trentham," Paddy concluded.

The coverage broke away to follow Scotland Yard Inspector Allan Shepley as he explained the series of events that had led to the arrests after he and his men had landed in the Shetlands.

———

Rawlings continued to sit in front of his television, still amazed at what he had just seen. He didn't care if he got no work done today. He wanted to see the remainder of the broadcast.

And he would call her!

He glanced at his watch again . . . seven-thirty. She might be home by now, depending on how her interview had gone.

He would try. Paddy's triumph deserved a hearty congratulations.

✾ FIVE ✾

Patricia Rawlings awoke with the most profound sense of contentment. Though she had only had five hours sleep, she was too keyed up to remain in bed another second.

She leapt up as if the previous day's adrenaline were still pumping through her veins at full strength. She had just poured herself a cup of coffee when the phone rang. She heard her husband's voice on the line when she answered.

"Paddy!" exclaimed Rawlings. "I caught your performance on the telly—you were terrific."

"Thank you, Bill."

"I tried to call you several times this morning—er, last evening for you, that is."

"I was out late."

"But I mean it—I was really proud of you, Yankee accent and all."

"You know, for once," laughed Paddy, "I wasn't self-conscious about it."

"I only heard that tremble in your voice one time," kidded Rawlings.

"Okay, so I was nervous," rejoined Paddy lightly. "Who wouldn't be?"

"And an interview with Andrew Trentham—how did you pull that off?"

"A long story. But I haven't pulled it off yet. It's slated for this afternoon."

"Well, best of luck. I thought I saw a little silent eye contact between the two of you during your statement."

"It showed?"

"Only to someone who knows you."

"Well, let's just say that he and I became very well acquainted during this whole investigation.—But I have *you* to thank for getting us going in the first place," added Paddy, "with that connection between Reardon and World Resources, Ltd. Without that, all the rest of the pieces may never have come together."

"No extra charge," laughed Rawlings. "And from the way they tell it, you're an Internet genius now."

"Not exactly," laughed Paddy. "Remember Bert Fenton—you introduced us several years ago? He helped out on that end too."

"Good old Bert! I haven't thought of him in ages. He was always something of a hacker."

"Well, it paid off.—By the way, when are you due back? Still the same schedule as the last time we talked?"

"Yeah . . . a week, maybe two."

There was a pause. The reminder of Rawlings' return to London from his New Zealand assignment sobered both their thoughts toward the hazily defined status of their separation.

"You know, Paddy," said Bill after a moment in a more serious tone, "I know how it was when I left . . . but on my end, well, now that I've had some time to think things over, I wouldn't mind trying it again. If you want to, that is."

"I didn't say I *wanted* you to leave."

"I thought—"

"I don't know, it just seemed . . ."

Paddy did not complete the sentence. Another silence intervened, this time more lengthy.

"I still love you, Paddy," said Rawlings after ten or fifteen seconds. "I've missed you. And well, I'd like to see if we can make it work. I know it was a rough go, and we both thought maybe we'd made a mistake. But being here, you know . . ."

"I know, Bill. I've thought about it too. Things look different when you're apart for a while."

"Well then, what do you think?"

"Let's talk when you get back."

"I'll call as soon as I'm in."

"Need a ride from Heathrow?"

"I can take the tube."

"But you'll have luggage. Listen, I'll pick you up. Let me know when."

"All right, then. Thanks."

Another silence followed.

"Bill," said Paddy, "thanks for calling—your words mean a lot."

"I meant them—you were sensational."

"Thanks again."

"Right, then . . . see you in a couple weeks."

Paddy hung up the phone, then sat back down on her couch, and smiled. It was not a smile of triumph or victory . . . but of happy contentment.

What could account for the sudden change in how she felt? Was it because of what had happened yesterday, or that her heart had gradually grown more open to Bill again?

She wouldn't analyze it right now. There'd be time for that later. She would see how she felt when she saw Bill face-to-face.

Now she had to get organized and make final notes for her live interview with the Honorable Andrew Trentham!

※   S I X   ※

Andrew awoke the morning after the announcement outside Westminster Palace with a feeling of relief. At last it was over. Now he could focus his attention on the business of his party, the House of Commons, and the future of the country. With the King's speech to open Parliament only a week away, he really had to get busy.

Actually, though, it wasn't *quite* over. He still had the interview with Paddy.

He almost regretted having agreed to it. But a deal was a deal. And Paddy had certainly earned her wings on this one. Without her digging, none of this plot may ever have come to light. The Stone might still be missing, the murder of an MP unsolved. The country owed Paddy Rawlings a debt of gratitude, and an interview was the least he could do to help repay it.

He thought back with a smile to their first journalistic encounter a year before. Paddy had come a long way since then, and now here she was in the spotlight.

Andrew's thoughts returned to the opening of Parliament. It would be like no opening in memory, with three party leaders and deputy leaders behind bars and a major scandal swirling at the highest levels of government.

And, Andrew realized, it could well be historic for other reasons. He had caught wind of serious talks between the prime minister and Dugald MacKinnon of the SNP. Some rumors suggested that Barraclough might be close to a concession on some of the SNP's long-standing demands.

He'd have to leave all that to Barraclough for the minute. Right now he had an interview to prepare for.

※   S E V E N   ※

As the cameras rolled, Paddy and Andrew did their best to put the personal elements of the story aside and speak to one another as the professionals they were. This was not easy in that the two of them together, and Paddy's Internet sleuthing, as Andrew called it, had been so pivotal in what had transpired.

But that aspect of the story would have to wait. Paddy had, in fact, already been contacted by several major magazines with offers for an exclusive from *her* point of view. But today she had to do her job, which was to interview Andrew Trentham about *his* role in the story as the dramatic events had broken wide open.

"So, Mr. Trentham," said Paddy after the introductory phase of the on-camera discussion, "we heard yesterday a brief chronology of events from Inspector Shepley. But I think everyone wants to hear what it was like for you, a politician and a layman, as it were, to find yourself in the middle of a harrowing Scotland Yard arrest."

"It was more than a little frightening," replied Andrew with a laugh. "I mean, I would consider myself as brave as the next man, but I have to tell you—when the guns came out, I wanted to run for cover!"

"And did you run?" asked Paddy.

"Not exactly. I believe I held my ground. But not from bravery . . . I think I was too afraid to move!"

"I doubt that!" The interviewer smiled as the camera moved back and forth between them. "The way I hear it, you remained anything but glued to the spot."

"It's the truth," agreed Andrew with another light laugh. "After we landed in the Shetlands and were making arrangements and loading into the cars, with all of Inspector Shepley's men checking their guns and talking about where to sneak up and when to fire if it came to that . . . I seriously began to wonder if I was in over my head. I mean, suddenly I realized bullets might start flying, and I could be right in the middle of it."

"And did bullets fly?" asked Paddy.

"Only one . . . and thankfully not toward anyone."

———

Alastair Farquharson's call had come while they were still in the air, through a satellite phone transfer arranged by Scotland Yard for Andrew's mobile number. As soon as Andrew had the big Scotsman on the line, he handed the phone to Shepley, who took down the information while he perused a detailed map of the Shetlands in his lap. A minute or two later, he handed the phone back to Andrew.

"We've got the site located," he said. "Near the Moul of Eswick, east coast on South Nesting Bay. That still doesn't tell us if anyone will be there. But it's where we'll start."

"Have they heard anything from the laird or his daughter?" asked Andrew.

"No," replied Shepley. "Farquharson said the lady, Mrs.—What's her name?"

"Gordon, Mrs. Gordon."

"Right. He said Mrs. Gordon knew nothing more than he told you before. She thought they were to meet their solicitor somewhere in Lerwick today, then drive up to the property."

"When were they supposed to meet?"

"Don't know," answered Shepley.

They were on the ground thirty minutes later and crammed into the waiting police vehicles, speeding north out of Lerwick fifteen minutes after that.

The laird's property of approximately eighty-seven acres comprised a stretch of isolated coastline about a third of a mile long, which narrowed as it came inland some half a mile. The result was an irregular sort of rectangle of no visible value, yet of apparent importance to World Resources, Ltd.

The narrow road from Catfirth out to the Moul of Eswick did not actually extend as far as the property. They would have to walk the last quarter mile on foot, then another half mile to the bluff where the land dropped off to the sea. Nothing about the site as it appeared on the map would indicate singular value, except that the shoreline curved in a semicircle and thus formed a protected bay within the larger South Nesting coastline. The only other feature of interest was that an oil-production platform lay in the sea three miles straight off the Moul of Eswick.

As they drove close, the cars slowed. Andrew, in the lead automobile with Inspector Shepley, saw three vehicles parked beside the road ahead, including the maroon BMW Andrew had seen pulling into the Houses of Parliament just two days before.

"That's Ramsey's car, all right," said Shepley to Andrew. "So far it looks like your information was on the mark. He must have left immediately after you saw the car the other day."

Andrew glanced about anxiously but saw no sign of Ginny, her father, or anyone else.

As quietly as possible, they parked the cars and got out. Not a tree was in sight, only an endless expanse of rolling peat moor. It was as quiet and isolated a spot as Andrew could imagine. He couldn't understand how the property brought in the meager income it did, unless there were sheep about someplace.

Shepley conferred briefly with his men. One was already making for a rise in the rocky landscape with a pair of binoculars. After a minute, he hurried back down and joined the others again.

"They're over there all right, Inspector," he said, "out at the coast—a thousand, maybe twelve hundred, yards away."

"How many?" asked Shepley.

"Looks to be five or six . . . couldn't tell for certain."

Andrew crowded in a little closer to listen.

"Is there a young woman with them?" he asked.

"Yeah, I think I saw what could be a female . . . rather short—red hair."

"Do they know we're here?" asked the inspector before Andrew could get in another question.

"Didn't look like it. They were standing close together talking. Didn't look my way."

"All right, then, let's go," said Shepley. "We'll have to split up, make for the coast on either side of them, keeping out of sight—"

As he spoke, he pointed to indicate a two-pronged approach.

"—Blenkinsop, you stay behind and temporarily disable their cars, then head straight over the ground between us. Give us a ten-minute lead. We'll work our way to the shore, then approach from opposite directions under cover of the bluff. Everyone got it?"

Nods followed around, and they struck out.

"Trentham, you come with me," said Shepley. "Everyone keep low. Stay in the hollows of the moor."

They reached the rocky coastline without much difficulty after some twelve or fifteen minutes. Thankfully the bluff overlooking the sea was not a sheer one. They were able to crouch low enough among its uneven rocks and protrusions to begin making their way gradually westward, along a line parallel to the water, toward the small party. As they drew near, Andrew caught occasional glimpses of the backs and heads of the individuals involved. By and by voices drifted faintly toward them, though now, at the edge of the sea, a brisk wind and pounding waves made it difficult to hear.

At length Shepley paused, crouched lower yet, and turned to Andrew and the three agents with them.

"We're close enough now," he whispered. "We'll give it another few minutes to make sure the others are in place. Then we'll get up over the ledge as quickly as we can and hope the element of surprise does the trick. What's your read of the thing, Burford?"

"Won't know until we get them in plain sight, Inspector," said Shepley's assistant softly. "If Blenkinsop's in place, as well as the boys on the other side, we ought to have them surrounded. They won't have anyplace to go."

As they waited, Andrew strained to listen, though they could only make out fragments of the conversation through the wind.

". . . if you don't, you'll be staying here . . ."

". . . treacherous coastline . . . anything can happen . . . food for the gulls . . ."

"Tell them, Strang . . . have to sign . . ."

". . . no good refusing . . ."

". . . offering five times what it's worth . . ."

". . . dinna ken what ye—"

Andrew realized this last was the laird's voice. His Highland temper was obviously up.

"—no goin' t' sell t' the muckle likes o' a pack o' thieves . . ."

"All right," said Shepley glancing at his watch. "Sounds like it's getting heated . . . let's bust up this little party."

"Just make sure no one gets hurt," said Andrew.

"Relax, Trentham. We know our business."

"But—"

Already they were on the move. Andrew scrambled up the jagged slope to follow.

They burst quickly onto the flat of the bluff. Even as Andrew scurried to follow, Shepley was running forward, gun in hand.

"All right, everyone," he shouted, "stay exactly where you are! No one move—we have you surrounded."

From the other side, another three agents ran toward them. Within seconds a half-circle was stretched around the conspirators, pinning them against the sea bluff.

Exclamations and a few imprecations sounded in surprise. As he ran forward behind Shepley, Burford, and the others, Andrew recognized four of his parliamentary colleagues, including one party leader and two deputy leaders, one of whom was his own. Ginny and her father were there as well, along with a man he did not know holding a small sheaf of papers.

"What in the world, Inspector!" began Tory leader Miles Ramsey, arguably the second most powerful man in the country. "What in blazes is the meaning of this?"

"I think you know well enough, Mr. Ramsey," answered Shepley, slowing and walking calmly toward him, gun still in hand.

"We are merely conducting a business arrangement with these good people. This gentleman is Dobson Strang, solicitor from Aberdeen. He will tell you—"

"We know all about what you are doing, Ramsey," interrupted Shepley. "We are here on other business than a real estate transaction, namely the theft of the Stone of Scone and the murder of Eagon Hamilton."

Andrew glanced toward Ginny but could not catch her eye. If she recognized him under the circumstances and without his beard, she did not show it.

"Don't be ridiculous. I haven't the slightest idea what you're talking about," said Ramsey. "This gentleman here, Mr. Finlaggan Gordon, controls this land on behalf of his clan, and we are simply engaged in negotiations to purchase—"

"'Tis a lie!" now interrupted Ginny's father, emboldened to speak his mind even more by the arrival of reinforcements. "'Tis more like thievin' than negotiations, ye foul blackguard!"

"We happen to know that Mr. Reardon—" Shepley began, still addressing Miles Ramsey, but now turning in Reardon's direction, "was involved with the theft of the Stone. Mr. Trentham here is an eyewitness. We have had a bulletin out for Mr. Reardon's arrest since June."

At the word "Trentham," both Ginny's and her father's faces lit in sudden recognition, though neither said a word. Shepley motioned to two of his men, who now walked to either side of the LibDem deputy leader and grasped his two arms.

"I had nothing to do with Hamilton's murder," said Reardon nervously. "You can't pin that part of it on me. I didn't even know he and—"

"Shut up, you fool!" shouted Ramsey, losing grip on his calm political persona. "They've got nothing on us."

"I don't know what part you have in all this, Mr. Burslem," said Shepley, addressing Ramsey's vice-chairman, "but I'm sure we'll find out.—What about you, Ferguson?" he went on, turning toward the SNP deputy leader. "We know you were involved in the Stone theft."

"I know nothing about the murder," sputtered Ferguson. "The Stone, maybe, but I wasn't alone. There was Dwyer and Reardon and all the rest. But Hamilton—"

Suddenly a gun was in Ramsey's hand. In a single motion, he ran several steps to his right before anyone could stop him and grabbed Ginny with his left hand. A surprised scream escaped her lips.

"Let go o' me, ye rascal!" she cried, squirming and trying to resist.

"Shut up, you little minx!" spat Ramsey, clutching her small frame all the more tightly. "—Now stand back, Inspector. Clear your men away or the girl—"

But he did not finish.

Almost without thinking, Andrew broke into a run and sprinted straight toward them.

"Let her go, Ramsey!" he shouted.

Taken by surprise, Ramsey's grip on Ginny loosened momentarily. She wriggled free, turned and kicked him as hard as she could in the shin, then ran to her father just as Andrew crashed into the Tory leader as if it had been a rugby match.

Both men tumbled to the ground. An explosion of gunfire sounded as the pistol flew from Ramsey's hand and landed several feet away.

Even Shepley's men were taken by surprise with Andrew's sudden attack, but now they hurried to help. While one secured Ferguson, two more now ran forward and pulled Andrew from the top of Ramsey.

"You all right, Trentham?" said Shepley.

"Yeah, I think so," replied Andrew, brushing himself off.

"You were lucky that bullet didn't find you. That was the most foolhardy move I've ever seen. You'd never last at the Yard."

Andrew laughed. "That's good. This kind of business is far too dangerous for me."

Two of Shepley's men dragged Ramsey to his feet. Before he knew it, his wrists were handcuffed behind his back.

"I tell you, you can't pin the murder on us!" cried Ferguson as he, too, felt the steel cuffs clamp over his wrists. "Talk to Ramsey. He'll tell you all about it—"

"I said to shut up, you idiot," growled Ramsey.

"We'll sort it all out later.—All right, Mr. Strang," said Shepley, turning to the solicitor, "what do you know about all this?"

As they spoke, suddenly Ginny ran toward Andrew almost as vigorously as he had toward Ramsey. Before she realized what she was doing, she found herself in his arms.

"That was so brave o' ye," she said.

Andrew did not reply, but simply enjoyed the moment by giving her an extra reassuring squeeze.

Behind them, the laird now approached, patting Andrew on the shoulder and greeting him warmly.

"Ye're a right braw lad, Mr. Trentham," he said, "gien ye dinna mind me callin' ye by yer real name."

"Of course not," laughed Andrew. "I just wish I had told it to you when we first met."

"'Tis all behind us noo. Dinna ye worry yersel' aboot it again."

"What about the woman you told us about before?" Shepley asked Andrew.

"Oh, right, Blair—they call her Fiona."

"Where's the woman called Fiona?" said the inspector, turning back toward his prisoners.

"He stashed her in a cottage not far from here," said Ferguson, nodding his head in Ramsey's direction.

"What for?" asked Shepley.

"He said she'd watch the girl if he had to put her on ice for a while to convince her father to cooperate."

"I see . . . so we have a planned kidnapping to add to everything else. What about it, Ramsey?"

As the inspector continued to grill the conspirators, Ginny gradually came to herself, embarrassed for her impulsive actions. She stiffened and pulled away from Andrew's arms.

"Why did ye du this?" she said to Andrew, backing away.

"What do you mean?" asked Andrew, still smiling and unaware of what she was thinking.

"Why did ye come here?" she said.

"Because you were in trouble," replied Andrew, "not to mention that we learned that man there may be a killer. I was worried about you."

"But hoo did ye ken whaur we were?" she added insistently.

"Alastair Farquharson telephoned me. He saw the maroon car and was worried. He thought maybe I could help."

"Why the muckle lunk!" exclaimed Ginny, her temper rising—toward Alastair, toward Andrew, toward everyone. "He had no right t' du it."

"Even if he was trying to help you?"

"We Gordons can tak care o' oursel's, thank ye verra much," she huffed. "Besides, wha kens whether we can believe ye or no?"

"What are you talking about?" laughed Andrew, bewildered by the turn the conversation had taken.

"Ye're an Englishman!"

"And that makes me a liar?" said Andrew incredulously. What in the world could have aroused this sudden change within her?

"I dinna ken aboot that, but I ken ye're no friend o' Scotland."

"Why would you say that?"

"'Tis what the papers say."

"And you believe everything you read?"

Ginny was silent a moment.

"How do you know any of that?" asked Andrew. "Maybe I am *trying* to be a friend, and you won't let me."

"Noo ye're jist tryin' t' confuse me wi' yer smooth Englishman's tongue!"

"Ginny, ye're bein' a perfect nincompoop," scolded the laird. "Ye can at least give the lad a chance t' explain himsel'. He's proven himsel' oor friend today. He could hae been shot, as weel as yersel'. 'Twas a brave thing he did. Seems ye're bein' a mite hard on him whether or no, like ye say, he's a friend t' Scotland."

"Well, he'll have t' prove it t' me!"

She turned and stormed off, hiding the hot tears that were already clouding both her vision and her good sense. The laird turned to Andrew, now embarrassed himself.

"Ye'll have t' forgive the lass. She's a mite hotheaded by nature, an' more'n a wee bit confused at the minute."

"Confused," repeated Andrew. "Confused about what?"

"Why aboot ye yersel', lad—dinna ye see it wi' yer ain twa eyes? She doesna ken whether t' love ye or hate ye. So all she can du is blow off steam through that fiery red head o' hers, an' say foolish things she'll regret one day."

Before the conversation could go further, Inspector Shepley again walked toward them.

"Everyone all right here?" he said.

"We're fine, Inspector," replied Andrew. He introduced him to the laird. The agent and the Scotsman shook hands.

"Right," said Shepley. "Well, we've about got it wrapped up here, so let's be off. I'll want to talk to you further, of course, Mr. Gordon."

They turned and followed Shepley's men back across the moor toward the cars. Ginny kept her distance, and she and Andrew did not speak again.

⬚   E I G H T   ⬚

The King's speech at the state opening of Parliament in late November did not offer a great many surprises. Labour's program for the following twelve months was not unlike what everyone had expected and what Prime Minister Richard Barraclough had predicted. In keeping with the centuries-old formality of the occasion, no mention was made of the parliamentary scandal that had so recently rocked the world.

There was, however, one item in the King's address which took the entire United Kingdom by surprise: Home rule for Scotland would be put on the agenda for debate in the House of Commons. The SNP had lobbied strenuously and successfully, and the Right Honorable Richard Barraclough had at last consented.

"My government," stated the King, "will introduce a bill to provide increased independence for Scotland, to be phased in over a period of several years, with an end in view of complete autonomy."

As His Majesty King Charles III read out the simple statement, buried two-thirds of the way through a speech whose monotone was only slightly less uninspiring than his mother's, he seemed completely unfazed by the historic implications of his words.

But Dugald MacKinnon and his colleagues were exultant. After years of trying, they had finally succeeded in bringing the issue of Scots independence before Parliament.

What the prime minister's actual plans in the matter were, he had divulged to no one. Did he really intend to proceed with debate and a vote on the matter? Or did he think the Scottish Nationalists could be bought off by simply inserting the item in the speech and then proceeding to ignore it?

Only time would tell.

———

As Andrew sat listening, his thoughts drifted to Malcolm and Margaret. Things had certainly shifted for Scotland during their reign too. Was another such era of dramatic change coming for Caledonia?

So much he read about Margaret and Malcolm reminded him of himself and Ginny—except in reverse.

He was the sedate Englishman who came north and found himself face-to-face with a tempestuous Highland Celt. He might not exactly be a saint, but he could probably be forgiven that. And on the other side of it, he supposed that to draw a parallel between the diminutive Leigh Ginevra Gordon and huge old ruthless Malcolm Canmore—

What am I thinking? Andrew asked himself.

Even if the comparison *were* apt, he had thus far been no more successful at subduing her Celtic temperament than Margaret had Malcolm's. What did it matter anyway? He might never see Ginny again. Her Highland temper was directed in the opposite direction from Malcolm's. Whereas Malcolm loved Margaret, she seemed to hate the very sight of him. He had begun at least ten letters to her since they had seen each other in the Shetlands, but they had all ended up in the bin.

Andrew glanced up. The King was still speaking. He tried to force himself to pay attention.

———

The Labour prime minister and the leader of the Scottish Nationalist Party listened too, with very different responses. But neither Richard Barraclough nor Dugald MacKinnon realized what deep and dramatic changes were taking place within the heart of their longtime colleague and new party leader Andrew Trentham—changes that could ultimately make him either an ally or a foe in the approaching debate on the matter of Scottish home rule. Nor did they realize that he rather than either of them would become the focal figure in the Commons when the division came to a head.

If the Honorable Andrew Trentham did not know what he himself planned to do in the matter, he had certainly been giving it considerable thought, much of which now involved his own very personal reasons for being interested in Scotland and its future.

⊠   N I N E   ⊠

Andrew went back to his flat that same evening thinking that he had to try to write Ginny again. He simply could not let more time pass without trying to explain himself to her.

After sitting a moment, he took down the volume in which he had read the story of Malcolm and Margaret, opened it and stared for a long minute at the color portrait of the two together under a tree, the saintly Queen's hand resting gently upon her husband's. There was no way to know how accurate the representation might be—no doubt it was colored by centuries of romantic mists that had embellished the legends. Yet the painting of the two ancient lovers was so compelling! How different their personalities had been, yet they had been devoted to one another.

He replaced the book and made his way to the desk, sat down, and pulled out a sheet of his monogrammed stationery.

Dear Ginny, he wrote. *I know it has been a couple of weeks since—* Andrew's hand stopped.

It was no use. He *still* didn't know what to say! He had to say something . . . but what?

He sighed as slowly the paper crumpled in his fist, then remained on the top of the table as a twisted reminder of his uncertainty.

He rose again and this time went straight to his bedroom. It was late, anyway. Tomorrow was just a few hours away.

Andrew awoke a little before seven. It was still dark out. He had tried to resume his morning and evening routine of the previous spring since his return to the city. But all was so changed now. He was not in the same curious and eager frame of mind as when the exploration into Scotland's history, poetry, and music had been so fresh. Everything had now taken on more weighty overtones—both personally and nationally. It was difficult to read Burns with the same exuberant innocence as before. Now he felt like he was a star-crossed lover in one of the bard's poems!

What a momentous year it had been. If he thought his life as an MP had been hectic *before*—now he was a party leader, and the demands on his time and energy and commitments had increased tenfold.

His whole outlook had changed as well. He *knew* Scotland now—knew it personally. Caledonia had become his friend. He knew its past and its people. He had listened to its music. He knew more than a few of its moors and hills better than places in Cumbria only a few miles from his home. And had he not so entirely bumbled his handling of the incident at Ballochallater, he would probably have said he was falling in love with a certain Highland lass.

That, of course, was the most significant change in his perspective. He not only loved *Scotland*, he cared for a *Scot.* A beautiful, intriguing, maddening Scot.

There could be no denying that the politics of Scotland were changing as well. Andrew felt the storm clouds on the horizon perhaps more keenly than any man in England. He knew he must brace himself in readiness. For there was one thing of which he could be certain—whenever the storm broke, he would be right in the middle of it.

⌗   T E N   ⌗

It was early December, with the nip of winter in the air, when Paddy and Bill Rawlings agreed to meet early one morning for a walk in Regent's Park and then have breakfast together.

Bill had been back a week now, and they had seen one another every day. The time together had been good, Paddy thought to herself, better than she had expected. She was remembering what she liked about Bill—his easygoing nature, his enthusiasm about his work, but also his willingness to *stop* working from time to time and enjoy a holiday. Because she shared her days with a pack of workaholics—and tended a bit that way herself—she found herself enjoying Bill's lower-key presence.

But something about Bill had changed too. She couldn't exactly put a finger on what it was, but she liked it. He was the same old Bill, and yet somehow he seemed more settled, more grounded, more confident in what he wanted. Stronger, somehow—in a way that caused her pulse to quicken when she saw him.

Could it be that she was falling in love again with her very own husband?

Andrew had dropped by unexpectedly one evening and she'd been able to introduce them. The discovery of several mutual acquaintances in their respective fields of journalism and politics gave them more than enough to talk about, and the two men hit it off quickly. Somehow that fact warmed Paddy's heart in a way she couldn't explain.

The feel of frost on her face as she left the flat turned Paddy's thoughts away from Bill and Andrew and reminded her instead of visiting her grandmother in Boston at this time of year. Of being at home in Upstate New York. A momentary pang of nostalgia surged through her.

There might even be snow on the ground by now, she thought.

The melancholy lasted but a minute. This was home now. She would not go back except to visit, even if someone came up and handed her a one-way ticket to the States with the offer of a cushy network job.

For some reason winter always brought her reminders of the past. It was probably the holiday season that did it. When time for Thanksgiving came around every year, she could not keep from thinking of the old stories of the pilgrims and Indians. Then the sweet melancholy would engulf her and linger through Christmas. She realized she had been especially lonely these last two seasons without Bill—though she had worked hard to ignore the feelings.

A gust of wind whipped up, sending dried fallen leaves swirling in a miniature tornado at her feet. Paddy gave a kick at them in instinctual pleasure to be out in the elements on a day such as this. She was nearly alone in the park, for it was early, and the morning was easily the coldest of the season thus far. The sky was covered over in a thick gray that looked and felt as if the overspreading clouds had settled over the whole island for a lengthy stay.

She pulled her coat tightly up around her neck, thinking with a smile about the morning last spring when she had orchestrated her so-called chance meeting with Andrew.

But then quickly her reflections drifted back to her own situation. It would be good if she and Bill could get things worked out in the next couple weeks. She didn't particularly want to spend another Christmas alone. And as she thought about it, she realized she wanted to spend the holidays with him.

As if in answer to her thoughts, in the distance she saw two men approaching.

"Look who I ran into," said Bill with a wide smile on his ruddy face when he saw Paddy walking toward them.

"Andrew . . . good morning!" exclaimed Paddy. "Back to your old early-morning wandering practices, I see."

"Not every day, but when I can."

"How did you two hook up?" she asked, turning around and joining them at Bill's side. She always had to stretch a bit to keep up with his lanky stride. "I thought I was the one who arranged chance meetings like this."

Andrew roared. "You don't mean to tell me you *arranged* that last spring!"

"What's all this?" said Bill, glancing back and forth between the two.

Now Paddy laughed, reddening slightly.

"Let's just say that I used my reporter's wiles to ambush the Honorable Mr. Trentham, even before I became a sleuth and detective in the matter of the Stone of Scone."

"Aha, so it all becomes clear!" said Andrew.

"My apologies," said Paddy, "although I'm not really sorry."

"I suppose neither am I," rejoined Andrew. "—Well, I'll leave you two here."

"No, wait," said Bill as Andrew turned and began to walk off. "Why don't you join us for breakfast?" As he spoke he glanced inquiringly toward Paddy.

"Yes . . . do, Andrew," she said nodding. "That would be great."

Thirty minutes later, the three were seated in Cachao enjoying coffee, tea, and croissants—a more Italian or French version of the morning repast than English—and the subject had gotten around to the upcoming holidays.

"If I can just make it to the Christmas recess," Andrew was saying, "it will give me a chance to catch my breath. The opening of any session is hectic, but this has been doubly so."

"What *will* you do for Christmas?" asked Paddy.

"I hope to make a quick trip up into Scotland—sort of on my way, if you can call it that," replied Andrew. "Then I'll spend several days with my mum and dad in Cumbria."

"How is your mother doing?" said Paddy.

"Very well. Which reminds me . . . I need to get you up again to Derwenthwaite for a visit. I'm afraid the old girl's still annoyed with me for running you off last time. Perhaps the two of you could come up together for the New Year."

"I, uh, don't know," said Paddy, glancing toward Bill, then back at Andrew. "We haven't even made Christmas plans yet, much less for the week after."

"But if that's an invitation," added Bill, "then we certainly shall talk about it."

"It *is* an invitation," said Andrew. "I know my parents would both be delighted."

▨   E L E V E N   ▨

For the third time in four months, Andrew found himself driving into the small Highland village of Ballochallater.

How different were the circumstances now, and how gray and brown the hillsides that had so recently been adorned by the royal purple garment of Caledonia. Snow now covered the highest crests and was piled at both sides of the road. The cold here at this time of year was bitter, far worse than in Cumbria. Andrew found himself wondering how the ancients had managed to survive so far north.

He had already determined not to make an effort to talk to Ginny. If she did not want to see him, he would respect that. He had finally written her. Beyond that, he would leave whatever happened next between them in her hands. But he had two things of importance to discuss with the laird, and he could not postpone them no matter how his feisty daughter felt.

From his correspondence with the laird, he imagined everyone in Ballochallater would know in advance of his coming. If not, by the time he checked into *Craigfoodie* and had enjoyed supper with Alastair Farquharson at the Heather and Stout, every man and woman for miles would be talking of his presence.

On this occasion, however, he was relieved to draw friendly nods and greetings from a good many of the villagers, though a few expressions indicated uncertainty about his motives.

The next morning, he had an appointment with the laird. On his last visit, he had gladly walked the half-mile distance to the castle. Today, with a light snow beginning to fall and the temperature several degrees below zero Celsius, he paid his bill to Mrs. Stirrat, then climbed in his car for the short drive.

T W E L V E

Three hours later, after a conversation he would never forget, Andrew rose to take his leave from Laird Finlaggan and his wife. Already he felt he had known them both all his life. He would not be able to rest until he had seen the laird and his friend Duncan MacRanald enjoying tea and oatcakes face-to-face.

"Thank you, Mrs. Gordon," he said, offering his hand. "Your hospitality, as always, warms the heart. I appreciate it very much."

She brushed aside his hand, and Andrew found himself swallowed up in her motherly arms. When he stepped back two or three seconds later, he realized she had tears in her eyes. The good woman turned and made a hasty exit toward the kitchen. The laird accompanied Andrew outside to his car.

"Ye'll hae t' take it slow, laddie," he said. "The snow's comin', an' it'll be piled on the road afore nightfall."

———————

At the window of her room, peeking from behind the curtain so she wouldn't be seen, Ginny Gordon watched them leave the house together. A perfect hurricane of confusing emotions swirled about inside her.

For the last three hours she had done everything imaginable to summon the internal fortitude to go downstairs and talk to Andrew. But every time she approached the door, something had held her back. Not a few pillows, several childhood stuffed animals, two books (one poetry, one animal physiology), and one vase of dried heather had been hurled across the room in the interim during the ebb and flow of her ranting tirades against her own indecision.

And now he was leaving!

Andrew and her father were shaking hands . . . he was walking toward his car . . . he opened the door and got in—

Suddenly she spun around, threw open the door, bolted through it, and ran for the stairs.

———————

Outside, Finlaggan Gordon watched the young Englishman he had grown to think a great deal of slowly pull out of the castle drive. The tires of his car crunched in the quarter inch of new white powder as he turned onto the highway.

Suddenly behind him the door swung open with a crash. Footsteps ran toward him on the snow-covered gravel. He turned to greet them.

"Ginny," he said, "ye're a wee late gien ye were thinkin' o' sayin' goodbye."

"He's gone!"

"Ay. What did ye think, lass? There's his car jist disappearin' doon the road."

"What fer did ye let him go!" she cried. "Didna ye ken I wanted t' see him?"

"Ye sure got a mixed-up way o' showin' it, lass. He thinks ye canna stand the sight o' him."

"And maybe I canna!" she yelled, turned, and stomped off a few steps. "Maybe I do jist hate him, the confounded Sassenach!"

"Ginny, ye're bein' a bigger fool than I ever saw ye—an' ye've ne'er been a fool! But noo ye're jist talkin' nonsense."

Ginny froze in place, drawing herself up to her full height, the picture of righteous indignation. The next minute, she spun around and ran toward her father. He opened his arms to receive her. But if he thought she was seeking comfort, he was mistaken. She began pounding with her little fists against his chest.

"Why'd ye let him go, Papa? Why'd ye let him go!"

Her father did his best to draw her struggling frame toward him, patting her gently on the shoulders and speaking soothing words. Gradually she calmed and let his embrace enfold her as when she was young.

"Oh, what's wrong with me?" she wailed. "I'm behavin' like sich a ninny!"

"Lass, I think ye're confused 'cause yer head sees an Englishman, but yer hert sees a Scot."

"He's no Scot, Papa—he's jist a Sassenach!"

"No, Ginny, he's no Sassenach. He's a Gordon."

"A *Gordon*! Hoo can ye say sich a thing, Papa!"

"'Tis true, Ginny. He jist told us himsel'. His name's Andrew Gordon Trentham."

Now Ginny pushed herself away and stared at her father with wide, tear-stained eyes. Then she carefully turned and half ran back into the house. She managed to get up the stairs to her room before the tears started again. Then she threw herself onto her bed.

"I canna fall in love with an Englishman!" she cried. "I just canna!"

———

In the distance, between the village and the castle, his cap and shoulders covered with falling snow, the village blacksmith watched the drama unfold. In spite of the distance, he realized what had just passed between the laird and his daughter.

He turned and walked back toward his workshop, revolving in his mind what he now knew he must do.

⬚ T H I R T E E N ⬚

Bill Rawlings was already waiting downstairs in the lobby of the BBC building when Paddy emerged from the elevator doors. His well-worn trench coat and gigantic umbrella, hastily furled, still dripped from the downpour outside.

"Bill, what on earth are you doing way out here?" she asked. The BBC headquarters at White City in Shepherd's Bush were at least a twenty-minute train ride from the apartment Bill had sublet from a friend.

"I thought you might fancy a drive in the countryside," he answered. "On a lovely day like this, who could resist?" With a straight face, he gestured gallantly through the glass doors toward the soggy brown-and-gray landscape outside.

Amused, Paddy followed his gesture. From her desk, she had been watching the cold, slanting rain all morning. "Perhaps we could have a picnic," she commented wryly. "We'll put the top down on the Mercedes."

Bill pretended to be hurt. "You don't believe me."

"What, that we're going for a picnic in the rain in your nonexistent Mercedes?"

"Ah, but I didn't say it was a Mercedes."

"But, Bill, you don't have a car."

"Correction. *Didn't* have a car. A responsible married man with a responsible job and a promotion needs a way to get around, don't you think?"

It took a minute for the words to sink in.

"Bill!" Paddy exclaimed after a moment. "You got the promotion?"

"Right," he said in the fake Liverpudlian drawl that always made her laugh. "And don't forget the car."

"What I thought, actually," he said, dropping the accent, the tenderness of his lopsided smile pulling at Paddy's heart, "was that a car might come in handy for a lovely Christmas trip up north . . . and perhaps a bit of a second honeymoon. If you're interested, of course . . ."

Paddy didn't answer immediately. She just stood gazing into his dear, familiar face, realizing for the first time in a long while that she *wanted* to see that face beside her every morning when she woke.

Neither spoke for several long moments. Then Bill added, very softly, "So what about it, Paddy? Want to see the car?"

The next instant she was in his arms, heedless of the wet, dripping raincoat.

The new year came.

Paddy and Bill Rawlings, who had celebrated Christmas together as a re-newed commitment to their marriage, took the train north and spent two days with Andrew and his family at Derwenthwaite. Nothing had proved such a healing tonic to Mrs. Trentham during the months of her recovery as the lively talk of politics and journalism and recent events in London. By the end of the holidays her speech had improved noticeably, and her eyes shone with a spark of the same fire that had blazed during her years in the Commons.

Andrew, Bill, and Paddy all returned to London together.

Though it was still midwinter, the change of year caused Andrew to look forward and give even more focused attention to the Scottish issue.

The woman called Fiona had been located, arrested, and brought back to London. Like Ferguson and Reardon, she was eager to save her own skin and only too happy to talk. Soon Malloy and Fogarty, who also had been instrumental in the theft of the Stone, were also behind bars. The druid Amairgen Dwyer, however, continued to elude Scotland Yard's most concerted efforts to locate him.

The Conservative leader Miles Ramsey still professed his innocence, though he stepped down temporarily from his party's leadership. But evidence continued to mount against him in the murder, including a match of the partial fingerprint painstakingly lifted from the sgian-dubh murder weapon, as well as information provided by his former accomplices.

Perhaps knowing that to apply pressure would prove futile in the long run, the SNP had not made contact with Andrew since the King's speech. But new Conservative Party leader Archibald Craye, who had served as Miles Ramsey's second-in-command for several years, was doing his best in the suddenly altered political landscape to woo Andrew's affiliations in the direction of a new alliance in the Commons. The stakes were high, for if he succeeded, the SNP would be denied its coveted objective, and the Labour government of Richard Barraclough—held partly through coalition with Andrew's Liberal Democrats—would surely tumble.

As the new year progressed and as generally noncontroversial legislation worked its way through the parliamentary process, Andrew knew that eventually forces would converge to bring home rule to the front burner. When that time came, Barraclough, Craye, and Dugald MacKinnon would all do their best to convince him to side with them.

⚑   F I F T E E N   ⚑

Meanwhile, Andrew's walks, reading, and research now took the course of a dedicated search, motivated not merely out of curiosity but out of mounting commitment to make certain he possessed the historical detail necessary to make a wise decision for the country.

As the backward threads of his own genealogy became clearer, Andrew found himself swept up in the drama of Scotland's independence on two levels at once—historical and contemporary.

He had managed to trace his own family's line several generations further toward the present. Having discovered Foltlaig, Fintenn, Donnchadh, Dallais, Breathran, and Fionnaghal, now the name *Darroch* suddenly arrested his attention in his twelfth-century research. Darroch and the sons of Darroch were no Gordons. But the fact that circumstances had forced one of Darroch's sons to move from Fife to the heart of the Gordon district indicated potential links with the Gordon name that Andrew found intriguing.

It was a period of Scotland's history, like today, when change had been imposed upon its people by forces from the south. Norman feudalism had sent the young MacDarroch, descendent of Fionnaghal, northward to a region known as Strathbogie. And right in the middle of Strathbogie now sat the town of Huntly—where the colorful blue sign had made him wonder if his family had roots everywhere in Scotland!

UNITED SCOTLAND

AND ITS REGIONS

CAITHNESS

SUTHERLAND

ROSS

The Isles

BUCHAN

Strathbogie/Huntly

MORAY

Aberdeen

ATHOLL

MAR

ARGYLL

ANGUS

STRATHEARN

FIFE

Stirling

Dunfermline

Forth

Edinburgh

Glasgow

Clyde

LOTHIAN

STRATHCLYDE

Berwick

Alnwick

CARRICK

NORTHUMBRIA

GALLOWAY

Annandale

Carlisle

Solway

CUMBRIA

9

NORMANIZATION OF
THE NORTH

A.D. 1172

✖ ONE ✖

A poor Scots woman sat up on the bed where she was lying.

"Are you certain?" she asked.

"The signs are unmistakable, Nara," replied the midwife at her side.

A moan of despair escaped the woman's lips. Her name meant "happy," but this news made her anything but. The joy of childbirth had already visited her twice within the last five years. But times were different now. For weeks she had prayed she was wrong.

It was silent a moment in the small cottage. At length the young mother spoke.

"How long?" were her only words.

"From what you have told me, six or seven months," replied the other. "But perhaps as few as five."

Nara nodded.

"And how long before he will know?"

"You will feel that better than I. Another month, perhaps two."

"Then I must tell him soon."

The midwife rose.

"Thank you for your discretion, Odharnait," said the woman, rising too and walking toward the table. "Do not forget the bread," she added, handing the midwife two fresh loaves. "No one must know the other reason you came until I tell Darroch."

"You may count on my silence."

As soon as the large woman left with her loaves, Nara sat down on the edge of the bed again. What were they going to do? They did not have enough to eat as it was.

And now another hungry mouth was on the way!

❊   T W O   ❊

Times were severe that winter of 1172.

The cold had come early. Vegetables had grown to but half their normal size. Snowfall in the late autumn had been heavy. And the cow that Darroch, Nara's husband, depended on to give milk to his small family had finally outlived its ability to be useful upon the earth and expired.

Now he could neither feed his children nor pay his rent to the earl for his sparse plot of hard earth. It wasn't much, but out of it he encouraged a few poor things to grow, and it had produced enough grass to give sustenance to the cow while she lived and still provided bugs for the chickens. He had never known good times, nor had his father before him. But this was surely the worst year of them all. If they did not starve, they would likely freeze to death before winter was past.

And now his wife was again with child. It could not have come at a worse time. She had just told him yesterday, though he had already begun to suspect it.

Darroch, son of Donnuill, who dwelt with his family west of the Ochil Hills, knew that he had come from the bloodline of the old Scots King called MacAlpin as well as the holy man Fineach-tinnean macAedh, though he knew nothing of his connection to the rising new clan of Donald in the west whose influence would spring from Somerled, Lord of the Isles.

Notwithstanding the blood of past kings and conquerors, poets and priests, that flowed in his veins, poverty for Darroch was a consuming reality. These days, the only nobility that mattered in Scotland spoke French and English. The amber blood of one's Celtic heritage and one's Gaelic tongue—whatever their *past* glories—counted *now* for little. Even what he knew of his lineage seemed to be of little practical value in his life. Though he was by nature a thoughtful and even philosophical man, his life had taught him well the impossibility of putting one's genealogy on the table for hungry mouths. Bread, turnips, kale, and milk to feed his family—these had to be of primary concern to Darroch MacDonnuill. And this year he knew he had too little of any of them to last the winter.

❈   T H R E E   ❈

What should have been an occasion of great rejoicing five months later was for poor Darroch MacDonnuill only a further reminder that there were too many mouths and not enough to put in them.

All at once the number of those mouths he must feed had grown, not by one . . . but by *two!*

Even the midwife Odharnait had not foreseen this!

When the startling fact was known, at last the mother's heart could not help reflecting on the meaning of her name. They might all starve, thought Nara, but what a gift for the Almighty to bestow upon a woman—to choose her to give birth to twins! It had not been an easy labor, but now her months of anxiety gave way to the fullness of a mother's joy.

That his wife should bear twin sons—both of whom, by the look of them, would grow into strapping lads—was an improbability that could not altogether penetrate Darroch's consciousness before it was confirmed a second time by the midwife. With a great smile on her face, the ruddy-cheeked, buxom woman turned back toward the bedchamber, leaving poor forlorn MacDonnuill with an expression of hopeless incredulity on his suddenly very pale face.

Whatever the development may have indicated in approbation of his own virility, all Darroch knew was that all of a sudden he was the father of *four* . . . and poorer than ever.

At no time and in no place does the arrival of twins fail to occasion heightened interest in the mystery of birth and the hand of Providence in the affairs of men. Word of the simultaneous appearance of two young MacDonnuill offspring therefore spread quickly through the tiny village. Thence, like widening ripples in a quiet mountain pool, it moved out through the countryside—from cottage to cottage, from mouth to mouth—until at length it arrived to the ear of the lord of the region, Duncan II, earl of Fife.

Himself a twin whose identical mate had died at birth, Lord Duncan had harbored a lifelong fascination with the phenomenon of multiple birth. Upon hearing the news that twins had been born in his region, he immediately set out to investigate.

Toward the end of July, therefore, in the year 1173, when the lads were three months of age, Darroch MacDonnuill heard a tumult of horses early one afternoon outside his poor cottage. He rose to investigate the clatter and found Lord Fife himself at the door, inquiring if he might set eyes on Donnuill's twin sons.

Trembling lest the laird mention the upcoming rent, for which he had not a penny laid aside, Darroch fearfully complied.

※   F O U R   ※

Though great influences had come north to Scotland in Margaret's train, it had been the *sons* of the Canmore and the Saint—they of the English names, whose faces no longer looked toward their Celtic past—who actually accomplished the most widespread Normanization of the land of their heritage.

Malcolm and Margaret's youngest son, David, more than any of his brothers, had been responsible for permanently altering Scotland's cultural landscape. Bred in English ways, educated largely in the south, and having spent much time in France, David the Saint was a thoroughly English and Norman lord. His marriage to a rich Norman heiress made him the English King's brother-in-law and one of the most powerful barons in all Britain. He encouraged both Normans and Anglo-Saxons to settle in the north, desiring to bring Scotland fully into the flow of modern Europe. Devout and as religious as his mother and a great benefactor of the church, David I would nevertheless be remembered primarily as the man who turned Scotland over to Norman hands.

Every aspect of Scottish society was changing during these years. Under the Norman system of feudalism, *land* became the sole determinative commodity, the essential unit by which all things were measured. With control of land went authority over every aspect of the lives of those living upon it.

All the realm belonged to the King. In the King's hand was thus power to grant use of land according to his will. Twelfth-century kings, therefore, granted *fiefs*, or "holdings of land," to loyal noblemen they could trust. By this means, kings maintained their domains, kept them free from invasion or rebellion, and profited from them.

Landholding nobles were responsible to make their land pay. This they accomplished by dividing their land into smaller *fiefdoms*, which they leased to *vassals* lower than themselves. This practice provided them with means to raise the tribute they owed to those over them and to line their own pockets in the process.

Each nobleman was lord over his own particular domain—giving protection to his vassals, while profiting from them. Large fiefs usually contained within them any number of smaller fiefs, while overall the King remained lord of the land.

It was an ingenious scheme, allowing every level of the nobility a certain degree of autonomy to profit from his judicious exercise of power, as long as he kept the one above him happy. Universal law, as it would one day be known, did not exist. Each fiefdom was a law unto itself, with its landholding nobleman serving as constable, judge, and jury all in one.

Alas, however, for those at the bottom, where the peasantry labored to eke out a meager living. These vassals at the bottom level of the feudal system had no rights and privileges except those granted them by their lord, who served as both landlord and magistrate. Each paid the master above him, who paid his, who in turn paid his . . . all the way back up to the earls and dukes who held huge tracts of land and who were obliged to make *their* tribute to the King.

FIVE

Duncan II's visit to admire Darroch MacDonnuill's new twins was brief. The son of Donnuill would not set eyes on the earl again for seven years. Yet almost immediately after the visit, circumstances for the poor household began to brighten.

For one thing, he managed to keep his rent paid—how, Darroch never quite understood. If, as was said, twins brought good fortune, Gachan and Beath had certainly brought it to Darroch's humble cottage.

A cow had been given him when the boys were four months old by a farmer in the next village. The circumstances were peculiar, MacDonnuill admitted, but he was not one to turn away such a needed gift. The poor man's perplexity mounted when, only months following, a calf was born. Surely there was some mistake. The farmer could not *intentionally* have meant him to have a fertile beast.

When the calf was three weeks old, therefore, with rope around its slender, hairy neck, Darroch made the long walk out into the countryside to the farm on the other side of the earl's estate to explain what mistake had been made, to thank the man again for his generosity, and to return the newborn.

No, answered the man, seemingly surprised only by MacDonnuill's appearance, not by the existence of the calf. Good fortune followed the gift. Calf and mother belonged entirely to Darroch.

Protestation proved useless. At length Darroch turned and began the thirty-minute return walk clutching the end of the rope, still too bewildered to rejoice in his newfound circumstances of plenty. Two beasts—this was wealth indeed!

Nor were the benefits of the newly smiling face of fortune occasioned by the twins' birth entirely bovine in origin. Not only did more milk flow into the mouths of his children—there were also more eggs to accompany it. From several sources, even a few with whom MacDonnuill possessed not so much as a passing acquaintance, began arriving gifts of a chicken or two. The givers had heard, they said, of the boys' birth and of the difficult straits in which the father and mother found themselves. It was only fitting, they added, that neighbors and kinsmen do what lay in their power to help. They hoped Darroch and Nara would accept their humble gifts.

"I don't know what to think," the baffled father said to his wife as she sat nursing the two infants.

"Then don't think," she urged him with a mother's innate practicality. "God has blessed us. It is up to us to accept His blessings with thankful hearts."

S I X

The intrinsic societal change in western European culture to a land-based feudal system involving landowners and tenants, noblemen and peasants, had brought with it an inevitable class hierarchy extending from the lowest vassal-peasant all the way up to the King. The more entrenched the system grew, the more advantage was taken of those at the lower levels of the societal ladder. The poorest eventually became little more than serfs, or slaves, to a wealthy aristocratic elite, which included its own hierarchy within itself.

To endure, feudalism needed a mechanism to insure faith between the various echelons of the developing society. If the loyalty of a landholding noble began to waver, the King might strip him of his land and give it to another who *would* be loyal. Thus, by the authority of his position at the top rung of the feudal ladder—and his ability to bestow wealth and power—did the King rule his kingdom and command the loyalty of those under him. This process of keeping a vassal in submission, financially bound and morally indentured to his lord, was the mortar which held the whole system together.

Sealing the bargain between King and nobles—and those nobles in turn with those under them—the ceremony of homage thus became foundational. It was essentially a statement of the terms of loyalty and submission—including both financial and military obligation—upon which the entire system rested.

To give homage, a vassal went to both knees, clasped his hands, placed them between the hands of his lord, and solemnly declared himself bound as his "lord's man," promising to keep faith with him, to bear arms with him against all others, with the proviso—if the lord did not happen to be the King—"except the faith that I owe to the King."

The King, or lord, on his part, essentially said in return, "By virtue of your homage, I grant you a portion of land in my kingdom to hold *for* me, as my man. You may develop and improve and profit from it and in every way treat it as your own. Certain fees will be required of you, for I too must profit. You must keep what I have granted secure and maintain order on my behalf. And you must help me in battle when I require it and do whatever I may call upon you to do, for you are my man."

Feudalism offered an efficient decentralized system for maintaining order in distant regions of a kingdom where dwelt potentially fractious and unruly native populations.

Subjugation of the diverse peoples inhabiting the land was accomplished by placing loyal noblemen at vital strongholds along strategic routes throughout the country. There, fortified by castles and defenses,

noblemen of varying rank were able to administer their fiefs, rein in dissi-
dent subjects, and squelch whatever uprisings might occur, thus keeping
the kingdom intact on behalf of the King. To these ends, castles began to
be built upon raised earthen mounds throughout Scotland.

And what, meanwhile, of those to whom the lands of Caledonia had
belonged for hundreds of years? Gradually they were given to others—
parceled out among the vassals of the King, just as other tribal societies
around the world would later be dispossessed by those with the power to
control the direction of progress.

Such transformations were slow and gradual. Not only Englishmen
and Normans were granted lands from Scottish kings. Celtic earls with
Pict and Scot heritage also rose to prominence—or retained their power
under the new system. Nevertheless, the imposition of a feudal land system in the north brought more and more Norman blood into the great
blending of bloodstreams that had characterized Scotland's past.

▓   S E V E N   ▓

The earl's factor called on Darroch MacDonnuill one day when the
twins were nearly a year of age. The serious expression on the man's face
struck a cold dread in the poor father's soul. Timidly Darroch listened
while the factor explained that an error of long past and untraceable date
had been discovered. It was with great regret that he had the duty to
inform MacDonnuill that the rent on his cottage—

Poor Darroch was by this time trembling for what must be about to
come.

The rent had been found excessively high, the factor went on, and
was, therefore, as of this quarter year, reduced to an amount which he
went on to specify. On the earl's behalf, regret and apologies were suitably expressed. In exchange for the error, the factor further had the duty to
inform him that there would be no payments *whatever* required for the
next six quarters, after which time, payment of the proper, and lower,
amount would commence.

MacDonnuill stood as one stunned, still trembling, though now with
disbelief, as the dust from the hooves of the factor's mount retreated in
the distance. How was it possible for so much grace to arrive at the door-

step of one man in such a short time! Nara was right. Truly had Isaac's blessing fallen upon him from the hand of God, and he had been given freely of both heaven's manna and the abundance of the earth.

The sense of blessing increased as the twins grew. By the age of seven, the two boys were sturdy, cheerful lads, devoted to one another, and able to assist their older brother and sister with many of the tasks about the place. Darroch and Nara watched their family grow with grateful hearts.

❖   E I G H T   ❖

When David I, son of Malcolm Canmore and Queen Margaret, had come to Edinburgh in 1124 to assume the throne after his years in England and France, he had distributed large grants of land among many Anglo-Normans who had been his friends in the south. He bestowed upon them rank and privilege, introducing names into Scotland that would play pivotal roles in its future. An enormous flood of Norman nobility surged into Scotland during the twenty-nine years of David's reign.

Much of Scotland's land changed hands during that time. In the very year of his coronation, the new King's friend Robert de Brus was granted a charter for the lands of Annandale, across the Solway from Carlisle. Through David's gifts the families Bailleul, Comyn, Gordon, Fraser, Boswell, Seton, fitzAlan (who would become the King's hereditary high stewards), and many others, already landowners in England, were given charters for huge tracts throughout the north.

Scotland's clans, meanwhile—which in former years had occupied nearly all the land north of the Solway-Tweed line—seeing domains that had been theirs for centuries taken away and given into the hands of a French-speaking aristocracy, retreated into the Highlands where they might hope to make a living while preserving their language and their way of life.

But though the ancient Celtic way of life was gradually being swept away, the dynamism of Celtic energy and individuality entered silently and invisibly into the hearts and bloodlines of the newcomers and changed *their* essential personality. If the Norman newcomers were not of pure Celtic extraction, they came ultimately to behave in strangely similar ways, becoming *less* English and *less* Norman the longer they remained in the north . . . and *more* Scot.

As these changes occurred, loyalties within Scotland's nobility became increasingly divided. Many landholders were bound in loyalty pledges to both England's *and* Scotland's kings, for they held estates both north and south of the Solway and Tweed. Conflict became inevitable, for in the feudal system there could be but a single King who was *owner* of all lands and to whom *all* were bound. Malcolm's homage to William the Conqueror opened to dispute the question of who was ultimately lord over the northlands—the King of Scotland . . . or the King of *England!*

Relations between the south and the north remained generally friendly—for there was much intermingling of noble and royal families—until David I's second grandson, William, came to the Scottish throne in 1165, seventy-two years after old Malcolm Canmore's death.

The spirit of his great-grandfather now rose up within the heart of the new King, called "the Lion." Many might have thought William the Lion was a reincarnation of the Canmore himself. For in temperament and thirst for territorial conquest there could be no mistaking that he was of old Malcolm's lineage.

This new King first negotiated a formal treaty with France, which would later be called the Auld Alliance. Then, nine years after being crowned on the Stone of Scone, William the Lion proceeded to invade England to retrieve lands that had been taken from Scotland during the recent reign of his brother.

William the Lion was obviously of the opinion that no *Scottish* King was vassal to an *English* crown.

But William's invasion of England was of short duration. The Scottish King was taken prisoner at Alnwick, where his great-grandfather had been stabbed in the eye with the point of a traitor's lance. He was then taken to Falaise, where in 1174 he performed the greatest homage of all.

With his life at stake, William swore to hold all Scotland as Henry's vassal. He thus declared every person in Scotland the feudal servant of the English King Henry II and all Scotland Henry's fiefdom.

Whatever ambiguity might have existed in Malcolm's act of homage, that of William the Lion was mortifyingly clear. With good reason was it called the humiliation of Falaise. For the next fifteen years, Henry II lorded it over William at every opportunity, making him *feel* the weight of his sovereign overlordship.

❈ N I N E ❈

In 1180, six years after the reduction of his rents, Darroch MacDonnuill discovered that the hand of blessing was of much nearer origin than the heavens to which he had first attributed his changing fortunes.

He was well aware that his lord Duncan had gone to fight the English with the King called the Lion. Though Darroch heard that the King's army had been defeated, he knew little about the situation other than that the laird had since returned and that English troops occasionally passed by on their way to Duncan's castle. Certainly he had never heard of the Treaty of Falaise or the fact that, as a result, many of Scotland's castles were now in English hands.

When Darroch saw the earl's carriage again approaching his dwelling, no fear rose this time within his breast. He was happy to see the earl healthy and well after a war in which many Scottish knights and lords had lost their lives. A rent payment was due, but the fact was no cause for alarm these days. That the earl should come for it himself was unusual, but then since the birth of his boys *everything* about MacDonnuill's tenancy on the earl's land had been out of the ordinary.

MacDonnuill put down his tools and walked from the field where he had been working toward the carriage that had drawn up beside his cottage. Stepping out, Earl Duncan greeted him warmly, then asked if he might have a few words.

The poor man hesitated, then invited the earl into the cottage. Only Nara, his wife, was inside.

"I come to you with an opportunity, MacDonnuill," said the earl, moving straight to the point. "I know times are difficult for men in your position."

"Your generosity in the matter of the rent has been of great help, sir," said Darroch.

"Indeed," rejoined the earl, "that is precisely why I have come—to offer you an opportunity to continue things as they are."

"To continue—"

"Yes, so that I do not find it necessary to raise your yearly obligation back to what it was before."

"I . . . I understood there had been an error . . . that I now pay the correct amount."

"Tut, tut, MacDonnuill. That was merely my factor's way of explaining it. I thought you understood that I had purposely *lowered* your rent and given you a year and a half for free on top of it."

"I . . . it . . . it was most generous of you, sir," stammered Darroch. He was uncertain of the earl's meaning, but he felt an approaching discomfort. He looked over to his wife and felt an even deeper unease at the expression on her face—as though she had been seized by a premonition of doom.

"I told you when I visited before that I would do what I could to make things easier for you, on account of your twins."

"You have been most kind, my lord."

"Ah, yes, of course—but you see, now we must evaluate matters again."

The earl paused briefly, then added, "How *are* the boys?"

"The twins?"

"Of course—yes, the twins."

"Very well, sir—healthy and growing and strong."

"Good, I am delighted to hear it—and the eldest, what is his name?"

"Gachan."

"Yes, of course—Gachan, a fine lad. What would you say, Mac-Donnuill, if I told you I was prepared to make a gentleman of young Gachan?"

"I . . . I don't know . . . but how would—"

"It is my wish to take your son into my household, MacDonnuill," interrupted the earl. "I could make use of a bright, hardworking lad. He would be my servant at first, of course. But if he shows himself to be a good learner and hard worker, there is no reason why he should not in time be given advantages."

"But . . . but why would you do this . . . for us?"

"I have always fancied twins. I told you I am one myself. I took a liking to your lads straightaway. I would like company as well for my younger son, David, who is seven. His brothers are considerably older."

The earl paused and waited.

"It is . . . certainly," hesitated Darroch after a moment, "an opportunity for the boy. But . . . but I do not see, sir, how we could do without him. Your offer is most kind, sir. But I think my wife and I would prefer that he remain with us."

"I see," nodded the earl. "But if your rent were to go up to the previous amount . . . or should circumstances force me to raise it higher—I am certain you see that this is an opportunity not only for your son, but also for your family ... to continue without the burdens some others on my land have to carry. Times have changed, you see. The English thumb is heavy upon us these days after Falaise."

Darroch MacDonnuill was not a brilliant man, but slowly the earl's meaning became clear.

"The cow ... the chickens?" he asked at length.

"Yes, yes—it was my doing," replied the earl. "I thought you knew, MacDonnuill. I told you I would see to your sons. I said that same day that I would find an opportunity to help them. I thought my intent was unmistakable. Unfortunately, at this time I only have need for one of the boys."

Darroch had hardly paid attention to the earl's words at the time. Now he recalled them, and they stung with sudden new import.

In truth, the earl of Fife was not a cruel man. He was indeed a generous landlord by the standards of the day. What he had done in easing MacDonnuill's burden and what he now expected in return carried no intent of duplicity, but was born out of a compassionate heart. If he could improve the boy's station and give the family a decent life in the process, what else would they be but grateful?

At the same time, if the man was obstinate, the earl was sufficiently a man of his times that he was not above employing the force of his position to get what he wanted. And he had spoken truthfully about the changing times. English soldiers, in fact, were at that moment garrisoned at his very castle.

"But ... but if I decline your offer?" Darroch now said timidly to the earl.

"Then I fear times may become difficult for you, MacDonnuill," replied the earl, eyeing the peasant keenly.

Nothing more was said. The earl rose and left the cottage.

Four days later, the notice arrived for Gachan to be ready, with whatever possessions he desired to bring with him, in seven days. Personal clothing, other than what he wore, would be unnecessary. He would be provided for.

A carriage, the communiqué concluded, would arrive for him at precisely twelve o'clock noon.

▨ T E N ▨

On the night prior to his son's departure, a father whose heart was full left his cottage and wandered out alone into fields that he and others like him worked to feed their families. His was not a life that fostered introspection, but now he knew he must find a place to be alone.

Darroch MacDonnuill held no bitterness for the difficulty of his existence. Life was arduous for everyone except lords and earls who owned the land—that was simply the order of life. Men of his station expected no different. So Darroch did not think himself ill used, even though his heart wrenched at the thought of sending his son away. All things considered, Lord Fife was a reasonably generous and tolerant man, and he seemed sincere in his desire to help Gachan.

MacDonnuill's thoughts turned to his four children.

The birth of the twin boys had indeed brought blessing, even though at the time he had misunderstood its implication. He had secretly harbored the thought ever since that perhaps they might do great things, that one or both of his sons might rise high, perhaps even become a knight, maybe even fight at the King's side.

And now—who could tell? Might not this opportunity for Gachan to enter the earl's household be the fulfillment of that very dream? Only a fool would ignore the possibility. Such chances came to peasants like him only once in a lifetime . . . and then only to the most fortunate.

Gachan would go far, mused Darroch, if the earl truly gave him the chance—if he was not merely desirous of adding a boy servant to his household.

And what of Beath, the father reflected. What would the future hold for him? Was it not possible that Gachan could reach a position where he could help his brother as well?

As Darroch MacDonnuill walked on alone, gradually the heritage of the Celt stirred his heart to quicker pulse. The passion of past holy men rose up within him, and suddenly the entreaty burst forth from his lips:

"God . . . take care of my sons!"

They were the only words of spontaneous prayer Darroch had ever uttered in his life, except for what he repeated by his wife's side at Mass. The sound of his own voice almost frightened him with the boldness of his request—that he, humble Darroch MacDonnuill, might presume to address God himself and make petition on his own behalf.

Yet the words had been spoken. He could not take them back. And the brief prayer seemed to alleviate the anxiety of his soul.

He turned back toward his home. He must speak with the boys. But first there was something else he had to do.

He ducked into the cottage, sought out the small box where he and his wife kept what few items they considered valuable, removed the item he wanted, then went in search of tools. He needed only a hammer and a sharp blade.

A short time later, father and twin sons walked along the same ground the father's steps had recently trod. The twins were yet young. How could they fully understand the import of such a moment? Yet they would reflect upon this evening many times in later years and recall to mind their father's solemn injunctions.

In the cottage, Nara now walked to the door to gaze after the three retreating figures—her tall husband and the two boys on either side of him. She would like to hear the words passing between them. But she knew that the injunctions of this night were those a father alone must pass on. Her mother's heart would say good-bye in its own way. But this occasion belonged to the men—her husband and his sons. As she watched, her heart swelled in gratitude that the man she loved cared about preserving the heritage from which they had both come.

"This is a historic land, my two sons," MacDonnuill began. "We come of stock that has dwelt upon it longer than the memories of men are able to see clearly. My father, and my grandfather before him, told of those in our lineage who came before and of the land they tamed—before the English, before the French, even before the Norsemen. It is now time I tell you again what was passed on to me. I want you to know of your pedigree so that you will feel what blood flows in your veins and so that never will love for Caledonia's past leave you. The King on the throne—William, the man they call the Lion—is but part Scot, and in his heart he's more of a Norman than a Scot. What is to become of old Caledonia—who can tell? That is why you must know, so that you may preserve the old ways and the old legends and tell them to your sons and your daughters."

"Why do you tell us now, Papa?"

"Because tomorrow your brother leaves us, Beath," replied Darroch. "We may not be together, the three of us, like this again."

With tears already beginning to well up in their eyes at the shocking words, they sat down. Gently the father sat down with them and explained. He answered their questions to the best of his ability—where Gachan would live, what he would do while there at the earl's estate, when he would visit. Finally, when the questions had dwindled into troubled silence, he began to tell them stories. He recounted every old tale he could remember from his own father and grandfather—of Dallais and Breathran, and of Donnchadh who had met his death at the hands of the Vikings. Then, gazing more distantly back, he told them of their links to the first King of Scotland, still further back to the times of Columba and Maelchon, and finally, though by now the mists were overlaid with mere legend, to fragmentary accounts of ancient Cruithne himself.

The twins listened for two hours.

It was not the first time they had heard the ancient legends. On this occasion, however, they listened with heightened interest. Never had they heard it all recounted together, as one connected narrative, which, in spite of many fragments and personalities and the distinct directions of its many offshoots, was in reality a single epic stretching across thousands of years. Nor had they before heard their father speak with such eloquence. On this evening they hardly recognized his voice. A spirit seemed to have come over him from another time. He spoke as with the power of the bard, even with the authority of a King.

"And now, my sons," Darroch concluded, laying his hands on both the boys' heads, "as your father, I bless you both. May your lives be full of the blessing of this land. Yours is an inheritance of no earthly kingdom. It is not one of wealth or possession or rank. Such has not been allotted to the house of Darroch MacDonnuill. Yours is an inheritance more permanent. It is a legacy no one can take from you. Never forget your birthright. In you flows blood strong, thick, and rich as the brown waters which trickle down from the Highlands. It gives the descendents of Caledonia something no other people on earth possess."

"What, Papa?" asked young Gachan.

"Our heritage, my son . . . the inheritance and blood of our ancients! Scotland is the land of our forefathers. Now it rests with you to carry that heritage forward into new generations."

The boys sensed the solemnity of the moment and were silent.

Their father now removed a small leather pouch from around his neck, opened it, and took out two identical objects of great antiquity.

"Though you two are the youngest of my offspring," he said, "a compulsion has come over me to place this into your hands. I have shown it to you before, but as you can see, I have severed its links into two equal lengths. I know little of the history of this relic except that it has been considered sacred in our family for generations—so sacred that we would not part with it even when we had no food. Some say it was once worn about the neck by an ancient King, though it seems heavy to have been put to such a use. After what I have done to it, though, such a function will no longer be possible. Whether it has *earthly* value, I am not expert enough to know. I have already told you something of how it came into my father's possession and thus into mine."

He paused in his speech, then handed one half of the weighty silver chain to Gachan, the other to Beath.

"Take these, each of you now possessing half of what until a brief time ago was *one*," he said. "Let it be a reminder of the things I have told you—a reminder that wherever the fortunes of life take you, you will always be one. Never forget the ancient lesson of the white stag. Do not forget the two brothers of the Caledonii. Though they were two, they were *one*. So are the two of you, my sons—as shown by these links you each now carry. Now *you* must carry forward that ancient brotherhood of Caledonia."

✦ ELEVEN ✦

The day for parting came. That there had been a week to prepare for it, and to explain the necessity for the change to the children, in no way lessened the trauma of the moment for the poor mother and father.

Darroch himself stood watching the carriage disappear with stoic resignation. Nara wept. And the suddenly destitute Beath hung his head like a forlorn puppy that had lost its master, wondering what would become of him.

The family endured the day of Gachan's departure, however, and the next . . . and the next after that.

These were days when necessity was too severe to worry long about happiness. Life therefore continued, as it always manages to do. Hardship was the essential building block of survival. Where work is to be done, and *is* done, even heavy anxieties eventually relinquish their hold on heart and brain.

And the earl was not an unkind man. He allowed young Gachan to return to his old home one day each month. Though these happy intervals brought a return of sadness, the rest of the family gradually accustomed themselves to the new arrangement, and all five came to relish the visits more than dread their end.

Their sadness was also alleviated to see the bright expression on Gachan's face at his arrival back home after his first month with the earl. He too had cried as he left and was fearful at what might become of him.

Now he came with reports of being well fed—the clothes he wore certainly gave indication that he was far from neglected—and of spending much time with the earl's son, which boded well. He was cared for, they learned, by an old woman and her husband who lived in a house attached to the castle. The woman had once been a lady's maid to Lady Duncan, and now her husband tended the earl's horses.

"But I cannot understand him, Father," said Gachan. "He speaks a funny language."

"Gaelic," said the father, "as my own father and his father spoke. It is the tongue of our ancient people, Gachan. Is the man a Highlander?"

"I don't know, Papa. I only know that when he speaks to his wife or the horses, the sound is very strange."

Darroch smiled. He could not have hoped for better. That his son was in the care of an old Highland couple warmed his heart.

"Are you with the man every day?"

"Yes, Papa. He shows me all about the horses, and I help him keep the stables clean and the horses fed."

Such a prospect would even have delighted Nara if only it had come when the boy was older. For such a family to place one of its children in the stables of the earl was good fortune indeed. Even now, if she could not *delight* in it, she saw much ground for a quieter form of thankfulness. Thus Darroch, Nara, and the two brothers and one sister who remained readily accustomed themselves to the change.

✖   T W E L V E   ✖

Several years passed.

Gachan, son of Darroch and Nara, was now twelve and happily

growing as a bright and capable stable assistant to Calum Dhuibh. The old Highlander was delighted to discover that the boy was also of Highland stock and spoke to him in the Gaelic tongue at every opportunity.

He also taught him the ways and secrets of the stables, and the young boy learned eagerly. The smell of manure was offensive to the sensitive nostrils of the earl's youngest son. To Gachan, combined as it was with all the other evocative sensations of Lord Duncan's stables, it was of the aroma of heaven.

The sound of old Dhuibh's step behind him intruded into Gachan's daydreams one morning as he tossed another load of straw and dung from his fork to the cart.

"How're the arms, laddie?" said the stableman kindly in the soft language Gachan had come to understand.

"Tolerably well," he answered, "—the dung's no heavier today than every other."

"Sit down, lad," said Dhuibh. "I would tell you of one who lived in the old times, in the hills not so far from here. He would be your own kin, I think, just like he's mine."

Gachan listened as one entranced while the melodic Gaelic tongue of the Highlander spun out the tale, then broke into the gently mysterious chant of an ageless bardic melody.

Fàgaidh mi ùpraid, sùrd, agus glagarsaich,
Dh' fhaicinn an fhuinn anns an cluinnteadh a' chagararsaich
Chi mi na mór-bheanna,
Chi mi na coireachan.
Chi mi na coilltean, chi mi na doireachan,
Chi mi na maghan bàna, as toraiche,
Chi mi na féidh air làr nan coireachan
Falaicht' ann an trusgan de ched.
O chi, chi mi na mór-bleanna,
O chi, chi mi na mór-bleanna,
O chi, chi mi na coireachan,
Chi mi na sgoran fo ched.

I will leave confusion, hurry, and clatter,
To see the land where whispering can be heard.
I will see the big mountains,
I will see the valleys.

I will see the woods; I will see the groves,
I will see the fair and fertile fields.
I will see the stag at the foot of the hollows
Enshrouded in a mantle of mist.
Oh, I will see, see the big mountains,
Oh, I will see, see the big mountains,
Oh, I will see, see the corries,
I will see the peaks under the mist.

Silence fell in the stable, broken only by the gentle shuffling sounds of the horses in their stalls. They likewise seemed to have been calmed by the spell of the otherworldly crooning.

"Our lord the earl's of the old blood himself," remarked the groom.

"He is not a Norman like they say are most of the earls?" asked an inquisitive Gachan.

"Nay—he's no Norman. He comes of the same stock as I do, and you do yourself. 'Tis even said his line goes back to the Pictish kings. He's a man we can take pride in serving. Why, lad, 'tis the earl of Fife who holds the hereditary right to crown our kings at Scone."

"Did Earl Duncan crown King William?" asked Gachan in astonishment. The very thought struck the young man with awe. If it were true, it would give him a link to the King himself.

"Ay, he did, lad . . . ay, he did. Our earl may be the King's man, but he's also the man that made a King o' William."

The link to royalty was thus established in the boy's brain, and ever afterward deepened his loyalty to both his lord and the Scottish King.

"Who's to say?" Dhuibh mused, at length picking up a fork to help Gachan with the remainder of his pile. "When I'm gone, you might yourself become groom t' the earl. And maybe one day, when he goes to see the King, you'll hold the reins of the King's own horse."

The old man's words penetrated the heart of his young assistant. Gachan said little for the rest of the afternoon. Visions of kings and horses and battles filled his youthful imagination, with himself in the middle of them, a great sword in his right hand, a cape of burgundy flying from his shoulders, a vest of leather protecting his chest while he acted as groom to a majestic King of the future, ready when the summons should come to follow his master into battle.

The old Highlander's prophetic words would not be fulfilled within Gachan's lifetime. But they would not be so far wrong with respect to one of the boy's descendents, to whom would be passed the love both these two felt for the magnificent beasts upon which kings rode into battle.

Another five years passed, and another bitter parting was in store for the family of Darroch MacDonnuill.

Gachan and Beath, Darroch's twin sons, were now seventeen, but the fact that they were nearly men could not alleviate the anguish of what they were informed would soon happen.

This time Gachan would be taken not merely a few miles distance from the family, but far to the north of the country. Old Dhuibh, said Gachan, was eager for the change because it would mean a return to the region from which his people had come. But only sorrow greeted the news on the part of Darroch MacDonnuill's family. All Darroch, Nara, their older son and daughter, and especially Beath, could think was that they would probably never see Gachan again.

Word had been delivered through the earl's factor.

King Henry II of England was dead. After a long period of occupation, the English were now withdrawing from Scotland. The new King Richard of England, called the Lionhearted, had renounced the feudal superiority given his predecessor by William the Lion and had removed his troops. The humiliation of Falaise was broken.

As a result, however, great resistance to the King of the Scots had suddenly sprung up among many Highland and island clans. Even though he was Malcolm Canmore's great-grandson and thoroughly Scottish by blood, William the Lion was also thoroughly Norman by custom. This fact caused him great difficulty in keeping down native resistance to his rule, especially in the northern region of Moray.

The King had resolved, therefore, to send his man Duncan, earl of Fife, to the region, to a certain valley known as Strathbogie. There, in that predominantly Celtic region, the earl would act as lord on behalf of the King, to prevent further outbreaks of the clans against him. In return for the earl's service, the King would provide him with a huge tract of land to administer as his own. Dhuibh, who could speak the old tongue to the natives should it become necessary, would accompany him north.

"What . . . what does all this mean?" asked Darroch when the factor was through.

"That the earl will be removing from Fife," answered the man, "to take up residence in Strathbogie."

"Permanently?"

"The earl will maintain his residence here, for he will remain, of course, the earl of Fife. But he will take much of his household with him."

"And our son?" asked the fearful wife.

"The earl's stable staff, as I said," replied the factor, "will go north, and thus Dhuibh's stableboy must go as well."

"When. . . ?" was the only word Nara could utter.

"Four months."

Tears waited until the man had left, then flowed freely.

What Dhuibh had told Gachan some years earlier was entirely true. The earl himself was not a Norman. His ties of race were closely linked with MacDonnuill's own, for he came of the same Celtic stock as many of his vassals. But Duncan was a practical man. He had long ago embraced the new order and adopted Norman ways. Why should he not better his own position, just as he had offered opportunity for betterment to Darroch MacDonnuill for *his* son? It would profit nothing to resist change as the rebels continued to do in the remote Highland regions.

Change *was* coming—that was clear enough. Year by year, old tribal chieftainships were being forced to come under the dominion of the King of Scotland. Duncan, earl of Fife, would fit in with the new scheme and take what was offered him, even if it meant having to squelch rebellion on the part of his Celtic kinsmen.

After all, if he refused William's offer, Strathbogie would go to some Norman knight.

※   F O U R T E E N   ※

The first objective on Lord Duncan's part in the far north country would be to construct an impenetrable fortress.

He chose as the most defensible site one between the two rivers, the Bogie and the Deveron, some half a mile from where the former emptied into the latter. The location offered a strategic position along the route stretching from Aberdeen and Kildrummy to Elgin and Inverness. This gave the earl control over the wide valley on behalf of Scotland's King. Near the banks of the Deveron, therefore, he would erect a great timber tower to serve as his castle.

Designs were drawn up, and the earl moved most of his staff and family to Strathbogie and into temporary quarters in the village near the site of the future fortress. By the time wagons, tools, horses, supplies, and other equipment were brought in, laborers, quarrymen, carpenters, and assorted craftsmen enlisted for the undertaking, and the digging of trenches and foundations was begun, two years had passed.

All work ceased during the winter months. In those far northern regions, the snow piled high, and the ground froze solid as granite. No dirt could be dug or hauled for the castle mound until the cold months had passed.

But eventually a new summer came to the valley and work resumed. The earl of Fife was enjoying the bright sunshine—a treat after the long months of winter overcast—as he rode toward the construction site where Gachan MacDarroch was working.

Young Gachan was now a strapping and muscular twenty-year-old youth—with the looks and intelligence of a man of thirty. Never had the earl been happier that he had made the twin one of his household. If the truth were known, the young fellow was twice the man his own son was. The two boys had forged a decent friendship in their early years but no longer saw much of one another. Young David had spent several years in England and had been less than indifferent over the prospect of returning north. He now showed little enthusiasm over the plans that were under way. Gachan, meanwhile, had become an increasingly valuable worker—all the more so now that the huge project was progressing.

The earl reined in his horse and dismounted, then walked toward the ditch where twenty or thirty men were digging. The young son of Darroch pulled himself up from the depths of the hole and strode toward him with a smile. It was a warm day, and sweat poured down his dirt-smeared chest.

"Ho, Gachan!" greeted the earl, thinking again what a manly specimen he was. If he had had a daughter, he would already have married her to him!

"Hello, my lord," said Gachan. "The foundation for your new home advances nicely!"

"And you, it appears, have been working harder than all the rest!" laughed Duncan, looking him up and down. "Though I should find nothing so unusual in that!"

"Your men all work hard," rejoined the young man with a smile. "We shall complete this portion of the trench by tomorrow. The motte I would say will then be about half the height you desire. Then we shall begin with the moat, which will give us sufficient dirt to complete the motte."*

"And the second mound, for the bailey?"*

"Will be under way by week's end."

"Well, I shall be away in Fife for two, perhaps three weeks. I leave in the morning. I am placing you in charge of the completion of the motte. Hector will be engaged gathering lumber, overseeing the work at the quarry, and making plans for beginning the construction. I need a man here on the site at all times. I have decided to make you that man."

"I am honored you feel you may trust me, my lord."

"I *know* I may trust you, Gachan," returned the earl.

———

By summer's end, both the tall conical motte, with its steeply sloping sides, and the much more extensive but lower mound encircling it were completed. Atop the former would be erected the earl's castle. On the larger would sit the enclosed bailey, whose walls would contain a number of separate buildings, including servants' quarters, kitchen, cellars, chapel, and stables.

※   F I F T E E N   ※

The construction of all the buildings for the castle complex took several years.

Gachan continued to show himself faithful and rose steadily in the service of Duncan, earl of Fife and now lord of Strathbogie.

As construction neared completion, while Gachan was supervising a critical joint where roof and one of the chimneys met, high atop what

---

* *Motte*—the mound upon which a castle tower was built.
* *Bailey*—a palisade or enclosure surrounding the motte in which were constructed outbuildings associated with the castle itself.

would soon be the castle, a voice called from below.

"Gachan . . . you have a visitor."

Puzzled who would ask for him rather than for the factor, Gachan finalized his instructions to the two men with him, then began his descent. It took him three or four minutes to reach the ground by use of several ladders. He turned and walked down the steep slope of the motte. The assistant who had delivered the message pointed out a large, broad-shouldered man, a peasant worker by the look of him, standing some distance away with back turned, watching the progress of one of the bailey walls.

Gachan walked toward the stranger.

"I am Gachan MacDarroch—" he began as he approached.

The newcomer turned. Gachan gave a start as his vocal cords seized him. Standing in front of him was an exact image of himself!

Both stared awestruck for a moment. Then a smile gradually broke across his visitor's face.

The next instant they were in one another's arms, sharing an affectionate embrace accompanied by manly tears of love.

"Beath!" Gachan exclaimed to his twin. "How . . . how did you know where to find me?"

"It was not hard," replied his brother. "Strathbogie is not difficult to locate from Aberdeen. Everyone for miles knows of you the moment I mention the earl. Never Pharaoh had so loyal a Joseph. They thought I *was* you!" he laughed.

"But this is too wonderful!" said Gachan as they stepped back. "When did you grow so large and tall—so strong?" he exclaimed.

Beath laughed.

"At the same time you did."

"But it has only been, what, four years?"

"Five—and you have changed as much as I. Just look at you—and gaffer over all the construction!"

"The factor is an excellent man too. But you are right. The earl places great trust in me."

"With good reason, my brother, I am certain."

"How are Mother and Father?" asked Gachan.

Beath's face fell.

"That is why I am here," he said. "Father is ill. He has been asking about you. I told him I would find you."

"Is his life in danger?"

"It is possible," answered Beath gravely. "The end is not imminent, but we believe is approaching."

"I will be there at the soonest the earl can part with me. I will leave before winter."

"How can you be certain Lord Duncan will grant your request?"

"The earl is a fair man. He will let me go. And Mother?"

"Very well—strong and healthy."

"Ewan and Letitia?"

"Ewan and his wife have two sons and a daughter. Letitia remains with me at home, but a man in the village fancies her. I do not doubt it will soon be only myself left to care for Father and Mother."

Gachan took in the news of his family with many emotions. It broke his heart to be so far from them. But it could not be helped that his life was in Strathbogie now.

⊠   S I X T E E N   ⊠

Beath and Gachan remained together four days, during which time Beath joined his brother on the construction site. Those were times of great rejoicing, hard work, laughter, and a newfound manly comradeship to replace that childhood friendship they had left behind fifteen years earlier. Early the morning following Beath's arrival, the two were out before any of the other laborers, working together on the troublesome chimney joint, discussing the best method to insure that not one of the ten billion drops which would fall on that roof during the coming winter's rains would penetrate the inner walls of the house.

When the earl came to inspect the premises midway through the morning, he was surprised to see *two* Gachans standing before him! A young man himself no longer, the earl was steadily advancing toward that second childhood into which all must grow, and many emotions from his own past now revisited him with increasing regularity.

He glanced back and forth between the identical faces and physiques with a look of bewildered astonishment. Then, unexpected by any of the three, tears slowly filled his eyes. Beholding so vividly the close relationship between these two, the great man realized again his own loss so many years before. Surely Gachan and his brother possessed, each within the other, a wealth no power or worldly title could buy. Perhaps one or two tears resulted as well from the realization—how clear does much become in old age to which the eyes of *self* are oblivious in youth—that he had himself caused in these two the same separation which all his life had stung him with regret.

Coming quickly to the rescue of the master he had grown to love, Gachan now explained with a beaming smile.

"It is my brother, my lord!" he said.

The two shook hands—the earl who had crowned the King of Scotland and Gachan's humble peasant brother. They were instantly friends.

"He journeyed north to tell me that our father is ill," said Gachan as his smile faded.

"Then you will return to the south with your twin immediately."

"I must see to the completion of the roof and the bailey wall," replied Gachan. "Beath assures me there is no impending danger to our father."

"You must go regardless," insisted the earl.

"I would have your family snugly inside your new home before winter's first snowfall," rejoined Gachan. "Then, with my lord's gracious leave, I shall return home to spend the winter with my family in the south."

"I see when I am beaten," laughed Lord Duncan. "All right, then. I agree to your plan, and most heartily."

Beath departed for Fife at the end of his four-day visit. On the first night of his return journey, he stopped at an inn in Aberdeen, for which accommodation the earl himself had insisted on paying. As he opened the small parcel in which were packed his few clothes and other traveling necessities, twelve silver coins tumbled onto the floor. They had been wrapped inside a cloth containing provisions for the journey which Gachan had given him from the earl's kitchen.

Beath smiled. His brother had indeed risen high in the King's service. But he had not forgotten his humble roots, nor had his affection for his family diminished. What wealth this was!

———

The castle at Strathbogie was completed on schedule. Afterward, in the autumn, young Gachan returned to Fife—and great was the rejoicing of his entire family to greet him. He spent the winter in his childhood home. And when their father, Darroch, died the following spring, Beath and Gachan were sitting on either side of his bed, one of his hands resting within the gentle clasp of each.

The twins' sister, Letitia, married within the year. Beath continued to live in the same cottage where he had been born, caring for his mother. He did not marry till he was forty-one. Neither did he nor any of the other sons or daughter of Darroch want for anything, for the earl of Fife grew more and more generous as his years advanced.

Upon his return to Strathbogie, Gachan assumed the duties of overseeing the new and expanded stables at the castle. Dhuibh was by now an old man and able only for the smallest of tasks. The earl, however, continued to show Dhuibh and his wife kindness for their years in his service. They lived out their days happily and contentedly in two small rooms attached to the stables.

         ▩   S E V E N T E E N   ▩

As the twelfth century gave way to the thirteenth, a well-ordered feudal system under Scotland's landowning aristocrats was solidly in place. Clan rebellion continued to be beaten back by William the Lion's successors. Norman blood and customs continued to spread throughout the land.

The Gaelic language, already intermingled with Norse, now became steadily infused and corrupted by Anglo-Saxon, or "Inglis" as it would come to be called—the old and new tongues mingling in a way that would ultimately produce a unique hybrid *Scots* dialect of its own.

The *character* of the Scots people was becoming intermingled as well, with the vigor and independence of the Celt proving hard to vanquish.

The new century demonstrated increasingly, in fact, that the lords and nobles who came to Scotland after the Norman Conquest were allowing the spirit of the Highlands to infect them. They became ever more intent upon securing and consolidating their own power and feudal holdings than upon strengthening the crown of Scotland. As the year 1066 retreated further into the past, in truth the descendents of the Norman newcomers behaved more and more like native Scots themselves.

Though many of these nobles held lands in England as well as Scotland, by the thirteenth century the individualistic Celtic blood in their ancestry rose to predominate. Brown peat ran stronger than sea blue, and the clans continued to thrive.

While their neighbors and relations south of the border were learning to pride themselves on being *English*, the descendents of Cruithne, Folt-laig, and Maelchon would forever be MacDonald or Forbes, Campbell or MacLeod, Douglas or Moray . . . or Bruce, Balliol, and Comyn.

But that they were all Scots together mattered little when disputes arose.

In the year 1284, more than a hundred years after the births of Darroch MacDonnuill's twin sons, arose the greatest dispute it is possible for a monarchy to face—an empty throne. King Alexander III of Scotland was dead, and all three of his children had preceded him to the grave—two sons and his daughter, Margaret, who had married the King of Norway and become that nation's Queen.

The heir to the throne of Scotland, therefore, appeared to be Alexander's three-year-old granddaughter, also named Margaret, whose birth had ended the life of the Norwegian Queen, her mother.

Complications and disputes set in immediately.

Two Scottish lords put themselves forward and laid claim to the throne in place of Margaret—stating that no female could inherit the kingdom. The first was the aging Robert Bruce, lord of Annandale, a region just north of Carlisle, who held large estates in both England and Scotland. His Scottish lands had been granted to the Bruce family by David I in 1124, and his own father had married David's great-grand-daughter. That made Bruce a direct descendent of David I, and therefore of Malcolm Canmore and Margaret—a lineage that Bruce might well trace all the way back to Kenneth MacAlpin. It was a strong claim.

But John Balliol, lord of Galloway, stepped in to contest Bruce's claim. He *also* was in David I's direct line, with nearly identical descent. *He* not Bruce, insisted Balliol, ought to be made King.

The Scottish Parliament listened to the plea of both claimants, but decided only that peace should be kept and the "nearest by blood must inherit."

The nearest blood remained three-year-old Margaret. And she remained in Norway.

EIGHTEEN

The prospects in Scotland were not bright for a child-queen, a foreign one at that, hovered about by jealous regents and nobles scrambling for power.

To make matters worse, south of the border a strong English king, Edward Plantagenet, great-uncle of the so-called Maid of Norway, possessed his *own* claim to the rule of Scotland—a claim not only of descent, but of homage. For even though Richard the Lionhearted of England had repudiated the subjection of Scotland accorded in the Treaty of Falaise, his successors, when it suited them, continued to consider Scotland *de facto* among their dominions.

By loose interpretation of an oath sworn to him some years before by Alexander—a statement of homage similar to the one Malcolm Canmore swore to William the Conqueror—Edward found justification in considering himself Lord Paramount over all Scotland. He was also, conveniently, Alexander's uncle. Did not his position give *him* as strong a right to the Scottish throne as a Norwegian toddler?

The English King, therefore, was added to the list of claimants, now grown to four. The young Margaret, Maid of Norway, was by all rights Queen—but Bruce, Balliol, and Plantagenet were not far behind with their claims.

Scotland's nobles were not eager to give Edward I of England a more secure foothold than he already had. But neither did they relish placing the kingdom in the hands of either Bruce or Balliol. A nervous parliamentary council of lords and clergymen therefore hastily convened to appoint a regency to rule Scotland in Margaret's name, before Edward should press his own potential rights in the matter.

This regency represented the strongest of Scotland's aristocracy and included the great-grandson of the earl of Fife, who had raised Gachan, son of Darroch, so high from his humble birth. These regents—called guardians—were William Fraser; Robert Wishart; Duncan, earl of Fife; Alexander Comyn; James the Steward; and John Comyn. For obvious reasons, neither of the chief Scottish contenders for the throne was included.

The powerful Bruce family—Bruce the elder, at seventy-seven, and his son, also Robert Bruce, earl of Carrick—resented being omitted from the ruling council of guardians. They began to gather men and arms. The growing dispute over the throne now appeared capable of sending the country into civil war.

Within three years, the situation in Scotland had grown delicate and grave. By 1289, King Eric of Norway, concerned for his young daughter's future and safety in Scotland, appealed to Edward in England for protection and assistance.

N I N E T E E N

Edward had already established himself as a skillful mediator on the Continent and had many allies within the aristocracy of Scotland. Many Scots, therefore, followed the lead of the Norwegians and turned to Edward as the strongest individual involved, as well as the most likely to effect a harmonious solution. The blood ties between the three royal families were viewed not as a difficulty, but as a potentially unifying factor.

Edward was only too glad to help facilitate in Scotland's difficulty—on one condition . . . that the Scots acknowledge his claim to be Lord Paramount over their kingdom, which was no more, he said, than their dead King himself had done. And Alexander had indeed given homage to Edward after the fashion of Malcolm Canmore. But now once again the critically ambiguous interpretation of this event surfaced. Was such homage only for lands held by the Scottish King in England? Or was it rendered for the *entire* kingdom of Scotland?

Edward knew exactly where he stood on the issue. He had not pressed the matter during Alexander's lifetime. But with Alexander now dead and unable to dispute what had been said, and with the Scottish throne up for grabs, the English King was ready at last to assert his claim to rule all of Scotland.

To strengthen his claim, Edward now brought up a subject that he and Alexander had discussed before the Scots King's death—the prospect of a royal marriage between the infant Margaret and the English King's young son and heir, also named Edward, who was a year younger than the infant Queen of Scotland. Edward preferred to seize the throne peacefully if he could. What better way than by marriage? It was a plan certain to resolve any future disputes once and for all.

Discussions were arranged between the three nations—England, Norway, and Scotland. Negotiations proceeded in great detail. A treaty was at length concluded which firmly established Margaret as heir and Queen of Scotland and provided for the marriage between her and young Edward. The Maid would sail from Norway to England to be placed in the custody of her great-uncle Edward, who would send her north to Scotland to rule when *he* judged the time fit and the nation at peace.

This final provision extended the unclear homage a dramatic step further and established a vital precedent that would come back to plague the Scots time and again: *the manifest right of the English King to intervene in Scotland's affairs.*

The *Scottish* Queen had been placed under the authority of the *English* King, who would *himself* decide what was to be done and when to do it. Edward might intervene whenever and however he chose.

The line between Scottish independence and English sovereignty thus grew all the more vague. Edward's overlordship, left unresolved during Alexander's reign, thus remained precariously ill defined.

The Scots did insist upon, and were granted, a declaration that *appeared* to insure independence. It guaranteed that Scotland was separate and divided from England and that its rights, laws, liberties, and customs were wholly and inviolably preserved for all time. However, to this promise were added words which kept English hands still vying for control: "Saving always the right of our lord King," added the document, "and of any . . . that has pertained to him . . . or which ought to pertain to him in the future."

Even in this attempt to clarify the relationship of Scotland to the English King, ambiguity deepened. Scotland had been guaranteed "separation" from England—but not *independence.*

The treaty of November 1289, signed at Salisbury, had compromised the future liberty of their nation. The Scots nobles did not yet realize how seriously.

One fact in the entire matter, however, was *not* ambiguous: Edward's ambitions were clear enough. That he instigated no immediate hostile activity made the concession appear less serious than it was. But with the signing of the treaty, Edward's desire to be recognized as Lord Paramount over Scotland had been committed to writing.

At the end of September in the year 1290, seven-year-old Margaret, Maid of Norway, Queen of Scotland, and the implied ward of the King of England, set sail from Norway on her way to England.

The crossing was windy and rough. The child became deathly sick. The ship reached the Orkney Islands safely, but within days young Margaret was dead.

Years of schemes, negotiations, and treaties were suddenly for naught. If the Scottish throne had been in doubt before, now ambition surfaced from many new quarters.

Scottish affairs were thrown into instant turmoil. Whereas before there had been four, now at least a *dozen* contenders immediately claimed right to the throne of ancient Caledonia.

Strife appeared unavoidable.

※　T W E N T Y　※

But a century before, when Gachan MacDarroch was making his move north into the region of Strathbogie, the people of Scotland could not have foreseen that their country was moving toward such a fate. For most, as they accustomed themselves to the Normanization of their land, life remained more or less as it had been—each small fiefdom doing its best to feed and protect its own.

In Strathbogie, the twin who had found favor in the earl's eyes continued to prosper. When he was twenty-eight, Gachan met the daughter of a baron from Lothian. The man had traveled northward with his daughter to visit the earl.

The baron's daughter and earl's assistant were married the following year. The earl had built for them a small house in the village. Knowing of Gachan's love for horses, an adjoining stable was constructed as soon as the house was complete. The earl's wedding gift to the young couple was a fine roan mare and a black stallion with white forelegs.

Gachan's four sons and two daughters all inherited their father's love for horses. Every one of the youngsters would have been content to make his or her home in a stable forever. Gachan, who over the years had taken up the farrier's trade, attempted to pass along his skills to his sons. His third son, Cein, took to it with greater proficiency than the others and made it his lifelong profession.

The farrier trade continued to be passed down through the family to Gachan's grandchildren and to a certain great-grandson, who would still be plying the art in Strathbogie a hundred years later.

Love for horses continued in the family. One of the grandsons, rather than being known as MacDarroch—as were Gachan and the rest of Darroch's descendents—took for himself the name Killop, called by some Philop, or "lover of horses."

The many generations of *his* descendents, in after years, would be known by both the names *MacKillop* and *Philops*.

10

NORTHWARD TOWARD THE FUTURE

░ O N E ░

Prime Minister Richard Barraclough may have been an idealist during his youthful political career. What Labourite wasn't? The Labour Party had been founded on idealism and change.

But he was also a realist, Barraclough realized as he looked up from his desk at Number Ten Downing Street. He had become more so since occupying this office.

The fact was, reaching the pinnacle of political power changed one. Suddenly there were no more mountains to climb. All his life he had imagined what it would be like to get to the top. He had worked and struggled to get here. But then everything changed. Now he found himself looking down the slope on the other side, wondering what course his life might take after he left the summit.

What permanent legacy would he leave behind?

Would there be any lasting change in this great nation for which people would look back and say, "Richard Barraclough was responsible for that. He had courage to move the country in a bold new direction"?

The prime minister rose and walked slowly about the office. The hour was late, and most of the city was quiet.

He glanced toward the framed mirror on the opposite wall, then approached more closely to take stock of the face looking back at him. The lines of age had begun to show more noticeably around his eyes. His hair had certainly grayed since he had taken office. Reaching this summit of political power not only changed your outlook, he thought. It aged you!

Barraclough smiled pensively. One thing was certain—he would not last forever at the top. No one did. He was at the apex, but how long would it be his to enjoy? Margaret Thatcher had had eleven years. But not all PMs were so lucky. Wilson and Macmillan had both served for six. Even the great men Disraeli and Churchill had only been PM for nine years, and many of Barraclough's predecessors had served terms of five years or less. There were no guarantees . . . except that one day you were sure to be gone.

Political cycles came and went. He had ridden into this office on a wave of anti-Tory sentiment. But that wouldn't last, either. The Tories would come to power again, and Labour again after them, and on it would go—up and down, cycle following cycle. That's how a free democratic system worked. It was the same in America, with the reins of control passing back and forth between Republicans and Democrats over the years.

He turned from the mirror back toward his desk. His eyes fell on the framed copy of the Magna Carta on the wall behind it, one of the greatest documents of freedom in the history of the world. Even though its intended meaning in 1215 may have been less idealistic than once thought, its symbolic meaning provided the foundation for the growth of democracy itself. Beside it hung a portrait of President Reagan and Premier Gorbachev—a remnant from his predecessor he had decided to keep—another fitting image of the triumph of liberty in this new age.

He considered the implications of the two eras of history depicted on that section of wall—the thirteenth and the twentieth centuries.

What an astounding thing it was, as both reminded him, to *relinquish* power rather than fighting tooth and nail to hold it.

How distinct was that principle, as represented by the two images on his wall, from the force that drove such men as Alexander, Caesar, Napoleon, and Hitler. It was the difference between trying to *grasp and seize and maintain* power versus *giving up* power for the sake of a greater good.

Gorbachev was truly one of the heroes of the twentieth century, thought Barraclough. His genius lay in recognizing the need to *lay down* power and *let go* of the Soviet behemoth in favor of its smaller constituent states. The basis for his standing in history was not in gaining power, as so many autocrats perceived their destiny, but in yielding back independence to those very regions his predecessors had conquered. And in so doing, he might well have single-handedly prevented another world war and holocaust.

Barraclough turned again and walked slowly across the floor to the window, where he stood gazing out into nighttime London.

The decision facing him was not one of such epic proportions as encountered by Gorbachev in the 1980s. But perhaps in its own way it was similar. The USSR had been an accumulation of separate states, each with its own individuality, history, and ethnicity. The Kremlin held it together for seventy years. But Gorbachev and Yeltsin after him ultimately recognized that to continue doing so was futile. They saw the future. They recognized that progress required the *relinquishment* of that centralized power. In Gorbachev, for the first time, a Soviet premier saw the necessity of freedom. As a result, he stepped to the front rank of history, insuring his legacy as one of the truly great men of the last century.

It had been the same recognition of the need for freedom of indigenous peoples throughout the world that led to the breakup of the British Empire during the last century. As a result, dozens of former colonies—from India and Nigeria and the Gold Coast to Rhodesia and the Sudan—were now sovereign and independent nations.

Funny, thought Barraclough—in this modern era of the late twentieth and now twenty-first century, two seemingly opposite trends were manifesting themselves throughout the world.

On one hand, power and autonomy were being granted to small states previously included in larger conglomerates and to colonies that had been part of larger empires. The world's new nations over the last fifty years were too numerous to count—from those of the British Commonwealth to those of the former USSR and even the new Balkan countries that had resulted after the breakup of the Soviet Union. In every instance, power was being returned, or, as they said in Britain, *devolved*, to smaller levels of autonomy.

Yet at the same time, the joining of states into larger units, as the United States had paved the way for more than two centuries earlier, was now coming even to Europe. Who would have guessed, even in the days that the Soviet Union was breaking up, that the European Union would have developed so far?

Barraclough paused in his thoughts as he continued to stare out into the dark London night. He knew it wasn't because of Rhodesia, the Balkans, Belarus, or Kazakhstan that he had been unable to sleep on this night.

What was really on his mind was this nation whose center was located in this very city, even this very room.

What of *Britain's* future?

That was the question most heavily on his mind, and which had been keeping him awake lately.

What of their *own* nation, this accumulation of islands just off the western shores of the European continent known as the United Kingdom of Great Britain and Northern Ireland? Because the UK was a democracy, did that reduce the imperative to look toward the future with less idealism and realism?

Then came the question that had been nagging at him: Was their collection of states in its own way just as diverse as those of other nations whose separate parts were now independent?

If Britain was the world's first and primary democracy from which had sprung all the world's democracies—from the United States more than two centuries ago to the most recent explosions of democratic nationhood around the globe—what role ought Britain to play to insure that no people is coerced into the submission of an artificial nationhood?

And in that light, was Britain's democratic foundation, example to the free world though it was, actually faulty?

Which model ought to serve as beacon for the future of the United Kingdom and its four disparate parts: England, Wales, Scotland, and Northern Ireland?

And just as important, Barraclough wondered, what ought to be his role in determining that future?

It was an uncomfortable question.

How many politicians had the guts to do what Gorbachev had done—relinquish their standing even in their own countries and parties to do what the future required?

Might he be such a one? Did he have that kind of guts if it came to it?

Barraclough sighed, turned from the window, and walked back to his desk.

He needed someone to talk to . . . someone who could help him put all this in perspective.

But who? His own party colleagues would doubtless only be able to see the politics of the thing. They were still on the way up, many of them still hopeful of someday occupying this same room where he was alone with his thoughts. Because of that, how objective could they possibly be? Perhaps it was inevitable that vision was clouded by politics until one reached this point.

But however he did it, whomever he talked to, he had to look beyond politics . . . to posterity.

If history was beckoning, he had to make sure he was hearing what it was trying to tell him.

❧ T W O ❧

The request to visit Number Ten was not altogether unexpected, in that they were now the two leaders of a coalition government for a new session of Parliament. But from the tone in the PM's voice on the telephone, Andrew Trentham had the feeling that something other than politics as usual was on Richard Barraclough's mind.

He was shown into the prime minister's private study. The door closed behind him. No one other than Barraclough was present.

"Thank you for coming, Andrew," said the PM as they shook hands.

"Of course, Prime Minister," replied Andrew. They took seats.

"It's a terrible shock about Miles and all the others," said Barraclough. "I would never have expected such a thing possible."

"Nor I," rejoined Andrew.

"It just shows, I suppose, that power does corrupt as they say, and that we cannot be too careful. Always vigilant, and all that."

"The Americans had their wake-up call with Nixon and Clinton," remarked Andrew. "I guess now it's our turn."

A brief pause followed.

"I know we have spoken with one another many times in the past, Andrew," the prime minister began in a new vein, "as all politicians do. I am sure you and I will become much closer in the coming session, as you are now the leader of Labour's coalition partner. But that is not what is on my mind today."

"I had that feeling," smiled Andrew.

"I asked you here," the prime minister continued, "because I need someone to talk to on another level, as a colleague . . . or a friend, perhaps, but also as one who understands the stakes of what I am facing. I think you do, because what I am contemplating may in the end rest as much upon your shoulders as on mine."

"I'm not sure I follow you, Prime Minister."

"These days I find myself reflecting on the trends and tides of history, Andrew," Barraclough continued seriously, "and on what may be required of us at this juncture—particularly with respect to the furthering of home rule and devolution. I suppose, in a way, I need your help as I try to come to terms with this very complex issue."

At the words, Andrew realized that the PM was talking about the same questions he had been grappling with for months. He listened as Barraclough went on briefly to recount the nature of his quandary.

"So, which is the case in the UK?" the PM asked at length. "Is this another Rhodesian situation, a USSR, in which independence and autonomy truly belong in the hands of distinct cultural entities—namely, in our case, Wales, Scotland, and Northern Ireland? Or are we like the United States, where our future lies in the *unity* of our smaller parts? Which is the appropriate model, Andrew? Do you see my dilemma? They point to very different futures."

"Yes, Prime Minister, I think I understand what you are wrestling with," replied Andrew. "These very questions have been a great deal on my mind as well in recent months."

"Oh?" intoned Barraclough. "I am curious to know your thoughts."

"It is a long story," Andrew said. "You may find, as I have, that Scottish history contains at least some of the answers we're looking for."

"The past holding the key to the future, as they say."

"Exactly."

"Why do you say that?"

"Because Scotland's history is like no other, Prime Minister. I know we've all studied it in school. But we are taught about Scotland from an English perspective, almost as if—and there we come to the nub of it, I suppose—as if Scottish history isn't as important. I'm not sure we ever really get to the essence of what makes a Scot a Scot."

"An interesting phrase. What *does* make a Scot a Scot?" asked Barraclough.

"In a word, I would say it is their heritage, their history."

"And why is that?"

"Because it is a very distinctive history, one that in a way I find more fascinating than the history of the English. It is in that history one discovers—at least I feel I have begun to find such—answers to some very important contemporary questions, such as the issue of sovereignty."

"All right then, Andrew," said the prime minister, "you have succeeded in getting my attention. Give me a history lesson. Tell me what makes a Scot a Scot and why a Scot is different from an Englishman . . . and what that distinction ought to mean to us now, today."

Andrew went on to recount his pilgrimage into the history of Scotland, touching on his own personal roots, finally explaining how his search had come to influence his thinking on the issue his election to the leadership of the Liberal Democratic Party had so amplified—that of how far devolution ought to go in Scotland, and even of whether it should progress all the way to home rule and complete independence.

The discussion that followed was spirited and enlightening and left both men on far more intimate terms than when they had begun. Most of their discussion centered around the philosophical distinction between the two opposite trends: one, the *distribution* of power into smaller sovereign entities, and two, the *coalescing* of power into larger governmental units.

"I am absolutely fascinated with all you have told me, Andrew," Barraclough said at length. "I have never before seen the thing with such clarity. Your explanation of Culloden and its aftermath puts everything in such a different light. I do not think it insignificant that in the case of the United States, notwithstanding its civil war, in the beginning the states *chose* to come together into a larger national framework. As you make clear, that was certainly not the case in our own country. In the case of Scotland in particular, we—or England, I should say—*forced* unity by conquest."

"Right," rejoined Andrew. "Though Scotland's Parliament technically voted for the union in 1707, it was a vote coerced by bribery and the sword. I think the argument could be made that the choice was never really put fairly into Scotland's hands—or, if it was, it has never been revisited in light of modern times. In other words, do we not owe Scotland the same consideration that was given India, say, or the many other Commonwealth nations that now rule themselves—reexamining the situation for a new era?"

"A persuasive argument. You do know your Scottish history."

"As I said, I've been studying it a great deal recently," smiled Andrew. "If we are going to make an important decision about Scotland's future, I want to know as much as I can about its past. I feel I have to. We must do what is best for Scotland—not, as our predecessors did, what is best for England. So as I said before, in my opinion Scotland's history is the key to this whole issue, from Bannockburn to Culloden."

"The implication, then," Barraclough went on, thinking as he spoke, "seems to be that our situation actually more parallels that of the Soviet Union than the U.S. Would you agree?"

"Perhaps, in that England *conquered* Scotland and subdued its people rather than giving it the same level of choice that the American states exercised at the beginning of their democracy . . . yes, I see what you mean."

"It certainly casts the history of our union into a new light," said Barraclough, shaking his head.

Another twenty or thirty minutes of discussion went by.

"If it is true," Barraclough was saying, "that our union is based on conquest rather than choice, it hardly seems a fit foundation for the world's leading democracy, does it, Andrew?"

"No, it really does not."

"Well then," the prime minister said after a silent moment, "I wonder if it is not time to rectify that wrong in light of the twenty-first century."

"What are you suggesting, Prime Minister?"

"That perhaps it is time to let the nation's representatives decide the future of our constituent parts. Perhaps it is time we redress that conquest you spoke of and give Scotland the *choice* we denied it centuries ago."

"Specifically . . ." said Andrew, letting his voice trail off. He did not want to put words in the prime minister's mouth, but his heart immediately began to beat more rapidly. He had sensed it might come to this eventually, but he hadn't anticipated its happening so soon.

"I know most thought the statement in the King's speech about home rule was a mere token gesture to the SNP on my part," Barraclough went on. "Perhaps it was at the time. The SNP was on my back, and I felt I had to do something. But lately I've been thinking . . . and talking with you has helped clarify my thoughts in so many ways. I wonder, therefore, if perhaps we ought not let it languish, but bring it to the forefront. The history, as you've been saying, makes a compelling case for Scottish freedom—a case that I think we can no longer ignore."

Barraclough glanced at the clock on his desk.

"Two-ten—I had no idea it was so late!" he said. "It appears we are going to have to bring this to an end. If we don't get over to the Palace, we will be late for this afternoon's session."

He rose and shook Andrew's hand.

"I want you to know how appreciative I am, Andrew. Though I had no idea of the research you had been doing on the matter, I had the feeling you were the right man to talk to. This discussion has been most stimulating and enlightening. I'm especially grateful for what you have told me about your Scottish ancestry. That may have more to do with what is before us than you probably realized at the outset."

"Thank you, Prime Minister," Andrew nodded. "I'm glad you felt free to call. If there is anything more I can do, please do not hesitate."

"History may be knocking on our door, Andrew, yours and mine. We cannot ignore its summons. But we'll resume that discussion another time.— I've got just a couple quick calls to make before I go. If you'd like to wait a few minutes, you can ride over with me."

"No, I came on foot," replied Andrew. "The sun's out, and I think I have time to walk. Besides," he added, "I need a few minutes myself to put this into perspective before we are bombarded by the business of the day. You've suddenly elevated this issue to a level even I wasn't quite prepared for . . . at least not so soon."

Barraclough laughed. "Thank you again, Andrew. You've helped me a great deal."

❧ T H R E E ❧

As Andrew walked along Whitehall, his brain was spinning in what seemed a thousand directions at once.

Thoughts of Ginny intruded as he replayed the past two hours. Any mention of Scotland reminded him of her. She was the one and perhaps the most important element in his own "Scottish story" that he had not divulged to Barraclough.

Once he had the Scottish situation settled, Andrew realized, he would have to resolve his own personal crisis with Ginny. Neither would be easy. Although he tried to keep his focus on the issues at hand, more and more he was finding himself distracted by thoughts of her. He was even beginning to live with the fact his feelings for her would not go away. But what good was that when she obviously hated him? On top of all that, she was still involved with Alastair Farquharson.

As if in response to his thoughts, after he had crossed Bridge Street and was approaching the gate into New Palace Yard and the members' entrance, he saw a familiar hulking figure pacing the sidewalk twenty or thirty yards in front of him.

Andrew slowed, thinking at first that his eyes must be playing some trick. The fellow was dressed in a black suit that appeared two sizes too small, choking him at neck and waist. Both buttons were stretched uncomfortably tight across his midsection. The sleeves of the jacket, as well as the trousers, were two or three inches short, and he wore great work boots that seemed more in keeping with a construction site than the front entrance of Parliament. One of the guards at the gate was keeping a close watch on him, for the fellow could not help standing out like a sore thumb.

Andrew drew closer, then stopped five yards away, staring dumbfounded. The man saw him and turned, his face brightening.

"Alastair Farquharson!" Andrew exclaimed in a tone of both question and disbelief. "Is it really you?"

"Ay, Mr. Trentham," replied Alastair, lumbering toward him with three gigantic strides. " 'Tis me all right."

"But . . . I don't understand—what are you doing in the middle of London?"

"Luikin' fer ye, Mr. Trentham. I've been walkin' aboot in front o' this place fer two days, hopin' I'd see ye."

"I can hardly believe it!" laughed Andrew. "Well, it seems you've found me at last. But surely you didn't come here just to see me."

"Ay, I did."

"Why, then? Is something going on I should know about?"

"In a manner o' speakin', perhaps. But 'tis no emergency, gien that's what ye mean. I jist came all this way t' talk t' ye, Mr. Trentham. Though noo that I'm here, I'm feelin' a mite foolish aboot it. Ye're an important man, an' canna hae time fer the worries o' sich as me, an' I've ne'er been in London afore, an' 'tis a mite overwhelmin'."

"Where are you staying?" asked Andrew, still trying to place the two disparate images together in his mind—Alastair Farquharson and Parliament Square, London.

"At a hostel o'er in Earl's Court."

"Not anymore," said Andrew. "Tonight you're staying with me."

"I couldna du that, Mr. Trentham."

"Nonsense, it's already decided. I will call my housekeeper at our first break. But you still haven't told me what was so important to bring you all this way."

" 'Tis Ginny, Mr. Trentham. I've got t' talk t' ye aboot Ginny."

"But you say nothing is the matter?"

"No, nothin' like that."

"Hmm, right . . . well, I'm nearly late for Commons as it is," said Andrew glancing at his watch. "I was hurrying inside just now when I saw you."

He paused and thought a moment.

"Mr. Farquharson," he said, "can you be back here sometime around six o'clock this evening?"

"Gien ye say so, Mr. Trentham."

"Dress warmly because we may run late. One never knows. But wait for me, even if I'm not here till eight. When we adjourn, I'll come straight to this same gate. Then we'll go to my flat."

"'Tis kind o' ye, Mr. Trentham. But 'tis no trouble fer me t' stay at the hostel."

"You just be here, Farquharson, and wait for me. We'll have something to eat—and we can talk."

❋ F O U R ❋

At eight-fifteen that evening, Andrew Trentham, MP, and Alastair Farquharson, blacksmith, sat down to a simple, yet in the latter's eyes lavish, tea at the kitchen table in Andrew's flat. Alastair had not eaten since early in the afternoon, having hovered in front of the Houses of Parliament from five o'clock until Andrew's appearance just before seven-thirty, and the big man was clearly famished. He quickly did justice to the spread of meats and cheeses, breads and jams, that Mrs. Threlkeld had waiting for them upon their arrival.

"This is more kind o' ye than I can say, Mr. Trentham," said Alastair, slabbing a third slice of bread with butter, then scrutinizing the meat tray for a suitable addition to top it with. "I canna imagine an important man like yersel' jist takin' in people off the streets like this."

Andrew laughed. "No, I have to admit I don't make a custom of bringing home tourists from the front of the Palace. But I was once shown the same hospitality by your laird when I was a stranger in your village and said something very similar about it to his wife. So perhaps this is my way of returning the favor."

"Yer mentionin' o' the laird brings me t' mind o' why I came, Mr. Trentham," said Alastair.

"You mentioned Ginevra. Is there some difficulty. . . ?"

"Ay, 'tis aboot Ginny more than the laird. An' in a manner o' speakin', ye might say there's a difficulty. . . ."

Alastair paused and stared down at the half-finished slice of bread and meat on his plate.

"'Tis hard t' talk aboot, Mr. Trentham," he said after a moment. "T' speak o' a yoong lady ye care aboot's ne'er an easy thing, an' I'm not noted in Ballochallater fer bein' what a body'd call eloquent wi' my tongue. I read a lot, though folks dinna ken't. I like buiks an' stories an' such. But doon inside I'm still jist a workin' man, an' I du most o' my talkin' wi' my hands. But I care aboot her, ye see. Ginny an' I've kenned each other since we were bairns, an' I hope I luv her like a sister, whate'er else may be in my hert toward her. So ye see, I gotta say what I came t' tell ye."

Again he paused, squirming uncomfortably in his chair.

"Please go on," said Andrew. "You have nothing whatever to fear from me."

"Weel, ye see, Mr. Trentham," Farquharson struggled to continue, "'tis jist that Ginny's no been the same since, ye ken . . . since the wee Games in oor village last summer."

"Why, did something happen? Was she hurt? I didn't see—"

"Naethin' like that, Mr. Trentham," interrupted Alastair. "Dinna ye see what I'm tryin' t' say t' ye? 'Twas when *ye* came an' stopped by an' then spent those days wi' the laird an' his guid wife, Mrs. Gordon."

"Not been the same, you say?"

"No the same at all. She's been a mess, gien ye want t' ken—laughin' one minute, cryin' the next, snappin' at folks, not eatin' fer days, gaein' off on long walks alone sayin' she doesna want t' see anyone, an' behavin' so peculiar t' me as t' drive a puir man crazy. She's been a most perplexin' woman since then, Mr. Trentham, an' the laird an' Mrs. Gordon an' Alexander Buchan—that's her partner in the surgery—dinna ken what t' du wi' her."

"But what has caused—" Andrew began.

Alastair glanced across the table with such a strange expression that it stopped Andrew in midquestion.

"I thought ye kenned what I've been tryin' t' tell ye," said Alastair. "Dinna ye unnerstan'—she's been different since the day ye came t' Ballochallater . . . *yersel'*. Dinna ye see what I'm sayin'? 'Tis jist this . . . I'm o' the mind that she luvs ye, Mr. Trentham."

The words jolted Andrew momentarily speechless. It was the last thing Andrew had expected to hear.

"But I don't understand," he said after a few seconds. "What about *you*, Alastair? I thought you and she . . ."

"Ne'er mind aboot me," replied Alastair. "Ay, I hoped one day she might luv me. An' she's a nice enough lass, but I ken weel enough that she doesna luv me—not in the way folks mean the word. An' e'en gien that canna be, I want what is best fer her, ye see. . . ."

He paused and drew in a deep breath.

"Noo I reckon I'm come t' what brought me all the way south t' the big city in hopes o' speakin' wi' ye, Mr. Trentham," he went on. "I dinna ken gien ye luv her or no. But I'm hopin' ye du, 'cause gien ye luv her, ye're a man that can take her oot o' Ballochallater, Mr. Trentham. An' though a part o' me's maybe a wee bit sad t' realize I'm no the one her hert's been achin' fer, the ither part o' me's happy fer her. She's a fine yoong lady, an' she deserves more o' the world than t' stay all her life taking care o' dogs an' pigs in a wee village like Ballochallater. She's too special fer that, oor red-haired Ginny—intelligent, and spirited too. I've always thought she ought t' hae been born t' grit things. An' ye see, I want that fer her—grit things. I want a bigger world fer her. I ken that world only in my buiks. But she deserves t' be part o' that world hersel'. But sich as me, I'll ne'er be able t' offer her a bigger life—t' travel, t' see the world. I canna be those things t' her. I'm jist a humble blacksmith. But the minute ye came, I saw the change in Ginny. Sae what I'm sayin' is jist this: I ken she loves ye. I want the best fer her, an' I think ye're it. An' I'd be happy t' see her wi' ye. Noo, I ken that's a long speech, an' I hope ye'll forgive my long-winded tongue that's no sae wise as yer Parliament frien's, but 'tis what I came t' tell ye."

Andrew sat dumbfounded both by the unexpected torrent of words and by their import. This was a turn of events he had not expected!

It was silent a few minutes. At last he smiled pensively.

"Do not let anyone ever say you're not gifted with your words, Mr. Farquharson," he said, then paused again. "But what is so baffling about what you say," he resumed more seriously, "is that Ginny said she never wanted to see me again. From what she has said and the way she has acted, I assumed she could not stand the sight of me."

"I dinna ken hoo much ye ken aboot women, Mr. Trentham. I'm thinkin' it must be a heap more'n me. But the way I see it, when women rant an' fuss an' storm, 'tis a sure sign they're in luv. Ye must ken that. I see it wi' all the silly lassies o' the village when they're walkin' by my shop frae the school. An' in Ginny's case, though she's older, 'tis much the same. She's had things her own way fer so long, she doesna ken what t' make o' what she's feeling noo, which is love fer yersel' gien I'm no mistakin' it—least 'tis hoo the thing appears t' me. She's all o' a sudden vulnerable-like, gien that's the word I want—all nervous and jittery and thinkin' aboot ye an' no kennin' what t' du aboot it. She's no alt'gither in control o' hersel', an' she finds it a mite fearsome, I'm thinkin'. She doesna ken what t' do but git angry wi' ye. 'Tis one o' those luv-hate kind o' relationships I read aboot in a book once, though it sounded like a bit o' psychological haggis t' me. But noo that I've seen Ginny these last months, I'm thinkin' that's what she's got—a case o' the luv-hate sickness, gien ye want t' call it that. The way I see it, she thinks she hates the Andrew Trentham she reads aboot in the newspapers—the *image* o' Andrew Trentham frae Parliament an' London an' all, but she's in luv wi' the *man* she kenned that was under her papa's roof those few days."

"But they're the *same* me," said Andrew.

"Ay, but she doesna ken it. So ye've got t' show her. Ye've got t' show her that the man's the same man all the way through. Ye see, Mr. Trentham, Ginny's never been in luv afore, not even wi' me. That might sound strange to ye, but 'tis true. She was in school all those years, and then she was back an' startin' in practice. An' we went t' the Heather an' Stout fer years an' danced t'gither an' had fun. But dancin's no the same as bein' in luv—nor the best way o' findin' oot gien a body be one ye want t' spend yer life wi'.'"

Andrew glanced up into Alastair's face, still reeling and probing the gentle honest face for insight.

"Ay, I ken what ye're thinkin'," said the big man. "But 'twas never really luv she felt fer me. 'Twas maybe luv I had fer her—I dinna rightly ken. She likes me all right, as a friend, but no, Mr. Trentham, 'tis not luv. But she's in luv noo, an' it's made her all topsy-turvy inside. That's why ye've got t' help her, Mr. Trentham—ye got t' help her ken what she's feelin' . . . what it is she's feelin' fer yersel'."

Andrew continued to sit in bewilderment. Slowly he began to chuckle, then broke into laughter.

"At first I thought you were going to tell me to stay away from your girl," he said. "Now suddenly you tell me that you hope I'm in love with her! It will take me a while to put all you've said into order in my brain."

"I'm sorry I put ye into sich a perplexity, but ye see, I couldna rest until I told ye."

Two days later, after a tour of London as the special guest of one of its most important politicians, Alastair Farquharson was sitting on a train on his way back to Scotland, considerably relieved in mind and heart. What he would tell Ginny if she asked where he had been, he wasn't sure. But no one in Ballochallater had known his destination when he left the village four days before, and he hoped he could keep it that way.

Meanwhile Andrew had more than enough to think about on both the political and the relational fronts that were now facing him, though he determined to be in no hurry to resolve the dilemmas concerning either.

One thing was for certain—the timing of this sudden new personal perplexity was surely inconvenient!

❊   F I V E   ❊

Whatever Andrew might have intended to do with regard to Ginny, his plans on that and every other front were preempted by the prime minister himself.

It was in the third week of March, a month following Andrew's discussion with him at Number Ten, that Richard Barraclough released the stunning announcement that took everyone in the nation by surprise—Dugald MacKinnon and his SNP colleagues along with Andrew Trentham.

The first wind Andrew had of it was from Paddy Rawlings the night before.

The telephone rang in his flat that evening just before nine.

"Andrew . . . it's Paddy."

"Paddy!" exclaimed Andrew, "—hello. Haven't talked to you in a while. How are you doing—or should I ask, how are you and Bill doing?"

"Actually, we're doing great," replied Paddy. "I'm very happy. But that's not what I called about.—Do you know anything about the prime minister's announcement?"

"No . . . what announcement?"

"I just heard, from Kirk Luddington no less. Something big is apparently up—no one knows exactly what. We just received word of a press conference being put together for tomorrow."

"I'd heard nothing about it. Must be very last minute. There was no mention of it this evening—we adjourned a little before eight."

"All right, I suppose we'll all have to wait until tomorrow."

"What time's the thing set?"

"Twelve-thirty . . . in front of Number Ten."

They chatted a few more minutes, then Andrew hung up. Not five minutes later, the telephone rang again. It was the prime minister.

"Andrew, it's Richard."

"Hello, Prime Minister."

"I've scheduled a press conference for tomorrow."

"I just heard."

"Word does travel in this city!" laughed Barraclough.

"I have a close friend in the press."

"In any event, I plan to talk about some of what you and I discussed last month. I would like you to stand with me, if you don't mind."

"Not at all. It would be my privilege."

"As a matter of fact, why don't you come to Number Ten for lunch, say at eleven-thirty. We can chat further. I've scheduled the announcement for twelve-thirty."

"I'll be there."

❈   S I X   ❈

Neither the fifteen-hour advance notice of the event, however, nor the hour's lunch with the prime minister totally prepared Andrew for the impact of the words as he stood beside the prime minister listening to Barraclough read through his text.

"Thank you all for coming on such short notice," the PM began. "I have a brief prepared statement to read, after which Mr. Trentham and I will take a few questions."

He paused, cleared his throat, then began to read from the single typed sheet in front of him.

"It is my intention to call upon the government to bring before the House of Commons, as outlined in our agenda in November, a bill calling for the continued devolution of power to Scotland over the course of the next several years. I believe such to be the right course of action historically. England and Great Britain are proud to have brought democracy to the world, and I believe we must continue leading the way of freedom in this new millennium. I am speaking of far more than merely the ongoing program of devolution as previously understood.

"I have not yet spoken with either my cabinet or the leaders of the SNP."

As he listened, Andrew's mind reeled. He had told the prime minister he sensed it might come to this in the end. But now suddenly the reality broke in upon him that the incredible thing could actually happen . . . and soon!

"—so a specific schedule and timetable will have to be determined at a later date," Barraclough continued. "But the overall objective will be for London to gradually turn more and more of Scotland's affairs over to the

Scottish Parliament in Edinburgh, especially those issues of importance to the Scottish people—with an end in view, at the culmination of this process, and if the Scottish Parliament and Scottish people so approve, of complete independence from the UK, and autonomous, sovereign nationhood."

The prime minister stopped.

The crowd outside his residence at Number Ten Downing Street remained silent a second or two, as if collectively stunned by what they had just heard.

Then gradually a murmuring began to circulate, which rose within moments to a great hubbub of scurrying and talk and shouted questions.

Within an hour, news of the announcement had circled the globe.

❊   S E V E N   ❊

In the month following, all news throughout the UK was dominated by the Scottish story.

Interviews, personality profiles, historical specials, and rampant speculation filled every television network and were the subject of pub talk from Land's End to John O'Groats. It was all the Commons could do to conduct its other business.

The matter was of course discussed informally—heatedly and energetically—by the members of Parliament at every opportunity, even before the formal legislation was introduced. At length, the bill was drawn up by the prime minister and his party leaders and submitted to the Commons, where it went through its initial reading and then to committee. It appeared a final vote would be called for sometime toward the middle to end of April, at which time the future of both Scotland and the UK would be determined.

Early predictions indicated that the vote would generally follow party lines, though such was by no means assured.

At this point, most Labour MPs appeared in favor of the measure, as obviously were the members of the Scottish Nationalist Party. Tory sentiment, as predicted, ran against. If major defections within Labour's ranks occurred, however, the voting balance could be seriously upset.

If such did not happen, it appeared that Andrew Trentham and the Liberal Democrats would hold the deciding bloc of votes—determining not only what the future of Scotland would be, but whether the government of Richard Barraclough would continue to stand . . . or fall.

⊠   E I G H T   ⊠

As the critical vote neared, Andrew knew that he needed to get away from London and distance himself from the mounting pressure and media attention upon him. He had to think the entire issue through one more time—perhaps review the stories he had read to make sure he was heeding their lessons aright. This was the most important vote of his life, and he could not make a mistake. The rest of his party was looking to him for leadership. Most had already pledged their support and would back his decision.

And as his party looked to him, the entire country was watching and holding its breath.

He drove north to Derwenthwaite during the Easter holiday in the second week of April. He knew the burden upon him was now much greater than merely getting in touch with his personal roots. He had to make a historic decision about the future of a nation. Somehow fate had chosen him to occupy a determinative role in that process.

Early on the morning after his arrival, he found himself once more walking the rocky, overgrown pathway up the hill toward Bewaldeth Crag. He had been back to Derwenthwaite on a number of occasions during the past year and had even walked these hillsides. But today he purposed exactly to follow the steps of that previous day a year ago February that had led him, for the first time in years, to Duncan MacRanald's cottage.

He climbed steadily over rocks and heath, walking stick in hand. But his mind was far away from the familiar paths that climbed up over open heathland and wound over the folding ridges of the Skiddaw range. Instead, he recalled to mind everything that had happened since that visit—all he had read, what he had learned and thought about, every discussion with the old Scotsman, his entire historical pilgrimage through ancient Caledonia. Now he needed to put it all into an overarching perspective—to decide once and for all what were the contemporary lessons of that quest.

When he had come out merely to enjoy the morning on that fateful day and then begun thinking about Scotland, he could never have foreseen the events that would soon gather upon the horizon of his life. Everything had changed in the fourteen months since a southern breeze and the peat smoke from Duncan's chimney had beckoned him backward in time.

And everything, it seemed, was about to change again. The Scottish Bill, as it was called, had had its first reading seven weeks ago. The next reading and final vote were set to take place immediately after the Easter recess. The entire country was talking feverishly about the pros and cons—and what would be the outcome for Britain in either case.

Was Caledonia's destiny now to chart a new course in the millennium as a sovereign nation again as of old?

The prime minister's announcement last week was clear: "Upon resumption of our duties" he had said, "we will have the second reading of the legislation for Scottish Home Rule. I have allocated eight hours for debate, after which, if called for by the opposition, the House will divide."

He had just a matter of days to sort it out for the last time.

Andrew stopped for a short rest after ascending the ridge that overlooked the sea. On a clear day, he would have been able to see the coast of Scotland just twenty miles over the firth. But today's clouds swirled damply across the water, and the opposite coast was invisible in the mist. So Andrew continued his walk, reflecting on the byways of his youth and on his own Scottish heritage, which he had traced during the past year. He was more certain than ever of his Scottish roots and of the mist-clouded beginnings of his own Gordon lineage—stretching back into the Celtic origins of Caledonia itself.

As on so many occasions before, his steps again on this day led him to Duncan MacRanald. He knocked on the door to the old, familiar cottage today with purpose and resolve. Though the Scottish vote was most heavily on his mind, Andrew also remained curious as to whether it was possible to connect the story of the twelfth-century twins from the Gordon district to the threads of his own past. He had wanted to talk to Duncan ever since learning of Gachan and Beath, the twin sons of the hardworking peasant Darroch MacDonnuill.

The old Scotsman and the young member of Parliament talked late into the afternoon. On this occasion, no snowstorm nor message from the south nor ancient book brought an end to the discussion, and they continued until every detail had been unraveled to Andrew's satisfaction.

"So what you are telling me," he said at length, "is that my people originally came from Strathbogie too . . . from the town called Huntly, with one branch migrating from there down to the upper Speyside and the region of Cliffrose Castle?"

"Ay. Lady Fayth was born an' bred in the valley o' the Spey at the place called Cliffrose."

"And then a hundred and fifty years ago, she came south to Cumbria when she married my great-great-grandfather?"

"Ay—Lord John. 'Tis frae the twa o' them ye git yer twa names—the Gordon an' the Trentham."

"And your own people came with Lady Fayth?" asked Andrew.

"Ay, laddie. We been servin' yer family all this time."

Duncan went on to explain the solemn pledge that his own great-grand-mother, as lady's maid, had made to Lady Fayth herself when she accompanied her to Cumbria for the marriage.

"She remained in Lady Fayth's service?"

"Ay, and her daughter after her t' Lady Fayth's daughter Lady Ravyn, an' then t' Lady Kimbra. It's been a pledge my people hae honored this mony a year since, which is why I always took sich a keen interest in yersel', laddie—'cause it was a solemn vow ne'er t' let yer Scots past drap oot altogether frae yer sicht."

"It almost did," laughed Andrew.

"Ay," smiled Duncan. "But I was aye watchin' ye . . . waitin' for the chance t' speak . . . tellin' ye the auld stories."

"That you did," nodded Andrew with a smile of revelation, realizing at last how many things about old Duncan MacRanald suddenly fit together and how deep the connections between the two families had been.

"I kenned ye was the one t' bring yer heritage back alive," Duncan added. "I kenned the auld tales would git under yer skin in time . . . Caledonia always does."

"So I have discovered," replied Andrew with a pensive nod and smile. "Indeed it does."

A pause intervened.

"But now the matter has far more import than simply my own roots," Andrew went on. "The future of all Scotland is at stake."

"Ay, I've been followin' the matter wi' keen interest, as ye ken—even readin' the newspapers frae time t' time."

Andrew laughed—Duncan's refusal to keep up with the news had become a bit of a joke between them. Then he paused, reflecting on the idea that had come to him on his walk over the hills to the cottage. "There is a man I would like you to meet, Duncan," he said at length "—a Scotsman like you, a Highlander. I would like to get the two of you together for a talk, to help me sort everything out and put the question into the perspective I need for a final decision. May I bring him down?"

"Certainly, laddie. My door's open t' any man or woman, an' t' a Scotsman most o' all."

As Andrew walked down the hillside toward Derwenthwaite an hour later, he felt content and complete. What a heritage indeed was his, personally and politically—a heritage of history and of blood. At last he could feel the pieces starting to come together.

All except for Ginny, that was.

Leigh Ginevra Gordon was a puzzle all her own.

But he mustn't cloud his duty to his country with confusing matters of the heart. As difficult as it was, he must keep them separate . . . for now.

Before he could resolve either dilemma, however, he needed to see Ginny's father. He and Duncan and people like them were what this vote was all about.

The two old Scotsmen together in Duncan's cottage. . . . what better way to come to terms with what he ought to do? He would telephone Ballochallater the minute he got back to the Hall.

❈　N I N E　❈

Laird Finlaggan Gordon arrived at Derwenthwaite two days later. He had left to drive south the morning after Andrew's call.

He hit it off with Andrew's parents immediately. The four of them spent one of the most enjoyable evenings together Andrew could ever remember. His father was in rare form, talking and laughing as if their guest were a long-lost relation, as indeed—who could tell?—he might be. No longer ambivalent, as he once had been, Harland Trentham now seemed genuinely enthusiastic about his Scottish heritage. Andrew's mother, her speech now more than ninety percent restored, kept directing the discussion toward its political implications and the impending vote of which they all now felt such an intrinsic part and toward which she expressed surprising openness, given her Tory sympathies. The ideas and perspectives of her experience gave Andrew a number of valuable points to consider.

Andrew and the laird walked across the fields to Duncan's cottage the following morning a little before noon. If the telephoto lenses of the press were watching now, thought Andrew, just let them try to figure out what *this* was all about!

As he knew could not be helped, Duncan MacRanald and Finlaggan Gordon were instantly the best of friends. When they began talking intently in the old Scots tongue both loved, Andrew could scarcely understand a word, but laughed aloud in pure enjoyment as he listened.

The three talked into the afternoon, enjoying pot after pot of tea and a double batch of Duncan's orange oatcakes, which he had made for the occasion. Andrew shared his dilemma and decision with these two old Scots, explaining everything that was on his mind and the factors he felt he must consider in making a wise judgment in the case, posing a hundred questions, to which they did their best to give unbiased answers.

"I'm thinkin' there's but one place where ye'll find the answer t' the biggest question o' all, lad," said Laird Gordon at length.

He glanced at Duncan.

"Ye ken where I'm meanin', eh, Duncan, gien I'm no mistakin' the luik in yer eyes."

"I'm thinkin' ye're meanin' where the legend o' the Bruce still lives."

"Ay. I see we're o' one mind on it."

"Where then?" said Andrew, glancing back and forth questioningly between the two Scotsmen.

" 'Tis t' Stirling ye've got t' gae," said the laird, "an' work this oot by yersel'."

"Ay," added Duncan. "I've dune what I can fer ye, laddie, an' ye've been a good listener all these years. But noo that ye ken yersel' as a Scot, ye must spend some time wi' the Bruce. Ye've got t' make yer decision alone, wi' the ancients luikin' doon on ye. Ye got t' hear what they would tell ye, laddie. No one can du it fer ye. 'Tis a road ye must walk in the quiet o' yer own hert—wi' the Lord, an' wi' history."

Andrew nodded. He immediately recognized the wisdom of Duncan's words, and in that realization his decision was made.

He must drive to Stirling.

If his entire way was not clear, at least he was confident in what should be his next step. As Duncan had once read to him from an old book, "We do not understand the *next* page of God's lesson book; we see only the one before us. When we understand the one before us, only then are we able to turn the next." Thankful for this clarification of his own "next page," Andrew rose to leave. Already the sun was beginning to disappear behind the hills that enfolded Duncan's cottage.

"I believe it is time we should head back down to the Hall," he told the laird.

"I think I'll jist stay here wi' Duncan a wee bit longer," said Gordon. "I can find my own way back, I'm thinkin'."

"Why dinna ye spend the night, Laird?" asked the old shepherd. "Ye can hae my bed."

"I couldna du that, Duncan, lad. Jist gie me a tartan, an' I can sleep anywhere."

"Jist like wee Andrew used t' du."

"One request, Laird," said Andrew, pausing at the door. "When you go home, I think I would prefer you said nothing of our conversation to Ginny."

"Why's that, lad?"

"I can't say exactly. Maybe it's because I want her to know me on the basis of who I am rather than what I may or may not do for Scotland."

He paused and chuckled briefly.

"And who can tell?" he added. "It may be that the vote I feel compelled to make in the end will anger her even more than what I have done thus far."

"Weel, I'll honor yer request, lad, whate'er ye decide. 'Tis the least I can du."

Andrew turned again to go. As he was closing the door, the last words he heard behind him came from the laird's mouth. "I think I'll jist hae anither drap o' tea, Duncan, lad," Ginny's father was saying, "an' one or twa more o' those orange oatcakes."

Andrew smiled, his heart warmed by the bonds of friendship he was leaving behind in the cottage.

The two Scotsmen talked late into the night. Neither later divulged to Andrew the subjects touched on between them. But the lifelong friend of the one and the daughter of the other, and what might be their future together, came in for a good share of the evening's conversation.

❈ T E N ❈

The mood in the private room of the Burn and the Bush in Knightsbridge was subdued. Dugald MacKinnon and his SNP colleagues, still reeling from the arrest of their deputy leader, Baen Ferguson, knew they needed to maintain a low profile amid the firestorm of speculation regarding Scotland's future.

None had anticipated that Prime Minister Barraclough would so soon put into their very laps the thing some of them had been hoping and fighting for all their political lives. Yet now they found themselves in a position, because of the scandal of the two crimes involving parliamentary leaders, where to lobby too strenuously for passage of the bill could backfire.

"As I noted a year ago, Dugald," said Gregor Buchanan, "when I was congratulating you and toasting your success, your strategy with Barraclough seems to have succeeded beyond our wildest expectations. I only wish there was something we could do to push the vote forward."

"My concern exactly," rejoined Lachlan Ross more soberly than usual. Even the Glaswegian was not drinking much tonight. "Here we are at the threshold, yet if the vote fails, it will be extremely difficult to revisit the matter again for years."

"And there is nothing we can do to insure passage," put in Archibald Macpherson. "We obviously need help from the other parties and the undecided members."

"Not to mention that a defeat could reverse our own party's advances in recent years," put in William Campbell, the new deputy leader in Ferguson's place.

Gradually eyes turned toward MacKinnon.

"As I said on that earlier occasion, gentlemen," he began at length, "all we can do is wait and hope that history thrusts up a new hero in our midst, a man who will not fear the challenge of what is before us."

It was silent several long moments. A few sipped at their glasses as they pondered their leader's words.

"Are you referring to Andrew Trentham?" asked Buchanan at length.

"Perhaps . . . but only time will tell if he has the courage of a Bruce."

"There is a rumor circulating that he is half Scot himself," said Campbell.

"I've heard that as well," added Macpherson.

"Is there anything to it?"

"I don't know, though there were also reports that he spent a good deal of time in Scotland last summer."

"Some kind of spiritual rebirth, the way I heard it," put in Ross.

"Rumors mean nothing," spoke up MacKinnon. "I of all people know that the sheets can't be trusted. That story linking Trentham and me last summer had no basis in fact. Half of what they put in *my* mouth wasn't accurate, so why should we believe anything they said about him?"

"He was probably just on holiday," commented Macpherson. "People do visit the north, you know, for reasons that have nothing to do with the so-called Scottish question."

"True enough, but I have the feeling there was more to it."

"Why do you say that, William?"

"Because I also heard that he's gone north again for the recess and may be in Scotland even now."

"Perhaps we should have someone keep an eye on him," suggested Ross.

"It would be pointless, Lachlan," replied MacKinnon. "If there's one thing I've learned about Andrew Trentham, it's that he's his own man. Pressuring him will be less than useless. Even if he is a Scot, he will have to make up his own mind. And if our future rests with him now . . . all we can do is hope that Caledonia will speak its magic to him."

▓ E L E V E N ▓

Two mornings later, promptly after breakfast, Andrew was on his way north.

As he paused at the gate, the contingent of reporters scrambled toward his car with a flurry of questions.

"Where are you going, Mr. Trentham . . . do you have a statement . . . any further developments on the Scottish issue . . . have you been in contact with the SNP. . . ?"

"Gentlemen and ladies, please," laughed Andrew, doing his best to quiet them. "I have no comment yet. You will have the news at the same time as everyone else. As far as my itinerary is concerned, I'm simply off for a brief personal respite before the storm breaks upon me again."

"Where, Mr. Trentham?"

"Tell you what," replied Andrew, smiling to himself, "—contact Patricia Rawlings of BBC 2." Even if he hadn't told Paddy anything, this ought to raise her stock in the minds of her fellow journalists. He'd telephone her the first chance he got and give her fair warning. "Ms. Rawlings knows how to reach me if it becomes necessary," he added. "Any statements I have will be released through her."

As the members of the press assimilated this unexpected bit of news, Andrew accelerated and then sped off down the winding road away from Derwenthwaite and toward the highway. He drove a little faster than was his custom in hopes of preventing any of them from being able to follow.

As he drove north into Scotland yet again a little over an hour later, this land of his ancestors once so foreign and unfamiliar was now a beloved part of the world he felt he was beginning to know as well as Cumbria. As strong as was the urge to head first to Ballochallater, he felt he must heed the advice of Duncan and the laird and visit the site of Robert Bruce's historic encounter with Edward II of England undistracted by trying to sort out his feelings for Ginny. He had to be fair to his duty to the country. He would resolve the one issue first, then deal with the other.

As Andrew crossed the northern border, the words of the prime minister came back to him from a recent conversation after the surprise press conference.

"You realize what this means," Barraclough had told Andrew. "Our Labour-LibDem coalition is at stake. The Tories will surely fight us on this. It may come down to the two of us in the end . . . and no one else."

Now, as he motored north with a heart and brain full of many and varied sensations, Andrew had a feeling the prime minister was right. At any rate, he knew he was on the verge of something historic—for himself . . . and for the entire nation.

But he would not go directly to Stirling. Instead he would approach it as he had throughout his investigation—by reliving every story and legend in which he had become immersed during the previous fourteen months, placing each now against the contemporary backdrop of Parliament's pending decision. If it took several days, even a week, so be it . . . even if his return to London was delayed. This was no matter that could be rushed. He must do the right thing and take whatever time was necessary to find out what that was.

Andrew now realized that he had not just been encountering isolated fragments from the past, each story interesting but separate. He saw that in reality it had been one single story all along—the sweeping saga of a land and its people, and whether their freedom was still a thing that mattered as it had in days of old. To find out, he would once more revisit the sites where Scotland's history had come alive for him.

Driving north on the now-familiar roads, he recalled to mind the tale out of Duncan's old book of the Wanderer and his son that had so captivated him as a boy.

As the terrain became lonelier and more mountainous, his thoughts drifted north to dwell on last summer's sojourn into the desolate Highlands where Cruithne and Fidach had hunted and erected their monument from hich the stone of destiny had been hewn. With poignancy he called to mind their mutual pact not to allow unity and brotherhood to disappear from Caledonia. If only it might be so again—not in Caledonia only, but throughout the world.

The open expansive moor of Rannoch turned his reflections toward the ancient Pict warriors Foltlaig and Maelchon, who had battled to preserve Caledonia's freedom from the Romans. Then, as he turned and began the descent from the high plateau down again into Glencoe, the story of Ginevra and Brochan came back to his heart and mind with all the vividness and drama as when he first visited this haunting region. He spent the night in the legendary valley, and the next morning he again walked along the River Coe and climbed up to Signal Rock, where he stood a few quiet moments before returning to his car and again heading north.

As he went on this day, he recalled the courage of Columba as he had ventured along this very route through the glen of Loch Ness to face the ancient Pict King of Inverness. Another visit to Culloden brought again to life his own bonds of descent with Sandy and Culodina of Cliffrose and his kilted ancestor Kendrick Gordon, Sandy's father, whose portrait hung back in his home at Derwenthwaite, and whose links to Duncan's family had recently been made clear to him.

From Culloden, Andrew drove around the northeastern coast with now a new destination he had passed through but not visited before—the town of Huntly in the center of the Gordon district. By the time he arrived, it was late in the day. He booked a room in a bed-and-breakfast, with plans to tour the ruins of Huntly Castle in the morning.

After a dinner on the small historic town square, he returned along cobbled streets to the B & B, where the headline of a newspaper in the sitting room of the establishment caught his eye: "Scottish Vote Too Close to Call." He took the paper to his room and there read the article.

> The outcome of the most historic vote to face the House of Commons in a century looks to remain uncertain down to the very end. Though Prime Minister Richard Barraclough has publicly instructed his own Labour MPs to vote their consciences rather than their party, even if it means splitting with him, it yet appears that most will adhere to party lines.
>
> With approximately 275 Labourites on the record as favoring the measure and 270 Conservatives against, the final outcome will therefore likely be determined by the largest two of the remaining parties, the SNP and the Liberal Democrats.
>
> No doubt exists as to where the SNP stands. Adding its 21 votes to

Labour's, the vote stands at 296 in favor to 270 against, with 42 un-decideds and uncounted MPs from the remaining parties, as well as 51 Liberal Democrats. With the LibDems reportedly voting as a bloc, any-thing could happen. If they come down opposing the measure, and with 15 MPs representing unionist sentiments and certain to vote nay, the Scottish Bill will surely fail.

Liberal Democratic leader Andrew Trentham could not be reached for comment. Scottish Nationalist spokesman Dugald MacKinnon re-leased a statement yesterday in which he expressed his hope that the Liberal Democrats, as well as all undecided MPs, will look to the future and . . .

Andrew set down the paper and sighed. Even this far away from London, he could not escape the mounting pressure.

The article reminded him of Paddy. He had forgotten to call her. He would try right now.

After a morning in Huntly and a thoughtful walk about its magnificent castle ruins, Andrew drove to Aberdeen, where he spent the rest of the day and another night. The following morning, thinking of Dallais and Breathran and the fact that Kenneth MacAlpin was remembered for uniting Scotland into a nation while their royal links to Scotland's kingship were forgotten, he drove south along Scotland's east coast to Scone and finally to Dunfermline, where so many changes had come to Scotland. After a quiet and reverent walk through Dunfermline Abbey and a thoughtful minute or two beside the tomb of Robert the Bruce, he walked outside to the shrine of St. Margaret, where she and King Malcolm were buried.

Leaving Dunfermline, Andrew crossed the Firth of Forth to spend the remainder of the day in Edinburgh, viewing one final time the legendary Celtic stone that had been responsible for energizing his quest, once again resting safely in its well-guarded home in the heart of Edinburgh Castle. Leaving the Crown Room, he walked across the cobbled courtyard to the tiny chapel built by Queen Margaret. He was glad it was empty. He went inside and sat down on one of the plain benches, soaking in the quietness of the ancient stone walls.

"Lord," he prayed quietly, "I can think of no more suitable setting to reflect on all that Scotland's history means than right here, high above this city in its castle fortress, and in St. Margaret's Chapel. If this land is again to be an independent nation, ruled from this very city . . . if Edinburgh is meant to take its place among the modern capitals of the free world, then show me clearly. I ask for your help in this most important thing I have ever done."

Five days had now passed since his departure from Derwenthwaite. Only one stop remained, the single most important destination—the one toward which he had been bound all along.

He would have to get back soon. The House of Commons had reconvened yesterday. But still he felt he could not rush this important business he was on. He had been in private contact with Barraclough, keeping him abreast of his movements. They would not vote without him, and he must not return until he was ready.

From Edinburgh on the following morning, therefore, at last Andrew drove toward the center and strategic hub of Scotland.

Stirling had always been a magnet to history, and now the old city at Scotland's crossroads was drawing him, as if there—and *only* there—could be found the resolution and culmination to Caledonia's epic story.

Rather than entering the city, Andrew drove to the village immediately to its south. He pulled in at the Bannockburn visitor's center, following two tourist buses into the lot, then parked and went inside.

He had no beard this time, but by pulling his cap low and his coat high around his neck, by looking down and keeping to himself, he managed, as he had on most occasions these last weeks, to get through the day mostly unrecognized.

Leaving the throngs a few minutes later with a couple of pamphlets under his arm, Andrew walked out through the treelined avenue up the slight incline to the battle monument. The exhibition building behind him was full of interesting artifacts and a hundred books he would like to examine. But it wasn't data that Andrew was seeking today. No mere facts would satisfy this quest. He had to be alone, to drink in the spirit of the place . . . and also to pray.

※   T W E L V E   ※

Paddy Rawlings heard Kirk Luddington and her editor, Edward Pilkington, talking in the latter's office for some ten minutes before the buzzer on her own telephone rang. She answered it, then rose and obeyed the summons. The moment she was inside, Pilkington nodded for her to close the door behind her.

"Do you know where Andrew Trentham is?" asked the editor when the three of them were alone.

"Why would I know?" shrugged Paddy.

"It's no secret that you and he are chummy," replied Pilkington. "Our man at his place up in Cumbria specifically heard him say he would be in touch with you before he disappeared. I thought you two talked every day."

"Hardly that."

"We need to know," now said Luddington in an importune tone.

"Look, Paddy," said Pilkington, "this is no time to play it coy. I put you on camera after the arrests were made, but you're not going to be able to ride that story forever. All markers are in. This might even be a bigger story yet. I want to know what you know."

"Honestly . . . nothing."

"Nobody in town's seen Trentham for days. The vote's coming up, and he's the center of the whole thing. You're our ticket to some kind of inside scoop. I can't believe you don't have something. Are you saying he *hasn't* contacted you?"

"I didn't say that."

"So he *has*?"

"He called me a couple days ago."

"From where?"

"He didn't say. He just wanted to alert me to the comment he'd made, that's all—that he had put the rest of the press on to me to get them off his back." She smiled at the thought. "But he didn't divulge a thing," she added. "Honestly, he's keeping this one to himself all the way."

"Where do you *think* he is?"

Paddy paused before answering.

"I'm sure he's in Scotland, Mr. Pilkington," she answered softly after a moment.

"Could you contact him?"

"I have his private mobile phone, if that's what you mean."

"Then call him, Rawlings," interjected Luddington. "Why are you stalling?"

"I'm sorry," answered Paddy, "I can't do that."

"What if I make you?" said Pilkington.

"I'm sorry, then I would have to say that I *won't* do it."

"Even if it costs you your job?"

"That's right. I will not disturb him. I think I know well enough what he is doing—and we have to respect that. He needs to resolve this alone, and I will not interfere. You can fire me if you want, but I will *not* contact him."

Paddy rose and left the editor's office.

✼   T H I R T E E N   ✼

Andrew had driven across a small bridge fifteen minutes earlier, whose simple sign noting the "Bannock Burn" signaled his arrival at the historic intersection of Scottish history two miles south of Stirling. And now, as he walked, he quietly approached a point overlooking the site of that ancient battle where British history had been changed.

Andrew slowed, gazing down across the gently sloping plain, allowing the quiet impulses of destiny to speak their faint words . . . that he might feel the legend.

Scotland was famous for her historic memorials. Its National Trust had probably done as much, if not more, than anyone else to preserve the heritage of this land. In a book or on a map of Scottish places of historical significance, one might easily find a thousand sites noted, from a few piled stones to magnificent castles to exquisitely excavated prehistoric ruins. Andrew had visited many such centers last summer.

But none was fuller or richer—none contained more symbolism and significance—than the precise spot where Andrew Trentham now stood.

To his left, a six-acre field of well-kept grass gently eased down toward the small river called the Bannock. The outlook had obviously been altered through the passage of seven centuries. For one thing, there would have been many more trees back then. The low valley of the burn wound through what was called the Tor Wood, below New Park, though few woodsy areas were now to be seen there. Such changes, however, did not prevent the mood of the past from yet imbuing the surroundings with an aura of history to be found at few other locales where men have set the stamp of their footprint for their descendents to remember.

Andrew glanced in the opposite direction.

In the distance, singularly situated at the very heart of Scotland, Stirling's castle rose out of the valley floor itself, as if the ground had burst apart one day and exploded upward with granite, growing of itself the mighty gray fortress-flower that sat proudly atop it.

Andrew stood silent a long time, gazing out over castle and burn, all but overwhelmed by the sense of *convergence* he felt here.

He had been to Iona, Culloden, and Glencoe, Balmoral and Loch Lomond, the Galloway Hills, the Western Isles, Scone, and Dunfermline. He had walked Edinburgh's Royal Mile and St. Andrews' sandy shoreline. He had climbed Scotland's highest peaks and stood overlooking massive cliffs on the wildest of its seascapes. He had toured castles of magnificence and visited humble crofters' cottages. He had enjoyed some of Scotland's finest cultivated gardens and walked its loneliest Highland moors.

But here in the center of it all, where geography itself seemed to demand a reckoning . . . *here* did the history of a proud people draw together into an inevitable and dramatic climax.

Andrew walked the rest of the way to the battle monument. Slowly he made his way around the circular area, reading the posted information with patriotic and historic reverence.

Leaving the circle after a few minutes, he walked on farther toward the giant bronze statue of Robert Bruce himself. In the same way that the castle to the north emerged from the rocks of the valley, the silent, massive sentinel from the past seemed to grow up from out of the surrounding terrain.

Andrew approached, then stared upward at the majestic, silent figure of bronze. The expression of fearlessness on Bruce's face, looking down from out of his helmet of mail, was so lifelike as to compel an observer to silence, commanding all to behold the mighty hand that subdued the north and vanquished its enemies. The wide eyes and flared nostrils of the mighty beast underneath likewise compelled—not hushed submission like its master, but terror, lest any stand in its path and be crushed beneath the onslaught of its powerful hooves. Truly were horse and rider one, fit symbol of that independent spirit of a proud nation who could not forever remain under the rule of another.

For several long minutes he stood as one transfixed, gazing now into the face of the rider, now into the fearful eyes of the beast, quieting himself to hear what his heart told him about his own impending decision.

Then slowly he turned and made his way once again toward the overlook down across the river valley where the momentous events had taken place. He paused at the crest, and there stood as visions gradually pervaded his brain—visions of the living men whom the statues had been fashioned to remember.

The huge grassy expanse spread out before him. A warm breeze whispered across his cheeks, though he could but faintly hear its message.

He breathed in deeply and squinted imperceptibly. What must this sight have been like . . . back then?

What did Bruce and his commanders *feel* on the eve of battle?

Off in the distance, if he tried, Andrew could just imagine the fearsome cadence of the hooves and feet as Edward's army of seventeen thousand advanced northward toward the badly outnumbered Scots under Bruce's command. Was that a faint dust cloud from their movement in the south, gradually growing larger as the great horde approached?

He imagined himself not merely standing now, but astride a great, black equine beast of battle . . . watching . . . waiting . . . wondering what fate the hours ahead boded . . . and whether Providence would be smiling upon him when this day was done.

Were any of *his* ancestors present here on that fateful day?

If so, how did they come to be there?

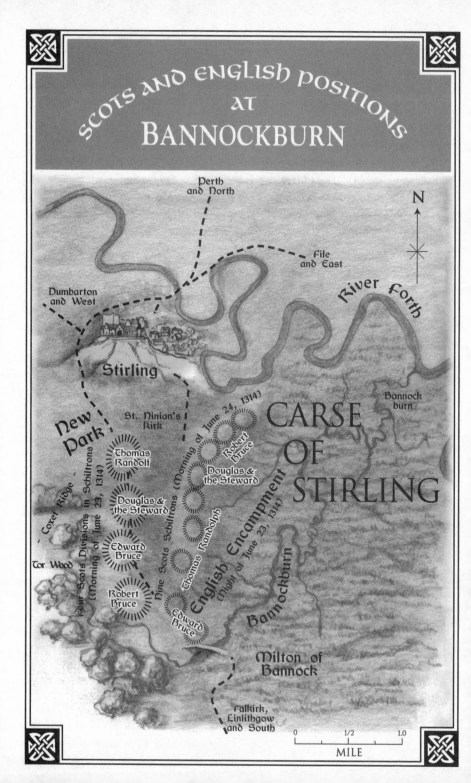

11

STATURE OF A HERO

A.D. 1314

☒ ONE ☒

November 1307

The morning was young. A thin fog hung low over the region, suspended as from a gigantic web woven by invisible celestial spiders between the encircling hills. Thin white wisps of smoke stretched straight up from the rooftops below until they met the layer of fog, then bent parallel to the earth from which they had come, more literally than figuratively, then blended into the airy blanket of white.

Except for the fog and smoke, all was brown and gray. Autumn came early to this region, and it was now November of the year 1307. The snows had not yet arrived. But the precursory cold gave clear warning they were not far away, stripping the trees of every reminder of the summer recently past. A more distinctively dreary atmosphere it would have been difficult to imagine.

In the early hour, what few noblemen and ladies made their residences in this out-of-the-way place pulled thick coverings and blankets around them. Those of less fortunate means were by now stirring. Their energies, however, were expended mostly upon feeding their dying fires with fresh peats in the vain attempt to forestall the approach of winter. The very thought of the months ahead brought shivers to the bone.

There was no village, only a scattering of cottages, mostly of turf, some of stone and wood, spreading into the countryside in all directions from the castle called the Peel of Strathbogie, with some slight aggregation at close distance to one another between the Peel and the banks of the Bogie a mile or two distant.

All was quiet, except for a light booted step tramping through this cluster of cottages. The sound echoed off a dull brown dirt street with an imperative of urgency matched by the look on the face of the fleet-footed boy making it.

Besides the merging of the two rivers between which he ran, the terrain in this valley of the Bogie, or *Strathbogie*, was unremarkable. The confluence of the Deveron into the waters of the Bogie provided a strategic position in the north which, before these troubled times that were now upon them, had given John, earl of Strathbogie, control over the wide valley just as it had more than a hundred years ago when his great-grandfather Duncan, earl of Fife, had come north to build the castle here. That the present earl himself, as well as his son, was at that moment being held in an English prison for aiding the very man now seeking the shelter of his castle in no way diminished the importance of this location.

It was not for any of these reasons, however, that the boy ran through the rough streets on this morning. He was running because a certain visitor had just arrived in their village.

❋   T W O   ❋

1290–1292

When Scotland's throne was suddenly vacated in 1290 by the death of young Margaret, Maid of Norway, the list of claimants to follow her had represented some of Scotland's most prominent families—mostly of Norman blood, but several tracing their ancestry all the way back to the kings of the Picts.

The strongest of such links came from the houses of Bruce, Balliol, Hastings, the Count of Holland, and Comyn. The principal players were unscrupulous and brutal, and none had qualms about killing to secure Scotland's throne. Such had been the Scots way before. Such it would be again.

Chief among them were still Robert Bruce the elder and John Balliol, both descendents from Malcolm and Margaret through their son David.

Two generations hence, it would be said that the choice of these two had been obvious from the beginning.

> Said they, the heir by the nearest male
> Was Robert the Bruce, of Annandale,

The Earl of Carrick; he alone
Was rightful claimant to the throne. *

At the time, however, it was anything but clear. Civil war appeared imminent.

King Edward Plantagenet of England still had many friends in Scotland during this time of confusion and unrest. Again, therefore, came an appeal to Edward for help. A letter was sent to the English King by William Fraser, Bishop of St. Andrews and one of the original guardians appointed after Alexander's death—a man who was no friend of the house of Bruce. The bishop informed Edward that Robert Bruce was marshaling an army and was on his way to Perth to seize control of the country. The earls of Mar and Atholl were also collecting forces. Sides were beginning to form. The situation was grave.

Bishop Fraser begged Edward to come north to the border and there choose between the claimants. The English King's intervention, the bishop felt, was necessary to avoid a bloody and savage civil war throughout Scotland. Fraser concluded his communication to London by noting particularly that favor toward John Balliol on Edward's part would be rewarded thereafter with special loyalty on Balliol's part toward the English crown.

The hint was more than obvious, and Edward seized upon it. This was exactly the opportunity he had been waiting to exploit.

The English King marched north. When he arrived, he lost no opportunity to remind the Scots that he had agreed to involve himself because of his position as "overlord of the land of Scotland." He therefore requested acknowledgment of such right and position by all the Scottish nobles involved.

After some delay, all the claimants to the throne acceded to Edward's sovereignty and agreed to accept his choice for King. Robert Bruce, now eighty, and as much Englishman as Scot, was perfectly willing to grant Edward this concession in exchange for the crown. Likewise, Balliol was as loyal to Edward as any duke or baron in London.

Piece by piece, the ambivalent claimants parceled away Scotland's freedom in hopes of obtaining the prize of power in the land. Edward

*From John Barbour, *The Bruce*, originally written in 1395. Translation 1964 by Archibald A. H. Douglas (William MacLellan & Co.)

played the situation to his advantage, gradually assuming complete control of Scotland until a King should be chosen. He now took the further step of ordering the arrest of all who refused to take an oath of allegiance to him as King of England and sovereign of Scotland.

Then followed a complex proceeding involving legal experts throughout the land, each supporting of the various claimants. Edward presided over the intricate arguments on behalf of the twelve parties seeking the Scottish throne.

The deliberations took sixteen months. Edward's final adjudication, passed down in November of 1292, declared John Balliol Scotland's King. Balliol was crowned at Scone on the last day of that month. The new Scots King joined Edward for Christmas at Newcastle and the following day knelt and did homage to him.

Scotland had a King once more, one who had bowed the knee in submission to Edward of England. The dispute over succession *appeared* over.

Alas, it had only begun.

THREE

November 1307

None of the facts of his country's successionary crisis mattered, nor were even known, to twelve-year-old Donal, son of Fergus, farrier and ironsmith to absent Lord John of Strathbogie, as he panted his way through the chilly morning air from the castle to the cottage he and his father had left an hour before while yet the night was black. Nor was the lad thinking at the moment that his own great-great-grandfather had helped build the castle. In the years since, new earls had risen up who knew not the name of Gachan, son of Darroch, and how he had been brought from a distant fiefdom and had risen high in the lord's service. Thus the lineage of the house of Donnuill had sunk back to what it was before, and his numerous descendents in the land of the north called Strathbogie were once again peasants. One thing that had not changed was the strain's love for horses, which remained strong in both Fergus and his son.

"Yoong Donal, Fhearghis's son, whaur be ye bound in sich a hurry?"

came the voice of a man gathering peats from the stack alongside his cottage.

But the breathless boy did not stop to answer. The man's eyes continued to follow with inquisitive stare until the lad burst at length through the door of his own house some distance farther down the street.

"Donal ... Donal! What is it, then?" exclaimed his mother, busy at the hearth in the center of the dirt floor. "Are ye bein' chased by wolves?"

"No, Mama," the boy panted. "Papa sent me."

"Why didna he come himsel'? The gruel's nigh cooked."

"He sent me t' fetch his cap an' some tools, an' said fer me t' dress warm, too, and t' tell ye we'll be gone the day."

"Whate'er for, Donal?" asked the woman, not knowing whether to be alarmed or anxious for the oatmeal she had only just boiled. "What aboot yer breakfast, lad?"

"He told me t' eat enough t' last me the day afore I came back. He said they'd give him somethin' frae the laird's kitchen."

"But why, Donal?"

"The castle's got a visitor, Mama."

※ F O U R ※

1294–1296

John Balliol, of loyal Norman and English blood, chosen by the King of England to succeed to the Scottish throne, occupied the position of King of Scotland for four years.

To say he *ruled* Scotland would stretch the truth, for he was weak, timid, and ineffectual—Edward's vassal in every way, and treated by the English King with contempt and humiliation. That he accepted such a role so meekly made him despised by the Scottish nobility as well. Gradually support of Scotland's leading men began to swing away from Balliol and in the direction of the house of Bruce.

Meanwhile, Edward faced problems on other fronts and was eager to forget the troublesome Scots. War broke out between England and France in 1294. Balliol, as Edward's vassal, was ordered by the English King to mobilize men and to raise money for the war effort.

By now, however, Scottish resistance to the English King and his northern vassal was stiffening. Edward, who had been viewed as an ally by many Scottish nobles a short time earlier, was now increasingly regarded as Scotland's chief adversary. Gradually the realization dawned upon the Scots that they had relinquished more of their independence than they had intended.

As the years passed, the relationship between the two nations grew seriously strained. Edward was determined not merely to possess the title of "overlord of the land of Scotland," but to *exercise* that overlordship. With his ultimatum for troops and money, Edward's demands became intolerable.

A breaking point had been reached.

It was clear that the independence of Scotland, and potentially the entire course of its future, was at stake. There was far from unanimity among the Scots lords, however, about what ought to be done to resecure control of Scotland into their own hands.

The aged Robert Bruce was now dead. But his son and grandson, both likewise Roberts, had in no wise forgotten the family's claim to the Scottish throne. Yet the family of Bruce, of Norman root, was not pure Scot at all, but *Anglo-Scot*, with large holdings in both England *and* Scotland, and therefore of mixed motive in the affair. Loyalty had less to do with nationalistic fervor than with what might be lost if one chose the wrong side.

The Bruce family was hardly alone in this circumstance. Most noted Scots families, in fact, held lands in Yorkshire, Cumbria, and Northumbria. John Balliol likewise had a strong interest in remaining loyal to England, for he possessed lands in seventeen English shires which brought him over five hundred pounds yearly in rents.

Economics, therefore, as well as loyalties of blood, pulled all the principal players in many directions.

With his own circle of loyal nobles strenuously resisting Edward's demands, at last John Balliol stiffened himself to oppose the English King. He sent word to Edward refusing the demand for troops and money. Furthermore, he declared that his homage and all the promises he had made to the English King had been given under threat of violence and were therefore void. The following year, the Scots concluded a treaty with France, resuming the Auld Alliance of 1165.

Crisis quickly mounted.

Enraged at Balliol's refusal to support his war efforts and still more at the treaty Balliol had concluded with France, Edward promptly seized Balliol's estates in England, then amassed an army and marched north to teach the rebellious Scots a lesson in submission they would not soon forget. Hardly prepared to fight for Balliol, the Bruces crossed the border to meet Edward and pledge their loyalty—a fleeting commodity indeed during these times—confident that after his victory, they would again be able to pursue *their* claim to the Scottish throne.

Balliol responded to Bruce's treason by seizing the Bruce lands of Annandale, near Carlisle, and giving them to Balliol's ally and brother-in-law, John Comyn, who was also earl of Buchan, north of Aberdeen.

Caledonia's newest fight for independence had thus begun with the house of Bruce taking up arms on the *English* side of the conflict.

King Edward I of England crossed the border at Berwick in March of 1296 and massacred most of that city's inhabitants. His army marched on to Dunbar, where Scottish forces were soundly defeated. Accounts of merciless hangings, countless rapes, and savage murders, were recounted by an embittered Scots populace. The English King continued on throughout Scotland, seizing control of the important castles, in what amounted to a brutal homage-gathering tour. Thousands of names filled the so-called Ragman Roll, which legally recorded these pledges. The Scots leaders who refused to sign were imprisoned.

In July Balliol was forced to sign a document confessing his folly, and surrendering his entire realm to Edward, acknowledging the English King to be overlord of the land and people of Scotland. Balliol was publicly disgraced—crown, ring, scepter, sword and even most of his clothes taken from him. Because of this humiliation and his weakness as a King, he became known as *Toom Tabard*—the empty robe.

The fight was over in just a few months. The brutal invasion produced its chilling effect. The names of a majority of Scots nobles were to be found on the Ragman Roll, having sworn their loyalty, yet again, to the King of England.

Edward now proceeded to remove the ancient royal Stone of Coronation from Scone and take it with him to England. With it he sent Balliol ignominiously south to the Tower of London. He would never return to Scotland.

Caledonia had been stripped of its right even to have a King. Its former ruler was now in prison, its legendary Celtic stone in England. By the time Edward returned south, the north had been plundered and disarmed and was securely in the hands of an English occupation army from Inverness to the Tweed. Scotland was leaderless and paralyzed.

In the wake of Edward's smashing victory, the two younger Robert Bruces, father and son—Edward's brief allies—now returned across the border from Carlisle to reclaim their Annandale lands from their Comyn enemies and to take their place again in Scotland as *Edward's* men.

The Bruce-Plantagenet alliance, however, would not be a permanent one.

※   F I V E   ※

November 1307

What visitor's the laird got, Donal?" asked the boy's mother as she spooned out a bowlful of thick porridge for her son.

"A man Papa says is in danger," answered the boy.

"What's he doing here?"

"Papa said he came in the middle o' the night. He's at the castle noo, lying on his deathbed, Papa says. The laird's people are tendin' him, but it's up t' Papa t' reshoe the horses o' his men an' sharpen their weapons. Papa says there isna muckle time, an' he needs me t' help him."

"Why the danger, Donal? Be the man an outlaw? What fer's the castle o' Strathbogie helpin' an enemy o' the kingdom, gien that's what he be?"

"I dinna ken, Mama. Papa says he's bein' chased by the King o' England an' half the nobles o' Scotland. But Papa says *he's* the rightful King. Papa says he's the man Earl John left to fight wi'."

"What's his name, Donal?"

"Papa called him the earl o' Carrick, Mama."

The woman sucked in a sharp breath of air and brought her hand to her chest. "Robert the Bruce!" she exclaimed, in mingled awe and fear. "I winna hae ye at the castle, Donal," she added firmly. "The man's a murderer, whether oor earl's friend or no!"

"Papa called him the King."

"The King o' what? He murdered Red John Comyn in the verra sicht o' God, and noo he has half o' England an' Scotland thirstin' fer his head! He's a godless man, Donal."

"What will I tell Papa, Mama?" asked Donal.

Calming, the woman thought a moment. "Weel, sit ye doon an' eat your gruel," she said after a moment, "and let me think. I dinna guess I can keep ye frae what yer father asked o' ye. Still, I dinna like the thought o' my son around a man that would take another's life on the verra altar o' God's kirk an' then make himself King, though it cost his family their life an' freedom—no, no, he's no righteous man in my eyes, Donal."

Though he hadn't an idea what she meant, the boy had already taken his mother's words to heart and was sitting at the humble table to await the gruel she proceeded to slop into a wooden bowl as she spoke.

In time he would understand everything his mother was talking about, and far more, about the man who would be King called Robert the Bruce.

⌘ S I X ⌘

1297

Steadily the embers of resentment smoldered in Scotland against Edward of England and his occupation forces, which filled the north.

Yet the Scots had no one around whom to rally. The elder Bruce was dead. His son had taken up arms for Edward. The disgraced King, John Balliol, sat prisoner in the Tower of London.

A new leader was needed to fan the coals into life.

In 1297 such a man appeared. His name was William Wallace.

The anger of the Scots broke into flame when young Wallace, the son of a Scottish knight, became involved in an argument with the English sheriff of Lanark. The dispute ended with the sheriff dead and Wallace on the run. He was immediately declared a murderer and an outlaw against the English crown—and he willingly took on the rebel's role.

Suddenly all the pent-up resentment against England gathered and rallied around Wallace. Outlaw bands of rebels flocked to join the insurgency against Edward's rule and the English occupation.

Within months, Wallace and his rebels were raiding English-held castles and striking against garrisons of English soldiers. Using guerrilla tactics, they hit the enemy quickly, then disappeared into the Scottish wilds.

In time, more and more recruits flocked to the cause, intent upon freeing Scotland from English dominion. Scottish lords joined the fight along with peasants. James the Steward, James Douglas, and Bishop Wishart of Glasgow gathered men and arms. Andrew de Moray led forces in the recapture of many key castles in the north.

In July of 1297, less than a year after Edward had squashed the whole of Scotland, he received notification from Hugh Cressingham, his treasurer in Scotland, that the whole land was in turmoil and that the Scots were ousting English officials everywhere.

Edward did not believe the reports of Scottish insurrection could be as serious as Cressingham reported. Hadn't he dealt with the Scots last year and received fealty oaths from thousands of Scots lords and nobles? Besides, he was busy fighting the French and did not want to be bothered at the moment with the irksome northland. The next month, Edward sailed for the Continent.

But nothing could stop the war for freedom that Wallace had begun. He and his supporters continued to storm triumphantly through Scotland, eventually taking back most of the significant castles from English hands. In the King's absence, Cressingham amassed the English forces and marched to meet Wallace and Moray.

The armies met at Stirling Bridge, where Wallace's rebels completely routed the English. Cressingham was killed, the castle of Stirling surrendered, and the government of Scotland was back in Scots' hands. On behalf of Lord John Balliol, King of Scotland, the Scottish nobility appointed William Wallace as guardian of the kingdom of Scotland and commander of its armies.

Edward returned from the Continent, learned what had happened, and in a fury immediately marched north.

Wallace awaited this renewed assault near Falkirk. He deployed his army in four large oval groupings called *schiltrons*, in which the men were drawn tightly together in bristling hedgehog formations, standing or kneeling two or three deep and pointing eight- to ten-foot spears outward so as to make penetration into their ranks impossible.

At Falkirk, however, though the formation succeeded in blunting the initial attack, English archers were able eventually to exact a heavy toll on the thickly grouped spearmen, and the tight formations were broken apart. English horsemen rode in, killing and disbursing the confused Scots. Wallace's own cavalry, placed to the rear of the schiltrons, proved ineffective. Falkirk resulted in a disastrous defeat for the Scottish rebel forces.

Wallace and those who were able fled. The bright flame of independence was extinguished as rapidly as it had ignited. The power of the brilliant leader was destroyed, and Wallace went into hiding.

⬚ S E V E N ⬚

1297–1304

Biding his time throughout William Wallace's rebellion had been a certain Robert Bruce, grandson of the former contender for the throne, and now, at twenty-three, the earl of Carrick in his own right.

His grandfather had died two years earlier, but the aging lord of Annandale had been convinced to the end that his right to the Scottish throne was just and legitimate. After Balliol's selection he had drawn up a document transmitting his claim to his posterity, both to his son and his heirs, according them "full and free power to sue for the realm, and to prosecute the right which pertains to him in this matter, in the way that seems best to him."

The old man's son did not share his passion to pursue the throne. But the eyes of the young grandson gleamed with thoughts of the prize he believed was rightfully his. When the father resigned his earldom shortly thereafter, leaving title and headship of family to a son barely out of his teens, the flame of his desire began to burn more brightly still.

In 1297, with the nation in full revolt and with no King of Scotland on the throne, twenty-three-year-old Robert Bruce—the third successive generation of the old Norman family to share the name—awaited developments. He had not actively participated with Wallace, for Wallace was fighting to secure a return of John Balliol to the throne—yet he had been inspired by Wallace's courage and intrigued by Wallace's cause.

More than anything, he wanted to rule the land of Scotland. But now he was beginning to consider what kind of a nation he wanted to rule—not an occupied land humiliated by her captors and ruled by the whims of a southern King, but a proud and free nation of her own.

In the meantime, with Balliol still in England and Wallace in hiding, it seemed that young Bruce's opportunity might be at hand. Increasingly he was being recognized as one on whom the mantle of Scots leadership might rest. And yet he was not without rival—for many nobles in the land considered the claims of young John Comyn, lord of Badenoch, called John the Red, to be equal to those of the earl of Carrick. *

Increasingly, in the eyes of the northland's leading nobles, hope for the future leadership of Scotland had come to rest upon the shoulders of these two young men—the son and grandson of the two prominent contenders from 1286. Now, eleven years later, these two hereditary rivals were appointed as joint "guardians of the kingdom."

It was an arrangement doomed to failure from the start.

Old feuds do not die easily. Not only were Robert Bruce and Red Comyn each jealous of the other's potential power and resentful of each other's claims, but they also quickly grew to hate one another personally. To make matters worse, each young man was possessed of a quick temper that easily flared to violence.

Their antipathy erupted during a council of war in 1299. Accusations of treason were made. Comyn seized Bruce by the throat, and the two men had to be pulled apart.

Partly as a result of this discord, the guardianship was reorganized. A bishop was added, then young Bruce was ousted the following year. Consequently he made a renewed peace with Edward. He saw it as politically necessary, though his heart was not in the arrangement.

For five years Scotland was in the hands of the guardians, and its army managed with occasional success to harass the occupying English troops. Robert Bruce, however, involved himself little in the northern kingdom's affairs, though he watched developments with keen interest. As years went by, he felt more and more discomfort over his ties to the south. He was gradually coming to see himself, first and foremost, as a Scot. Part of him yearned to take up the cause of freeing Scotland. But hothead though he might be, Robert the Bruce also had a keen sense of strategy. It was clear to him that his wisest strategy for the moment was to watch and wait. So he bided his time, keeping eyes and ears open for his best opportunity.

---

* Note that two different branches of the Comyn family figure in this story. John the Red Comyn was earl of Badenoch. His kinsman, John Comyn, earl of Buchan, was the descendent of the Comyn who had once been given the Bruce lands of Annandale by Edward I. Robert the Bruce contended against each of these John Comyns—Badenoch and Buchan, in turn.

By 1304 Edward had worn down the Scots. Many nobles were surrendering and making renewed submission to Edward. Then, after trips abroad to rally support, William Wallace suddenly resurfaced.

By now, however, circumstances had changed, and fate quickly turned against the man who so recently had rallied a nation. Wallace was arrested by English soldiers the following year near Glasgow, taken to London, tried for treason, and convicted.

The brief hero of Scotland was dragged through the streets, hanged, cut down while still alive, sliced into quarters, his heart cast into a fire, the four sections of his body sent to Perth, Berwick, Newcastle, and Aberdeen. His head was placed on a pike and displayed above London Bridge.

Finally, thought Edward, his vexing and annoying troubles with Scotland must be over.

EIGHT

November 1307

The clanging of a massive hammer against a large iron anvil resonated with metallic ring throughout the small enclosure. While his father pounded the red-hot horseshoe into its final shape, young Donal, given new energy by the breakfast gruel in his stomach, vigorously pumped the bellows of the forge, keeping the fire hot, thankful on a cold day such as this to be inside the laird's farrier's shed.

"The man's in rum condition, Donal lad," sighed Fergus. "They say he mayna live the night."

"But he's the *King*, Papa," said the boy, unable to place the two things in his mind at the same time—as if the fact of kingship insured immortality. Unconsciously he relaxed his hand.

"Pump, Donal," exhorted his father. "I canna bend the iron gien the coals be not red."

Donal's tired arm swung back into motion.

"Kings has t' die like ither folk, Donal," said his father, now addressing his son's former uncertainty.

"Will he die, Papa ... while he is here?" asked the boy in a fearful tone. The fact that, across the court and high up in the tower a man lay so close to the unknown beckonings of eternity seemed to hallow the very walls off which clanked the sounds of his father's hammer.

"I think not, Donal. They say he's restin' well an' will be astride his horse again by Christmas Day."

"Is what Mama said true, Papa?"

"What did she say?"

"That the man's a murderer."

"I canna say, lad. That he's killed I dinna doobt, more than once. He's a warrior an' a fighter, a commander o' armies, Donal. That's why he's King. 'Tis why oor ain laird went t' join him, though some say it will cost him his life. The throne's no won wi'oot fightin'."

"Why, Papa?"

The man was silent a moment. The question was profound in its very simplicity.

"I dinna ken, Donal," Fergus replied at length.

"But who's he fightin', Papa?"

"John Comyn, earl of Buchan."

"I thought you said it was the English King."

"Edward o' England's been the enemy o' Scotland fer many a year. But noo the lords in Scotland are fightin' among themselves. Sometimes that's the way it is."

"Will it always be so, Papa?"

Again Fergus did not reply immediately. A long silence intervened. Both bellows and hammer fell idle from their respective duties.

"'Tis an auld legend, laddie," the father said at length, "that comes from oot of the hills. It says that it will be so . . . until the white stag appears again in Scotland."

"The white stag—what's that, Papa?"

"Sit ye doon, lad. I'll tell you aboot it."

Fergus set down his hammer and took a seat on the edge of a rough rail of wood. Donal scrambled onto the makeshift bench beside him and gazed up into the blackened face of the father he loved.

"The legend is said t' have begun years ago when oor distant fathers lived in the hills t' the west, when the land wasna yet called Scotland."

"What was it called?" asked Donal.

"Back then, it was known as *Caledonia*."

❊ N I N E ❊

1305–1306

At long last, in 1305, Edward I breathed with relief.

William Wallace, leader of the resistance, was dead. The King of England had received loyalty oaths from most of Scotland's leaders. John the Red Comyn seemed favorably disposed toward peace. Robert Bruce had caused no trouble for three or more years. Scotland and its leadership again seemed to have been subdued.

Yet truly was Edward called "The Hammer of the Scots," for as heavy as the ironworker Fergus's mallet had been the blows by which he had attempted to subdue them. And though the land had seemed momentarily quiet, his harsh methods had not been forgotten.

The execution of William Wallace did *not* blunt Scottish resistance as Edward hoped. The spirit of Scottish independence would never die. And by now, unknown to Edward . . . young Robert Bruce had plans.

He was as convinced as his grandfather that the most legitimate claim to the kingship of Scotland belonged to the name Bruce. More than ever, Scotland *needed* a King—and *he* was the rightful heir to that throne. The time at last seemed ripe to step forward and take control of the struggle for independence . . . and at the same time make his bid for the crown.

If he was to be successful, however, he would need somehow to deal with his bitterest enemy. With Wallace dead, John the Red Comyn of Badenoch was the most powerful leader in Scotland.

Robert Bruce by now was a formidable man of thirty-one. Comyn was about the same age. The fathers of both had died two years earlier. They were thus now heads of families with vast holdings, and both were in earnest about their claims to the Scottish throne. Having already unsuccessfully attempted to share power, the two men were now archrivals, and all Scotland was aware that bad blood flowed between them.

Comyn, serving as one of Scotland's guardians, clearly occupied the stronger position. The son of Balliol's sister as well as in the direct descent of Malcolm III's brother, who had succeeded him as the King, Red John saw himself the undisputed heir to Balliol's ill-fated kingship.

Young Robert the Bruce realized that his own claim to the crown would have no chance of succeeding unless he could somehow negotiate with Comyn. But given their past history, would that be possible? What could he offer that might gain Comyn's support—though the very thought of offering anything to that arrogant upstart made his skin creep? And Balliol had to be considered as well. The old King was now living in France and had not given up hope of a return.

Unlikely as the prospects seemed, thought Bruce, he *had* to find some way to swing Comyn to his side and out of Balliol's camp. In the past few years he had become convinced that the only hope for Scotland's future lay in ousting the English. And leadership of the cause against the English, to be effective, had to be united. They mustn't fragment. Only united could they hope to defeat Edward.

He would set up a meeting with Comyn, Bruce thought to himself, to discuss the future. Both he and Red John were older now. Surely there was some way to patch up their differences and gain Comyn's critical backing.

The meeting was arranged for the tenth of February, 1306. The place would be Greyfriars' Church in Dumfries. So great was the mistrust between the two men, and so high the possibility of treachery, that only in a church might they perhaps be able to discuss matters of such importance without fear for their lives.

Robert the Bruce arrived in Dumfries with a mingled sense of anticipation and unease. More than ever, he believed that the future of his kingdom depended on this meeting. But still he dreaded the prospect of trying to negotiate with Red John Comyn.

Red John and his contingent rode up to the chapel not long after Bruce and his own men had dismounted. The tension between the two groups was obvious. The two priests who had waited for them outside the chapel glanced around uneasily. The sounds and motions behind him told Bruce that his followers had stealthily unsheathed their knives.

Quickly he motioned to his men to stay where they were. He and Red John would enter the church alone.

Red John Comyn gave a similar motion to his nervous men. A quivering silence held while the two young heirs who would rule Scotland walked into the church alone to weigh the future of a nation.

Once they were inside, the discussion did not last long. Immediate disagreement flared.

"What would it take to win you over to my side, John?" Bruce asked. "I need your support."

"*My* support!" laughed Comyn derisively. "What of my claim to the kingship? Do you expect me to simply abandon it?"

Bruce was silent.

"After all the loyalty oaths you have signed to Edward," Comyn went on, "why don't you go to him?"

The retort hit uncomfortably close to home, especially because there was some truth in it. But Bruce forced down his rising irritation and replied evenly. "You must understand how it is. One pledges loyalty when English swords are at his throat. It means nothing."

"They were hardly at your throat when you and your father rode out to intercept Edward in '96!" shot back Comyn. "Nor, I suspect, all the other times."

"I was young and had little say in the matter. But I tell you, my loyalty is to Scotland."

"Do you speak for your father and grandfather?"

"I speak only for myself."

"And you now claim such pledges meant nothing?"

"I say only that expedience occasionally demands such measures," answered the Bruce in a tight voice. The man seemed intent on needling him. "One makes peace in order to fight another day."

"Ha! You did more than merely *pledge* loyalty. You and your father, and his father before him, took arms in Edward's cause and *fought* against all the rest of us—against my family . . . against your own King!"

"The same might be said of your people," retorted Bruce.

"Years ago, perhaps—but not in my generation. None has betrayed our cause as greatly as the house of Bruce. Or, should I say, the house of treason!"

Young Robert's face flushed with fury.

"How dare you!" he cried.

"While the loyal name of Comyn has fought and shed blood against the English for ten years," his rival went on, clearly taunting him, "you and your father and grandfather drifted back and forth to whatever side of the conflict suited your purposes. *I* have been fighting Edward—*you* have been protecting your lands. You have sacrificed nothing for Scotland!"

With great effort, Bruce attempted to quell once more the rising passion of his blood.

"Be that as it may," he said in measured tone, "I remain the legal heir to its throne."

"Your claim is no nearer than my own. I am directly in line from Donald Bane. I have been one of Scotland's guardians. And I am next to follow in the Balliol line."

"Both your claim and that of Balliol are more distant than that of the Bruce."

"A Balliol is King. Where does that leave the Bruce?"

"Balliol's claim was always weak. I will be Scotland's *next* King."

"And yet it is I who have support among the nobles—more than you could dream of."

"You will never be King!" said Bruce a little more heatedly.

"We shall see," said the redheaded man.

"I tell you, the crown belongs to me," insisted Bruce, clenching and unclenching his fists. "And I am now asking for your support. Are you with me or against me?"

"Ha!" spat Comyn. "You are not worthy of the throne!"

"I *will* be Scotland's King!"

"Betrayal of our cause is in your family's blood!"

"Are you calling me a traitor again, Red Comyn?" shouted Bruce, stepping toward his rival, "as you did seven years ago!"

"I do not have to call you one," replied Comyn, reaching for the sheath that hung at his side. "Your own deeds betray you and reveal you for the traitor you are!" Suddenly his hand flew toward the handle of his dirk.

What happened in the seconds that followed was over quickly. The next thing that the men gathered outside knew, Bruce had emerged from the church, dagger in hand dripping red with blood.

Realizing what had happened, Comyn's men drew their swords. Bruce's complied in kind.

Dust flew, horses reared and whinnied, and a brief skirmish ensued. A minute later two of Comyn's men lay dead on the dirt, while the rest fled for their lives.

Bruce's men, meanwhile, ran into the church. They found Red John Comyn lying crumpled and bleeding on the floor inside. Quickly they moved to finish what their master had begun, then ran quickly back outside almost the same moment as the horrified priests rushed in to discover what had happened.

It had all happened so quickly. A negotiation had become a murder—and on holy ground. It was not at all what had been intended, but it was done.

There would be no going back.

———

While his brothers proceeded to seize Dumfries Castle, Bruce now rode straight to Glasgow to beg absolution from Bishop Wishart—partly from his own discomfort that his rash deed had occurred on sanctified soil, but also because religious protocol must be observed if he was to have a chance of reaching his objective. In addition, it would not hurt to receive spiritual sanction for what would follow.

He obtained the absolution.

A decision of great import now faced Robert Bruce. He could flee to the hills and allow himself to become an outlaw and renegade after the fashion of Wallace. Or he could attempt a much bolder stroke.

He chose the latter.

This time there would be no councils, no committees, no discussions, no turning over decisions into the hands of an enemy king. There would be no *negotiations* over who held the right of kingship, no guardianships. He would discuss the matter with no one.

What he was about to do was for the good of the country. Only led by a strong King could Scotland defeat Edward of England. Only led by a strong King could Scotland win back the freedom Edward had stolen from it. He would *take* the kingship that belonged to him by right of blood and descent from Scotland's past kings.

Within but a few weeks of the murder of Red John Comyn, therefore, Robert Bruce was on the way to Scone with what support he could muster.

TEN

1306

That young Robert Bruce had committed murder was only the half of it.

That he had committed murder in a church was a sacrilege against God and the church, and great was the outcry that rose up against him— in England, on the Continent, even in Scotland. Notwithstanding his own bishop's absolution, excommunication from the pope resulted three

months later. Balliol loyalists and Comyn kinsmen alike expressed out-
rage over the crime.

There was therefore no time for Bruce to lose. He was determined to
have himself crowned King before anyone could move to stop him.

At Scone he assembled a small but not inconsequential gathering that
included his four brothers, who had already been seizing castles with their
men on his behalf, as well as Bishops Wishart and Moray and Lamberton
and two of Scotland's Seven Earls.

To give the hurried ceremony the sanction of legitimacy, Countess Isabel of Buchan, sister of the laird of Strathbogie Castle, was summoned.
That her husband, the earl of Buchan, was nearest kinsman to the Red
Comyn and a staunch Bruce adversary might be considered a strange
fact. But she was of the family MacDuff, sister to the earl of Fife, now
lord of Strathbogie. To her family had gone the hereditary right to crown
the kings of Alba for centuries.

Whatever Countess Isabel thought personally of Robert the Bruce, in
this case she evidently decided that the blood of her clan came before
marital loyalty. Her brother and nephew sat in an English prison. Therefore she determined to do her part to break Edward's tyranny. She stole
her husband's horses, sneaked away from home, and rode to Scone to do
her duty to clan and race and nation.

On March 25, 1306, therefore, Robert Bruce was crowned King of
Scotland.

The Stone of Destiny, stolen by Edward of England, still sat in Westminster Abbey. A substitute was quickly quarried, and Bruce took his
place upon it. Edward had also taken the royal crown and scepter, ring
and sword. Bruce wouldn't worry about those just now.

In the name of the past kings of Scotland, Countess Isabel stepped
forward to place a circlet of gold upon the head of Robert Bruce, earl of
Carrick.

"I declare you commander of the Scottish army," she said solemnly,
"and by consent of the realm and by God's grace, Robert I, King of the
whole of the kingdom of Scotland and sole guardian of its lands and people, in the name of God the Father, and the Son, and the Holy Ghost."

Bruce rose, clasped the hands of the few witnesses and accepted their
good wishes, then sighed with relief, as if a weight had been removed from
his shoulders. He was glad this part of the struggle was over. As to a
crown . . . he would see about having a new one made at the soonest pos-

sible convenience. Also a royal surcoat. He must, after all, *look* the part of King.

Whether or not he was *legitimately* King of Scotland would be argued around many hearths for some time to come.

As always, Scotland's nobles were divided on the matter of Bruce's kingship. Some supported him, but many swore vengeance for the blood he had shed and the enormity of his presumption in seizing the throne. Kinsmen and allies of the Comyn-Balliol faction were numerous and powerful and vowed that whatever he might call himself, the young Bruce would never *reign* as King. They would kill him before they would let him rule.

And so, of course, would Edward of England, if given a chance.

He had made himself King, but Robert Bruce knew his life was in danger from many sources. From Scone, therefore, he fled into hiding, adopting the former tactics of the great guardian martyr Wallace. He would continue to wage war guerrilla-style against the English occupation of the north, hoping gradually to consolidate the support of Scotland's doubting nobles. His following would have to be built. Bruce was willing to do so slowly.

Considering all that was against the Bruce, it is perhaps surprising that support did indeed begin to come in from among Scotland's influential landowners, including James Douglas and the earl of Atholl. But it was not yet sufficient to wrest back lands from English control nor even to quell the hostile opposition throughout Scotland from Bruce's own countrymen. In mid–1306, after an unsuccessful attempt to capture Perth from the English, the fugitive King and his followers took refuge in the central Highlands.

Enraged at Bruce's slap in the face against English sovereignty, a furious Edward yet again marched north with his own twenty-three-year-old son, namesake, and heir, sending out orders to his commanders ahead of him to round up Bruce's supporters—and to show no mercy. In accordance with this order, one of Bruce's brothers and his brother-in-law were captured and hanged. Bruce's wife and daughter and sisters were taken from Kildrummy Castle—where Bruce had left them, he thought, in safety—and imprisoned. The Countess of Buchan, who had installed him at Scone, was confined to a small tower in Berwick Castle. Sixteen other of Bruce's supporters were tried at Newcastle and hanged.

The future looked dark. Against such odds, the new King of the Scots went into deep hiding, disappearing into the west and island regions. He was not seen or heard from for the rest of the year.

The English King Edward himself, now almost sixty-eight years old and ill, but determined to lead the search for the traitor Bruce and personally preside over his hanging, proved unable to continue the journey. He paused to winter in Carlisle.

For years ever after the tale would be told that during his travels, while hiding on Rathlin Island, Bruce observed the persistence of a spider. Six times did the tiny creature attempt unsuccessfully to swing from one beam to another. Not until the seventh did it gain its objective.

The visual lesson, the story goes, inspired Bruce to persevere under the adversity then facing his cause.

⬚   E L E V E N   ⬚

January–October 1307

Bruce emerged from hiding early in the year 1307 far to the south of Scotland, then marched through his own lands of Carrick trying to muster support. He found himself, however, still hemmed in by enemies on all sides. Two more of his brothers were taken prisoner by English troops and executed. Yet again, after only a few months, Bruce took to the hills.

Early in the summer of 1307, Edward of England resumed his march north. Though still frail from his illness, he had himself helped into the saddle and led his army north out of Carlisle.

But he was too weak to continue. Only three miles from the Scottish border, on the sands of the Solway, still determined with his last ounce of strength to subdue the rebellious Highlanders of the north, Edward I of England had to be lifted from his horse and taken to shelter in the village.

Frustrated, but knowing he was dying, Edward made but one last request—that his heart be carried to the Holy Land and his bones go in his stead at the head of the army until all of Scotland and its rebels had been wholly subdued and Robert Bruce the traitor was dead.

When the final words of his adversary were conveyed to the Scottish King, Bruce could not help but smile.

"I fear the dead bones of the father more than I fear the living flesh of the son," Bruce replied.

Those were prophetic words indeed regarding Edward II of England. A far weaker monarch than his father, he who would have been husband to the Maid of Norway was hardly a worthy successor to the Hammer of the Scots, who died on July 7, 1307.

The first decision of Edward II's reign, in fact, gave Robert Bruce the kingdom of which Edward I had spent his life trying to deprive him. The English army was ordered to turn around and march south. Young Edward had decided to take neither his father's bones *nor* the English army across the border.

Though Scotland was still largely occupied by the English, the removal of immediate threat of another invasion meant that Bruce could turn his attention to the consolidation of his own power against the remaining Comyn-Balliol relatives and loyalists among the Scottish nobility.

Bruce therefore marched immediately from his lands in the southwest into northern Scotland, with three thousand men under his command, to face another John Comyn, this one the earl of Buchan. The years of running and fighting and hiding, however, had exacted their toll. Bruce was by this time so worn down by the prolonged strain of travel and battle that he fell sick and could scarcely command.

Buchan, alerted to the threat, raised his own army . . . and waited.

In early November the army of Bruce, plagued by desertion and near starvation, halted at Slioch just west of the valley of the Bogie.

When the news reached Buchan, the report was clear.

"Bruce himself is sick, my lord," said the scout. "He sits on a litter from morning till night, hardly able to eat."

Comyn nodded with interest. If Bruce should die, or if he could attack and manage to kill the usurper, it was entirely probable that he himself, as heir to the Comyn legacy, could emerge as the new King of Scotland.

This was indeed a fortuitous turn of events.

"And the disposition of his troops?" the earl asked.

"His men are said to be starving," the man replied, "and are deserting in droves. His force shrinks daily."

More good news, thought Buchan. He required only another moment's deliberation.

"Then the time has come for us to attack," said the earl enthusiastically. "We will put an end to this imposter of a King once and for all!"

Buchan advanced with his army of fifteen hundred men. Of Bruce's force, but a thousand or less remained. The future of a kingdom hung in the balance—and fewer than three thousand soldiers were present to decide it.

Buchan's army marched to within sight of Bruce's encampment, where Buchan ordered his own camp be made. An early snow had begun to fall and continued sporadically through the night. Men on both sides were cold and dispirited. Buchan's force continued to grow, and as he made final plans he took hope in Bruce's rumored illness.

Comyn went out to survey his adversary the following morning. Suddenly there appeared Robert Bruce across the fields, sitting boldly on horseback at the front of his army.

"What is Bruce doing there?" Comyn called to his commander.

"I do not know, my lord. Shall I order the attack?"

Buchan sat astride his mount perplexed. Suddenly he was filled with doubts as to the success of a strike. For several long minutes he sat while his commander waited, peering at the tall figure of the self-crowned King across the white field of snow.

"It . . . it is some ploy," he murmured at length, still debating within himself.

If the report of sickness had been false, Buchan thought, what of the reports of desertion? What if all the reports were spurious—ploys to lure him into battle?

He sat pondering but a few minutes more, then decided. He would not fall for the ruse and be drawn into Bruce's trap. He would wait.

He turned his horse. "Give orders to postpone the attack," he said, then rode back toward his tent.

Meanwhile, out of the sight of Buchan, Bruce's brother Edward helped the King, in a near state of collapse, out of the saddle. The gambit had sapped every ounce of strength he possessed.

"We must rush him to shelter, where he can recover," said Edward Bruce. "If he dies now, the kingdom is lost."

"Where will he be safest, my lord?" asked the attendants and commanders.

"Prepare the litter as comfortably as possible," replied Bruce's brother. "Make the King warm with what plaids you can gather from the men. We will make for the Peel of Strathbogie. It's not far. Earl John has been one of our loyal supporters. Even though he is himself in prison, his people will give us shelter."

❧ T W E L V E ❧

December 11, 1307

"Is the King better, Papa?" asked an eager voice the instant the tired iron-monger entered the cottage.

"Ay, he's said t' be recoverin', Donal lad," replied Fergus.

"A murderer—no King," muttered the mother.

"He's o' the blood o' auld King David I, guidwife, an' auld Malcolm and Margaret afore him," said Fergus. "And crowned at Scone by the Lady Isabel. That makes him oor King, whate'er else he'll be."

She returned him no comment, and Donal's father continued in a somber tone.

"If yer words be true, wife," he said, "he's not the only murderer sittin' on a throne, as all Scots have kenned weel enough this mony a year."

She looked toward him with concern and seemed to know his meaning even before he spoke it. Fergus met her inquisitive gaze with a nod.

"Oor ain John's been executed in prison by that blackguard King o' England," he said. "I jist heard the ill news."

"Och, no!" she moaned, eyes filling with tears. "Oor ain puir laird! But why?"

"On account o' Isabel's hand in crownin' the Bruce at Scone, the way they tell it. She's John's ain sister, an' the man had t' exact his vengeance."

"Will it ne'er end—the killin', the killin'?"

"Not till the matter o' Scotland's freedom be settled once an' fer all," rejoined her husband prophetically.

❧ T H I R T E E N ❧

December 22, 1307

It was a week before Christmas of the year 1307. Robert Bruce had been recuperating for five weeks at the castle of the earl of Strathbogie, whose descendents had been given the lands by William the Lion.

As his brother had predicted, Robert Bruce recovered sufficiently at Huntly to again take his position at the front of his men. But his constitution remained weak, and he could only sit on horseback for brief periods. His army remained encamped where the sick-litter had left it in November a few miles from Huntly.

Now, with Christmas approaching, the earl of Buchan appeared to be gathering his forces for the attack he had delayed before.

Bruce and his brother strode toward the stables three days before Christmas, about to take leave of the King's temporary refuge.

"In what condition are our horses?" Bruce asked.

"Mostly well ironed," replied his brother. "We have made use of the laird's smith."

As if in response to the words, the clank of metal on metal interrupted their conversation. The King's ear perked up at the sound. He turned and made his way toward the smithy's shed, from which the metallic echo had originated.

Bruce walked inside. A rugged-looking man stood beside a hot forge, pounding a bar of iron into the round over the flat top of a great anvil.

Fergus glanced up, arresting his arm in midstroke. He knew at once who had paid him this impromptu visit. He set down the hammer and bowed toward the King.

The Bruce dipped his head respectfully toward the farrier.

"I understand you have helped maintain the equipment of my small army," Bruce said. "I want to offer you my sincere thanks."

Fergus nodded in acknowledgment, though he could find no words to speak.

"You are a patriot for your kingdom," Bruce added, then turned with his brother and left the darkened enclosure.

▨   F O U R T E E N   ▨

December 25, 1307

An urgent beating sounded upon the wooden door.

Groggily, Fergus MacDarroch groped for a candle, then stumbled toward the door.

Who could possibly—

His thoughts remained uncompleted as he opened the door. In front of him stood a man he had never seen before.

"I come in the name of King Robert of Scotland," said the stranger with importance in his voice. "The King's smith has deserted. The King sent me to ask if you would join with him in the fight for Scotland's freedom."

Already Fergus was dressing clumsily, the decision made even as the request was spoken. He had been summoned by the King!

"What aboot . . . my tools . . . a cart? I must prepare coals—"

"You will require nothing," interrupted the King's messenger. "All is in readiness. We possess cart, a horse to pull it—we need only you."

Fergus nodded, then closed the door and went back inside to complete his preparations.

"Come . . . come, Donal!" called the rousing voice only a few moments later.

The imperative voice of his father startled his young son awake from a deep sleep. It was Christmas morning, and still dark outside.

Donal struggled to make himself come awake, though it was cold and all his senses fought against it.

"Come, my son—the King an' his men hae left the castle. The enemy marches on Strathbogie!"

"What . . . what will we do, Papa? Will they hurt us . . . what enemy?" he asked, still sleepy and confused.

"Comyn of Buchan. No, he will not hurt us—he only wants t' kill the King. We must gae wi' him."

"With who?"

The boy was sitting on the edge of his bed now, while his father did his best to dress him in haste.

"With the King."

"But why, Papa?"

"His own farrier hae deserted 'im. I must be ready with iron and hot coals and a ready hammer gien his horses' feet need help during battle."

"You, Papa—are ye gaein' wi' the King?"

Now was Donal awake in earnest.

"Ay, an' ye'll gae wi' me. I spoke wi' him—with the King himsel'. His man is waitin' outside noo."

By now the wife had wandered toward them with a candle in her hand, hearing the ending fragments of the conversation.

"Dinna be a fool, Fergus MacDarroch," she said. "The man's a murderer—he's no worth fightin' fer. I'd sooner ye'd take the Buchan's side."

"Yer ain people come frae east o' here where Comyn's lord," said the husband. "But mine's frae Fife, they say, and afore that the west. My ain grit-grandfather Gachan MacDarroch, 'tis said, helped the first lord o' Strathbogie build the verra castle where oor ain John, rest his soul, lived till the English King took him south t' kill him. If the King o' the Scots be my laird's King, then he's aye my King too."

"King!" spat the woman. "The man's King in his own eyes maybe, but no in the sicht o' God. He killed Buchan's kinsman for his ill-gotten crown."

"Well, Buchan's not gaein' t' be King whate'er comes o' Bruce, guid-wife. Gien the earl kills Bruce, yoong Edward o' England will make himsel' King again. And I'll die sooner than bow t' an Englishman. No, wife, the Bruce is a Scot an' he's my King, an' I'll serve him when he calls."

"An' gien he takes ye to the grave wi' him?" retorted the wife, now more angry than worried.

"Then I say it'd be an honor fer a man t' die fer one wha fought fer the freedom o' Scotland. 'Tis not mony a man gets such a chance. 'Tis what makes heroes o' them."

"An' fools," remarked the wife in a muttered outburst of boldness.

"What's that ye say?"

"I say Donal's no gaein' wi' ye."

"Wha's gaein' t' pump the bellows?"

"No, my laddie!" asserted the woman.

"We'll let the boy decide, then," said the father.

"I must gae, Mama," interjected Donal, now fully awake and eager to take his place as a man at his father's side. "He's the King."

❖   F I F T E E N   ❖

Though by now Bruce's army numbered a mere seven hundred men, there were at least two present on that fateful winter's birthday of the Lord who had not been with the King when he arrived in the region.

The ironmonger Fergus MacDarroch was determined to make sure the horses of the King's army were well shod. He joined the army of the King for a mere day, but that was enough to draw his son into the ongoing saga of their land and its people.

The earl of Buchan was not so much routed as surprised by the events of that Christmas battle.

Bruce's force proved small but stouthearted, and Buchan was unable to budge them from their positions. The battle of Slioch, therefore, proved inconclusive.

During its final moments, chance fighting resulted behind the lines when Comyn's men broke through Bruce's rear flank, endangering for a brief time the supply carts, grooms, and other noncombatants. Bolting horses, in fear from the fighting erupting about them, overturned the smith's wagon. Caught unexpectedly in the sudden stampede, the man who had put shoes on the horses of the King's men during his brief stay at Strathbogie was trampled by fleeing hooves and thrown under the wheel of the errant cart.

By midday Buchan broke off the fight. He would go for reinforcements, leaving his scouts to keep an eye on Bruce and his movements.

Upon the earl's departure, Bruce's forces immediately set about assessing casualties and preparing for the next assault. The King, still weak from his illness, rode toward the rear of the force to lie down and rest. He reined in his mount when he observed a boy standing alone and crying. He swung his horse in the boy's direction, then stopped and dismounted, wondering what one so young was doing so close to the field of battle.

"What is it, lad?" asked the King.

"My father's dead," said Donal, struggling to stop crying.

Glancing around and now seeing the overturned horseshoeing cart and the broken form under it where a few men were seeking to extricate the body and put the wagon upright, suddenly the King perceived the truth. The boy's father was the same man whom he had met in the castle—and whom he had sent for this morning to join his cause and help with the ironwork.

Perhaps made tender by the weakness of his own body, Bruce's heart smote him with compassion for the boy whom his request had made suddenly fatherless.

He turned and with a gesture signaled some of his men to make haste in removing the body. Dismounting, he knelt and peered into Donal's face. He placed one of his great hands to the boy's cheek and wiped away the tears streaming down them.

"Your father is a hero, son," he said softly and sincerely. The voice was large and deep and resonated with a strength of authority in the boy's grief-stricken ears. "He gave his life for the land of the Scots," Bruce continued. "He loved it no less than I do myself. You must be proud of him, son. Your father will be remembered as a great man in the battle for our freedom."

Donal struggled to draw in a quivering breath and managed to steady himself. The very timber of command calmed him, though he did not know who was speaking to him.

"What is your name, lad?" asked Bruce.

"Donal . . . Donal, son of Fergus MacDarroch."

"It is a worthy and noble name. How old are you, then?"

"Twelve."

Donal gazed up miserably into the eyes of the man who had stopped to speak to him.

Behind them, a rider rode up. "You are wanted, King Robert," said the man. "Your brother asks if you desire that the fleeing Buchan be pursued eastward."

Suddenly the truth broke in upon the son of Fergus that he had been speaking to none other than the King of Scotland himself. A light came into his eyes as the King now rose. Now indeed did the voice that had spoken to him penetrate with even deeper power into the soul of young Donal MacDarroch.

"No, do not pursue," said the King to the rider. "Tell my brother we will feign to cross the mountains toward Mar, but then circle back in the direction of Inverurie."

Again Bruce looked down at Donal, still standing speechless.

Gently he placed his huge hand on the boy's head, patted it twice, then handed the reins of his horse to him.

"How would you like to feed my horse, young Donal, son of Fergus?"

———

Later that Christmas night, cursing the man she would go to her grave calling a murderer, the widow of the man who had shod King Robert the Bruce's horses lay weeping and unable to sleep.

Her son, too, wept in his bed that night. But despite his tears, the disconsolate woman's twelve-year-old son had become a man that day. His father had fallen. But in the wake of tragedy a King had crowned the light brown locks of his hair with the gentle touch of his hand, and his voice had spoken into his soul. Henceforward would he gladly serve the man his father had counted it an honor to die for.

He had heard what the King had said about the direction of his army. As soon as he could, he would ride after the great man.

The King in whose service Fergus MacDarroch had given his life had a rendezvous with history approaching. Now had his son also been drawn into those events . . . and would, before he reached twenty, take his own share in that coming destiny.

SIXTEEN

1309

Fortunately, Donal's eyes did not witness Bruce's final defeat of the earl of Buchan outside Inverurie—or the raping, burning, and wasting of Buchan's lands, or the cruel killing that accompanied it. With the blood feud over, Bruce had finally destroyed the power of the Comyns. Only a few more opponents remained to be pacified, and within two years the Scottish throne was his without contest.

By the time King Robert convened his first Parliament at St. Andrews in 1309—made up largely of northerners, Highlanders, and representatives from Celtic families and clans from whom most of his support came— young Donal MacDarroch, who had once been handed the reins to the King's horse, had left his mother in Strathbogie to follow the army of *the Bruce*. If he might just help with the great man's horse again, thought Donal, he would be happy. The King's groom was the first acquaintance he made upon arriving at the camp, where he then served for several years without again speaking with Robert Bruce or even seeing him close by.

He had no reason to believe the King knew of his presence, but that fact in no way diminished his loyalty.

SEVENTEEN

1311

Are the horses well fed, lad?" asked a lanky man in his early sixties, ambling toward the pen he and his young assistant had fashioned out of ropes an hour or two before.

Most of the men of the army took care of their own horses. But the old Highlander Aonghuis had been the groom of Robert Bruce's father, and never more loyal servant could a king have to attend his own mount and those of his commanders. Aonghuis treated the creatures as if they were his children.

But the man was aging, and was therefore glad enough for the help of the young fellow who had joined the King's regiment. Aonghuis was never sure exactly where the boy had come from. He was certainly too young to be in the army. Appearing one day, the boy had simply begun cleaning up after the horses, rubbing them down, and making himself so useful that the old groom had seen no reason to send him away. Day after day, the boy had proved so helpful with chores and shown such a keen eye to the needs of horseflesh that none grudged him a share of the food or a plaid under which to keep warm at night.

Recruits came and went regularly in a mobile army such as this, and most of the time no one asked many questions. When one gave himself to the King, however, it was counted a worthy service and not taken lightly. Everyone could tell instantly that this particular boy was one who knew horses and loved them—and was fiercely loyal to the King.

As time passed, Aonghuis could hardly remember a time when the lad *hadn't* been his assistant.

The boy, now sixteen, turned and came walking toward him.

"All fed and content," he replied with a smile in a deep, masculine voice. He tossed the empty bucket he was carrying onto the back of a cart, where it landed near the sack of oats from which he had been filling it.

"And watered?"

"Ready for the night," said Donal.

The son of Fergus MacDarroch had indeed grown remarkably in the years since death had taken his father. Though the expression upon his face yet hovered delicately between youth and manhood, in his carriage and strength it was clear that the latter had overtaken the former.

Donal had seen much since joining King Robert Bruce's following— things no youth ought to see unless he is indeed prepared for the arrival of manhood. Death and blood may be required to fashion a kingdom, but they are grievous sights even for those who can endure them.

With most of Scotland's nobles and clergy at last lining up in support behind him, Robert Bruce now turned his attention again toward the English and set about removing them from the north. Many key castles—Edinburgh, Perth, Stirling, Dundee, Banff, Dunbar, Berwick, and two dozen others—were still solidly in the hands of English garrisons. The fact that many could be reached from the south by sea insured fresh recruits and supplies and thus greatly added to the difficulty of removing the English presence.

The castles had to be besieged one at a time. This Bruce proceeded to do, with the notable help of his brother Edward and his staunch friend and ally James Douglas.

Edward II, on the verge of a civil war with his own nobles in England, did little to aid his garrisons in the north. His determination to hold Scotland under his thumb was not so passionate as had been his father's. Though fierce and bitter fighting was required, one by one its fortresses were gradually reclaimed by Bruce as he gradually wrested Scotland out of English hands.

"The King will march south tomorrow," said Aonghuis as he and Donal replaced the feed in the wagon, then walked slowly around the perimeter of the enclosure to inspect the knots and make sure they were secure. "Have ye e'er been to England, lad?"

"No," said Donal.

"Are ye going with us?"

"Why would I not?"

"I thought wi' the army headin' off t' raid south o' the border, maybe ye'd be wantin' t' return t' yer home."

"I'm the King's man now," replied Donal. The look in his eye and the sound of his voice arrested the old groom's attention. They were those of a man, not of a youth. "Wherever King Robert goes," he added, "that is my home now."

As his groom had said, the King and his two generals began raiding southward into England in 1311—ransacking, burning, and exacting ransom from English landowners in exchange for truce. Casualties generally were light for the Scots in these brief campaigns into Northumberland. One of the heaviest proved the loss, not in battle but to the strain of age and lingering illness, of the King's aging groom.

The morning after Aonghuis's death, the King walked to the stables. Bruce had been with the faithful old man the previous night in the sick wagon. Now, ten hours later, he came in search of his mount, expecting to saddle and tend the animal himself until arrangements could be made for a replacement.

He was met instead by a young man, sixteen or seventeen by the looks of it, who handed him the two strips of leather. The horse connected to them was fully saddled and obviously well groomed, appearing fed and watered.

Bruce took the reins slowly, with puzzled expression, glancing up and down at the young fellow, then pausing to peer deeply into his eyes.

"I know you, do I not?" he said at length. "Are you Aonghuis's assistant?"

"Yes, my lord," replied the youth.

"But . . . there is something else—something familiar in your eyes. I noticed it when I took the reins from your hand."

Donal smiled.

"You once handed these very reins," he said, "to a lad who had just lost his father."

The light of recognition and remembrance broke over Bruce's hard-chiseled face.

"I remember the day perfectly!" he exclaimed. "A brave and worthy man, your father."

"Thank you, sir."

"And you? You have been with my army—?"

"Three or four years, my lord," answered Donal.

"I must apologize for not realizing it, nor speaking to you sooner. It would seem you have grown into quite a man since last our paths crossed."

Donal did not reply.

"Well, MacDarroch," said Bruce after a moment, "it seems I shall not have to look far for my new groom—that is, if you want the assignment."

"I would be more honored than I can say."

"Spoken like a brave son of Scotland!"

The King took the reins, mounted, and rode away. From that day forward, Donal MacDarroch took the place of the departed Aonghuis as Bruce's groom.

The struggle against the English continued. One by one, Scotland's castles fell into the hands of the Bruce.

✣ E I G H T E E N ✣

1313–1314

These were days when loyalty was everything, yet loyalty could be fleeting. Allegiances must be chosen with an eye to the future, and great were the risks of miscalculation. While King Robert Bruce gradually reclaimed Scotland, the fortunes of two Scottish families shifted dramatically as each weighed the odds of probable outcome and chose two very different paths to walk.

A certain Adam de Gordon, descended from a Norman family that had been granted lands near the village of Huntly in Berwickshire two or three generations earlier, had all his life been loyal to the English King. In 1313, however, he defected to the Scottish King's cause. Robert Bruce, not one to forget loyalty, would suitably reward Gordon's timely change of heart.

A very different altering of sympathies took place in the region of Strathbogie where Bruce's groom had been born. There, the new earl David turned against the very King who seven years earlier found refuge one Christmas season at the castle which he now called home and which the ancestor of that groom had helped build. It was a foolish decision on the part of the scion of the family who had crowned Bruce King, and one for which young Lord David would pay dearly.

Perth fell to the Scots in January of 1313. Robert Bruce himself, heavily outfitted in armor, led his men into the icy waters of the castle moat, then scaled the wall with the great weight of his armor on his back and himself led the bitter fighting inside.

Dumfries, Lochmaben, Dalswinton, and Loch Doon followed. By mid-year, most of Scotland was back in the hands of her King.

But Stirling Castle, held by English troops, seemed impenetrable. Edward Bruce besieged the high fortress for months. Yet while the rest of the country gradually came into his brother's possession, the younger Bruce could not overcome the mighty rock at the center of the nation.

In the summer of 1313, Stirling's English commander, Sir Philip Mowbray, weary of the siege, offered cunning terms for a temporary peace: He would surrender Stirling to the Bruces *if* he was not relieved by an English army appearing within three miles of the castle by Midsummer's Day the following year. Edward Bruce, unsuccessful with all other attempts, accepted Mowbray's terms and called off the siege.

While the truce halted fighting at Stirling, there was no letup against the few other English-held garrisons. Early in 1314 came the daring capture of the great fortress of Edinburgh. While a handful of attackers led by commander Thomas Randolph diverted attention near the main gate, thirty men crept in the middle of the night along a treacherous path up the northern cliff face of the rock behind, scaled the castle walls, and opened the gates to Randolph's men.

By the summer of 1314, only one castle still remained in the hands of the English—the great fortress of Stirling, where fighting had ceased now for a year. More than a few battles had been fought through the years at this critical juncture where the geography of the land forced a confluence of all things.

Now again did all eyes focus upon Stirling.

Nothing could have suited the English better than Edward Bruce's agreement with Mowbray, which gave the English King an entire year to prepare for a renewed invasion. Edward II had responded to the terms by raising the greatest army ever to march upon England's troublesome northern neighbor. He mustered his forces at Berwick in early June, then set out to relieve Mowbray's command and take Scotland back once and for all.

A climax was inevitable. Two kings and all the forces each could assemble would meet, and the future of two kingdoms would be decided.

NINETEEN

June 1314

The evening was warm.

Midsummer was approaching as inexorably as Edward's army was marching north. Destiny drew nearer as surely as day followed night. Every man in Bruce's army felt it.

Robert Bruce felt it most keenly of all. The King of a nation that was at last united behind him walked out toward the makeshift stables of the encampment in the serene hours of the gloaming.

It was early June. The year was 1314.

The first person Bruce encountered as he approached the enclosure where the horses were kept was his groom. An urge came over him to talk to the youth who had served him so well ever since old Aonghuis's death.

"Well, Donal MacDarroch, son of Fergus the farrier," said the Bruce casually, yet with an edge of seriousness in his tone as well, "I have been listening for weeks to the counsel of my lords and earls. What do *you* think—shall we live to see the end of this summer which is now upon us?"

"Of course we shall, my lord King."

"You sound more confident than most of my generals," smiled Bruce, though the upward turn of his lips could not dispel the wrinkles of doubt which continued to plague his forehead.

Donal said nothing. For a few moments, all that could be heard was the shuffling of horses' hooves behind them, broken by an occasional snort from their large fleshy lips.

"You have surely heard the reports," Bruce went on after the pause. "Edward mustered, some say, twenty thousand men to relieve Stirling Castle. We scarcely have a third that number."

Donal nodded. He also had heard the reports.

"And you remain confident?"

Once more Donal nodded.

"You are a young man of few words," remarked Bruce.

"I would not render an opinion unsought, my lord."

"Wise words for one of tender years. But now I *do* ask—what would *you* do, son of Fergus, if you were my general? If I gave into your hands the disposition of our men against Edward's vast host, how would you respond?"

"I would be loath to presume to advise one whose generalship has already won Scotland," replied Donal.

Bruce broke into a chuckle, which gradually gave way to laughter.

"You are not merely wise—you are also a diplomat, I see!" he said. "But I ask your opinion sincerely. I have consulted my men. I am not without ideas of my own. But I am curious what a groom might say. You have shown yourself a stout and intelligent fellow. No harm will come to you even should you counsel retreat. So again I ask—what would you do?"

A long silence this time intervened. The evening was peaceful. The King had never spoken to his groom in such a manner.

"Are you committed to engage the English King?" asked Donal at length.

"No," replied Bruce thoughtfully. "In the face of such odds, wisdom may in fact dictate retreat rather than engagement. I will not so lightly throw away all we have gained. We would be foolish to fight if the cause were doomed from the start."

"But you are willing to fight?"

"Certainly," answered the King quickly, as if the question was an affront. Donal did not flinch. Bruce's eyes continued to probe the young face.

Another silence ensued. Donal considered his words with care.

"Position and strategy will be everything," he said at length.

Now it was Bruce's turn to nod without comment. He was a master of both, and his groom knew it. By now every lord in Scotland who had attempted to hold out against him knew it.

"The English *cannot* be defeated unless the position of battle greatly favors you," Donal continued.

Again came the thoughtful kingly nod.

"If Edward of England is determined to march upon Stirling," continued Donal, "it would seem that the most likely—the *only*—position from which you could possess such an advantage would be if his army were on the Carse of Stirling."*

"Edward is no fool," rejoined the King. "His scouts know the danger of that marshland as well as we. He would never willingly choose to fight from such unsuitable ground."

"But if he could be enticed upon it . . ." suggested Donal.

"Are you suggesting an attack before he reaches the Bannock?" asked Bruce. "How would we then confine him to the southeast of the carse when he is coming from Falkirk? If we crossed the bridge at Milton, Edward could spread out in a semicircle around us and force *us* back into the carse—or into the waters of the Bannock!"

"But if you could lure *Edward* to cross at Milton?"

"Do you mean bring his army across the bridge onto the carse?"

Donal nodded.

"But how?" said Bruce. "Why would he cross the bridge and put his army with its back to the river? He would never cross."

---

* *Carse*—extensive flat, rutted, wet alluvial land lying along the banks of a river.

"Unless you lured him across under false pretense."

"Again I say, *how*?"

"By massing on the ridge between Tor Wood and St. Ninian's kirk and then feigning retreat. And, perhaps, by then standing out yourself, alone . . . to goad the English after you."

Bruce took in the words calmly but seriously. He had been discussing options along such lines with his brother, but the pretended retreat and the use of himself as bait were new ideas.

Gradually his head began to nod.

"He has scouts, as you said," Donal went on. "They will know that my lord Randolph commands the vanguard and you, my lord, command the rear guard. If you position my lord Randolph's battalion toward the castle—at St. Ninian's, perhaps—and yours, my lord, nearest Milton, the scouts will report to Edward that our direction is likely west, *away* from engagement."

Bruce continued to nod, then smiled.

"Luring him, in effect, to *chase* us across the bridge and onto the carse . . . luring him to chase *me*."

"That is how I see it, my lord."

"It is a bold strategy, young MacDarroch," he said. "So daring it might just work—or else get me killed! I shall have to bring you to my commanders and let them hear it from you."

"Across the Bannock at Milton is the nearest route to the castle. Surely that will be King Edward's objective."

"I am certain you are correct. By then he will be highly confident, which will add to our advantage. He will assume retreat to be my best option."

Donal did not comment further. He had offered his thoughts on the matter. Now it was time to let the King determine how best to meet the approaching enemy.

"Do you recall the day when I first saw you?" asked Bruce after both men's thoughts had strayed in different directions from battle strategy.

"How could I forget, my lord? It was the day my father was killed."

"Which I have always regretted."

"He taught me to honor my King," said Donal. "His death no longer counts a grief in my memory. He served you and died without fear. I hope I am worthy to walk in his footsteps."

"Do you trust me, Donal?" asked the King.

"Of course, my lord."

"You would go wherever I ordered you?"

Donal nodded.

"Are you afraid of what might lie ahead?"

"I do not fear death, my lord," he said. "Though I must confess I fear what it may be like to die. Some deaths are very painful."

"In war, nearly all. Do you count yourself a brave young man, son of Fergus?"

"That would depend on what you consider bravery, my lord."

Bruce thought a moment.

"To meet the foe gamely and not shrink from the battle—even in the face of fear," he replied after a moment.

Donal considered his words.

"I do not know if I can answer you then, my lord," he said finally. "I have not faced battle as your men have. I have only observed it from a distance. Therefore, I cannot count myself courageous, for I have not been tested with the foe—and possibly death—staring me in the eye."

"Wisely spoken. Though I do believe I detect bravery even in such an admission."

"I pray that whenever the test comes, I shall, as you say, not shrink in the face of fear."

"I am sure you shall face it with courage."

Bruce eyed his groom another moment, as if sensing such a moment approached for the young man as surely as his adversary marched to meet them.

He said nothing, however, but turned and made his way back to his own tent.

❈   T W E N T Y   ❈

The night was late. It was Saturday night, the twenty-second of June, shortly before eleven.

The strategy was decided. The ground the Scots would occupy to face the English had been chosen with care and cunning.

After arriving earlier that same day, Bruce's army had been divided into four oval spear-ring schiltrons and placed to insure maximum protection throughout the area called New Park, just above Tor Wood. The left flank was led by Thomas Randolph, that nearest him commanded jointly by the Steward and Douglas, the next by Edward Bruce. The right flank schiltron was commanded by the King himself.

The men of Bruce's own division had dug a series of pits and trenches, each a foot wide and three feet deep, between the trees of Tor Wood and the water of the Bannock, then covered them with brush, to protect the critical right flank of the army against the horses of the English cavalry.

Now, at this late hour, the throng of men under their four commands were either asleep or soon would be. Edward's army would arrive on the morrow, and the future of a nation would be decided. If the English marched straight on and could be lured across the bridge at Milton and onto the carse, the schiltrons and pits of the Scots would be ready for them. If the English waited on the solid ground of the other side of the river, where and how the battle would be fought must remain in doubt for now.

The King had called his most trusted advisors, the commanders of the other three battalions, to his tent for final discourse: his brother Edward, James Douglas, who commanded young Walter the Steward's battalion, and Thomas Randolph. One other also was present.

An unsteady flame flickered low in the late summer's night.

Bruce had just spoken, saying he had decided to ride out upon the plain alone, in plain view of the English vanguard, as soon as it reached the bridge. To do so would set a tone, he said, of bold defiance. He would let them see him, he said, as a single rider, hoping the sight might entice them across the bridge to do battle.

All depended on which side of the river they could engage the English, on whether the larger English force stopped short of the Milton bridge or continued across. Bruce's daring idea of going out alone, he hoped, would tip the balance in their favor.

"I argue against this last, my lord King," said Douglas. "Your marching out to challenge them as you describe is unwise."

"Why do you say so? Give me your reason, Douglas," said the King.

"They may send an entire regiment, or perhaps a troop of longbowmen."

"The first across the bridge will be their heavy cavalry," replied the King. "I am sure of it."

"One man against many will invite their attack."

"They will not attack en masse, for it will take hours to get all their troops across. The bridge is narrow. I would only challenge their van."

"One man against even a small contingent would not be able to stand."

"It will not be a division, I tell you, so let them attack," insisted the King. "I want to anger Edward and thus cloud his judgment. If I can anger him so that he does not stop to consider the danger of crossing, but thinks only of sending his men after me, then I will have been successful—especially if he thinks we are retreating and charges after us. Then, once his cavalry is on the carse, and while his foot soldiers are just getting across and spreading out between their horses and the stream, we will turn back on them. It is our only chance of success."

"What if they make camp on the far side, and do not come across the bridge to take your bait?"

"Then we will have to devise another strategy. That is one of the reasons I must do as I have proposed—so that they do not stop and make camp before crossing."

"I salute your courage, my lord, but the enemy's superior strength demands that such courage be sustained throughout the charge. You must be there to give heart to our men when time for the major battle comes."

It required courage on the part of the lieutenant as well to raise the specter of doubt on the night prior to battle.

"If you die, my lord, Scotland is doomed," Douglas added. "None other can unite the country and lead its clansmen and nobles as you have done."

"What if we could somehow lure them to make camp on the carse itself?" now asked Randolph.

"Impossible," declared Edward Bruce. "Even Edward of England is not that big a fool. No commander would order his men to make camp on such a bog. It would be suicide."

The tent grew silent.

Douglas had voiced the reservation several of the King's high-placed officers held in their hearts concerning Bruce's final suggestion.

Bruce sat motionless, staring into the thin flame of the candle, pondering what lay ahead. Douglas had been prudent in saying he must not act rashly. How many might the English have when they marched out the Roman Road from Tor Wood tomorrow? Reports varied widely. His four schiltrons contained but fifteen hundred men each. They would almost certainly be seriously outnumbered.

In truth, he had not yet decided to engage the English in battle at all. The doubts which had surfaced in his conversation with his groom continued to nag at his brain. He must *not* allow a repeat of Wallace's defeat at Falkirk. If the English proved too many, retreat was the most prudent policy. He had all of Scotland except Stirling. He could not throw everything away in a foolishly fought battle they could not hope to win.

That was one of the reasons he had chosen this high position near St. Ninian's and New Park. He had to keep his troops well away from the swampy carse. The alignment of the battalions was only partially to feign retreat. It was also to make retreat possible should it prove necessary. His army might well have to beat their way back west in the middle of the night.

If independence for this nation required temporary retreat to avoid massacre, Robert the Bruce would not hesitate to order it. He had no desire to martyr either himself or his men so that he might become a hero like Wallace. For though Wallace was a hero, Wallace was also dead. Scotland needed her King alive, or there would be no freedom . . . nor any kingdom at all.

Bruce, however, did not openly state his own doubts just now. The silence continued several minutes.

At length the King turned his head unexpectedly toward his groom, a youth who looked no more than twenty standing behind the others.

"And you, young MacDarroch," he said, "what advice would *you* give your King on the eve of battle? You have heard the objection. What does your stout heart tell you in the matter?"

Whatever the reaction of the nobles around the tent to the King's asking such a one to render opinion on the momentous proceeding, their faces displayed nothing. They had already grown accustomed to the King's fondness for the groom and had hidden their astonishment at Bruce's asking him to join this conclave.

"My lord Douglas speaks wisely, my lord King," replied Donal after a momentary wait, and with a confidence in excess of his years, "when he warns care on your part. He speaks truth when he says your courage will be required as long as the battle wages."

A brief pause followed.

"And it *shall* be so given, I am confident," Donal went on, if possible even more boldly. "Of one thing I am certain: the English King under-estimates his opponent. So I say, my lord King Robert, go out to meet the battle as you suggest—perhaps mounted on one of our small horses. Let them ride against you on their huge destriers in their hauberks of mail. They will grow stupidly confident in their own might. Let them think you are in retreat. Then let them discover whom they have chosen for an ad-versary . . . and what manner of man rules over Caledonia."

"Bravely spoken," commented Bruce.

Donal stood motionless.

"Would you ride beside me to await them, MacDarroch?" asked the King, thinking back to the words they had exchanged earlier.

"With honor, my lord King."

The Bruce waited but a moment more, then turned his piercing gaze back to the nobles gathered with him.

"It is decided, then," he said decisively. "If this stalwart youth places such confidence in me as to answer thus without a tremble of fear in his voice, shall I begin to doubt myself? No, I will meet them as proposed, whomever they send to dispatch me—and on a palfrey, as MacDarroch suggests."

"And then?" asked the King's brother. "If they cross the bridge, will we engage them immediately?"

"No, Edward, that is the one thing we must *not* do," replied Bruce. "If we succeed in luring them across, we must allow most of their force to get over the bridge before engagement. Otherwise we will spend our-selves, possibly with great loss, and the remainder of Edward's force can then march over and easily rout us. No, we must defeat their whole army . . . or decline the engagement altogether."

The words revealed his continued wavering on the question of whether there would be a battle fought at all.

He glanced around at his commanders. Each in his turn nodded sol-emn consent. No one questioned whether the King's final words meant he was considering a midnight withdrawal.

Again there was silence. The candle burned low.

Robert Bruce spoke once more. "The time has at last arrived," he said softly, but with the fervor of the great warrior-heart rising to fullness in his breast, "when the interloping Sassenach must be sent back across the border not for a mere day, or year, or season . . . but forever. What we could not achieve with Edward's father now rests with us to do on this occasion.

It is for this season that we have fought for twenty years. The moment has come for us to lay claim once more to the land of our fathers, the land of our Kings, the land of our heritage, the land of our birthright."

There was another pause, this time brief. Then Bruce added:

"Hail, Caledonia! We pledge here and now, that you shall not be taken from your own people again!"

⌗   T W E N T Y · O N E   ⌗

Bruce's army slept but little after the fateful conclave of its leadership in the King's tent.

At four o'clock on the morning following, an ethereal mist hovered over the lowlands surrounding Stirling. Trumpets sounded among the host, summoning the Scots to Mass.

By the time the many clergy had completed administering Communion to the soldiers, the morning had dawned bright and warm. It would be a hot Sunday. Breakfast for the troops was ordered: bread and water. They were a Spartan race and would dine according to the severity of their present calling.

Donal MacDarroch had been lying awake, it seemed, for most of the hours between leaving the King's tent and the sound of the trumpets. It was a relief to rise at last. Mass completed, he ate his bread in haste. He must be ready when the King required him. He set about immediately saddling the small gray horse that would lead the battle.

Bruce met first with Douglas and his marischal Robert Keith, ordering them to ride swiftly toward Falkirk that he might have a reliable firsthand report on the enemy's position and strength. He then went in search of his groom.

"My mount is ready, I see, MacDarroch," said the King. "Well done. Now that the day has arrived, are you afraid?"

"No, my lord," answered Donal.

"If you were, would you say?"

"No, my lord."

"You remember your father?"

"I remember."

"He lost his life in my cause."

"A worthier one he could not have given his life for, my lord."

"And if such should be your fate?"

"I will try to meet it with courage and say the same."

Bruce eyed the young man with steadily mounting approval.

"Last night you said you would go out with me to meet the enemy—even if I went alone."

"Yes, my lord."

"Now that the day of battle has dawned, will you make the same answer? You do not now want to stand behind the army with the supply wagons and other grooms?"

"No, my lord. As I said, I would go at your side with honor."

"So you shall, then," declared the King. "I shall *give* you that honor. Besides," he added, "*should* I fall—if Douglas is right and it proves a fool's gambit—you are perhaps the only one I could trust to drag me back to safety! What say you to that, young MacDarroch?"

"You will not fall, my lord," answered Donal. "But I shall count it a privilege to ride out with you."

"Good, then prepare a mount for yourself as well—though you shall stay well behind me and remain out of danger unless, as I say, I am un-seated."

He took the reins Donal had been holding, mounted, and rode off to inspect the honeycomb screen of holes his troops had dug that would pro-tect his men if the English did attack today. In the front of them, along the road from Milton, had also been scattered spiked iron calthrops. If King Edward attacked, his horses would pay a heavy price. Pleased with what he saw, Bruce rode to each of the four battalions to give final en-couragement to his men.

Douglas and Keith returned from their reconnaissance mission several hours later. They appeared haggard and worn.

"Their force is as an unending sea," said Douglas. His voice contained obvious dismay. "—Countless riders . . . infantry stretching all the way to Edinburgh, say some of the scouts."

He paused to take a swallow of water from the tin handed him by Keith. Bruce gravely contemplated his words.

"How many has King Edward in all?" asked Bruce.

"Twenty thousand . . . fifty thousand—who can tell?" said Keith.

"How far off?"

"Close—the leading van approaches within two or three miles."

"How aligned?"

"Medium cavalry, probably six thousand, several hundred mounted Welsh archers, three or four thousand armored knights on destriers."

"The cavalry leads?"

Keith nodded.

"And the infantry?"

"Well back, several miles—behind the horsemen," replied Douglas, "spreading behind farther than any of our scouts could see—a numberless horde, to Falkirk and beyond."

Bruce again took in the words. If they caused fear, his facial expression did not show it. In his own mind he could not help wondering if retreat now indeed loomed as his best option. It seemed impossible that young MacDarroch's plan could succeed.

After a moment he spoke.

"Good . . . what you say is good news. The battle will be one of infantry."

"But King Edward brings his cavalry first to meet us."

"Yes, exactly as we wish! Were he to attack with his infantry, their superior numbers would doom us from the outset. But with *our* infantry against *his* cavalry, we will carry the day. We will choose the high ground and fight where *we* decide to fight. Then we must make certain their footmen remain penned up *behind* their horsemen. Their cavalry will be useless on the carse, and their infantry will not be able to get at us. What is the condition of their horses and men?"

"Weary, very weary—that much is clear. They have marched hard from Tweeddale and Lauderdale. They are hot and exhausted, and slept little last night."

"More good news! I am more confident than ever, despite their numbers."

The King paused, then added in a subdued tone, "Keep what you have seen to yourselves. Spread the word that the English are in disorder."

Bruce turned, mounted, and rode off to address the battalions that had been ordered to assemble so that the King could be heard by as many as possible.

To himself, Bruce wished he were truly as confident as he had displayed to his commanders—and as he was about to sound to his men.

※ T W E N T Y · T W O ※

The Scottish force stood to arms while their King, Robert the Bruce, rode up and down before them. For seventeen years, some of these men had fought behind him. This day represented the culmination of all they had struggled for. Robert Bruce had almost entirely ousted the English presence from Scotland, but all would be for naught if he could not gain control of Stirling.

As he went, Bruce spoke with many of the men individually, encouraging and exhorting. A commanding figure of a man, the King sat astride a small gray horse. He was fully clad in light chain mail from neck and head to legs and arms. A great outer surcoat of bright yellow and red flowed down from his shoulders, upon the chest of which was emblazoned the red lion rampant, the emblem of the Scottish crown. A sword of great weight hung at his side. He also wore his crown. He would discard it prior to heavy fighting. But for now it was a needful symbol of what they were attempting to do—secure a kingdom from foreign occupation.

At last he began to address his men.

"You faithful soldiers," he said in loud voice, "have been with me, some of you, for years, through victories and retreats. We have scaled the walls of Perth and Edinburgh. We have steadily rid our land of the English intruder. But all has been preliminary to this day. The greatest army ever assembled on this soil has invaded and now marches toward us. On this day will Scotland stand or fall."

He paused to allow the weight of his words to sink in.

"With the help and by the grace of God," he continued, "we shall prevail. The *Brecbennoch* accompanies us, with the bones of our dear St. Columba. We shall, therefore, send this mighty host back across the border whence it came. It is an exhausted and hungry army, for its supply train lags far behind. The leading van is led by Gloucester, the King's own nephew, a child of little more than twenty who has never fought a battle in his life. I tell you, it is an army unprepared to give its all, and thus, whatever its numbers, we shall defeat them. This is our land. We know the ground. We are rested and ready. Therefore, we win . . . or—"

Already a cheer had gone up in response, drowning out his words. He waited until it had subsided.

"But I would not deceive you," Bruce went on. "United though we may be, we are few in number beside the English host. There will be loss of life. Such cannot be avoided. Some of you now hearing my words may be dead before the setting of today's sun. Certainly Scots blood will be shed along with English. As I said, either we win, or we die."

A solemn silence now replaced the revelry.

"So I speak now to each individual man among you. Remain with me not a moment longer unless you are prepared to die for Scotland's freedom. I now give you the choice, without fear of reprisal, to leave the field of battle and return to home and family. In good faith, I will thank you for standing by me until this day and will wish you godspeed. Nor will your fellows mock or jeer you. If you have not the heart to face the battle knowing your own blood may be required to make Scotland free, you must act now, for united against the enemy we must remain."

He paused.

Not a muscle moved to disturb the deathly silence between Milton and the New Park. No horse stirred.

It became clear not a single man of them intended to avail himself of the King's offer. Gradually the rumble of a renewed cheer began to rise over the throng. It grew into great shouts of readiness and eager support.

Bruce smiled, allowed the celebration to continue a moment, then raised his hand high. "Thank you, my faithful!" he cried. "Now, for God and St. Andrew—and for Scotland!"

Again a cheer rose as Bruce sent his men back to take up their positions in their battalions.

The wait did not last much longer. The first of the English troops had already been seen on the south side of the burn.

TWENTY-THREE

Sir Humphrey de Bohun, the English earl of Hereford, rode silently along at the head of an unending column of horsemen. Beside him, his nephew Henry—in full battle armor and holding a long and heavy lance—appeared more prepared for a jousting tournament than combat. He was young and eager, thought Hereford, but such preparations would do him little good in battle.

Hereford had told him so this morning, but Henry hadn't listened. Youth was not inclined to heed the counsel of its elders, preferring instead its own reckless schemes and ideas.

The very thought of someone half his age giving *him* orders still kept the earl's blood at a simmering boil.

It had been with more disbelief than anger that Hereford had first heard the King's words at Berwick: "I am appointing the earl of Gloucester high commander for the invasion of Scotland and the relief of Stirling Castle."

Pembroke, Clifford, Beaumont, and the other commanders were as stunned as he by Edward II's decision, but no word of objection broke the silence. Gloucester, the King's nephew, was obviously a royal favorite, and, Hereford had to admit, not without some skill and courage. But he was barely old enough to grow a beard, much less head an invasion of such proportion. Worse—he had never so much as commanded a single battle! He would as soon put his *own* nephew Henry de Bohun in command—though that would be equally disastrous.

It wouldn't surprise him, Hereford thought to himself, if neither of the two young men—his nephew Henry and the King's nephew Gloucester—lived through this day. Both were idiots and mere boys.

Ever since his appointment, Gloucester had been lording it over the others, taking special delight as they marched north in exercising his heavy-handed command over the man who should rightfully have been in charge—he himself, the earl of Hereford and high constable of England. Hereford felt as if he had been demoted to the status of foot soldier from the way the young Gloucester spoke to him, never heeding his counsel, never even asking for his recommendations.

Hereford glanced ahead to where his young rival led the front column, or van, at the head of the army.

The young fool, he thought, *thinking he will defeat Robert Bruce with sheer force of numbers.*

Hereford knew better. Anyone with an ounce of sense would know better! But the King wasn't listening to him these days, and he had learned the impossibility of trying to talk sense into Gloucester's brain. The boy had grown so puffed up by his own importance that he thought he was invincible.

Hereford sighed.

Maybe Bruce would be discouraged by their numbers and retreat.

It was a good sign that the Scots had let Mowbray through this morning from Stirling. The governor of Stirling had given his English allies a reasonably reliable report of Bruce's position. Edward's army of reinforcements had arrived within the appointed time, with one day to spare. Technically, Hereford supposed, the moment Edward II and Mowbray had shaken hands, the transfer was made. The terms of the bargain from the previous year had been met, and Edward of England had gotten the best of Edward Bruce's deal. What was the point of an engagement now?

Only pride.

King Edward was not about to march so far with such a gigantic force just to turn around and return to England. No, he would take Stirling and hold it—both castle and town—and thus maintain his grip upon Scotland. If Bruce and his small army got in the way, they would be destroyed.

Thus, Gloucester's order this morning had been that they would march across the bridge at Milton and continue straight on. The river was only two or three miles from the castle. Tonight they would sleep in beds in Stirling Castle!

An hour ago they had stopped for a final rest before reaching Milton. Hereford had ridden back, surveying and speaking with the men in both columns. Distressed by what he saw, he had returned to the front to attempt one final time to reason with the young earl.

"I believe the men and horses are so parched and weary that we should encamp for the night south of the burn," he urged.

"What, so close to our objective? We are almost in sight of the castle. Why should we stop when we are so close?"

"Bruce and the Scots stand between Milton and Stirling. That will not be so easy a two miles as these last."

"Nonsense," said Gloucester. "When we arrive and begin crossing the bridge, they will disburse."

"I doubt that Robert Bruce will retreat. He has not shown himself to be easily cowed by the sight of Englishmen."

"Fortunately," rejoined Gloucester with bite in his tone, "*you* are not in command—"

Hereford knew the bitter fact all too well, and hardly needed to be reminded.

"—and I say we have suffered too much in this heat to stop now. We shall continue straight into Stirling!" he added with emphasis.

"You will not wait for the King?"

Hereford's question brought Gloucester up short. He thought for a moment.

"You and I will lead an advance party across in two columns of five hundred men each. Once we have secured the north bridgehead, we will give orders for the rest of the main van to follow. No, I think we will not wait for the King. We will have Stirling secure by the time he reaches Milton."

"If the Scots attack?"

"They will not."

"If they do?" asked Hereford again.

"Then you wait until Pembroke reaches the burn before engagement."

"Is that an order, sir?" The tone was unmistakable in its intended implication.

"That *is* an order, my lord Hereford!" replied Gloucester angrily.

It was an absurd strategy, now thought Hereford, recalling the conversation as he rode along. But he had done his best, and now they were nearly to Milton . . . with a mere boy in command of the entire English army!

▪   T W E N T Y - F O U R   ▪

The columns led by jealous and competitive rivals, the earls of Gloucester and Hereford, reached the narrow bridge of Milton.

Without even a pause, the iron hooves of Gloucester's heavy destrier started across and soon echoed on the wooden planks, followed within minutes by hundreds more, clomp-clomping across in their relentless advance upon Stirling.

From where he watched under cover of trees, Robert Bruce's pulse began to quicken.

They were crossing the bridge!

He could hardly believe his good fortune. He had hoped and planned for this moment but hardly dared imagine that the English would fall right into his trap.

He turned and ran for his horse. It was time to prepare for the next phase of his daring plan.

———

Thirty minutes later, Hereford, with his nephew at his side, led his advance column across the Milton bridge. Sir Robert Clifford had already brought three hundred men across and was now making along the flat meadowland of the carse, escorting Sir Philip Mowbray back to Stirling. The main van was starting to cross behind them.

"You see, my lord," said a gloating Gloucester, riding up to the earl of Hereford as they clomped over the wooden planks, flushed in the apparent success of his command, "there is nothing to worry about! We shall be inside the castle within the hour."

Hereford hated to admit it, but maybe the young blackguard was right.

But wait—up the hill toward the New Park was a small regiment of Scots moving toward the wood. Why hadn't he seen them before?

"My lord!" Hereford called after Gloucester.

But Gloucester had seen them now too.

"After them!" he cried, kicking his heels into the flanks of his horse and galloping forward. "They retreat!"

Suddenly the Scots regiment disappeared. There emerged from the wood a single Scots horseman.

Gloucester reined in, momentarily confused about what to do. Hereford likewise brought his column to a halt. They were across the bridge now and on the edge of the carse. They continued to look up at the solitary figure on the hill—out in the open in front of them. What could he be doing?

The Scotsman stood his ground, unmoving on a small gray Highland pony, facing the charge. A silence of uncertainty followed.

Beside Hereford, suddenly his nephew recognized the lone Scotsman who had come out to meet them.

"It's the Bruce!" he cried. "It's Bruce himself . . . and alone!"

Just as suddenly, he dug his spurs into the sides of his mount and bolted forward at full gallop.

"Stop—stop, Henry!" cried Hereford. "Don't be a fool!"

But his nephew was as unheeding of his cautions as the earl of Gloucester. Here was a moment for heroism. Young de Bohun would seize it for himself.

———

Up the hill, Bruce saw the charge . . . and waited.

He had no lance, and his sword remained sheathed. His only weapon was the light battle-axe in his hand. Hardly a match for the charging rider's lance point if it struck its mark.

On de Bohun came, in full armor, his lance taking deadly aim at Bruce's chest. The English troops paused in their march to watch the drama unfold. Still Bruce sat without moving. The lanceman charged close and closer...

At the last possible instant, suddenly Bruce kicked and wheeled his small mount aside. Barely avoiding the spear tip with which the young Englishman would have ended his life, he deftly maneuvered with yank of reins and kick of boots, clutching tight the handle of his weapon.

No heroism would come to Hereford's nephew that day, only a defeat to fuel the morale of the Scots to new heights. For as he jerked himself to the side, Bruce rose up in his stirrups, lifting his arm high in the air. Bringing the tip of his axe down with great force as de Bohun missed his mark and thundered past, Bruce drove the steel blade through the young man's helmet and bone in a single blow.

The skull was split from crown to chin. Blood spurted out. What was left of the mangled body slumped to the ground in a pool of red.

Bruce spun his light horse around. Even as he did, a battalion of screaming Scots charged forward down the hill.

Stunned by what they had witnessed, Gloucester immediately ordered retreat. Hereford, face ashen and with stomach lurching, did his best to recover himself and get his men back over the bridge they had just crossed. Meanwhile, down the hill into the carse, Thomas Randolph's division of Scots was attacking Clifford's party, which found itself trapped in bog as it likewise attempted to get back to the bridge.

Leaving the ensuing attack to his men, Bruce rode back toward his groom, patiently awaiting what might be required of him.

"It seems I shall not need you to drag me away after all, Mac-Darroch," he said as he rode up to Donal, positioned some forty feet behind. "Your recommended strategy has dispatched one Englishman, at least, which I hope bodes well for what follows. But I have broken a good battle-axe—and they are retreating back across the bridge. I fear we have sprung our trap too soon. We may not get another chance."

The retreat was indeed well under way. The onrushing Scots suddenly seemed to the English a huge host. Within minutes the startled and dismayed English horsemen were so disbursed that they were spread out in confusion among the holes and spiked balls of iron. Horses reared and screamed. Spears seemed to be coming at them from all sides. It was a far messier retreat than had been the approach.

Knocked from his horse, the young earl of Gloucester picked himself up, mortified but happy to find himself unwounded, ran after his mount, managed to reseat himself in the saddle, and now made for the bridge in full and inglorious retreat.

Within two hours, the entire advance party of King Edward's army was safely back on the south side of the burn, licking its wounds.

The earl of Hereford, however, took no pleasure in the failure of his rival's strategy. What mattered his pride when such a hideous death had come to his nephew and the house of Bohun?

T W E N T Y - F I V E

Bruce's men withdrew up the slope to their previous positions.

They knew they had attacked too soon. The unexpected charge of Hereford's idiotic nephew had thrown their whole plan into disarray. Now there seemed no hope of luring the English back across and onto the carse as previously planned. Perhaps, thought Bruce as he watched the vast English army continue to arrive and pause on the far side of the river with the retreating vanguard, retreat would now indeed be the most prudent course for him as well.

The sultry day wore on. Steadily the English army continued to arrive, spreading out and halting short of the bridge, gradually choking and congesting the entire south bank of the burn. They would not make Stirling today, as predicted by the earl of Gloucester. More importantly, they had little opportunity to water their parched horses, for the south bank of the Bannock was steep and in many places inaccessible.

For hours there was no change. The English horses grew thirstier and thirstier but were unable to reach the river's edge from the steep south bank.

As the afternoon gave way to evening, the van of the English army, which had remained stationary for hours, gradually began again to move forward. Rather than making camp where they were, it appeared they would attempt to get at least a portion of their huge army across the burn before nightfall.

Still Bruce was watching every move of his enemy. This movement now, so late in the day, puzzled him. They were not actually going to start across the bridge again . . . not so late in the afternoon.

But as he gazed, a mass of men and horses and wagons began gradually to crowd across the Bannock Burn. Bruce and his commanders watched from their overlook, their perplexity mounting. What could possibly be Edward's design? Where was he planning to *put* these men for the night?

Surely the English King was not thinking of a dusk battle? If he still had hopes of making Stirling, he could not do so without encountering the Scots again. There was scarcely dry land enough on this side of the Bannock to hold such a colossal force. Edward's vast supply of horses, as well as fifteen or more thousand men, were parched and dry, it was true, and on this side there was certainly water to be had in plenty. But it still seemed a monstrously foolish move to cross the Bannock now.

The low meadowland between the Bannock Burn and the River Forth amounted to little more than a waterlogged plain, crossed by a thousand runnels and veins, creating a boggy carse of water and marshland. Had Edward's scouts given him wrong information about this land? Surely this was a gigantic blunder! There could be no more treacherous place for them to put up, hemmed in on three sides by water, mud, and mire.

The astonishment of the Scots observers mounted. After leaving the bridge, the English columns bent to the north and moved down into the marshy carse, slowly picking their way through pools and ponds and ditches and streamlets and bogs, while behind them the rest of the English host followed. Were they trying to effect a large circular approach to the town?

But no! The front troops were now stopping. The soldiers were unsaddling their mounts, pitching tents, and gathering materials for fires. The English army was making camp for the night in the middle of the Carse of Stirling!

Robert Bruce wouldn't have believed it if he wasn't witnessing it with his own eyes!

As night began to fall and campfires sprang up, there could be no doubt that the English army was in the middle of the carse to stay.

But for how long? And what should the Scots do now? Everything about their planned strategy had now changed. Now there was no need to feign retreat. The English were already across the river. Now it was just a matter of where to attack . . . and when. And the most nagging quandary of all was whether the crossing had been effected in order that the English could attack the *Scots* in the middle of the night.

The question plagued Robert Bruce long into the darkness as he paced back and forth, eyeing the fires in the distance, afraid that any moment one of the English commanders would suddenly awaken to the peril of their position and order a relocation.

Bruce's gravest fear continued to be that the English had perhaps chosen their ground in readiness for a dawn attack.

Leading with their cavalry and now well away from the pits and calthrops, they might possibly move out of the carse and onto the incline. Then *they* would have the advantage, and he would have no choice but to consider retreat.

If only . . . if only they remained where they were throughout the night!

Bruce and his groom had agreed that the carse was the only place where an engagement could successfully be waged. If he could just spring a trap and attack the English while they were yet in the midst of the carse and mostly surrounded by water, his inferior numbers could exploit the terrain to their maximum advantage.

All he could do was wait for dawn . . . and hope.

Thus it was that the Scottish King passed the night, vacillating between fear of being attacked and trembling with anticipation at the incredible trap the English had laid for themselves.

If only he had time to spring it!

🢒   T W E N T Y - S I X   🢒

A mile away, on the Carse of Stirling, within the silk enclosures of the tent of King Edward II, the atmosphere was less anxious.

"When would you have the bugles sound, my lord King?" asked the recently appointed commander over the forces, Edward's own nephew of but twenty-four years.

"The men are exhausted, are they not?" said Edward.

The earl of Gloucester nodded. "But both men and beasts are recovering by quenching their thirst."

"There is a great deal of water here, to be sure. The encampment was well chosen. And you—have you recovered from today's blow?"

"Yes, sir," replied Gloucester with imperceptible wince, not wanting to be reminded that he had been unseated. The thought of it, however, also reminded him that he had not had it so bad as Bohun.

"And Hereford?" said the King. "Tell me, Gilbert, are you and he . . ." Edward let the tone of his voice complete the sentence for him.

"The earl is a soldier," replied Gloucester. "He will obey orders even when they come from one so many years his junior as myself."

The King nodded. A moment later, the object of their discussion, along with the earl of Pembroke and Sir Robert Clifford, entered the King's tent. The English high command was now assembled.

"I am grieved to hear of your nephew's death, Humphrey," said the King.

"Thank you, my lord," replied Hereford with a grave nod. "It was a foolhardy move, even though Bruce was alone. My nephew underestimated the man the Scots call King . . . which mistake I hope *you* will not make, my lord King," he added with obvious significance.

"I do not think any of us in this tent underestimate Bruce, my lord Hereford," rejoined the son of the Hammer testily. He knew well enough that the veteran high constable was annoyed at his appointing Gloucester over him as commander for this campaign. Everyone knew it.

"Perhaps," said Hereford. "I pray it is so. But I must again lodge the most urgent protest against our position. We are enmeshed in a bog, my lord. We must get out of it before engagement."

"The site has been chosen, the men are already resting comfortably, horses have had their fill to drink for the first time in days, and here we shall remain," replied Edward firmly.

Hereford sighed. "At least, then," he added resignedly, "swing the infantry troops around to the west so they might encamp between the horsemen and the Scots. As it is, our infantry is hemmed in between our cavalry and the river. They are trapped."

An outburst, half of astonishment, half of derision, burst from the mouth of young Gilbert de Clare of Gloucester.

"What?" he laughed. "Would you pen in the horsemen behind fifteen thousand foot soldiers! The way up the hill to the west must be kept clear so that I may make an attack with my cavalry. You have your logistics exactly backward. Our horsemen will attack up the hill, and the foot soldiers will follow. They are not trapped as you say. All is exactly as it should be."

Hereford sighed in frustration. The earl was too inexperienced to understand the danger. Today's debacle had proved that well enough. Unfortunately, the young fool had the King's ear.

"So then," Hereford said to the King, vouchsafing no answering comment to his youthful commander's ridicule, "it has been decided to attack?"

"Nothing has been decided," replied Edward. "We shall see how the Highlanders dispose themselves in the morning. Perhaps we shall awaken and find they have disappeared. Then the way will be clear for us to march straight into Stirling and take control of the castle, the town—and all of Scotland."

"Impossible," said Hereford. "I know Robert the Bruce better than that. We will awake to find him no farther away than he is at this moment. Perhaps even closer."

"Reports today indicate that Bruce's forces appear to be withdrawing. Their van is on the far side from us."

"They hardly withdrew today. Have you considered that their position might be intentional, to trick us?"

"I do not believe it for a moment. Today it was *you* who appeared reluctant to engage, not Bruce," said Clifford to the earl of Hereford. "I needed more support."

"I was under orders," shot back Hereford, "*not* to attack until the earl of Pembroke should reach the burn."

Hereford's irritation had by now turned to seething anger. He had been furious all afternoon over Gloucester's bungling of the initial encounter and silently blamed the King's nephew for the death of his own.

A heavy silence descended over the gathering.

"In any event," Hereford resumed, calming himself, "I must emphasize my strong conviction that Bruce will *not* withdraw and that we *must*, therefore, protect our western flank with infantrymen."

"And I state again that I must have the west open, therewith to attack the Scots with my cavalry," repeated Gloucester.

"And if the Scots should attack us first?" queried Hereford.

"Impossible!" insisted Gloucester, again with a laugh. "We outnumber them four to one. They will not attack."

"Three to one at the most," interposed the former high constable.

"Three, four—what difference?" said the King, tiring of the dispute between the two. "Bruce will never attack—of that I am convinced. He is a coward, and he knows this battle for control of Stirling is already ours. My father knew him a coward, and I know him a coward. Whenever there is a threat, he retreats to the safety of his idiotic Highlands. We have seen it time and again. His deployment before Stirling is a gigantic ruse."

"And today?" queried Hereford.

"He merely hopes to scare us off. But I shall not be intimidated by the brute. The initiative lies entirely with us, I tell you. The only thing remaining to be known is how many of his own the Bruce is prepared to sacrifice before he flees back into the hills. I say we sleep well tonight, and tomorrow, when our men and horses are refreshed, we move on to Stirling and wrest control of this land once and for all from Robert Bruce. We have finally arrived at the very heart of Scotland. He who controls Stirling controls the north. We are safely across the burn and need but march the remaining two miles to the castle. If Bruce proves stubborn, then we shall attack and rout him. His paltry force of foot soldiers will be no match for our cavalry. I tell you, the battle of Stirling is already won!"

None responded further. The King had made his will explicit.

The order was given not to rouse the men by trumpet until half past six. They needed a good night's sleep.

T W E N T Y · S E V E N

Humphrey de Bohun of Hereford left Edward's tent some minutes later and walked slowly back to his own. It was late and as dark as it would get. His men were exhausted, and he heard snoring all around him.

He stopped and looked out westward, up the hill away from their camp. There the distant fires of the Scots camp twinkled like a hundred earth-stars.

What will the morrow bring? Hereford thought.

Bruce was a shrewder man than either Edward or Gloucester gave him credit for. Against Hereford's own foolhardy nephew he had today shown clearly enough what he thought of retreat. Young Henry had possessed the same advantage over Bruce's small light battle-axe as Edward's army possessed in numbers over the Scots. Bruce had not retreated a step, and now Henry was dead.

Hereford sat down to remove his soggy boots. He had stepped in four or five bogs and small streams, one to his knees, before arriving back at his tent. This marshland was an evil place, he thought to himself. A gloomy sense of foreboding passed over him.

But there was nothing he could do. He had voiced his cautions. Neither the King nor his would-be commander had heeded them.

He lay down with a sigh. It was time to see what sleep he could manage. Tomorrow's fate would have to decide itself.

TWENTY-EIGHT

A mile and a half from where the earl of Hereford slept uneasily, Robert Bruce paced anxiously about, squinting down across the incline at the English in the same way that Edward's displaced high constable had earlier eyed him.

What were the English planning?

Bruce knew but one thing—that he could not wait for Monday morning to dawn. His most important ally was surprise. The strategic position of the two armies offered him an unthinkable advantage, more than he had dared dream of. If he would seize it to full measure, he must move before the sun.

This time it would not be trumpets that would awaken his men, but whispers.

Sometime between three and four in the morning, Bruce personally shook his commanders awake.

"Up . . . rouse the host—prepare your men as quietly as possible."

It was a simple order, and soon whispering circulated quietly through the camp, effecting a stirring that took considerably longer than one done with the assistance of bugles.

It was the day of the Feast of St. John the Baptist, and again the morning began with Mass. Once more the night's fast was broken with bread and water.

The King sought his mount—this time a sturdy war horse—which was saddled and ready, held by his groom.

"The morning of battle has come, MacDarroch," he said, taking the reins from his groom. "It seems your suggested ploy has worked. Edward has been lured across the Bannock. Now we must see what we can do with him."

He paused, took the reins, then added, "The clergy, packhorses, porters, and other grooms are already making their way to the high ground on the ridge north of St. Ninian's. The attack will be visible from there. Will you join them?"

"As I said before, I will march at your side if you will have me."

"I believe you," said Bruce. "But a good groom is difficult to find. I would be loath to lose you."

"The decision is yours," replied Donal. "I will do as you command. But if you will have me among your men, my lord, I will take my place with those who fight for Scotland's freedom."

"You are the bravest groom I have ever met," remarked the Bruce.

"You spoke the words two nights ago in your tent, my lord."

"What words?"

"You said it was time to lay claim to the birthright of the land of our fathers. Though royal blood does not flow in my veins as yours, no less is Scotland the land of *my* fathers and *my* heritage. No less, therefore, am I prepared to die for the freedom of my land and defend the honor of its name."

The Bruce stood as one transfixed by the words, listening as to a Celtic prophet rather than to the nineteen-year-old who had charge of his horse. The words penetrated the King's heart, as if giving voice to the courage he prayed the rest of his force likewise felt. He found himself momentarily speechless.

At last the King spoke. "Hail Caledonia!" he said. No other words seemed appropriate.

"*Hail Caledonia!*" repeated Donal.

The two men clasped hands, the King of the land and the young groom who was descended from another who might have ruled Caledonia, but chose instead to roam its Highlands. The eyes of the two met, as if in that moment a silent bond had made of them equals.

Robert Bruce now mounted, swung his horse around, and rode to the head of the army.

He had already made the situation plain to his commanders, and they now began to marshal their men according to the plan.

The schiltrons of the four divisions would leave their high defensive positions to form a tightly compacted arc stretching from the ridge at St.

Ninian's around to the bridge across the Bannock at Milton. If they could move this arc forward while the English were yet spread out on the south of the carse, and if Edward Bruce could bring his division far enough along the road to his right, preventing retreat across the bridge over which they had come the evening previous, the vastly superior English army would find themselves hemmed in on three sides by water.

As silently as possible, the Scots commanders moved their divisions into position—Edward Bruce on the far right closest to Milton, Randolph next to him, Douglas and the Steward next, with King Robert following slightly back and far to the left near St. Ninian's.

The misty gray light of dawn had still not given way to sunrise when the silent advance began on foot down the mile-long gradual incline toward where the English camp still slept. No sounds disturbed the morning air. Hushed footsteps crept across the soft terrain, betraying nothing of their approach toward the Bannock Burn.

⌗   T W E N T Y - N I N E   ⌗

The earl of Hereford had been awake since shortly after four.

He was exhausted, but could not sleep. Never had he felt so trapped.

Dawn was coming at the edge of the eastern sky. He could lie still no longer. Even though he had been stripped of command, his senses still reacted as a leader. He must be up to assess the situation.

He rose, pulled on his wet boots, and strode out into the misty pale light.

All was silent. Most of the army still slept. It was an eerie quiet, he thought, that spread out over the flatland. The sensation did nothing to dispel the anxiety that had plagued him all night. Picking his way through the bog, finding patches of dry earth as best he could, he walked to the western limit of the camp near the edge of the meadow where the ground began to rise.

It was from this side that he intuitively sensed danger. To the west lay the high ground, the hard dry earth . . . and to the west was encamped the Scots army.

He reached the sentry outposts.

"My lord," one of the guards greeted him.

Hereford nodded.

"Any sign of activity?" he asked, tilting his head westward.

"All is quiet, sir," answered the man.

The earl glanced about, then continued along the sentry line, greeting the guard units somberly as he went, straining his eyes and ears for any hint of danger.

The sense of eeriness deepened. A presence was about . . . an invisible presence. He did not like the feel of this morning air. Light from the coming sun was just beginning to send a thin orange line up the horizon behind him. Hereford, however, was preoccupied with thoughts of what might be approaching from the opposite direction.

He glanced again westward, for the dozenth time.

He could make out no fires from the Scots camp. He had not realized it before, but all was deathly quiet up the hill where the night before had been scattered *hundreds* of campfires.

Unconsciously Hereford's step turned onto the carse west of the sentry outposts. Slowly he began to walk toward the plain.

Something *was* wrong! He could feel it, but he could not identify—

Suddenly he arrested his steps and froze. A chill swept down his spine.

Had he detected movement out against the gray horizon, mingled with the dark shapes of trees in New Park?

He squinted.

Panic surged through his frame as he unconsciously sucked in a sharp breath of shock.

The entire host of Scots was moving against them!

Hereford turned and sprinted back for the closest sentry unit.

"Sound the alarm!" he cried.

The guard hesitated.

"Blow your trumpet, man—Bruce is upon us!"

Within seconds, as Hereford made for the main camp, the sound of bugles broke the stillness—first one, then two, then everywhere trumpets sounded shrilly through the thin fog.

Already King Edward and the earl of Gloucester had leapt to their feet to see what was the commotion.

※ T H I R T Y ※

The moment Bruce heard the English bugles, he knew the element of surprise must be grabbed quickly if it was to weigh to his advantage.

No one had seen the form of Hereford, but it didn't matter. They had been spotted. They must push the charge immediately.

Within seconds Bruce's own trumpeters were sounding the alerting flourish.

Onward they came, running now, down the plain . . . toward destiny.

———

From the carse, in the midst of which he and his nephew still did not fully divine their great peril, England's Edward II stood surrounded by his commanders. It was light enough now to see the approaching Scots army. Yet still the astonished King did not believe they would actually attack.

"They . . . they will not fight—*surely* they do not mean to engage us?" he said in continuing disbelief. "They are on foot. They will not go against a fully mounted cavalry!"

Edward's commanders gave no response to his words.

At last the grim truth began to dawn on them—even as their thousands of troops rushed to ready themselves for battle—that closer heed should have been given to Hereford's warnings of the previous night.

"*Will* they fight?" the King said again.

At last one of his men replied.

"They will fight," said Ingram de Umfraville. The measured determination of the tone of his voice left no further doubt in the rest of their minds. If anyone would know the disposition of the Scots, it was Ingram. He had once been a guardian of Scotland but had joined Edward's cause and was now Bruce's enemy.

"They will fight," he repeated almost to himself. "You may depend on it."

※ T H I R T Y - O N E ※

Robert the Bruce, self-proclaimed King of Scotland, was about to wage battle to determine whether the kingship he had claimed at Scone eight years before would endure or whether it would end with the spilling of his own blood into the waters of the Bannock.

He spurred his mount quickly to the front of his men, dismounted, took the *Brecbennoch* of St. Columba from the hands of Abbot Bernard, then sank to one knee.

"In the name of God and John the Baptist, and with the help of St. Andrew of Scotland, we hereby commence battle for the just cause of Scotland's freedom and independence!"

He rose and turned to face his army. Already half of them had sunk to their knees and were intoning the Lord's Prayer, some in murmurs, others in shouts.

The other half, motivated less from piety and more with sound battle instincts, took opportunity of the brief halt to tighten the formations of their schiltrons and sink their spears into the ground toward the English horsemen who were already massing.

Suddenly the King of England came to attention where he stood with his generals. He peered excitedly into the distance.

"Look!" he cried, pointing westward. "I *knew* they would not risk it. They will not engage. See, they have stopped. They yield already!"

His companions followed his gesture. There could be little doubt a sudden change had indeed come among the ranks of the Scots. But what?

"They have seen the size of our force and know that to advance further is suicide," Edward went on excitedly. "Look, I tell you—they kneel there, on the open plain! They plead for mercy."

"Not from you, my lord King, I fear," said Hereford, whose eyes on this morning proved sharper than the King's, just as his senses had been on the previous night.

"What do you mean?" barked Edward.

"They pause to kneel, it is true," replied the earl. "But it is to God they pray, not the King of England."

———

Bruce handed the *Brecbennoch* back to the Abbot. He remounted his steed, then drew out his large two-handed sword and raised it aloft over his head.

"God be with you!" shouted Bruce. "For Scotland, for honor—and for freedom!"

A great cry went up. The host of Robert the Bruce surged forward.

They were already well down the slope toward the carse and found the footing increasingly difficult—but not so bad as the English cavalry found it as soon as it was mounted and attempted to move toward the advancing Scots.

Even as the Scots were praying and gathering themselves, the young earl of Gloucester—perhaps to show himself a better commander on this than on the day before and to rectify his contribution to the now-apparent colossal blunder of positioning—was frantically rallying his squadrons. He set his sights on his first objective: the bridge at Milton. His company had bivouacked nearest it and would have the best chance to seize and hold the bridgehead against any Scottish attempt to escape. Already Gloucester was leading his men toward it with trumpets blasting away.

The going for the hoofed beasts beneath them, however, was nearly impossible. Hereford's warnings had underestimated the trouble many times over. The English troops had come across here to make camp last evening easily enough, keeping in single file and managing to probe their way by circuitous pathways on dry ground. But now, suddenly, in attempted charge, the same route became impassable. Everywhere through the marsh lurked streams and sump holes, ditches, and marshy ground that acted like quicksand for the heavy-footed creatures.

From the west, Edward Bruce had observed Gloucester's ploy and immediately recognized the bridge as his objective. He must secure it first!

The moment the elder Bruce lowered his sword, the brother of the King sent his division sprinting for the bridge. The enemy was mounted, it was true. But through the carseland, bounding and jumping and vaulting over brooks and canals and puddles, the Scots came on foot from the opposite site and made much quicker work of it. Bruce's men reached the bridge in a yelling human tide about the same time as a handful of Gloucester's mounted soldiers.

Now the eight- and ten-foot poles by which they had formed their schiltrons proved to be effective offensive weapons as well. Jabbing and thrusting at both riders and beasts, the Scots soon dispatched Gloucester's advance party. Terrified and wounded horses screamed and kicked and reared, then sprinted off riderless to safety, while the blood of their masters gave the Scots their first victory and temporary control of the bridge.

The earl of Gloucester himself, however, and much more of his cavalry were arriving on the scene rapidly.

"Into schiltrons!" shouted Edward Bruce.

Well practiced at the exercise, his battalion hastened into two ovals next to each other at the very entry to the bridge. Thrusting their long lances into the ground and angling them in an outward fan all round, Bruce's men presented two huge battlefield hedgehogs to the English horsemen, and at the end of each quill stood an angry Scot!

No solid ground existed on which the horsemen could assemble into a widespread attack position. Lead riders plunged at the Scots, but swords and even lances were too short to penetrate the schiltrons. From behind them their comrades were arriving. But as the horses pushed their way forward, they gradually shoved the first arrivals straight into the deadly spears.

Gloucester's cavalry attack fell apart into chaos. Circling the twin hedgehogs, nowhere could they find an opening by which to penetrate, while one by one the long poles of the Scots poked and stabbed and knocked the riders away. Panicked and whinnying horses plunged and reared.

Sensing that an opportunity for heroism had befallen him, the impulsive nephew of the King circled around to the opposite side, ordered his men away, then spurred his horse forward and straight into the narrow gap between the two schiltrons. He would break their flank himself. His men would follow and overwhelm them!

But his confused and constricted battalion did not follow. Seeing him suddenly alone and isolated, the screaming Scots pikemen attacked and drove the earl of Gloucester from his horse, then broke forward in a wild melee.

"Stop—don't kill him!" cried Edward Bruce behind them. "It's Gloucester. We'll need him for ransom!"

It was too late. The earl had fallen, run through with more than a dozen spears and swords.

The battle was only minutes old, and already the King's nephew had gone to join Hereford's.

THIRTY-TWO

Meanwhile, to Edward Bruce's left, the line of Scots under Randolph and Douglas advanced down the hill. Seeing their advantage over the cumbersome struggling English cavalry, they came quickly now, keeping their flank tight and unbroken, spears leveled toward the enemy.

Randolph's division first came to the support of Edward Bruce, routing the rest of Gloucester's force. The eager Highlanders gave no mercy, their dirks and swords and longpoles clashing into metal breastplates until the blood burst through the very armor itself. By the time Gloucester's cavalry, without its leader, managed to retreat into the carse for a respite, already the pools and streams about Milton were stained with red.

And the battle had only begun.

From the beginning, the English position was hopeless. On foot, and with their longpoles advancing before them, the Scots gradually pushed the English horsemen farther and farther back into the Bannock.

Had the English met the advancing Scots with their vastly superior infantry, hand-to-hand combat would have hugely favored the southern invaders. But the fifteen thousand English foot soldiers found themselves hemmed in behind the cavalry, as Hereford had warned, trying to muster but confined along the bank of the Bannock. The English archers and Welsh longbowmen, who might have broken both offensive and defensive schiltroned positions, were also wedged in behind the cavalry and thus unable to enter the battle.

With the advantage all on their side, the Scots army continued its methodical advance.

Randoph and Douglas now marshaled their men into two mobile schiltrons each and began moving behind hundreds of long protruding pikes, slowly, inexorably over whatever terrain they encountered. Finally, to the left, Robert Bruce's division formed into its three mobile ovals, completing the line of nine schiltrons stretching in an arched bow northward from the bridge.

As the morning advanced, the nine hedgehog schiltrons continued the slow push, compressing and engaging the English cavalry, whose only advantage lay in attack, into a gradual, protracted retreat back ... back ... with nowhere to go but into the waters of the Bannock Burn. The infantry, those vast numbers who might have conquered Scotland for King Edward, could not even *see* the Scots for their own horsemen.

Steadily the battle wore on. And as the English staggered rearward, still more bodies fell. All morning they fell, and blood flowed, and the grass of the Carse of Stirling turned color, and even the burn of the Bannock flowed red. It was a horrible sight, but more horrible to hear, for death was everywhere.

A nation was being born . . . but *men* were dying.

Two companies of King Edward's archers at length managed to slip up alongside the Forth toward higher ground. From this position they hoped to inflict damage behind the Scots lines.

But the keen eye of Robert the Bruce spotted the maneuver. He sounded the attack for his own light cavalry, under Robert Keith, to sweep round from the left of the main force, intercept the archers, and turn them back.

Still forward drove the Scots schiltrons, compressing what remained of the English cavalry tightly back against its own frustrated but immobile infantry.

Time wore on, and exhaustion gradually began to pull at both Scots and English. Most of the horsemen had realized the uselessness of their mounts and by this time were on the ground, attempting to fight by hand. Terrified horses, left riderless, tried to escape. But everywhere men were in the way. Everywhere was bog. Nowhere could man or beast move.

Neither plan nor formation ordered the English steps. All was a chaos of mud and water and blood. Speared horses crushed the living. Frantic hooves inflicted as many wounds as Scottish swords. Fallen bodies lay everywhere. Still Bruce drove his men to beat the English back, butchering the foe as they went, hour after bloody hour.

Even now, the Scots were badly outnumbered. If somehow the English King could rally his men, and bring the infantry forward, Bruce might yet be defeated.

But in the confusion and chaos, neither Edward nor his generals were capable of altering the terrible momentum of defeat. Their men began to break rank. To the rear, and facing the threat of being crushed by the horses of its own cavalry, the infantry began to flee.

There was nowhere to go but back—back across the Bannock Burn.

Looking out beyond the fray, from upon the hill at New Park, the English commanders suddenly saw a wave of Scots reinforcements streaming down the hill toward the battle-carse. Their knighted horsemen saw it too.

Horses turned . . . and the English retreat was on.

"On them!" rose up great exultant cries from the schiltrons. "On them! They fail!"

For the English it was now every man and beast for himself. Seventeen thousand soldiers had encamped on the carse the previous night. Perhaps three or four thousand bodies lay dead. But the greatest carnage was yet to come.

Some of the infantry had already found a place to ford the burn, a deep stream even in summer. But now came the deluge of swarming thousands, scrambling over one another, horses trampling men, men's boots burying their comrades under the brown-red water. The retreat became a chaos of frantic pandemonium. And behind the fleeing English came the Scots with their long spears, running now to slay all who remained.

And from the hill behind swarmed the reinforcements who had turned the tide—peasants and neighboring Scots men and women accompanying the priests and the porters and cooks and grooms of Bruce's own army—running into the fray with banners of tartan tied to tree branches and cloth strips from poles, running with their knives and crude spears . . . every man and woman wanting to have a part of their nation's fight for independence.

By now the burn was choked with the dead and trampled and dying. Men and horses crossed frantically over bridges made from the bodies of their fellows. Those who somehow got across made for Stirling or the surrounding farmland.

With five hundred mounted knights led by Pembroke, Edward II made good his escape toward Stirling Castle, to which Mowbray had managed to flee with a small band the previous day. But now the governor refused his King entry. Edward turned and hastily made for Linlithgow, then Dunbar, where he boarded a ship back for England. What remained of his army was left to find its own way south to the border and beyond.

What his father, the Hammer, might have done, Edward II had no idea. But he had had enough! Let the Scots have their nation—and their King!

He had been soundly defeated, and knew it, and was not inclined to press the point further.

THIRTY-THREE

In the aftermath of Bannockburn, Bruce's troops plundered Edward's forsaken camp and found booty of magnificent proportions—food, supplies, silver, gold, wine, religious vestments, pay-chests, armor, and weapons. It was almost enough, in one place, to elevate Robert Bruce's new Scottish kingdom to the temporary status of a wealthy nation.

The earl of Hereford was captured attempting his escape. In a bargain with the English, he was later traded for Bruce's wife and daughter and a number of other Scots prisoners.

Bruce's throne was now secure, both within and without. Back in London, however, Edward's familial pride again asserted itself, and he refused to acknowledge either Scotland's independence or her King.

The years following Bannockburn offered opportunity for Robert Bruce to reward the loyalty of his followers.

After coming over to his cause from northeastern England, Adam de Gordon was chosen one of the King's envoys to the pope in 1320, bearing to Rome the Declaration of Arbroath, which begged the intervention of John XXII in the ongoing attempts by the English King to subdue the freedom of the Scottish people. It was a noble yet defiant document, signed by nearly forty Scottish earls and barons, expressing in writing exactly what the battle of Bannockburn had achieved by the sword—the determination of the Scots to live as a free and independent people.

When Gordon returned from the Continent, he was given the lordship over one hundred twenty square miles of lands in Strathbogie, which lands had been forfeited by David of Strathbogie for his defection against the King. Adam de Gordon removed himself to his new estates and named the village which had grown up near the castle after his home in Berwickshire. The village in the heart of Strathbogie would forever after be known as Huntly.

Donal MacDarroch continued in Bruce's service. He married in 1324, and in gift the King made a landowner of him, adding the title of baronet along with the property. Donal continued as a member of the King's personal guard.

In 1327, King Edward II of England was overthrown and murdered by his wife and her lover, then succeeded on the English throne by his son, Edward III. In the following year, a treaty of peace was signed between the two nations at Northampton. In signing it, the new Edward formally recognized Scotland as a sovereign land, and Robert Bruce as its rightful King.

Bruce had conquered.

Scotland was a free and *independent* nation!

Donal MacDarroch's daughter, Helen, became a Gordon in 1347, when she married a certain John de Gordon, grandson of Robert Bruce's envoy to the pope.

Thus it was that in time the grandson of the Bruce's groom, a certain Cailean Darroch Gordon—whose descendents would eventually lead the Gordon strain to Cliffrose on the banks of the Spey—came into the world less than two miles from where Donal himself had grown up and where, as a lad, he had first run through the streets with the name of the earl of Carrick on his lips.

That had been a long time before when, as an old man, Donal recalled the incident.

"My mother hated the man," he said to the young Gordon grandson on his knee. "But my father," he said with a faraway sigh and happy smile, "my father knew a king when he saw one . . . and knew what an honor it was to serve him, to be known as the King's man."

Donal's thoughts drifted back, many memories now filling his mind.

The world was a far different place now than then. Because of the man he and his father had served, the Scots had been a free people since that time, and subject to no King but their own.

> The daring invaders, they fled or they died . . .
> Thus bold, independent, unconquer'd, and free,
> Her bright course of glory for ever shall fly,
> For brave Caledonia immortal must be.[*]

---

[*] From Robert Burns, "Caledonia."

12

CLIMAX IN WHITEHALL

—————————————— ※ ——————————————

※ O N E ※

The fading sounds of the campaign still echoed in the ear of Andrew Trentham's imagination as he stood overlooking the ancient battle plain above the burn known as the Bannock.

How long he remained transfixed, gazing back in his mind's eye through the mists of history, he could not have said. As he relived the old story, and the part his own recently discovered ancestor had played in it, visions of momentous events pervaded his brain. Truly no place on earth at this moment could contain more symbolism and significance to him than the precise spot on which Andrew now stood. Everything around him spoke of heroic precedent, of men who had placed the stamp of their footprint upon the byways of history for their descendents to follow. Truly had the legacy of a proud people here converged in a pinnacle of triumph.

Cailean Darroch Gordon.

The very sound of the name in his ears as he whispered it sent a tingle down his spine—grandson of the great Donal MacDarroch, baronet, son of Fergus . . . groom to the King.

Andrew glanced down again at the guidebook he had been reading in the midst of his reflections, tracing the roots of the ancient families connected with Bruce during that time.

Here was the link he had so long sought between the Gordon name and the previous ancestry he had unraveled. It had taken Adam de Gordon's friendship with Robert Bruce to bring the Gordon name into prominence.

He would have to return for another visit to Huntly and the great castle, the Peel of Strathbogie, which he now realized his ancestor, the twin Gachan son of Darroch, had helped build. There Robert Bruce had lain ill that

Christmas season, and there Fergus MacDarroch had first set eyes on the man for whom he would give his life.

It was his own ancestor, Donal MacDarroch, who had ridden at Bruce's side, who had held the reins of his horse and perhaps even his sword.

He was heir to the Gordon name, through Lady Fayth to Sandy and Culodina and Kendrick and Aileana Gordon all the way back to Cailean Darroch Gordon and, beyond him, to Donal MacDarroch and the twins Gachan and Beath . . . and Dallais and Breathran . . . and Fintenn and Maelchon and Foltlaig . . . and all the way back to Cruithne, ancient chief of the Caldonii.

He was heir to them all! Their heritage now had come to rest all these years later . . . on him!

He, Andrew Trentham, was a Scot. And he was proud to call himself a Scot! These were *his* people.

The amount of Scots blood in his veins may have been a relatively small percentage. But henceforth would he walk in that heritage proudly—whatever the amount.

He stood in the descent of those ancient men of valor who had fought for freedom and won independence for this kingdom they loved.

If he, Andrew Trentham, was to be worthy of such a legacy, worthy to follow in those footsteps, how could he do other than summon his *own* courage . . . and continue the battle so bravely begun?

He took in one final deep draft of the warm air, now understanding the message of the breezes blowing up from the valley of the burn.

History had been changed here once. Why should not this be the place for the beginnings of a *new* victory for a *new* generation of the descendents of Robert the Bruce . . . and the descendents of Cruithne and Foltlaig and Donal?

The quiet impulses of destiny were permeating through Andrew as he stood. He pulled out his worn volume of Burns, opened it, found the passage he was looking for, then began reading, as if the words were mingled with the drum cadence of soldiers marching.

> Scots, wha hae wi' Wallace bled,
> Scots, wham Bruce has aften led,
> Welcome to your gory bed,
>   On to victorie!

Now's the day, and now's the hour:
See the front o' battle lour,
See approach proud Edward's power—
    Chains and slaverie!

Wha will be a traitor knave?
Wha can fill a coward's grave?
Wha sae base as be a slave?—
    Let him turn, and flee!

Wha for Scotland's King and Law
Freedom's sword will strongly draw,
Freeman stand or freeman fa',
    Let him follow me!

The words echoed in Andrew's ear as if Robert the Bruce were calling out through the centuries . . . *to him!* These were the words he had been meant to hear.

Let him follow . . . let him follow me!

He had felt the legend . . . and now realized that its mantle was passing to him.

The spirit of Bannockburn had accomplished its work.

Andrew knew what course lay before him. It was time for him to mount his *own* battle steed, face the approaching army of events, and stand for the freedom and independence of his people—the Scots!

The great King Robert was only a silent monument now, presiding, it was true, over his former realm with the strength of legend, yet powerless within himself any longer to move events.

That charge must rest with others. Now he, Andrew Trentham, had to step into the footprints left behind and carry the banner of history forward, not knowing what would be the result any more than Bruce could have been assured of his victory as he overlooked the English encampment.

He *would* face the challenge as Bruce had, resolved Andrew, and let his progeny decide the outcome. He would do what he had to do, confident in the knowledge that his cause was true . . . hoping posterity would judge him kindly.

Andrew turned, and with a determined look of purpose on his countenance and a swelling sense of rising triumph welling up within his heart, strode from the symbolic mount of battle.

It was time for him to carry out the destiny which had been borne to his shoulders by the winds of history.

⚘   T W O   ⚘

The scene in the House of Commons was alive with expectation. Clearly, something extraordinary was at hand.

No one would argue this, however, simply because the erudite British body was noisy. To do so would be as logical as heeding a Scottish sheepherder's forecast of an uncommon event on the basis of his observation that rain was falling. Neither noise in the Commons nor rain in the Highlands could be considered worthy of note.

Today's hubbub in the chamber, however, buzzed with a different quality. The weather report was uncertain, though some predicted a thunderstorm the likes of which Whitehall had rarely witnessed.

Murmurs had circulated throughout the Palace of Westminster all day. Whispered conversations, overheard tidbits, snatches of speculation, and last-minute machinations both by the Tories and the SNP had all mounted in number and intensity as the hour had approached. Increasingly, they centered on the still-missing Andrew Trentham.

When was he expected? No one knew for certain. There were rumors, of course, but most of it bordered on gossip rather than fact. Even Maurice Fraser-Smythe, his new deputy leader, and other LibDem colleagues had not heard from him in days.

Some of the more enterprising among the press had attempted to follow his movements since the speedy getaway from his home in Cumbria a week earlier and were making the most of their discoveries. One of the tabloids had it that he had finally succumbed to the pressure and had gone north to "find himself," describing the journey in mystical religious phrases and likening his movements to a Tibetan pilgrimage. A photograph, inconclusive but purported to be of the LibDem leader, showed a man walking alone at the top of an unidentified rocky peak. Another of the papers claimed that the young MP had fallen in love and was moving about secretively in order to keep his clandestine love affair from the press. Someone claimed to have an informant on the staff of one of Edinburgh's prestigious kilt and bagpipe makers, who possessed a story he would sell for a handsome price.

Kirk Luddington of BBC 2, even more determined to be the first journalist to uncover the real story since the incident with Rawlings in their editor's office, had spent a small fortune on informants in the attempt to trace Trentham's steps, but with only sketchy results.

Most of Trentham's parliamentary associates did not believe the reports and innuendoes that were mounting hourly in one tabloid after another. Yet it could truthfully be said that a good many of them *did* wonder what was going on inside the Cumbrian MP's head.

Those closest to the situation rigorously denied any allegations in the directions of scandal, mysticism, stress, lunacy, or religion. Yet none were absolutely sure quite what was going on with the LibDem leader. And Fraser-Smythe had admitted off the record that, yes, there were peculiarities he had noticed lately. Trentham *had* behaved with a certain detachment, saying odd things, quoting poetry, dropping enigmatic historical references to ancient men and women, most of whom he had never heard of.

And now, with the second reading, debate, and division imminent, the Honorable Gentleman from Cumbria seemed to have disappeared from London without a trace, exacerbating rumor and speculation to greatly heightened levels. Could a second LibDem leader be doomed to the same fate as Eagon Hamilton? suggested one of the seamier rags. Was a *new* parliamentary scandal brewing? Or had perhaps Trentham been more involved in the previous affair than was known at the time?

Not only was the critical approaching vote newsworthy in its own right, a genuine uncertainty existed concerning the outcome: The critical block of deciding votes was held by an MP no one had seen hide nor hair of in five days!

Most of the vote on the matter was well established by now and had been running in the papers and television broadcasts all week. Labour was solidly together with the Scottish Nationalists, with but a handful of defections, but the Ulster MPs were against the bill, along with all but five of the Conservatives. The four Welsh Plaid Cymru members seemed to be leaning toward dividing on the Labour side, and the three votes of the SDL seemed a solid yea, while the Democratic Unionists would clearly be against the measure. The *aye* votes appeared to stand, therefore, between 310 and 315, and the *nays* between 292 and 297. Both sides were well short of the 326 needed for a majority.

Home rule for Scotland would therefore indeed be decided by the Liberal Democrats, as would the future of Richard Barraclough's government.

But still no one had seen the Liberal Democrat leader.

No one even knew for certain if he was back in London, although it was being circulated through the chamber that he *had* been heard from and was on his way toward the city.

⁂   **T H R E E**   ⁂

The hour at which the House of Commons was to convene for the day approached.

It was five minutes before the two-thirty stroke of Big Ben atop the famed tower overlooking Westminster. Inside, the noisy hubbub of men and women gradually began to gravitate and jostle toward their respective seats on the two sides of the hall. Most of the two front benches were already full with the cabinet and its shadow, while the multitude of backbenchers on both sides moved toward their positions.

At precisely one minute before the half hour, as if the moment had been chosen for maximum impact—though in actual fact it was the traffic on London's snarled Great Northern Circle and a last-minute telephone call that were responsible for the climactic moment of high drama—suddenly the doors opened, and in strode the Honorable Andrew Gordon Trentham.

A hush of stunned disbelief spread through the six hundred fifty men and women present.

The Liberal Democratic leader was fully adorned with the blue-and-green kilt of the dress Gordon tartan reaching to the middle of his kneecap, knee-high wool stockings holding a jewel-cased sgian-dubh against his right calf, and a leather sporran with hanging horsetail hair swinging from the front of his kilt as he walked, dress Argyle jacket of solid light green wool and silver buttons, and a matching Glengarry bonnet atop his head.

For a moment time seemed to stand still. Every man and woman in the chamber was spellbound.

Andrew strode purposefully forward, the cadence of his step the only sound, nodded respectfully toward the speaker, the prime minister, and Archibald Craye of the opposition, then finally proceeded to take his seat with his Liberal Democratic colleagues.

The palpable silence lasted but a few seconds.

Suddenly Dugald MacKinnon of the SNP was on his feet. His prophecy had been fulfilled. Their new hero had come!

He burst into applause. His small contingent of Scottish Nationalists now stood with him. A clapping of hands erupted, followed by their cheers. More MPs entered into the ovation, joined now by spectators from the public gallery.

Bedlam broke out.

A great scurrying from the reporters' gallery above the speaker's seat gave indication that the biggest news story in all Europe, perhaps all the world, had just exploded wide open.

One look at Andrew Trentham's face told all. It had been almost three centuries since the Act of Union between England and Scotland in 1707.

And now the Scots were about to have their independence again!

※   F O U R   ※

Far to the north, in a small Highland village known by the name Ballochallater, a breeze had recently sprung up, signaling that the afternoon was on the wane.

It was not the weather that was on the mind of a certain Finlaggan Gordon, however, but the astonishing news to which he was listening on the telephone from a friend in Edinburgh at that very moment.

"But there canna weel be time," he now said.

The voice at the other end of the line, talking excitedly and hurriedly, replied. Gordon glanced to his right at the clock on the wall as he listened.

The voice completed its plea. Gordon was silent a moment, thinking.

"Weel," he said at length, "we'll see aboot it—ye say he's leaving from Auld Reekie at six?"

The caller spoke a brief clarification.

"Ay—six sharp. Gien we come, we winna be late."

Gordon hung up the phone and hastened immediately in search of wife, daughter, and son.

"Ye winna believe what I hae t' tell ye," he said the moment he saw Ginny. "'Twas Angus MacLeod on the telephone, an' jist as I've been tellin' ye, it seems ye might hae been a bit hard in yer jeedgment o' oor frien' frae last year wha called himsel' Trent."

"What is it, Papa?" asked Ginny. She knew from the tone of her father's voice that the call had been serious.

"Sit ye all doon," he replied, glancing about as now his wife and Shorty also approached. "I'll tell ye. But we got t' make it fast, 'cause Angus has a frien' wha has a plane fuelin' in the reekin' city as we speak, an' gien ony o' ye're gaein' wi' me, we haena a second t' spare."

"Papa, what are ye talkin' aboot?" persisted Ginny.

"Kennin' that ye're a mite more darin' ahind the wheel than me or Shorty," said the laird, "I'm askin' ye, Ginny, gien ye're finally ready t' put away the nonsense o' yer anger aboot Andrew Trentham, an' then hoo fast ye can drive us t' Edinburgh—an' git us there in one piece!"

※   F I V E   ※

Frantically Paddy Rawlings fumbled with her earring. But her fingers were too sweaty and trembling to make the tiny thing behave.

There!—she had it.

Now for a last check of her makeup and outfit.

She looked herself over in the mirror, up and down from head to feet. She had worn this navy blue suit only once before. She was so flustered she could hardly get the jacket on. She had to stop perspiring, or her blouse would cling. She couldn't wipe the beads of moisture from her forehead or she would smear her foundation.

"Bill . . . Bill, come in here," she called out. "—How do I look . . . is everything okay?"

"Smashing—you'll knock 'em dead," replied Rawlings, walking in and glancing over her shoulder into the mirror. "Just don't let anyone see that you're nervous."

"Yeah, right . . . thanks for nothing!"

"Come on, Paddy—you look terrific," he added, kissing the back of her neck.

"I wish I felt terrific," she sighed.

Paddy turned her attention again to the mirror for a last check. They would make her face over, of course, before she stepped in front of the lights and the camera, but she wanted to arrive on the scene looking as much the part as possible.

She had hardly believed her ears when she answered the phone at her desk four and a half hours ago—a few minutes after two earlier in the day.

"Paddy," said the familiar voice she knew in an instant, "—it's Andrew Trentham. Do you still want that story I promised you last year?"

"Why . . . why—yes, of course, Andrew," she answered. "What's up? Where are you?"

"All I can say is, stay near your phone. Today's the day."

"What should I do?" she asked, unable to hide her excitement.

"Just be around. I'll try to get word to you," he said. "But if I can't . . . well, as I said, just be around."

Paddy hung up the receiver with shaking hand. For the remainder of the afternoon she was unable to concentrate on her duties with any attention at all and remained altogether oblivious to the commotion, phone calls, and comings and goings around Edward Pilkington's office. The fact that she did not see Kirk Luddington all afternoon scarcely occurred to her.

By five forty-five, still having heard nothing further from Andrew, she began to grow anxious.

She rose and walked toward Pilkington's office. For one of the few times in this extraordinarily busy day, her boss was alone and awaiting the six o'clock news hour, hoping nothing would happen now that would be too late to make the early broadcast.

"What is it, Rawlings?" he asked.

"That story I told you about several months ago," she said, "it could be anytime, maybe even later this evening."

"What story?"

"On Andrew Trentham—the up close and personal inside look."

"I'm afraid you're too late," he said with a smile of sympathetic irony.

"What do you mean?" she asked.

"That's everyone's story now," he replied. "Every journalist in London is waiting for it to break."

"I don't . . ." said Paddy in a confused voice, "—what do . . . I don't understand you."

"Don't you know what's going on, Rawlings?"

"No, I don't suppose I do."

"The whole country's flocking to Westminster."

"But . . . why?"

"Because of your friend Trentham. The thing's about to explode wide open. Commons is debating right now, and the vote will come sometime this evening."

"You promised to give me a chance on camera."

"I gave you that shot in November with the announcement of Ramsey's arrest. Besides, what I said when we first discussed it was that I would put you on camera *if* you brought me something no one else had," rejoined Pilkington. *"Everyone's* going to have this Trentham story before the night's out."

As the truth began to dawn on her that she was waiting at the wrong place, Paddy half turned to go. Then she caught herself. She would not give up so easily.

"But this is my story," she said. "Mr. Trentham said he would give *me* an exclusive."

"When did he tell you that?" asked Pilkington, leaning forward imperceptibly with suddenly heightened interest.

"Earlier this afternoon—about two."

"Today?"

Paddy nodded.

The newsman sat back, screwing his face into an expression of hurried mental regrouping. This was a twist he hadn't expected. "All right," he said after a pause, "maybe you *will* get another chance in front of the lights after all."

"Is a cameraman ready?" asked Paddy, her mind jumping into action.

"Our whole film crew is already over there, Rawlings. Don't you understand? This thing has been building for hours."

"Then I'm on my way!" she said, spinning the rest of the way around and taking several quick strides toward the door.

"Not so fast, Rawlings," called out Pilkington behind her. "You're not going in front of any camera of mine looking like that. Get yourself to your flat, take a cold shower, calm down, and then put on your best. If you're on the level with what you've told me, the whole world will be watching. If you're lucky, the climax will wait for you."

"You'll notify them that the story's mine?"

Pilkington nodded.

"You just get over to Parliament Square within an hour—Kirk is already there. If it breaks before you get there, I won't be able to keep him from doing the lead."

"I'll be there," she said. "Just remember—the personal interview is mine."

▨   S I X   ▨

If the scene in the chamber of the House of Commons was laden with significance when, to the incredulity of his fellows, the Honorable kilt-clad
member of Parliament had walked so briskly and confidently through its
doors, the spectacle in Parliament Square when Parliament dismissed some
seven hours later could be described as nothing less than a pandemonium the
likes of which British politics had not seen since the end of the Second World
War.

Every television station in Great Britain—and cameramen from at least
fifty stations in the States—was represented. Reporters and photographers
were on hand from every nation in Europe. Writers and photojournalists
from newspapers and magazines of stature stood alongside those from sleazy
tabloids.

They had all expected news today—but no one had anticipated *this*!

Even the highly competitive Kirk Luddington was in rare form, joking
and laughing and sharing exaggerated experiences with colleagues he might
have avoided on other occasions.

Though the debate lasted only about six hours, it was time enough for
news of Trentham's dramatic entry to spread throughout London to Scotland and around the world. From his kilted appearance, no doubt remained
as to how he intended to cast his vote!

All afternoon and evening, therefore, Scots had been gathering. Through
London a firestorm of rumor had spread through the Scottish community—
from Scotch House in Knightsbridge and on Regent's Street to the Scottish
Travel Bureau off Trafalgar Square to Scottish gift shops and grocers and
thence to Scottish country dance groups and congregations of Scottish Pres-
byterians. Wherever there were Scots, the news spread quickly.

Old Robert the Bruce might well have invaded for all their excitement!
By the thousands they prepared to join in the march or celebration or whatever was going to happen—like the onlookers at Bannockburn who wrapped
their scarves around sticks and branches and joined Bruce's charge. No one
wanted to miss out on *this*!

Musty kilts and tartans, long in disuse, were dug from boxes and dusted
off. . . . Scarves, sweaters, old pins and brooches and caps—anything Scottish—were brought out for the occasion. And the rest of the senses were
brought into the celebration too. Bagpipes and pennywhistles began to be
heard throughout the city. Oatcakes and shortbread, twelve-year-old Glenfid-

dich and *ran Mór* and Columba Cream flowed off the shelves of markets in
a flood as Scots made ready to unleash their festive mood.

About the dinner hour they began to descend upon the center of Westminster and continued to fill the underground and buses and taxis in greater
and greater numbers as the evening progressed.

The London regiment of the 144th Division of the Royal Highlanders
had been notified and was on hand in full regalia, as were the 98th Pipe and
Drum Corp and the Southern England Highlanders and nearly every Scottish
organization in the south of England, from a regiment of the Gordon Highlanders to the pipe band of the Royal Scots Guard. The musicians Alistair
MacDonald, the Alexander Brothers, and Valerie Dunbar had all flown in and
were strumming and singing and entertaining the crowd.

Though the vast majority of those gathering were London Scots, across
the nation phone and fax lines were operating at full capacity. Shortly after
news broke of Trentham's entry into Parliament, therefore, great crowds
began flying, driving, and riding on buses and trains down from the north.
Every available flight from all major and minor Scottish airports was full, and
tremendous standby lines clogged the terminals. The situation was the same
at train and bus stations, though most of those travelers could not hope now
to get to London before evening.

Everyone with a drop of blood—real or imaginary—linking them to the
most insignificant scion of the Scottish royal house or to the chieftainship of
any clan sought means to get themselves to the city, that their presence might
do its part to seal and sanction the great cause of Scotland. Not a private
plane or charter was left on the ground north of the Solway or the Tweed
after about seven o'clock that evening.

The single message melting the telephone lines to the north was a simple
one: *Come to London however you can get here! Bannockburn is about to happen all over again!*

At least five hundred bagpipers from across Britain, representing nearly a
hundred clans and septs, had joined together, clad in their multicolored kilts,
prepared to sound out to the strains of "Scotland the Brave" with such vigor
that they would be heard up and down the Thames, maybe all the way to St.
Paul's.

Certainly they would be heard by the thousands of Scots who now filled
the grounds of St. Margaret's and Westminster Abbey and lined the sidewalks
all the way across both sides of Westminster Bridge, down Parliament and
Whitehall Streets to Downing Street, and spreading along Great George

Street as far as St. James's Park. What unsuspecting tourists happened to be out were soon overwhelmed by the colorful, boisterous throng.

Eventually the whole of central Westminster was so congested with pedestrians that sometime after eight o'clock the police had no choice but to close off the circle around Parliament Square to cars, taxis, and bus traffic and allow the growing and restive throng to pour into the streets.

▨ S E V E N ▨

Three there were who would *not* be among the throng of celebrants that evening.

During Andrew's final hours with his mother and father at Derwenthwaite the day before, he had paid one final visit to Duncan MacRanald, telling him what he was returning to London to do. He had hoped to persuade the old Scotsman to travel south with him. Duncan had been such an important part of all that had happened, and Andrew wanted him to share in it.

But MacRanald would have none of it, nor could Andrew hope to change his mind. He would be happier here, Duncan said, among the hills, within sight of Scotland's ridges. He did promise, however, actually to read the local paper for the next few days.

Then Andrew returned across the hills to Derwenthwaite.

"Are you and Mum planning to go down to London with me tomorrow?" he asked his father as soon as he located him.

"We hadn't really decided, son," Harland Trentham replied. "I think your mother would like to be there, but the trip would surely tax her. To tell the truth, I would be more comfortable remaining here. But what would you like us to do? From the sound of what you plan to do, all eyes will be upon you. You're the man of the hour now. I'm sure we could manage it if you really want us there."

Andrew thought a moment.

"How about your inviting Duncan to the Hall for dinner with you and Mum, so he could watch the newscast with you on the telly?"

"Would he come?"

"I don't know. Be convincing."

"It sounds like a capital idea," said Mr. Trentham. "I like that much better than a long trip with your mother. We'll do it—it will be fun. I'll ride out and invite him this very afternoon."

And now, as the London streets filled to bursting with people and noise and anticipation, after a wonderful dinner and a warm rekindling of childhood affection, Harland and Lady Trentham sat with their honored but humble guest watching the BBC's coverage of events as they unfolded outside the Palace of Westminster in London.

Clustered throughout the room also sat the rest of the household staff. This was no time for ceremony or rank. Their own Andrew was about to make history. Something about the occasion seemed to demand that they all share it together.

The former Tory firebrand Waleis Bradburn Trentham would have given anything to be present outside the Palace where she had spent so many years at the center of Parliament's affairs. If she had been stronger, nothing would have kept her away. But the spirited, politically minded lady had learned much in the past year about acceptance—and now she accepted her diminished circumstances with a good grace that still surprised those who knew her best. She was happy for her son and contented herself with watching the proceedings quietly with husband and friends.

When Andrew's figure first came on the screen some minutes later in full Highland attire, every eye in the sitting room at Derwenthwaite Hall filled with tears, Duncan MacRanald wept most freely of all.

※　E I G H T　※

It was the alert and roving eye of Kirk Luddington himself who saw the light above Big Ben go out just before nine-thirty that evening, signaling that Parliament was adjourned. Whatever the result, the vote had been cast.

He gave a great shout to his crew, and immediately all other news agencies followed. By the time the first MPs made their appearance a few minutes later, Luddington and a hundred more reporters were ready for them.

When Andrew Trentham exited the Palace of Westminster, still clad in the tartan of his Gordon clan, the screech and wail of the pipes threatened to drown out the chiming of Big Ben himself ringing out the time of nine-thirty.

Now rose a clamor from the loyal and jubilant Scots—from London, from everywhere!—awaiting their modern-day Robert Bruce. They hoped he had, if not sent the usurper back over the border, then invaded England at the heart of its dominance, and with stealth and cunning was about to carry off the victory . . . and the blue-and-white flag of St. Andrew back to Edinburgh.

At least with such importance would the nationalistic Scottish papers imbue the Commons vote on the morrow.

The film crews—everywhere now—madly tried to obtain footage of the incredible phenomenon. Most were running live reports, though they had to share the momentous event with what was estimated as ten thousand spectators.

Paddy Rawlings saw that her ambitious colleague had no intention of relinquishing either his microphone or his lead role in front of the BBC's lights. With a shove of final encouragement from Bill at her side, at last she stepped forward just as the cameras were about to switch on.

"I'll take it from here, Kirk," she said, reaching forward and laying her hand on the microphone.

He looked at her in astonishment, then broke into a laugh. The message from Pilkington had come two hours ago, but he had not believed the American neophyte would press the matter if he made it difficult enough for her.

"Don't worry, Rawlings," he said. "I'll open and get us rolling, then give you the mike after a bit."

"No deal, Kirk. The story's mine, the interview's mine. You know it as well as I do."

"But you don't—"

"*Mine*, Kirk—now stand aside gracefully before *you* are embarrassed in front of our colleagues."

Incredulous, Luddington loosened his grip on the microphone. As Paddy's fingers closed around it, a surge of adrenaline swept through her.

Slowly Luddington backed a few steps away, even as the lights flashed upon his inexperienced colleague. The producer called his technicians into action.

Paddy drew in a deep breath, then turned to face the camera with every appearance of poise and confidence.

"For those of you who have just joined us," she began without concern for her accent, "we are standing across the street from the Palace of Westminster, where the House of Commons has just adjourned from a historic session voting on what is known as the Scottish Bill, calling for a progressive phasing in of full sovereignty and independence for Scotland. The doors are open and the members are now filing out. . . ."

She had only begun her opening remarks when she saw that Andrew was crossing the street and moving in her direction. Signaling to the cameraman to follow, and continuing to speak into the camera, Paddy began moving, hoping to intersect with him. But the crowd was so thick as to make movement nearly impossible.

"Mr. Trentham . . . Mr. Trentham!" shouted thirty reporters at once.

Above the tops of a hundred heads, however, Andrew was glancing this way and that, looking for only one face among them all. At last he spotted her.

Paddy knew from the contact of his eyes and the smile he cast her that *she* had been the island in the sea of faces he had been searching for, and that the look was meant to convey, *Don't go away . . . I'll be with you eventually!* She stumbled with her words momentarily, but quickly recovered and went on.

Finally Andrew managed to inch his way through the crowd, ignoring the pleas of Paddy's many competitors and the dozens of microphones being shoved toward him. A few minutes more, and he emerged through the thick mass of people.

He nodded and smiled to Paddy and her husband, who was struggling to keep near her.

"Bill," he said as they shook hands.

"Congratulations!" returned Bill. "It looks like you've set something off!"

But already Paddy was pulling Andrew by the elbow and trying to turn him toward her cameraman. Seconds later she began to speak, attempting to introduce him.

As she held her microphone toward him, gradually the din subsided.

"This is a great day," said Andrew in a triumphant voice, "not only for Scotland, but for all the UK and for the cause of free sovereignty everywhere."

The pause that followed gave opening for twenty questions called out simultaneously, accompanied by shouts and cheers and bagpipes throughout the throng behind. Andrew dismissed them with a wave of the hand.

"I will answer but one question," he said. "That is to tell you the decision of the Commons on the matter under consideration—the answer is *Yes!* . . . Scotland *shall* have her independence again!"

Shouts behind him erupted.

"I will make a further statement," he added, seeking still to be heard before his voice was overwhelmed, "in my interview later this evening with Patricia Rawlings."

Andrew and Paddy exchanged knowing smiles. Both of their triumphs on this day, in many ways, had been won together.

Andrew tried to step away. Immediately, without foresight or planning, a processional emerged out of the bedlam, with Andrew Trentham at its head and five hundred pipes wailing behind him. Photographers and reporters followed, doing their best to press close to the man who had suddenly become the most talked-about individual in the whole land.

But his protective piping Highland *schiltron* would have none of it and now closed ranks around him. Onward they proceeded, to strains of "Scotland the Brave," "Amazing Grace," and "Flower of Scotland," while the loyal Scots celebrants followed in their train much as the Highlanders had followed Bonnie Prince Charlie through Edinburgh.

The procession made its way around Parliament Square, then around Westminster Abbey and finally, ten or fifteen minutes later, back to the front of the Palace near the unchanging countenance of Winston Churchill's gruff and unimpressed presence.

※　N I N E　※

As he approached the statue and the procession slowed, to his disbelief Andrew looked ahead to see the tiny smiling red-crowned figure of Leigh Ginevra Gordon standing awaiting his triumphant return at the head of his victorious trail of admirers.

"Ginny!" exclaimed Andrew, breaking into a laugh of incredulity and running toward her.

"I couldna let ye hae yer moment o' victory wi'oot sharin' it wi' ye," she said, flashing the wide smile he had pictured so many times in his mind's eye since last seeing its reality when they were together on the peak of Lochnagar. "But I hardly ken yer face wi'oot yer beard! I only saw ye twice wi'oot it, an' the last time was frae up in my window when ye was talkin' t' my father, an' I was too mixed up o' mind t' take a guid luik at ye."

Andrew burst into another laugh, this time of delight. The next moment, though neither had planned it, she was in his arms.

"I cannot tell you how glad I am to see you!" said Andrew. "I intended to leave tomorrow for Ballochallater, and this time I did not intend to take no for an answer. I was going to *make* you see me whether you wanted to or not."

"Please," groaned Ginny, "dinna remin' me what a goose I've been." She was nearly yelling to be heard. "I'm sorry, an' I winna treat ye so rude ever again. I hope ye can forgive a lassie her confusion."

"All is forgiven," said Andrew, "—on one condition."

"An' jist what might that be?"

"That you will accompany me once again to the top of Lochnagar."

"In that case, Mister Andrew Trentham—though I'm still a wee bit partial t' the Andy Trent—ye hae my promise that I'll gae there wi' ye the very day ye set foot again in Ballochallater."

Ginny stepped back as Andrew released her, and now Andrew saw the small entourage that had come with her.

"Alastair . . . Shorty!" he exclaimed. "You're all here!"

He and Alastair Farquharson shook hands. Their eyes met briefly as Alastair nodded and smiled. Andrew leaned toward the big man and lowered his voice.

"I thought you told me you were never coming back to the big city," he said.

"I couldna weel miss all this," replied Alastair. "An' noo that I ken the place like an expert, 'tis nae so fearsome.—An'," he added more softly, "I'm happy fer ye an' Ginny."

Andrew smiled, gave the big hand another squeeze, then turned again toward Ginny.

"But . . . but how did you—?" laughed Andrew.

"In the airplane o' a friend o' Angus MacLeod's," she answered, "—wha phoned t' tell us what ye'd dune."

"How long have you been here?"

"We only jist noo got here through the crowd."

Behind her, Andrew now saw Ginny's father standing by, fully clad in Gordon kilt to match his own.

Andrew took two or three steps toward him.

"Well, laird," he said, smiling now himself, "what do you think of the city?"

"A mite ower big fer the likes o' us! But it still has a few things t' recommend it."

"And now you see the result of my conversation with you and Duncan!" he rejoined.

"So dinna keep us in suspense," said Ginny with a grin. "Hoo did ye vote?"

"Let me just say this—the Commons is still in a state of shock," laughed Andrew. "Labour's government is secure, but I can't say the same for the *United* Kingdom."

"'Tis a braw muckle tartan ye'll be sportin'," said Ginny's father, gesturing toward Andrew's kilt.

"Ay, isna it noo?" rejoined Andrew gaily. "An' 'tis aye my ain. Do ye suppose that makes ye yersel' my ain chief too, laird?"

Ginny and her father laughed heartily.

"Not bad fer a Sassenach," said Ginny with a mischievous smile.

"I doobt anyone'll call him a Sassenach after tonight, Ginny," corrected her father.

Ginny slipped her hand into Andrew's arm, and the two of them began a second victory march around Parliament Square. Laird Finlaggan Gordon took Andrew's left arm, and they were followed by Shorty and Alastair and the rest of the Scots. As they passed them again, Andrew hailed Bill and Paddy Rawlings, gesturing for them to join in at the front of the procession. Paddy handed her microphone to an astonished Kirk Luddington, and she and Bill now ran and fell into step beside Andrew, Ginny, and her father.

Behind them, the rising crescendo of chanting and cheering drowned out any further hope of conversation.

At first Andrew could not make out what was being said. Then finally the words of all those who had followed him in the procession around the cathedral began to come clear.

Hail, Caledonia! rose the words of the Scottish throng.

Hail, Caledonia! . . . Hail, Caledonia!

Then gradually the chants turned to song, and before long the entire spectacle of ten thousand voices joined in the massive singing, to the accompaniment of two or three hundred bagpipes, of "Scotland the Brave."

It was only too bad, Andrew thought as they walked with the throng of singing Scots following behind, that Sandy and Kendrick Gordon and their wives . . . and Ginevra and Brochan . . . and Robert the Bruce and his groom Donal . . . and Gachan and Darroch and Fionnaghal and Malcolm Canmore and Queen Margaret . . . and Dallais and Breathran and Kenneth MacAlpin . . . the priests Columba and Fintenn . . . Maelchon and Foltlaig and Cruithne and Fidach . . . even the ancient Wanderer and his sons and grandsons—if only *they* could all witness this moment of crowning triumph for the people who had come after them.

And then again, reflected Andrew further, *perhaps they all are here among us in spirit . . . watching after all!*

He hoped they would be pleased by what he had done.

Therefore, since we are surrounded by so great a cloud of witnesses, let us throw off every encumbrance that hinders us . . . and let us run with perseverance the race set before us.

—Hebrews 12:1

EPILOGUE

L̲ate summer had come once again to the Highlands of Scotland.

The annual Games at the Spittal o' Ballochallater—just two years after the appearance in the small Scottish village of a mysterious Englishman going by the name of Andy Trent—was such as the region had never seen. It had been billed as the most important Highland Games event of the year, and had even rivaled the Edinburgh Tattoo in publicity. No one who attended was disappointed.

The surrounding hillsides could not have been more resplendent in their royal garb of purple, as if all Scotland's kings and queens from the past were gazing down and giving their sanction to the proceedings.

So many visitors and guests came from throughout Scotland, Cumbria, and London that traffic clogged roads throughout all the central Highlands. And when was the last time the prime minister and half of Parliament had attended any event in Scotland, much less a small celebration in such an out-of-the-way place that a year ago would have been lucky to boast more than a hundred or two people?

Of course, it was not often that a Highland Games was put to use as a backdrop for the most celebrated public wedding in Scotland in decades, one which would unite one of the country's most famous and admired politicians with a feisty Highland veterinarian, whose bright orange-red crown barely reached up to the Honorable Gentleman's shoulder.

Ever since the announcement had been made several months after the historic vote in Parliament, and shortly after one of Andrew Trentham's many visits to Ballochallater, during which a very significant conversation with Leigh Ginevra Gordon was held on the slopes of Lochnagar, the country had talked of nothing else. By the time the long-awaited wedding approached, the name *Ginny Gordon* was nearly as well known as that of her husband-to-be. Women throughout the kingdom were in love with her.

The list of honored guests was so long that there was no room in the village to put them all up: Andrew's parents, Harland and Lady Waleis Tren-

tham, Duncan MacRanald, William and Patricia Rawlings, Andrew's London
housekeeper, Dorothea Threlkeld, Prime Minister Richard Barraclough, Dugald MacKinnon and other members of the SNP, many of Andrew's Liberal
Democratic colleagues, and dozens more. Every man, woman, and child of
Ballochallater, of course, considered *themselves* the most honored guests of
all, though they did not have to travel to attend. Did they not know, they
insisted to one another, that the laird's daughter was bound to make her
mark on the world one day? They had foreseen it all along.

Duncan and the Trenthams enjoyed rooms in the castle with the laird and
Mrs. Gordon. Bill and Paddy Rawlings stayed at the Craigfoodie Bed-and-
Breakfast. The most surprising accommodation was that of Prime Minister
Richard Barraclough. In a private conversation with Andrew he had expressed
his wish, as he put it, to mingle with the genuine and humble people of the
region rather than stay in an expensive hotel thirty-five miles away in Perth.
The Scottish issue and their conversations leading up to the vote, he said, had
stimulated his interest in the north, and he was eager to know its people on
a more intimate basis than as a stuffy politician from faraway London. Prime
Minister Barraclough and his wife, therefore, had been guests for two nights
in the home of blacksmith Alastair Farquharson, who, upon their departure,
had a standing invitation to Number Ten Downing Street, for as long as Richard and Mrs. Barraclough remained in residence.

The wedding took place at ten o'clock on Saturday morning. Following
the outdoor ceremony the Games began, with the new Mr. and Mrs. Andrew
Trentham officiating as honorary hosts. Andrew had debated long and hard
about whether to wear the English morning coat or full Highland regalia. In
the end it was his mother who helped him decide. She said, meaning more
than the mere words indicated, "The past is behind you, Andrew. It is time
to move forward in your father's heritage. The old kilted Highlander's dress
in the gallery is your standard now."

So he again donned the kilt and jacket he had worn into Parliament that
fateful day a year earlier.

Ginny looked stunning beside him in her mother's heavy satin wedding
gown, which had been packed away in blue paper for thirty-five years, then
brought out and altered down to size. She had her dress tartan scarf pinned
to her left shoulder with an amethyst brooch, and the tartan sash came round
her back and was pinned again at her waist on the right. Somehow—Andrew
couldn't tell how—there were green ribbons woven all through her hair, with
sprigs of purple heather tucked into the strands. She carried a bouquet of

more heather combined with white baby's breath and more green ribbons. Behind her, dressed in a simple frock of lavender, walked young Margaret, Ginny's niece, leading two shaggy terriers on a leash. Faing and Fyfe walked with sprightly dignity, relishing the attention, each showing off the sprig of heather tucked decoratively in its collar.

There wasn't a single photo or snapshot taken that day that didn't turn out magnificently. How could they not—with such subjects and such a color-ful backdrop?

After the wedding proper, the Games commenced with even more good spirits than was usual. Alastair Farquharson had made a shorter and lighter caber to accompany the full-size log—in order to enable Lowlanders the ex-perience of participation in the uniquely Scottish caber toss. Andrew took second place to a surprisingly strong and agile William Campbell of the SNP. In addition to the usual races and athletic contests, special fundraising men's and women's Parliamentary editions of both the 2.8-mile and 200-meter run were held, whose publicly announced entrants beforehand included Andrew Trentham, Richard Barraclough, Sally Lutyens, Maurice Fraser-Smythe, and Lachlan Ross, all of whom were successful in persuading many of their more reluctant colleagues to join in on the day of the event.

In all other aspects the Games had been conducted as usual, with mer-chants' booths and sheep shearing and Highland dance competitions, tables of local handcrafts and edibles, and *much* music. The press was on hand in droves, but this was one occasion on which no one seemed to mind.

At four o'clock in the afternoon—earlier than was customary for the ben-efit of the couple of honor—a great feast of roast lamb managed to feed all the hungry mouths in attendance. Country dancing to the live music of one of Edinburgh's best-known box and fiddle bands followed, during which An-drew successfully organized a gigantic Gay Gordons encircling the entire castle.

At seven o'clock on the evening of the happy day, to great cheers and well wishes, the bride and groom departed for the first stop on their two-week honeymoon, the beautiful valley of Glencoe. From there they would pay a leisurely visit to the other places Andrew had encountered in his private search and had not had a chance to show Ginny during the months of their courtship. Now he could explain to her in full how they had all contributed to make a Scotsman of him.

———

Ten days later, two hikers whose faces had been on nearly every television and in the pages of every newspaper in Britain made their way up a steep slope in the desolate northern Highland regions of Sutherland. That they were alone was a relief, for wherever they went they were recognized. Their notoriety, however, had not diminished the enjoyment of their time together.

Panting heavily from the climb, they paused for a breather.

"Now do you see why I wanted to bring you here?" said Andrew, gesturing about.

"Ay, I do," replied Ginny. " 'Tis an even wilder view than frae Lochnagar, though that mountain will always be even more dear t' my hert noo as the place ye speired me t' marry ye. But I aye see what ye mean. I've lived my life doon in the central Highlands—'cept fer my vet-school years in Glasgow, of course—but this is stark indeed."

"I am certain," Andrew went on, "that we are somewhere in the vicinity of Laoigh, where the Caledonii brothers made the first monument of stones and where the ancient chiefs were buried. Just imagine, Ginny, if we could find it!"

"But hoo could we, Andrew? It doesna seem possible."

"I don't know, I suppose we would need a guide—someone who knew where it was—or a sign given to us somehow. But you're probably right. Too much time has passed. Maybe we will never know the exact location. But I will always dream of it and wonder if it still exists . . . somewhere."

They sat down on a large flat stone, breathing more easily now, and gazed about in contented silence.

"Ye've made me a happy lass, Andrew Trentham," said Ginny after a minute or two, slipping her arm into his. "Ken ye that?" she added, looking up into his eyes.

"I think so," smiled Andrew, leaning over to kiss her gently. "And you have done the same for me. I never dreamed that my search for roots would lead me to a wife—and one from my own clan, at that!"

"So, Andrew," Ginny continued, "noo that ye're an admitted Scot, an' prood o' the fact, an' noo that we're finally married, 'tis high time we didna jist talk aboot the future like we've been doin' fer six months—noo we've really got t' *decide* what we're gaein' t' du. Ye're not really plannin' t' mak me learn t' speak civil English an' become a London lady, are ye? I dinna think I could abide it."

Andrew laughed with delight.

"I've told you before and I'll tell you again," he said. "Even if I stay in the Commons and we have to spend half the year in London, don't you dare become English! I married a Scots lass, and a *Scot* I want her to remain."

"I'm aye relieved t' hear it."

"But I am still wondering," Andrew continued, "if perhaps I ought to relocate to Scotland. We could live up here all year round, and you could even keep your practice if you want to."

"I ken hoo ye've talked aboot it, Andrew, but Alexander already expects that I'll be leaving the practice, fer the present at least. My place is with you noo, where'er that taks us."

"Perhaps when the transfer of power to Edinburgh is complete," said Andrew, "I could stand for the Scottish Parliament. Who knows," he added laughing, "I might even become prime minister of Scotland someday!"

"I dinna ken what t' think o' that, Andrew. Du ye think the country'd hae the likes o' *me* fer the wife o' a prime minister?"

"And why not?" laughed Andrew.

"I'm a bit outspoken fer politics, dinna ye think?"

"All the women of the country love you, Ginny. Just like that woman at the market yesterday, wanting *your* autograph, not mine."

"Ay, she was a dear," smiled Ginny at the memory, "wi' sich a bashful look on her round face as she walked up t' me. Although I dinna think I'll ever git used t' folks wantin' me t' sign my name. 'Tis a mite strange fer a simple country lass like me."

"You are just what Scottish politics needs, Ginny—an outspoken prime minister's wife! I tell you, you're going to be the most famous Trentham before much longer.—No wait . . . I have an even better idea! *You* shall become prime minister of Scotland!"

"Andrew!" laughed Ginny playfully. "Dinna make sport o' sich a thing."

"I'm serious. . . . yes—I like it. I shall leave the Commons in London and become the *husband* of the Scottish prime minister!"

"It canna be quite so easy, I'm thinkin'?" said Ginny, still laughing at the outlandish notion.

"No, not so easy at all. We'd have to get you elected to the Scottish Parliament first. Times have changed since Robert the Bruce—it's not just for the taking anymore. And there could still be problems because of me."

"What du ye mean?"

"I'm sure many Scots still think of me as a Sassenach."

"Not after what ye've dune fer Scotland," rejoined Ginny.

"Then you would be sure to win hands down!"

Another reflective silence went by. Far off in the distance, partway up the slope of an adjoining hill, a faint movement caught Andrew's eye. He stood and squinted.

Yes, something was there! Something large, something . . .

"Ginny," he said excitedly, "could you please grab the binoculars out of my backpack!"

"Why, what du ye—"

"Hurry—I'll show you."

Twenty seconds later he was fumbling frantically with the focus dial. The next thing Ginny heard was an exhaled exclamation of wonder and disbelief.

"What is it, Andrew!"

"Here—look for yourself." His voice quivered. "I don't believe it . . . tell me I'm not crazy!"

He handed her the binoculars and pointed with his hand and arm. She put the lenses to her eyes and moved them about until she found what Andrew was pointing at. A gasp of astonishment now also escaped her lips.

"I canna believe what I'm seein'!" she said. "I always thought the white stag was jist legend! But Andrew, it *is* white . . . or are my eyes playin' a trick on me?"

"It looked white to me, unless the sun—"

"Luik, Andrew!" interrupted Ginny. "The creature's turnin' an' walkin' away."

"Yes, I see it!"

"Here—take the binoculars," she said. "See noo—it's luikin' back . . . I think it sees us!"

"Right, I see . . . yes, it's gazing straight up here . . . no, there he goes again, walking away, into that little thicket of woods."

"He must mean fer us t' follow, Andrew—come!" cried Ginny, jumping up and grabbing Andrew's hand.

"It's too far, Ginny. We could never hope to keep up with him."

"If he means us t' follow, then he'll wait—an' if we dinna follow," Ginny added, urging him on, "we may never hae the chance again."

Hand in hand they began running down the slope opposite that which they had descended.

Andrew needed no more convincing. Even if the attempt proved unsuccessful, seeing it once was enough for a lifetime. His ancient predecessors had not set eyes on the white stag again after their encounter in Muigh-bhlaraidh

Ecgfrith. But if their blood indeed flowed through him, he must, like Fidach, never abandon the quest.

Five minutes later, Andrew and Ginny were hurrying eagerly through the valley with a carefree abandon reminiscent of Cruithne and Fidach themselves, then scrambling up the slope opposite where they had seen the great beast disappear. If he had indeed beckoned them toward the legendary stones of antiquity, then perhaps these two would be blessed to complete in their time what the two brothers of old had begun in theirs.

As they went, though no human eyes saw the direction of their retreating footsteps, in truth these two modern Caledonian pioneers were not alone.

The cloud of witnesses joining in their pilgrimage came not only from ancient times, but was also made up of those many thousands like Andrew Trentham whose discovery of their Scottish heritage had opened new worlds of adventure into both the past *and* the present.

And like Andrew's, their quest was one that has no end, and whose next chapter may be standing across the glen on the next Highland ridge. For the glory of Scotland never fades, but lives and ever renews itself in the hearts of all who will forever love those magnificent northern reaches, whose souls are set singing at mere mention of that land known to the ancients . . . as Caledonia.

> Hark, when the night is falling,
> Hear! Hear the pipes are calling
> Loudly and proudly calling,
> Down thro' the glen.
> There where the hills are sleeping,
> Now feel the blood a-leaping,
> High, as the spirit of the
> Old Highland men.
>
> High in the misty Highlands,
> Out by the purple islands,
> Brave are the hearts that beat
> Beneath Scottish skies.
> Wild are the winds to meet you,
> Staunch are the friends that greet you,
> Kind as the love that shines
> From fair maiden's eyes.

Towering in gallant fame,
Scotland my mountain hame,
High may your proud standards gloriously wave.
Land of my high endeavor,
Land of the shining silver,
Land of my heart forever,
Scotland the brave.

APPENDIX A
Ancestry of Andrew Gordon Trentham

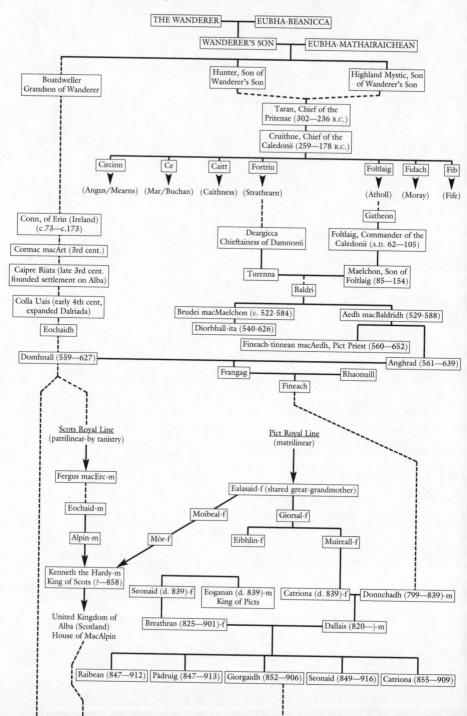

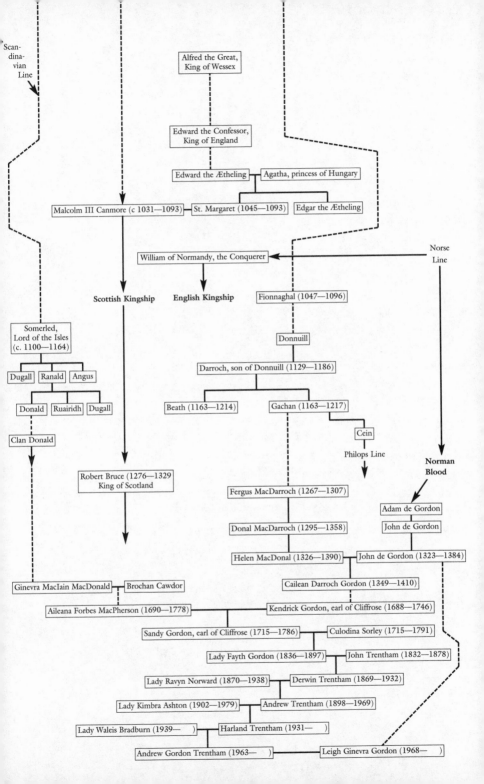

Political Allignment in the Lower House of the
British Parliament Following General Election (Fictional)

			Party Leader
Labour (Socialist) Party	285	Members of Parliament	Richard Barraclough
Conservative Party (Tories)	277	"	Miles Ramsey/Archibald Craye
Liberal Democratics (Lib Dem)	51	"	Andrew Trentham
Scottish Nationalist Party (SNP)	21	"	Dugald MacKinnon
Miscellaneous MPs and Speaker	25	"	Various
Total MPs in House of Commons	659	(Needed for Coalition and Majority Vote—326)	

❊   ❊   ❊

Party Breakdown of MPs in House of Commons Since 1974

	1974 (Feb)	1974 (Oct)	1979	1983	1987	1992	1997	(Fictional)
Labour	301	319	268	209	229	270	418	285
Conservative	296	276	339	397	375	336	165	277
Liberal Democrat	—	—	—	—	—	20	46	51
Liberal	14	13	11	17	17	—	—	—
Scottish Nationalist	7	11	2	2	3	3	6	21
Social Democrat	1	—	—	6	5	—	—	—
Plaid Cymru	2	3	2	2	3	4	4	4
Democrat Unionist	—	—	3	3	3	3	2	2
SDLP	1	1	1	1	3	4	3	3
Sinn Fein	—	—	—	1	1	—	2	2
Ulster Popular Unionist	—	—	—	1	1	1	—	1
Ulster Unionist	11	10	6	10	9	9	10	10
UK Unionist	—	—	—	—	—	—	1	1
Independent	1	1	2	—	—	—	1	1
The Speaker	1	1	1	1	1	1	1	1
	635	635	635	650	650	651	659	659

NOTES AND BIBLIOGRAPHY

Those who have read the first volume of CALEDONIA: LEGEND OF THE CELTIC STONE, will by now be well familiar with my particular method of blending fact and fiction in order to help bring to life various historical eras. If you have not read it, I recommend both that book and its appendices to you, for *Legend of the Celtic Stone* and *An Ancient Strife* are truly a single story.

In order somewhat to clarify what I have called the "blurry line between story and history, fact and fiction," I hope the following brief remarks will be helpful.

Aileana and Kendrick, Sandy and Culodina Gordon are fictional, though most of those involved in the buildup and aftermath to the battle of Culloden are historical individuals. The movements of Prince Charles Edward Stuart, the infighting among his staff, and the disastrous details of the battle itself are factually accurate.

The character of Kendrick Gordon is very loosely modeled after one Cluny MacPherson, at first a somewhat reluctant convert to Bonnie Prince Charlie's cause, but later one of his staunchest supporters and closest friends. The location of Cliffrose Castle along the banks of the Spey in the region just west of the Cairngorms known as Badenoch sits at the former site of Cluny Castle. Culodina's father and Tullibardglass Hall are entirely fictional.

Ill-fated though it was, the brief shining moment of Prince Charlie's fame remains one of the most romantic and legendary periods of Scottish history. Had I the time—and would my editors allow me another hundred pages!—I would have loved to follow Sandy Gordon's movements in more detail during those frantic months in hiding with the prince. Stories abound of narrow escapes, disguises, midnight getaways, treacheries, and triumphs. And those months did actually culminate in two weeks of hiding out high above Loch Ericht on Ben Alder in a fully outfitted and elaborate "tree house" known as Cluny's Cage and made famous by Robert Louis Stevenson. Some maps of Scotland now note the site as "Prince Charlie's Cave." This hideout was used by many Jacobites, including Cluny and the prince, for several years after the rebellion and is known for hiding not only the prince, but also a sizeable Jacobite treasure.

When financial help from France in the form of a huge stash of gold coins belatedly arrived on the western shores of the Highlands to aid in the Jacobite rebellion, the battle was over and the prince on the run. Its only immediate impact was to make a few chiefs wealthy men, probably including MacPherson himself. What was not stolen at the outset was taken inland to Loch Arkaig and thence to Cluny's Cage to prevent the English from getting their hands on it. This Treasure of Loch Arkaig, as it was called, was buried somewhere in the vicinity and never seen again. In the 1950s, several gold Spanish coins were discovered in the hooves of limping cattle in the region of Loch Arkaig.

Unfortunately the most fictionalized portion of the story lies in this: Very few of the leading Jacobites, such as the fictional Sandy Gordon, ever lived normal lives in Scotland again. Men such as Cluny MacPherson and Lord George Murray and hundreds of others were hunted down ruthlessly by the English. Those who were not killed either spent the rest of their lives in exile on the Continent or were imprisoned and their homes and lands confiscated. Sadly, the "happy ending" enjoyed by Sandy and Culodina in the afteryears is not as true to the facts as one might hope.

The village of Spittal o' Ballochallater and its inhabitants are fictional.

The specific genealogy of Kenneth MacAlpin is fictional as well. Nothing is known beyond the fact that he became joint King of the Picts and the Scots in 843, and this may have been accomplished through ties from his mother to the Pict royal line. Donnchadh, Dallais, Breathran, and Steenbuaic are all fictional. The later fictionalized history of Steenbuaic (or *Stonewycke*), however, I have written of elsewhere, in partnership with Judith Pella, in two collections entitled *The Stonewycke Trilogy* and *The Stonewycke Legacy*.

The character of Fionnaghal is fictional, although most of the portrayal of Margaret and Malcolm III, including many of the incidents recorded, is based on fact. St. Margaret washed the feet of many and ministered to the needy both in the village surrounding the castle and in the great hall of the castle itself. She is also said to have given them her jewelry, sat outside the castle so people could come to her, and to have fed nine orphans daily with her own spoon. King Malcolm did indeed, upon at least one occasion, kneel with his wife and wash the feet of a beggar.

Darroch and Nara MacDonnuill, their twin sons, and their descendents Fergus and Donal are fictional.

Duncan, earl of Fife, however, did in fact construct the first castle in Strathbogie in the late twelfth century. His descendents offered the castle to Robert the Bruce in which to recuperate prior to the Christmas battle of Slioch against the earl of Buchan. A later earl of Strathbogie turned against Bruce prior to Bannockburn, and ultimately the lands were taken from him by the King, who granted them to Adam de Gordon of Huntly in Berwick-shire. The castle of Strathbogie, therefore, received both a new owner and a new name, and from that time until the present, that region of Scotland has been called, as it is today, "the Gordon District." The village became Huntly, where what has managed to survive of Strathbogie Castle remains to this day, magnificent even in collapse and decay—one of the truly impressive castle ruins in Scotland. The motte (earthen mound) raised in the late 1100s by Earl Duncan II still stands.

Robert the Bruce, of course, and his commanders, as well as those of the English, are all factual, as are generally the events leading up to and including the battle of Bannockburn itself.

The marriage between the Gordon strain and the fictional lineage of MacDonnuill/MacDarroch/MacDonal is fictional, as are the characters of Helen MacDonal and Cailean Darroch Gordon.

Several poems of Robert Burns have been cited. In the approximate order of their appearance, I have quoted from the following: "A Winter Night," "The Winter Is Past," "Yon Wild Mossy Mountains," "My Heart's in the Highlands," one modified stanza at the end of chapter 11 from "Caledonia," and "Scots, Wha Hae."

The Gaelic lullaby sung to the children by Aileana in chapter 3 is from "A Fairy Lullaby" (*An Cóineachan*), taken from *The Minstrelsy of the Scottish Highlands* (arr. Alfred Moffat, translation by Lachlan MacBean).

The Gaelic Lord's Prayer in chapter 3 is taken from *Scottish Lore and Folklore* by Ronald Macdonald Douglas.

The Gaelic ballad sung by Calum Dhuibh in chapter 9 was adapted from the song *Chi Mi Na Mór-bheanna* ("I Will See the Big Mountains") by John Cameron, from *The Gaelic Echo* (Summer 1992).

As I did in the earlier volume, I would again express my indebtedness to the eminent Scottish historian John Prebble, author of many wonderfully readable accounts, whose *Lion in the North* I heartily recommend. His defin-itive account, simply entitled *Culloden*—as does all his work—illuminates the personal story of all the principal players of the drama. It was one of the most helpful of all the books of my research and, as I said before, is simply the best history you will find anywhere.

In addition, the following books were extremely helpful in my research for *An Ancient Strife*.

Barbour, John. *The Bruce*. Originally written in 1395. Translated by Archibald A.H. Douglas in 1964. Reprint, William MacLellan.

Barke, James. *Poems and Songs of Robert Burns*. London: Fontana/Collins, 1955.

Blaikie, Walter, ed. *Origins of the Forty-Five*. Edinburgh: Scottish History Society, 1916.

Bold, Alan. *Scotland's Kings and Queens*. London: Pitkin Pictorials, 1980.

Bonnie Prince Charlie. London: Pitkin Pictorials, 1973.

Cannon, John and Ralph Griffiths. *The Oxford Illustrated History of the British Monarchy*. Oxford: Oxford University Press, 1988.

Carruth, J.A. *Scotland the Brave*. Norwich: Jarrold & Sons, 1973.

Crowl, Philip. *The Intelligent Traveller's Guide to Historic Scotland*. New York: Congdon & Weed, 1986.

Dickinson, William Croft. *Scotland from the Earliest Times to 1603*. Edinburgh: Thomas Nelson & Sons, 1961.

Donaldson, Gordon. *Scotland: The Shaping of a Nation*. London: David & Charles, 1974.

Douglas, Ronald Macdonald. *Scottish Lore and Folklore*. New York: Crown, 1982.

Ferguson, William. *Scotland: 1689 to the Present*, vol. 4 of *The Edinburgh History of Scotland*. Edinburgh: Oliver & Boyd, 1968.

Fisher, Andrew. *A Traveller's History of Scotland*. Gloucestershire, UK: Windrush Press, 1990.

Kybett, Susan. *Bonnie Prince Charlie*. New York: Dodd, Mead, 1988.

Lindsay, Maurice, ed. *Modern Scottish Poetry*. London: Faber & Faber, 1946.

Macdonald, Donald J. *Clan Donald*. Loanhead, Scotland: Macdonald Publishers, 1978.

MacKintosh, John. *Scotland: From the Earliest Times to the Present Century*. 1890. Reprint, Freeport, New York: Books for Libraries Press, 1972.

Maclean, Fitzroy. *A Concise History of Scotland*. London: Thames and Hudson, 1970.

Martine, Roddy. *Scottish Clan and Family Names*. Edinburgh: Mainstream Publishing, 1992.

McGrigor, Mary. "St. Margaret of Scotland." *Scottish World,* Winter 1992.

McNie, Alan. *Clan Gordon.* Jedburgh, Scotland: Cascade Publishing, 1983.

Nicholson, Ranald. *Scotland: the Later Middle Ages,* vol. 2 of *The Edinburgh History of Scotland.* Edinburgh: Oliver & Boyd, 1974.

Parliament. London: Her Majesty's Stationery Office, 1991.

Parliamentary Elections. London: Her Majesty's Stationery Office, 1991.

Prebble, John. *Culloden.* Martin Secker & Warburg, Ltd., 1961.

———. *The Lion in the North.* London: Penguin Books, 1971.

Ritchie, Anna. *Scotland BC.* Edinburgh: Scottish Development Department, 1988.

Scots Kith and Kin. Glasgow: HarperCollins, 1953.

Simpson, W. Douglas. *Huntly Castle.* Edinburgh: Her Majesty's Stationery Office.

Tranter, Nigel. *Robert Bruce: The Path of the Hero King.* London: Hodder & Stoughton, 1970.

Whitaker's Concise Almanack, 1999. London: Whitaker & Sons, 1999.

For those of you not familiar with my other work, I might just add here a brief biographical note.

My own love affair with Scotland began more than thirty years ago with my discovery of the writings of a nearly forgotten Scotsman, George Mac-Donald (1824–1905). A contemporary of England's greatest Victorian novelists and poets whose immense popularity in his day on both sides of the Atlantic rivaled that of Dickens himself, MacDonald produced more than fifty books of enormous variety, including novels, poems, fantasies, children's stories, sermons, essays, and literary criticism. Yet I found that the passage of time had not treated MacDonald so kindly as it had many of his contemporaries. The attempt to lay my hands on MacDonald's work proved daunting. Only four or five of his titles were then in print and his literary reputation, once so widespread, had all but vanished.

Happily that situation is now reversed. MacDonald's work—especially his wonderful Scottish stories!—is again widely available.

If you love Scotland, MacDonald is the master storyteller of the land. Whatever you may have enjoyed in my attempt to bring Caledonia to life, you will find, and more besides, in George MacDonald. Five titles deserve special attention as being what I would call classically Scottish: *The Baronet's Song, The Laird's Inheritance, The Highlander's Last Song, The Maiden's Bequest,* and *The Fisherman's Lady.* I have also written a biography entitled

George MacDonald, Scotland's Beloved Storyteller. These titles have all been published by Bethany House.

As I said when we began this quest together, in a magical sense we are all Scots together, and Andrew Trentham's story is a universal one. We *all* have roots that stretch back into antiquity, even all the way to those intrepid wanderers who first explored and peopled our lands. As I look over Andrew's genealogy, therefore, fictional though it may be, a tingle of excitement surges through me to realize that we *all* possess just such a family tree—if only we knew how to trace it far enough backward in time. I wrote this tale not just to tell the story of one individual, but in a sense to tell the story of all men and women. I hope you will consider it your story, too, as I feel it is mine.

I hope and pray that your own personal Caledonian adventure, like Andrew's and Ginny's, never ends, and that you will follow your own white stag to whatever discoveries lie ahead for you in the ancient land of the Wanderer.

As always, I welcome comments from readers. I may be reached—and a list of available George MacDonald titles may be obtained upon request—either through the publisher or at P.O. Box 7003, Eureka, CA 95502, USA.

Books by Michael Phillips

Best Friends for Life (with Judy Phillips)
The Garden at the Edge of Beyond
A God to Call Father†
Good Things to Remember
A Rift In Time†
Hidden in Time†
*The Stonewycke Legacy**
*The Stonewycke Trilogy**

CALEDONIA

   Legend of the Celtic Stone   *An Ancient Strife*

THE JOURNALS OF CORRIE BELLE HOLLISTER

*My Father's World**   *Sea to Shining Sea*
*Daughter of Grace**   *Into the Long Dark Night*
On the Trail of the Truth   *Land of the Brave and the Free*
A Place in the Sun   *A Home for the Heart*

      Grayfox (Zack's story)

THE JOURNALS OF CORRIE AND CHRISTOPHER

The Braxtons of Miracle Springs   *A New Beginning*

MERCY AND EAGLEFLIGHT†

Mercy and Eagleflight   *A Dangerous Love*

THE RUSSIANS*

The Crown and the Crucible   *Travail and Triumph*
A House Divided

THE SECRET OF THE ROSE†

The Eleventh Hour   *Escape to Freedom*
A Rose Remembered   *Dawn of Liberty*

THE SECRETS OF HEATHERSLEIGH HALL

Wild Grows the Heather in Devon *Heathersleigh Homecoming*
Wayward Winds   *A New Dawn Over Devon* (2001)

*with Judith Pella   †Tyndale House